N is for Noose
'Full marks to Grafton for storytelling and stamina.
No other crime writer so consistently delivers the goods'
Literary Review

O is for Outlaw
'One of the more humane and empathic sleuths on
the block, Grafton's heroine is also genuinely
believable, full of quirks and all too human
foibles which help the reader identify with her . . .
Absolute top form'
Time Out

P is for Peril
'Intricate and exciting, with plot turns and twists
mostly unguessable. Grade A entertainment'
Literary Review

Q is for Quarry
'As cogent and witty as ever,
with images as sharp as a tack'
Literary Review

R is for Ricochet
'Book by book, this may be
the most satisfying mystery series going'
Wall Street Journal

S is for Silence
'Sue Grafton knows what she's doing'
New York Times

Sue Grafton has become one of the most popular female crime writers, both here and in the US. Born in Kentucky in 1940, the daughter of the mystery writer C. W. Grafton, she began her career as a TV scriptwriter before Kinsey Millhone and the 'alphabet' series took off. Her first novel, *A is for Alibi*, was inspired by Sue's own divorce: *'For months I lay in bed and plotted to kill my ex-husband, but I knew I'd bungle it and get caught so I wrote it in a book instead.'*

Sue freely confesses that Kinsey is her alter ego: 'I think of her as the person I might have been had I not married young and had kids; she is that stripped down piece of my personality.' She writes one book a year and plans to take Kinsey all the way through the alphabet to Z when Kinsey will be forty years old.

She lives and writes in Montecito, California, and Louisville, Kentucky.

Also by Sue Grafton

A is for Alibi
B is for Burglar
C is for Corpse
D is for Deadbeat
E is for Evidence
F is for Fugitive
G is for Gumshoe
H is for Homicide
I is for Innocent
J is for Judgment
K is for Killer
L is for Lawless
M is for Malice
N is for Noose
O is for Outlaw
P is for Peril
Q is for Quarry
R is for Ricochet
S is for Silence

Keziah Dane
The Lolly Madonna War

Sue Grafton

G is for Gumshoe

&

H is for Homicide

&

I is for Innocent

PAN BOOKS

G is for Gumshoe first published 1990 by Henry Holt and Company, New York.
First published in Great Britain 1990 by Macmillan.
First published in paperback 1991 by Pan Books.
H is for Homicide first published 1991 by Henry Holt and Company, New York.
First published in Great Britain 1991 by Macmillan.
First published in paperback 1992 by Pan Books.
I is for Innocent first published 1992 by Henry Holt and Company, New York.
First published in Great Britain 1992 by Macmillan.
First published in paperback 1993 by Pan Books.

This omnibus first published 2007 by Pan Books
an imprint of Pan Macmillan Ltd
Pan Macmillan, 20 New Wharf Road, London N1 9RR
Basingstoke and Oxford
Associated companies throughout the world
www.panmacmillan.com

ISBN 978-0-330-45237-3

3 5 7 9 8 6 4 2

A CIP catalogue record for this book is available from
the British Library.

Printed and bound in Great Britain by
Mackays of Chatham plc, Chatham, Kent

G is for
Gumshoe

For Molly Friedrich and Geoffrey Sanford . . . who carve a path through the jungle for me

The author wishes to acknowledge the invaluable assistance of the
following people: Steven Humphrey; Eric S. H. Ching; Deputy
District Attorney Harvey Giss, County of Los Angeles; Joe Driscoll,
Driscoll & Associates Investigations; Noel Waters, District Attorney,
Carson City, Nevada; Ms. Terry Roeser, Nevada State Public
Defender; Richard and Vicki Windsor; Allen Glanze, Stano
Components; Lucy Thomas, Reeves Medical Library, Cottage
Hospital; Bobbie Kline, Nursing Director, Cottage Hospital
Emergency Room; Karen Nelson, Pathology Department, Cottage
Hospital; Lieutenant Tony Baker, Santa Barbara County Sheriff's
Department; Robert Simonet, Director of Security, Four Seasons
Biltmore; Sergeant Dennis Prescott and Detective Lawrence Gillespie,
Santa Barbara County Coroner's Office; Pepper Breault, Santa
Barbara County Court Recorder; Ken Orrock, deputy sheriff,
Imperial County; Bob Hall; and Carter Blackmar.

▶▶▶ Three things occurred on or about May 5, which is not only Cinco de Mayo in California, but Happy Birthday to me. Aside from the fact that I turned thirty-three (after what seemed like an interminable twelve months of being thirty-two), the following also came to pass:

1. The reconstruction of my apartment was completed and I moved back in.
2. I was hired by a Mrs. Clyde Gersh to bring her mother back from the Mojave desert.
3. I made one of the top slots on Tyrone Patty's hit list.

I report these events not necessarily in the order of importance, but in the order most easily explained.

For the record, my name is Kinsey Millhone. I'm a private investigator, licensed by the State of California, (now) thirty-three years old, 118 pounds of female in a five-foot six-inch frame. My hair is dark, thick, and straight. I'd been accustomed to wearing it short, but I'd been letting it grow out just to see what it would look like. My usual practice is to crop my

1

own mop every six weeks or so with a pair of nail scissors. This I do because I'm too cheap to pay twenty-eight bucks in a beauty salon. I have hazel eyes, a nose that's been busted twice, but still manages to function pretty well I think. If I were asked to rate my looks on a scale of one to ten, I wouldn't. I have to say, however, that I seldom wear makeup, so whatever I look like first thing in the morning at least remains consistent as the day wears on.

I'd been living since New Year's with my landlord, Henry Pitts, an eighty-two-year-old gent whose converted single-car garage apartment I'd been renting for two years. This nondescript but otherwise serviceable abode had been blown sky-high and Henry had suggested that I move into his small back bedroom while my place was being rebuilt. There is, apparently, some law of nature decreeing that all home construction must double in its projected cost and take four times longer than originally anticipated. This would explain why, after five months of intensive work, the unveiling had finally been scheduled with all the fanfare of a movie premiere. I was uneasy about the new place because I wasn't at all sure I'd like what Henry had come up with in the way of a floor plan and interior "day-core." He'd been very secretive and extremely pleased with himself since he'd gotten city approval for the blueprints. I was worried that I'd take one look at the place and not be able to conceal my dismay. I'm a born liar, but I don't do as well disguising what I feel. Still, as I'd told myself many times, it was his property and he could do anything he pleased. For two hundred bucks a month, was I going to complain? I doesn't think so.

I woke at six o'clock that Thursday morning, rolled out of bed and into my running clothes. I brushed my teeth, splashed some water on my face, did a perfunctory hamstring stretch, and headed out Henry's back door. May and June, in Santa Teresa, are often masked by fog—the weather as blank and dreary as the white noise on a TV set when the broadcast day is done. The winter beaches are stripped bare, massive boulders exposed as the tides sweep away the summer sand. We'd had a rainy March and April, but May had come in clear and mild. The sand was being returned as the spring currents shifted, the beaches restored for the tourists who would begin to pour into the town around Memorial Day and not leave again until Labor Day weekend had come and gone.

This dawn was spectacular, early morning clouds streaking the sky in dark gray tufts, sun tinting the underbelly an intense rose shade. The tide was out and the beach seemed to stretch toward the horizon in a silvery mirror of reflected sky. Santa Teresa was lush and green and the air felt soft, saturated with the smell of eucalyptus leaves and the newly cut grass. I jogged three miles and was home again thirty minutes later in time for Henry to sing "Happy birthday to yooouuu!" as he pulled a pan of freshly baked cinnamon rolls out of the oven. Being serenaded is not my favorite activity, but he did it so badly, I could only be amused and gratified. I showered, pulled on jeans, a T-shirt, and my tennis shoes, and then Henry handed me a gift-wrapped jeweler's box that contained the newly minted brass key to my apartment. He was behaving like a kid, his lean, tanned face wreathed in shy smiles, his blue eyes glinting with barely suppressed excitement. In a two-person ceremonial procession, we walked from his back door, across the flagstone patio, to the front door of my place.

I knew what the exterior looked like—two stories of cream-colored stucco with rounded corners in a style I'd have to call Art Deco. Numerous hand-crankable windows had been installed and there was new landscaping, which Henry had done himself. To tell you the truth, the outward effect was unprepossessing, which I didn't object to a bit. My prime anxiety had always been that he'd make the apartment too fancy for my taste.

We took a few minutes to survey the site, Henry explaining in detail all the hassles he'd gone through with the City Planning Commission and the Architectural Board of Review. I knew he was just dragging out the explanation to pump up the suspense and, in truth, I was feeling anxious, just wanting to get the whole thing over with. Finally, he allowed me to turn the key in the lock and the front door, with its porthole-shaped window, swung open. I don't know what I'd expected. I'd tried not to conjure up fantasies of any kind, but what I saw left me inarticulate. The entire apartment had the feel of a ship's interior. The walls were highly polished teak and oak, with shelves and cubbyholes on every side. The kitchenette was still located to the right where the old one had been, a galley-style arrangement with a pint-size stove and refrigerator. A microwave oven and trash compactor had been added. Tucked in beside the kitchen was a stacking washer-dryer, and next to that was a tiny bathroom.

In the living area, a sofa had been built into a window bay, with two royal blue canvas director's chairs arranged to form a "conversational grouping." Henry did a quick demonstration of how the sofa could be extended into sleeping accommodations for company, a trundle bed in effect. The dimensions of the main room were still roughly fifteen feet on a side, but now there was a sleeping loft above, accessible by way of a tiny spiral staircase where my former storage space had been. In the old place, I'd usually slept naked on the couch in an envelope of folded quilt. Now, I was going to have an actual bedroom of my own.

I wound my way up, staring in amazement at the double-size platform bed with drawers underneath. In the ceiling above the bed, there was a round shaft extending through the roof, capped by a clear Plexiglas skylight that seemed to fling light down on the blue-and-white patchwork coverlet. Loft windows looked out to the ocean on one side and the mountains on the other. Along the back wall, there was an expanse of cedar-lined closet space with a rod for hanging clothes, pegs for miscellaneous items, shoe racks, and floor-to-ceiling drawers.

Just off the loft, there was a small bathroom. The tub was sunken with a built-in shower and a window right at tub level, the wooden sill lined with plants. I could bathe among the treetops, looking out at the ocean where the clouds were piling up like bubbles. The towels were the same royal blue as the cotton shag carpeting. Even the eggs of milled soap were blue, arranged in a white china dish on the edge of the round brass sink.

When the inspection tour was complete, I turned around and stared at him, speechless, a phenomenon that made Henry laugh aloud, tickled with himself that he'd executed his scheme so perfectly. Close to tears, I leaned my forehead against his chest while he patted at me awkwardly. I couldn't ask for a better friend.

He left me alone soon afterward and I went through every cabinet and drawer, drinking in the scent of the wood, listening to the phantom creaking of the wind in the rafters overhead. It took me fifteen minutes to move my possessions in. Most of what I owned had been destroyed by the same bomb that flattened the old place. My all-purpose dress had survived, along with a favorite vest and the air fern Henry'd given me for Christmas. Everything else had been pulverized by black powder, blasting caps, and shrapnel. With the insurance money, I'd bought a few odds and ends—jeans and jumpsuits—and then I'd tucked the rest in a money market account, where it was merrily collecting interest.

At 8:45, I locked up, looked in on Henry briefly, and fumbled my way through yet another thank-you, which he waved away. Then I headed to the office, a quick ten-minute drive into town. I wanted to stay home, circling my house like a sea captain preparing to embark on some fabulous voyage, but I knew for a fact I had bills to pay and telephone calls to return.

I dispensed with several minor items, typing up a couple of invoices for two standing accounts. The last name on the list of phone calls was a Mrs. Clyde Gersh who had left a message on my machine late the day before with a request to get in touch at my convenience. I dialed her number, reaching for a yellow pad. The phone rang twice and then a woman picked up on the other end.

"Mrs. Gersh?"

"Yes," she said. Her tone held a note of caution as if I might be soliciting contributions for some fraudulent charity.

"Kinsey Millhone, returning your call."

There was a split second of silence and then she seemed to recollect who I was. "Oh yes, Miss Millhone. I appreciate your being so prompt. I have a matter I'd like to discuss with you, but I don't drive and I'd prefer not to leave the house. Is there any chance you might meet with me here sometime today?"

"Sure," I said. She gave me the address and since I didn't have anything else on the books, I said I'd be there within the hour. There didn't seem to be any particular urgency to the matter, whatever it was, but business is business.

The address she'd given me was in the heart of town, not far from my office, one of the older blocks of single-family residences on a quiet tree-lined street. A tangle of shrubs formed a nearly impenetrable wall that separated the property from street view. I parked out front and let myself in through a creaking gate. The house was a shambling affair, two stories of dark green shingle set sideways on a lot dense with sycamores. I climbed pale gray wooden porch steps still fragrant with a recent repainting. The screen was open and I moved to the front door and pushed the bell, surveying the façade. The house was probably built in the twenties, not elegant by any means, but constructed on a large scale: comfortable, unpretentious, once meant for the middle class— out of reach for the average buyer in the current real estate market. A house like this would probably sell for over half a million these days and then require remodeling to bring it up to snuff.

An obese black woman, in a canary-yellow uniform with white collar and cuffs, let me in. "Mrs. Gersh's out on the upstairs porch," she said, indicating a staircase directly ahead. She lumbered off, apparently trusting me not to lift any cut-glass knickknacks from the occasional table to the right of the entranceway.

I had a momentary glimpse of the living room: a wide painted brick fireplace flanked by built-in bookcases with leaded-glass doors, lots of cotton shag carpeting in a much-trampled off-white. Creamy-painted wainscoting ran halfway up the wall with a pale print wallpaper above, extending across the ceiling in an inverted meadow of wildflowers. The room was shadowy and cried out for table lamps. The whole house was muffled in silence and smelled of cauliflower and curry.

I went up. When I reached the first landing, I saw that a second set of stairs branched down into the kitchen, where I could see a kettle bubbling on the stove. The maid who'd admitted me was now standing at the counter, chopping cilantro. Sensing my gaze, she turned and gave me an idle look. I moved on up.

At the top of the stairs, a screen door opened onto a broad, flat porch ringed with wooden planters filled with bright pink and orange geraniums. The main street, two blocks over, ebbed and flowed with traffic noises as sibilant as the sea. Mrs. Gersh was stretched out on a chaise longue, a plaid lap robe arranged across her legs. She might have been taking the air in a deck chair, waiting for the social director to advise her of the day's shipboard activities. She had her eyes closed, a Judith Krantz novel face-down on her lap. The branches of a weeping willow draped long, lacy limbs across one corner of the porch, which was dappled in shade.

The day was mild, but the breeze seemed faintly chilly up here. The woman was stick-thin, with the dead-white complexion of someone profoundly ill. She struck me as the sort of woman who, a hundred years ago, might have spent long years in a sanitarium with a series of misdiagnoses stemming from anxiety, unhappiness, laudanum addiction, or an aversion to sex. Her hair was an icy blond, harshly bleached, and sparse. Bright red lipstick defined the width of her mouth and she wore matching bright red polish on nails cut short. Her Jean Harlow eyebrows had been plucked to an expression of frail astonishment. Her eyes were defined by false lashes that lay against her lower lids like sutures. I judged her to be in her fifties, but she might have been younger. Disease is an aging process in itself. Her chest was sunken, with breasts as flat as the flaps on an envelope. She wore a white silk blouse, expensive-looking pale gray gabardine slacks, vivid green satin slippers on her feet.

"Mrs. Gersh?"

She was startled, eyes flying open in a blaze of blue. For a moment, she seemed disoriented and then she collected herself.

"You must be Kinsey," she murmured. "I'm Irene Gersh." She held out her left hand and clutched mine briefly, her fingers wiry and cold.

"Sorry if I frightened you."

"Don't worry about it. I'm a bundle of nerves. Please. Find a chair and sit. I don't sleep well as a rule and I'm forced to catnap when I can."

A quick survey showed three white mesh lawn chairs stacked together in one corner of the porch. I lifted the top chair, carried it over to the chaise, and sat down.

"I hope Jermaine will have the presence of mind to bring us tea, but don't count on it," she said. She shifted into a more upright position, adjusting the lap robe. She studied me with interest. It was my impression that she approved, though of what I couldn't say. "You're younger than I thought you'd be."

"Old enough," I said. "Today's my birthday. I'm thirty-three."

"Well, happy birthday. I hope I didn't interrupt a celebration."

"Not at all."

"I'm forty-seven myself." She smiled briefly. "I know I look like an old hag, but I'm relatively young . . . given California standards."

"Have you been ill?"

"Let's put it this way . . . I haven't been well. My husband and I moved to Santa Teresa three years ago from Palm

Springs. This was his parents' house. When his father died, Clyde undertook his mother's care. She passed away two months ago."

I murmured something I hoped was appropriate.

"The point is, we didn't need to move here, but Clyde insisted. Never mind my objections. He was raised in Santa Teresa and he was determined to come back."

"I take it you weren't enthusiastic."

She flashed a look at me. "I don't like it here. I never did. We used to come for visits, maybe twice a year. I have an aversion to the sea. I always found the town oppressive. There's an aura about it that I find very dark. Everybody's so smitten with the beauty of it. I don't like the attitude of self-congratulation and I don't like all the green. I was born and raised in the desert, which is what I prefer. My health has deteriorated since the day we arrived, though the doctors can't seem to find anything wrong with me. Clyde is thriving, of course. I suspect he thinks this is a form of pouting on my part, but it's not. It's dread. I wake up every morning filled with debilitating anxiety. Sometimes it feels like a surge of electricity or a weight on my chest, almost overwhelming."

"Are you talking about panic attacks?"

"That's what the doctor keeps calling it," she said.

I murmured noncommittally, wondering where this was all going to lead. She seemed to read my thoughts.

"What do you know about the Slabs?" she asked abruptly.

"The Slabs?"

"Ah, doesn't ring a bell, I see. Not surprising. The Slabs are out in the Mojave, to the east of the Salton Sea. During the Second World War, there was a Marine base out there. Camp Dunlap. It's gone now. All that's left are the concrete foundations for the barracks, known now as the Slabs. Thousands of people migrate to the Slabs every winter from the North. They call them snowbirds because they flee the harsh Northern winters. I was raised out there. My mother's still there, as far as I know. Conditions are very primitive . . . no water, no sewer lines, no city services of any sort, but it costs nothing. The snowbirds live like gypsies: some in expensive RVs, some in cardboard shacks. In the spring, most of them disappear again, heading north. My mother's one of the few permanent residents, but I haven't heard from her for months. She has no phone and no actual address. I'm worried about her. I want someone to drive down there and see if she's all right."

"How often does she usually get in touch?"

"It used to be once a month. She hitches a ride into town and calls from a little café in Niland. Sometimes she calls from Brawley or Westmorland, depending on the ride she manages to pick up. We talk, she buys supplies and then hitchhikes back again."

"She has an income? Social Security?"

Mrs. Gersh shook her head. "Just the checks I send. I don't believe she's ever had a Social Security number. All the years I remember, she supported the two of us with housework, which she did for cash. She's eighty-three now and retired, of course."

"How does mail reach her if she has no address?"

"She has a post office box. Or at least, she did."

"What about the checks? Has she been cashing those?"

"They haven't showed up in my bank statement, so I guess not. That's what made me suspicious to begin with. She has to have money for food and necessities."

"And when did you last hear from her?"

"Christmas. I sent her some money and she called to thank me. Things were fine from what she said, though to tell you the truth, she didn't sound good. She does sometimes drink."

"What about the neighbors? Any way to get through to them?"

She shook her head again. "Nobody has a telephone. You have no idea how crude conditions are out there. These people have to haul their own trash to the city dump. The only thing provided is a school bus for the children and sometimes the townspeople raise a fuss about that."

"What about the local police? Any chance of getting a line on her through them?"

"I've been reluctant to try. My mother is very jealous of her privacy, even a bit eccentric when it comes right down to it. She'd be furious if I contacted the authorities."

"Six months is a long time to let this ride."

Her cheeks tinted slightly. "I'm aware of that, but I kept thinking I'd hear. Frankly, I haven't wanted to brave her wrath. I warn you, she's a horror, especially if she's on a tear. She's very independent."

I thought about the situation, scanning the possibilities. "You mentioned that she has no regular address. How do I find her?"

She reached down and picked up a leather jewelry case she'd tucked under the chaise. She removed a small envelope and a couple of Polaroid snapshots. "This is her last note. And these are some pictures I took last time I was there. This is the trailer where she lives. I'm sorry I don't have a snapshot of her."

I glanced at the pictures, which showed a vintage mobile home painted flat blue. "When was this taken?"

"Three years ago. Shortly before Clyde and I moved up here. I can draw you a map, showing you where the trailer's located. It'll still be there, I guarantee. Once someone at the Slabs squats on a piece of land—even if it's just a ten-by-ten pad of concrete—they don't move. You can't imagine how possessive people get about raw dirt and a few creosote bushes. Her name, by the way, is Agnes Grey."

"You don't have any pictures of her?"

"Actually, I don't, but everyone knows her. I don't think you'll have a problem identifying her if she's there."

"And if I find her? What then?"

"You'll have to let me know what kind of shape she's in. Then we can decide what course of action seems best. I have to say, I chose you because you're a woman. Mother doesn't like men. She doesn't do well among strangers to begin with, but around men she's worse. You'll do it then?"

"I can leave tomorrow if you like."

"Good. I was hoping you'd say that. I'd like some way to reach you beyond business hours," she said. "If Mother should get in touch, I want to be able to call without talking to your machine. An address, too, if you would."

I jotted my home address and phone number on the back of my business card. "I don't give this out often so please be discreet," I said, as I handed it to her.

"Of course. Thank you."

We went through the business arrangements. I'd brought a standard contract and we filled in the blanks by hand. She paid me an advance of five hundred dollars and sketched out a crude diagram of the section of the Slabs where her mother's trailer stood. I hadn't had a missing persons case since the previous June and I was eager to get to work. This felt like a routine matter and I considered the job a nice birthday present for myself.

I left the Gersh house at 12:15, drove straight to the nearest McDonald's, where I treated myself to a celebratory Quarter Pounder with Cheese.

2

By one o'clock I was home again, feeling smug about life. I had a new job, an apartment I was thrilled with . . .

The phone began to ring as I unlocked the door. I snatched up the receiver before my answering machine kicked in.

"Ms. Millhone?" The voice was female and unfamiliar. The hiss in the line suggested the call was long-distance.

"Yes."

"Will you hold for Mr. Galishoff?"

"Sure," I said, instantly curious. Lee Galishoff was an attorney in the public defender's office in Carson City, Nevada, whom I'd worked with some four years back. At the time, he was trying to track a fellow named Tyrone Patty, believed to be in this area. An armed robbery suspect named Joe-Quincey Jackson had been arrested and charged with attempted murder in the shooting of a liquor store clerk. Jackson was claiming that Tyrone Patty was the triggerman. Galishoff was very interested in talking to him. Patty was rumored to have fled to Santa Teresa, and when the local police weren't able to locate him, Galishoff had contacted the investigator for the Santa Teresa public defender's office, who in turn had referred him to me. He filled me in on the situation and then sent me the background information on Patty, along with a mug shot from a previous arrest.

I traced the subject for three days, doing a paper chase through the city directory, the crisscross, marriage licenses, divorce decrees, death certificates, municipal and superior court records, and finally traffic court. I picked up his scent when I came across a jaywalking ticket he'd been issued the week before. The citation listed a local address—some friend of his, as it turned out—and Patty answered my knock. Since I was posing as an Avon sales rep, I was fortunate I didn't have to deal with the lady of the house. Any woman in her right mind would have known at a glance I didn't have a clue about makeup. Patty, operating on other instincts, had shut the door in my face. I reported his whereabouts to Galishoff, who by then had found a witness to corroborate Jackson's claim. A warrant was issued through the Carson City district attorney's office. Patty was arrested two days later and extradited. The last I'd heard, he'd been convicted and was serving time at the Nevada State Prison in Carson City.

Galishoff came on the line. "Hello, Kinsey? Lee Galishoff. I hope I didn't catch you at a bad time." His voice was booming, forcing me to hold the receiver eight inches from my ear. Telephone voices are deceptive. From his manner, I'd always pictured him in his sixties, balding and overweight, but a photograph I'd spotted in a Las Vegas newspaper showed a slim, handsome fellow in his forties with a shock of blond hair.

"This is fine," I said. "How are you?"

"Good until now. Tyrone Patty's back in county jail, awaiting trial on a triple murder charge."

"What's the story this time?"

"He and a pal of his hit a liquor store up here and the clerk and two customers were shot to death."

"Really. I hadn't heard that."

"Well, there's no reason you would. The problem is, he's pissed at us, claims his life was ruined the day he was put away. You know how it goes. Wife divorced him, kids are alienated, the guy gets out and can't find a job. Naturally, he took to armed robbery again, blasting anybody in his way. All our fault, of course."

"Hey, sure. Why not?"

"Yeah, well, here's the bottom line. Apparently, couple weeks ago, he approached another inmate on a contract murder plot involving the two of us, plus the DA and the judge who sentenced him."

I found myself pointing at my chest as I squinted into the receiver. "Us, as in me?" My voice had gotten all squeaky like I was suddenly going through puberty.

"You got it. Fortunately, the other inmate was a police informant who came straight to us. The DA put a couple of undercover cops on it, posing as potential hit men. I just listened to a tape recording that would chill your blood."

"Are you serious?"

"It gets worse," he said. "From the tape, we can't tell who else he might have talked to. We're concerned he's been in touch with other people who may be taking steps we don't know about. We've notified the press, hoping to make this too hot to handle. Judge Jarvison and I are being placed under around-the-clock armed protection, but they thought I better pass the information on to you. You'd be smart to contact the Santa Teresa police to see about protection for yourself."

"God, Lee. I can't imagine they'd provide any, especially on a threat from out of state. They don't have the manpower *or* the budget for that." I'd never actually called the man by his first name before, but I felt a certain privilege, given what I'd just heard. If Patty was the plotter, Galishoff and I were fellow plottees.

"We're actually facing the same situation here," he said. "The sheriff's department can't cover us for long . . . four or five days at best. We'll just have to see how things stand after

15

that. In the meantime, you might want to hire somebody on your own. Temporarily, at any rate "

"A bodyguard?" I said.

"Well, somebody versed in security procedures."

I hesitated. "I'd have to think about that," I said. "I don't mean to sound cheap, but it would cost me a fortune. You really think it's warranted?"

"Let's put it this way—*I* wouldn't chance it, if I were you. He's got six violent priors."

"Oh."

"Oh, indeed. The insulting part is he isn't even paying that much. Five grand for the four of us. That's less than fifteen hundred bucks apiece!" He laughed when he said this, but I didn't think he was amused.

"I can't believe this," I said, still trying to take it in. When you're presented with bad news, there's always this lag time, the brain simply unable to assimilate the facts.

Galishoff was saying, "I do know a guy, if you decide that's what you want. He's a local P.I. with a background in security. At the moment, he's burned out, but I know he's excellent."

"Just what I need, somebody bored with his work."

He laughed again. "Don't let that dissuade you. This guy's good. He lived in California years ago and loves it out there. He might like the change of scene."

"I take it he's available."

"As far as I know. I just talked to him a couple days ago. His name is Robert Dietz."

I felt a little jolt. "Dietz? I know him. I talked to him about a year ago when I was working on a case."

"You have his number?"

"It's around here someplace, but you might as well give it to me again," I said.

He gave me the number and I made a note. I'd only dealt with the man by phone, but he'd been thorough and efficient, and he hadn't charged me a cent. Really, I owed him one. I heard a buzz on Galishoff's end of the phone.

He said, "Hang on a sec." He clicked off, was gone briefly, and then clicked on again. "Sorry to cut it short, but I got a call coming in. Let me know what you decide."

"I'll do that," I said. "And thanks. Keep safe."

"You, too," he said and he was gone.

I set the receiver down, still staring at the phone. A murder contract? How many times had someone tried to kill me in the last year? Well, not *that* many, I thought defensively, but this was something new. Nobody (that I knew of) had ever put out a contract on me. I tried to picture Tyrone Patty chatting up the subject with a hit man in Carson City. Somehow it seemed strange. For one thing, it was hard to imagine the kind of person who made a living that way. Was the work seasonal? Were there any fringe benefits? Was the price discounted since there were four of us to whack? I had to agree with Galishoff—fifteen hundred bucks was bullshit. In the movies, hit men are paid fifty to a hundred thou, possibly because an audience wants to believe human life is worth that. I suppose I should have been flattered I was included in the deal. A public defender, a DA, and a judge? Distinguished company for a small-town private eye like me. I stared at Dietz's number, but I couldn't bring myself to call. Maybe the crisis would pass before I had to take any steps to protect myself. The real question was, would I mention this to Henry Pitts? Naaah. It would just upset him and what was the point?

When the knock at the door came, I jumped like I'd been shot. I didn't exactly flatten myself against the wall, but I exercised a bit of caution when I peered out to see who was there. It was Rosie, who owns the tavern in my neighborhood. She's Hungarian, with a last name I don't pronounce and couldn't spell on a dare. I suppose she's a mother substitute, but only if you favor being browbeaten by a member of your own sex. She was wearing one of her muumuus, this one olive green, printed with islands, palm trees, and parrots in hot pink and chartreuse. She was holding a plate covered with a paper napkin.

When I opened the door, she pushed it toward me without preamble, which has always been her style. Some people call it rude.

"I brought you some strudel for your birthday," she said. "Not apple. It's nut. The best I ever made. You' gonna wish you had more."

"Well, Rosie, how nice!" I lifted a corner of the napkin. The strudel had a nibbled look, but she hadn't snitched very much.

"It looks wonderful," I said.

"It was Klotilde's idea," she said in a fit of candor. Rosie's in her sixties, short, top-heavy, her hair dyed the utterly faux orange-red of new bricks. I'm not certain what product she uses to achieve the effect (probably something she smuggles in from Budapest on her biannual trips home), but it usually renders her scalp a fiery pink along the part. She had pulled the sides back today and affixed them with barrettes, a style much favored in the five-year-old set. I'd spent the last two weeks helping her find a board-and-care facility for her sister Klotilde, who'd recently moved to Santa Teresa from Pittsburgh, where the winters were getting to be too much for her. Rosie doesn't drive and since my apartment is just down the street from her little restaurant, it seemed expedient for me to help her find a place for Klotilde to live. Like Rosie, Klotilde was short and heavyset with an addiction to the same hair dye that tinted Rosie's scalp pink and turned her tresses such a peculiar shade of red. Klotilde was in a wheelchair, suffering from a degenerative disease that left her cranky and impatient, though Rosie swore she'd always been that way. Theirs was a bickering relationship and after an afternoon in their presence, I was cranky and impatient myself. After checking out fifteen or sixteen possibilities, we'd finally found a place that seemed to suit. Klotilde had been settled into a ground-floor room in a former two-family dwelling on the east side of town, so I was now off the hook.

"You want to come in?" I held the door open while Rosie considered the invitation.

She seemed rooted to the spot, rocking slightly on her feet. She becomes coquettish at times, usually when she's suddenly unsure of herself. On her own turf, she's as aggressive as a Canada goose. "You might not want the company," she said, demurely lowering her eyes.

"Oh, come on," I said. "I'd love the company. You have to see the place. Henry did a great job."

She wiggled once and then sidestepped her way into the living room. She seemed to survey the room out of the corner of her eye. "Oh. Very nice."

"I love it. You should see the loft," I said. I set the strudel on the counter and quickly put some water on for tea. I took her through the place, up the spiral steps and down, showing her the trundle bed, the cubbyholes, the pegs for hanging clothes. She made all the proper noises, only chiding me mildly for the meagerness of my wardrobe. She claims I'll never get a beau unless I have more than one dress.

After the tour, we had tea and strudel, working our way through every crispy bite. I cleaned the plate of flaky crumbs with a dampened fingertip. Her discomfort seemed to fall away, though mine increased as the visit went on. I'd known the woman for two years, but with the exception of the last couple of weeks, our entire relationship had been conducted in her restaurant, which she rules like a dominatrix. We didn't have that much to talk about and I found myself manufacturing chitchat, trying to ward off any awkward pauses in the conversation. By the time we finished tea, I was sneaking peeks at my watch.

Rosie fixed me with a look. "What's the matter? You got a date?"

"Well, no. I've got a job. I have to drive down to the desert tomorrow and I need to get to the bank."

She pointed a finger and then poked me on the arm. "Tonight, you come to my place. I'm gonna buy you a glass of schnapps."

We left at the same time. I offered to drop her off, but the tavern's only half a block away and she said she preferred to walk. The last I saw of her the mild spring breezes were billowing through her muumuu. She looked like a hot-air balloon shortly before lift-off.

I headed into town, detouring by way of the automated teller machine at my bank, where I deposited Mrs. Gersh's advance and pulled a hundred bucks in cash. I circled the block and parked my car in the public lot behind my office. I confess this news about a hit man had made me conscious of my backside and I suppressed the urge to zigzag as I went up the outside stairs.

In my office, I picked up my portable typewriter, some files, and my gun, then stopped into the California Fidelity Insurance offices next door. I chatted briefly with Darcy Pascoe, who doubles as the company's secretary and receptionist. She had helped me on a couple of cases and was thinking about changing fields. I thought she'd be a good investigator and I was encouraging her. Being a P.I. beats sitting on your ass at somebody else's front desk.

I moved on to Vera Lipton's cubicle, completing my rounds. Vera's one of those women men are mad about. I swear it's not anything in particular she does. I suppose it's the air of total confidence she exudes. She likes men and they know it, even when she sasses them. She's thirty-seven, single, addicted to cigarettes and Coca-Cola, which she consumes throughout the day. You'd think that would offend the health nuts, but it doesn't seem to cause dismay. She's tall, probably a hundred and forty pounds, a redhead who wears glasses with big round lenses, tinted gray. I know none of this sounds like the girl of your dreams, but there's something about her that's apparently tough to resist. She's not in any way promiscuous, but if she goes to the supermarket, some guy will strike up a conversation with her and end up dating her for months. When the relationship's over, they usually remain such good friends that she'll match him up with someone she knows.

She was not at her desk. I can usually track her by the smell of cigarette smoke, but today I was having trouble picking up the scent. I cleared a chair and sat down, taking a few minutes to flip through a handbook on insurance fraud. Wherever there's money, somebody finds a way to cheat.

"Hello, Kinsey. What are you up to?"

Vera came into the cubicle and tossed a file onto her desk. She was dressed in a denim jumpsuit with shoulder pads and a wide leather belt. She sat down in her swivel chair, reaching automatically into her bottom drawer where she keeps an insulated cold pack filled with Cokes. She took out a fresh bottle and held it up as a way of offering me one.

I shook my head.

She said, "Guess what?"

"I'm afraid to ask."

"Take a look around and tell me what you see."

I love this kind of quiz. It reminds me of that game we used to play at birthday parties in elementary school where somebody's mom would present a tray of odds and ends, which we got to look at for one minute and then recite back from memory. It's the only kind of party game I ever won. I surveyed her desk. Same old mess as far as I could see. Files everywhere, insurance manuals, correspondence piled up. Two empty Coke bottles . . . "No cigarette butts," I said. "Where's the ashtray?"

"I quit."

"I don't believe it. When?"

"Yesterday. I woke up feeling punk, coughing my lungs out. I was out of cigarettes, so there I am on my hands and knees, picking through the trash for a butt big enough to light. Of course I can't find one. I know I'm going to have to throw some clothes on, grab my car keys, and whip down to the corner before I can even have my first Coke. And I thought, to hell with it. I've had it. I'm not going to do this to myself anymore. So I quit. That was thirty-one hours ago."

"Vera, that's great. I'm really proud of you."

"Thanks. It feels good. I keep wishing I could have a cig-arette to celebrate. Stick around. You can watch me hyper-

21

ventilate every seven minutes when the urge comes up. What are you up to?"

"I'm on my way home," I said. "I just stopped by to say hi. I'll be gone tomorrow and we'd talked about having lunch."

"Shoot, too bad. I was looking forward to it. I was going to fix you up."

"Fix me up? Like a blind date?" This news was about as thrilling to me as the notion of periodontal work.

"Don't use that tone, kiddo. This guy's perfect for you."

"I'm afraid to ask you what that means," I said.

"It means he isn't married like *someone* I could name." Her reference was to Jonah Robb, whose on-again, off-again marriage had been a source of conflict. I'd been involved with him intermittently since the previous fall, but the high had long since worn off.

"There's nothing wrong with that relationship," I said.

"Of course there is," she snapped. "He's never there when you need him. He's always off with what's-her-face at some counseling session."

"Well, that's true enough." Jonah and Camilla seemed to move from therapist to therapist, switching every time they got close to a resolution of any kind; "conflict habituated," I think it's called. They'd been together since seventh grade and were apparently addicted to the dark side of love.

"He's never going to leave her," Vera said.

"That's probably true, too, but who gives a shit?"

"You do and you know it."

"No, I don't," I said. "I'll tell you the truth. I really don't have room in my life for much more than I've got. I don't want a big, hot love affair. Jonah's a good friend and he comes through for me often enough . . ."

"Boy, are you out of touch."

"I don't want your rejects, Vera. That's the point."

"This is not a reject. It's more like a referral."

"You want to make a sales pitch? I can tell you want to make a sales pitch. Go ahead. Fill me in. I can hardly wait."

"He's perfect."

" 'Perfect.' Got it," I said, pretending to take notes. "Very nice. What else?"

"Except for one thing."

"Ah."

"I'm being honest about this," she replied righteously. "If he was totally perfect, I'd keep him for myself."

"What's the catch?"

"Don't rush me. I'll get to that. Just let me tell you his good points first."

I glanced at my watch. "You have thirty seconds."

"He's smart. He's funny. He's caring. He's competent . . ."

"What's he do for a living?"

"He's a doctor . . . a family practitioner, but he's not a workaholic. He's really available emotionally. Honest. He's a sweet guy, but he doesn't take any guff."

"Keep talking."

"He's thirty-nine, never married, but definitely interested in commitment. He's physically fit, doesn't smoke or do drugs, but he's not obnoxious about it, you know what I mean? He isn't holier-than-thou."

"Unh-hunh, unh-hunh," I said in a monotone. I made a rolling motion with my hand, meaning get to the point.

"He's good-looking too. I'm serious. Like an eight and a half on a scale of one to ten. He skis, plays tennis, lifts weights . . ."

"He can't get it up," I said.

"He's terrific in bed!"

I started laughing. "What's the deal, Vera? Is he a mouth breather? Does he tell jokes? You know I hate guys who tell jokes."

She shook her head. "He's short."

"How short?"

"Maybe five four and I'm five nine."

I stared at her with disbelief. "So what? You've dated half a dozen guys who were shorter than you."

"Yeah, well secretly, it always bothered me."

I stared at her some more. "You're going to reject this guy because of that?"

Her tone became defiant. "Listen, he's terrific. He's just not right for me. I'm not making a judgment about him. This is just a quirk of mine."

"What's his name?"

"Neil Hess."

I reached down and pulled a scrap of paper from her wastebasket. I took a pen from her desk. "Give me his number."

She blinked at me. "You'll really call him?"

"Hey, I'm only five six. What's a couple of inches between friends?"

She gave me his number and I dutifully made a note, which I tucked in my handbag. "I'll be out of town for a day, but I'll call him when I get back."

"Well, great."

I got up to leave her office and paused at the door. "If I marry this guy, you have to be the flower girl."

3

I bypassed my run the next morning, anxious to hit the road. I left Santa Teresa at 6:00 A.M., my car loaded with a duffel, my portable Smith-Corona, the information about Irene Gersh's mother, my briefcase, miscellaneous junk, and a cooler in which I'd tucked a six-pack of Diet Pepsi, a tuna sandwich, a couple of tangerines, and a Ziploc bag of Henry's chocolate chip cookies.

I took Highway 101 south, following the coastline past Ventura, where the road begins to cut inland. My little VW whined and strained, climbing the Camarillo grade until it reached the crest, coasting down into Thousand Oaks. By the time I reached the San Fernando Valley, it was nearly seven and rush-hour traffic had crammed the road solidly from side to side. Vehicles were changing lanes with a speed and grace that I think of as street surfing, complete with occasional wipeouts. Smog veiled the basin, blocking out the surrounding mountains so completely that unless you knew they were there, you might imagine the land to be flat as a plate.

At North Hollywood, the 134 splits off, heading toward Pasadena, while the 101 cuts south toward downtown L.A.

On a map of the area, the heart of Los Angeles looks like a small hole in the center of a loosely crocheted pink shawl that spreads across Los Angeles County, trailing into Orange County to the south. Converging freeways form a tangle, with high-rise buildings caught in the knot. I've never known anyone who actually had business in downtown Los Angeles. Unless you have a yen to see Union Station, Olvera Street, or skid row, the only reason to venture into the neighborhood around Sixth and Spring is to check out the wholesale gold mart for jewelry or the Cooper Building for name-brand clothing discounted to bargain-basement prices. For the most part, you're better off speeding right on by.

You'll notice that I'm skipping right over the events of Thursday night. I will say that I did, indeed, stop by Rosie's for the drink she'd promised, only to discover that she and Henry had arranged a surprise birthday party for me. It was one of those mortifying moments where the lights come up and everybody jumps out from behind the furniture. I couldn't believe it was happening. Jonah was there, and Vera (the rat—who hadn't breathed a word of it when I'd seen her earlier), Darcy and Mac from CFI, Moza from down the block, some of the regular bar patrons, and a former client or two. I don't know why it seems so embarrassing to admit, but they had a cake and actual presents that I had to open on the spot. I don't like to be surprised. I don't like to be the center of attention. These were all people I care about, but I found it unnerving to be the object of so much goodwill. I suppose I said all the right things. I didn't get drunk and I didn't disgrace myself, but I felt disconnected, like I was having an out-of-body experience. Reflecting on it now in the privacy of my car, I could feel myself smiling. Events like this always seem better to me in retrospect.

The party had broken up at ten. Henry and Jonah walked me home and after Henry excused himself, I showed Jonah the apartment, feeling shy as a bride.

I got the distinct impression he wanted to spend the night, but I couldn't handle it. I'm not sure why—maybe it was my earlier conversation with Vera—but I felt distant and when he moved to kiss me, I found myself easing away.

"What's the matter?"

"Nothing. It's just time for me to be alone."

"Did I do something to piss you off?"

"Hey, no. I promise. I'm exhausted, that's all. The party tonight just about did me in. You know me. I don't do well in situations like that."

He smiled, his teeth flashing white. "You should have seen the look on your face. It was great. I think it's funny to see you caught off-guard." He was leaning against the door, with his hands behind his back, the light from the kitchen painting one side of his face with a warm yellow glow. I found myself taking a mental picture of him: blue eyes, dark hair. He looked tired. Jonah is a Santa Teresa cop who works the missing persons detail, which is how we'd met almost a year ago. I really wasn't sure what I felt for him at this point. He's kind, confused, a good man who wants to do the right thing, whatever that is. I understood his dilemma with his wife and I didn't blame him for his part in it. Of course, he was going to vacillate. He has two young daughters who complicate the matter no end. Camilla had left him twice, taking the girls with her both times. He'd managed to do all right without her, but the first time she crooked her little finger, he'd gone running back. It had been push-pull since then, double messages. In November, she'd decided they should have an "open marriage," which he figured was a euphemism for her screwing around on him. He felt that freed him up to get involved with me, but I was reasonably certain he'd never mentioned it to her. How "open" could this open marriage be? While I didn't want much from the relationship, I found it disquieting that I never knew where I stood. Sometimes he behaved like a family man, taking his girls to the zoo on Sunday afternoons. Sometimes he acted like a bachelor father, doing exactly the same thing. He and his daughters spent a lot of time staring at the monkeys while Camilla did God knows what. For my part, I felt like a peripheral character in a play I wouldn't have *paid* to see. I didn't need the aggravation, to tell you the truth. Still, it's hard to complain when I'd known his marital status from the outset. Hey, no sweat, I'd thought. I'm a big girl. I can handle it. Clearly, I hadn't the slightest idea what I was getting into.

"What's that expression?" he said to me.

I smiled. "That's good night. I'm bushed."

"I'll get out of here then and let you get some sleep. You've got a great place. I'll expect a dinner invitation when you get back."

"Yeah, you know how much I love to cook."

"We'll send out."

"Good plan."

"You call me."

"I'll do that."

Truly, the best moment of the day came when I was finally by myself. I locked the front door and then circled the perimeter, making sure the windows were securely latched. I turned out the lights downstairs and climbed my spiral staircase to the loft above. To celebrate my first night in the apartment, I ran a bath, dumping in some of the bubblebath Darcy had given me for my birthday. It smelled like pine trees and reminded me of janitorial products employed by my grade school. At the age of eight, I'd often wondered what maintenance wizard came up with the notion of throwing sawdust on barf.

I turned the bathroom light off and sat in the steaming tub, looking out the window toward the ocean, which was visible only as a band of black with a wide swath of silver where the moon cut through the dark. The trunks of the sycamores just outside the window were a chalky white, the leaves pale gray, rustling together like paper in the chill spring breeze. It was hard to believe there was somebody out there hired to kill me. I'm well aware that immortality is simply an illusion we carry with us to keep ourselves functional from day to day, but the idea of a murder contract was inconceivable to me.

The bathwater cooled to lukewarm and I let it galumph

away, the sound reminding me of every bath I'd ever taken. At midnight, I slid naked between the brand-new sheets on my brand-new bed, staring up through the skylight. Stars lay on the Plexiglas dome like grains of salt, forming patterns the Greeks had named centuries ago. I could identify the Big Dipper, even the Little Dipper sometimes, but I'd never seen anything that looked even remotely like a bear, a belt, or a scuttling crab. Maybe those guys smoked dope back then, lying on their backs near the Parthenon, pointing at the stars and bullshitting the night away. I wasn't even aware that I had fallen asleep until the alarm jolted me back to reality again.

I focused on the road, glancing down occasionally at the map spread open on the passenger seat. Joshua Tree National Monument and Anza-Borrego Desert State Park were blocked out in dark green, shaped like the pieces of a giant jigsaw puzzle. The national forests were tinted a paler green, while the Mojave itself was a pale beige, mountain ranges shaded in the palest brushstrokes. Much of the desert would never be civilized and that was cheering somehow. While I'm not a big fan of nature, its intractability amuses me no end.

At the San Bernardino/Riverside exit, the arms of the freeway crisscross, sweeping upward, like some vision of the future in a 1950s textbook. Beyond, there is nothing on either side of the road but telephone lines, canyons the color of brown sugar, fences of wire with tumbleweeds blown against them. In the distance, a haze of yellow suggested that the mesquite was in bloom again.

Near Cabazon, I pulled into a rest stop to stretch my legs. There were eight or ten picnic tables in a grassy area shaded by willows and cottonwoods. Rest rooms were housed in a cinderblock structure with an A-line roof. I availed myself of one, air-drying my hands since the paper towels had run out. It was now ten o'clock and I was hungry, so I pulled out my cooler and set it up on a table some ten yards from the parking lot. The virtue of being single is you get to make up all the rules. Dinner at midnight? Why not, it's just you.

Lunch at 10:00 A.M.? Sure, you're the boss. You can eat when you want and call it anything you like. I sat facing the road, munching on a sandwich while I watched cars come and go.

A kid, maybe five, was playing with an assortment of Matchbox trucks on the walkway while his father napped on a bench. Pop had a copy of *Sports Illustrated* open across his face, his big arms bared in a T-shirt with the sleeves torn out. The air was mild and warm, the sky an endless wash of blue.

On the road again, I passed the wind farms, where electricity is generated in acre after acre of turbines, arranged in rows like whirligigs. Today, gusts were light. I could watch the breezes zigzag erratically through the turbines, visible in the whimsical twirling of slender blades, like the propellers on lighter-than-air craft. Maybe, when man is gone, these odd totems will remain, merrily harvesting the elements, converting wind into power to drive ancient machines.

Approaching Palm Springs, the character of the road begins to change again. Billboards advertise fast-food restaurants and gasoline. RV country clubs are heralded as "residential communities for active adults." Behind the low hills, mountains loom, barren except for the boulders bleached by the sun. I passed a trailer park called Vista del Mar Estates, but there was no *mar* in view.

I took Highway 111 south, passing through the towns of Coachella, Thermal, and Mecca. The Salton Sea came into view on my right. For long stretches, there were only the two lanes of asphalt, powdery dirt on either side, the body of water, shimmering gray in the rising desert heat. At intervals, I would pass a citrus grove, an oasis of shade in a valley otherwise drubbed by unrelenting sun.

I drove through Calipatria. Later, I heard area residents refer to a town I thought was called Cow-pat, which I realized, belatedly, was a shortened version of Calipatria. The only landmark of note there is a building downtown with one brick column that looks like it's been chewed on by rats. It's actually earthquake damage left unrepaired, perhaps in an effort to pacify the gods.

Fifteen miles south of Calipatria is Brawley. On the outskirts of town, I spotted a motel with a VACANCY sign. The Vagabond was a two-story L-shaped structure of perhaps forty rooms bracketing an asphalt parking lot. I rented a single and was directed to room 20, at the far end of the walk. I eased my car into the space out in front, where I unloaded the duffel, the typewriter, and the cooler.

The room was serviceable, though it smelled faintly of eau de bug. The carpet was a two-toned green nylon in a shag long enough to mow. The bedspread and matching drapes were a green-and-gold floral print, flowering vines of some kind climbing up parallel trellises. The painting above the double bed showed a moose standing in lakewater up to his knees. The painted mountains were the same shade of green as the rug—just a little decorating hint from those of us in the know. I put a call through to Henry to tell him where I was. Then I dumped my belongings, christened the toilet bowl, and took off again, tracking north as far as the little hamlet of Niland.

I pulled in to what would have passed for a curb had there been a sidewalk in view. I asked a leather-faced rancher in a pair of overalls for directions to the Slabs. He pointed without a word. I took a right turn at the next corner and drove another mile and a half through flat countryside interrupted only by telephone poles and power lines. Occasionally, I crossed an irrigation canal where brown grasses hugged the banks. In the distance, to the right, I caught sight of a hillock of raw dirt, crowned by an outcropping of rock painted with religious sentiments. GOD IS LOVE and REPENT loomed large. Whatever was written under it, I couldn't read. Probably a Bible quote. There was a dilapidated truck parked nearby with a wooden house built on the back, also painted with exhortations of some fundamentalist sort.

I passed what must have served as a guard post when the original military base was still functioning. All that remained was a three-by-three-foot concrete shell, only slightly bigger than a telephone booth. I drove onto the old base. A few

31

hundred yards down the road, a second guardhouse had been painted sky blue. Evergreens were outlined on the face of it, with WELCOME TO painted in black letters on the roof line and SLAB CITY in an arch of black letters on white, with white doves flying in all directions. GOD IS LOVE was lettered in two places, the paint job apparently left over from the sixties when the hippies came through. Nothing in the desert perishes—except the wildlife, of course. The air is so dry that nothing seems to rot, and the heat, while intense through much of the year, preserves more than it destroys. I'd passed abandoned wood cabins that had probably been sitting empty for sixty years.

Here, in the endless stretch of gravel and dirt, I could see numerous vans, a few automobiles, many with doors hanging open to dispel the heat. Trailers, RVs, tents, and pickup trucks with camper shells were set up in makeshift neighborhoods. The wide avenues were defined by clumps of creosote and mesquite. Only one roadway was marked and the sign, propped up against a stone, read 18TH ST.

Along the main road, one of the world's longest flea markets had been laid out. The tables were covered with odds and ends of glass, used clothing, old tires, used car seats, defunct television sets, which were being sold "cheep." A hand-lettered sign announced HOLES DUG & ODD JOBS. There was not a buyer in sight. I didn't even catch sight of any residents. A United States flag flew from a hand-rigged pole and I could see state flags as well, all snapping in a hot wind that whipped up the dust. Here, there were no TV antennas, no fences, no telephone poles, no power lines, no permanent structures of any kind. The whole place had a gypsy air, varicolored awnings offering protection from the midday sun. The silence was broken by an occasional barking dog.

I pulled over to the side of the road and parked my car, getting out. I shaded my eyes and scanned the area. Now that my eyes had adjusted to the harsh light, I could see that there were actually people in view: a couple sitting in the open doorway of their mobile home, a lone man passing from one

32

aisle of vehicles to the next. No one seemed to pay any attention to me. The arrival and departure of strangers was apparently so commonplace that my presence elicited no interest whatever.

About fifty yards away, I spotted a woman sitting in a rectangle of shade formed by a bright red and orange parachute that had been strung up between two campers. She was nursing a baby, her face bent to the sight of the infant. I approached, stopping about fifteen feet away. I wasn't sure what constituted personal turf out here and I didn't want to trespass.

"Hi," I said. "I wonder if you could give me some help."

She looked up at me. She might have been eighteen. Her dark hair was pulled up in a ragged knot on top of her head. She wore shorts and a cotton shirt, unbuttoned down the front. The baby worked with such vigor that I could hear the sucking noise from where I stood. "You lookin' for Eddie?"

I shook my head. "I'm trying to find a woman named Agnes Grey. Do you happen to know her?"

"Nunh-unh. Eddie might. He's been out here a lot longer than me. Is she permanent?"

"I understand she's been out here for years."

"Then you might check at the Christian Center down here on the left. Trailer with a sign out listing all the activities. Lot of people register with them in case of emergency. What'd you want her for?"

"She has a daughter up in Santa Teresa who hasn't heard from her for months. She asked me to find out why her mother hasn't been in touch."

She squinted at me. "You some kind of detective?"

"Well, yeah. More or less. I'm a friend of the family and I was down in this area anyway so I said I'd check it out." I took out the two snapshots Irene Gersh had given me. I moved over and held them out so she could see. "This is her trailer. I don't have a picture of her. She's an old woman, in her eighties."

The girl tilted her head, looking at the photographs. "Oh,

yeah, that one. I know her. I never heard her real name. Everybody calls her Old Mama."

"Can you tell me where to find her?"

"Not really. I can tell you where her trailer's at, but I haven't seen her for a while."

"Do you remember when you saw her last?"

She thought about it briefly, screwing up her face. "I never paid much attention so I can't really say. She goes stumping up and down out here when she needs a ride into town. Everybody's real good about that, if your car's broke or something and you gotta have a lift. She's kinda weird though."

"Like what?"

"Uh, well, you know, she has these spells when she talks to herself. You see people like that jabbering away, making gestures like they're in the middle of an argument. Eddie took her into Brawley couple times and he said she was all right then. Smelled bad, but she wasn't out of her head or anything like that."

"You haven't seen her lately?"

"No, but she's probably still around someplace. I been busy with the baby. You might ask somebody else. I never talked to her myself."

"What about Eddie? When do you expect him back?"

"Not till five, I think he said. If you want to check her trailer, go down this road about a quarter mile? You'll see this old rusted-out Chevy. That's called Rusted-Out Chevy Road. Turn right and drive till you pass these concrete bunker things on the left. They look like U's. I don't know what they are, but her trailer's in the next lot. Just bang on the door loud. I don't think she hears good from what Eddie said."

"Thanks. I'll do that."

"If you don't find her, you can come on back here and wait for him, if you like. He might know more."

I glanced at my watch. It was just 12:25. "I may do that," I said. "Thanks for the help."

4

The trailer on Rusted-Out Chevy Road was a sorry sight, bearing very little resemblance to the snapshot I had in my possession, which showed an old but sturdy-looking travel trailer, painted flat blue, sitting on four blackwall tires. From the picture, I estimated that it was thirty-some years old, built in the days when it might have been hitched to the back of a Buick sedan and hauled halfway across the country. Now, spray paint had been used to emblazon the siding with the sort of words my aunt urged me to hold to a minimum. Some of the louvres on the windows had been broken out and the door was hanging on one hinge. As I drove by, I saw a unisex person, approximately twelve years of age, sitting on the doorsill in ragged cutoffs, hair in dreadlocks, finger up its nose, apparently mining the contents. I passed the place, did a U-turn and doubled back, pulling over to the side of the road in front. By the time I got out, the doorsill was deserted. I knocked on the doorframe.

"Hello?" I sang. Nothing. "Heellloo."

I peered in. The place was empty, at least the portion I could see. The interior, which had probably never been clean, was littered now with trash. Empty bottles and cans were discarded in a heap where a fold-down table should have been. Dust coated most surfaces. The banquette on the right looked like it had been chopped up for firewood. The doors on the kitchen cabinets had all been removed. Cupboards were empty. The tiny four-burner butane-fueled stove looked like it hadn't been used for months.

I glanced to my left, moving down a short passage that led to a small bedroom in the back. A door on the right opened onto a bathroom, which consisted of a defunct chemical toilet, a ragged hole in the wall where a basin had once been attached, and a length of pipe sticking out above a shower pan filled with rags. The bedroom contained a bare mattress and two sleeping bags zipped together and left in a wad. Someone was living here and I didn't think it was Irene Gersh's mom. I peered through the window, but all I saw outside was a buff-colored stretch of desert with a low range of mountains ten or fifteen miles away. Distances are deceptive out here because there aren't any reference points.

I picked my way back to the front door and stepped out, circling the trailer. Around the corner, a bucket lined with a plastic bag served as a makeshift outhouse. There were several bags like it, tied at the top and tossed together in a pile, a black fly manufacturing plant. Across the road, there was a concrete pad where a Winnebago was moored. Beside the RV, there was a pickup truck mounted with a camper shell. The pad itself was cracked, weeds growing up through the crevices. A Weber grill had been set out and the smell of charcoal lighter and smoking briquettes drifted across the road to me. Near the grill, there was a folding table surrounded by mismatched chrome chairs. As I crossed the road, a woman emerged from the trailer carrying a tray loaded with a foil-covered plate, condiments, and utensils. She was in her forties, slim, with a long, weathered face. No makeup, salt-and-pepper hair cropped short. She wore blue jeans and a flannel shirt, both faded to a pale gray. She went about her business, ignoring my approach. I watched her put five fat hamburger patties on the grill. She moved over to the table and began to set it with forks and paper plates.

"Excuse me," I said. "Do you know the woman who lives over there?"

"You related?"

"I'm a friend of the family."

"About time somebody took an interest," she said snappishly. "What's going on over there is a low-down disgrace."

"What *is* going on over there?"

"Kids moved in. You can see they trashed the place. Loud parties, loud arguments, fights breaking out. We all make it a point to mind our own business out here, but there's limits."

"What about Agnes? What happened to her? Surely, she's not still living there."

The woman cocked a head toward the Winnebago. "Marcus? You want to come out here, please? Woman's asking about Old Mama."

The door to the Winnebago opened and a man peered out. He was of medium height, small-boned, with warm skin tones suggesting Mediterranean origins. His hair was dark, combed back from his face. His nose was short and straight, his lips very full. His dark eyes were fringed with black lashes. He looked like a male model in an Italian menswear ad. He stared at me for a moment, his expression neutral.

"Who're you?" he asked. No accent. He wore pleated pants at, l the sort of ribbed undershirt old men wear.

"I'm Kinsey," I said. "Agnes Grey's daughter asked me to drive out here and check on her. Do you have any idea where she is?"

He surprised me by holding out his hand to introduce himself. We shook. His palm was soft and hot, his grip firm.

"I'm Marcus. This is my wife, Faye. We haven't seen Old Mama for a long time. Like, months. We heard she got sick, but I don't know for sure. Hospital in Brawley. You might see if she's there."

"Wouldn't somebody have notified her relatives?"

Marcus stuck his hands in his pockets with a shrug. "She might not've told them. This's the first I knew she had family. She's a real private person. Like a recluse almost. Minds her own business as long as you mind yours. Where's this daughter live?"

"Santa Teresa. She's been worried about Agnes but she didn't have a way to get in touch."

Neither of them seemed impressed with the sincerity of Irene's concern. I changed the subject, looking back at the trailer across the road. "Who's the little gremlin I saw sitting on the front step?"

Faye spoke up, her tone sour. "There's two of them. Boy and a girl. They came by a few months ago and staked the place out. They must have heard it was empty because they moved in pretty quick. Runaways. Don't know how they survive. Probably stealing or whoring, whichever comes first. We asked them to clean up the sewage, but of course they don't."

Clearly, *sewage* was a euphemism for the bags of sewage. "The kid I saw couldn't have been twelve years old," I said.

Faye answered. "They're fifteen. Boy is, at any rate. They act like wild animals and I know they do drugs. They're always picking through our garbage, looking for food. Sometimes, other kids come by and camp out with them. Word must be out they have a place to crash."

"Can't you report 'em to the cops?"

Marcus shook his head. "Tried that. They vamoose the minute anybody shows up."

"Could there be a connection between Agnes's disappearance and their moving in?"

"I doubt it," he said. "She'd been gone a couple months by the time they got here. Somebody might have told them the trailer was empty. They never seemed to worry about her showing up. I know they've torn the place apart, but there's not much we can do."

I gave him my card. "This is my number in Santa Teresa. I'll be down here a couple of days seeing if I can get a line on her. After that, you can reach me at this 805 area code.

Would you give me a call if she gets in touch? I'll try to check back with you before I leave town, in case you've heard from her. Maybe you'll think of something that might be of help."

Faye peered over his shoulder at the card I'd given him. "A private detective? I thought you said you were a family friend."

"A hired friend," I said. I had started back to my car when he called my name. I turned and looked at him.

"There's a sheriff's substation in Niland, right next to the old jail on First. You might check with the deputy. There's always a possibility she's dead."

"Don't think it hasn't occurred to me," I said. His gaze held mine briefly and then I moved on.

I headed back toward the township of Niland, 145 feet below sea level, population twelve hundred. The old jail is a tiny stucco structure with a shake roof and an ornamental iron wheel attached to the wooden porch rail. Next door, not ten feet away, is the new jail, housed in the sheriff's substation, also stucco and not much wider than the width of one door and two windows. An air conditioner hung out of a window around on the side. I parked out in front. A note was taped to the front door. "Back at 4:00 P.M. In emergency or other business talk to Brawley deps." Not a clue about how to contact the Brawley sheriff's department.

I stopped at a gas station and while the tank was being filled, I found a pay phone and checked the dog-eared directory that was chained to the wall, looking up the telephone number of the Brawley sheriff's department. From the address listed, I had to guess it wasn't far from my motel on Main. In a quick call, I learned that Sergeant Pokrass, the deputy I should be talking to, was presently at lunch and would be back at one o'clock. A glance at my watch showed it was 12:50.

The sheriff's substation is a one-story stucco building with a red tile roof, located right across the street from the Brawley Police Department. There were two white sheriff's cars parked in the narrow lot. I went in through a glass door. A

Pepsi machine dominated the corridor. To the left of the entrance was a closed door that, according to the sign, led to a courtroom. On the other side of the hallway were two small offices with an open door between them. The interior was polished brown linoleum, Formica countertops, light wood desks, metal file cabinets, swivel chairs. There were two deputies and a civilian clerk in sight, the latter on the telephone. The low murmur of conversation was underscored by the steady, low ratchet of the police radio.

Deputy Pokrass turned out to be a woman in her thirties, tall and trim, with sandy hair cut short, glasses with tortoiseshell rims. The tan uniform seemed designed for her: all function, no frills. There was very little animation to her face. Her eyes were a penetrating brown, rather cold, and her manner, while not actually rude, was on the abrupt side of businesslike. We didn't waste a lot of time on pleasantries. I stood at the short counter and filled her in on the situation, keeping my account brief and to the point. She listened intently, without comment, and when I finished she picked up the telephone. She called the local hospital, Pioneers Memorial, and asked for the patient billing and accounting department, her voice warming only slightly in her conversation with someone named Letty on the other end. She pulled a yellow legal pad closer and picked up a pencil sharpened to a perfect point. She made a note, her handwriting full of angular downstrokes. I was sure that, even at the age of twelve, she'd never been the type to make a little happy face when she dotted an *i*. She hung up the phone and used a straightedge to tear off the strip of paper on which she'd written an address.

"Agnes Grey was admitted to Pioneers on January 5, through emergency after the paramedics picked her up outside a downtown coffee shop where she collapsed. Diagnosis by the admitting physician was pneumonia, malnutrition, acute dehydration, and dementia. On March 2, she was transferred to Rio Vista Convalescent Hospital. This is the address. If you locate her, let us know. Otherwise you can come back in and fill out a missing persons report. We'll do what we can."

I glanced at the paper, then folded it and put it in my jeans pocket. "I appreciate your help." By the time I got the sentence out, she'd turned away, already back at work on the report she was typing. I used my proffered hand to scratch my nose, feeling the way you do when you wave back at someone who turns out to be waving happily at someone else.

On the way to my car, it occurred to me that the admissions officer at the convalescent home might be reluctant to give me information on Agnes Grey. If she was still a patient, I could probably get a room number and whip right in. If she'd been released, things might get trickier. Medical personnel aren't as chatty as they used to be. Too many lawsuits over the right to privacy. Best not blow my chances, I thought.

I went back to the Vagabond, where I unzipped the duffel and removed my all-purpose dress. I gave it a shake. This faithful garment is the only dress I own, but it goes anyplace. It's black, collarless, with long sleeves and a zipper down the back, made of some slithery, miracle fabric that takes unlimited abuse. You can smush it, wad it up, sit on it, twist it, or roll it in a ball. The instant you release it, the material returns to its original state. I wasn't even sure why I'd brought it— hoping for a hot night on the town, I suppose. I tossed it on the bed, along with my (slightly scuffy) low-heeled black shoes and some black panty hose. I took a three-minute shower and redid myself. Thirteen minutes later I was back in the car, looking like a grown-up, or so I hoped.

The Rio Vista Convalescent Hospital was set in the middle of a residential area, an old two-story stucco building painted a tarnished-looking Navajo white. The property was surrounded by chain-link fence, wide gates standing open onto a parking lot. The place didn't look like any hospital I'd ever seen. The grounds were flat, unlandscaped, largely sealed over in cracked asphalt on which cars were parked. As I approached the main entrance, I could see that the brittle blacktop was limned with faded circles and squares of some

41

obscure sort. It wasn't until I'd passed through the main doors and was standing in the foyer that I knew what I'd been looking at. A playground. This had once been a grade school. The lines had been laid out for foursquare and tetherball. The interior was nearly identical to the elementary school I'd attended. High ceilings, wood floors, the sort of lighting fixtures that look like small perfect moons. Across from me, a water fountain was still mounted on the wall, white porcelain with shiny chrome handles down low at kiddie height. Even the air smelled the same, like vegetable soup. For a moment, the past was palpable, laid over reality like a sheet of cellophane, blocking out everything. I experienced the same rush of anxiety I'd suffered every day of my youth. I hadn't liked school. I'd always been overwhelmed by the dangers I sensed. Grade school was perilous. There were endless performances: tests in spelling, geography, and math, homework assignments, pop quizzes, and workbooks. Every activity was judged and criticized, graded and reviewed. The only subject I liked was music because you could look at the book, though sometimes, of course, you were compelled to stand up and sing all by yourself, which was death. The other kids were even worse than the work itself. I was small for my age, always vulnerable to attack. My classmates were sly and treacherous, given to all sorts of wicked plots they learned from TV. And who would protect me from their villainy? Teachers were no help. If I got upset, they would stoop down to my level and their faces would fill my field of vision like rogue planets about to crash into earth. Looking back on it, I can see how I must have worried them. I was the kind of kid who, for no apparent reason, wept piteously or threw up on myself. On an especially scary day, I sometimes did both. By fifth grade, I was in trouble almost constantly. I wasn't rebellious—I was too timid for that—but I did disobey the rules. After lunch, for instance, I would hide in the girls' rest room instead of going back to class. I longed to be expelled, imagining somehow that I could be free of school forever if they'd just kick me out. All my behavior netted me were trips to the office, or endless hours in a little chair placed in the hall. A public scourging, in effect. My aunt would swoop down on the principal, an avenging angel, raising six kinds of hell that I should be subjected to such abuse. Actually, the first time I got the hall penalty, I was mortified, but after that, I liked it pretty well. It was quiet. I got to be alone. Nobody asked me questions or made me write on the board. Between classes, the other kids hardly looked at me, embarrassed on my behalf.

"Miss?"

I glanced up. A woman in a nurse's uniform was staring at me. I focused on my surroundings. I could see now that the corridor was populated with wheelchairs. Everyone was old and broken and bent. Some stared dully at the floor and some made mewing sounds. One woman repeated endlessly the same quarrelsome request: "Someone let me out of here. Someone let me up. Someone let me out of here . . ."

"I'm looking for Agnes Grey."

"Patient or employee?"

"A patient. At least she was a couple of months back."

"Try administration." She indicated the offices to my right. I collected myself, blanking out the sight of the feeble and infirm. Maybe life is just a straight shot from the horrors of grade school to the horrors of the nursing home.

The administration offices were housed in makeshift quarters where the principal's office had probably been once upon a time. A portion of the large central hallway had been annexed and was now enclosed in glass, providing a small reception area, which was furnished with a wooden bench. I waited at the counter until a woman emerged from the inner office with an armload of files. She caught sight of me and veered in my direction with a public-relations smile. "May I help you?"

"I hope so," I said. "I'm looking for a woman named Agnes Grey. I understand she was a patient here a few months ago."

The woman hesitated briefly and then said, "May I ask what this is in connection with?"

I took a chance on the truth, never guessing how popular I was going to be as a consequence. I gave her my card and then recited my tale of Irene Gersh and how she'd asked me to determine her mother's whereabouts, ending with the oft-repeated query: "Do you happen to know where she is at this point?"

She blinked at me for a moment. Some interior process caused a transformation in her face, but I hadn't the faintest idea how it related to my request. "Would you excuse me, please?"

"Sure."

She moved into the inner office and emerged a moment later with a second woman, who introduced herself as Mrs. Elsie Haynes, administrator of the facility. She was probably in her sixties, rotund, with a hairstyle that was whisker-short along the neck and topped by a toupee of ginger-colored curls. This made her face appear too large for her head. She was, however, smiling at me most pleasantly. "Miss Millhone, how very nice," she said, holding out her hands. The handshake consisted of her making a hand sandwich with my right hand as the lunch meat. "I'm Mrs. Haynes, but you must call me Elsie. Now how can we be of help?"

This was worrisome. I usually don't get such receptions in my line of work. "Nice to meet you," I said. "I'm trying to locate a woman named Agnes Grey. I understand she was transferred here from Pioneers."

"That's correct. Mrs. Grey has been with us since early March. I'm sure you'll want to see her, so I've asked the floor supervisor to join us. She'll take you up to Mrs. Grey's room."

"Great. I'd appreciate that. Frankly, I didn't expect to find her here. I guess I thought she'd be out by now. Is she doing okay?"

"Oh my, yes. She's considerably better . . . quite well . . . but we *have* been concerned about continued care. We can't release a patient who has noplace to go. As nearly as we can tell, Mrs. Grey doesn't have a permanent address and she's never admitted to having any next of kin. We're delighted to hear that she has relatives living in the state. I'm sure you'll want to notify Mrs. Gersh and make arrangements to have her transferred to a comparable facility in Santa Teresa."

Ahh. I felt myself nodding. Her Medi-Cal benefits were running out. I tried a public-relations smile of my own, unwilling to commit Irene Gersh to anything. "I'm not sure what Mrs. Gersh will want to do. I told her I'd call as soon as I found out what was going on. She'll probably need to talk to you before she makes any decisions, but I'm assuming she'll ask me to drive Agnes back to Santa Teresa with me."

She and her assistant exchanged a quick look.

"Is there a problem with that?"

"Well, no," she said. Her gaze shifted to the doorway. "Here's Mrs. Renquist, the ward supervisor. I think she's the person you should properly discuss this with."

We went through another round of introductions and explanations. Mrs. Renquist was perhaps forty-five, thin and tanned, with a wide, good-natured mouth and the dusky, lined complexion of a smoker. Her dark auburn hair was pulled back in a knot shaped like a doughnut, probably supported by one of those squishy nylon devices they sell at Woolworth's. The three women seemed to hover about me like secular nuns, full of murmurs and reassurances. Within minutes, Mrs. Renquist and I were out in the corridor, heading toward the ward.

5

■ 37 ■ ■ 32 ■ ■ 32 ■ I heard Agnes Grey before I ever laid eyes on her. Mrs. Renquist and I had climbed the wide curving stairs to the second floor. We proceeded down the upper hallway without saying much. The character of the grade school was still oddly evident, in spite of the fact that extensive remodeling had been done to accommodate current use. The former classrooms had been quite large, with wide, multipaned windows stretching almost ceiling to floor. Light streamed in through glass embedded with chicken wire. The woodwork had been left in its original state, varnished oak aged to a glossy russet shade. Up here, the worn wood floors had been covered with mottled white vinyl tiles and the once spacious rooms had been partitioned into cubicles, containing two beds each. The walls were painted in shades of pale green and blue. The place was clean, if impersonal, the air perfumed with intimate body functions gone sour. Old people were visible everywhere, in beds, in wheelchairs, on gurneys, huddled on hard wooden benches in the wide corridor; idle, insulated from their surroundings by senses that had shut down over the years. They seemed as motionless as plants, resigned to

infrequent watering. Anyone would wither under such a regimen: no exercise, no air, no sunlight. They had outlived not
only friends and family, but most illnesses, so that at eighty
and ninety, they seemed untouchable, singled out to endure,
without relief, a life that stretched into yawning eternity.

We passed a crafts room where six women sat around a
table, making potholders out of nylon loops woven on red
metal frames. Their efforts were as misshapen as mine had
been when I was five. I never liked doing that shit the first
time around and I didn't look forward to having to do it
again at the end of my days. Maybe I'd get lucky and be
struck down by a beer truck before I was forced into such
ignominy.

The recreation room was evidently just ahead, as I'd picked
up the blast of a television set turned up loud enough for
failing ears, a PBS documentary by the sound of it. The
banging and shrieking suggested tribal rites somewhere in a
culture not given to quietude. We turned left into a six-bed
ward where a series of curtains were all that separated one
patient from the next. At the far end of the room, like the
origins of the Nile, I could see the source of the uproar. It
wasn't a television set at all. Without even asking, I knew this
was Agnes. She was stark naked, dancing a dirty boogie on
the bed while she accompanied herself by banging on a bedpan with a spoon. She was tall and thin, bald everyplace
except her bony head, which was enveloped in an aureole of
wispy white fuzz. Malnutrition had distended her belly, leaving her long limbs skeletal.

The lower portion of her face had collapsed on itself, jaw
drawn up close to her nose in the absence of intervening
teeth. She had no visible lips and the truncated shape of her
skull gave her the look of some long-legged, gangly bird with
a gaping beak. She was squawking like an ostrich, her bright,
black eyes snapping from point to point. The minute she
caught sight of us, she fired the bedpan in our direction like
a heat-seeking missile. She seemed to be having the time of
her life. A nurse's aide, maybe twenty years old, stood by

47

helplessly. Clearly, her training had never prepared her for the likes of this one.

Mrs. Renquist approached Agnes matter-of-factly, pausing only once to pat the hand of the woman in the next bed who seemed to be praying feverishly for Jesus to take her very soon. Meanwhile, Agnes, having asserted herself, was content to march around on the bedcovers saluting the other patients. To me, it looked like a wonderful form of indoor exercise. Her behavior seemed far healthier than the passivity of her wardmates, some of whom simply lay in moaning misery. Agnes had probably been a hell-raiser all her life, and her style, in old age, hadn't changed a whit.

"You have a visitor, Mrs. Grey."

"What?"

"You have a visitor."

Agnes paused, peering at me. Her tongue crept into view and then disappeared again. "Who's this?" Her voice was hoarse from screeching. Mrs. Renquist held out a hand to her, helping Agnes down off the bed. The nurse's aide took a clean gown from the nightstand. Mrs. Renquist shook it out and draped it around Agnes's scrawny shoulders, pushing her arms into the sleeves. Agnes submitted with the complaisance of a baby, her rheumy-eyed attention still focused on me. Her skin was speckled with color: pale brown maculae, patches of rose and white, knotty blue veins, crusty places where healing cuts formed fiery lines of red. The epidermal tissue was so thin I half-expected to see the pale gray shapes of internal organs, like those visible on a newly hatched bird. What is it about aging that takes us right back to birth? She smelled sooty and dense, a combination of dried urine and old gym socks. Right away, I started revising the notion of driving back to Santa Teresa in the same tiny car with her. The aide excused herself with a murmur and made a hasty getaway.

I held out a hand politely. "Hello, Agnes. I'm Kinsey Millhone."

"Hah?"

Mrs. Renquist leaned close to Agnes and hollered my name so loud that two other old ladies on the ward woke up and began to make quacking sounds. *"Kinsey Millhone. She's a friend of your daughter's."*

Agnes drew back, giving me a suspicious look. "Who?"

"Irene," I yelled.

"Who asked you?" Agnes shot back, peevishly. She began to work her lips mechanically, as if tasting something she'd eaten fifty years before.

Mrs. Renquist repeated the information, enunciating with care. I could see Agnes withdraw. A veil of simplicity seemed to cover her bright gaze and she launched abruptly into a dialogue with herself that made no sense whatever. "Keep hush. Do not say a word. Well, I can if I want. No, you can't. Danger, danger, ooo hush, plenty, plenty. Don't even give a *hint* . . ." She began a warbling rendition of "Good Night, Irene."

Mrs. Renquist rolled her eyes and a short, impatient sigh escaped. "She pulls this when she doesn't feel like doing what you want," she said. "She'll snap out of it."

We waited for a moment. Agnes had added gestures and her tone was argumentative. She'd adopted the quarrelsome air of someone in a supermarket express line when the customer at the register tries to cash a paycheck. Whatever universe she'd been transported to, it did not include us.

I drew Mrs. Renquist aside and lowered my voice. "Why don't we leave her alone for the time being," I said. "I'm going to have to put a call through to Mrs. Gersh anyway and ask her what she wants done. There's no point in upsetting her mother any more than we have to."

"Well, it's whatever you want," Mrs. Renquist said. "She's just being ornery. Do you want to use the office phone?"

"I'll call from the motel."

"Be sure we know how to get in touch with you," she said, with a faint note of uneasiness. I could see a hint of panic in her eyes at the notion that I might leave town without making arrangements for Agnes's removal.

"I'll leave the motel number with Mrs. Haynes."

I drove back to the Vagabond, where I put in a call first to Sergeant Pokrass at the sheriff's department, advising her that Agnes Grey had indeed turned up.

Then I placed the call to Irene Gersh and filled her in on her mother's circumstances. My report was greeted with dead silence. I waited, listening to her breathe in my ear.

"I suppose I better talk to Clyde," she said finally. She did not sound happy at having to do this and I could only imagine what Clyde's reaction would be.

"What do you want me to do in the meantime?" I asked.

"Just stay there, if you would. I'll give Clyde a call at the office and get back to you as soon as possible, but it probably won't be till around suppertime. I'd appreciate it if you'd drive back out to the Slabs and put a padlock on Mother's door."

"What good is that going to do?" I said. "The minute I'm gone, the little turds will break in. The louvres in one window are already gone. Frustrate these kids and they'll tear the place apart."

"It sounds like they've already done *that*."

"Well, true, but there's no point making life any more difficult."

"I don't care. I hate the idea of trespassers and I won't abandon the place. She may still have personal belongings on the premises. Besides, she might want to go back when she's feeling like herself again. Did you talk to the sheriff? Surely there's some way to patrol the area."

"I don't see how. You know the situation better than I do. You'd have to have an armed guard to keep squatters out and what's the point? That trailer's already been trashed."

"I want it locked," she said with an unmistakable edge.

"I'll do what I can," I said, making no attempt to disguise my skepticism.

"Thank you."

I gave her the telephone number at the Vagabond and she said she'd get in touch with me later on. I changed back into jeans and tennis shoes, hopped in the car, and headed over to a hardware store where I bought an oversize padlock of cartoon proportions that weighed about three pounds. The clerk assured me it would take a blasting cap to pop it off the hasp. What hasp, I thought? While I was at it, I bought the

whole mechanism—hinged metal fastening and the corresponding staple—along with the tools to install the damn
thing. Nothing was going to keep those kids out. I'd seen at
least two holes punched into the trailer shell. All they'd have
to do was enlarge one and they could crawl in and out like
rats. On the other hand, I was getting paid to do this, so what
did I care? I picked up some nails and a couple of pieces of
scrap lumber and returned to my car.

I drove north on 111, doing the eighteen-mile return trip
to the Slabs. Offhand, I couldn't recall the name of the road
I was looking for so I kept my speed down and spent a lot of
time peering off to my right. I passed a grove of date palms
on my left. Beyond, in the far distance, I could see the vivid
green of fields under cultivation. Somehow the countryside
looked different, but it wasn't until I spotted the sign reading
SALTON SEA RECREATION AREA that I realized how far I'd over-
shot the mark. The road to the Slabs had to be ten miles back.
I spotted a gravel side road ahead on the left and I figured it
was as good a place as any to make the turnaround. An old
high-sided truck was approaching, kicking up a trail of dust
in spite of the fact it was only moving ten miles an hour.

I slowed for the turn, checking my rearview mirror. A red
pickup truck was barreling down on me, but the driver must
have noted my change in speed. He veered right, cutting
around me as I gunned the engine, scooting out of his path.
I heard the faint pop of a rock being crushed under my
wheel, but it wasn't until I'd done the U-turn and was back on
111, that I felt the sudden roughness in the ride. The flap-
flap-flapping sound warned me that one of my back tires was
flat.

"Oh great," I said. Clearly, I'd run over something more
treacherous than a rock. I pulled over to the side of the road
and got out. I circled my car. The rim of my right rear wheel
was resting on the pavement, the tire forming a flabby rubber puddle underneath. It must have been five or six years
since I'd changed a tire, but the principles probably hadn't
changed. Take the jack out of the trunk, crank the sucker till
the weight is lifted off the wheel, remove the hubcap, strug-

gle with the lug nuts, pull the bad wheel off and set it aside while you heft the good one into place. Then replace all the lug nuts and tighten them before you jack the car down again.

I opened my trunk and checked my spare, which was looking a bit soggy in itself. I wrestled it out and bounced it on the pavement. Not wonderful, but I decided it would get me as far as the nearest service station, which I remembered seeing a few miles down the road. This is why I jog and bust my hump lifting weights, so I can cope with life's little inconveniences. At least I wasn't wearing heels and panty hose and I didn't have glossy fingernails to wreck in the process.

Meanwhile, the flatbed had turned out onto the highway and had come to a stop a hundred yards behind me. A dozen male farmworkers hopped off the back of the truck and rearranged themselves. They seemed amused at my predicament and called out suggestions in an alien tongue. I couldn't really translate, but I got the gist. I didn't think they were giving any actual pointers on how to change a flat. They seemed like a good-natured bunch, too weary from the short hoe to do me any harm. I rolled my eyes and waved at them dismissively. This netted me a wolf whistle from a guy grabbing his crotch.

I tuned them out and set to work, cussing like a stevedore as the flatbed pulled away. At times like this, I tend to talk to myself, coaching myself through. It was midafternoon and the sun was beating down on me. The air was dry, the quiet unbroken. I don't know the desert well. To my untutored eye, the landscape seemed unpopulated. At ground level, where I sat wielding my crescent wrench, all I could see was a dead mesquite tree a few feet away. I've been told that if you listen closely, you can hear the clicks of the wood-boring beetles that tunnel through the dead wood to lay their eggs.

I settled down to work, letting the isolation envelop me. Little by little, I became accustomed to the stillness in the same manner that eyes become accustomed to the dark. I picked up the drone of an occasional insect and noticed then the foraging warblers catching bugs on the fly. The true citizens of the Mojave emerge from their lairs by night: rattlesnakes and lizards, jackrabbits, quail, the owl and the Harris hawk, the desert fox and the ground squirrel, all searching for prey, angling to eat each other in a relentless predatory sequence that begins with the termites and ends with the coyote. This is not a place I'd want to unroll my sleeping bag and lay my little head down. The sun spiders alone will scare you out of ten years' growth.

By 3:20, I'd successfully completed the task. I rolled the flat tire around to the front of the car so I could hoist it into my trunk. I could hear a foreign body rattle around inside, a rock or a nail by the sound of it. I checked for the puncture, running my fingers around the circumference of the tire. The hole was in the sidewall—a ragged perforation not quite the size of my little fingertip. I blinked at it, feeling chilled, not wanting to believe my eyes. It looked like a bullet hole. An involuntary sound escaped as I was overtaken by one of those rolling shudders you experienced as a kid on leaving a dark room. I lifted my head. I surveyed the countryside. No one. Nothing. Not another car in sight. I wanted out of there.

I hoisted the tire and shoved it into my trunk. Swiftly, I gathered the jack and my crescent wrench, moved around to the driver's side and got in. I started the engine and rammed into gear, pulling back onto the highway. I drove faster than I should have, given the condition of my spare, but I didn't like the idea of being out there by myself. It had to have been the guy in the pickup truck. He'd passed me just as the blowout occurred. Of course, a rock might have caused the damage, but I couldn't think how it could have penetrated the sidewall, leaving such a nice neat hole in its wake.

The first service station I passed was out of business. The gas pumps were still standing, but the windows were broken and graffiti, in a garland, had been sprayed along the foundation. Local advertisers were using the supporting columns for their poster art and a real estate company announced in bold print that the property could be leased. Fat chance.

53

On the outskirts of Niland, at the intersection of Main Street and the Salton Highway, I found a small station selling one of those peculiar brands of gasoline that make your car engine burp. I put some air in the spare tire and dropped off the flat.

"I've got some business to take care of at the Slabs," I said. "Any way you can do this in the next hour and a half?"

He studied the tire. The look he gave me suggested that he'd come to the same conclusion I had, but he made no comment. He said he'd pull the tire off the rim and have it patched by the time I returned. I was guessing I'd be back by five o'clock. I didn't want to imagine myself out in the desert once the sun went down. I gave him a ten for his trouble and told him I'd pay for the repair when I got back. I hopped in my car and then leaned my head out in his direction. "Where's the road to the Slabs?"

"You're on it," he said.

I took Main to the point where it becomes Beal Road, approaching Slab City this time with a sense of familiarity. I felt safer out here. There seemed to be more people about at this hour: an RV pulling into a site, kids being dropped off in a snub-nosed yellow school bus. Now the dogs were out, leaping joyously at the sight of all the children home from school. When I reached Rusted-Out Chevy Road, I turned right and soon Agnes Grey's blue trailer appeared just ahead. I parked short of the place and pulled my tools out of the backseat. Thoroughly paranoid by now, I took out my little Davis semi-automatic and tucked it into the waistband of my blue jeans at the small of my back. I grabbed an old cotton shirt and pulled it on over my T-shirt, gathered up the lumber, the padlock, and the latch, and approached the trailer on foot.

The gremlins were in residence. I could hear the murmur of their voices. I reached the front door, unable to avoid the gravel crunching underfoot. The voices were silenced instantly. I leaned against the frame, peering in at an angle. For all I knew, I'd get whacked with a two-by-four. Instead, I found myself face-to-face with the dreadlocked creature I'd spied earlier that day. A second scummy face appeared beside the first. I'd been informed by the neighbors that one was the boychick and one was the girl. I was guessing this one to be male, but I truly couldn't discern any sex-based differences. Neither had facial hair. Both were young, with the unformed features of cherubs, tatty mops on top, ragged clothes below. Neither smelled any better than Agnes had.

The boy and I eyed each other and swelled up in the manner of apes. So ludicrous. We were both the same size—five six, neither one of us over a hundred and twenty pounds. Little banty-weight toughs. One possible difference was that I was willing to kick the shit out of him and I didn't think he was prepared to do likewise. With a glance at his companion, he rocked back on his heels, hands in his pockets as if he had all day. He said, "Hey, Poopsie. What the fuck are you doin' here?"

I felt my temper flash. My nerves were already on edge and I didn't need any aggravation from a little punk like him. "I own this place, ass eyes," I said snappishly.

"Oh really? Let's see you prove it."

"No problem, *Poopsie*. I've got the deed of trust." I pulled the gun out of my waistband and held it with the barrel up. It wasn't loaded, but it looked good. If I'd had my old Colt, I could have cocked it for effect. I freely confess—while I can intimidate little boys, I'm not that good with the grown ones. "Get lost," I said.

The two of them fell all over each other trying to scramble out the back. The trailer shook with their trampling feet and then they were gone. I ambled down the passageway and peered into the bathroom. As I suspected, they were using a hole in the wall as an emergency exit.

The first thing I did was board up their escape route, pounding nail after nail into the flimsy bathroom wall. Then I used a handheld drill to set the screw holes for the hasp I was mounting. I can't say I worked with any astonishing skill, but I got the job done and the physical labor improved my mood. It felt good to smash things. It felt good to sweat. It felt good to be in control of one small corner of the universe. As long as I was here, I did a quick search, looking to see if there was anything of Old Mama's left. I couldn't find a thing. The cupboards were bare, closets stripped, the various nooks and crannies emptied of her possessions. Most of them had probably been sold at the flea market on the road coming in.

I went out to the VW and snagged the 35-millimeter camera I keep in the rear well. I had part of a roll of film left and I snapped off as many photos of the place as I could. I didn't think Irene Gersh was going to "get it" otherwise. She had talked as if her mother might retire here in her golden years.

Before I popped the padlock into place, I bundled up the gremlins' sleeping bags and miscellaneous belongings and left them by the front step. Then I went across the road and told Marcus what I'd done. As I returned to the trailer, I spotted a slice of crawl space underneath, makeshift storage, where a few items had been crammed. I got down on my hands and knees, reaching back among the bugs and spiders, and pulled out a couple of dilapidated cardboard boxes. One was open and contained a motley collection of rusted garden tools: trowels, a spade, a short hoe. The second box had the top flaps closed, sections interlocked to secure the contents without anything actually being sealed shut. I pulled the flaps back and checked inside. The box contained numerous pieces of china wrapped in newspaper, a child's tea set. It didn't even look like a full set to me, but I thought Irene or her mother might like to take a look. Certainly, I wasn't eager to leave the dishes for the gremlins to raid. I closed the box up again. I snapped the padlock shut on the trailer door. I had no hope whatever of keeping the little buggers at bay, but I'd tagged the necessary bases. I toted the box to my car and shoved it in the backseat. It was still light when I left the Slabs, but by the time I picked up my tire and headed back into Brawley, it was fully dark.

In my pocket was the .38 slug the mechanic had removed from the tire. I really wasn't sure what it signified, but as I'm keenly aware of the obvious, I had a fair idea.

6

I went back to the Vagabond and got cleaned up. I made a wad of my overshirt and tucked it in the duffel, pulled on a fresh T-shirt and buckled on my shoulder rig. I put my briefcase on the bed beside me while I took out a box of PMC cartridges and loaded my .32, which I tucked snugly under my left arm. A threat on your life is a curious thing. It seems, at the same time, both abstract and absurd. I didn't have any reason to disbelieve the facts. I was on Tyrone Patty's hit list. Some guy in a pickup had shot out my tire on an isolated stretch of road. Now, it could have been a wholly unrelated prank, but I suspect if the flatbed full of farm-workers hadn't pulled up behind me, the guy in the pickup might have circled back and plugged me. God. Saved by a truckload of Mexicans making obscene digital remarks. I might have been abducted or killed outright. Instead, prov-identially, I was still in one piece. What I was having trouble with was figuring out what to do next. I knew better than to go to the local cops. I couldn't tell them the make, the model, or the license number of the truck itself and I hadn't gotten a good look at the driver's face. Under the circumstances, the cops might sympathize, but I didn't see what they could offer in the way of help. Like the Santa Teresa police, they'd be long on concern and short on solutions.

What then? One alternative was to pack my car and head back to Santa Teresa "toot sweet." On the other hand, it didn't seem smart to be out on the road at night, especially in territory like this, where it was possible to drive for ten miles without seeing a light. My friend in the pickup had already tried for me once. Better not offer him a second opportunity. Another possibility was to put a call through to the Nevada private eye and ask for some help. The community of private investigators is actually a small one and we're protective of one another. If anyone could offer me assistance, it would be someone who played the same game I did with the same kind of stakes. While I pride myself on my independence, I'm not a fool and I'm not afraid to ask for backup when the situation calls for it. That's one of the first things you learn as a cop.

In a curious way, this still didn't feel like an emergency. The jeopardy was real, but I couldn't seem to make it connect to my personal safety. I knew in my head the danger was out there, but it didn't feel dangerous—a distinction that might prove deadly if I didn't watch my step. I knew I'd be wise to take the situation seriously, but I couldn't for the life of me work up a sweat. People in the early stages of a terminal illness must react the same way. "You're kidding . . . who, me?"

After the phone call from Irene Gersh, I'd have to come up with a game plan. In the meantime, as I was starving, I decided I might as well grab a bite of supper. I zipped on a windbreaker, effectively concealing the shoulder holster and the gun.

On the far side of the road was a café with a blinking neon sign that said EAT AND GET GAS. Just what I needed. I crossed the highway carefully, looking to both sides like a kid. Every vehicle I saw seemed to be a red pickup truck.

The café was small. The lighting was harsh, but it had a comforting quality. After years of horror movies, I'm inclined to believe bad things only happen in the dark. Silly me. I elected to sit against the rear wall, as far from the plate-glass window as I could get. There were only six other patrons and they all seemed to know one another. Not one of them seemed sinister. I studied a clear plastic menu with a slip-in mimeographed sheet reproduced in a blur of purple ink. The items seemed equally divided between cholesterol and fat. This was my kind of place. I ordered a Deluxe Cheeseburger Platter, which included french fries and a lily pad of lettuce with a slice of gas-ripened tomato laid over it. I had a large Coke and topped it all off with a piece of cherry pie that made me moan aloud. This was the cherry pie of my childhood, tart and gluey with a lattice top crust welded in place with blackened sugar. It looked like it had been baked with an acetylene torch. The meal left me in a chemical stupor. I figured I'd just consumed enough additives and preservatives to extend my life by a couple of years . . . if I didn't get killed first.

On the way back to my room, I stopped by the motel office to see if there were any messages. There were two from the convalescent home and a third from Irene, who had called about ten minutes before. All three were marked URGENT. Oh, boy. I tucked the slips into my pocket and headed out the door. Once out on the walkway, I stopped dead in my tracks, struck by the eerie sensation that I was being watched. A silvery feeling traveled my body from head to toe, as chilling as a trickle of melting snow down the back of my neck. I was acutely aware of the glowing windows behind me. I eased out of range of the exterior lights and paused in the shadows. The parking lot was poorly illuminated and my motel room was at the far end. I listened, but all I could hear were the noises from the highway—the whine of trucks, the sonorous blast from a speeding semi warning vehicles in its path. I wasn't sure what had alerted me, if anything. I peered into the dark, turning my head from side to side, eyes averted as I tried to pinpoint discreet sounds against the obliterating fog of background noise. I waited, heart thumping in my ears. I didn't like what this business was doing to my head. Faintly, I picked up the musical tinkling of a little kid giggling somewhere. The tone was impish. high-pitched, the helpless snuffling of someone being tickled unmercifully. I sank down on my heels beside a wall of thick shrubbery.

A man appeared from the far end of the parking lot, walking toward me through the shadows with a kid perched on his shoulders. He had his arms raised, in part to secure the child, in part to torment him, digging the fingers of one hand into his ribs. The kid clung to the man, laughing, fingers buried in his hair, his body swaying in a tempo with his father's walking pace, like a rider mounted on a camel. The man ducked as the two of them turned into a lighted passageway, an alcove where I'd seen the soft drink and ice machines. A moment later, I heard the familiar clunking sound of a can of soda plummeting down the slot. The two emerged, this time hand in hand, chatting companionably. I let my breath out, watching them round the corner to the exterior stairs. They appeared again on the second floor where they entered the third room from the end. End of episode. I wasn't even aware that I'd taken my gun out, but my jacket was unzipped and it was in my hand. I stood upright, tucking my gun away. My heartbeat slowed and I shook some of the tension out of my arms and legs, like a runner at the end of an arduous race.

I returned to my room along the narrow drive that ran behind the motel. It was very dark, but it felt safer than traversing the open parking lot. I cut around the end of the building and unlocked my door, reaching around to flip the light on before I slipped inside. The room was untouched, everything exactly as I'd left it. I locked the door behind me and closed the drapes. When I sat down beside the bedtable and picked up the telephone, I realized my underarms were damp with sweat, the fear like the aftershock of an earthquake. It took a moment for my hands to quit shaking.

I called Irene first. She picked up instantly, as if she'd been hovering by the telephone. "Oh, Kinsey. Thank God," she said when I identified myself.

"You sound upset. What's going on?"

"I got a call from the convalescent home about an hour ago. I had a long chat with Mrs. Haynes earlier this afternoon and we've made arrangements to have Mother flown up by air ambulance. Clyde has gone to a great deal of trouble to get her into a nursing home up here. Really, it's a lovely place and quite close to us. I thought she'd be thrilled, but when Mrs. Haynes told her about it, she went berserk . . . absolutely out of control. She had to be sedated and even so, she's raising hell. Somebody's got to go over there and get her calmed down. I hope you don't mind."

Hell, I thought. "Well, I don't want to argue, Irene, but I can't believe I'd be of any help. Your mother hasn't the faintest idea who I am and, furthermore, she doesn't care. When she saw me this afternoon, she threw a bedpan across the room."

"I'm sorry. I know it's a nuisance, but I'm at my wit's end. I tried talking to her myself by phone, but she's incoherent. Mrs. Haynes says sometimes the medication has that effect; instead of calming these older patients down, it just seems to rev them up. They have a private-duty nurse driving up from El Centro for the eleven-o'clock shift, but meanwhile, the ward's in an uproar and they're begging for help."

"God. All right. I'll do what I can, but I don't have any training in this kind of thing."

"I understand," she said. "I just don't know who else to ask."

I told her I'd head on over to the hospital and then I hung up. I couldn't believe I'd been roped into this. My presence on a geriatric ward was going to prove about as effective as the padlock on the trailer door. All form, no content. What really bugged me was the suspicion that nobody would have even *suggested* that a boy detective do likewise. I didn't want to see that old lady again. While I admired her spunk, I didn't want to be in *charge* of her. I had my own ass to worry about. Why does everybody assume women are so nurturing? My maternal instincts were extinguished by my Betsy Wetsy doll. Every time she peed in her little flannel didies, I could feel my temper climb. I quit feeding her and that cured it, but it did make me wonder, even at the age of six, how suited I was for motherhood.

It was in this charitable frame of mind that I proceeded to the Rio Vista. I drove with an eye to my rearview mirror to see if anyone was following. I watched for pickup trucks of every color and size. I thought the one I'd seen was a Dodge, but I hadn't been paying close attention at the time and I couldn't have sworn to it.

Nothing untoward occurred. I reached the convalescent hospital, parked my car in a visitors' slot, walked back through the front entrance and headed for the stairs. It was ominously quiet. No telling what Agnes was up to. It was only 8:00 P.M. but the floor lights had already been dimmed and the facility was bathed in the muted rustle and hush of any hospital at night. The old sleep restlessly, pained limbs crying out. Nights must be long, filled with fretful dreams, the fear of death, or, worse perhaps, the certainty of waking to another interminable day. What did they have to hope for? What ambitions could they harbor in this limbo of artificial light? I could sense the hiss of oxygen in the walls, the pall of the pharmaceuticals with which their bodies were infused. Hearts would go on beating, lungs would pump, kidneys filtering all the poisons from the blood. But who would diagnose their feelings of dread, and how would anyone provide relief from the underlying malady, which was despair?

When I reached the ward, I could see that Agnes's bed was the only one with a light. A male aide, a young black, set his magazine aside and tiptoed in my direction with a finger to his lips. We spoke briefly in low tones. The medication had finally kicked in and she was dozing, he said. Now that I was here, he had his regular duties to attend to. If I needed anything, I could find him at the nurses' station down the hall. He moved out of the room.

62

I crossed quietly to the pool of bright light in which Agnes slept. The counterpane on her bed was a heavyweight cotton, harsh white, her thin frame scarcely swelling the flat coverlet. She snored softly. Her eyes seemed to be opened slightly, lids twitching as she tracked some interior event. Her right hand clutched at the sheet, her arthritic knuckles as protuberant as redwood burls. Her chest was flat. Coarse whiskers sprouted from her chin, as if old age were transforming her from one sex to the other. I found myself holding my breath as I watched her, willing her to breathe, wondering if she'd sail away right before my eyes. This afternoon, she'd seemed sassy and energetic. Now, she reminded me of certain old cats I've seen whose bones seem hollow and small, who seem capable of levitating, so close are they to fairylike.

I glanced at the clock. Twelve minutes had passed. When I looked back, her black eyes were pinned on my face with a surprising show of life. There was something startling about her sudden watchfulness, like a visitation from the spirit world.

"Don't make me go," she whispered.

"It won't be so bad. I hear the nursing home is lovely. Really. It'll be much better than this."

Her gaze became intense. "You don't understand. I want to stay here."

"I do understand, Agnes, but it's just not possible. You need help. Irene wants you close so she can take care of you."

She shook her head mournfully. "I'll die. I'll die. It's too dangerous. Help me get away."

I felt the hair stiffen along my scalp. "You'll be fine. Everything's fine," I said. My voice sounded too loud. I lowered my tone, leaning toward her. "You remember Irene?"

She blinked at me and I could have sworn she was debating whether to admit to it or not. She nodded, her voice tremulous. "My little girl," she said. She reached out and I took her shaking hand, which was bony and hot, surprisingly strong.

"I talked to Irene a little while ago," I said. "Clyde's found a place close by. She says it's very nice."

63

She shook her head. Tears had leaped into her eyes and they trickled down her cheeks, following deeply eroded lines in her face. Her mouth began to work, her face filled with a pleading she couldn't seem to articulate.

"Can you tell me what you're afraid of?"

I could see her struggle, and her voice, when it came, was so frail that I had to rise slightly from my chair to catch what she was saying. "Emily died. I tried to warn her. The chimney collapsed in the earthquake. The ground rolled. Oh, I could see . . . it was like waves in the earth. Her head was bashed in by a brick. She wouldn't listen when I told her it was dangerous. Let it be, I said, but she had to have her way. Sell the house, sell the house. She didn't want roots, but that's where she ended up . . . down in the ground."

"When was this?" I asked, trying to keep the conversation afloat.

Agnes shook her head mutely.

"Is that why you're worried? Because of Emily?"

"I heard the niece of the owner of that old house across the street died several years ago. She was a Harpster."

Oh, boy. We were really on a roll here. "She played the harp?" I asked.

She shook her head impatiently. Her voice gathered strength. "Harpster was her maiden name. She was big in the Citizens Bank and never married. Helen was an ex-girlfriend of his. She left because of his temper, but then Sheila came along. She was so young. She had no idea. The other Harpster girl was a dancer and married Arthur James, a professional accordion player who owned a music shop. I knew him because we girls at the Y used to go over to his place and he would play for us after he locked the door," she said. "It's a small world. The girls said their uncle's house was their second home. She might still be there if he left it to her. She'd help."

I watched her carefully, trying to understand what was going on. Was there really something she was too frightened to talk about? "Was Emily the one who married Arthur James?"

"There was always some story . . . always some explanation." She waved a hand vaguely, her tone resigned.

"Was this in Santa Teresa? Maybe I could help you if I understood."

"Santa came over special and gave us all a stockingful of goodies. I let her have mine."

"Who, Emily?"

"Don't talk about Emily. Don't tell. It was the earthquake. Everyone said so." She extracted her hand and a veil of cunning dropped over her eyes. "My arthritis is in my shoulder and knee. My shoulder has been broken two times. The doctor didn't even touch it, just X-rayed. I had two cataract operations at least, but I never had to have a tooth filled. You can see for yourself." She opened her mouth.

Sure enough, no fillings, which is not that big a deal when you have no teeth.

"You look like you're in pretty good shape for someone your age," I said gamely. The subject was careening around like conversational pinball.

"Lottie was the other one. She was a simpleton, but she always had a big smile on her face. She didn't have the brains God gave a billy goat. She'd go out the back door and then she'd forget how to get back in. She'd sit on the porch steps and howl like a pup until someone let her in. Then she'd howl to get back out again. She was the first. She died of influenza. I forget when Mother went. She had that stroke, you know, after Father died. He wanted to keep the house and Emily wouldn't hear of it. I was the last one and I didn't argue. I wasn't really sure until Sheila and then I knew. That's when I left."

I said, "Unh-hunh," and then tried another tack. "Is it the trip that worries you?"

She shook her head. "The smell when it's damp," she said. "Never seemed to bother anyone else."

"Would you prefer to have Irene fly down and travel back with you?"

"I worked cleaning houses. That's how I supported Irene

all those years. I watched Tilda and I knew how it was done. Of course, she was dismissed. He saw to that. No financial records. No banks. She was the only casualty. It was the only time her name was ever in the papers."

"Whose name?"

"You know," she said. Her look now was secretive.

"Emily?" I asked.

"Time wounds all heels, you know."

"Is this your father you're talking about?"

"Oh dear, no. He was long gone. It would be in the footing if you knew where to look."

"What footing?"

Her face went blank. "Are you talking to me?"

"Well, yes," I said. "We've been talking about Emily, the one who died when the chimney fell."

She made a motion as if to lock her lips and throw away the key. "I did it all to save her. My lips are sealed. For Irene's sake."

"Why is that, Agnes? What is it you're not supposed to tell?"

She focused a quizzical look on me. I was suddenly aware that the real Agnes Grey was in the room with me. She sounded perfectly rational. "Well, I'm sure you're very nice, dear, but I don't know who you are."

"I'm Kinsey," I said. "I'm a friend of your daughter's. She was worried when she didn't hear from you and she asked me to come down and find out what was going on."

I could see her expression shift and off she went again. "Well, no one knew that. No one even guessed."

"Uh, Agnes? Do you have any idea where you are?"

"No. Do you?"

I laughed. I couldn't help myself. After a moment, she began to laugh, too, the sound as delicate as a cat sneezing. Next thing I knew, she'd drifted off to sleep again.

7

I did not sleep well. I found myself thinking about Agnes, whose fears were contagious and seemed to set off worries of my own. The reality of the death threat had finally filtered down into my psyche, where it was beginning to accumulate an energy of its own. I was sensitive to every noise, to changes in room temperature as the night wore on, to shifting patterns of light on venetian blinds. At 1:00 A.M., a car pulled into a parking slot near my room and I found myself instantly on my feet, peering through the slats as a couple emerged from a late-model Cadillac. Even in heavy shadow, I could tell they were drunk, clinging to one another in a hip-grinding embrace. I moved away from the window, my senses heightened by anxiety as the two of them fumbled their way into the room next to mine. Surely, if they were killers they wouldn't postpone my demise for the noisy grappling that started up the minute the bolt shot home. The bedframe began to thump relentlessly against the adjoining wall like a kid drumming his heels. There were occasional lulls while the woman offered up suggestions to her hapless companion. "Hop on up here like a puppy dog," she would say. Or "Get that old bald-headed thing over here."

On my side of the wall, the picture of the moose would start to rattle out another little tap dance. I had to reach up and hold it, lest the frame jounce right off the hook and smack me in the face. She was a screamer, sounding more like a woman in labor than one in love. The tempo picked up. Finally, she uttered a little yelp of astonishment, but I couldn't tell if she came or fell off the bed. After a moment, the smell of cigarette smoke wafted through the walls and I could hear their murmured postmortem. Twelve minutes later, they were at it again. I got up and took the picture off the wall, stuffed a sock in each cup of my bra and tied it across my head like earmuffs, with the ends knotted under my chin. Didn't help much. I lay there, a cone over each ear like an alien, wondering at the peculiarities of human sex practices. I would have much to report when I returned to my planet.

At 4:45, I gave up any hope of getting back to sleep. I took a shower and washed my hair, returning to the room wrapped in a motel towel the size of a place mat. As I pulled on my clothes, she was beginning to yodel and he was yipping like a fox. I had never heard so many variations on the word *oh*. I locked the door behind me and headed out across the parking lot on foot.

The smell of desert air was intense: sweet and cold. The sky was still an inky black with strands of dark red cutting through the low clouds at the horizon. I was nearly giddy from lack of sleep, but I felt no sense of endangerment. If someone were waiting in the bushes with an Uzi, I would leave this world in a state of sublime innocence.

The lights in the café were just blinking on, vibrant green neon spelling out the word CAFE in one convoluted loop, like a squeeze of tooth gel. I could see a waitress in a pale pink uniform scratch at her backside at the height of a yawn. The highway was empty and I crossed at a casual pace. I needed coffee, bacon, pancakes, juice, and I wasn't sure what else, but something reminiscent of childhood. I sat at the far end of the counter, my back against the wall, still mindful of the plate-glass window and the gray wash of dawn light outside. The waitress, whose name turned out to be Frances, was probably my age, with a country accent and a long tale to tell about some guy named Arliss who was systematically unfaithful, most recently with her girlfriend, Charlene.

"He has really tore himself with me this time," she said, as she plunked down a bowl of steaming oatmeal in front of me.

By the time I finished eating, I knew everything there was to know about Arliss and she knew a lot about Jonah Robb.

"If it was me, I'd hang on to him," she said, "but now not at the expense of meeting this doctor fella your friend Vera wants to fix you up with. I'd jump right on that. He sounds just real cute to me, though personally I've made it a practice not to date a man knows more about my insides than I do. I went out with this doctor once? Actually he's a medical student, if the truth be known. First time we kissed, he told me the name of some condition arises when you get a pubic hair caught down in your throat. Tacky? Lord God. What kind of person did he think I was?" She leaned on the counter idly swiping it with a damp rag so she'd look like she was busy if the boss stopped in.

"I never heard of a doctor dating a private eye, have you?" I said.

"Honey, I don't even know any private eyes, except you. Maybe he's tired of nurses and lab technicians and lady lawyers and like that. He's been dating Vera, hasn't he? And what is she, some kind of *insurance* adjuster . . ."

"Claims manager," I said. "Her boss got fired."

"But that's my point. I bet they never sat around having long heart-to-heart chats about medical malpractice, for God's sake. He's bored with that. He's looking for someone new and fresh. And think of it this way, he probably doesn't have any communicable diseases."

"Well, now there's a recommendation," I said.

"You better believe it. In this day and age? I'd insist on a blood test before the first lip lock."

The front door opened and a couple of customers came in. "Take my word for it," she said, as she moved away. "This guy could be it. You could be Mrs. Doctor Somebody-or-other by the end of the year."

I paid my check, bought a newspaper from the vending machine out front, and went back to my room. All was quiet next door. I propped myself up in bed and read the *Brawley News,* including a long article about "palm gardens," which I learned was the proper term for the groves of date palms strung out on both sides of the Salton Sea. The trees, exotic transplants brought in from North Africa a century ago, transpire as much as five hundred quarts of water a day and have to be pollinated by hand. The varieties of dates—the Zahid, the Barhi, the Kasib, the Deglet Noor, and the Medjool—all sounded like parts of the brain most affected by stroke.

As soon as it seemed civilized, I called the convalescent hospital and talked to Mrs. Haynes about Agnes Grey. Apparently, she'd been as docile as a lamb for the remainder of the night. Arrangements for her transport to Santa Teresa by air ambulance had been finalized and she was taking it in stride. She claimed she couldn't even remember what had so upset her the day before.

After I hung up, I put a call through to Irene and passed the information on to her. Agnes's outburst still felt unsettling to me, but I didn't see what purpose my apprehension might serve.

"Oh, Mother's just like that," Irene said when I voiced my concern. "If she's not raising hell, she feels she's somehow remiss."

"Well, I thought you should know how fearful she was. She sure raised the hair on the back of my neck."

"She'll be fine now. Don't be concerned. You've done a wonderful job."

"Thanks," I said. As there didn't seem to be any reason to

remain in the area, I told her I'd be taking off shortly and would give her a call as soon as I got back to town.

I packed my duffel, gathered up my briefcase, the portable typewriter, and miscellaneous belongings, and locked everything in the car while I went up to the front office to settle my bill.

When I returned, the lovers were just emerging from the room next door. They were both in their fifties, a hundred pounds overweight, dressed in matching western-cut shirts and oversize blue jeans. They were discussing interest rates on short-term Treasury securities. The slogan painted on the Cadillac's rear window read: JUST MERGED. I watched them cross the parking lot, arms around each other's waists, or at least as far as they would go. While the car warmed up, I pulled my little .32 out of the briefcase where I'd tucked it the night before and transferred it to my handbag on the passenger seat.

I cut over to Westmorland, taking 86 north. I drove the first ten miles with a constant check on the rearview mirror. The day was sunny and the number of cars on the road was reassuring, though traffic began to thin some by the time I reached Salton City. I fiddled with the car radio, trying to find a station with more to offer than static or the price of soybeans, alfalfa, and sugar beets. I caught a flash of the Beatles and focused briefly on the radio while I did some fine-tuning.

It was when I glanced up again, with an automatic reference to the traffic behind me, that I spotted the red Dodge pickup bearing down on me. He couldn't have been more than fifty yards back, probably driving eighty miles an hour to my fifty-five. I uttered a bark of surprise, jamming my foot down on the accelerator in a futile attempt to get out of his path. The engine nearly stalled out with the unexpected surge, shuddering a hop, skip, and a jump before it leaped ahead. The front grill of the pickup appeared at my rear window, completely filling the glass. It was clear the guy meant to crawl right up my tailpipe, crushing me in the process. I jerked the steering wheel to the right, but not fast enough. The Dodge caught my rear fender with a smashing blow, spinning me in a half circle that left me facing south instead of north. I slammed on the brakes and the VW skittered along the shoulder, throwing up a spray of gravel. My handbag seemed to leap into my lap of its own accord. The engine died. I turned the key in the ignition and willed the car to start. Dimly, I registered the now empty highway. No help in sight. Where had everybody gone? Just up ahead on my left, a soft-packed dirt road followed the curve of an irrigation canal that bordered a fallow field, but there was no ranch house visible and no signs of life.

Behind me, the Dodge had made a U-turn and was now accelerating as it headed straight at me again. I ground at the starter, nearly singing with fear, a terrified eye glued to my rearview mirror where I could see the pickup accumulating speed. The Dodge plowed into me, this time with an impact that propelled the VW forward ten yards with an ear-splitting *BAM*. My forehead hit the windshield with a force that nearly knocked me out. The safety glass was splintered into a pattern of fine cracks like a coating of frost. The seat snapped in two and the sudden liberation from my seat belt slung me forward into the steering wheel. The only thing that saved me from a half-rack of cracked ribs was the purse in my lap, which acted like an air bag, cushioning the blow.

The other driver threw the pickup into reverse, then punched on the gas. The truck lurched back, then forward, ramming into me like a bumper car. I felt the VW leave the ground in a short flight that ended in the irrigation ditch, plumes of runoff water splatting out in all directions. I narrowly avoided biting my tongue in half as I bounced against the headliner and then off the dashboard. I put a hand on my mouth and checked my teeth automatically, making sure I hadn't lost any. The car seemed to float briefly before it settled against the muddy bottom. The runoff water in the ditch was only three feet deep, but both doors had popped open and silty water flooded in.

On the shoulder of the road, my assailant got out of the pickup and moved around to the rear, a tire iron in his right hand. Maybe he thought a death by bludgeoning was more consistent with a car wreck than a bullet in the brain. He was a big man, white, wearing sunglasses and a baseball cap. Mewing in panic, I fumbled in my handbag for my gun and rolled out of the VW. I crouched, shielded by the car as I jacked a shell into the chamber. I propped the barrel of the gun on the roof and steadied the sites with both hands.

Miraculously, I saw the guy toss the tire iron in the bed of the pickup as he slid back under the steering wheel and slammed the door. The window was rolled up on the passenger side, where a sheet of paper had been affixed. Like an eye test, I made out the top line of print which read AS IS, with several lines of print below; the temporary sticker from a used car lot. I thought I saw a face peering out at me briefly as the engine roared to life and the truck peeled out. I felt a jolt of recognition, which I didn't have time to process. The pain descended and I felt the blackness close in, narrowing my vision to a long, dark barrel with a glinting bull's-eye of daylight at the far end. I took a deep breath to clear my head and looked up in time to catch one last glimpse of the pickup as it headed north toward Mecca. The license plate had been caked with mud. No numbers were visible.

Two cars went by on the road, heading south. The driver in the second car, a vintage Ford sedan, seemed to do a double take, catching sight of the VW, which sat in the canal partially submerged. He braked to a stop and began to back up, transmission whining in reverse. The adrenaline surging through my system crested like a wave and I began to shake. It was over. I found myself weeping audibly, from pain, from fear, from relief.

"Need some help?" The old man had angled his car onto the shoulder of the road and rolled his window down. Dimly, I realized he was probably obscuring any tire tracks left by the Dodge, but the gravel shoulder seemed too hard-packed to take a print. To hell with it. I was safe and that's all I cared about. I shoved the gun in my bag and staggered to my feet, wading across the canal toward the road. I scrambled up the embankment, tennis shoes slipping in the mud. As I approached the sedan, the old man studied the knot on my forehead, my disheveled hair, my blood-streaked face, my blue jeans sopping wet. I wiped my nose on my sleeve, registering the streak of blood that I'd mistaken for tears. I swayed on my feet. I could feel the goose egg protruding from the middle of my forehead like I was suddenly sprouting a horn. Pain thundered in my head, and for the first time, nausea stirred. I crossed to his car, watching his concern mount when he saw how shaky I was. "Sister, you're a mess."

"Is there any way you can get the highway patrol out here? Somebody just ran me off the road."

"Well, sure. But don't you want a lift somewhere first? You look like you could use some medical attention. I just live up the road a piece."

"I'm fine. I just need a tow truck . . ."

"Young lady, you listen here. I'll give the sheriff a call and get a tow truck out, too, but I'm not going to leave you standin' here by the road."

"I don't want to leave my car."

"That car's not going to budge and I'm not either unless you do as I say."

I hesitated. The VW was totaled. The entire back end appeared foreshortened, the right rear fender crushed. The car had been suffering from countless dings and dents anyway, the beige paint oxidized to a chalky hue, highlighted with rust. I'd had the car nearly fifteen years. With a pang of regret, I turned back to the sedan, hobbling around to the passenger side. I felt like I was leaving a much-loved pet behind. I'd apparently banged my left leg from the knee right up my thigh and it was already stiffening up. When I finally dared to pull my jeans down, I was going to find a bruise the size and color of an eggplant. The old man leaned across and opened the door for me.

"I'm Carl LaRue," he said.

"Kinsey Millhone," I replied. I slid in, slouching down on the base of my spine so I could rest my head against the seat. Once I closed my eyes, the nausea subsided somewhat.

The sedan eased out into the highway again, heading south about a quarter of a mile before we made a left turn onto a secondary road. I sincerely hoped this was not part of some elaborate ruse, the old man in cahoots with the guy in the pickup truck. I flashed on the AS IS sticker in the window, the glimpse I'd had of someone peering out at me. Gingerly, I sat up, remembering where I'd seen the face. It was at the rest stop where I'd eaten lunch on the way down to the desert. There'd been a kid there, a boy maybe five, playing with a Matchbox toy. His father had been napping with a magazine laid across his face . . . a white guy, with big arms, in a T-shirt with the sleeves ripped out. Once I made the connection, I knew I'd actually seen them twice. The same man had crossed the darkened motel parking lot with the kid perched up on his shoulders as they headed for the Coke machine. I felt a chill ripple through me at the recollection of how he'd tickled the kid. What sang in my memory was the peal of impish laughter, which seemed now as dainty and evil as a demon's. What kind of hit man would bring his kid along?

8

▶▶ ▶▶ ▶▶ While Mr. LaRue put a call through to the
county sheriff's department, I found myself folding up like a
jackknife on the lumpy couch in his living room, overwhelmed by sleepiness. My head was pounding. My neck was
stiff from whiplash, my rib cage bruised. I felt cold and little,
as I had just after the accident in which my parents were
killed. In a singsong voice, inexplicably, my brain began feeding back to me the text I'd read in the morning paper. "Palms
grow to 70 feet and can produce 300 pounds of dates. A
mature palm will grow 15 to 18 bunches of dates. Each cluster, when the fruit has reached the size of a pea, must be
protected with brown paper covers to ward off birds and
rain. . . ." What I couldn't remember anymore was where I
was or why I hurt so bad.

Carl was shaking me persistently. He'd apparently placed a
call to the hospital emergency room and had been told to
bring me in. His wife, whose name kept slipping away, had
soaked a washcloth in ice water so she could dab the dirt and
crusted blood off my face. My feet had been elevated and I'd
been wrapped in a down comforter. At their urging, I roused

myself and shuffled out to the car again, still wrapped in the puffy quilt like a bipedal worm.

By the time we reached the emergency room, I had come out of my stupor sufficiently to identify myself and make the correct answers to "How many fingers am I holding up?" and similar neurological pop quizzes I took while lying flat on my back. The ceiling was beige, the cabinets royal blue. Portable X-ray equipment was wheeled in. They X-rayed my neck first, two views, to make sure it wasn't broken, and then did a skull series, which apparently showed no fractures.

I was allowed to sit up then while a young doctor peered at me eye to eye, our breaths intermingling with a curious intimacy as he checked my corneal reflexes, pupil size, and reaction to light. He might have been thirty, brown curly hair receding from a forehead creased with fine horizontal lines. Under his white jacket, he wore a buff-colored dress shirt and a tie with brown dots. His aftershave lotion smelled of newly cut grass, though his electric mower had missed a couple of hairs just under his chin. I wondered if he realized I was noting his vital signs while he was noting mine. My blood pressure was 110 over 60, my temperature, pulse, and respirations normal. I know because I peeked every time he jotted anything down. In a box at the bottom of the page, he scrawled the words "postconcussional syndrome." I was happy to realize the accident hadn't impaired my ability to read upside down. Various forms of first aid were administered and most of them hurt, including a tetanus shot that nearly made me pass out.

"I think we should keep you overnight," he said. "It doesn't look like you sustained any major damage, but your head took quite a bump. I'd be happier if we could keep an eye on you for the next twelve hours, at any rate. Anybody you want notified?"

"Not really," I murmured. I was too battered to protest and too scared to face the outside world anyway. He moved out to the nurses' station, which I could see through an interior window shuttered for privacy by partially closed rust-red venetian blinds. In the corridor, a sheriff's deputy had appeared. I could see horizontal slats of him chatting with the young female clerk who pointed over her shoulder to the room where I sat. The other cubicles in the emergency room were empty, the area quiet. The deputy conferred with the doctor, who evidently decided I was fit enough to answer questions about how my car came to be sitting in an irrigation ditch.

The deputy's name was Richie Windsor, one of those baby-faced cops with an uptilted nose and plump cheeks reddened by sunburn. He had to be a rookie, barely twenty-one, the minimum age for a sheriff's deputy. His eyes were hazel, his hair light brown and cut in a flattop. He hadn't been at it long enough to adopt the noncommittal, paranoid expression that most cops assume. I described the incident methodically, sparing no details, while he took notes, interjecting occasional enthusiastic comments in a borrowed Mexican accent. "Whoa!" he would say, or "Get real, kemosabe!" He seemed nearly envious that someone had tried to kill me.

When I finished my recital, he said he'd have the dispatcher broadcast a "be on the lookout" in case the Dodge was still somewhere in the area. We both knew the chances of intercepting the man were slim. If the guy was smart, he'd abandon the vehicle at the first opportunity. As the deputy turned to leave, I found myself snagging impulsively at his uniform sleeve.

"One thing," I said. "The doctor wants me here overnight. Is there any way we can keep my admission under wraps? This is the only hospital in the area. All the guy has to do is call Patient Information and he'll know exactly where I am."

"Good point, *amigo*. Let me see what I can do," he said. He tucked his pen away.

Within minutes, the admissions office had sent a young female clerk over with a wheelchair, a clipboard full of forms to be completed, and a patient identification strip in a cloudy plastic band, which she affixed to my wrist with a device that looked like a hole punch.

Carl LaRue and his wife had been sitting patiently in the corridor all this time. They were finally ushered in to see me while last-minute arrangements were being made for a bed. The deputy had apparently cautioned the old couple about the situation.

"Your whereabouts is safe with us," Carl said. "We won't say a word."

His wife patted my hand. "We don't want you to worry now. You just get you some rest."

"I appreciate everything you've done," I said. "Really. I can't thank you enough. I'd probably be dead if you hadn't come along."

Carl shifted uncomfortably. "Well, now. I don't know about that. I'm happy to be of help. We got kids of our own and we'd want somebody helping them under similar circumstances."

His wife tucked her arm in his. "We best get a move on. They'll want to put you to bed."

As soon as they departed, I was whisked up to the second floor by freight elevator to a private room, probably on the contagious-disease ward where no visitors were allowed. It was only three in the afternoon and the day looked like it'd be a long one. I didn't get zip for painkillers because of the head injury, and I wasn't allowed to sleep lest I slip into some coma from which I might never wake. My vital signs were checked every hour. The meal carts were long gone, but a kindly nurse's aide found me a cup of muscular cherry Jell-O and a packet of saltines. I pictured the ward clerk filling out a charge slip for twenty-six dollars. I could probably hold my hospital bill down to seven or eight hundred bucks, but only if I didn't need a Band-Aid or a safety pin. I had insurance, of course, but it offended me to be charged the equivalent of the down payment on a car.

My eye lighted on the telephone. There was a telephone book in the bottom of the nightstand. I looked up the area code for Carson City, Nevada (702 all locations, in case you really want to know), dialed Information, and got the listing for Decker/Dietz Investigations, which I dialed in turn. The phone rang five times. I half-expected a service to pick up or a machine to kick in, but someone picked up abruptly on the sixth ring, sounding brusque and out of sorts. "Yes?"

"May I speak to Robert Dietz?"

"I'm Dietz. What can I do for you?"

"I'm not sure if you remember me," I said. "My name is Kinsey Millhone. I'm a friend of Lee Galishoff's and he suggested I get in touch. I called you about a year ago from Santa Teresa. You helped me locate a woman named Sharon Napier . . ."

"Right, right. I remember now. Lee said you might call."

"Yeah, well it looks like I'm going to need some help. I'm in Brawley, California, at the moment in a hospital bed. Some guy ran me off the road—"

He cut in. "How bad are you hurt?"

"I'm okay, I guess. Cuts and bruises, but no broken bones. They're just keeping me for observation. The car was totaled, but a passing motorist came along before the guy could finish me off—"

Dietz broke in again. "Where's Brawley? Refresh my memory."

"South of the Salton Sea, about ninety minutes east of San Diego."

"I'll come down."

I squinted, unable to repress a note of surprise. "You will?"

"Just tell me how to find you. I have a friend with a plane. He can fly me into San Diego. I'll rent a car at the airport and be there by midnight."

"Well, God, that's great. I mean, I appreciate your efficiency, but tomorrow morning's fine. They're probably not going to let me out before nine A.M."

"You haven't heard about the judge," he said flatly.

"The judge?"

"Jarvison. They got him. First name on the list. He was gunned down this morning in the driveway of his house."

"I thought he had police protection."

"He did. From what I understand, he was supposed to be sequestered with the other two but he wanted to be at home. His wife just had a baby and he didn't want her left alone."

"Where was this, in Carson City?"

"Tahoe, fourteen miles away."

Jesus, I thought, it must have happened just about the same time the guy here was after me. "How many people did Tyrone Patty hire?"

"More than one from the sound of it."

"How's Lee doing? Is he okay?"

"Don't know. I haven't talked to him. I'm sure security on him is tight."

"What about the killer? Did he get away?"

"She. Woman posing as a meter reader in a little truck across the street."

I could feel outrage flash through me like a fever. "Dietz, I hate this. What the hell is going on? The guy who tried to kill me brought his *kid* along." I took a few minutes then to fill in the details. He listened intently, asking questions now and then to clarify a point. When I finished, a short gap in the conversation suggested he had paused to light a cigarette. "You have a gun?" he asked. I could almost smell the smoke drifting through the line.

"In my handbag. A little thirty-two. It's not much of a weapon, but I can hit where I aim."

"They let you keep that?" he said with disbelief.

"Hey, sure. Why not? When you check into a hospital, you get quizzed about meds. Nobody thinks to ask about your personal firearms."

"Who knows you're there?"

"I'm not sure. It's a small town. I asked the deputy to keep it quiet, but word gets around. Actually, I was feeling secure until I talked to you."

"Good. Stay nervous. I'll get there when I can."

"How will you find me? They're not going to let you roam around up here in the dead of night."

"Don't worry about it. I got ways," he said.

"How will I know it's you and not another one of Tyrone Patty's little friends?"

"Pick a code word."

"Dill pickle."

He laughed. "What's that supposed to mean?"

"Nothing. That just popped into my head."

"Dill pickle. Around midnight. Be careful with yourself."

After I hung up, I eased out of bed and crept out to the nurses' station, clutching my hospital gown shut with one hand behind my back. Three nurses, a ward clerk, and an aide sat behind the counter. All five looked up at me, eyes straying then to a spot just behind me. I turned. The rookie deputy was sitting on a bench against the wall. Sheepishly, he lifted a hand, a blush creeping up his face.

"You caught me. I'm burnt," he said. "I thought maybe somebody oughta keep an eye on you in case this dude comes back. I hope you don't mind."

"Are you kidding? Not at all. I appreciate your concern."

"This's my girlfriend, Joy . . ."

The nurse's aide flashed a smile at me and I was introduced to the other four women in turn. "We've alerted security," one of the nurses said. "If you want, you can get some sleep now."

"Thanks. I could use some. There's a private eye named Robert Dietz, who said he'd be here later on. Let me know when he gets here and make sure he's alone." I told them the code word and his estimated time of arrival.

"What's he look like?"

"I don't know. I never met the man."

"Don't worry about it. We'll take care of it," Richie said.

I slept until dinnertime, sat up long enough to eat a plate of hospital food concealed under an aluminum hubcap. My vital signs were checked and I slept again until 11:15 that night. At intervals, I was aware of someone taking my pulse, fingers cool as an angel's pressed against my wrist. By the time I woke, someone had retrieved some of my belongings from the car. The portable typewriter and my duffel were tucked against the wall. I clenched my teeth and slid out of bed. When I bent over to unzip the duffel, my head pounded like a hangover. I pulled out fresh jeans and a turtleneck and laid them on the bed. The drawer in my bedtable held soap, toothbrush, toothpaste, and a small plastic bottle of Lubriderm. I went into the bathroom and brushed my teeth, grateful that all of them were present and accounted for. I took a long, hot bath in a tub with handholds affixed to the wall at every conceivable point. I needed them. Getting in and out of the bathtub only made me aware of multi-hurt places distributed randomly all up and down my bod.

While I dried myself off, I checked myself in the mirror, disheartened by the sight. In addition to the bruise on my forehead, my eyes were now dark along the orbital ridge and streaked with red underneath, perfect for Halloween only six months away. My left knee was purple, my torso sooty-looking with bruises. Combing my hair made me wince, sucking air through my teeth. I moved into the other room and took my time getting dressed, resting between articles of clothing. The process was exhausting, but I plugged on doggedly. Whatever damage I'd sustained in the accident was taking its toll.

I stretched out on the bed again with a glance at the clock. Midnight straight up. I figured Dietz would arrive any minute now. Somehow I assumed he'd want to hit the road right away, which suited me fine. If I'd suffered a concussion, it must have been mild. I wasn't even sure I'd lost consciousness and I wasn't aware of any post-trauma amnesia—though, of course, if I'd forgotten something that thoroughly, how would I really know? My head still hurt, but so what? That might go on for weeks and in the meantime, I wanted out. I wanted someone in charge—preferably someone with a big gun and no hesitation about using it. I noticed I was skipping right past the notion of Judge Jarvison.

The next thing I was aware of was the soft pinging of the hospital paging system and the rattle of the breakfast carts out in the corridor. It was morning and some female was addressing me. It took me a minute to remember where I was.

"Miss Millhone? Time to take your temperature . . ." I automatically opened my mouth and she slipped a cold, wet thermometer under my tongue. I could taste lab alcohol that hadn't been rinsed off properly. She took my blood pressure, holding my right arm against her body while she secured the Velcro cuff. She placed the silver dollar of the stethoscope against the crook of my arm and began to pump the cuff. I opened my eyes. She was not one I'd seen before: a slender Chicana with bright red lipstick on a plump mouth, her long brown hair pulled up in a ponytail. Her eyes were pinned to the gauge as the needle descended counterclockwise. I assumed my blood pressure was normal, as she didn't gasp aloud. It would help if they'd tell you things about yourself now and then.

I turned my head toward the window and saw a man leaning against the wall, arms folded across his chest. Dietz. Late forties. Five ten, maybe 170, in jeans, cowboy boots, and a tweed sport coat with a blue toothbrush protruding from the breast pocket like a ballpoint pen. He was clean-shaven, his hair medium length and showing gray around the ears. He was watching me with expressionless gray eyes. "I'm Dietz." Husky voice in the middle range.

With a ripping sound, the aide removed the blood-pressure cuff and made a note in my chart. With my free hand, I took the thermometer out of my mouth. "What time'd you get in?"

"One fifteen. You were out like a light so I let you sleep."

The aide took the thermometer and studied it with a frown. "You didn't keep this in long enough."

"I don't have a fever. I was in an accident," I said.

"The charge nurse is gonna fuss at me if I don't get a temp."

I tucked the thermometer in the corner of my mouth like a cigarette, talking to Dietz while it bobbled between my lips. "Did you get any sleep?"

"In this place?"

"As soon as the doctor comes, we can get the hell out of here," I said. "The guy with the kid was in the same motel. I think we ought to go back and see what we can find out from the desk clerk. Maybe we can pick up the license number of his truck."

"Sir, I'm gonna have to ask you to wait in the hall."

"They found the truck. I called the county sheriff from a pay phone when I got in. The vehicle was abandoned outside San Bernardino. They'll go over it for prints, but he's probably too smart for that."

"What about the local car lots?"

"We can try it, but I think you're going to find out the truck's a dead end."

The aide was getting restless. "Sir . . ."

He flicked a look at her. I started to object, but Dietz pushed away from the wall at that point. "I'll go down to the lounge and grab a cigarette," he said.

By 10:35, he was helping me ease my battered bones into the passenger seat of a bright red Porsche. I watched him move around the front of the car and slide in on the driver's side.

"You rented this?"

"It's mine. I drove down. I didn't want to wait for my buddy with the plane. He couldn't leave soon enough."

I snapped on the seat belt and settled into the low, black leather seat. He fired the engine up with a rumble and pulled out of the parking lot, adjusting the air conditioner. The compact interior of the car smelled of leather and cigarette smoke. With the tinted windows rolled up against the desert heat, I felt insulated from the harsh realities of the spare countryside.

"Where we headed?"

"The body shop where your car was towed."

"Will it be open on Sunday?"

"Now it is."

"How'd you manage that?"

"I called the emergency number. The guy's meeting us there."

86

We headed into Brawley to an auto body shop that was housed in a converted gas station just off the main street. My VW was parked in a side lot, surrounded by chain-link fence. As we pulled into the service area, the owner emerged from the office with a set of keys in hand. He unlocked the padlock on the chain-link fence and rolled the gate back. Dietz pulled into the lot and parked the car, placing a restraining hand on my arm as I moved to open the door.

"Wait till I come around," he said. From his tone, I didn't think good manners were at stake. I did as I was told, watching the way he positioned himself as he opened the car door for me, shielding my exit. The owner of the station didn't seem to notice anything unusual in the interaction between us. Dietz handed him a folded bill, but I couldn't see what denomination it was. Large enough, apparently, that the man had agreed to meet us here on a day when the place was ordinarily closed.

We circled my car, surveying the damage. There was scarcely a spot on it that wasn't affected in some way.

"Looks like she got banged up pretty good," the owner said to Dietz. I didn't know if he was referring to me or the vehicle. I wrenched open the buckled door on the passenger side and emptied the glove compartment, tucking the registration in my purse, tossing out the collection of ancient gasoline receipts. I still had some personal belongings in the backseat: law books, a few hand tools, my camera equipment, odds and ends of clothing, a pair of shoes. Many items had tumbled onto the floor in the course of the attack and were now sodden with the muddy water from the ditch. I checked the much-abused box of old china and was gratified to find that nothing had been broken. I loaded what I could into the trunk of Dietz's Porsche. What I didn't immediately toss, I packed in a large cardboard box that the shop owner obligingly rustled up out of the shop. I tucked the box of dishes into the larger box. I wrote a check for the towing, arranging at the same time to have everything shipped to me in Santa Teresa. I'd file a claim with my insurance company as soon as I got back, though I couldn't believe the car would net me much.

Ten minutes later, we were heading north on 86. As soon as we were under way, Dietz put a cigarette between his lips and flicked open a Zippo. He hesitated, glancing over at me. "My smoking going to bother you?"

I thought about being polite, but it didn't make much sense. What's communication for if it isn't to convey the truth? "Probably," I said.

He lowered the window on his side and tossed the lighter out, flipped the cigarette out after it, and followed both with the pack of Winstons from his shirt pocket.

I stared at him, laughing uncomfortably. "What are you *doing*?"

"I quit smoking."

"Just like that?"

He said, "I can do anything."

It sounded like bragging, but I could tell he was serious. We drove ten miles before either of us said another word. As we approached Salton City, I asked him to slow down. I wanted him to see the place where the guy in the Dodge had caught up with me. We didn't stop—there wasn't any point— but I didn't feel I could pass the spot without some reference to the event.

At Indio, we pulled into the parking lot of a small strip shopping mall where a Mexican restaurant was tucked between a VCR repair shop and a veterinarian.

"I hope you're hungry," Dietz said. "I don't want to stop once we hit the outskirts of Los Angeles. Sunday traffic is the pits."

"This is fine," I said. The truth was I felt tense and needed the break. Dietz handled the car well, but he drove aggressively, impatient every time he found himself behind another vehicle. The highway was only two lanes wide and his passing style had me clinging to the chicken stick. His attention was constantly focused on the road ahead and behind, watching (I surmised) for suspicious vehicles. He kept the radio off and the dead quiet in the car was broken only by the thump of his fingers tapping out a beat on the steering wheel. He had the kind of energy that set me on edge. It might not have been objectionable in the open air, but in the confines of the car, I felt crowded to the point of claustrophobia. The idea of having him at my side twenty-four hours a day for any length of time at all was worrisome.

We pushed through glass doors into a long, blank rectangular space that had evidently been designed for retail sales. A clumsy partition separated the kitchen from the dining area where a few tables had been arranged. Through the doorway, I could see a stove and battered refrigerator that might have come from a garage sale. Dietz told me to wait while he strolled through to the rear, where he checked the back door. The place was chilly and echoed when we scraped back our chairs to sit down. Dietz angled himself so he could keep an eye on the car through the plate-glass windows in the front.

Someone peered out of the kitchen at us with uncertainty. Maybe they thought we were from the health department inspecting for rat turds. There was some sort of whispered consultation and then a waitress appeared. She was short and heavyset, a middle-aged Mexican in a white wraparound apron decorated with stains. Shyly, she tried out her language skills. My Spanish is limited to (approximately) three words, but I could swear she offered to serve us squirrel soup. Dietz kept squinting and shaking his head. Finally, the two of them rattled at each other in Spanish for a while. He didn't seem fluent, but he managed to make himself understood.

I studied him casually while he fumbled with his vocabulary. He had a battered look, his nose slightly flattened, with a knot at the bridge. Mouth wide and straight, turning lopsided when he smiled. His teeth were good, but my guess was that some of them weren't his. Looked too even to me and the color was too white. He turned back to me.

"The place just opened yesterday. She recommends the menudo or the combination plate."

I leaned toward him, avoiding her bright gaze. "I don't eat menudo. It's made with tripe. Have you ever seen that stuff?

It's white and spongy-looking . . . all these perforations and bumps. It's probably some internal organ human beings don't even have."

"She'll have the combination plate," he said to her blandly. He held up two fingers, ordering one for himself.

She shuffled away in huaraches that she wore with white socks. She returned moments later with a tray that held glasses, two beers, a small dish of salsa, and a basket of tortilla chips still sizzling with lard.

We snacked on chips and salsa while we waited for our lunch.

"How do you know Lee Galishoff?" I asked. The beer bottle had a little piece of lime resting on the top and I squeezed some in. Both of us ignored the glasses, which were still hot from a recent washing.

Dietz reached for his cigarettes before he remembered that he'd thrown them out. He caught himself and smiled, shaking his head. "I did some work for him, hunting down a witness on one of his first trials. After that, we started playing racquetball and became good friends. What about you?"

I told him briefly the circumstances through which I'd ended up tracking Tyrone Patty for him. "I take it you've done security work before."

He nodded. "It's a lucrative sideline, especially in this day and age. Tends to limit your personal life, but at least it's relief from straight private-eye work, which is a yawn, as you know. Last week I sat for six hours looking at microfiche in the tax assessor's office. I can't stand that stuff."

"Lee told me you were feeling burned out."

"Not burned out. I'm bored. I've been doing it for ten years and it's time to move on."

"To what?" I asked. The beer was very cold and made a nice contrast to the fiery salsa, which was making my nose run. I kept dabbing surreptitiously with a paper napkin, looking like a junkie in need of a fix.

"Don't know yet," he said. "I got into the business in the first place by default. Started out doing repos, serving papers, stuff like that for a guy who eventually took me into his agency. Ray hated doing fieldwork—too rough for his taste— so he did all the paperwork and I dealt with the deadbeats. He was the cerebral type, really had it up here." He tapped his temple.

"You're using past tense. What happened to him?"

"He dropped dead of a heart attack ten months ago. The guy jogged, worked out lifting weights. He married this gal, gave up alcohol and cigarettes, gave up dope, gave up staying out all night. Bought a house, had a baby, happy as a pig eating shit, and then he died. Forty-six. A month ago, his widow started talking like she expected me to step in and fill the gap. It's bullshit. No thanks. I had her cash me out."

"You've lived in California?"

He gestured dismissively. "I've lived everywhere. I was born in a van on the outskirts of Detroit. My mother was in labor and the old man didn't want to stop. I got hauled all over hell and gone as a kid. Pop worked the oil rigs so we spent a lot of time in L.A. . . . this was in the late forties, early fifties when the big boom was on. Texas, Oklahoma. It was dangerous damn work, but the money was good. Pop was a brawler and a bully, very protective of me as long as I was tough myself. He was the kind of guy who'd get in a bar fight and tear the place apart . . . just for the hell of it. If he had a clash with the boss or decided he didn't like what was going on, we'd pack up and hit the road."

"How'd you manage to go to school?"

"I didn't if I could help it. I hated school. I couldn't see the point. To me, it all looked like preparation for something I didn't want to do anyway. I was never going to work in a feed store so why did I have to know how many bushels in a peck? Is that an issue that comes up for you? Two trains leaving different cities at sixty miles an hour? I couldn't sit still for junk like that. Nowadays they call kids like me hyperactive. All those rules and regulations, just for the sake of it. I couldn't stand it. I never did graduate. I ended up with an equivalency degree. Took some kind of written test that I aced without ever cracking a book. The system's not designed for transients. I liked phys ed and shop, woodworking, auto mechanics . . . stuff like that. But nothing academic. Doesn't make any sense unless you start at the beginning and work straight through. I always showed up in the middle and had to leave before the end. Story of my life."

Lunch arrived and we paused to study our food, trying to figure out what it was. Rice and a puddle of refrieds, something folded with cheese leaking out, something flat. I recognized a tamale because it was wrapped in a corn husk. This was real basic fare—no parsley, no orange slice twisted open and resting on the top. My plate was so hot, I could have used it to iron a shirt. The cook appeared from the kitchen shyly bearing a stack of steaming flour tortillas wrapped in a cloth. The two hospital meals had left my taste buds craving astonishment. I wolfed the food, slowing only long enough to suck down another cold beer. Everything was excellent, the sort of flavors that make you whimper. I reached the finish line slightly in advance of Dietz and wiped my mouth on a paper napkin. "What about your mother? Where was she all this time?"

He shrugged, mouth full, waiting till he could speak. "She was there. My granny, too. The four of us traveled in an old station wagon with our gear shoved in the back. Everything I know my mom or my granny taught me in a moving vehicle. Geography, geology. We'd buy these old textbooks and work our way through. Usually, they'd be drinking beers and cutting up, laughing like lunatics. I thought that was neat and learning was a hoot. Put me in a classroom, I withered from the quiet."

I smiled. "You were probably the kind of kid I was afraid of in school. Boys mystified me. I never understood where they were coming from. When I was in fifth grade, we used to give these plays every Friday afternoon. Improvisational stuff we'd rehearse in the cloak room. The girls would always do love stories full of tragedy and self-sacrifice. The boys had sword fights . . . lots of mouth noises and bumping. They'd stagger against the wall and then fall down dead. I couldn't figure out why that was fun. I didn't much like what the girls did, but at least people weren't getting stabbed with imaginary rapiers."

He smiled. "Were you raised in Santa Teresa?"

"I've lived there all my life."

He shook his head in mock amazement. "I couldn't even list all the places I've been."

"Were you in the service?"

"I was spared that, thank God. I was too young for Korea and too old for Vietnam. I'm not sure I could have passed the physical in any event. I had rheumatic fever as a kid . . ."

The waitress returned and started clearing our plates.

"Can you tell me where the ladies' room is?" I said to her.

"*Gracias,*" she said, smiling at me happily while she loaded the tray.

"*El cuarto de damas?*" Dietz supplied.

"Oh *sí, sí!*" She laughed at herself when she understood her mistake. She gestured toward the kitchen. I pushed back my chair. Dietz made a move as though to accompany me, but I stopped him. "God, Dietz. There are limits here, you know?"

He let it pass, but I noticed that he watched me carefully as I moved toward the back door. The *damas* did their business in a mop closet in the rear. While I was washing my hands afterward, I caught sight of myself in a shard of mirror that was propped up on the sink. I looked worse than I had the night before. My forehead was black and blue, my eye sockets smudged now with lavender. The red streaks beneath my eyes made it look like I had conjunctivitis. The dry desert climate had affected my hair, causing it to look like something I'd swept up from under the bed. I couldn't believe I'd been out in public without having people shriek and point. My head was starting to pound again.

By the time I reached the table, Dietz had paid the bill. "You okay?" he asked.

"You don't happen to have any pain pills, do you?"

"I have some Darvocet in the car."

He bought a can of Coke and we took it with us when we left. I watched him scan the parking lot as he unlocked the car. He opened the door for me, waiting until I was safely tucked in before he moved around to the driver's side. Once in his seat belt, he searched the glove compartment for the vial of pills.

"Let me know if this doesn't do the job. I've got prescriptions for everything." He checked a label or two, found what he was looking for, and shook a pill out onto his palm. I murmured a thank-you. He popped the can of Coke open for me and I washed the medication down. Within minutes, the pain began to recede. Shortly after that, I fell asleep.

I woke as we crossed the Ventura County line. I could smell the ocean before I even opened my eyes. The air was moist and briny, the surrounding countryside lush with green, a peculiar juxtaposition of junipers and palms. After the lean monotony of the desert, the coastal vegetation seemed lavish and strange. I could feel every cell in my body respond, drinking in the damp. Dietz glanced over at me. "Better?"

"Much." I sat up and ran my hands through my hair, scratching at the flattened strands. The medication had erased the pain, but I was feeling slightly out of it. I leaned my head back again and slouched down on my tail bone. "How's the traffic been?"

"We're through the worst of it."

"If I don't get a shower soon, I'll have to kill myself."

"Twenty-five miles to go."

"No sign of a tail?"

His gaze crept up to the rearview mirror. "Why follow us? He probably knows where you live."

"A happy thought," I said. "How long is this whole thing likely to go on?"

"Hard to say. Until he gives up or gets caught."

"And who's doing that?"

He smiled. "Not me. My job's to look after you, not catch bad guys. Let's leave that to the cops."

"And what's my responsibility in all of this?"

"We'll talk about that in the morning. Most of what I want is 'obedience without whining.' Very few women master it."

"You don't know me very well."

He peered over at my face. "I don't know you at all."

"Well, here's a hint," I said dryly. "I was raised by my mother's sister. My folks were killed in an accident and I went to live with her when I was five. This is the first thing she ever said to me . . . 'Rule number one, Kinsey . . . rule number one . . .'—and here she pointed her finger right up in my face—'No sniveling.' "

"Jesus."

I smiled. "It wasn't so bad. I'm only slightly warped. Besides, I got even. She died ten years ago and I sniveled for months. It all came pouring out. I'd been a cop for two years and I gave that up. Turned in my uniform, turned in my nightstick . . ."

"Symbolic gesture," he interjected.

I laughed. "Right. Six months later, I was married to a bum."

"At least the story has a happy ending. No babies?"

I shook my head. "Not a one."

"With me, it's just the opposite. I never had a wife, but I've got two kids."

"How'd you manage that?"

"I lived with a woman who refused to marry me. She swore I'd leave her in the end and sure enough that's what I did."

I stared at him for a while, but he subsided into silence. Soon afterward, the outskirts of Santa Teresa began to speed into view and I felt an absurd rush of joy at the notion of home.

10

We found a parking spot for the Porsche two doors down from my place and unloaded the trunk. By the time we pushed through the gate and rounded the corner to the rear, Henry had emerged from his back door to welcome me home. He stopped in his tracks, his smile faltering as his eyes shifted from my face to Dietz's. I introduced the two of them and they shook hands. Belatedly, I remembered what my battered visage must look like.

"I was in an accident," I said. "A guy ran me off the road. I had to leave the car in Brawley and Dietz gave me a ride back."

Henry was visibly dismayed, especially as he was in possession of only half the tale. "Well, who was the fellow? I don't understand. Didn't you file a report with the police down there?"

I hesitated, uncertain how much detail to get into at this point. Dietz settled the matter for me. "Let's go inside and we'll fill you in on the rest of it." He was clearly uneasy about standing around in the open air, exposed to view.

I unlocked the door and pushed it open, moving into the

apartment with Henry behind me and Dietz at the rear, herding us like a sheepdog.

"I'll just be a second. I want to get things squared away," I said to Henry. And then to Dietz, "Henry designed the place. It was just finished two days ago. I've spent exactly one night here."

I set my duffel down and cranked open a window to let in some fresh air. The apartment still smelled of sawdust and new carpeting. The space felt like a Barbie-doll penthouse in its own carrying case: scaled-down furniture, built-ins, spiral staircase, the loft visible above.

"I brought your mail in," Henry said, his eyes on my guest. He sat down on the couch, perplexed at the liberties Dietz seemed to take. The contrast between the two men was interesting. Henry was tall and lean, the blue eyes in his narrow, tanned face giving him the look of an ascetic; someone otherworldly, aged and wise. Dietz was compact, more muscular, a pit bull of a man with a thick chest and a brazen manner, his face marked by life, as if he'd had lessons hammered into him since birth. Henry had a stillness about him where Dietz was restless and energetic, the air around him charged with a curious tension.

Dietz circled the place without comment, automatically checking security, such as it was. I had latches on the windows, but not much else. He pulled the shutters closed, checked closets, peered into the downstairs bath. He snapped his fingers, idly popping them against his palms in a gesture that suggested some inner agitation. His manner was authoritative and Henry shot a look at me to see how I was taking it. I made one of those faces that said, Your guess is as good as mine, pal. It's not like I enjoyed someone taking over like this, but I wasn't fool enough to protest with my life on the line.

I turned my attention to the mail. Most of it looked like junk, but before I could sort it properly Dietz removed the stack from my hands and set it on the counter.

"Let it be till I can take a look at it," he said.

Henry couldn't stand it. "What's going on here? I don't understand what this is about."

"Someone's been hired to kill her," Dietz said unceremoniously. I don't think I would have been so blunt, but Henry didn't fall backward on the couch in a faint so maybe he's not as easily upset as I assume. Dietz filled in the picture, laying out the circumstances by which the Carson City DA's office had first gotten wind of Tyrone Patty's assassination plot. "The police in Carson City are doing what they can to control the situation up there. Obviously, Kinsey's position is a little bit more perilous . . ."

"Why's she here at all?" Henry burst out. "Why not take her someplace out of town?"

"I was out of town," I said, "and what good did it do? Three people knew where I was going and the guy was right there. Hell, he even managed to get there before I did at the first rest stop on the road." I told him briefly about spotting my assailant at the rest area near Cabazon.

"There has to be someplace," Henry said stubbornly.

"Frankly, I think we're better off right here as long as we take a few elementary precautions," Dietz said. "I've got a portable alarm system with me . . . receiver, siren, 'panic button' for her in case someone tries to break in and I'm not actually on the premises. If it seems useful, we can wire in pressure mats for selected doorways, both here and at your place. I want us all to keep an eye out for strangers. And that includes the mailman, gas man, delivery people, meter readers . . . anyone." He turned to look at me. "We'll vary your schedule as much as possible. Take a different route to and from the office every day. I'll be with you for the most part, but I want you to understand the basic strategy. Stay away from public places and public events. By the same token, I don't want you anyplace isolated or remote."

"What about jogging, or going to the gym?"

"Stow that for now. Any guy with a canvas bag could probably walk into the gym."

"Should I have a gun?" Henry asked, moving right into cops-and-robbers mode.

"Henry, you hate guns!"

"It may come to that, but I doubt it," Dietz said to Henry, ignoring me completely. "We're looking at prevention. With luck, we won't have anybody to shoot at."

"Hey. Excuse me. Do you guys mind if I voice an opinion?" Dietz turned to me.

I said, "If the guy in the truck wants to kill me, he'll kill me. I'm willing to be careful, but let's don't go nuts here."

Dietz shook his head. "I disagree. He'll do it if you're foolish and give him the chance, but he's not getting paid enough to stick his neck out."

I turned to Henry, filling him in. "He's a cut-rate killer. Fifteen hundred bucks."

Dietz amplified. "For that kind of money, he's not going to hang around for long. If he's quick about it, it may be worth it to him. Otherwise forget it. It's not cost-effective."

"Yeah," I said. "We don't want him to get chewed out by his accountant."

Dietz said, "Listen. The guy's trying to make a buck. Every day he's in Santa Teresa, it's costing him something. Food, lodging, gasoline. If he has a kid with him, the expenses mount up." He was rattling his car keys. "I'm going over to the police station and have a chat with the cops. You have any plans for tonight?"

I started to answer when I realized he was talking to Henry. I raised my hand like a schoolkid. "I don't mean to be argumentative, but could I have a vote?" I hated being so obnoxious, but this was driving me nuts. These guys were riding right over me.

Dietz smiled at me briefly. "Sorry. You're right. I have a tendency to overorganize."

I murmured something, backing down of course. The truth was I didn't have any idea what to do. I just didn't want to be pushed around.

Dietz put his keys in his pocket. "What about groceries? Let me know what we need and I can stop by a supermarket on my way back."

I didn't even have to look. The refrigerator was empty and my cupboards were bare.

"Any requests?"

"Whatever you want. I don't really cook."

"Me neither. We'll have to fake it. I want us eating in whenever possible. While I'm gone, please stay here and keep the door locked. We'll set up the alarm in the morning first thing. I don't want you going out. And no answering the telephone. You have a machine on it?"

I nodded.

"Let the machine pick up."

"I can stay with her if you think it's wise," Henry said.

Dietz looked at me to check my reaction. The guy was a quick study. I'd have to give him that.

"I'd like to have some time by myself," I said. Who knew when I'd ever get to be alone again?

Dietz was apparently willing to honor the request. Henry offered to cook for us, but I really didn't feel up to it. I was tired. I was sore. I was irritable. I just wanted to grab a quick supper and go to bed. My culinary repertoire was limited to peanut-butter-and-pickle sandwiches and hot sliced hard-boiled egg with lots of mayonnaise and salt. I'd have to quiz Dietz later on his specialties. Surely, he could do something.

I showered while Dietz was gone, remembering numerous items I wished I'd asked him to pick up. Wine for one. I gave my hair a quick shampooing, feeling antsy and distracted. The sound of running water masked other sounds in the apartment. Someone could be breaking one of my windows out and I wouldn't hear it. I should have had Henry baby-sit. I cut the shower short, wrapped myself in a towel, and peered over the loft railing. Everything looked just as it had before— no broken window, no bloodied hand reaching through to turn the latch.

I put on jeans and a fresh shirt, found clean sheets in the linen closet and made up the sofa bed. It was odd to have a houseguest even in the guise of a bodyguard. I wasn't used to living in the place by myself, let alone with a guy I'd only met that day.

I unpacked the duffel and tidied up the living room. Dietz had told me not to answer the telephone, but he hadn't said anything about phoning out. It was only 6:15. I needed the comfort of business as usual.

I put a call through to Mrs. Gersh. "Irene? This is Kinsey Millhone. I just wanted to touch base and check on your mother. Is she up here yet?"

"How nice of you. Yes, she is. Mother arrived about three this afternoon," she said. "We had an ambulance meet her at the airport and take her right to the nursing home. I just got back from seeing her, as a matter of fact, and she seems fine. Tired, of course."

"The trip must have been hard on her."

Irene's voice dropped slightly. "They must have sedated her, though nobody said as much. I expected her to be raising Cain, but she was very subdued. At any rate, I can't tell you how grateful I am you were able to locate her, and so quickly, too. Even Clyde seems relieved."

"Good. I'm glad. I hope everything works out."

"What about you, dear? I heard about your accident. Are you all right?"

I squinted at the phone with puzzlement. "You heard about that?"

"Well, yes. From your associate. He called here this afternoon, wondering when you'd be home."

All of my internal processes came to a dead halt. "What associate?"

"I don't know, Kinsey. I thought you'd know that. He said he was a partner in your agency. I really didn't catch the name." A note of doubt had crept into her voice, probably in response to the chilly note in mine.

"What time was this?"

"About an hour ago. I told him I hadn't heard from you, but I was certain you'd be driving back this afternoon. That's when he mentioned that you'd had an accident. Is something wrong?"

"Irene . . . I don't have a partner. What I have is some guy hired to kill my ass. . . ."

I could practically hear her blink. "I don't understand, dear. What does that mean?"

"Just what it sounds like. A hit man. Someone hoping to murder me for money."

There was a pause, as if she were having to translate from a foreign tongue. "You're joking."

"I wish I were."

"Well, he seemed to know all about you and he sounded very nice. I never would have said a word if he hadn't seemed so familiar."

"I hope you didn't give him my home address or phone number," I said.

"Of course not. If he'd asked me that, I'd have known something was amiss. This is awful. I feel terrible."

"Don't worry about it. It's not your fault. If you hear from the guy again, or from anyone else, please let me know."

"I will. I'm so sorry. I had no idea . . ."

"I understand. There was no way you could know. Just get in touch with me if you hear from him again."

After I hung up, I went into the downstairs bathroom and stood in the tub, looking out the window at the street. It was not quite dark, that hazy twilight hour when light and shadow begin to merge. Lights in the neighborhood were beginning to come on. A car passed slowly along the street and I found myself pulling back. I didn't actually whimper, but that's how I felt. It was amazing to me how quickly I was losing my nerve. I consider myself a capable person (*ballsy* is the word that comes to mind), but I didn't like the idea of this guy breathing down my neck. I returned to the living room, where I circled restlessly in a space scarcely bigger than a nine-by-twelve rug.

At 6:45 there was a tap at the door. My heart volunteered an extra beat just to speed the adrenaline along. I peered through the porthole. Dietz was standing on the doorstep, his arms loaded with groceries. I unlocked the door and let him in. I took one bag of groceries while he put the other on the kitchen counter. I'm not sure what expression I had on my face, but he picked up on it. "What's wrong?"

My voice sounded abnormal, even to my own ears. "Some guy called the woman I was working for and asked about me. He told her about the accident and asked if I was back in town yet."

Dietz's hand moved toward the pocket where he'd kept his cigarettes. He flashed a look of annoyance, apparently meant for himself. "How'd he know about her?"

"I have no idea."

"Shit!"

"What'd the cops have to say?"

"Not much. At least they know now what's going on. They'll have the beat car cruise by at intervals."

"Whoopee-do."

"Cut the sarcasm," he said irritably.

"Sorry. I didn't know it would come out like that."

He turned back to one of the grocery bags, pulling out a garment that looked like the blue vests we'd worn in high school sports to distinguish one team from another. "Lieutenant Dolan suggested you wear this. It's a bulletproof vest, a man's, but it should do the job. Some rookie left it behind when he quit the force."

I took the thing, holding it up by one Velcro strap. It was heavier than it looked and it had all the sex appeal of an ace bandage. "What about you? Don't you need one of these?"

Dietz was taking his jacket off. "I've got one in the car. I'm going to clean up. We'll talk about supper in a bit."

I put groceries away while he showered in the downstairs bathroom. Judging from the items he'd bought, he must have snagged two each from every department he passed. I hadn't been in the apartment long enough to decide where anything should go, so I amused myself with paper goods and staples, cans, condiments, spices, and household cleaners. Fortunately, he'd had the presence of mind to buy a bottle of Jack Daniel's, two bottles of white wine, and a six-pack of beer. I'm ashamed to say how cheered I was by the sight. Given my current level of anxiety, I wasn't above a nip of alcohol. I put the beer away and got out the corkscrew.

The bathroom door opened and Dietz came out, dressed in jeans and a dress shirt, his feet bare, the scent of after-shave wafting toward me in a cloud. He was toweling his hair dry and it stood out around his head like straw. The gray in his eyes was as clean as ice. He spotted the radio on the kitchen counter and turned it on, tuning in a country-western song with lots of major chords and a rocking-horse rhythm that would probably drive me mad. My problem with country music is that I try to avoid the very situations the lyrics lament. However, having objected to his cigarettes, I didn't feel comfortable protesting his taste in music as well. He probably wasn't any happier with the proximity than I was.

I poured wine in a glass. "Want some?"

"Of course!"

I handed him the glass of wine and poured a second for myself. I felt like we should drink a toast to something, but I couldn't think what. "Are you hungry? I notice you picked up some bacon and eggs. We could have that if you like."

"Fine. I wasn't sure what else to get. I hope you're not a vegetarian. I should have asked."

"I eat anything . . . well, except tripe," I said. I set the wineglass on the counter so I could get out the eggs. "Scrambled all right? I'm terrible at fried."

"I can cook 'em."

"I don't mind."

"It shouldn't be your responsibility. I'm not here as a guest."

I hate bickering about who's going to be nicer. I got out the skillet and tried a new subject. "We never talked about money. Lee didn't mention your hourly rate."

"Let's not worry about that. We'll work something out."

"I'd feel better if we came to some agreement."

"What for?"

I shrugged. "I don't know," I said. "It's just more business-like."

"I don't want to charge you. I'm doing this for fun."

I turned and stared at him. "You think this is fun?"

"You know what I mean. I've chucked the business anyway so this one's on me."

"I don't like that," I said. "I know you mean well, and believe me, I appreciate the help, but I don't like to feel indebted."

"There's no debt implied."

"I'm going to pay you," I said, testily.

"Great. You do that. My rates just went up. Five hundred bucks an hour."

I stared at him and he stared back. "That's bullshit."

"That's *my* point. It's bullshit. We'll work something out. Right now I'm hungry so let's quit arguing."

I turned back to the skillet with a shake of my head. The joy of being single is you always get to have your own way.

I went up to bed at nine, exhausted. I slept fitfully, aware that Dietz was up and prowling restlessly well into the night.

105

11

I woke automatically at 6:00 A.M. and rolled out of bed for my early morning run. Oh, wow, shit, hurt. I was sucking air through my teeth, on my hands and knees, staring at the floor when I remembered Dietz's advisory. No jogging, no lifting weights. He hadn't said a word about getting out of bed. I was clearly in no condition to work out anyway. The second day of anything is always the worst. I staggered to my feet and hobbled over to the loft rail, peering down at the living room. He was up. The sofa bed had been remade. I caught the smell of fresh coffee and a glimpse of him sitting at the kitchen counter with the L.A. *Times* open in front of him, probably wishing he could have his first cigarette of the day. From my perspective, foreshortened, his face seemed to be dominated by his furrowed brow and jutting chin, his body topheavy with bulky shoulders and biceps. He reversed the pages, flipping to the middle of the metro section, which is where all the juicy Los Angeles crime is detailed. I eased out of his line of sight, climbed into bed again, and spent a few minutes staring up through the skylight. A marine layer had blanketed the Plexiglas dome with white. Impossible to tell yet what kind of day it would be. It seldom rains here in May. Chances were the clouds would lift and we'd have sunshine, mild breezes, the usual lush green. Sometimes perfection ain't that easy to bear. Meanwhile, I couldn't lie here all day, though I was tempted, I confess.

If I went downstairs, I'd have to be polite and interact with Dietz, making small talk of some as yet undetermined sort. New relationships are daunting, even when they're short-term. People have to trade all those tedious details about their previous lives. It made me tired to consider the sheer weight of the exchange. We'd touched on the preliminaries in the car coming home, but we had reams of data to cover yet. Chitchat aside, Dietz might turn on the radio again . . . more Roy Orbison. I couldn't face that at 6:05 A.M.

On the other hand, it was my house and I was hungry, so why shouldn't I go downstairs and eat? I didn't have to talk to him. I pushed the covers back and got up, limped into the bathroom and brushed my teeth. My face was still a Technicolor wonder, a rainbow of bruises after a shower of blows. I wiggled my eyebrows and studied myself. The contusion on my forehead was shifting subtly from dark blue to gray, my blackened eyes lightening from lavender to an eerie green. I've seen eye shadow in the same shade and it always puzzles me why women want to look like that. "I got belted in the chops last night," is what it says. My hair was, as usual, mashed from the night's sleep. I'd showered the night before but I hopped in again, not for the sake of cleanliness, but hoping to improve my mood. Having Dietz under the same roof was making my skin itch.

Once I pulled on jeans and an old sweatshirt, I dumped my dirty clothes in the hamper, tucked the empty duffel in the closet, and made the bed. I went downstairs. Dietz murmured a good morning without lifting his eyes from the sports page. I helped myself to some coffee, poured a bowl of cereal with milk, grabbed the funnies, and toted it all into the living room, where I sat, bowl in hand, spooning cereal into my mouth absentmindedly while I read the comic page. The funnies never make me laugh, but I read them anyway in hopes. I caught up with Rex Morgan, M.D., the girls in Apartment 3G, and Mary Worth. It's comforting how slowly life moves in a comic strip. I hadn't read the paper in maybe four days and the professor was just now looking startled at something Mary'd said to him. What a wag she was. I could tell he was disconcerted by the wavy lines around his head.

Dimly, I was aware that Dietz had opened the front door and stepped out into the backyard. When I finished my cereal, I washed my bowl and spoon and left them in the dish rack. Hesitantly, I moved to the front door and peered out, feeling like a housebound cat discovering that a door has inadvertently been left ajar. Was I allowed outside?

The marine layer was already beginning to dissipate, but the yard had that bleached look that a mist imparts. The foghorn was bleating intermittently—a calf separated from its mother—in the still morning air. The strong scent of seawater saturated the yard. Sometimes I half expect the surf to be lapping at the curb out front.

Dietz was hunkering near the flower beds. Henry had put in some bare root roses the year before and they were in full bloom: Sonia, Park Place, Lady X, names giving no clue about the final effect. "Aphids," he said. "He should buy some ladybugs."

I leaned against the doorframe, too paranoid to venture all the way out into the yard. "Are we going to talk about security again or did we cover it last night?"

He got to his feet, turning his attention to me. "We should probably discuss your schedule. Any standing appointments? Massage, beauty salon?"

"Do I look like someone with a standing appointment at a beauty salon?"

He studied my face with curiosity, but refrained from comment. "The point is, we don't want your movements predictable."

I rubbed my forehead, which was still smarting to the touch. "I gathered as much. Okay, so I cancel my masseuse, bikini wax, and the weekly pedicure. Now what?"

He smiled. "I appreciate your cooperation. Makes my job easier."

"Believe me, I'm not interested in being killed," I said. "I do need to go in to the office."

"What time?"

"Doesn't matter. I want to pick up my mail and get some bills paid. Minor stuff really, but I don't want to put it off."

"No problem. I'd like to see the place."

"Good," I said, turning to go back inside.

"Kinsey? Don't forget the body armor."

"Right. Make sure you wear yours, too."

Upstairs, I dutifully stripped off my sweatshirt and slipped on the bulletproof vest, pressing the Velcro straps into place. Dietz had told me this particular vest offered threat-level-one protection, which was good against a .38 Special or less. Apparently, he was assuming a hit man wouldn't use a 9-millimeter automatic. I tried not to think about garrotes, head wounds, blasted kneecaps, the penetrating power of ice picks—any one of a number of assaults not covered by the oversize bib I wore.

"Make sure it's tight enough," Dietz had called up from below.

"Got it," I said. I had pulled the sweatshirt on over the vest and checked myself in the mirror. I looked like I was eleven years old again.

At 8:45, we moved through the front gate. Dietz had gone out first to check the car and scan the street. He returned, motioning me forward. He walked slightly in front of me, his stride brisk, his eyes alert as we traversed the fifty paces to his Porsche. The whole maneuver had an urgency about it that made me feel like a rock star. "I thought a bodyguard was supposed to be inconspicuous," I said.

"That's one theory."

"Won't everybody guess?"

He looked over at me. "Let's put it this way. I'm not interested in advertising what I do, but if this guy's watching us, I want him to understand just how hard his job is going to be. Most attacks occur suddenly and at very close range.

I'll try not to be obnoxious, but I'm sticking to you like glue."

Well, that answered that.

Dietz drove with his usual determination. He was a real A-type personality, one of those guys who lives like he's always late for some appointment, irritated at anybody who slows him down. Bad drivers caught him by surprise, as though they were the exception instead of the rule. I directed him to the downtown area, which, fortunately, was only ten minutes away. If he noticed I was bracing myself between the dashboard and the door frame, he didn't mention it.

At the entrance to the parking lot, he slowed the car, surveying the layout. "Is this where you usually park?"

"Sure, the office is right up there."

I watched him calculate. He was clearly hoping for a way to change my routine, but parking farther away was only going to make the walk longer, thus exposing us for an extended period. He pulled in, handed me the ticket, and found a parking space. "Anything looks weird," he said, "speak up right away. Any sign of trouble, we'll get the fuck out."

"Right," I said. It was amazing what this "we" business was doing to my head. I wasn't famous for letting guys tell me what to do and I was hoping I wouldn't get used to it.

Again, he came around to the passenger side and opened the door, his gaze sweeping the lot as I emerged into the open air. He took my elbow, walking me rapidly across the lot to the back stairs. I wanted to laugh. It felt like having a parent march you up to your room. He entered the building first. The second-floor corridor was deserted. California Fidelity offices weren't open yet. I unlocked my office door. Dietz stepped in ahead of me and took a quick look around, making sure there weren't any goons lurking behind the furniture.

He scooped up the mail that had piled up on the floor just under the slot. He sorted through it quickly. "Let me tell you what we're looking for, in case I'm not here to do this. An unfamiliar return address, or one done by hand. Anything marked personal, extra postage due to weight, oil stains . . ."

"A bulky package with a fuse hanging out the side," I said.

110

He handed me the stack, his expression bland. It's hard to warm to somebody who looks at you that way. Apparently, he didn't think I was as funny as I thought I was. I took the stack of mail and sorted through it as he had. Much of it was third-class, but I did have a few checks coming in—all with return addresses I could identify on sight. Together we listened to the few messages on my machine. None were threatening. Dietz wanted time to acquaint himself with the building and its environs, so he went off to inspect the premises while I put on a pot of coffee.

I opened the French doors and paused, suddenly reluctant to step out on the balcony. Across the street, I could see the tiers of the parking garage and it occurred to me that anyone could drive up two levels, park, and get a bead on me. I wasn't even sure a high-powered rifle would be required. You could almost throw a rock from there and pop me in the noggin. I stepped away from the doors, withdrawing into the shadowy safety of the office. I really hated this.

At 9:05, I put a call through to my insurance agent and reported the accident. She said there was no blue book on the VW because of its age. It looked like I was going to be lucky if I picked up two hundred bucks on the claim, so there was no point in having the car towed. Finding an adjuster in Brawley who would go out and take a look was almost more trouble than the car was worth. She said she'd check into it and get back to me. This conversation failed to fill me with happiness. I have a savings account, but the purchase of a car would seriously deplete my funds.

Dietz returned to the office in time to intercept Vera, who had stopped in to say hello on her way into the office next door.

"My God, what happened to you?" she said when she saw my face.

"My car ended up in an irrigation ditch down in Brawley," I said. "This is Robert Dietz. He was nice enough to drive me back. Vera Lipton, from the offices next door."

They shook hands briefly. She was wearing a black leather miniskirt that fit her like automobile upholstery and made a creaking sound when she eased into one of my client chairs. Dietz moved over and parked a hip on the edge of my desk. It was amusing to watch them size each other up. Unknown to Vera, Dietz was viewing her as a potential assassin while I suspect she was evaluating his qualifications for a roll in the hay—whether hers or mine, I couldn't say. From her expression, she assumed he'd picked me up hitchhiking and since she considers me hopelessly conservative when it comes to men, I thought the possibility might lend me a certain stature in her eyes. I tried to look like the kind of woman who'd flag down a stranger on the road, but she wasn't interested in me—she was studying him. I was going to have to call this doctor friend of hers so we could double-date.

She reached into her handbag automatically and pulled a cigarette from a pack of Virginia Slims. "I'm not smoking this. I just need to hold it," she said when she caught my look. "I quit last week," she added in an aside to him.

I glanced at Dietz to see what his reaction would be. He hadn't had a cigarette now for over twenty-four hours, a personal best perhaps. Fortunately, he seemed to be sidetracked by the pheromones wafting through the air like perfume. Vera didn't actually drape one long leg across the chair arm, but there was something provocative about the way she sat. As often as I've seen her operate, I've still never figured out exactly what she does. Whatever the behavior, most men will begin to sit, lie down, and fetch like trained pups.

"I hope you're not forgetting the dinner tomorrow night," she said. She knew from my face I hadn't the faintest idea what she was talking about. "For Jewel. Retirement," she said, keeping it simple for those of us who'd suffered brain damage.

"Oh, that's right! I completely forgot. Really, I'm sorry, but I just don't see how I can make it," I said, with visual reference to Dietz. He was never going to permit my attendance at a public affair. Vera caught the look and said to Dietz, "You're invited, of course. Jewel's leaving the company after twenty-five years. Attendance is mandatory . . . no ifs, ands, or buts."

112

"Where's it being held?" he asked.

"The Edgewater Hotel. A private dining room. Should be very elegant. It's costing enough."

"How many people are we talking about?"

Vera shrugged. "Maybe thirty-five."

"Invitation only?"

"Sure. It's California Fidelity employees and guests. Why?"

"Can't do it," I said.

"I think we can manage it," Dietz said at the same time. "It will help if there's been no advance publicity."

Vera looked from one of us to the other. "What's going on?"

Dietz filled her in.

I waited, feeling oddly irritated, while they went through the catechism of disbelief and assurances. Vera expressed all the requisite attitudes. "God, that's awful. I can't believe things like that actually go on. Listen, if you guys don't want to risk it, I'll understand."

"I'll want to check it out, but we'll see how it looks. Can we let you know in the morning?" Dietz said.

"Of course. As long as I know by noon, it shouldn't be any problem."

"What time's the dinner?"

"No-host cocktails at seven. The dinner's at eight." Vera glanced at her watch. "Oops. I gotta scoot. It's been nice meeting you."

"You, too."

She moved toward the door.

"Oh, and Vera . . . ," he said. "We'd prefer to keep this quiet."

She pulled her glasses down on her nose, looking at him over the rims. There was an elegant pause while she raised a brow. "Of course," she said—the word *asshole* implied. There was something flirtatious in the very way she left the room. Lord, she was really going all out for this guy.

Dietz seemed to color. It was the first time I'd seen him disconcerted by anything. The most unlikely men turn out to be suckers for abuse.

When the door closed behind her, I turned on Dietz with an outraged tone. "I thought you said no public events!"

"I did. I'm sorry. I can see I caught you by surprise. I don't want to interfere any more than I have to. If this is something you want, then let's find a way to do it."

"I'm not going to risk my life for something like that!"

"Look. There's no way we can eliminate every possibility of attack. I'm here to reduce the likelihood, that's all. The *president* goes out in public, for God's sake," he said. His tone shifted. "Besides, I'm not convinced the guy we're dealing with is a pro. . . ."

"Oh, great. He might be a lunatic, instead."

Dietz shrugged matter-of-factly. "If we play our cards right, you'll be safe enough. The guest list is restricted and these are people you know. Once we scope it out, the question boils down to, do you want to go or not? You tell me. I'm not here to dictate the terms of your life."

"I don't know yet," I said, somewhat mollified. "The dinner's no big deal, but it might be nice to be out."

"Then let's see what it looks like and we'll decide after that."

By noon, I'd wrapped up my business and locked my files again. The phone rang just as Dietz and I were heading out the door. I started to answer, but he held a hand up, stopping me. He picked it up. "Millhone Investigations." He listened briefly. "Hold on." He passed the phone to me.

"Hello?"

"Kinsey, this is Irene Gersh. I'm sorry to be a bother. You're busy I know . . ."

"No problem. What's up?"

"Mother's disappeared. I don't suppose she's been in touch with you."

"Well, no, but I'm not sure she'd know who to call if she wanted to. I only saw her twice. How long's she been gone?"

"Nobody really knows. The supervisor at the nursing home swears she was there at breakfast time. An aide took her to the dining room in a wheelchair and then went off to take

114

care of someone else. She told Mother she'd just be a minute, but when she turned around Mother'd left her wheelchair and had taken off on foot. Nobody dreamed she could get very far. I guess they scoured the building and grounds and now they've started searching the neighborhood. I'm on my way over but I thought I'd check with you first, just in case you knew anything."

"I'm sorry, but I haven't heard from her at all. You need some help?"

"No, no. There's really no need at this point. The police have been notified and they have a patrol car cruising the area. So far there's no sign of her, but I'm sure she'll turn up. I just didn't want to overlook the possibility that she might be with you."

"I wish I could be more help. We've got an errand to run, but we can check with you later and see what's going on. Give me the address and telephone number at the nursing home." I tucked the phone against my shoulder while I made a note on a piece of scratch paper. "I'll give you a call when we get back."

"Thank you. I appreciate your concern."

"In the meantime, don't worry. I'm sure she's somewhere close."

"I hope so."

I told Dietz what was going on as we headed down the back steps. I was half-tempted to have him take me over to the nursing home, but it didn't feel like a real emergency. He wanted to see the Edgewater and check the arrangements for the banquet. He suggested I call Irene from the hotel as soon as he was done. It made sense and I agreed, though I knew for a fact if I were on my own, I'd have done it the other way. I was feeling distracted and, for once, his driving style didn't bother me. It was hard to imagine where Agnes could have gone. I knew she was capable of raising hell when it suited her, but Irene had made it sound like she was resigned to the move. I had to shrug to myself. Surely, she'd turn up.

12

I leaned my head back on the seat, staring out the car window while Dietz circled the area surrounding the hotel. I could see that he was committing various routes to memory, getting a sense of the sections of the road where we might be vulnerable to attack. I wasn't that interested in attending the dinner. Now that I thought about it, what the hell did I care? Jewel was a nice lady, but I really didn't know her well. I wasn't feeling that good and—just to get basic—I didn't have a thing to wear. The all-purpose dress—the only one I owned—had been in my car at the time of the accident. In the auto body lot down in Brawley, I remembered packing soggy items in a cardboard box, which hadn't arrived in Santa Teresa yet. When the dress did get here, it was probably going to smell like a swamp, complete with primordial life forms wiggling out of the wet. I could always ask Vera to lend me some rags. She towered over me, outweighing me by a good twenty pounds, but I'd seen her wearing a sequined tunic cut right to her crotch. It would probably hit me at the knee. Not that I could wear a skirt in my current condition, of course. I was sporting a bruised leg that made me look like spoiled fruit. On a more optimistic note, once I strapped on my body armor, what difference would it make that her bazookas were twice the size of mine?

Dietz had apparently satisfied himself with the general layout of the neighborhood and we were getting down to the particulars. He pulled into the Edgewater parking lot and turned his Porsche over to a parking attendant, passing the guy a folded bill. "Keep the car up here close and let me know if anyone takes an interest."

The attendant glanced down at the bill. "Yessir! Hey, sure!"

Dietz and I moved toward the entrance.

"Why so quiet?" he asked as he steered me through the lobby by the elbow like the rudder of a boat.

I pulled my arm away automatically. "Sorry," I murmured. "I've been thinking about the banquet and it's put me in a bad mood."

"Anything I can help with?"

I shook my head. "What's this feel like to you?"

"What, the job?"

"Yeah. Trailing around with me everywhere. Doesn't it get on your nerves?"

"I don't have nerves," he said.

I turned and scanned his face, wondering if that was really true.

He hunted down the hotel manager and had a long talk with him about the banquet room, the closest medical facility, and matters of that ilk. I would have jettisoned the whole plan, but by now we'd invested so much time and energy, I felt I was obligated to follow through. Meanwhile, Dietz was triggering all the disagreeable aspects of my personality. I was beginning to remember certain personal traits that had probably contributed to my divorces. I prefer to believe it was all *their* fault, but who are we trying to kid here . . .

I left Dietz in the manager's office and wandered down the corridor. Just off the hotel lobby, there were little shops where rich people browsed, looking for ways to spend money without having to leave the premises. I went into a clothing boutique and circled the place. The merchandise seemed unreal to me, outfits laid out with all the color-coordinated accessories. My notion of accessories is you wear your gym socks with matching rims. The air smelled of one of those movie-star perfumes that cost a hundred and twenty bucks an ounce. Just for laughs, I checked the sale rack. Even marked down, most items cost more than my monthly rent. I crossed to the section where the evening wear was arranged: long skirts in brocade, tops stiff with sequins, everything embroidered, hand-stitched, hand-painted, appliquéd, beaded and otherwise bejeweled. The saleswoman glanced over at me with a practiced smile. I could see her expression falter slightly and I was reminded, yet again, how unnerving my appearance must be to those unprepared for it. I was hoping I looked like I'd just had cosmetic surgery. A little nose bob, eye tucks. For all she knew I was holing up here with some sugar daddy until the swelling went down.

Dietz appeared in the doorway and I moved in his direction. As usual, he grabbed me by the elbow without ceremony and marched me down the hall. He was brusque, distracted, probably mentally several moves ahead. "Let's have lunch."

"Here?" I said, startled. I'm more the Burger King type myself.

"Sure, why not? It'll cheer you up."

We'd reached the entrance to the hotel restaurant, a vast room enclosed in glass, with polished red tile floors and white wicker furniture. The room was dense with greenery: palms and rubber plants, potted ficuses lending an air of tropical elegance. The patrons were actually very casually dressed: tennis outfits, golf shirts, and designer sweats. Dietz was wearing the same jeans and tweed sport coat he'd worn for two days, while I was in my jeans and tenny-bops. No one seemed to pay the slightest attention to us, except for the occasional look of curiosity that flickered to my face.

He spotted a sheltered table near a fire exit with a sign

prominently displayed above it: THIS DOOR MUST BE KEPT UNLOCKED DURING BUSINESS HOURS. Perfect if needed to make a fast getaway. The service area nearby was being used as a station for linen and flatware. A waitress had been sentenced to folding napkins into cloth boats.

"How about that one," he said. The hostess nodded and led the way, showing us to our seats without questioning his taste.

She handed us two oversized menus bound in leather. "Your waiter will be right with you," she said and moved away. I'll admit I checked the menu with a certain curiosity. I'm used to fast-food chains where the menus feature glossy photos of the food, as if the reality itself is bound to disappoint.

The edibles here were itemized on a quarto of parchment, handwrit by some kitchen scribe who had mastered Food-speak. ". . . lightly sauced pan-smoked filets of free range veal in a crib of fresh phyllo, topped with squaw bush berries, and accompanied by hand-formed gaufrettes of goat cheese, wild mushrooms, yampa root, and fresh herbs . . ." $21.95. I glanced at Dietz, who didn't seem at all dismayed. As usual, I could tell I was completely out of my element. I hardly ever eat squaw bush berries and yampa root.

I checked the other patrons. My view was actually half-obscured by a Boston fern. Next to the plant stand was a cylindrical cage in which finches were twittering. There were small bamboo baskets affixed to the wire sides and the little birds hopped in and out with strips of newspaper, making nests. There was something charming about their bright-eyed busyness. Dietz and I watched them idly while we waited for our waiter.

"You know anything about crows?" he asked.

"I'm not much on birds."

"I wasn't either until I met one personally. I used to have a crow named Albert. Bertie, when I got to know him better. I got him when he was just a little guy and had him for years. A young crow doesn't navigate well and they'll sometimes crash-land. They're called branchers at that age—that's about all they can do, lumber awkwardly from branch to branch. Sometimes they get stuck and they wail like babies until you get 'em down. Bertie must have bitten off a bit more than he could chew and he'd tumbled to the ground. I had a cat named Little John who brought him in, squawking hellishly. LJ and I had a tussle to see who was going to take possession. Fortunately for Bertie, I won the contest. He and the cat became friends later, but it was touch-and-go for a while there. LJ was pissed off because he thought this was Thanksgiving dinner and I was getting in his way . . ."

Dietz looked up. The waiter was approaching, dressed like an usher at a wedding, complete with white gloves.

"Good afternoon. Something to drink before lunch?" The waiter's manner was circumspect and he avoided making eye contact.

Dietz turned to me. "You want a drink?"

"White wine," I said.

"Chardonnay, sauvignon blanc?" the waiter asked.

"Chardonnay."

"And you, sir?"

"I'll have a beer. What do you have imported?"

"Amstel, Heineken, Beck's dark, Beck's light, Dos Equis, Bohemia, Corona . . ."

"Beck's light," Dietz said.

"Are you ready to order?"

"No."

The waiter stared at Dietz, then nodded and withdrew.

Dietz said, "We probably won't see him for half an hour, but I hate being bullied into ordering."

He picked up his story again about Bertie the crow, who liked to take long walks on foot and lived on a diet of M&M's, hard-boiled eggs, and dry cat food. While Dietz talked, his gaze shifted restlessly around the room. He seldom looked at faces, always at hands, checking for concealed weapons, sudden movements, signals perhaps. Some underling arrived, bearing our drinks, but the waiter didn't return. Dietz scanned the dining room, but there was no sign of him. Twenty minutes passed. I could see Dietz take note and in a surge of uneasiness, he finally tossed a bill on the table and got up. "Let's get out of here. I don't like this."

"Do you see everything as part of some plot?" I asked, trotting after him.

"That may be all that keeps the two of us alive."

I shrugged to myself and let it go at that. When we reached the front entrance, the Porsche was parked right up against the shrubs. He snagged the keys off the board himself and helped me into the car. He got in on his side and fired up the engine.

We drove home along the beach. I was exhausted and my head was starting to pound. When we got to my apartment, Dietz hauled out his portable alarm system, which he showed me how to arm and disarm. He affixed it to the door.

"I'll tell Henry to keep an ear tuned while I'm out . . ."

"You're going off somewhere?" I felt a little bubble of panic arise, testimony to how quickly I'd come to depend on him for my sense of personal safety.

"I want to have another chat with Lieutenant Dolan. He said he'd talk to the Carson City DA and try to get an ID on this guy with the kid. Somebody must have heard of him. Maybe we can pick up a mug shot and at least figure out what he looks like. I'll be back in half an hour. You'll be fine here. Get some rest. You look beat."

He took off while I downed a pain pill and headed up to the loft. I had promised to call Irene and I could feel the tiny voice of my conscience whining deep within. The phone rang just as I was pulling off my shoes. Dietz had told me not to answer it if he wasn't there, but I couldn't help myself. I leaned across the bed and picked up the receiver.

It was Irene Gersh. "Oh good, it's you. I'm calling from the nursing home. I'm so glad you're there. I was afraid you were still out."

"We just got in. I was thinking I should call you, but I hadn't worked up the energy."

"Is this a bad time?"

"It's fine. Don't worry about it. What's happening?"

"Nothing. That's the point. I'm sorry to be such a pest, but I'm just beside myself. Mother's been gone now for eight hours and there's simply no sign of her. Clyde feels maybe we should get out and check the neighborhood ourselves."

"Sounds smart," I said. "You need any help knocking on doors?" In that split second my concern for Agnes's safety overrode my worries about myself.

"Thank you. We'd appreciate it. The longer Mother's on the loose, the more frightened I get. Somebody must have seen her."

"You'd think so," I said. "When do you need me there?"

"Soon if you could. Clyde called from work and he's on his way over now. If it's not too much trouble . . ." She gave me an address in the eleven hundred block of Concorde.

"I'm on my way," I said and hung up. I put a quick call through to Lieutenant Dolan's office and left word for Dietz to meet me at the nursing home, reiterating the address. That done, I picked my way carefully down the stairs. I craved action. My whole body was seizing up in the wake of the accident and my joints felt stiff with rust. Certain postures caused excruciating pains to shoot through my neck, causing me to murmur, "Ow, ow, ow." I was hoping the painkiller would do its work before long.

I found a jacket and my handbag, checked to make sure my little .32 was accounted for, and headed for the door, searching for my car keys in the outside leather pouch. Where the hell were they? I stopped dead, perplexed, and then it dawned on me. I didn't *have* transportation. My VW was still down in Brawley at the auto body shop. Well, hell, I thought.

I turned on my heel, picked up the phone again, and called a cab. By that point, I had already begun to internalize some of Dietz's precautions. I knew better than to loiter outside on the curb in plain sight. I waited, dutifully standing in the tub in the downstairs bathroom, where I could look out the window until the cab appeared in front. For the second time, I snatched up my jacket and my handbag. When I opened the front door, the alarm system went off, scaring me so badly that I nearly wet my pants.

Henry's back door banged open and he came running out with a meat cleaver in his hand. All he had on was a pair of turquoise briefs and his face was pale as bread dough. "My God, what happened? Are you all right?"

"Henry, I'm fine. I accidentally set off the alarm."

"Well, get back inside. You scared the hell out of me. I was about to take a shower when that damn thing went off. Why are you out here? Dietz said you were napping. You look awful. Go to bed." His panic had rendered him a little cranky, I thought.

"Would you quit worrying? There's no cause for hysteria. Irene Gersh called me and I'm on my way over to the nursing home to help look for her mom. I've got a cab waiting out in front."

Henry grabbed my jacket. "You'll do no such thing," he said snappishly. "You can wait till Dietz gets back and go over there with him."

I could feel my temper climb in response to his. I grabbed the jacket back, the two of us tugging like kids in a school-yard. The cleaver he was holding made it treacherous work.

The second time he reached for the jacket, I held it up and away from him. "Henry," I said warningly. "I'm a free human being. Dietz knows I'm going over there. I called Dolan's office and talked to him myself. He's on his way."

"You did not. I know you. You're lying through your teeth," Henry said.

"I *did* call!"

"But you didn't *talk* to him."

"I left a message. That's just as good."

"What if he never gets it?"

"Then you can tell him where I am! I'm going."

"No, you're not!"

I had to argue for five minutes before I was allowed to leave the premises. Meanwhile, the cab driver had already tooted twice and he appeared from around the corner looking for his fare. I don't know what he must have thought when he caught sight of us . . . me with my battered face, Henry in his Calvin Klein skivvies with a cleaver in his mitt. Fortunately, Henry knew the guy and after earnest reassurances on all sides, he finally consented to my departure. He didn't like the idea, but there wasn't much he could do.

The cabbie was still shaking his head with mock disgust. "Get some pants on, Pitts. You could get arrested like that."

By the time I reached the nursing home on the Upper East Side, it was nearly two o'clock. I realized as the cab pulled up that I knew the neighborhood. Rosie and I had combed the entire area, looking for a board-and-care for her sister, Klotilde. The houses, for the most part, were built on a grand scale: rambling interiors with high ceilings, oversize windows, wide porches, surrounded by massive oaks and old, shaggy palms.

In contrast, the nursing home from which Agnes had disappeared was a two-story Victorian structure with a carriage house in the rear. The frame siding was a pale gray, with the trim done in fresh white. The steeply pitched roof was made of slate tiles, overlapping like fish scales. At the second-story level, a raw-looking L of decking and a set of wooden stairs had been added as a fire escape. The house sat on a large corner lot, the property shaded by countless trees, dotted with flower beds, and bordered with shrubs, which were pierced by the protruding upright arrows of an ornamental iron fence. There were several cars visible in the small parking lot in the rear.

Irene had apparently been watching for my arrival. I paid the driver and emerged from the cab in time to see her moving toward me down the front walk, followed by a gentleman I assumed was Clyde Gersh. Again, I was struck by the aura of illness that surrounded her. She was stick-thin and seemed unsteady on her feet. The shirtwaist dress she wore was a jade-green silk that only emphasized the unearthly pallor of her skin. She'd clearly gone to some trouble with her appearance, but the effect was stark. Her foundation makeup was too peachy a shade, and the false lashes made her eyes jump out of her face. A swath of blusher high on each cheek gave her the look of someone in the throes of a fever. "Oh, Kinsey. God bless you." She reached for me with trembling hands that were cold to the touch.

"How are you, Irene? Is there any sign of her?"

"I'm afraid not. The police have taken the report and they've issued one of those . . . oh, what do you call them . . ."

Clyde spoke up. "A 'be on the lookout' bulletin."

"Yes, that's it. Anyway, they'll have a patrol car cruising the neighborhood. I'm not sure what else they can do for the time being. I'm just sick."

Clyde spoke up again, extending his hand. "Clyde Gersh."

Irene seemed flustered. "Oh, I'm sorry. This is Miss Millhone. I don't know what I was thinking of."

Clyde Gersh was probably in his late fifties, some ten years older than his wife. He was tall and stooped, wearing an expensive-looking suit that seemed to hang on his frame. He had a thinning head of gray hair, a lined face, his brow knotted with concern. His features had the droopy quality of a man resigned to his fate. His wife's state of health, whether real or self-induced, must have been a trial to him. He'd adopted an air of weary patience. I realized I had no idea what he did for a living. Something that entailed a flexible schedule and wingtip shoes. A lawyer? Accountant?

The two of us shook hands. He said, "Nice to meet you, Miss Millhone. I'm sorry for the circumstances."

"Me, too. I prefer 'Kinsey,' if you would. What can I do to help?"

He glanced apologetically at his wife. "We were just discussing that. I'm trying to talk Irene into staying here. She can hold down the fort while we get out and bump doors. I told the director of this two-bit establishment he'll have a lawsuit on his hands if anything's happened to Agnes. . . ."

Irene shot him a look. "We can talk about this later," she

said to him. And to me, "The nursing home has been wonderful. They feel Mother was probably confused. You know how willful she is, but I'm sure she's fine. . . ."

"Of course she is," I said, though I had my doubts.

Clyde's expression indicated he had about as much faith as I did. "I'm just heading out if you'd care to join me," he said. "I think we should check the houses along Concorde as far as Molina and then head north."

Irene spoke up. "I want to come, Clyde. I won't stay here by myself."

An expression of exasperation flickered briefly in his face, but he nodded agreement. Whatever opposition he may have previously voiced, he now set aside, perhaps in deference to me. He reminded me of a parent reluctant to discipline a kid in front of company. The man wanted to look good. I glanced along the street for some sign of Dietz.

Irene caught my hesitation. "Something wrong, dear? You seem worried."

"Someone's meeting me here. I don't want to take off without leaving word."

"We can wait if you like."

Clyde gestured impatiently. "You two do what you want. I'm going on," he said. "I'll take this side and you can take that. We'll meet here in thirty minutes and see how it looks." He gave Irene's cheek a perfunctory kiss before he headed off. She stared after him anxiously. I thought she was going to say something, but she let the moment pass.

"Would you like to tell someone at the nursing home where we'll be?"

"Never mind," I said. "Dietz will figure it out."

13

We started with the house diagonally across from the nursing home. Like many others in the neighborhood, it was substantially constructed, probably built in the early years of the century. The façade was wide, the two-story exterior shingled in cedar tinted with a pale green wash. A prominent gabled porch sat squarely in the center, matching large bay windows reflecting blankly the sprawling branches of an overhanging oak. I thought I saw movement in an upstairs window as we came up the walk. Irene was clinging to my arm for support. Already, I could tell she was going to slow me down, but I didn't have the heart to mention it. I was hoping her anxiety would ease if she could help in the search.

I pressed the bell, which jangled harshly. Moments later, the front door opened a crack and a face appeared, an older woman. The burglar chain was still judiciously in evidence. Had I been a thug, I could have kicked the door open with a well-placed boot.

"Yes?"

I said, "Sorry to bother you, but we're talking to everybody in the neighborhood. An elderly woman's disappeared from the nursing home across the street and we're wondering if you might have seen her. About seven this morning. We think that's when she left."

"I don't get up until eight o'clock these days. Doctor's orders. I used to get up at five, but he says that's ridiculous. I'm seventy-six. He says there's nothing going on at that hour that I need to know about."

"What about your neighbors? Have you heard anybody mention . . ."

She waved an impatient hand, knuckles speckled and thick. "I don't talk to them. They haven't cut that hedge in the last fifteen years. I pay the paperboy to come in once a month and trim it up. Otherwise, it'd grow clear up through the telephone wires. They have a dog comes over in my yard, too. Does his business everywhere. I can't step a foot out without getting dog doodie on my shoe. My husband's always saying, 'Pee-you, Ethel. There's dog doodie on your shoe again.' "

I took out one of my business cards, jotting the number of the nursing home on the back. "Could I leave you my card? That way if you hear anything, you can give me a call. We'd appreciate your help."

The woman took it reluctantly. It was clear she didn't have much interest in geriatric runaways. "What's this woman's name?"

"Agnes Grey."

"What's she look like? I can't very well identify someone I've never laid eyes on before."

I described Agnes briefly. With Irene standing there, I couldn't very well suggest that Agnes looked like an ostrich.

"I'll keep an eye out," she said. And then the door closed.

We tried the next house, and the next, with about the same results. By the time we reached the corner, forty-five minutes had gone by. It was slow work and so far, unproductive. No one had seen Agnes. We headed east on Concorde. A UPS truck approached and we waited on the curb until we'd seen it pass. I put a hand under Irene's arm as we crossed the street, supervising her safety as Dietz supervised mine.

A fine tremor seemed to be vibrating through the dark green silk of her dress. I studied her uneasily. Years of bleaching had left her hair a harsh white-blond, very thin, as if she'd succeeded finally in eliminating any whisper of color from the wispy strands. She had no brows to speak of, just two brown lines she'd penciled in by hand, wide arcs like a child might have drawn on a happy face. I could see that she might have been considered a beauty once upon a time. Her features were fine, the blue eyes unusual in their clarity. One of her false lashes had come loose, sticking out like a tiny feather. Her complexion was too pale to seem healthy, but the texture of her skin was remarkable. She reminded me of an obscure one-role movie actress of the forties—someone you're surprised to find alive after all these years. She put a trembling hand on mine, her fingers so icy that I drew back in alarm. Her breathing was rapid and shallow.

"Irene, my God. Your hands are like ice. Are you all right?"

"This happens now and then. I'll be fine in a minute."

"Let's find you a place to sit down," I said. We were approaching a three-story clapboard house, tall and narrow with a porch on three sides. The yard was sunny, with the grass newly mown and not much attention to the flower beds. I knew it was a board-and-care because Rosie and I had been given the address. I'd never actually seen the inside of the house. Once Rosie realized there was no wheelchair access, we had crossed it off our list. I remembered the owner as an energetic fellow in his seventies, pleasant enough, but apparently not equipped to handle anyone who wasn't ambulatory. I'd already opened the shrieking iron gate and I could see the front curtain move as someone peered out. This seemed to be a neighborhood where people were on the watch. I couldn't believe Agnes had managed to get even half a block without someone spotting her.

We reached the front porch and Irene sank down on the bottom step. She put her head between her knees. I put a hand on the back of her neck, peering closely at her face. I could hear the wheezing in her throat.

"You want to lie down?"

"No, please. I'll be fine. It's my asthma acting up. I don't want a fuss made. Just let me sit here for a bit."

"Just slow your breathing down, okay? You're starting to hyperventilate. I don't want you passing out."

I checked the street for Clyde, but he was nowhere to be seen. I climbed the steps and crossed to the front door. The owner of the board-and-care emerged just as I was preparing to ring the bell.

He was a man who might have been hefty in his youth. Once-muscular shoulders had softened with age, sloping beneath his shirt. He was clean-shaven and balding, his extended forehead giving him a look of babyhood. He had pouches under his eyes and a mole stuck to his left cheek, like a raisin. "Something I can help you with?" His eyes strayed to Irene and I found my gaze following his. If she fainted, I was going to have a real problem on my hands.

"She'll be all right. She's feeling light-headed and just needs to sit down for a bit," I said. "A woman's disappeared from the nursing home down the block and we're checking with the neighbors, hoping someone's seen her."

He had focused on my face, surveying me quizzically. "You look familiar. Do I know you?"

"Kinsey Millhone," I said. "I was here a couple of weeks ago with a friend of mine—"

"Right, right, right. I remember now. Spunky little red-head with a sister in a wheelchair. I was sorry we couldn't accommodate her. She the one who's missing?"

"No. This is someone else," I said. I held a hand up above my own head, describing her again. "Tall, very thin. She's been gone since early this morning and we can't seem to get a line on her. I can't believe she got far."

"Some of those old folk move fast," he said. "They can fool you if you don't keep an eye out. Wish I could help you, but I've been working in the back. Have you called the police?"

"They were notified first thing. I understand they've searched this whole area. We thought we'd try again."

"Happens occasionally, especially in this neighborhood. Usually they turn up."

"Let's hope. Thanks, anyway."

His gaze strayed back to Irene still sitting on the bottom step. "How about a glass of water for your friend?"

"She'll be okay, but thanks," I said. I closed the conversation with my usual request for assistance. "Here. Let me leave you my card. If you see the woman or talk to anyone who might have noticed her, could you let me know? If I'm not available, you can always call the nursing home."

He took my card. "Certainly," he said. Someone spoke to him from inside, a feeble voice, faintly petulant. He excused himself and went in.

I helped Irene up. We made our way down the walk and out the gate. She was shaky on her feet, her face drawn and tense.

"I really think I ought to take you back," I said.

She shook her head emphatically. "Not yet. I'm feeling better." She straightened her back as if to illustrate the point.

I could see a fine mist of sweat beading on her forehead, but she seemed determined to go on. I had my doubts, but there wasn't much I could do. "One more, then," I said, "and then we'll check back with Clyde."

The house next door was a blocky bungalow with a low-pitched roof, a story and a half sheathed in fawn-brown clapboard. The porch was open and wide, the overhang supported on squat brick stanchions with wooden railings between. We were heading up the walk when I saw one of the wooden porch rails split, raw wood opening up like a flower blossoming. I heard a popping sound and glass broke. I jumped, thinking that some shift in the earth was causing the structure to snap apart. I heard Dietz's Porsche roar around the corner to our left. I turned to look for him and registered peripherally the UPS delivery truck still idling at the curb. The UPS man was coming up the walk behind us. He was

131

smiling at me and I felt myself smile automatically in response. He was a big man, muscular, clean-shaven, with blond curly hair, stark blue eyes in a tan face, full mouth curving into dimpled cheeks. I thought I must know him because he seemed glad to see me, his eyes soft, the look on his face both sensual and warm. He moved nearer, bending toward me, almost as if he meant to kiss me. He was so close I registered the heady bouquet of his personal scent: gunpowder, Aqua Velva aftershave, and a whiff of Juicy Fruit chewing gum. I felt myself drawing back, perplexed. Behind me, wood snapped like a tree being cracked by lightning. I could see his face suffuse with heat, like a lover at the moment of his climax. He said something. I glanced down at his hands. He seemed to be holding the nozzle of a hose, but why would a UPS man wear gardening gloves? Light spurted from the hose. I blinked uncomprehendingly and then I understood. I grabbed Irene by the arm, nearly lifting her off her feet. I hauled her up the two low stairs and toward the front door. The occupant of the house, a middle-aged man, was opening the front screen, puzzled by the noise. I could tell from his expression he wasn't expecting company. I snagged him by his shirtfront and shoved him aside, pushing him out of the line of fire as I shouldered us through the door. A front window shattered, spraying glass across the floor. Irene and I went down in a heap. She was too surprised to shriek, but I could hear the wind being knocked out of her as she hit the bare hardwood floor. The door banged back on its hinges, exposing the hallway and the stairs. The owner of the house had taken refuge in the living room, crouched beside the sofa, his arms folded across his head. He reminded me of a little kid who believes he's invisible just because his eyes are squeezed shut. A bullet ripped a hole through the back wall. Plaster dust blew inward like a bomb going off, with a fine cloud rising in its wake.

There was silence. I heard someone running, pounding steps receding in the grass, and I knew instinctively that Dietz would give chase. Crouching, I duck-waddled my way into

132

the dining room and peered cautiously out the side window, eyes barely above the sill. I saw Dietz round the corner of the house and disappear. Behind me, Irene was beginning to wail, from fear, from injury, from shock and bewilderment. Belatedly, I felt a rush of adrenaline that made my heart thunder in my throat. My mouth went dry. I clung to the windowsill and laid my cheek against the cold wall, which was papered in cabbage roses, maroon and pink on a field of gray. I closed my eyes. In my mind, the moment was being played out all over again. First the man . . . that warm light in his eyes, mouth curving up in a familiar smile. The sense that he meant to kiss me, husky voice saying something, then the muzzle flash. From the sound, I knew he'd had a suppressor on the gun, but I'd seen light spurt out. Didn't seem likely in daylight unless my mind had somehow supplied the image out of past experience. How many shots had he fired? Five? Six?

Dietz came into the house, striding across the room. He was winded, tightly controlled, sweating, his manner grim. He pulled me to my feet, his face stony. I could feel his hands digging into my upper arms, but I couldn't voice a protest.

"Are you okay?"

He gave me a shake and I nodded, feeling mute. He set me aside like a rag doll and moved away, crossing to Irene who was weeping as piteously as a three-year-old. She sat on the floor with her legs spread, skirt askew, arms limp in her lap, her palms turned up. Dietz put an arm around her, pulling her close. He kept his voice low, reassuring her, bending down so she could hear. He asked her a question. I saw her shake her head. She was gasping, unable to say more than a few words before she was forced to stop for breath.

The owner of the house was standing in the hallway, his fear having given way to outrage. "What's going on here? What is this, a drug bust? I open my door and I nearly get myself killed! Look at the damages. Who's going to pay for this?"

Dietz said, "Shut up and call the cops."

"Who are you? You can't talk to me that way! This is a private residence."

I sank down on a dining room chair. Through the front window, I could see that neighbors had begun to congregate, murmuring anxiously among themselves—little groups of two and three, some standing in the yard.

What had the man said to me? I ran it back again: I'd heard Dietz's car rumbling in the street and that's when I'd turned, smiling at the man who was smiling at me. I could hear his words now, understood at last what he'd said to me as he approached—"You're mine, babe"—his tone possessive, secretive, and then the incredible sexual heat in his face. I felt tears rise, blurring my vision. The window shimmered. My hands began to shake.

Dietz patted Irene's arm and returned to me. He hunkered at my side, his face level with mine. "You did great. You were fine. There was no way you could have known that would happen, okay?"

I had to squeeze my hands between my knees so the shaking wouldn't travel up my arms. I looked at Dietz's face, gray eyes, the blunt nose. "He tried to kill me."

"No, he didn't. He tried to scare you. He could have killed you the first time, in Brawley on the road. He could have nailed you just now with the first shot he fired. If he kills you, the game is over. That isn't what he wants. He's not a pro. He's sick. We can use that to get him. Can you understand what I'm saying? Now we know his weakness."

"Yeah, it's me," I said, forever flip. Actually, I didn't understand much of anything. I'd looked into the face of Death. I'd mistaken him for a friend. Other people had tried to kill me—out of vengeance, out of hate. It had never really seemed personal until the man on the walk. No one had ever connected to me as intimately as he had.

I glanced over at Irene. Her respiratory distress, instead of subsiding, seemed to be getting worse. Her breathing was rapid, shallow, and ineffectual, the wheezing in her throat like two high-pitched notes on a bagpipe. Her fingertips were turning a shadowy blue. She was suffocating where she sat. "She needs help," I said.

Dietz turned to look at her. "Oh hell . . ."

He was on his feet instantly, striding across the room. The owner of the house was standing at the telephone, repeating his address to the police dispatcher.

Dietz said, "We need an ambulance, too," and then to Irene, "Take it easy. You'll be fine. We'll have help for you soon. Don't panic . . ."

I saw Irene nod, which was as much as she could manage.

In the midst of the confusion, Clyde Gersh appeared, drawn by the scattering of neighbors who were standing out in front. He told me later that when he saw the damages to the house his first thought was that Agnes had been discovered and had put up some kind of fight. The last thing he expected was to see Irene on the floor in the midst of a stage III asthma attack. Within minutes, the cops arrived, along with the paramedics, who administered oxygen and first aid, loaded Irene on a gurney, and hustled her away. In the meantime, I felt strangely removed. I knew what was expected and I did as I was told. I rendered a detailed account of events in a monotone, letting Dietz fill in the background. I'm not sure how much time passed before Dietz was allowed to take me home. Time had turned sluggish and it seemed like hours. I never even heard the name of the guy who owned the house. The last glimpse I saw of him, he was standing on the porch, looking like the sole survivor of an 8.8 earthquake.

14

When we got home, I fumbled my way up to the loft. I pulled my shoes off. I stretched out on the bed, propping the pillows up behind me while I took stock of myself. All the niggling aches and pains in my body were gone, washed away by the wave of adrenaline that had tumbled over me during the attack. I was feeling drained, lethargic, my brain still crackling while my body was immobilized. Downstairs, I heard the murmur of Dietz talking on the phone.

I must have dozed, sitting upright. Dietz appeared. I opened my eyes to find him perched on the bed beside me. He was holding some papers in one hand and a mug of tea in the other. "Drink this," he said.

I took the mug and held it, focusing on the heat. Tea has always smelled better than it tastes. I can still remember how startled I was as a kid when I was first allowed to have a sip. I glanced up at the skylight, which showed a circle of lavender and smoke. "What time is it?"

"Ten after seven."

"Have we heard from Clyde?"

"He called a little while ago. She's fine. They treated her and sent her home. No sign of Agnes yet. How are you?"

"Better."

"That's good. We'll have some supper in a bit. Henry's bringing something over."

"I hate being taken care of."

"Me, too, but that's bullshit. Henry likes to feel useful, I'm starving, and neither of us cook. You want to talk?"

I shook my head. "My soul's not back in my body yet."

"It'll come. I got a line on the guy from the L.A. police. You want to take a look?"

"All right."

There was a sheaf of LAPD bulletins, maybe six. I studied the first. WANTED FELONY TRAFFIC SUSPECTS. There were ten mug shots—like class photos—one circled in ballpoint pen. It was him. He looked younger. He looked pale. He looked glum—one of life's chronic offenders at the outset of his career. His name was Mark Darian Messinger, alias: Mark Darian; alias: Darian Marker; alias: Buddy Messer; alias: Darian Davidson. Male, Caucasian, thirty-eight years old, blond hair, blue eyes, tattoo of a butterfly on the web of his right hand (I'd missed that). His date of birth was July 7, Cancer, a real family man at heart. His California driver's license number was listed, his Social Security number, his NCIC file number, FBI number, his department report number, his warrant number. The arrest, apparently in the summer of 1981, was for violation of Vehicle Code Section 20001 (hit-and-run resulting in death) and Penal Code Section 192(3)(a) (vehicular manslaughter while driving under the influence). The photograph was an inch and a half wide square, taken straight on. It helped to see him shrunk down to Lilliputian proportions, the size of a postage stamp. He looked like a low-life punk, the black-and-white mug shot not nearly as sinister as the flesh-and-blood reality.

The second police bulletin read: ARREST FOR MURDER OF A POLICE OFFICER, Felony Warrant LACA, with a string of numbers, charging Penal Code Section 187(a) (murder) and Section 664/187 (attempted murder) with a six-line narrative attached. "On October 9, 1981, two Los Angeles police officers responded to a domestic disturbance during which the above suspect fired an unknown type semiautomatic at his common-law wife. When the police officers attempted to subdue him, suspect shot one of the officers in the face, resulting in his death. The suspect then fled on foot."

The names of two detectives, assigned to the case, were listed below that, along with several telephone numbers if information came to light. At the bottom of the page was a line in bold print. KINDLY NOTIFY CHIEF OF POLICE, LOS ANGELES, CALIFORNIA, it said. KINDLY KILL THIS MAN ON SIGHT, I thought.

The third bulletin was dated less than two months back. ONE MILLION DOLLAR ROBBERY INFORMATION WANTED. And there he was again, in a police composite drawing, this time with a mustache, which he must have shaved off in the interim. According to the victim's account, the suspect had followed a wholesale gold dealer into a gold exchange business in the Jewelry Mart section of downtown Los Angeles on March 25, where he relieved the victim of the gold he was transporting, valued in excess of $625,000. The suspect had produced a gun and robbed the victim and another employee of an additional $346,000 in gold "granules" and $46,000 in cash. Mark Messinger had been identified from fingerprints at the scene.

I leafed through the remaining bulletins. There was apparently no crime Mark Messinger was incapable of committing—the well-rounded felon with a major in murder and minors in armed robbery and assault with a deadly weapon. He seemed to operate with equal parts impulse and brute force. He didn't go in for the intellectual stuff, nothing with finesse. The million-dollar robbery was probably the most sophisticated thing he'd ever done.

"Now we know how he can afford to take on a cut-rate hit," I said.

Dietz tapped the paper, pointing to one of the last lines of print. A brief note indicated that the suspect was reported to have relatives in Santa Teresa. "That's how he knew Tyrone Patty. From here. They were cellmates in the county jail four years ago. I guess they kept in touch."

"Have the cops here talked to his family?"

Dietz nodded. "No luck. His father claims he hasn't talked to Messinger in years. He's probably lying, but you can't do much about that. Dolan says they delivered a stern lecture about aiding and abetting. The old man swore a Boy Scout oath he'd notify the cops if the guy showed up."

I could feel a knot of dread begin to form in my gut. "Let's talk about something else."

"Let's talk about fighting back."

"Tomorrow," I said. "Right now, I'm not in the mood."

"Drink your tea and get cleaned up. I'll see you downstairs."

Henry had put together a meal of comfort foods: succulent meatloaf with mushroom gravy, mashed potatoes, fresh green beans, homemade rolls, fresh lemon meringue pie, and coffee. He ate with us, saying little, watching me with worried eyes. Dietz must have cautioned him not to chide me for leaving the premises. It was clear Henry wanted to fuss, but he had the presence of mind to keep his mouth shut. I felt guilty anyway, as if the attempt on my life was something I had done. Henry studied the police bulletins, memorizing Mark Messinger's face and the details of his (alleged) crimes. "A nasty piece of work. You mentioned a little boy. How does he figure into this?" he said to Dietz.

"He kidnapped the kid from his common-law wife. Her name is Rochelle. She works in a massage parlor down in Hollywood. I talked to her a little while ago and the woman's a mess. The kid's name is Eric. He's five. He was enrolled in a day-care center in Rochelle's neighborhood. Messinger picked him up about eight months ago and that's the last she's seen of him. I got boys of my own. I'd kill anyone came after them." Dietz ate like he did everything else, with intense concentration. When he finished the last scrap of food, he sat back, patting automatically at the shirt pocket where he'd kept his cigarettes. I saw a quick head shake, as if he were amused at himself.

They moved on to other subjects: sports, the stock market, political events. While they talked, I gathered the empty plates and utensils and took them to the kitchenette. I ran a sinkful of soapy water and slid the dishes in. There's nothing so restful as washing dishes when you need to separate yourself from other folk. It looks dutiful and industrious and it's soothing as a bubble bath. For the moment, I felt safe. I didn't care if I ever left the apartment again. What was wrong with staying right here? I could learn to cook and clean house. I could iron clothes (if I had any). Maybe I could learn to sew and make craft items out of Popsicle sticks. I just didn't want to go out again. I was beginning to feel about the real world as I did about swimming in the ocean. Off the Santa Teresa coast, the waters of the Pacific are murky and cold, filled with USTs (unidentified scary things) that can hurt you real bad: organisms made of jelly and slime, crust-covered creatures with stingers and horny pincers that can rip your throat out. Mark Messinger was like that: vicious, implacable, dead at heart.

Henry left at ten o'clock. Dietz turned the TV on, waiting up for the news while I went back to bed. I stirred twice during the night, glancing at the clock; once at 1:15 A.M., and again at 2:35. The light was still on downstairs and I knew Dietz was awake. He seemed to thrive on very little sleep while I never got quite enough. The light coming over the loft rail was a cheery yellow. Anyone coming after me would be forced to contend with him. Reassured, I drifted off again.

Given my anxiety level, I slept well and woke with some of my old energy, which lasted almost until I got downstairs. Dietz was still in the shower. I made sure the front door was locked. I considered loitering outside the bathroom, listening to him sing, but I was afraid he'd catch me at it and perhaps take offense. I made a pot of coffee, set out the milk, the cereal boxes, and the bowls. I peered out one of the windows, opening the wooden shutter just a crack. All I could see was a slit of the flower bed. I pictured Messinger across the street with a bolt-action sniper rifle with a 10x scope trained so he could blow my head off the minute I stirred. I retreated to the kitchenette and poured some orange juice. I hadn't felt this threatened since my first day in elementary school.

Coming out of the bathroom, Dietz seemed surprised to find me up. He was wearing chinos and a form-fitting white T-shirt. He looked solid and muscular, without an ounce of extra fat. He disarmed the portable alarm system, opened the door, and brought the paper in. I noticed I was careful to hang back out of the line of fire. Some forms of mental illness probably feel just like this. I pulled a stool out and sat down.

He tossed the paper on the counter and then did a brief detour into the living room. He came back with the Davis, which he'd apparently taken from my purse. He placed it on the counter in front of me. He poured himself some coffee and sat down on the stool across from mine.

I murmured, "Good morning."

He nodded at the Davis. "I want you to dump that."

"What for?"

"It's a pocket pistol. Useless under the circumstances."

I resisted the temptation to say something flip. "I just got that!"

"Get another one."

"But why?"

"It's cheap and unreliable. It's not safe to carry with a round in the chamber, which means you have to keep the magazine full, the chamber empty, and the safety off. If you're in trouble, I don't want you having to rack the slide to chamber a round in order to put it into action. You can get a new holster while you're at it."

I stared at him. He didn't seem that impressed with the look I was giving him.

He said, "Where's the closest gun shop?"

"I don't have the money. You're talkin' five or six hundred bucks."

_ **141**

"More like eleven hundred for the gun you should have."

"Which is what?"

"Heckler & Koch P7 in nine-millimeter. You can get it used somewhere. It's the latest yuppie firearm. It looks good in the glove compartment of a BMW, but it's still right for you."

"Forget it!" I said.

This time he stared at *me*.

I felt myself faltering. "Even if I bought a gun today, I'd have to wait two weeks to pick it up."

"You can use the Davis until then, but not with those cartridges. You should be using a high-velocity hollow-point like the Winchester Silvertip or a prefragmented round like the Glaser Safety Slug. I suggest the Winchester Silvertip."

"Why those?" Actually it didn't matter. I was just feeling stubborn and argumentative.

He ticked his reasons off, using his fingers for emphasis. "It's less expensive for one thing and it's fairly widely used by law enforcement. With the underpowered thirty-two round, penetration is the most important—"

"All right. I got it," I said irritably. "Is that all you did last night? Sit around thinking up this stuff?"

"That's all I did," he said. He opened the paper and checked the front page. "Actually I have a Colt .45 out in the car. You can practice with both guns when we go up to the firing range."

"When are we doing that?"

"After the gun shop opens at ten."

"I don't want to go out."

"We're not going to let the guy affect your life this way." His gray eyes came up to mine. "Okay?"

"I'm scared," I said.

"Why do you think we're doing this?"

"What about the banquet?"

"I think we should go. He won't make another move for days. He wants you to think about your mortality. He wants your anxiety to mount until you jump every time the phone rings."

"I already do that."

"Have some breakfast. You'll feel better."

I poured my cereal and some milk, still brooding while I ate.

Dietz broke the silence, looking across the paper at me. "I want to say one thing again so listen carefully," he said. "A truly professional assassin kills either at close range or very long range. Up close, the weapon of choice would probably be a suppressed .22 long rifle with subsonic ammunition. From a distance, a bolt-action .308. Messinger is a bad-ass, but he's also an amateur. I'm going to nail him."

"What if he gets you first?"

"He won't." He went back to the sports section.

I felt better, I swear to God.

15

Dietz and I went to the office first. I checked my answering machine (no messages) while he glanced at the mail from the day before (no letter bombs). I locked up again and we went next door to the California Fidelity offices, where Vera was just getting in. She was wearing a two-piece outfit of red parachute material, long flowing skirt, blousy top with long sleeves and a red belt at the waist. Since I'd seen her yesterday, her hair had turned very blond, with streaks, and her glasses had changed to aviator shades with blue lenses. As usual she looked like the kind of woman any guy would love to jump out of an airplane with, an effect that wasn't lost on Dietz. She was carrying a garment on a hanger, covered by a cleaning bag. "Oh hi. You guys going tonight?"

"That's what we stopped by to tell you," I said. "Should I call the hotel?"

"I already did that," she said. "I figured you'd be there. This is for you." She indicated the cleaning bag. "Come on back to my office and you can take a look. This is girl stuff," she said to Dietz. "You still off cigarettes?"

"Day three," he said.

I hadn't realized he was counting.

"This is day seven for me," she said.

"How are you doing?"

"Not too bad. I've got all this manic energy. I feel amped. I must have counted on the nicotine to mellow me out. What about you?"

"I'm okay," he said mildly. "I like to do things to test myself."

"I'll bet you do," she said and laughed down in her throat. "We'll be back in a sec." She breezed on toward the back.

"Was that nasty, what you said to him? It sounded nasty," I asked, scurrying to keep up.

She glanced over her shoulder. "Listen, babycakes, when I get around to nasty you won't have any doubts."

She anchored the hanger over the edge of her cubicle and stuck an unlit Virginia Slim in her mouth, dragging on it cold. She closed her eyes, as if praying. "Oh God, for a light . . . for smoke . . . for the first heady hit of a cigarette . . ." She opened her eyes and shook her head. "I hate doing things that are good for me. Why did I decide to do this?"

"You were coughing up blood."

"Oh yeah. I forgot that part. Ah well. Take a look." She eased the plastic bag off the hanger. Under it was a black silk jumpsuit with spaghetti straps and a tiny belt. The matching jacket had a Mandarin collar and long sleeves. "What do you think?"

"It looks perfect."

"Good. Make sure it fits. Otherwise give me a call and I'll scare up something else. You can bring it with you at six and get dressed in my room. I'm staying at the Edgewater so I won't have to drive myself home afterward. I hate having to monitor my alcohol intake."

"Don't you have a date? I thought you'd be coming with Neil."

"I'm meeting him there. That way he's free to do anything he wants. I'll bring the jewelry tonight and maybe help you do something with your hair. I can tell I'm going to have to dress you."

"Vera, I'm not helpless."

145

"Of course you're not *helpless*. You're completely ignorant when it comes to clothes. I'll bet you've never even had your colors done."

I gave a little noncommittal shrug, trying to look like I had my colors done sometimes twice a week.

"Don't bother. You're a Summer. I can save you the fifty bucks. You shouldn't wear black, but to hell with it. You'll look great." She paused to study my face. "Very becoming, those bruises . . . especially the one turning green." She began to ease the plastic bag back over the outfit, unlit cigarette bobbing from the corner of her mouth. "How's it feel to spend twenty-four hours a day with a hunk?"

"You mean Dietz?"

Vera sighed and rolled her eyes. "No, I'm talking about Don Knotts. Never mind. You probably like him because he's competent, right?"

"Well, yeah. Isn't that the point?" I said. "You know what puzzles me? How come I'm surrounded by bossy people? Rosie, Dietz, Henry . . . now you."

"You're cute, you know that? You think you're such a hard-ass."

"I *am* a hard-ass," I said defensively.

"Neil's going to love you. Have you called him yet?"

"I haven't had a chance. We just got back."

"He's only coming tonight to meet you. Just remember. Don't eat."

I squinted at her. "How come? This is a retirement dinner, isn't it?"

"Suppose you want to go to bed with him."

"I don't," I said.

"But suppose you did."

"What's that got to do with eating dinner?"

She was losing patience with me, but stopped to spell it out. "Never go to bed with a guy after a big meal. Your stomach will pooch out."

"Why would I go to bed with a guy I can't have a big meal with first?"

"You can eat later, when you're married."

I had to laugh. "I'm not getting married later, but thanks for the tip."

"You're welcome. See you tonight."

I found Dietz sitting out by Darcy's desk, leafing through a pamphlet on uninsured losses. I took the outfit downstairs with us, tucking it carefully in his trunk when we reached the parking lot. "There's no way I'm wearing any body armor under this," I said.

Dietz made no comment and I took that for assent.

On our way to the firing range, we stopped by the gun shop and spent an hour bickering about guns. He knew far more than I did and I had to yield to his expertise. I left a deposit on an H&K P7 in 9-millimeter, filling out all the necessary paperwork. I ended up paying twenty-five bucks for fifty rounds of the Winchester Silvertips Dietz had insisted on. In exchange for my compliance, he had the good taste not to mention that all of this was his idea. I'd expected to find it galling to take his advice, but in reality, it felt fine. What did I have to prove? He'd been at it a lot longer than I had and he seemed to know what he was talking about.

Dietz drove up the pass in his little red Porsche like a man pursued. Maybe we were practicing for a car chase later on. The Porsche was not equipped with passenger brakes, but I kept my foot jammed to the floorboards in hopes. From where I sat, it looked like one of those camera's-eye views of the Indy 500, only speeding straight uphill. I was wishing I believed in an afterlife, as I was about to enjoy mine. Dietz didn't seem to notice my discomfiture. Since he was totally focused on the road, I didn't want to spoil his concentration with the piercing screams I was having to suppress.

The gun club was deserted except for the rangemaster, to whom we paid our fees. The May sun was hot, the breezes dry, scented with bay laurel and sage. The rains wouldn't come again until Christmastime. By August, the mountains would be parched, the vegetation desiccated, the timber primed for burning. Even now, looking down toward the valley, I could see a haze in the air, ghostly portent of the fires to come.

Dietz set up a B-27 human silhouette target at a distance of seven yards. I'd been practicing with the Davis at twenty-five yards, but Dietz just shook his head. "A .32's designed for self-defense inside fifteen yards, preferably inside ten. The round has to penetrate deeply enough to get to the vital organs and blood vessels, eight to ten inches in. The Silvertip has a better chance of getting far enough to make a difference."

"Nice business we're in," I said.

"Why do you think I'm getting out?"

I loaded the magazine on my little Davis while he detailed an exercise he referred to as a Mozambique drill. He had me start from the guard position: pistol loaded, round chambered, safety on, finger off the trigger, pointing at a forty-five-degree angle downward. "Bring the pistol up to shooting position and fire two quick shots into the upper chest, level with the sternum. Do a quick visual check to see where you've hit and then fire a third more careful shot into the head right around here," he said, indicating his eye sockets.

I put on my ear protectors and did as I was told, feeling self-conscious at first under his scrutiny. It was clear that in the years since the police academy, my skills had deteriorated. I'd come up here often, on an average of once a month, but I'd begun to think of it almost as a meditation instead of schooling in self-defense. Left to my own devices, I'd been neither rigorous nor exact. Dietz was a good teacher, patient, methodical, suggesting corrections in a way that never made me feel criticized.

"Now let's try it with your gun in your purse," he said when he was satisfied.

"How do you know all this stuff?"

He smiled faintly. "Weapons are a passion of mine. My first formal training in defensive pistolcraft was a class designed for certifying security guards to carry weapons on the job. The practical shooting part was minimal, but it did give me a fair grounding in the laws related to firearms. I went to the American Pistol Institute after that." He paused. "Are we up here to work or chat?"

"I get to choose?" I said.

Apparently not. He had me try the .45, but it was too much gun for me coming off the .32. He relented on that point and let me continue with the Davis. We went back to work, the smell of gunpowder perfuming the air as I concentrated on the process. I'd ceased to think about Mark Messinger as a person. He'd become an abstract—no more than a flat, black silhouette seven yards away—with a paper heart, paper brain. It was therapeutic firing at him, watching his midriff shred. My fearfulness began to fall away and my confidence returned. I fired at his paper neck and hit an inky artery. I pretended to tattoo my initials on his trunk. By the time we packed up and left the range at noon, I was feeling like my old self again.

We had lunch at the Stage Coach Tavern, tucked up against the mountain with a stream trickling down through the rocks close by. Live oak and bay laurel kept the tavern shrouded in chill shade. The quiet was undercut by the gossiping of the birds. Only an occasional car climbed the grade out in front, heading for the main road. Dietz was still vigilant—scanning the premises—but he seemed more at ease somehow, sipping beer, one foot propped up on the crude wooden bench where he sat. I was seated on his left with my back to the wall, watching as he did, though there wasn't much to see. There were only three other customers, bikers sitting at one of the rough plank tables outside.

We'd ordered the chili verde, which the waitress brought: two wide bowls of fragrant pork and green chili stew with a dollop of cilantro pesto on top and two folded flour tortillas submerged in the depths. This might be as close to heaven as a sinner could get without repenting first.

"What's your deal with California Fidelity?" he asked, between bites.

"They provide me office space and I provide them services

maybe two or three times a month. It varies. Usually I investigate fire and wrongful death claims, but it could be anything."

"Nice arrangement. How'd you set that up?"

"My aunt worked for them for years so I knew a lot of those guys. She used to get me occasional summer jobs when I was still in high school. I went through the academy when I was nineteen and since I couldn't actually join the PD till I was twenty-one, I worked as the CF receptionist. Later, after I finally left the police force, I joined a private agency until I could get licensed, and then I went out on my own. One of the first big investigations I did was for CF."

"A lot more women getting into it," he said.

"Why not? It's fun, in some sick sense. You end up feeling pretty hard-bitten sometimes, but at least you can be your own boss. It's in my nature. I'm curious at heart and I like sticking my nose in where it doesn't belong," I said. "What about you? What will you do if you leave the field?"

"Hard to say. I'm talking to a guy out in Colgate who sets up antiterrorist training exercises for military bases overseas."

"Simulated attacks?"

"That's right. Dead of night, he takes a crew in, breaches perimeter fences, infiltrates the compound, and puts the whole maneuver on film to show 'em where they need to beef up their defenses."

"Cops and robbers without the firepower."

"Exactly. All the hype and none of the jeopardy." He paused, mopping the bottom of his bowl with a folded tortilla. "You look like you've got all your ducks in a row."

"I feel that way," I said. "Vera would disagree. She thinks I'm hopeless. Too independent, unsophisticated . . ."

"What's the story on her?"

"I've never figured it out, to tell you the truth. She's the closest thing to a friend I've got and even then, I can't claim we know each other very well. I'm gone a lot so I don't socialize much. She tends to circulate in the singles scene, which I've never been good at. I do admire her. She's smart. She's got style. She doesn't take any guff . . ."

"What is this, a sales pitch?"

I laughed, shrugging. "You asked."

"Yeah, well she's one of those women I've never figured out."

"In what way?"

"Don't know. I never figured that out either. Just something about her puzzles me," he said.

"She's a good soul."

"No doubt." He finished cleaning his bowl without another word on the subject. It was hard to tell sometimes what he was really thinking and I didn't know him well enough to press.

16

We left for the hotel at six. Dietz had already cleaned up and was dressed for the occasion in casual pants, a dress shirt, patterned tie, and dark sport coat, cut western-style: broad across the shoulders, tapered at the waist. He was wearing black boots, visible where his cuffs broke, the toes polished to a hard shine. Under his sport coat, of course, he was wearing a Kevlar vest that would stop a .357 Magnum at ten feet. I'd also watched him strap on a holster that he wore behind the hip on his right-hand side, and into which he'd tucked his .45.

I'd showered and hopped right back in my jeans, turtleneck, and tennis shoes, intending to slip into the silk jumpsuit once I reached Vera's room. I'd tried it on quickly just before we left the house. The pants were slightly too long, but I'd bunched 'em up at the waist and that took care of it. I'd packed black pumps, panty hose, black underpants, and some odds and ends in a little overnight case. Dietz had excused me from the bulletproof vest, which would have looked absurd with spaghetti straps. The Davis was tucked in an outside pouch of my big leather handbag, which looked more like a diplomatic pouch than an evening purse. The normally bulky bag was further plumped up by the inclusion of a nightscope Dietz had asked me to carry. The scope only weighed about a pound, but it was the size of a zoom lens for a 35-millimeter camera and made me list to one side. "Why're we taking this thing?" I asked.

"That's my latest toy. I usually keep it in the car, but I don't want to leave it in the hotel parking lot. Cost me over three thousand bucks."

"Oh."

Dietz took a roundabout route, saying little. Despite his assurances that Mark Messinger would be laying off me for a day or two, he seemed on edge, which made my stomach churn in response. He was focused, intense, already vigilant. He pushed the car lighter in and then reached reflexively toward his cigarettes. "Shit!" he said. He shook his head, annoyed with himself.

He rounded a corner, downshifting. "Times like this I envy the guys who do government work," he remarked. "You'd have a squad of bodyguards. They've got unlimited manpower, access to intelligence sources, and the legal authority to kick butt. . . ."

I couldn't think what to say to that so I kept my mouth shut.

We pulled into the wide brick drive in front of the hotel and Dietz got out, slipping the usual folded bill to the parking attendant with instructions to keep the car within sight. It was still light outside and the landscape was saturated with late afternoon sun. The grass was close-cropped, a dense green, the lawn bordered with pink and white impatiens and clumps of lobelia, which glowed an intense, electric blue. On the far side of the road, the surf battered at the seawall, clouding the air with the briny smell of the thundering Pacific.

In addition to the Edgewater's sprawling main building, there were a line of bungalows at the rear of the property, each the size of the average single-family dwelling in my neighborhood. The architecture was Spanish-style, white stucco exterior, heavy beams, age-faded red tile roofs, interior courtyards. Under an archway that led to the formal gardens, a wedding party was beginning to assemble: five bridesmaids in dusty pink and a manic flower girl skipping back and forth with a basket of rose petals. Two young men in tuxedos, probably ushers, looked on, contemplating the efficacies of birth control.

As usual, Dietz took me by the elbow, keeping himself slightly in front of me as he walked us toward the entrance. I found myself scanning, as he did, the smattering of guests in the immediate vicinity. He was keyed up, eyes watchful as we entered the spacious lobby, which was flanked by two oversize imported rose marble desks. We approached the concierge and had a brief chat. Dietz had apparently had a second conversation with the management up front because shortly afterward, Charles Abbott, the director of security, appeared. Introductions went around. Abbott was in his late sixties and looked like a retired Fortune 500 executive in a three-piece suit, complete with manicured nails and a Rolex watch. This was not a man you'd ever refer to as Charlie or Chuck. His silver hair was the same tone as the pale gray of his suit and a diamond stickpin winked from the center of his tie. I had the feeling what he did now was lots more fun than whatever he did then. He led us over to a corner of the lobby where three big leather wing chairs were grouped together in the shelter of a ten-foot rubber plant.

Dietz had brought photocopies of the mug shots of Mark Messinger. "This is the guy we're worried about. I'd like to distribute these among the staff who'll be working the banquet tonight."

Abbott gave a cursory glance to the pictures before he handed them back. He had luminous blue eyes and made lots of eye contact. "Mr. Dietz, I have to remind you that we're not equipped to handle any kind of sophisticated security measures for a private citizen. We cooperate with the Secret Service when the occasion arises, but the hotel can't accept any liability in the event of some kind of unfortunate incident. We're here primarily to protect the safety of our registered guests. As long as I'm kept informed, we'll be happy to do what we can, but beyond that I can't promise much."

Dietz smiled. "I understand that," he said pleasantly. "This is purely precautionary on our part. We don't anticipate any problems, but it's wise to tag a few bases just to ensure that everything goes smoothly."

Abbott said, "Of course."

Dietz was on his best behavior, casual, relaxed. He must have really needed this man's help.

Abbott's expression was bemused. He looked like the kind of man who'd use a cigarette holder and a small gold Dunhill. "How else can I help? I can make one of my security staff available."

"I don't think that'll be necessary, but thanks. We do have a California Fidelity employee, Vera Lipton, registered here for the night. I'd like to have her room number and the names of guests occupying the rooms on either side of her. Is that something you can do?"

Abbott considered the request. Under the smooth and easygoing manner, there was ice and flint. "I don't see why not." He excused himself and moved over to the front desk. After a short conversation with the desk clerk, he jotted a note in a small leather notebook he'd taken from his right pocket. He returned, tore the leaf off, and handed it to Dietz.

"You know either of these couples?" Dietz asked.

"I know both. The Clarks have stayed here many times. Mr. and Mrs. Thiederman happen to be my aunt and uncle."

Dietz tucked the paper away and shook Abbott's hand. "Thanks. We appreciate this."

"Happy to be of help," the man said.

We moved down a carpeted hallway to the right, following the room numbers in descending order. Dietz kept an eye on the corridor behind us, the ever-present hand on my elbow for leverage. At any unexpected occurrence, he had a modicum of control.

Vera's room was located in the same wing as the banquet room. "Did you set this up?" I asked him when I saw how close it was.

"I didn't want you hiking the length of the hotel, getting there and back." He knocked once. There was a pause. My guess was that Vera was peering through the tiny fish-eye porthole in the door. We heard a bolt turn, and there she was, squinting at us from behind the burglar chain. She was in a green silk kimono with a lot of cleavage visible where the fabric gaped in front. She glanced down and pulled the yawning lapels together with one hand. "I kept the chain on. Wasn't that smart?"

Dietz said, "You're a peach, Vera. Now let us in."

She tilted her head, gaze angling down the hall. "How do I know somebody's not holding you at gunpoint?"

Dietz laughed. I looked at him quizzically. I'd only heard him laugh once. "Good point," he said.

I personally didn't think the point was that good, but nobody was asking me, right?

Vera closed the door so she could slide the chain off and then let us in. The room was enormous: king-size bed, king-size antique armoire housing a king-size television set. The dominant color was pale yellow: thick pale yellow carpet, wallpaper strewn with delicate white Japanese irises. The pattern of the wallpaper had been repeated in the polished cotton bedspread and matching polished cotton drapes, pulled back on brass rods. The sheers were closed, lights outside indicating that the room faced the entrance drive. The two upholstered chairs were done in pale green with white latticework cut on the diagonal. Through a doorway, I spied a bathroom that continued the color scheme: a vase of white silk flowers, fat yellow hand towels rolled up in a willow basket on the sink.

Vera had her personal effects on every conceivable surface: discarded clothing tossed on the bed, hanging clothes hooked on the closet door, which stood open to the room. There were cosmetics on the chest of drawers, hot rollers and a curling iron on the bathroom counter, a damp towel on the toilet seat. A suitcase open on the luggage rack revealed a frothy tumble of soft chiffon lingerie. A pair of panty hose had been flung on one of the upholstered chairs, sprawling there with the legs spread and the diamond-shaped cotton crotch looking like an arrow, pointing up. Dietz headed straight for the door to the adjoining room, making sure it was locked. Then he closed the drapes.

Vera crossed to the coffee table. She'd had a bottle of champagne delivered, resting in a frosted silver ice bucket with four champagne flutes on a tray. She picked the bottle up by the neck and began to loosen the foil. "Grab a seat. We can have a drink."

"Not for me, thanks. I have to work," he said. And then to me, "Keep the door locked. If the phone rings, you can answer it, but don't identify yourself. If it's someone you know, keep the conversation brief. Don't give out information of any sort to anyone. If you get a wrong number, let me know. It's probably someone checking to see if the room is still occupied." He glanced at his watch. "I'll be back at seven, straight up, to walk you over to the banquet room."

Once Dietz left the room, she held her arms up and shimmied. "Let's get down!" she said and then did a little bump and grind, accompanied by a whoop. She twisted the wire off the champagne bottle and draped a towel across the top, working the cork back and forth with both thumbs until it popped. She filled two flutes and handed me one. "I've already done my makeup," she said. "Why don't you hop in the shower while I get dressed. Then we'll do your hair."

"I've already showered. All I have to do is put on the jumpsuit and I'm done."

She gave me a look to let me know how wrong I was.

Under her critical gaze, I slipped out of my jeans and into the jumpsuit. She only winced a little bit at the sight of my bruises. Meanwhile, my facial expression was probably the equivalent of an ailing dog on its way to the vet's. Ugh. Makeup. I pulled the suit on and started tucking the pants up at the waist.

She smacked my hand. "Don't do that," she said. She knelt and turned my pant legs under to a length that suited her and then secured them with fabric tape she'd brought in her purse.

"You think of everything," I said.

" 'Prepared' is my middle name, honeybun."

Then she went to work on the rest of me.

I sat on the closed toilet lid with a towel around my neck, Vera's body inserted between me and the wall-to-wall mirror that ran along the countertop. "What are you going to do about the bruises on my face?"

"Trust me, kid."

She had bottles and powders, lotions, creams, goo in jars, brushes, applicators, sponges, Q-tips. She worked with her face very close to mine, issuing instructions. "Close your eyes. Now look up . . . God, quit blinking! You're making a mess." She painted on lipstick with a brush, her own lips forming the shape she wanted me to form with mine.

Forty minutes later, she stepped back, scrutinizing her handiwork. She twisted the lipstick back down in the tube. "Yeah. I like it," she said. "What do you think?" She moved aside so I could see my reflection in the mirror.

I looked at myself. Suddenly, I had these dramatic eyes, all the color of a maiden in the first blush of youth, dewy mouth, hair standing out in a dark windblown tumble. I cracked up.

"Go ahead and laugh," she said acidly. "You look damn good."

Dietz returned to the room at seven, glancing at us both without remark. Vera had done herself up in six minutes flat, her personal best she said. She was wearing a black dress with a low-cut top filled to the brim with bulging breasts, black hose with a seam up the back, black spike heels. She stopped dead in her tracks and put her hands on her hips. "What do you say, Dietz? Come on. Cough it out."

"You look great. No shit. Both of you look swell."

" 'Swell' doesn't even come close." And then to me, "I'll bet he still calls women 'gals.' "

"Not so far," I said.

Dietz smiled to himself, but refused to engage. He propelled us across the hall and down three doors into the safety of the banquet room, which was small and elegant: chandelier, white woodwork, walls padded in cream-colored silk. Six tables for six had been laid out with a spray of orchids as the centerpiece. Each table was numbered and I could see that place cards were set out, names in script.

Many of the CF employees were already there, standing together in groups of three and four, drinks in hand. I spotted Mac Voorhies and his wife Marie, Jewel and her husband (whom I'd only met once), Darcy Pascoe and her boyfriend, the (allegedly) dope-peddling mailman. Vera slipped her hand through Dietz's arm and the three of us circled the room while everyone was introduced to everyone else and we all promptly forgot who was who. I could see Vera doing an eyeball cruise, checking across the heads to see if Neil Hess had arrived yet. I was just hoping he'd be tall enough for her to spot.

Dietz bought us each a drink. His was a plain soda water with lime, mine a white wine, and Vera's a tequila sunrise. She sucked that one down and bought herself another. I watched her with interest. I'd never seen Vera so tense. She turned to Dietz. "God, how can you drink without smoking a cigarette?"

"This isn't alcohol."

She rolled her eyes. "That's even worse. I'm going to bum one," she said. "No, I'm not. Well, maybe one. A puff."

"Is that Neil?" I asked. A doctorish type was poised in the doorway, searching for a familiar face. Without a reference point, of course, it wasn't possible to tell just how short he was, but he looked okay to me. Pleasant face, dark hair cut stylishly. He wore a navy suit, pale blue shirt I could have bet would have monogrammed cuffs. The bow tie was unexpected—I hadn't seen one in years. Vera raised a hand. His face brightened when he spotted her. He made his way across the room while she moved to join him, tucking her arm in his when they connected at the midpoint. She had to bend a bit to talk to him, but the disparity in their heights didn't seem remarkable to me. I tried to picture him with his head on my pillow, but it really didn't wash.

17

▶▶ ▶▶ ▶▶ Vera, in charge of the seating, had of course set it up so that Neil Hess and I were together. She and Dietz were at the table to our left. Dietz had apparently interceded to some extent, arranging it so that I was secured in one corner of the room, facing the entrance. Dietz was seated with his back to me, facing the entrance as well so he could keep an eye on the door. Vera was on his left, fully visible to me while all I could see of him was the back of his head. Both tables flanked an emergency exit that the security director had assured Dietz would remain unlocked for us during the course of the banquet.

By eight, everyone had arrived and the assembled group settled at the tables like a flock of birds. The noise level had risen several decibels as a result of the alcohol consumed. These were company relationships and there was a sense of giddiness and unease at the sudden shift from business to social behaviors. The three-course dinner was served at a leisurely pace: a salad of baby lettuces, boneless chicken breasts sautéed with lemon and capers, miniature vegetables, hot breads, and finally a dense chocolate cake in a puddle of vanilla sauce. I ate like a forest animal, head coming up to check the door at any sign of movement, worried that Mark Messinger would show up with an Uzi and mow us down like weeds. Judging from the set of Dietz's shoulders, he was more relaxed than I, but then he was staring down the front of Vera's dress, a titillating distraction for any man.

I tuned into the conversation at the table. Neil and I had been seated with two underwriters and their wives, a foursome talking bridge with an intensity I envied. I gathered they'd just returned from some kind of bridge-oriented cruise in which baby slams and gourmet foods were served up in equal measure. Much talk of no-trump, double finesses, and Sheinwold, whose strategies they were debating. Since neither Neil nor I played, we were left to our own devices, a possibility Vera had probably calculated well in advance.

At close range, the man was attractive enough, though I saw no particular evidence of all the virtues Vera had ascribed to him. Nice hands. Nice mouth. Seemed a bit self-satisfied, but that might have been discomfort masquerading as arrogance. I noticed that when we talked about professional matters (his work, in other words) he exuded confidence. When it came to his personal life, he was unsure of himself and usually shifted the subject to safer ground. By the time the dessert came, we were still groping our way through various conversational gambits, casting about for common interests without much success.

"Where'd you go to school, Kinsey?"

"Santa Teresa High."

"I meant college."

"I didn't go to college."

"Oh really? That surprises me. You seem smart enough."

"People don't hire me for 'smart.' They hire me because I'm too dumb to know when to quit. Also, I'm a woman, so they think I'll work cheap."

He laughed. I wasn't being funny so I gave a little shrug.

He pushed his dessert plate aside and took a sip of coffee. "If you got a degree, you could write your own ticket, couldn't you?"

I looked at him. "A degree in what?"

"Criminalistics, I would guess."

"Then I'd have to go to work for the government or the local cops. I already did that and hated it. I'm better off where I am. Besides, I hated school, too. All I did was smoke dope." I leaned toward him. "Now can I ask you one?"

"Sure."

"How did you and Vera meet?"

He was almost imperceptibly disconcerted, shifting slightly in his seat. "A mutual friend introduced us a couple of months ago. We've been seeing each other ever since . . . just as friends, of course. Nothing serious."

"Oh yeah, right," I said. "So what do you think?"

"About Vera? She's terrific."

"How come you're sitting here with me, then?"

He laughed again, a false, hearty roar that avoided a reply.

"I'm serious," I said. His smile cooled down by degrees. He still wasn't addressing the issue so I tried it myself. "You know what I think it is? I got the impression she had the hots for you herself and didn't know how to handle it."

He gave me a look like I was speaking in tongues. "I have a hard time believing *that*," he said. He thought about it for a moment. "Anyway, she's a bit tall for me, don't you think?"

"Not at all. You look great together. I was watching when you came in."

He gave his head a slight shake. "I know it bothers her. She's never actually come out and said so, but—"

"She'll get over it."

"You think so?"

"Does it bother you?"

"Not a bit."

"Then what's the problem?"

He looked at me. His face was beginning to appeal to me. His eyes held a nice light, conveying qualities of sincerity and competence. He was probably the kind of doctor you could call at 2:00 A.M., a man who'd sit up with your kid until the fever broke. I was about to hike up my pant leg and show him my bruise, but it seemed kind of gross.

"You should hear the way she talks about you," I went on.

" 'Eight and a half on a scale of ten.' That's how she describes you. I swear to God."

"Are you kidding?"

"Neil, come on. I wouldn't kid about that. She's completely smitten with you. She just hasn't figured it out yet."

Now he laughed the kind of laugh that made his whole face light up. A boyish pleasure showed through and I could swear he blushed. He was really kind of cute. I glanced up in time to see Vera shoot me a stark look. I gave her a little finger wave and turned my attention back to him.

"I mean, what the hell are relationships about?" I asked.

"But she's never given any indication . . ."

"Well, I'm telling you for a fact. I've known her for ages and I've never heard her talk about a guy the way she talks about you."

He was taking it in, but I could tell he wasn't buying it.

"How tall are you?" I said. "You don't look short to me."

"Five seven."

"She's only five nine. What's the big deal?"

Mac Voorhies tapped on his glass with a spoon about then, saying, "Ladies and gentlemen, if I may have your attention . . ." He and Marie had been placed at table two, near the center of the room. Jewel and her husband were at the same table and I could see Jewel begin to squirm, anticipating the speech to come. Maclin Voorhies is one of the California Fidelity vice presidents, lean and humorless, with sparse, fly-away white hair and a perpetual cigar clamped between his teeth. He's smart and fair-minded, honorable, conservative, ill-tempered sometimes, but a very capable executive. The notion of being publicly praised by this man had already brought the color to Jewel's face.

The room gradually quieted.

Mac took a moment to survey the crowd. "We're here tonight to pay homage to one of the finest women I've ever been privileged to work with. As you all know, Jewel Cavaletto is retiring from the company after twenty-five years of service . . ."

There's something hypnotic about the tone and tenor of

an after-dinner speech, maybe because everyone's full of food and wine and the room's too warm by then. I was sitting there feeling grateful that Mac had bypassed the canned humor and was getting straight to the point. I don't know what made me look at the door. Everyone else was looking at Mac. I caught something out of the corner of my eye and turned my head.

It was the kid. I blinked uncomprehendingly at first, as if confronted with a mirage. Then I felt a rush of fear.

The only clear glimpse I'd ever had of him was that first encounter at the rest stop. Mark Messinger had been feigning sleep that day, stretched out on a bench with a magazine across his face while Eric knelt on the pavement with his Matchbox car, making mouth noises, shifting gears with his voice. I'd seen him again one night in the motel parking lot, his features indistinguishable in the poorly lighted alcove where his father had taken him to buy a soft drink. I'd heard his laughter echo through the darkness, an impish peal that reminded me of the shadowy underworld of elves and fairies. The last time I'd seen him, his face had been partially obscured behind the paper sticker on the passenger side of the truck in which his father tried to run me down.

He was small for five. The light in the corridor glinted on his blond head. His hair was getting long. His eyes were pinned on me and a half-smile played on his mouth. He turned to look at someone standing in the corridor just out of sight. He was being prompted, like a kid acting an unfamiliar part in the grade-school play. I could see him say, "What?" I didn't wait to see what the next line would be.

I grabbed my handbag and came up out of my seat, nearly knocking my chair over in the process. Dietz turned to look at me and caught the direction of my startled gaze. By the time he checked the entrance, it was empty. I bolted around Neil's chair, heading toward the hall, tagging Dietz's arm. "It's the kid," I hissed. His gun came out and he grabbed my arm, jerking me along behind him as he moved toward the door. Mac caught the commotion and stopped midsentence, looking up at us in astonishment. Other people turned to see what was going on. Some woman emitted a startled cry at the sight of Dietz's .45, but by then he'd reached the entrance and had flattened himself against the wall. He peered around the doorway to the right, glanced left, and drew back. "Come on," he said.

Still propelling me by the arm, he walk-raced us down the corridor to the left, our footsteps thudding on the tiled surface. I half-expected him to stash me in Vera's room while he ran reconnaissance, but instead he steered us toward the exit at the end of the hall. At the door, we stopped again abruptly while he made sure there was no one out there. The night air hit us like icy water after the warmth of the banquet room. We eased away from the light, hugging the shrubs as we rounded the corner, moving toward the parking lot.

"You're sure it was him?" he asked, his tone low.

"Of course I'm sure."

We were on a darkened walkway that bordered one of the interior courtyards. Crickets were chirring and I could smell the slightly skunky scent of marigolds. Voices up ahead. Dietz drew us into the shelter of some hibiscus bushes bunched against the building. I was clutching the Davis, my hand shoved down in the outside pocket of my shoulderbag. Dietz's fingers dug painfully into the flesh of my right arm, but that was the only indication I had of how tense he was. A couple passed, two of the bridesmaids I'd seen earlier. I could hear their long taffeta skirts rustle as they hurried by.

"Just what I need . . . a guy equipped with a Fourex," one was saying.

"Hey, come on. He's buff . . . ," the other said, voices fading as they turned through the archway to our left.

Dietz moved out onto the walkway, keeping me close. "We'll check the parking lot," he murmured. "I want to make sure the guy's not out there waiting for us."

There was a scattering of guests at the hotel entrance, waiting for their cars to be brought around by three white-jacketed valets who had spread out, at a trot, across the parking lot. The immediate area was washed by a wide spill of light. The windows along the wing to our left formed tall rectangles of yellow, casting soft oblongs of illumination on the grass below. Banana palms intersected the light source at intervals. To our right, against the darkness, a thick cluster of birds-of-paradise was highlighted in blue and green outdoor spots that made them look like a flock of beaky fowl staring intently into the middle distance. A car eased out of the driveway and turned right, headlights flashing across the upright supports of the seawall. The ocean beyond was a pounding presence limned in moonlight.

The back end of Dietz's red Porsche was in plain view, parked close to the line of shrubs that bordered the circular driveway.

Dietz motioned for the nightscope, which I dug out of my handbag. He held the scope to his eye, scanning the grounds. "Here. You look," he murmured and handed me the device. I peered through the scope, startled by the sudden eerie green clarity of the landscape. Where the black had seemed dense and impenetrable, there was now a fine haze of green, with objects outlined in neon. The kid was crouching in a thicket of ferns beside a palm tree. He was sitting on his heels, arms wrapped around his bony knees, which were bared in shorts. While I was watching, he lifted his head, peering toward the entrance, perhaps in hopes of catching sight of us. His young body conveyed all the tension of a game of hide-and-seek. I didn't see Messinger, but he had to be somewhere close. I touched Dietz's arm and pointed. He took the scope and scanned again.

"Got him," he murmured. He checked with his naked eye and then again with the scope. Without a word, we retreated, retracing our steps. We circled the main building, slipping into the hotel through a service entrance at the rear. Dietz used one of a bank of wall phones near the kitchen to call a cab, which picked us up on a side street behind the hotel minutes later.

18

By the time we got home it was nearly eleven o'clock and Dietz was in a foul mood. He'd been silent in the cab, silent as he unlocked the door and let us in. Impatiently, he stripped off his jacket. The right sleeve got hung up on his cuff link. He jerked it free, wadded the jacket up and flung it across the room, ignoring the fact that it didn't go that far. He went into the kitchenette, opened the bottle of Jack Daniel's, and poured himself a jelly glass of whiskey, which he tossed down.

I picked up the jacket from the floor and folded it across my arm. "It's not your fault," I said.

"The fuck it's not," he snapped. "I was the one who insisted we go tonight. It was stupid . . . way too risky . . . and for what? Messinger could have walked in there with an Uzi and mowed us all down."

Actually it was hard to argue that one, as the same thing had occurred to me. "What happened? Nothing happened."

He reached for a cigarette, but caught himself abruptly. "I'm going out," he said.

"And leave me here by myself?" I yelped.

He flashed a dark look at me, his fingers tightened on the glass until I half-expected him to crush it in his grip. Something about the gesture made my temper climb.

"Oh, for God's sake. Just cut it out, okay? The guy's showing off again. Big deal. He wants me nervous and he wants you kicking your own butt. Well, so far, so good. You storm out to buy a pack of cigarettes and he can step in and finish me off without any interference. Thanks a lot."

He was silent for a moment. He set the glass aside and leaned, stiff-armed, against the counter, head down. "You're right."

"Damn right I'm right," I said peevishly. "Lighten up and let's figure out some way to kill his ass. I hate chickenshit guys trying to shoot me. Let's get him first."

That gave his mood a lift. "How?"

"I don't know how."

There was a knock at the door and both of us jumped. Dietz whipped his gun out and motioned me into the kitchenette. He crossed to the front door and flattened himself against the wall to the right. "Who is it?"

The voice was muffled. "Clyde Gersh."

I moved toward the door, but Dietz waved me back with a scowl. He tilted his head against the doorframe. "What do you want?"

"Agnes was picked up. She's in the emergency room at St. Terry's and she's asking for Kinsey. We left a couple of messages on the answering machine, but when we didn't hear back, we thought we'd stop by. We're on our way to the hospital. Is she home yet?"

Dietz said, "Hang on." He pointed to the answering machine, which rested on the bookshelf behind the sofa. I eased across the room and checked the message light, which indicated that two calls had been recorded. I turned the volume down, pushed the auto playback button, and listened to the tape. The first message was from Irene, the second from Clyde, both saying much the same thing. Agnes had been found and was asking for me. Dietz and I exchanged a look.

He lifted his brows in a facial shrug. He flipped the porch light on, peered through the spyhole, and opened the door with caution. Clyde was standing by himself on the doorstep in a circle of wan light. Beyond him, all was darkness. The fog was rolling in and I could see faint wisps of it curling around the light. "Sorry for the inconvenience," he said. "I don't like to disturb people this late, but Irene insisted."

"Come on in," Dietz said, stepping back so Clyde could enter. Dietz closed the door behind him and motioned Clyde to have a seat, an offer Clyde declined with a brief shake of his head. "Irene's waiting in the car. I don't want to leave her too long. She's anxious to get over there."

He was looking weary, his baggy face weighted with anxiety. He wore a tan gabardine topcoat, hands shoved down in his pockets. His gaze flickered across Dietz's holster but he refrained from comment, as if mentioning the gun might be a breach of etiquette.

"How's Agnes doing? Has anybody said?" I asked.

"We're not really sure. The doc says minor cuts and bruises . . . nothing serious . . . but her heartbeat's irregular and I guess they put her on some kind of monitor. She'll be admitted as soon as we sign the paperwork. I gather it's nothing life-threatening, but the woman is eighty-some-odd years old."

"The cops picked her up?"

Clyde nodded. "Some woman spotted her, wandering in the street. She was the one who called the police. The officer who called said Agnes is disoriented, has no idea where she is or where she's been all this time. The doc says she's been talking about you since they brought her in. We'd appreciate your coming with us if it's not too much trouble."

I said, "Sure. Let me change my clothes. I don't want to go like this."

"I'll let Irene know you're coming," he said to me. And then to Dietz, "Will you follow in your car or ride with us?"

"We'll come in your car and grab a cab back," Dietz said.

I was on my way up to the loft, stripping off the black silk jacket as I went, kicking off my shoes. I leaned my head out over the railing. "Where'd they find her?"

Clyde turned his face up to mine with a shrug. "Same neighborhood as the nursing home . . . somewhere close by . . . so she didn't get far. I can't figure out how we missed her unless she saw us and hid."

"I wouldn't put it past her." I ducked back, peeling off the jumpsuit, hopping on one foot as I tugged my jeans on over the black panty hose. I put a bra on, grabbed a polo shirt out of the chest of drawers, pulled it on, and shook my hair out. I stepped into my high-top Reeboks and left the laces for later. I was clopping down the narrow staircase two seconds later, reaching for my shoulderbag.

"Let's hit it," I said, as Dietz opened the door.

Clyde's white Mercedes sedan was parked at the curb. Irene, in the front, turned a worried face toward us as we approached.

The fifteen-minute drive to St. Terry's was strained. Dietz and I sat in the backseat with Dietz angled sideways so he could check out the back window for any cars following. I was perched, leaning forward, arms resting on the front seat close to Irene, who clutched my hand as if it were a lifeline. Her fingers were icy and I found myself listening unconsciously for the wheezing that might signal another asthma attack. No one said much. The information about Agnes was limited and there didn't seem to be any point in repeating it.

The small parking lot in front of the emergency room was full. A black-and-white occupied the end slot. Clyde pulled up to the entrance and let us out, then went off to find parking on the street. Irene hung back, evidently reluctant to go in without him. She wore a lightweight spring coat, double-breasted, bright red, which she pulled around her now as if for warmth. I could see her peering off toward the streetlights, hoping to catch sight of him.

"He'll be with us shortly," I said.

She clung to my arm while Dietz brought up the rear. The double doors slid open automatically as we approached. We passed into the reception area, which was deserted as far as I could tell. I was struck by the silence. Somehow I'd expected activity, urgency, some sense of the medical drama that plays out in every ER: patients with broken bones, puncture wounds, cuts, insect bites, allergic reactions, and superficial burns. Here, the rooms felt empty and there was no indication of acute care of any sort. Perhaps it was the hour, perhaps an unpredictable lull in the ordinary course of events.

Irene and I waited at the curved front counter, a C-shape enclosing a desk papered with forms. To our immediate right were two patient registration windows, shuttered at this hour. On our left, there was a room divider with two pay phones on the near side and a waiting area beyond. I could see a color television set, tuned to a news show, the sound too low to register. Everything was done in muted blues and grays. All was in order, tidy and quiet. Through an open doorway, I caught a glimpse of the nurses' station, ringed by examining rooms. There was no sign of the police officer or hospital personnel.

Dietz was restless, snapping his fingers against the palm of his hand. He ambled over to the interior door and peered in, checking the layout, automatically eyeballing avenues of escape in case Messinger showed up again. The receptionist must have spotted him because she emerged from the rear moments later, smiling at us politely. "Sorry to keep you waiting. How may I help you?"

"We're here to see Agnes Grey," I said.

She was a woman in her forties, wearing ordinary street clothes: polyester pants, cotton sweater, rubber-soled shoes. A stethoscope, like a pendant, dangled from her neck. Her eyes were a rich chocolate brown, lending warmth to her face. She checked some papers on her desk and then looked up at Irene. "Are you Mrs. Gersh?"

"That's right," Irene said.

The woman's tone was pleasant, but I could see her smile falter. Her attitude suggested the carefully controlled neutrality you'd merit if the actual test results were not what you'd been led to expect. "Why don't you come on back and have a seat in the office," she said. "The doctor will be right with you."

Irene blinked at her fearfully, her voice close to a whisper. "I'd like to see Mother. Is she all right?"

"Dr. Stackhouse would prefer to talk to you first," she said. "Would you like to follow me, please?"

I didn't like it. Her manner was entirely too kindly and benign. She could have made any one of a number of responses. Maybe she'd been advised not to discuss medical matters. Maybe she'd been chastised for offering her opinion before the doctor could offer his. Maybe hospital policy forbade her to editorialize about the patient's condition for complicated reasons of liability. Or maybe Agnes Grey was dead. The woman glanced at me. "Your daughter's welcome to come with you . . ."

"You want me to come?" I asked.

"Yes, please," Irene said to me. Then to the receptionist, "My husband's parking the car. Will you tell him where we are?"

Dietz spoke up. "I'll let him know. You two go on back. We'll be right there."

Irene murmured a thank-you. Dietz and I exchanged a look.

The receptionist stood by the open door while we passed through. She led the way while we followed along a corridor with high-gloss white flooring. She showed us into an office evidently used by any doctor on duty. "It won't be long. Can I get you anything? Coffee? A cup of tea?"

Irene shook her head. "This is fine."

We sat down in blue tweed chairs with upholstered seats. There were no exterior windows. The Formica shelf-desk was bare. There was a gray leather couch showing doctor-size indentations in the cushions. As an impromptu daybed, it was slightly too short and I could see where his shoes had scraped against the arm at one end. A white Formica bookcase was filled with standard medical texts. The potted plant was fake, a Swedish ivy made of paper with curling vines as stiff as florist's wire. The only pictures on the wall looked like reproductions from *Gray's Anatomy*. Personally, I can do without all the skinless arms and legs. The saphenous vein and its branches looked like an overview of the Los Angeles freeway system.

Irene shrugged her coat off and smoothed the lap of her skirt. "I can't believe there weren't any papers to fill out. They must have admitted her."

"You know hospitals. They have their own way of doing things."

"Clyde has the insurance information in his wallet. Blue Cross, I think, though I'm not sure she's covered."

"Bill the nursing home," I said. "It's their responsibility."

We sat for a moment saying nothing. I wondered if this was what it felt like to have family. Geriatric crises, accompanied by homely discussions about what should be done with Granny. We heard footsteps in the hall and the doctor came into the room. I was half-expecting the receptionist with Clyde and Dietz in tow, so it took me a second to compute the expression on this guy's face. He was in his early thirties, with carrot-colored curly hair and a ruddy complexion. He was wearing an unstructured cotton shirt in a hospital green, V-neck, short sleeves, matching cotton pants, soft-soled baggy shoes. He had a stethoscope around his neck and a white plastic name tag that read, "Warren Stackhouse, MD." With his red hair and freckles, the surgical greens gave him a certain Technicolor vibrancy, like a cartoon character. He smelled like adhesive tape and breath mints and his hands looked freshly scrubbed. He was holding a manila folder, which contained only one sheet. He placed that on the desk, lining up the edges.

"Mrs. Gersh? I'm Dr. Stackhouse." He and Irene shook hands and then he leaned against the desk. "I'm afraid we lost her."

"Oh, for God's sake," Irene snapped. "Can't anybody keep track of her?"

Uh-oh, I thought, Irene wasn't getting it. "I don't think he means it that way," I murmured.

"Mrs. Grey went into cardiac arrest," he said. "I'm sorry. We did everything we could, but we weren't able to revive her."

Irene grew still, her face blank, her tone of voice nearly petulant. "Are you saying she's dead? But that's impossible. She couldn't be. You've made some mistake. Clyde said her injuries were minor. Cuts and bruises. I thought he talked to you."

I was watching the doctor and I could see him pick his words with care. "When she was first brought in, she was already showing symptoms of cardiac arrhythmia. She was confused and disoriented, suffering from exposure and stress. In a woman her age, given her fragile state of health . . ."

Irene let out a sigh, finally taking it in. "Oh, the poor thing." Her eyes filled with sudden tears, which spilled down her cheeks. Blotches of color had come up in her face and neck. She began to tremble uncontrollably, quivering like a wet dog in the midst of a bath. I grabbed her hand.

Clyde appeared in the doorway. From the look in his eyes, he'd been told what was going on. The receptionist had probably informed him as soon as he came in.

Irene turned beseechingly. "Clyde . . . Mother's *gone*," she said. She reached for him, coming out of the chair and into his arms. He seemed to fold her in against him. For the first time, I realized how tiny she was. I looked away, not wanting to intrude on their intimacy.

I saw Dietz through the open doorway, leaning against the wall. His posture was identical to my first sight of him. Cowboy boots, his tweed coat. The hospital down in Brawley. All he needed was the toothbrush in his pocket, sticking up like a fountain pen. His gaze moved casually to mine, moved to Irene, came back to mine and held. The look in his eyes was quizzical, perplexed. His expression shifted from self-assurance to uncertainty. I felt an unexpected flash of heat.

I broke off eye contact, feeling flushed. My gaze drifted back. He was still looking at me, with a wistfulness I hadn't seen before.

We all waited uncomfortably for Irene's tears to pass. Finally, Dr. Stackhouse moved toward the door and I followed. The two of us withdrew, moving out into the corridor. As we walked back to the emergency room, Dietz fell into step with us, placing his hand on the back of my neck in a way that made me feel curious and alert. It was a gesture of possession and the physical connection was charged with a sudden current that made the air between us hum.

Dr. Stackhouse shook his head. "God, I'm sorry. It was a lousy break. Are you her granddaughter? Someone's going to have to talk to the police officer."

I focused on the situation as if coming up for air. "I'm a friend of Mrs. Gersh's. Kinsey Millhone," I said.

He glanced at me. "The one she was asking for."

"So I'm told," I said. "Do you have any idea what it was?"

"Well, I can tell you what she said, but I don't think it means much. She kept saying it was summer. 'Tell her it used to be summer . . .' Is that significant?"

"Not to me," I said. In her mind, it was probably connected to the long rambling tale she'd told me down at the desert. Emily and the earthquake, the Harpster girls and Arthur James. "That's all she said?"

"That's the only thing I heard."

"Will there be an autopsy?"

"Probably. We put a call through to the coroner's office and a deputy's on the way. He'll talk to the pathologist and decide if it's warranted."

"Which pathologist? Dr. Yee or Dr. Palchak?"

"Dr. Palchak," he said. "Of course, the deputy may just go ahead and authorize us to sign the death certificate."

"What about Agnes? Can we see her?"

He nodded. "Of course. She's just down the hall here. Whenever Mrs. Gersh is ready, the nurse will take you in."

Agnes had been moved temporarily to a little-used examining room at the end of the hall. Once we were gone, she'd be wheeled down to the basement and left in the refrigerated darkness of the morgue. Dietz waited in the hall with Clyde while Irene and I stood silently beside the gurney on which her mother lay. Death had smoothed many of the lines from her face. Under the white sheeting, she seemed small and frail, her beaky nose protruding prominently from the peaceful folds of her face.

There was a discreet knock at the door. A young uniformed police officer came into the room and introduced himself. He'd brought Agnes in and he talked to Irene briefly about his encounter with her mother. "She seemed like a very nice person, ma'am. I just thought you might like to know she didn't give me any trouble . . ."

Irene's eyes brimmed. "Thank you. I appreciate that. Was she in pain? I can't stand to think about what she must have gone through."

"No, ma'am. I wouldn't say so. She might have been confused, but she didn't seem to be in pain or anything like that."

"Thank God for that. Did she ask for me?"

Color tinted his cheeks. "I couldn't say for sure. I know she mentioned somebody named Sheila."

"Sheila?" Irene said blankly.

"I'm pretty sure that was it. She did cry some. She said she was sorry to be a bother. I kept talking to her, telling her everything was fine. She quieted down after that and seemed all right till we got here. I know the staff did everything possible to save her. I guess sometimes they just go like that."

Irene's chin began to quiver. She pressed a handkerchief to her mouth while she shook her head, whispering. "I had no idea she was dying. My God, if we'd only hurried we might have been here in time . . ."

The officer shifted uneasily. "I'll step out in the waiting room and finish filling out my report. I believe the sheriff's deputy's out there now. He'll need some information as soon as you're up to it." He moved out into the hall, leaving the door ajar.

176

After a moment, Clyde came in. He put his arm around Irene's shoulder and walked her out toward the reception area. Before the door closed again, I caught a glimpse of the sheriff's deputy in the corridor, conferring with his STPD counterpart. I gathered the city police had reported the death to the county coroner's office since Agnes was listed as missing and the last hours of her life were still unaccounted for. The coroner would make a determination as to the circumstances, manner, and cause of death. If she should be classified as a homicide victim, the city police would assume responsibility for the criminal investigation. I was guessing the death would be considered "nonreportable" in coroner's terms, but that remained to be seen. An autopsy might be done in any event.

Alone with the body, I lifted one corner of the sheet, reaching for the cool, unyielding flesh of Agnes's left hand. Her knuckles were scraped. Two nails were broken. On her ring finger and her pinkie there was soil impacted under the nails. The receptionist came into the room behind me. I slipped her hand under the sheet again and turned. "Yes?"

"Mr. Gersh said to tell you he's taking his wife out to the car. The other gentleman is waiting."

"What happened to her personal effects?"

"There wasn't much. Dr. Stackhouse set aside the articles of clothing for disposition by the coroner. She didn't have anything else with her when she was brought in."

I scribbled a note to Dr. Palchak, asking her to call me. I left the message with the ER nurse as I passed the desk. Dietz wanted to call a cab, but Clyde insisted on dropping us back at my place. Irene cried inconsolably all the way home. I was grateful when Dietz finally unlocked the door and let us in. In the backseat of the Mercedes, he'd placed his hand beside mine, our little fingers touching in a way that made me feel my whole left side had been magnetized.

19

The minute I was inside, I headed for the loft, too exhausted to bother with social niceties.

"You want a glass of wine?" he asked.

I hesitated. I looked back at him, caught in midflight. I had one foot on the bottom step, my hand on the curved railing of the spiral staircase. "I don't think so. Thanks."

There was a pause. He said, "Are you all right?"

We were suddenly talking in ways that felt unfamiliar, as if each exchange had a hidden meaning. His face seemed the same, but there was something new in his eyes. Where before his gaze had been opaque, there was now an appeal, some request he couldn't quite bring himself to voice. Sexuality stirred the air like the blades of a fan. Exhaustion fell away. All the danger, all the tension had been converted into this, mute longing. I could feel the lick of it along my legs, seeping through my clothes: something ancient, something dark, humankind's only antidote to death. The heat seemed to arc through the space between us like a primitive experiment, born of night. This is what I understood: this man was like me, my twin, and suddenly, I knew that what I saw in him

was a strange reflection of myself—my bravery, my competence, my fear of dependency. I'd been with him three days,
separated by externals, neutered by survival instincts. Only
desire could render us brave enough to cross that distance,
but which of us would risk it?

I watched him lock the door. I watched him flick the lights
out and cross the room. I started up the spiral staircase,
turning at the third step. I held the railing, sank into a sitting
position as he approached. Dietz was before me, his face level
with mine. The room behind him was dark. Light spilled
down from the loft, illuminating his solemn face. He leaned
into the kiss, his mouth cold at first, his lips soft. My craving
for him was as tangible as a finger of heat driven up through
my core. I was lying on the stairs, metal risers cutting into my
back until pain and desire had blended into a single sensation. I stroked his cheek, touched the silky strands of his hair
while he buried his face against me, nuzzling my breasts
through my cotton T-shirt. We moved together in mock in-
tercourse, clothes on, bodies arching. I could hear the sound
of fabric on fabric, his breathing, mine. I reached down and
touched him. He made an inhuman sound, lifting away from
me, pulling me after him as he moved up the spiral staircase.
The bed was better and we undressed by degrees as we
kissed. The first shock of heat when he laid his naked flesh
along mine made him say, "Oh . . . sweet Jesus," very softly.
After that, there were no words until the moment of obliv-
ion. Making love with this man was like no other lovemaking
I've experienced . . . some external chord resolved at its peak,
ageless music resonating through our bones, the spilling of
secrets, flesh on flesh, moment after moment until we were
fused. I fell into a deep sleep, my limbs wound into his, and
never knew a waking until daylight came. At six o'clock, I
stirred, vaguely aware that I was alone in bed. I could hear
Dietz moving around downstairs. He had the radio on and I
caught strains of a Tammy Wynette tune poignant enough to
rip your heart out. For once, I didn't care.

At some point, the doorbell rang . . . the UPS man (a real

one) with the box I'd shipped up from Brawley. Dietz took delivery, as I was still dead to the world. Soon after that, the smell of perking coffee wafted up the stairs. I roused myself, made my bed, fumbled my way into the bathroom and brushed my teeth. I showered, washed my hair, and then got dressed, slipping into the jeans and shirt I'd worn the night before. No point in contributing either to the laundry pile just yet. I went downstairs.

Dietz was perched on a bar stool at the counter, the paper open in front of him, empty juice glass and cereal bowl pushed to one side so he could read. He reached a hand back. I put my arms around him from behind. He kissed me with a mouth so fresh, I could taste the cereal. "You okay?" he asked.

"Yes. You?"

"Mmm. Your package arrived."

The box was sitting just inside the door, addressed to me in my own writing. "Have you inspected this for incendiary devices?"

His tone was dry. "It's clear. Go ahead."

I got a paring knife from the kitchen drawer and slit the strapping tape. The articles were packed as I remembered them, my all-purpose dress close to the surface. I pulled it out and inspected it, relieved to find it in better shape than I'd hoped. It was only moderately encrusted with mold, though it did smell of swamp gas, a scent that hovered somewhere between spoiled eggs and old toilet bowls.

Dietz caught one whiff and turned to me, his face twisted with distaste. "What *is* that? Good God . . ."

"This is my best dress," I said. "I just need to throw it in the wash and it'll be fine."

I set it aside and worked my way through the remaining contents, removing tools and other odds and ends. In the bottom was the child's tea set, still packed in the carton I'd pulled from under Agnes Grey's trailer. "I should drop this off at Irene's," I remarked, placing the carton near the door. There were few, if any, personal items left to commemorate

Agnes Grey's eighty-three years on earth and I thought Irene might appreciate the articles.

Dietz looked up from his paper. "Which reminds me. Dr. Palchak called at seven thirty this morning with the autopsy results. She wanted you to call her whenever you got up."

"That was fast."

"That's what I thought. She says she likes to get in at five when she's got a post."

I dialed the number for St. Terry's and asked for pathology. I'd dealt with Laura Palchak maybe twice before. She's short, plain, heavyset, competent, hardworking, thorough, and very smart, one of several pathologists under contract to the county, handling postmortem examinations for the coroner's office.

"Palchak," she said when she came on the line.

"Hi, Laura. Kinsey Millhone. Thanks for responding to my note. What's the story on Agnes Grey?"

There was a brief pause. "The coroner's office will be contacting Mrs. Gersh a little later this morning so this is just between us, okay?"

"Absolutely."

"The autopsy was negative. We won't have the toxi results back for weeks, but the gross came up blank."

"So what's the cause of death?"

"Essentially, it was cardiac arrest, but hell . . . everybody dies of cardiac or respiratory arrest if you want to get right down to it. The point is there was no demonstrable organic heart disease and no other natural findings that contributed to death. Technically, we have to list cause of death as undetermined."

"What's that mean, 'technically'? I don't like the way you said that."

She laughed. "Good question. You're right. I have a hunch about this one, but I need to do some research. I've talked to the hospital librarian about tracking down an article I read a few years back. I don't know what made me think of it, but something about this situation rang a little bell."

"Like what? Can you fill me in?"

"Not yet. I'm having my assistant set up some tissue slides that I can probably take a look at by this afternoon. I have sixteen cases lined up before this one, but I'm curious."

"Do you need anything from me?"

"I do have a suggestion if you're open to this. I'm very interested in what happened to this woman during the hours she was missing. It would be a big help if you can find out where she was all that time."

"Well, I can try," I said, "but it may turn out to be a trick. Am I looking for anything in particular?"

"She had what looked like rope burns on her right wrist, torn and broken nails on her left—"

"Oh yeah, I saw that," I said with sudden recollection. "The knuckles on her left hand were scraped, too."

"Right. It's possible she was held someplace against her will. You might see if anybody has a potting shed or a greenhouse. I took some soil traces from her fingernails and we might find a match. She also had superficial abrasions and contusions across her back. I saw a kid just last week with similar marks on his thighs and buttocks. He'd been beaten with a coat hanger . . . among other things."

"Are you saying *she* was beaten?"

"Probably."

"Does Lieutenant Dolan know about this?"

"He and the police photographer were both present for the post, so he saw the same things I did. The truth is, there was no internal trauma and the injuries were too minor to be considered the cause of death."

"What's your theory then?"

"Unh-unh. Not till I do a bit of checking first. Call me this afternoon, or better yet, let me call you when I've seen what we've got here. By then you may have something to report yourself."

She hung up. I settled the receiver in the cradle and sat there, perplexed.

Dietz was watching me. From my end of the conversation, he could tell there'd been a shift. "What's wrong?"

"Let's pick up your car and go by Irene's. I'd like to talk to Clyde." I made a quick call to let them know we'd be stopping by and then called a cab. .

I detailed the situation on the way over to the hotel, Irene's carton in my lap. When we reached the Edgewater, Dietz took his time with the Porsche, inspecting the engine and the electrical system. This wasn't the same car-park attendant we'd dealt with the night before and while the kid swore no one had been near the car, Dietz didn't want to trust him.

"I doubt Messinger knows his ass from his elbow when it comes to bombs, but this is no time to be surprised," he said. I waited while he stretched out on the driveway, inching partway under the car so he could scrutinize the underside. Evidently, there were no unidentified wires, no visible blasting caps, and no tidy bundles of dynamite. Satisfied, he got up and brushed himself off, then ushered me into the passenger seat. Dietz started the car and pulled out of the lot.

For once he drove slowly, his expression preoccupied.

"What are you chewing on?" I asked.

"I've been thinking about Messinger and I wonder if it wouldn't be smart to talk to his ex-wife."

"Down in Los Angeles?"

"Or get her up here. We know he's got Eric with him, at least as of last night. She'd probably jump at the chance to get the kid back. Maybe we could help her and she could turn around and help us."

"How?"

Dietz shrugged. "I don't know yet, but it's better than doing nothing."

"You know how to get in touch with her?"

"I thought I'd drop you off and go talk to Dolan."

"Sounds good. Let's do that."

We parked in front of the Gershes'. Dietz held the carton for me while I extricated myself from the low-slung seat. When we reached the front porch, he left the carton by the door while I rang the bell. Our agreement was that I would wait here until he came back to pick me up. "Make it fast,"

I murmured. "I don't want to be stuck with Irene all day."

"Forty-five minutes max. Any longer, I'll call. Be careful." He backed me against the house with a kiss that made my toes curl, then gave a careless wave and moved off down the walk.

Jermaine opened the front door, stepping back to admit me as the Porsche ignition turned over and the car pulled away from the curb. I was still collecting myself, trying to look like a sober private investigator when, in truth, my drawers were wet. Jermaine and I made the proper mouth noises at one another. I could hear the telephone ring somewhere in the house. She heard it too and raised her voice, as if projecting to the rear of an auditorium. "I'll get it!" She excused herself, waddling toward the kitchen with surprising grace.

The house was otherwise silent, the living room veiled in shadow from the junipers along the property line. I crossed to one of the end tables and snapped on a lamp. I leaned sideways, peering through an archway to my left. Irene was sitting at a little desk in the solarium just off the living room. A small portable radio was playing classical music and I assumed that's why she hadn't heard the front doorbell. She wore a bathrobe and slippers, looking worse than she had the night before. Her complexion, always pale, had taken on the tone of skin bleached by adhesive tape. It was clear she'd wept a good deal and my guess was that she hadn't slept much. The false lashes were gone and her eyes seemed puffy and remote.

"Irene?"

Startled, she looked up, her gaze searching the room for the source of the sound. When she caught sight of me, she pushed herself to her feet, using the desk for leverage. She came into the living room on shaky feet, hands held toward me like a toddler on a maiden voyage, making little mewing sounds as if every step hurt. She clung to me as she had before, but with an added note of desperation.

"Oh, Kinsey. Thank goodness. I'm so glad you're here.

Clyde had a meeting at the bank, but he said he'd be back as soon as he could make it."

"Good. I was hoping to talk to him. How are you?"

"Awful. I can't seem to get organized and I can't bear to be alone."

I guided her toward the couch, struck by the sheer force of her neediness. "You don't look like you've slept much."

She sank onto the couch, refusing to let go of my hands. She clutched at me like a drunk, sloppy with excess, grief perfuming her breath like alcohol. "I sat down here most of the night so I wouldn't disturb Clyde. I don't know what to do. I've been trying to fill out Mother's death certificate and I discover I don't know the first thing about her. I can't remember anything. It's inconceivable to me. So shameful somehow. My own mother . . ." She was beginning to weep again.

"Hey, it's okay. This is something I can help you with." I held a hand up, palm toward her. "Just sit. Relax. Is the form in there?"

She seemed to collect herself. She nodded mutely, eyes fixed on me with gratitude as I moved into the adjacent room. I gathered up a pen and the eight-by-eight-inch square form from the desk and returned to the couch, wondering how Clyde endured her dependency. Whatever compassion I felt was being overshadowed by the sense that I was shouldering a nearly impossible burden.

20

▶▶ ▶▶ ▶▶ "Treat this like a final exam," I said. "We'll do the easy questions first and then tackle the tough ones. Let's start with 'Name of Decedent.' Did she have a middle name?"

Irene shook her head. "Not that I ever heard."

I wrote in "Agnes . . . NMI . . . Grey."

Irene and I sat with our heads bent together, meticulously filling in the meager information she had. This took a little over one minute and covered race (Caucasian), sex (female), military service (none), Social Security number (none), marital status (widowed), occupation (retired), and several subheadings under "Usual Residence." What distressed Irene was that she didn't know the year of her mother's birth and she didn't have a clue about where Agnes was born or the names of her parents, facts she felt anyone with an ounce of caring should have at her fingertips.

"Quit beating yourself, for God's sake," I said. "Let's work backward and see how far we get. Maybe you know more than you think. For instance, everybody's been saying she was eighty-three, right?"

Irene nodded with uncertainty, probably wishing the form

186

had a few multiple-choice questions. I could tell she was still agitated at the notion of her own ignorance.

"Irene, you cannot flunk this test," I said. "I mean, what are they going to do, refuse to bury her?" I hated to be flip, but I thought it might snap her out of the self-pity.

She said, "I just don't want to get it wrong. It's important to do it right. It's the least I can do."

"I can understand that, but the world will not end if you leave one slot blank. We know she was a U.S. citizen so let's put that down. . . . The rest of the information we can pick up from your birth certificate. That would tell us your parents' place of birth and their ages the year you were born. Can you lay your hands on it?"

She nodded, blowing her nose on a handkerchief, which she then tucked in her robe pocket. "I'm almost sure it's in the file cabinet in there," she said. She indicated the solarium, which she'd set up as a home office. "There's a folder in the top drawer labeled 'Vital Documents.' "

"Don't get up. You stay here. I'll find it."

I went into the next room and pulled open one of the file drawers. "Vital Documents" was a thick manila folder right in the front. I brought the entire file back and let Irene sort through the contents. She extracted a birth certificate, which she handed to me. I glanced at it briefly, then squinted more closely. "This is a photocopy. What happened to the original?"

"I have no idea. That's the only one I ever had."

"What about when you applied for a passport? You must have had a certified copy then."

"I don't have a passport. I never needed one."

I stared at her, amazed. "I thought I was the only person without a passport," I remarked.

She seemed faintly defensive. "I don't like to travel. I was always afraid of getting ill and not having proper medical help available. If Clyde had to travel overseas on business, he went by himself. Is that a problem?" My guess was that she and Clyde had argued about her position more than once.

"No, no. This will do, but it strikes me as odd. How'd you come by this one?"

She closed her mouth and her cheeks flooded with pink, like a sudden restoration to good health. At first, I thought she wouldn't answer me, but finally she pursed her lips. "Mother gave it to me when I was in high school. One of the more humiliating moments in my life with her. We were writing our autobiographies for an honors English class and the teacher made us start with our birth certificates. I remember Mother had trouble finding mine and I had to turn my report in without it. The teacher gave me an 'incomplete' ... the only one I ever got ... which just made Mother furious. It was awful. She brought it to school the next day and flung it in the teacher's face. She was drunk, of course. All my classmates looking on. It was one of the most embarrassing things I've ever been through."

I studied her with curiosity. "What about your father? Where was he in all this?"

"I don't remember him. He and Mother separated when I was three or four. He was killed in the war a few years later. Nineteen forty-three, I think."

I glanced down at the birth certificate, getting back to the task at hand. We'd really hit pay dirt. Irene was born in Brawley, March 12, 1936, at 2:30 A.M. Her father was Herbert Grey, birthplace, Arizona, white, age thirty-two, who worked as a welder for an aircraft company. Agnes's maiden name was Branwell, birthplace California, occupation housewife.

"This is great," I said and then I read the next line. "Oh wait, this is weird. This says she was twenty-three when you were born, but that would make her ... what, seventy now? That doesn't seem right."

"That has to be a typo," she said, leaning closer. She reached for the document and peered at the line of print as I had. "This is off by years. If Mother's eighty-three now, she would have been thirty-six when I was born, not twenty-three."

"Maybe she's much younger than we thought."

"Not *that* much. She was nowhere near seventy. You saw her yourself."

I thought about it briefly. "Well, it doesn't make any difference as far as I can see."

"Of course it does! One way or the other, we'd be off by thirteen years!"

I disconnected my temper. There was no point in being irritated. "We don't have any way to verify the information," I said. "At least that I can think of. Leave it blank."

"I don't want to do that," she said stubbornly.

I'd seen her in this mood before and I knew how unyielding she could be. "Do whatever suits. It's your business."

I heard a key in the lock. The front door opened and Clyde came in, dressed in his usual three-piece suit. He was toting the cardboard carton I'd brought. He crossed to the couch, murmured a hello to me, and placed the box on the coffee table. Then he leaned over to kiss Irene's cheek, a ritualistic gesture without visible warmth. "This was on the front porch—"

"That's Irene's," I said. "I found it under Agnes's trailer and had it shipped up. It arrived this morning." I pulled the box closer and opened the top flaps, reaching down among the nesting cups, which were still swaddled in newspaper. "I wasn't sure if this was a good time or not, but these were just about the only things the squatters hadn't ripped off."

I unwrapped one of the teacups and passed it over to Irene. The porcelain handle had a hairline crack near the base, but otherwise it was perfect: pale pink roses, hand-painted, on a field of white, scaled down to child-size. Irene glanced at it without comprehension and then something flickered in her face. A sound seemed to rumble up from the depths of her being. With a sudden cry of revulsion, she flung it away from her. Fear shot through me in reaction to hers. Clyde and I both jumped and I uttered an automatic chirp of astonishment. Her scream tore through the air in a spiraling melody of terror. As if in slow motion, the cup bounced once against the edge of the coffee table and cracked as neatly in two as if it'd been cut with a knife.

Irene rose to her feet, her eyes enormous. She was hyperventilating: rapid, shallow breathing that couldn't possibly be delivering enough oxygen to her system. I could see her begin to topple, eyes focused on my face. She clawed at me as she fell, pitching forward in a convulsion that rocked her from head to toe. Clyde grabbed her as she went down, moving faster than I thought possible. He eased her back onto the couch and elevated her feet.

Jermaine thundered into the living room, a dish towel in her hand. Her eyes were wide with alarm. "What's the matter? What's happening? Oh my God . . ."

Irene's eyes had rolled back in her head and she jerked repeatedly, wracked by some personal earthquake that sent shock waves through her small frame. The acrid scent of urine permeated the air. Clyde peeled his jacket off and went down on his knees beside her, trying to restrain her so she wouldn't hurt herself. Jermaine stood by spellbound, twisting the dish towel in her big dark hands, making anxious sounds at the back of her throat.

Gradually, the spasm passed. Irene began to cough, a tight unproductive sound that made me ache in response. The cough was followed by a high-pitched wheeze that helped to mobilize me again. I put a supporting hand under Irene's right arm and shot Clyde a look. "Let's sit her upright. It'll make her breathing easier."

We hefted her into a sitting position, a surprisingly awkward maneuver given how light she was. She couldn't have weighed more than a hundred pounds; but she was limp and dazed, her eyes moving from face to face without comprehension. It was clear she had no idea where she was or what was going on.

"You want I should call emergency, Mr. Clyde?" Jermaine asked.

"Not yet. Let's hold off on that. She seems to be coming around," he said.

A fine layer of perspiration broke out on Irene's face. She reached for me blindly. Her hands had that clammy feel to them, like a still-animated fish in the bottom of a boat.

Jermaine disappeared and returned moments later with a cold, damp rag that she passed wordlessly to Clyde. He wiped Irene's face. She'd begun to make small sounds, a weeping, hopeless and childlike, as if she were waking from a nightmare of devastating impact. "There were spiders. I could smell the dust . . ."

Clyde looked at me. "She's always been phobic about spiders . . ."

I picked up the two halves of the teacup automatically, wondering if she'd seen something in the bottom. I half-expected one of those old dead spiders lying on its back, legs curled in against its belly like a blossom closing up at twilight. There was nothing. Meanwhile, Irene was inconsolable. "The paint ran down the wall in horrible streaks. The violets were ruined and I was so scared . . . I didn't mean to be bad . . ."

Clyde made soothing noises while he patted her hand. "Irene, you're okay. It's fine now. I'm right here."

The look in her eyes was pleading, her voice reduced to a plaintive whisper. "It was Mother's tea set from when she was little . . . I wasn't supposed to play with it. I hid so I wouldn't get spanked and spanked. Why did she keep it?"

"I'm putting her to bed," he said. He eased one arm under her bent knees, put the other behind her, and lifted, not without some effort. He inched away from the coffee table, walking sideways till he was clear, and then he headed toward the stairs. Jermaine accompanied him, hovering close by to help steady the load.

I sank down on the couch and put my head in my hands. My heart rate was beginning to return to normal, no mean feat given the rush of adrenaline I'd experienced. Other people's fear is contagious, a phenomenon magnified by proximity, which is why horror movies are so potent in a crowded theater. I smelled death, some terrifying experience neither Irene nor Agnes could deal with all these years afterward. I could only guess at the dimensions of the event. Now that Agnes was dead, I doubted the reality would ever be resurrected.

I stirred restlessly, glancing at my watch. I'd been here only thirty minutes. Surely Dietz would return soon and get me the hell out of here. I leafed through a magazine that was sitting on the coffee table. At the back of the issue there was a whole month's worth of dinner menus laid out, totally nutritious, well-balanced meals for mere pennies a serving. The recipes sounded awful: lots of Tuna Surprise and Tofu Stir-Fry with Sweet 'n' Sour Sauce. I set the magazine aside. Idly, I picked up the halves of the teacup, rewrapped them in newspaper, and tucked them back in the box. I got up and crossed the room, setting the box by the door. No point in having Irene face that again. Later, if she was interested, I could always bring it back. I looked up to find Clyde coming wearily down the stairs.

21

He looked like a zombie. I followed as he crossed to one of two matching wing chairs and took a seat. He rubbed his eyes, then pinched the bridge of his nose. His dress shirt was wrinkled, the tiny blue pinstripe stained with sweat at the armpits. "I gave her a Valium. Jermaine said she'd stay with her until she goes to sleep."

I stayed on my feet, clinging to whatever psychological advantage I had in towering over him. "What's going on, Clyde? I've never seen anyone react like that."

"Irene's a sick cookie. She has been ever since we met." He snorted to himself. "God . . . I used to think there was something charming about her helplessness . . ."

"This goes way beyond helpless. That woman's terrified. So was Agnes."

"It's always been like that. She's phobic about everything—closed spaces, spiders, dust. You know what she's afraid of? The hook and eye on a door. She's afraid of African violets. Jesus, *violets*. And it just gets worse. She suffers from allergies, depression, hypochondria. She's half dead from fear and probably hooked on all the prescription drugs she takes.

I've taken her to every kind of doctor you can name and they all throw up their hands. The shrinks love to see her coming, but then they lose interest when the old voodoo doesn't work. She doesn't want to get better. Trust me. She's hanging on to her symptoms for dear life. I try to have compassion, but all I feel is despair. My life is a nightmare, but what am I supposed to do? Divorce her? I can't do it. I couldn't live with myself if I did that. She's like a little kid. I thought when her mother died . . . I thought once Agnes was gone, she'd . . . improve. Like a curse being lifted. But it won't happen that way."

"Do you have any idea what it is?"

He shook his head. He had the hopeless air of a rat being badgered by a cat.

"What about her father? Could this be connected to him? She says he died in the war . . ."

"Your guess is as good as mine," he said, smiling wistfully. "Irene probably married me because of him . . ."

"Wanting a father?"

"Oh sure. Wanting everything—comfort, protection, security. You know what I want? I want to live one week without drama . . . seven days without tears and uproar and dependency and neediness, without all the juice being drained right out of me." He shook his head again. "Not going to happen in my lifetime. It's not going to happen in hers either. I might as well blow my brains out and be done with it."

"She must have suffered some kind of childhood trauma—"

"Oh, who gives a damn? Forty years ago? You're never going to get to the bottom of it and if you did, what difference would it make? She is who she is and I'm stuck."

"Why don't you bail out?"

"Leave Irene? How am I supposed to do that? Every time I think of leaving, she ends up flat on her back. I can't kick her when she's down . . ."

I heard a tap at the front window. Dietz was peering in. I let out a deep breath. I was never so relieved to see anyone.

"I'll get that," I said and moved to the front door. Dietz came in, his gaze straying to Clyde, who had leaned his head against the back of the chair, eyes closed, playing dead. Dietz's mere presence caused the tension in the air to dissipate, but he could tell at a glance that all was not well. I lifted my brows slightly, conveying with a look that I'd fill him in once we were alone. "How'd it go?" I asked.

"Tell you about it in a minute. Let's get out of here."

I said, "Clyde . . ."

"I heard. Go ahead. We can talk later. Irene will sleep for hours. Maybe I'd be smart to get a little shut-eye myself."

I hesitated. "One question. Yesterday, when we were scouring the neighborhood for Agnes . . . do you remember anyone with a toolshed or a greenhouse on the property?"

He opened his eyes and looked at me. "No. Why?"

"The pathologist mentioned it. I said I'd get back to her."

He shook his head. "I was bumping front doors. There might have been a shed in somebody's backyard."

"If you remember something of the sort, will you let me know?"

He gestured a yes both dismissive and resigned.

I picked up the box and we walked out to the car. Dietz tucked me in the passenger seat.

"What's the matter, she didn't like the tea set?" he said. He shut the door on the passenger side and I was forced to hold my reply until he'd rounded the car and gotten in himself. He fired up the engine and pulled out. I gave him a quick rendition of Irene's collapse.

"What do you think she's sitting on?" he asked when I was done.

"Beats me. I can think of a few possibilities. Abuse of some kind, for one," I said. "She might have been a witness to an act of violence, or maybe *she* did something she feels guilty about."

"A little kid?"

"Hey, kids sometimes do things without meaning to. You never know. Whatever it is, if she has any conscious recollection, she's never mentioned it. And Clyde doesn't seem to have a clue."

"You think Agnes knew about it?"

"Oh sure. I think Agnes even tried to tell me, but she couldn't bring herself to do it. I sat with her late one night down in a Brawley convalescent home and she told me this long, garbled tale that I'm almost sure now had the truth embedded in it someplace. I'll tell you one thing. I'm not interested in driving back down to the desert to investigate. Forget that."

"Be pointless anyway after all these years."

"That's what Clyde says. What's the deal on Rochelle Messinger?"

Dietz pulled a slip of paper from his shirt pocket. "I got her number in North Hollywood. Dolan didn't want to give it to me, but I finally talked him into it. He says if we get a line on the guy, we're to stay strictly the hell away."

"Of course," I said. "What now?"

He looked over at me with his lopsided smile. "How about a Quarter Pounder with Cheese?"

I laughed. "Done."

We got back to the apartment at one o'clock, fully carbed up, our fat tanks on overload. I could feel my arteries hardening, plaques piling up in my veins like a logjam in a river, blood pressure going up from all the sodium.

Dietz tried calling Rochelle Messinger. When he got no answer after fifteen rings, he turned the phone over to me. I was aching for a nap, but I thought I'd better find out if Dr. Palchak had seen the slides yet. I didn't like the idea of cruising the neighborhood around the nursing home, bumping all those doors again. With luck, I wouldn't have to.

I put a call through to the pathology department at St. Terry's and had Laura Palchak paged. I had Irene's cardboard box on my lap, using it as an armrest. For ten cents, I would have put my head down and gone to sleep right there. Sometimes I long for the simplicity of kindergarten, which is where I learned to nap on command.

She picked up the phone on her end.

"Hi, Laura. Kinsey Millhone," I said. "I was wondering if you'd had a chance to examine the tissue slides."

"You bet," she said. There was a grim satisfaction in her voice.

"I take it your hunch turned out to be right on the money."

"Sure did. This is one I've never run across myself, but I remembered an abstract on the subject from a few years back. The hospital librarian tracked down the journal, which is on my desk somewhere. Hang on."

"What subject?"

"I'm getting to that. This is an article on 'Human stress cardiomyopathy' written by a couple of doctors in Ohio. Here we go. Catch this," she said. "Mrs. Grey suffered a characteristic damage to her heart—a cell death called myofibrillar degeneration brought on by fear-generated stress."

"Can you translate?"

"Sure, it's simple. When the body gets flooded with intolerable levels of adrenaline, heart cells are killed. The pockets of dead cells interfere with the normal electrical network that regulates the heart. When the nerve fibers are disrupted, the heart starts beating erratically and, in this case, that led to cardiac failure."

"Okay," I said cautiously. I had the feeling there was more. "So what's the punch line here?"

"This little old lady was quite literally scared to death."

"What?"

"It's just what it sounds like. Whatever happened to her in those hours she was gone, she was so badly frightened it killed her."

"Are you talking about her being lost or something more than that?"

"I suspect something more. The theory is that, under certain circumstances, the cumulative burden of psychological stress and pain can generate lethal charges in cardiac tissue."

"Like what?"

"Well, take a little kid. Her father beats her with a belt, ties her up, and leaves her bound in a vacant room overnight. Next morning, she's dead. The actual physical injuries aren't sufficient to cause death. I'm not talking about the stress levels most of us experience in the ordinary course of events. Without getting graphic about it, it's analogous to certain animal experiments relating focal myocardial necrosis to stress."

"You're telling me this is a homicide."

"In essence, yes. I don't think Dolan would consider it such, but that's my guess."

I sat for a moment while the information sank in. "I don't like this."

"I didn't think you would," she replied. "In the meantime, if you haven't figured out yet where she was, you might want to try again."

"Yes." I felt a heaviness in my chest, some ancient dread activated by the proximity to murder. I'd done my job efficiently. I'd tracked the woman down. I'd helped facilitate the plan to move her to Santa Teresa, despite her fears, despite her pleadings. Now she was dead. Was I inadvertently responsible for that, too?

After I hung up, I sat there so long I found Dietz staring at me with puzzlement. I was picking at the flaps of the cardboard box, peeling the first layer of paper away from the corrugation. I tried to imagine Agnes Grey's last day. Had she been abducted? If so, to what end? There'd been no demand for money. As far as I knew, there hadn't been contact of any kind. Who had reason to kill her? The only people she knew in this town were Irene and Clyde. Not beyond the possible, I thought to myself. Most homicides are personal crimes—victims killed by close relatives, friends, and acquaintances . . . which is why I limit mine.

Blindly, I looked down. The paper was coming loose from around the cup I'd rewrapped. The broken halves lay in a torn half-sheet of newsprint that was yellow with age. I blinked, focusing on the banner partially visible across the top. I tilted my head so I could read the newsprint. It was the business section of the *Santa Teresa Morning Press*, a precursor of the current *Santa Teresa Dispatch*. Puzzled, I removed the paper from the box and smoothed it across my lap. January 8, 1940. I checked the exterior of the box, but there were no postmarks and no shipping labels. Curious. Had Agnes been in Santa Teresa? I could have sworn Irene told me her mother had never been here.

I looked up. Dietz was standing right in front of me, hands on his knees, face level with mine. "Are you all right?"

"Look at this." I handed him the paper.

He turned it over in his hands, checking both sides. He noted the date as I had and his mouth pulled down in speculation. He wagged his head back and forth.

"What do you make of it?" I asked.

"Probably the same thing you do. It looks like the box was packed in Santa Teresa in January of nineteen forty."

"January eighth," I said, correcting him.

"Not necessarily. A lot of people save newspapers for a time at any rate. This might have been sitting in a stack somewhere. You know how it is. You need to wrap up some dishes and you grab a section from the pile."

"Well, that's true," I said. "Do you think Agnes did it? Was she actually *in* this town at that point?" It was a question we couldn't answer of course, but I needed to ask it anyway.

"You're sure the box was hers? She might have been holding it for someone else."

"Irene recognized the teacup. I could see it in her face for the half second before she started screaming."

"Let's see what else we've got here," Dietz said. "Maybe there's more."

We spent a few minutes carefully unpacking the box. Every piece of china—cups, saucers, creamer, sugar bowl, teapot with its rose-sprigged lid, some fifteen pieces in all—was wrapped in the same edition of the paper. There was nothing else of significance in the carton and the news itself didn't reveal anything of note.

I said, "I think we ought to get Irene out of bed and find out what's going on."

Dietz picked up his car keys and we were out the door.

• • • •

We rang the Gershes' bell, waiting impatiently while Jermaine came to the door and admitted us. I had pictured her tidying things in our absence, but the living room looked exactly as it had when we'd left it, a little more than an hour ago. The couch cushions were still askew where Irene's thrashing had displaced them, the birth certificate, death certificate, and the "Vital Documents" file still strewn haphazardly across the coffee table. I caught a whiff of drying urine. The characteristic silence had descended again, as if life itself here were muffled and indistinct.

When I asked to see Clyde or Irene, Jermaine's dark face became stony. She crossed her arms, body language echoing her manner, which was clearly uncooperative. She said Mrs. Gersh was sleeping and she refused to wake her. Mr. Gersh was having "a little lay-down" and she refused to disturb him, too.

"This is really important," I said. "All I need is five minutes."

I could see her face set with stubbornness. "No, ma'am. I'm not about to bother them poor peoples. You leave them lay."

I glanced at Dietz. The shrug was written in his face. I looked back at Jermaine and indicated the coffee table with a nod. "Can I pick up the papers I left here earlier?"

"What papers? I don't know nothin' about that."

"For now all I need are the forms Irene and I were working on," I said. "I can come back later for a chat with her."

Her gaze was pinned on me with suspicion. I kept my expression bland. "Go on, then," she said. "If that's all you want."

"Thanks." Casually, I crossed to the coffee table and picked up the birth certificate and the entire document file. Thirty seconds later, we were out on the porch.

"What'd you do that for?" Dietz said as we headed down the steps.

"It just seemed like a good idea," I said.

22

I asked him to pull around the corner and park in an alleyway. We sat there in the dappled shade of an overhanging oak while I sorted through the contents of the Gershes' "Vital Documents" file. Nothing looked that vital to me. There was a copy of the will, which I handed to Dietz. "See if this tells us anything astonishing."

He took the stapled pages, reaching automatically toward his shirt pocket. I thought he was looking for a cigarette, but it turned out to be a pair of reading glasses with half-rims that he'd tucked there instead. He put them on and then looked over at me.

"What?" he said.

I nodded judiciously. "The glasses are good. Make you look like a serious adult."

"You think so?" He craned so he could see himself in the rearview mirror. He crossed his eyes and stuck his tongue out, just to show how adult he could look.

He began leafing through the will while I glanced at insurance policies, the title to the house, a copy of the emission inspection information for a vehicle they owned, an American Express flight insurance policy. "God, this is boring," I said.

"So's this."

I looked over at him. I could see his gaze skimming down the lines of print. I returned to my pile of papers. I picked up Irene's birth certificate and squinted at it in the light.

"What's that?"

"Irene's birth certificate." I told him the story she'd told me about the autobiography for her senior English class. "Something about it bothers me, but I can't figure out what it is."

"It's a photocopy," he said.

"Yeah, but what's the big whoopee-do about that?"

"Let me take a look." He placed it up against the windshield, letting the light shine through. The heading read: STATE OF CALIFORNIA DEPARTMENT OF HEALTH VITAL STATISTICS, STANDARD CERTIFICATE OF BIRTH. The form thereafter was comprised of a series of two-line boxes into which the data had been typed. He held it close to his face, like a man whose eyesight is failing rapidly. "Lot of these lines are broken and the type itself isn't very crisp. We ought to check with Sacramento and track down the original."

"You think it's been tampered with?"

"It's possible. Dab some kind of correction fluid on the original. Type over the blanks and then make a copy. It couldn't be used for much, but it'd be sufficient for a school project. Maybe that's why it took Agnes a day to produce the damn thing. The point of certified copies is that they're certified, right?" He gave me that crooked smile, gray eyes clear.

"Wow, what a concept," I said. "Wonder what she had to hide?"

Dietz shrugged. "Maybe Irene was illegitimate."

"Right," I said. "Can you think of anyone we can contact in Sacramento?"

"Department of Health? Not right offhand. Why not check with the county recorder here and have them call?"

"You think they'd do that?"

"Sure, why not?"

"Well, it's worth a try," I said. "Besides, if we do the research now, Irene will pay for it. Wait two weeks and she'll forget she ever gave a damn."

"Let's give it a shot, then," he said. "You want me to look at any other documents?"

"Nope. That's it."

"Great." He handed me the will and the birth certificate, both of which I tucked back into the file. He started the car and headed out to the street.

"Where to?" I asked.

"Let's hit the office first and call Rochelle Messinger."

We parked in the back lot and went up the exterior stairs. Dietz was, as usual, paranoid about everyone within range. He kept a hand on my elbow, his gaze scanning the area, until we were safely in the building. The second-floor corridor was empty. As we passed the rest rooms, I said, "I need to pop into the ladies' room. You want the office keys?"

"Sure. I'll see you in a few minutes." Dietz started to check out the ladies' room and was greeted by a shriek of outrage. He moved on down the corridor while I went into the john.

Darcy was standing at one of the sinks, splashing water on her face. From her pasty complexion and the eyes pinched with pain, I gathered she was still hung over from the banquet the night before. She stared at herself in the mirror, hair mashed flat in two places. "You know you're really in trouble when your hair goes out on you," she remarked, more to herself than to me.

"What time did you get in?" I asked.

"It wasn't that late, but I'd been drinking anisette and I was wrecked. I started upchucking about midnight and haven't stopped yet," she said. She rubbed her face and then pulled her lower lids down so she could inspect the conjunctivas. "Nothing like a hangover to make you long for death . . ."

A toilet flushed and Vera emerged from one of the four stalls. She was buttoning up an olive and khaki camouflage outfit, a jumpsuit with big shoulder pads and epaulettes, looking like she was moments away from a landing on Anzio Beach. The glance she gave me was not friendly. "What happened to you last night?" she said waspishly. I was exhausted and my nerves were on edge, so her tone didn't sit well and neither did her attitude.

I said, "Well, jump right in, Vera. Agnes Grey died, among other things. I didn't get to bed till after three A.M. How about you?"

Vera crossed to the sinks, her high heels snapping against the ceramic tiles. She turned the water on way too hard and splashed herself. She jumped back. "*Shit!*" she said.

"Agnes Grey?" Darcy said. She was watching our reflections in the mirror, her expression wary.

"My client's mother," I said. "She dropped dead of a heart attack."

Darcy frowned. "That's weird."

"Actually it was weird, but how did you know?"

"Do you *mind*?" Vera said to Darcy pointedly. Apparently, she wanted to talk to me alone. It occurred to me belatedly that she and Vera had been discussing me just before I came in. Oh boy.

Darcy shot me an apologetic look. She dried her hands hastily under the wall-mounted blower, blotting the residual water on the back of her skirt. "See you later, gang," she said. She took her purse and departed with a decided air of relief.

The door hadn't closed behind her when Vera turned and looked at me. "I don't appreciate the crap you told Neil last night," she said. Her face was tense, her gaze fiery.

I felt a rush of heat go through me. I needed to pee, but it seemed inappropriate. "Really," I said. "Like what?"

"I am not *smitten* with him. We're strictly friends and that's all it is. Get it?"

"What are you in such a snit about?"

She leaned against the sink, a hand on her hip. "I introduced you to the man because I thought you'd get along with him, not to have you turn around and ... *manipulate* the circumstances."

"How did I do that?"

"You know how! You told him I had a crush on him and now he's behaving like an idiot."

"What'd he do, break it off?"

"Of course he didn't break it off! He *proposed* to me last night!"

"He did? Well, that's great! Congratulations. I hope you said yes."

Vera's mouth turned down at the corners and she burst into tears. I was taken aback. For a sophisticated woman, she was bawling like a little kid. I found myself with my arms around her, patting her awkwardly. It's not easy to comfort someone twice your size. She had to hunch down slightly while I raised up on tiptoe. It was not the full California body hug of longtime friends. Contact was limited to the upper portions of our torsos where we were linked like the two bowed wings of a wishbone.

"What am I gonna doooo?" she wailed into my right ear.

"You might think about getting married," I suggested helpfully.

"I caaaan't."

"Of course you can, Vera. People do it every day."

"I'm too old and too tall and he says he wants kids."

I could feel a laugh bubble up, but I resisted the urge to make a flip remark. I said mothering-type things, "There, there" and "It's all right." Remarkably, it seemed to work. Within a minute, she calmed down to a series of hiccups and sniffs. She let out a big sigh and then blew her nose noisily on a piece of shriveled Kleenex she found in her jumpsuit. She pressed the tissue to her eyes and then she did a quick burbling laugh while she checked her makeup. "When I saw you and Neil with your heads bent together last night I wanted to kill you."

"Yeah, I caught the look. I just wasn't sure what it meant," I said.

"And right about then, Mac started making his speech and next thing I knew you were gone. What was that about?"

I filled her in on (some, but not all of) my night's activities and then quizzed her on hers.

She spent the next few minutes detailing the portion of the banquet I'd missed. Neil had slipped over into Dietz's chair while Mac finished his speech. After-dinner drinks arrived. She was so upset with Neil because of his apparent interest in me, she started tossing down brandies and the next thing she knew, the two of them were back in her room making love. She started laughing again. "We didn't even make it to the bed. The maid came in to turn the sheets down and there we were *grappling* on the floor. We never even heard her knock. It turned out she was a patient of his at the clinic where he works. You know how you do when the phone rings and you're on the pot? He sort of scrambled to his feet and hobbled off to the bathroom with his trousers down around his knees."

"Vera, if I laugh now, I'll end up peeing in my pants." I gave her a quick pat and headed straight to the nearest stall, relieving myself while I talked to her across the top of the cubicle. "What happened to the maid? She must have been mortified," I said. "Her own doctor with his bum hanging out of his pants? My God."

"She was out of there like a shot and that's when he proposed. He started screaming it was my fault. He said if I'd marry him we could grapple on our own floor without all the interruptions—"

"The man's got a point."

"You really think so?"

I flushed the toilet and emerged. "Vera, do me a favor. Just marry the guy. He's a doll. You'll be deliriously happy for eternity. I promise." I washed my hands and dried them, grabbing up my shoulder bag. "Dietz is waiting for me. I gotta go or he'll think I've been kidnapped. I get dibs on maid of honor, but I won't wear dusty rose. Let me know when you set the date." When I left, she was staring after me with a dazed look on her face.

As I passed California Fidelity, I caught sight of Darcy at

the file cabinet behind the receptionist's desk. She was barely moving, apparently intent on cooling her fevered brow against the cold metal of the cabinet top where she'd laid her head. I detoured into the office. She managed to raise her eyes without moving her head. "Vera chew your ass out?"

"We're fine. She's getting married. You can be the flower girl," I said. "I need to know what you were talking about when I mentioned that Agnes died. You said it was weird. What was weird?"

"Oh, I wasn't referring to her death," Darcy said. "That's the name of a book."

"A *book*?"

"*Agnes Grey*. It's a novel by Anne Brontë, written in eighteen forty-seven. I know because it was the subject of my senior thesis at UNLV."

"You went to college in Las Vegas?"

"What's wrong with that? I grew up there. Anyway, I was a lit major and it was the only paper I ever wrote that netted me an A-plus."

"I thought the name was Charlotte Brontë."

"This is a sister. The youngest. Most people only know about the two older ones, Charlotte and Emily."

A chill tiptoed over me like a daddy longlegs. "Emily . . ."

"She wrote *Wuthering Heights*."

"Right," I said faintly. Darcy went on talking, waxing eloquent about the Brontës. I was sifting back through Agnes's account of Emily's death, the hapless "Lottie" who was simpleminded and couldn't remember how to get in and out the back door. Was her real name Charlotte? Could Agnes Grey's real name be Anne something, or was that strictly a coincidence? I moved back toward the corridor.

"Kinsey?" Darcy was startled, but I didn't want to stop and explain what was going on. I didn't get it myself.

When I got to my office, Dietz was just hanging up the phone. "Did you talk to Rochelle?" I asked, distracted.

"It's all taken care of. She's hopping in her car and heading straight up. She has a friend who runs a motel on Cabana called the Ocean View. I said we'd meet her there at four. You know the place?"

"As a matter of fact, I do," I said. The Ocean View had been the setting of my last and most enlightening encounter with an ex-husband named Daniel Wade. Not my best day, but liberating after a fashion. What had Agnes told me about Emily? She was killed in an earthquake. Down in Brawley or somewhere else? Lottie was the first to go. Then the chimney fell on Emily. There was more, but I couldn't remember what it was.

Dietz glanced at his watch. "What shall we do till she gets here? You want to pop by your place?"

"Give me a minute to think." I sat down in my client chair and ran my hand through my hair. Dietz had the good sense to hold his tongue and let me ruminate. At this point, I didn't even want to have to stop and bring him up to speed. Could Emily's death have been the event that precipitated Agnes Grey's departure from Santa Teresa? Had she actually been here? If the name Agnes Grey was a phony, then what was her real name? And why the subterfuge?

"Let me try this on you," I said to Dietz. I took a few minutes then to fill him in on Darcy's remark. "Suppose her name really wasn't Agnes Grey. Suppose she used that as a cover name . . . a kind of code. . . ."

"To what end?" he asked.

"I don't know," I said. "I think she wanted to tell the truth. I think she wanted someone to know, but she couldn't bring herself to say it. She was terrified about coming up to Santa Teresa, I do know that. At the time, I figured she was nervous about the trip—unhappy about the nursing home. I just assumed her anxiety was related to the present, but maybe not. She might have lived here once upon a time. I gather she and Emily were sisters and there was a third one named Lottie. She might have known some critical fact about the way Emily died. . . ."

"But now what? At this point, we don't even know what her real name was."

I held a finger up. "But we do know about the earthquake."

"Kinsey, in California, you're talking eight or ten a *year*."

"I know, but most of those are minor. This one was big enough that someone died."

"So?"

"So let's go to the public library and look up the Santa Teresa earthquakes and see if we can find out who she was."

"You're going to research every local earthquake with fatalities," he said, his voice flat with disbelief.

"Not quite. I'm going to start with January six or seven, nineteen forty . . . the day before that box was packed."

Dietz laughed. "I love it."

23

▶▶ ▶▶ ▶▶ The periodicals room at the Santa Teresa Public Library is down a flight of stairs, a spacious expanse of burnt-orange carpeting and royal blue upholstered chairs, with slanted shelves holding row after row of magazines and newspapers. A border of windows admits ample sunshine and recessed lighting heightens the overall illumination. We traversed the length of the room, approaching an L-shaped desk on the left.

The librarian was a man in his fifties in a dress shirt and tie, no coat. His gray hair was curly and he wore glasses with tortoiseshell frames, a little half-moon of bifocal in the lower portion of each lens. "May I help you?"

"We're trying to track down the identity of a woman who might have died in one of the Santa Teresa earthquakes. Do you have any suggestions about where we might start to look?"

"Just a moment," he said. He consulted with another of the staff, an older woman, and then crossed to his desk and sorted through a pile of pamphlets, selecting one. When he returned he had a local publication, called *A Field Guide to the*

Earthquake History of Santa Teresa. "Let's see. I can give you the dates for earthquakes that occurred in nineteen sixty-eight, nineteen fifty-two, nineteen forty-one—"

"That's a possibility," I said to Dietz.

He shook his head. "Too late. It would have been before nineteen forty if that newspaper has any bearing. What other dates do you show?"

The librarian flipped the booklet open to a chart that listed the important quakes offshore in the Santa Teresa channel. "November four, nineteen twenty-seven, there was a seven point five quake, but that was west of Point Arguello and the damage here was slight."

"No casualties?" Dietz asked.

"Evidently not. There was an earthquake in eighteen twelve that destroyed the mission at La Purisima. Several more from July to December nineteen oh-two . . ."

"I think we want something after that," I said.

"Well then, your best bet would probably be to start with the big quake in nineteen twenty-five."

"All right. Let's try that."

The man nodded and moved to a row of wide gray file cabinets, returning moments later with a box of microfilm. "This is April first through June thirtieth. The quake actually occurred on the twenty-ninth of June, but I don't believe you'll find a newspaper reference until the day after." He pointed to the left. "The machines are over there. Use the schematic diagram to thread the film."

"If I find something I need, can I get a copy?"

"Certainly. Simply position that portion of the page between the two red dots on the screen and press the white button in the front."

We sat down at one of four machines, placing the spool on the spindle to the left, slipping the film across the viewer and attaching it so that it would wind onto the spool on the right side of the machine. I turned the automatic-forward knob from off to the slow speed position. The first page of the paper came into view against a background of black. The edges of the pages were ragged in places, but for the most part the picture was clear. Dietz stood behind me, looking over my shoulder as I turned the knob to fast forward.

Days whipped across the screen in a blur, like a cinematic device. Now and then, I'd halt the process, checking to see how far we'd gone. April 22. May 14. June 3. I slowed the machine. Finally, June 30 crept into view. The big earthquake had occurred at 6:42 A.M. on June 29. According to the paper, the severity of the quake was such that the concrete pavement buckled and street signs were snapped as if they were threads. The reservoir broke and sent a flood of mud and water into Montebello. Gas and electric power were shut off immediately and in consequence, there was only one fire, easily contained. Many buildings downtown were badly damaged, the streetcar track was snapped, the asphalt pavement sank six inches in places. Residents slept outside that night and many cars were reported on the highway heading south. In all, there were thirteen fatalities. Both the dead and injured were listed. Sometimes ages and occupations were specified, along with home addresses if they were known. None among the dead seemed remotely related to the tale Agnes Grey had told me.

I was hand-cranking the machine by then, stopping the film at intervals so that we could scan each column. A prominent widow had been crushed to death when the walls of a hotel toppled in on her. The body of a dentist was removed from the ruins of his office building. There was no mention of anyone named Emily. "What do you think?" I said to Dietz.

He made a thumbs-down gesture. I rewound the microfilm and took it off the spindle. We returned the box of film to the main counter, consulting in low tones, trying to figure out what to try next, if anything. Dietz said, "What year was Agnes born?"

"Nineteen hundred, as nearly as we can tell . . . though there's some question. It might have been nineteen thirteen."

"So she would have been somewhere between twelve and

twenty-five in nineteen twenty-five. If you figure her sister was in a five- or six-year age range of her, she could have been any age from six to thirty."

"We didn't see a female earthquake victim even close to that," I said.

Dietz lifted his brow. "For all we know, Emily was the family dog."

The librarian approached, smiling politely. "Find what you were looking for?"

"Not really," I said. "Would you have anything else?"

He took up his field guide with patient interest in our plight. "Let's see here. Well ... it looks like there was an aftershock to that nineteen twenty-five earthquake. Here ... June twenty-nine, nineteen twenty-six ... exactly one year later to the day. One fatality. The only other earthquake of note would have been November four, nineteen twenty-seven, but there were no fatalities recorded in that one. Would you like to take a look at the one in 'twenty-six?"

"Sure."

We went back to the same machine, repeating the process of threading the film. Again, we flew through the calendar, time flashing by in a whir of gray. As we reached the end of the reel, I slowed the machine, hand-cranking my way from day to day, scanning one column at a time. Dietz was leaning over my shoulder, making sure I didn't miss anything. I was losing hope. I thought it was a good theory—hell, it was my *only* theory. If this didn't pay off, we were out of luck.

I read about Babe Ruth, who'd just hit his twenty-sixth homer of the season back in Philadelphia. I read about some woman whose six-year marriage was annulled when she found out her former spouse was still alive. I read about Aimee Semple McPherson's stout defense of her alleged kidnapping at the hands of strangers ...

"There it is," Dietz said. He put a finger on the screen.

I let out a yelp and laughed. Six library patrons turned around and looked at me. I put a hand across my mouth sheepishly. I peered at the machine. It was like a gift—such an unexpected pleasure—lines leaping off the page. The article was brief and the style faintly antique, but the facts were clear and it all seemed to fit.

WOMAN KILLED AS BRICKS FALL
Chimney Crushes Out the Life of Local Resident

Emily Bronfen, 29-year-old bookkeeper employed by Brookfield, McClintock and Gaskell, met death yesterday afternoon when bricks fell from a chimney at the family home, 1107 Sumner Street, and crushed her during an earth tremor at 3:20 P.M. The body was taken to the Donovan Brothers funeral parlor and will be cremated today at 4:00.

The Associated Press reported that the shock, which swung doors at Pasadena and swayed hanging electric light drops at Santa Monica, was also felt in Los Angeles, where occupants of office buildings noticed their swivel chairs doing a wild shimmy along the floor.

Ventura reported two separate shocks lasting about four or five seconds each. Santa Monica reported a second shock shortly after 7:00 last night.

L. L. Pope, Santa Teresa City Building Inspector, made the rounds of the city yesterday afternoon and reported that he found no damage to any building erected under provisions of the new building code. "There was very little structural damage of any kind," he declared. "It was virtually all confined to old fire walls, some of which were fractured in the earthquake of one year ago . . ."

I turned and looked up at Dietz. We locked eyes for a moment and his mouth came down on mine. I'd reached a hand up, closing my fist in his hair. He reached a hand down my shirt and rubbed his fingertips across my left breast.

"Print it," he said hoarsely.

"Oh God," I breathed.

At the counter, the librarian pulled his glasses down and peered at us over the rims.

Blushing, I straightened my collar and adjusted my shirt. I pressed the button. We picked up an invoice for the photocopy at the desk when we turned in the microfilm. We left the periodicals room without further reference to the two librarians, who seemed to be conversing together about some terribly amusing subject.

"Bronfen. I like that. It's close enough to Brontë," I said as I followed him up the stairs. "The parents must have been big on Victorian literature."

"Possibly," Dietz said. "I don't know what it proves at this point."

On the main floor, we checked back through various city directories. The 1926 edition showed a Maude Bronfen (occupation, widow) at the address listed in the paper. "Shoot," I said. "I was hoping we'd find Anne."

Dietz said, "Maude was probably their mother. What now?"

"Let's try the Hall of Records. It's just across the street. Maybe we can track down Irene's birth certificate."

We paid for the photocopy, left the library, and headed over to the courthouse, crossing the one-way street. Dietz had taken me by the elbow, his gaze divided equally among cars approaching from the left, pedestrians in the general vicinity, and possible vantage points in the event Mark Messinger had chosen this location to pick me off. "So what's the operating theory here?" I asked.

He considered that for a moment. "Well, if I were altering a document like that, I'd try to keep the changes to a minimum. There's less chance of screwing up."

"You think Irene's first name is real then?"

"Probably. I'd guess the attending physician, date, and time of birth are okay, too, along with the filing date and the name of the registrar or deputy."

"Why would Agnes change her age? That seems peculiar."

"Who knows? Maybe she was older than the guy and too vain to have it part of the public record. As long as you're altering reality, you might as well eliminate anything that doesn't suit."

The recorder division of the county clerk's office is in an annex to the Santa Teresa Courthouse, a ground-floor office in the northwest corner of the building. We cut across the big square of side lawn to the entrance, pushing through the fifteen-foot wood-and-glass door. The interior was comprised of an outer office with a counter running along our left, a glossy red tile floor, a table and chairs available for those filling out forms, and on the right, glass display cases mounted on the wall, filled with samples of foreign currency. Behind the counter was a large, open office space broken up by the ubiquitous "action stations" that seem to characterize every other office I've seen of late.

There was one couple at the counter ahead of us, apparently picking up a marriage license. The husband-to-be was one of those skinny guys with a narrow butt and tattoos all up and down his arms. The bride was twice his size and so pregnant she was already into her Lamaze. She clung to the counter, her face damp with perspiration, panting heavily while the clerk completed all the papers in haste.

"You sure you're okay? We can probably get a wheelchair from someplace," she said. The clerk was in her sixties and didn't seem anxious so much as intent on efficiency. Visions of lawsuits were probably dancing in her head. Also, she might not have been certified in midwifery. I wondered if Dietz had any experience in delivery.

The bride, at the pinnacle of a contraction, shook her head mutely. "I'm ... fine ... unh ... I'm fine ..." She had a gardenia pinned in her hair. I tried to picture the wedding announcement in the papers. "The bride, in a peau-de-soie maternity smock, was accompanied by her obstetrician ..."

"Judge Hopper's waiting for us upstairs," the husband said. He smelled of Brylcreem and cigarettes, his blue jeans pleated up around his waist with a length of rope.

The clerk handed over the certificate. "Why don't I have June get the judge on the phone and have him come down here?"

A second clerk, her eyes rolling, picked up the telephone

and made a quick call while the bride crept haltingly toward the door. She seemed to be singing to herself. "Uh . . . uh . . . unh . . ."

The groom didn't seem that distressed. He simply matched his pace to hers, his gaze pinned on her shuffling feet. "You're not breathing right," he said crossly.

The clerk turned to us. "What can I do for you folks?"

Dietz was still staring off at the departing couple with a look of uneasiness.

I held out the copy of the birth certificate. "I wonder if you can help us," I said. "We suspect maybe this birth certificate's been tampered with and we'd like to check for the original in Sacramento. Is there any way you can do that? I notice there are some file numbers."

The clerk held the paper at arm's length, her thumbnail moving from point to point across the document. "Well, here's your first problem right here. You see that district number? That's incorrect. This says Brawley on the face of it, but the district number's off. Imperial County would be thirteen something. This fifty-nine fifty indicates Santa Teresa County."

"It does? That's great," I said. "You mean you'll have a copy of it here?"

"Oh sure. That little two in the margin tells you the book number and this number here is the page. Just a minute and I'll have someone pull the microfilm. Machines are right through there. You just have a seat and someone will be with you directly."

We waited maybe five minutes and then the second clerk, June, appeared with a microfilm cartridge, which she loaded into the machine.

Once we located the page, it didn't take us long to find Irene's name. Dietz was right. The date and time of birth and the physician's name were the same on both documents. Irene's name, the ages of both parents, and her mother's occupation were also the same. Everything else had been altered.

Her father's name was Patrick Bronfen, his occupation car salesman. Her mother's first name was Sheila, maiden name Farfell.

"Who the hell is this?" I said with disbelief. "I thought her mother's name would be Anne."

"Isn't Sheila the name Agnes mentioned to the cop who brought her into emergency?"

I turned around and stared at him. "That's right. I'd forgotten."

"If it's true, it might imply that Agnes and Sheila are the same person."

I made a face. "Sure shoots our Brontë theory. But hey, check this." I pointed to the screen. The address listed was the same one given for Emily Bronfen, whose death had occurred ten years before Irene's birth—fourteen years before the tea set had been packed away in the box. I found myself squinting, trying to make sense of it. Dietz seemed equally mystified. What the hell *was* this?

24

▶ ▶ ▶ We paid eleven dollars and waited another ten minutes for a certified copy of Irene's birth certificate. I didn't think she'd believe us unless she saw it for herself. As we left the Hall of Records, I paused briefly at the counter, where the clerk who had helped us was sorting through a pile of computer forms.

"Do you have a city map?" I asked.

She shook her head. "The docent might have one at the information booth around the corner on the first floor," she said. "What street are you looking for? Maybe I can help."

I showed her the address on the birth certificate. "This says Eleven Oh-seven Sumner, but I've never heard of it. Is there such a street?"

"Well, yes, but the name was changed years ago. Now it's Concorde."

"Concorde used to be Sumner?" I said, repeating the information blankly. News to me, I thought. And then I got it. I lowered my head for a moment. "Dietz, *that's* what Agnes was talking about in the emergency room. She didn't say 'it used to be summer.' She was saying 'Sum*ner.*' That's where the nursing home is. She knew the street."

"Sounds good," Dietz said. He took me by the elbow and we pushed through the double doors, heading back to the public garage where his car was parked.

We were getting close to the answer and I was beginning to fly. I could feel my brain cells doing a little tap dance of delight. I was half-skipping, excitement bubbling out of me as we crossed the street. "I love information. I love information. Isn't this great? God, it's fun . . ."

Dietz was frowning in concentration as he scanned the walkway between the library and the parking structure, unwilling to be distracted from his assessment of the situation. We reached the three-story garage and started climbing the outside stairs.

"What do you think the story is?" he finally asked as we passed the second landing. I was straggling behind him, working hard to keep up. For a man who'd only quit smoking four days before, he was in remarkable shape.

"I don't know yet," I said. "Patrick could have been a brother. They lived at the same address. The point is, Emily did die in the earthquake just like Agnes said. Or at least that's how it looked. . . ."

"But what's it got to do with Irene Gersh? She wasn't even born then."

"I haven't figured that part out yet, but it has to fit. I think she witnessed an act of violence. It just wasn't Emily. Let's go to Eleven Oh-seven Concorde and see who lives there. Maybe we can get a line on this Bronfen guy."

"Don't you want to go talk to Irene about it first?"

"No way. She's too stressed out. We can fill her in afterwards."

I arrived at the top level of the structure, heart pounding, out of breath. One of these days, I was going to have to start jogging again. Amazing how quickly the body tends to backslide. When we reached the car, I shifted impatiently from foot to foot while Dietz went through his inspection routine with the Porsche, checking the doors first for any signs of a booby trap, peering at the engine, the underside of the chassis, and up along the wheel mounts. Finally, he unlocked the door on my side and ushered me in. I leaned across the driver's seat and unlocked his door for him.

He got in and started up the engine. "Lay you dollars to doughnuts, there's nobody left. If this traumatic event took place in January nineteen forty, you're talking more than forty years ago. Whatever happened, all the principal players would be a hundred and ten . . . if any were alive."

I held my hand out. "Five bucks says you're wrong."

He looked at me with surprise and then we shook hands on the bet. He glanced at his watch. "Whatever we do, let's be quick about it. Rochelle Messinger's due up here in an hour."

Pulling out of the parking structure, he cut over one block and headed left on Santa Teresa Street. Concorde was only nine blocks north of the courthouse, the same quiet tree-lined avenue Clyde Gersh and I had walked yesterday in our search for Agnes. Unless I was completely off, this had to be an area she recognized. Certainly, it was the address given for Emily Bronfen at the time of her death. It was also the house where Irene's parents resided at the time of her birth ten years later.

Dietz turned right onto Concorde. The nursing home was visible above the treetops, half a block away. I was watching house numbers march upward toward the eleven-hundred mark, my gut churning with a mixture of anticipation and dread. Please let it be there, I thought. Please let us get to the bottom of this . . .

Dietz slowed and pulled into the curb. He turned the engine off while I stared at the house. It was right next door to the place where Mark Messinger had caught up with me and sprayed the porch with gunfire.

I held a hand out to Dietz without even looking at him. "Pay up," I said, gaze still pinned on the three-story clap-board house. "I met Bronfen yesterday. I just figured out how I know him. He turned the place into a board-and-care. I met him once before when a friend of mine was looking for a facility for her sister in a wheelchair." I saw a face appear

221

briefly at a second-floor window. I opened the car door and grabbed my handbag. "Come on. I don't want the guy to scurry out the back way."

Dietz was right behind me as we pushed through the shrieking iron gate and went up the front walk, taking the porch steps two at a time. "I'll jump in if you need me," he murmured. "Otherwise, you're the boss."

"You may be the only man I ever met who'd concede that without a fight."

"I can't wait to see how you do this."

"You and me both." I rang the bell. The owner took his sweet time about answering. I really hadn't even formulated what I meant to say to him. I could hardly pretend to be doing a marketing survey.

He opened the door, a heavyset man in his seventies, diffuse light shining softly on his balding pate. It was strange how different he looked to me. Yesterday, his elongated forehead had lent him a babylike air of innocence. Today, the furrowed brow suggested a man who had much to worry him. I had to make a conscious effort not to stare at the mole on his cheek. "Yes?"

"I'm Kinsey Millhone. Do you remember me from yesterday?"

His mouth pulled together sourly. "With all the gun battles going on, it'd be hard to forget." His gaze shifted. "I don't remember this gent."

I tilted a nod at Dietz. "This is my partner, Robert Dietz."

Dietz reached past me and shook hands with Bronfen. "Nice to meet you, sir. Sorry about all the uproar." He put his left hand behind his ear. "I don't believe I caught your name."

"Pat Bronfen. If you're still looking for that old woman, I'm afraid I can't help. I said I'd keep an eye out, but that's the best I can do." He moved as though to close the door.

"I held a finger up. "Actually, this is about something else." I took the birth certificate from my handbag and held it out to him. He declined to take it, but he scanned the face of it.

His expression shifted warily when he realized what it was. "How'd you get this?"

The inspiration came to me in a flash. "From Irene Bronfen. She was adopted by a couple in Seattle, but she's instituted a search for her birth parents."

He squinted at me, but said nothing.

"I take it you're the Patrick Bronfen mentioned on her birth certificate?"

He hesitated. "What of it?"

"Can you tell me where I might find Mrs. Bronfen?"

"No, ma'am. That woman left me more than forty years ago, and took Irene with her," he said, with irritation. "I never knew what happened to the child, let alone what became of Sheila. I didn't even know she put the child up for adoption. Nobody told me the first thing about it. That's against the law, isn't it? If I wasn't even notified? You can't sign someone's child away without so much as a by-your-leave."

"I'm not really sure about the legalities," I said. "Irene hired me to see what I could find out about you and your ex-wife."

"She's not my ex-wife. I'm still married to the woman in the eyes of the law. I couldn't divorce her if I didn't know where she was." He gestured impatiently, but he was running out of steam and I could see his mood shift. "That wasn't Irene, sitting on my front porch steps yesterday, was it?"

"Actually, it was."

He shook his head. "I can't believe it. I remember her when she was this high. Now she'd have to be forty-seven years old." He stared down at the porch, brow knitting parallel stitches between his eyes. "My own baby girl and I didn't recognize her. I always thought I'd be able to pick her out of a crowd."

"She wasn't well. You really never got a good look at her," I said.

He looked up at me wistfully. "Did she know who I was?"

"I'm sure she didn't. I didn't realize it myself until a little while ago. The certificate says Sumner. It took us a while to realize the address was still good."

"I'm surprised she didn't recognize the house. She was almost four when Sheila took her. Used to sit right there on the steps, playing with her little dollies." He shoved his hands in his pockets.

It was occurring to me that Irene's asthma attack might well have been generated by an unconscious recognition of the place. "Maybe some of the memories will come back to her once she knows about you," I said.

His eyes had come back to mine with curiosity. "How'd you track me down?"

"Through the adoption agency," I said. "They had her birth certificate on file."

He shook his head. "Well, I hope you'll tell her how much I'd like to see her. I'd given up any expectation of it after all these years. I don't suppose you'd give me her address and telephone number."

"Not without her permission," I said. "In the meantime, I'm still interested in finding Mrs. Bronfen. Do you have any suggestions about where I might start to look?"

"No, ma'am. After she left, I tried everything I could think of—police, private investigators. I put notices in the newspapers all up and down the coast. I never heard a word."

"Do you remember when she left?"

"Not to the day. It would have been the fall of nineteen thirty-nine. September, I believe."

"Do you have any reason to think she might be dead?"

He thought about that briefly. "Well, no. But then I don't have any reason to think she's still alive either."

I took a small spiral-bound notebook from my handbag and leafed through a page or two. I was actually consulting an old grocery list, which Dietz studied with interest, looking over my shoulder. He gave me a bland look. I said, "The adoption agency mentions someone named Anne Bronfen. Would that be your sister? The files weren't clear about the connection. I gathered she was listed as next-of-kin when the adoption forms were filled out."

"Well now, I did have a sister named Anne, but she died in nineteen forty ... three or four months after Sheila left."

I stared at him. "Are you sure of that?"

"She's buried out at Mt. Calvary. Big family plot on the hillside just as you go in the gate. She was only forty years old, a terrible thing."

"What happened to her?"

"Died of childbed fever. You don't see much of that anymore, but it sometimes took women in those days. She married late in life. Some fellow named Chapman from over near Tucson. Had three little boys one right after the other, and died shortly after she was delivered of her third. I paid to bring her back. I couldn't believe she'd want to be buried out in that godforsaken Arizona countryside. It's too ugly and too dry."

"Is there any possibility she might have heard from Sheila in those few months?"

He shook his head. "Not that she ever told me. She was living in Tucson at the time Sheila ran off. I suppose Sheila might have gone to her, but I never heard of it. Now, how about you answer me one. What happened with that old woman who wandered off from the nursing home? You never said if she turned up or not."

"Actually she did, about eleven o'clock last night. The police picked her up right out here in the street. She died in the emergency room shortly afterward."

"Died? Well, I'm sorry to hear that."

We went through our good-bye exercises, making appropriate noises.

Walking back to the car, Dietz and I didn't say a word. He unlocked the door and let me in. Once he eased in on his side, we sat in silence. He looked over at me. "What do you think?"

I stared back at the house. "I don't believe he was telling the truth."

He started the car. "Me neither. Why don't we check out the gravesite he was talking about?"

25

They were all there. It was eerie to see them—Charlotte, Emily, and Anne—their gravestones lined up in date order, first to last. The markers were plain; information limited to the bare bones, as it were. Their parents, the elder Bronfens, were buried side by side: Maude and Herbert, bracketed on the left by two daughters who had apparently died young. Adjoining those plots, there was an empty space I assumed was meant for Patrick when the time came. On the other side were the three I knew of: Charlotte, born 1894, died in 1917; Emily, born 1897, died in 1926; and Anne, who was born in 1900 and died in 1940.

I stared off down the hill. Mt. Calvary was a series of rolling green pastures, bordered by a forest of evergreens and eucalyptus trees. Most of the gravestones were laid flat in the ground, but I could see other sections like this one, where the monuments were upright, most dating back to the late nineteenth century. The heat of the afternoon sun was beginning to wane. It wouldn't be dark for hours yet, but a chill would settle in as it did every day. A bird sang a flat note to me from somewhere in the trees.

I shook my head, trying to make the information compute.

Dietz had the good sense to keep his mouth shut, but his look said "What?" as clearly as if he'd spoken.

"It just makes no sense. If Sheila Bronfen and Agnes Grey are the same person, then why don't their ages line up right? Agnes couldn't have been seventy when she died. She was eighty-plus. I know she was."

"So the two aren't the same. So what? You came up with a theory and it didn't prove out."

"Maybe," I said.

"Maybe, my ass. Give it up, Millhone. You can't manipulate the facts to fit your hypothesis. Start with what you know and give the truth a chance to emerge. Don't force a conclusion just to satisfy your own ego."

"I'm not forcing anything."

"Yes, you are. You hate to be wrong—"

"I do not!"

"Yes, you do. Don't bullshit me—"

"That has nothing to do with it! If the two aren't the same, so be it. But then, who was Agnes Grey and how'd she end up with Irene Bronfen?"

"Agnes might have been a cousin or a family friend. She might have been the *maid* . . ."

"All right, great. Let's say it was the maid who ran off with the little girl. How come he didn't tell us that? Why pretend it was his wife. *He's* convinced Sheila took the child, or else he's lying through his teeth, right?"

"Come on. You're grasping at straws."

I sank down on my heels, pulling idly at the grass. My frustration was mounting. I'd felt so close to unraveling the knot. I let out a puff of air. I'd been secretly convinced Agnes Grey and Anne Bronfen were one and the same. I wanted Bronfen to be lying about Anne's death, but it looked like he was telling the truth—the turd. Out of the corner of my eye, I saw Dietz sneak a look at his watch.

"Goddamn it. Don't do that," I said. "I hate being pushed." I bit back my irritation. "What time is it?" I said, relenting.

"Nearly four. I don't mean to rush you, but we gotta get a move on."

"The Ocean View isn't far."

He clammed up and stared off down the hill, probably stuffing down a little irritation of his own. He was impatient, a man of action, more interested in Mark Messinger than he was in Agnes Grey. He bent down, picked up a dirt clod, and tossed it down the hill. He watched it as if it might skip across the grass like a pebble on water. He shoved his hands in his pockets. "I'll wait for you in the car," he said shortly and started off down the hill.

I watched him for a moment.

"Oh hell," I murmured to myself and followed him. I felt like a teenager, without a car of my own. Dietz insisted on my being with him almost constantly, so I was forced to trail around after him, begging rides, getting stuck where I didn't want to be, unable to pursue the leads that interested me. I doubled my pace, catching up with him at the road. "Hey, Dietz? Could you drop me off at the house? I could borrow Henry's car and let you talk to Rochelle on your own."

He let me in on my side. "No."

I stared after him with outrage. "No?" I had to wait till he came around. "What do you mean, 'No'?"

"I'm not going to have you running around by yourself. It's not safe."

"Would you *quit* that? I've got things to do."

He didn't answer. It was like I hadn't said a word. He drove out of the cemetery and left on Cabana Boulevard, heading toward the row of motels just across from the wharf. I stared out the window, thinking darkly of escape.

"And don't do anything dumb," he said.

I didn't say what flashed through my head, but it was short and to the point.

The Ocean View is one of those nondescript one-story motels a block off the wide boulevard that parallels the beach. It was not yet tourist season and the rates were still down, red neon VACANCY signs alight all up and down the street. The

Ocean View didn't really have a view of anything except the backside of the motel across the alley. The basic cinderblock construction had been wrapped in what resembled aging stucco, but the red tiles on the roof had the uniform shape and coloring that suggested recent manufacture.

Dietz pulled into the temporary space in front of the office, left the engine running, and went in. I sat and stared at the car keys dangling from the ignition. Was this a test of my character, which everyone knows is bad? Was Dietz *inviting* me to steal the Porsche? I was curious about the exact date Anne Bronfen had died and I was itching to check it out. I had to have a car. This was one. Therefore . . .

I glanced at the office door in time to see Dietz emerge. He got in, slammed the door, and put the car in reverse. "Number sixteen, around the back," he said. He smiled at me crookedly as he shifted into first. "I'm surprised you didn't take off. I left you the keys."

I let that one pass. I always come up with witty rejoinders when it's too late to score points.

We parked in the slot meant for room 18, the only space available along the rear. Dietz knocked. Idly, I felt for the gun in my handbag, reassured by its weight. The door opened. He was blocking my view of her and I had too much class to hop up and down on tiptoe for an early peek.

"Rochelle? I'm Robert Dietz. This is Kinsey Millhone."

"Hello. Come on in."

I caught my first glimpse of Rochelle Messinger as we stepped through the door into her motel room.

"Thanks for coming up on such short notice," Dietz was saying.

I don't know what I expected. I confess I'm as given to stereotyping as the next guy. My notion of ladies who work in massage parlors leans toward the tacky, the blowsy, and (face it) the low class. A tattoo wouldn't have surprised me . . . a hefty rear end, decked out in blue jeans and spike heels, tatty dark hair pulled up in a rubber band.

Rochelle Messinger was my height, very slim. She had flyaway blond hair, a carelessly mussed mop that probably cost her $125 to have touched up and snipped every four weeks. Her face was the perfect oval of a Renaissance painting. She had a flawless complexion—very pale, finely textured skin—pale hazel eyes, long fingers with lots of silver rings, expensive ones by the look. She was wearing an ice-blue silk blouse, a matching silk blazer, pale blue slacks that emphasized her tiny waist and narrow hips. She smelled of some delicate blend of jasmine and lily of the valley. In her presence, I felt as dainty and feminine as a side of beef. When I opened my mouth, I was worried I would moo.

"God, how'd you end up with a piece of shit like Mark Messinger?" I blurted out instead.

She didn't react, but Dietz turned and gave me a hard look.

"Well, I really want to know," I said to him defensively.

She cut in. "It's all right. I understand your curiosity. I met him one night at a party in Palm Springs. He was working as a bodyguard for a well-known actor at the time and I thought he had class. I was mistaken, as it turns out, but by then we'd spent a weekend together and I was pregnant—"

"Eric," I said.

She nodded almost imperceptibly. "That was six years ago. I'd been told I could never have children, so for me, it was a miracle. Mark insisted on marriage, but I refused to compound the initial error in judgment. Once Eric was born, I didn't even want him to see the child. I knew by then how twisted he was. He hired a high-powered attorney and took me to court. The judge awarded him visitation rights. After that, it was simply a matter of time. I knew he'd make a try for Eric, but there was nothing I could do."

So far, she'd left more unexplained than she'd managed to clarify, but I thought it was time to back off and give Dietz room to operate. By unspoken agreement, this was his gig in much the same way the Bronfen interview had been mine. Dietz was getting into work mode, his energy intensifying, restlessness on the increase. He'd started snapping the fingers of his right hand against his left palm, a soft popping sound. "When did you last talk to him?" Dietz asked her.

"To Mark? Eight months ago. In October, he picked Eric up at the day-care center and took him to Colorado, ostensibly for a weekend. He called me shortly after that to say he wouldn't be returning him. He does allow the boy to call me from time to time, but it's usually from a pay phone and the contact's too brief to put a trace on. This is the first time I've actually known where he was. I want my child back."

Dietz said, "I can appreciate that. We understand Mark has family in the area. Will they know where he is?"

She smiled contemptuously. "Not bloody likely. Mark's father denounced him years ago and his mother's dead. He does have a sister, but I don't believe they're on speaking terms. She turned him in to the police the last time he got in touch."

"No other relatives? Friends he might have tried to contact?"

She shook her head. "He's strictly solo. He doesn't trust a soul."

"Can you suggest how we can get a line on him?"

"Easy. Call all the big hotels. The cops quizzed me as to his whereabouts after the gold mart robbery. He'll be loaded and, believe me, he's the sort of man who knows how to treat himself well. He'll book himself into first-class accommodations somewhere in town."

Dietz said, "Do you have a telephone book?"

Rochelle crossed to the bed table and opened the drawer. Dietz sat down on the edge of the king-size bed and turned to the yellow pages. I could tell he was dying for a cigarette. Actually, if I were a smoker, I'd have wanted one myself. It was the same bed where I'd caught my ex-husband with a lover during the Christmas holidays. What a jolly season that was . . .

Dietz looked at me. "How many big hotels?"

I thought about it briefly. "There are only three or four that might appeal to him," I said, and then to her, "Will he be registered under his real name?"

"I doubt it. When he's on the road, he tends to use one of his aliases. He favors Mark Darian or Darian Davidson, unless he's got a new one altogether, in which case I wouldn't know."

Dietz had flipped through the yellow pages to the hotel/motel listings.

"Hey, Dietz?"

He looked up at me.

"I'd try the Edgewater first," I said. "Maybe his showing up at the banquet last night was just a piece of dumb luck."

He stared for a moment until the logic sank in. Then he laughed. "That's good. I like that." He found the number and punched it in, his attention focusing as someone picked up on the other end. "May I speak to Charles Abbott in security? Yes, thanks. I'll hold." Dietz put a palm over the mouthpiece of the receiver and used the interval to fill Rochelle in on events to date. He interrupted himself abruptly. "Mr. Abbott? Robert Dietz. We talked to you yesterday about security on the banquet . . . Right. I'm sorry to bother you again, but I need a quick favor. I wonder if you can check to see if you have a guest registered there. The name is Mark Darian or Darian Davidson . . . possibly some variation. Same man. We believe he'll have his little boy with him. Sure . . ."

Apparently, Dietz was on hold again while Charles Abbott checked with the reservations desk. Dietz turned to Rochelle and took up the narrative where he'd left it. She didn't seem to have any trouble following. Watching her, I began to realize how strung-out she was, despite the poised façade. This was a woman who probably didn't eat when she was under stress, who lived on a steady diet of coffee and tranqs. I'd seen mothers like her before—usually pacing back and forth in a cage at the zoo. No appearance of domestication would ever undercut the savagery or the rage. Personally, I was happy I'd never laid a hand on her pup.

By the time Dietz caught her up, her expression was dark. "You have no idea how ruthless he is," she said. "Mark is very, very smart and he has all the uncanny intuitions of a psychopath. Have you ever dealt with one? It's almost like a form of mind reading. . . ."

232

Dietz was on the verge of replying when Charles Abbott cut back in. Dietz said, "You do. That's right, the boy is five." He listened for a moment. "Thanks very much. Absolutely." He placed the receiver in the cradle with exaggerated care. "He's there with the kid. They're in one of the cottages out in back. Apparently, the two of them have just gone down to the pool to have a swim. I told Mr. Abbott there'd be no trouble."

She said, "Of course not."

"You want to call the police?"

"No, do you?"

From the look that passed between them, they understood each other exactly. She picked up a leather handbag from the bed and took out a little nickel-plated derringer. Two shots. I gave him a smirky look, but his expression was neutral. God, and he'd criticized *my* gun.

"What's your intention if we succeed in getting Eric back? You can't go home," he said to her.

"I have a rental car, which I'm dropping at the airport. My brother's a pilot and he'll pick us up at a charter place called Neptune Air. Mark and I used it once."

Dietz turned to me. "You know it?"

"More or less. It's this side of the airport on Rockpit Road."

He turned back to Rochelle. "What time's he flying in?"

"Nine, which should give us time enough. don't you think?"

"It should. What then?"

"I've got a place we can hole up for as long as we want."

Dietz nodded. "All right. It sounds good. Let's do it."

I held a finger up, snagging Dietz's attention. I tilted my head toward the door. "Could I have a word with you?"

He flicked a look at me, but made no move, so I was forced to charge on.

I said, "I've got something I want to check out and I need some wheels. Why can't I take the rental car while you two take the Porsche? You know where Messinger is and you're on your way over. I don't see why I need to be there."

There was a silence. I had to struggle not to jump in with a lot of pointless dialogue. I'm too old to beg and whine. I just couldn't picture us in a motorcade, driving across town to a kidnapping or a shootout with Mark Messinger. My presence was redundant. I had other fish to fry. Rochelle was loading her gun—both chambers. It was too ludicrous for words, but something about it gave me a leaden feeling in my gut.

I could see Dietz debate my request. In an odd flash of ESP, I knew he'd have felt safer if I were going with him. He held out his car keys, not quite making eye contact. "Take my car. There's a chance Messinger might spot us if we pull into the hotel parking lot in it. We'll take the rental car. What I said before goes. Nothing dumb."

"Same to you," I said, perhaps more sharply than I intended. "I'll meet you out at the charter place."

"Take care."

"You too."

26

It was 4:42 when I turned into the entrance to Mt. Calvary for the second time that day. A long line of eucalyptus trees laid lean shadows across the road. I passed through them as though through a series of gates as I wound my way up the hill. I turned left into a parking area near the office and pulled in beside a splashing stone fountain in a circle of grass. Bright orange goldfish darted among the soft, dark green filaments of algae. I locked the car. The tall carved wooden doors to the nondenominational chapel were standing open. The stone interior was dark.

I passed a double row of flat monuments, displaying various types of granite markers and styles of lettering. Hard to decide which I preferred at such a quick examination. I reached the office and pushed through the glass door. The reception area was empty, the desk bare except for a neat stack of postcards depicting the crematorium. What kind of person would you write to on one of those? I spotted a discreet sign saying PRESS BUZZER FOR SERVICE attached to a device about the size of an electric letter opener. I pressed a lever. Magically, a woman appeared from around the corner.

I wasn't really up on the fine points of cemetery ethics so, of course, I told a lie. "Hello. I wonder if you could help me . . ."

From the woman's expression, she was wondering the same thing. She was in her forties, dressed in prim office clothes: a gray wool dress with a touch of white at the neck. I was sporting my usual jeans and tennis shoes. "I certainly hope so," she said. She kept her judgment in reserve just in case I was rich and had a passel of dead relatives in need of lavish burial.

"I believe my aunt is buried here and I need to know the date she died. My mother's in a nursing home and she's worried because she can't remember. Is there some way to check?"

"If you'll give me the name."

"The last name is Bronfen. Her first name was Anne."

"Just a moment." She disappeared. It was hard to picture how she'd find the information. Was all this stuff on a computer somewhere? In some old file cabinet in the back? If the date and place of death didn't coincide with Bronfen's story, I was going to do some digging and see if I could come up with the death certificate. It might mean a few phone calls to Tucson, Arizona, but I'd feel better knowing what had really happened to Anne.

She returned in a remarkably short period of time, holding a white index card which she passed to me. There wasn't much on the face of it, but it was all pertinent. I soaked up the typed information in a flash. Surname, Chapman. Given name, Anne Bronfen. Age, forty. Birthdate, January 5, 1900. Sex, female. Color, white. Place of birth, Santa Teresa, California. Place of death, Tucson, Arizona.

Ah. Date of death, January 8, 1940. That was interesting. Date of interment, January 12, 1940. The space allotted to the funeral director had been left blank, but the lot number and the plot number were filled in.

"What's this?" I asked. I held the card out, pointing to the bottom line on which the word *cenotaph* had been handwritten in black ink.

236

"That's a commemorative headstone for someone who's not actually buried in that plot."

"She's not? Where is she?"

The woman took the card. "According to this, she died in Tucson, Arizona. She's probably interred there."

"I don't get it. What's the point?"

"The Bronfens might have wanted her remembered in the family plot. It's a great comfort sometimes to feel that everyone's together."

"But how do you know this woman's really dead?"

She stared at me. "Not dead?"

"Yeah. Don't you require any proof? Can I just come in here and fill out one of these cards and buy somebody a gravestone?"

"It's hardly that simple," she said, "but yes, essentially . . ."

She had launched into an explanation of the particulars, but I was on my way out.

I drove to the board-and-care in a state of suspended animation. All I'd really wanted was corroboration of Bronfen's tale, and here I was with another possibility altogether. Maybe Agnes Grey and Anne Bronfen *were* the same person after all. I thumbed my nose in Dietz's general direction as I turned right on Concorde.

I parked the Porsche at the curb and got out. For once, there was no little twitch of the curtain as I pushed through the gate. I went up the porch steps and rang the bell. I waited. Several minutes passed. I moved over to the porch rail and peered toward the back of the house. At the far end of the driveway, I spotted a single-car garage. Attached to it was a lath house and a dark green potting shed with a big handsome padlock hanging open in the hasp.

Behind me, I heard the front door opening. "Oh, hi. Is that you, Mr. Bronfen?" I said, turning my attention back.

The man in the doorway was someone else—a frail old fellow with an air of shuffling indecision. He was thin and bent, his shoulders narrow, his fingers twisted with arthritis. He wore a much-washed plaid flannel shirt, thin at the elbows, and a pair of pants that came halfway up his chest.

"He's out. You'll have to come again," he said. His voice was a pastel blend of raspiness and tremor.

"Do you have any idea what time he'll be back?"

"About an hour," he said. "You just missed him."

"Oh, gee, that's too bad. I'm the contractor," I said in this totally false warm tone I use. "I guess Mr. Bronfen's thinking about an addition to the shed out back. He asked me to take a look. Why don't I just go on out there and see what's what."

"Suit yourself," he said. He closed the door.

Heart thumping, I made a beeline for the backyard, figuring my time was going to be limited. Patrick Bronfen was not going to appreciate my snooping, but then, if I were quick about it, he'd never know. The shed was perched haphazardly on a concrete foundation that did a sort of zigzag between the single-car garage and the house. This looked like the sort of work that was done without permit and was probably not up to code. Given the slope of the side yard and the retaining wall at the property line, Bronfen probably should have had a team of civil engineers out here before he opened that first sack of Redi-Mix.

I removed the dangling padlock from the hasp and let myself in. The interior was probably eight by ten, smelling of loam, peat moss, and potting soil, overlaid with B1 and fish emulsion. There were no windows and the light level had dropped by more than half. I felt around in the gloom, trying to find a light switch, but apparently the shed wasn't wired for electricity. I groped through my handbag till I came up with a penlight and shone it around. The beam illuminated a large expanse of wall-mounted pegboard, hung with gardening tools. A mower leaned against the wall, its blades flecked with grass clippings. There was a six-foot workbench, its surface littered with clay pots, trowels, spilled potting soil, and discarded seed packs. Damp air clambered over my ankles and feet. Under the bench, I could see a gap in the rotting wood where a board had been pushed out.

To the right was an oblong wooden bin with a hinged lid, knee-high, the sort of unit where tools are stored. A square of newly cut plywood had been nailed across one end. Big plastic bags of bark mulch and Bandini 101 were stacked on top. One of the bags had a rip in the bottom and a trail of bark extended across the cracked cement floor. A pie-shaped wedge of track suggested that the bin had been dragged forward and then pushed back again. I thought about Agnes's torn knuckles and broken nails.

I lifted my head. "Hello," I said, just to check the sound level. The word was muffled, as if absorbed by the shadows. I tried again. *"Hello?"* No echo at all. I doubted the noise carried five feet beyond the shed. If I'd abducted a half-senile old lady, this would be a neat place to stash her till I decided what to do.

I balanced the penlight on the workbench and removed the twenty-five-pound bags from the top of the bin, stacking them to one side. When I'd cleared the lid, I opened it and peered in. Empty. I retrieved the penlight and checked the rough interior surface. The space was easily the size of a coffin and constructed so poorly that the air flow could probably sustain life, at least for a brief period. I ran the penlight from corner to corner, but there was no evidence of occupancy. I lowered the lid and restored the bags of mulch to their original positions. On my hands and knees, I checked the area around the bin. Nothing. I'd never be able to prove Agnes Grey had been here.

As I backed out of the space, I caught a whiff of foul air, musty and sweet, like a faint wisp of smoke. I felt my skin contract with recognition, hairs standing at attention along the back of my neck. I could feel my lips purse with distaste. This was the odor of dead squirrel trapped in a chimney, rotting gopher parts left on the porch by your cat, some creature guaranteed to perfume your nights until nature had completed the process of decomposition. Jesus. Where was it coming from?

I raised myself up on my knees and fumbled across the workbench until I found the trowel. I ducked under the bench again, running my fingers lightly along the shed's concrete footing. The material was porous, softening with age, the texture mealy. I found a patch of crumbling mortar and began to dig with the trowel, gouging out a pocket. I turned the penlight off and worked by feel, using both hands. Under the hardened outer shell, the stuff felt gritty and wet, as if the groundwater had somehow seeped in, undermining the concrete. The smell seemed stronger. There was something dead down here.

I tried the light again, working my way to the right where I could see two horizontal cracks. I began to chop away at the concrete, doing more damage to the trowel than I was doing to the footing. I pulled myself to my feet again, searching the workbench for a more effective tool. Up on the pegboard, I spotted a short-handled hoe with a pick on the backside of the blade. I crawled back to my little strip mine and began to hack in earnest. I was making so much damn noise, it was a wonder the neighbors didn't complain. A hunk of cement fell away. Tentatively, I scooped some of the debris off, using the pick to excavate. I felt resistance, some sort of root perhaps, or a length of rebar. I turned on the penlight again and peered into the space.

"Oh shit," I whispered. I was looking at the dorsal surface of a little finger bone. I scooted backward across the floor, bumping into the mower. I sucked air through my teeth as my banged elbow sang. The pain was a welcome diversion under the circumstances. I flicked the light off and scrambled to my feet. I shoved a bag of bark mulch in front of the hole and snagged my handbag.

I was making little whimpering sounds as I whipped out of the door again. I placed the padlock where it had been and danced away from the shed with a spasm of revulsion. For a moment, all I could do was shiver, slapping at my arms as if to aid circulation. I paced in a circle, trying to think what to do. I breathed deeply. God, that was vile. From the glimpse I'd had, the bone had been there for years. Whatever the odor, it wasn't emanating from *that*, but what else was down there? In the fading afternoon light, the zigzagging foundation seemed to glow. Someone had been adding outbuildings from time to time. First the lath house had been attached to the garage, then the potting shed had been attached to that. Extending from the side of the potting shed, there was a pad where firewood was stacked. If Anne Bronfen (in the guise of Agnes Grey) was accounted for, then the body had to be Sheila's. Bronfen claimed his wife had run away with Irene, but I didn't believe a word of it. I did one of those all-over body shudders, thinking about the finger. All of the flesh was gone. I gave my head a shake and took two deep breaths, disconnecting my sensibilities. There had to be other answers somewhere on the premises.

I went back to the front door and knocked. I waited, hoping fervently that Bronfen wasn't back. Eventually, the old fellow shuffled his way to the door and opened it a crack. I had to clear my throat, assuming what I hoped was a normal tone of voice.

"Me again," I chirped. "Could I come in and wait for Mr. Bronfen?"

The old gent put a gnarly finger to his lips, giving my request some thought. Finally, he nodded and backed away from the door awkwardly as if controlled by wires. I followed him into the house, quickly checking my watch. I'd been in the shed twenty minutes. I still had plenty of time if I could figure out what I was looking for.

The old man crept toward the living room. "You can have a seat in here. I'm Ernie."

"Nice to meet you, Ernie. Where did Mr. Bronfen go? Did he say anything to you?"

"No. I don't believe so. He'll be home directly I should think. Not long."

"Nice house," I said, peering into the living room. There I was, telling lies again. The house was shabby and smelled of cooked cabbage and peed-in pants. The furniture looked like it had been there since the turn of the century. The once-upon-a-time white curtains hung in limp wisps. The wall-paper in the hallway, with its motif of violets, fanned out in all directions like a bug infestation. Lucky for Klotilde she hadn't qualified for occupancy.

To the left, uncarpeted stairs led up to a second floor. I could see a dining room with a series of decorative plates on the wall. I moved toward the rear of the house, passing a small door that probably opened onto a little storage area under the stairs. Across from that was the basement door. "Is this the kitchen through here? I need to wash my hands." But I was talking to myself—Ernie had shuffled into the living room, forgetting me entirely.

The kitchen was the prototype "before" in any home remodeling magazine. Cracked tile counters, black and white floor tiles, brown woodwork, stained sink, a dripping faucet. Someone, in a jaunty attempt to update the place, had covered the original wallpaper with a modern-day vinyl equivalent: pale green fruits and vegetables intermixed with white and yellow daisies. Along the baseboard, the vinyl strip was curling up like a party favor. I checked the walk-in pantry. The shelves were lined with industrial-size cans of hominy and peas. I went in and stood there, looking out at the kitchen with the door half-shut.

Irene Bronfen had been four when she left. I hunkered down, smelling soot, my eyes level with the doorknob. I returned to the hallway. The door to the storage space beneath the stairs was kept locked. I wondered if she'd used it as a playhouse. I hunkered there, looking left toward the kitchen. Not much visible from that vantage point. Murders are, so often, domestic affairs. Alcohol is a factor in more than sixty percent. Thirty percent of the weapons in these murders are knives, which, after all, antedate gunpowder and don't have to be registered. As a matter of convenience, the kitchen is a favored location for crimes of passion these days. You can sit there with your loved ones, grabbing beers out of the fridge, adding ice to your Scotch. Once your spouse makes a smart remark, the stakes can escalate until you reach for the knife rack and win the argument.

I moved through the kitchen. At the rear of the house,

there was an enclosed wooden porch, uninsulated board and batten, where an antique washer stood. The water heater was out there, looking too small and decrepit to provide much hot water to the residents.

Irene at four had been somewhere in this house. I was willing to bet she'd been playing with the tea set. What had she told me? That the paint ran down the walls and ruined all the violets. I thought about her phobias: dust, spiders, closed spaces. I stood in the doorway, looking through the kitchen toward the hall. The ceilings were high, papered overall with the same repeating pattern of violets as the hall. The kitchen walls had been repapered, but not the ceiling itself. There must have been a time when it was the same throughout. I checked the baseboard near the stretch where the old icebox had once stood. In the wall above it was the square space with the little door to the exterior where the iceman had left his delivery. The next section of wall was a straight shot, floor to ceiling.

I could feel my attention stray to the portion of the vinyl paper that was loose along the bottom. I leaned over and peeled a corner back. Under it was a paper sprigged with roses. Under that layer came the paper with the violets again. I got a grip on the lower edge of the vinyl panel and I pulled straight up. The strip made a sucking sound as it raced up the wall, taking some of the sprigged paper with it. The rust-colored streaks were showing through, drab rivulets coursing through a field of violets, spatters of dull brown that had soaked into the paper, soaked into the plaster underneath. The blood had sprayed in an arc, leaping high along the wall, penetrating everything. Attempts to clean it had failed and the second coat of paper had been layered over the first. Then a third coat over that. I wondered if current technology was sufficiently sophisticated to forge the link between the blood here and the body that was buried in the footing. Lottie was the first to go. Her death must have been passed off as natural since she was buried with the rest. Emily must have come next, her skull "crushed" by falling bricks.

And Sheila after that, with a story to cover her disappearance. That must have been the killing Agnes and Irene witnessed. Bronfen had probably made up the story of Sheila's departure. I doubted there were any neighbors left who could verify the sequence of events. No telling what Bronfen had told them at the time. Some glib cover story to account for the missing.

Agnes had been in exile for years, protecting Irene. I wondered what had tempted her to return to the house. Perhaps, after over forty years, she thought the danger had passed. Whatever her motives, she was dead now, too. And Patrick—dear brother Patrick—was the only one left.

I heard the front door shut.

27

He stood in the kitchen doorway, a brown grocery bag in his arms. He wore a dark green sport shirt and wash pants, belted below his waist. He was wheezing from exertion, sweat beading his face. His gaze was fixed on the length of vinyl wallpaper that now lay on the floor, folded over on itself. His gaze traveled up the wall and then jerked across to mine. "What'd you do that for?"

"Time to take care of old business, my friend."

He crossed to the kitchen table and set the grocery bag down. He removed some items—toilet paper, a dozen eggs, a pound of butter, a loaf of bread—and set them on the table. I could see him try to settle on an attitude, the proper tone. He'd been rehearsing this in his mind for years, probably confident the conversation was one he could handle with a perfect air of innocence. The problem was, he'd forgotten what innocence felt like or how it was supposed to look. "What old business?"

"All the blood on the wall for one."

The pause was of the wrong length. "What blood? That's a redwood stain. I refinished a piece of porch furniture and

245

knocked the can off on the floor. Stuff sprayed all over, went everyplace. You never saw such a mess."

"Arterial blood will do that. You get a pumping effect." I tromped over the crumpled strip of paper, with a scrabbling sound, and washed my hands at the kitchen sink.

He put a half gallon of ice cream in the freezer, taking a moment to rearrange boxes of frozen vegetables. His rhythm was off. An accomplished liar knows how important the timing is in conveying nonchalance.

I dried my hands on a kitchen towel of doubtful origin. It might have been a part of a pillow case, a paint rag, or a diaper. "I drove over to Mt. Calvary and looked for Anne's grave."

"Make your point. I got work to do. She's buried with the family on the side of the hill."

"Not quite," I said. I leaned against the counter, watching him unload canned goods. "I went into the office and asked to see the interment card. You bought her a stone, but there's no body in the grave. Anne left town with Irene in January nineteen forty."

He tried to get huffy, but he couldn't muster any heat. "I paid to bring her all the way from Tucson, Arizona. If she wasn't in the coffin, don't tell me about it. Ask the fellow on the other end who said he put her there."

"Oh, come on," I said. "Let's cut to the chase. There wasn't any husband in Arizona and there weren't any little kids. You made that stuff up. You killed Charlotte and Emily. You killed Sheila, too. Anne was alive until late last night and she told me most of it. She said Emily wanted to sell the house and you refused. She must have pressed the point and you were forced to eliminate her just to end the argument. Once you got Emily out of the way, there was only Anne to worry about. Have her declared dead and you collect the whole estate. . . ."

He began to shake his head. "You're a crazy woman. I got nothing to say to you."

I crossed to the wall-mounted telephone near the hall door.

"Fine with me. I don't care. You can talk to Lieutenant Dolan as soon as he gets here."

Now he was willing to argue the point, any means to delay. "I wouldn't kill anyone. Why would I do that?"

"Who knows what your motivation was? Money is my guess. I don't know *why* you did it. I just know you did."

"I did not!"

"Sure you did. Who are you trying to kid?"

"You don't have a shred of proof. You can't prove anything."

"I can't, but somebody can. The cops are really smart, Patrick, and persistent? My God. You have no idea how persistent they are where murder's concerned. The whole of modern technology will be brought to bear. Lab techs, machinery, sophisticated tests. They've got experts out the wazoo and what do you have? Nothing. A lot of hot air. You don't stand a chance. Fifty years ago you might have fooled 'em, but not these days. You're up shit creek, pal. You are totally screwed . . ."

"Now see here. You wait a minute, young lady. I won't have that kind of talk used in my house," he said.

"Oh, sorry. I forgot. You've got standards. You're not going to tolerate a lot of smutty talk from me, right?" I turned back to the telephone. I had picked up the receiver when the window shattered in the back. The two acts came so close together, it looked like cause and effect. I pick up the phone, the window breaks out. Startled, I jumped a foot and dropped the phone in the process, jumping again as the handset thumped against the wall. I saw a hand come through the shattered window and reach around to unlock the door. One savage kick and the door swung back abruptly and banged against the wall. I had grabbed my handbag and was just reaching for my gun when Mark Messinger appeared, his own gun drawn and pointed at me. The suppressor created the illusion of a barrel fourteen inches long.

This time there was no smile, no aura of sexuality. His

blond hair stood out around his head in damp spikes. His blue eyes were as cold and as blank as stone. Patrick had turned, heading toward the front door in haste. Messinger fired at him casually, not even pausing long enough to form an intent, the shooting as simple as pointing a finger. *Spwt!* The sound of the silenced .45 semiautomatic was almost dainty compared to its effect. The force of the bullet drove Patrick into the wall where he bounced once before he fell. Blood and torn flesh bloomed in his chest like a chrysanthemum, shreds of cotton shirting like the calyx of a flower. I was staring at him mesmerized when Messinger grabbed me by the hair, hauling my face up within an inch of his. He shoved the barrel of his gun under my chin, pressing so hard it hurt. I wanted to protest the pain of it, but I didn't dare move. "Don't shoot me!"

"Where's Eric?" he breathed.

"I don't know."

"You're going to help me get him back."

Fear had pierced my chest wall like splinters. All the adrenaline was coursing upward to my brain, driving out thought. I had a brief image of Dietz with Rochelle Messinger. They'd evidently succeeded in plucking the kid from his father's grasp. I could smell chlorine from the swimming pool, mingled with Messinger's breath. He probably couldn't take his gun to the pool without calling attention to himself. I pictured him in the water, Eric on the side just waiting to jump in. If his mother appeared, he'd have run straight to her with a shriek of joy. By now they were probably barreling out to the airport. The plane had been chartered for nine to allow time for the snatch. I willed the thought away. Made my mind blank.

Messinger slapped me across the face hard, setting up a ringing in my head. I was dead. I wouldn't get out of this one alive. He shoved me toward the back door, kicking a chair out of my path. I caught sight of Ernie, the old guy, shuffling toward the kitchen. His expression was perplexed, especially when he spotted Patrick on the floor with the corsage of blood pinned to the center of his chest. Mark Messinger turned and pointed the gun at the old man.

"Oh don't!" I burbled. My voice sounded strange, high-pitched and hoarse. I squeezed my eyes shut and waited for the *spwt!* I looked back. The old fellow had pivoted and was shuffling away in panic. I could hear his howls echo down the hall, as frail and helpless as a child's. Messinger watched him retreat, indecision flickering in his eyes. He lost interest and turned his attention back to me. "Get the car keys."

I saw the bag where I'd dropped it on the floor near the phone. I pointed, temporarily unable to speak. I longed for my gun.

"We'll take my car. You drive."

He grabbed me by the head and buried his grip in my hair again, propelling me with a fury that made me cry out in fear.

"Shut up," he whispered. His face was close to mine as we descended the back stairs. I stumbled, grabbing at the rail with my right hand for balance. My heel slipped off the stair and I nearly went down. I thought he'd pull all my hair out, effectively scalping me with his closed fist, which held me like a vise. I couldn't look down, couldn't move my head to either side. I could feel the gravel driveway underfoot. I proceeded like a blind woman, hands out, using senses other than sight. The car was parked in the drive near the shed. I wondered briefly if a neighbor would spot our clumsy progress. Nearly dark now. In my mind's eye, I could see Rochelle's face. Please be on the plane, I thought. Please be in the air. Take Dietz with you forever and keep him somewhere safe. I pictured his impatience, his intensity. I willed him into a taxi, drove him away from the danger. I couldn't save him, couldn't even save myself this time around. Messinger yanked open the door on the passenger side and pushed me across the front seat. He was driving a yellow Rolls-Royce: walnut dashboard, leather upholstery.

"Start the car," he said. He got in after me, crowding close. He placed the barrel of the gun against my temple. He was breathing hard, his tension concentrated in his grip on the gun. If he shot me, I wouldn't feel it. I'd be dead before the pain could travel along my nerve ends and get the message to my brain. I willed the act, wanted it over with. "Do it," he said. I thought the voice was mine, so nearly did it mimic my thought.

"Start the fuckin' car!" His anger was erratic, sometimes fire, sometimes ice, his command of himself veering inexplicably from unbridled impulse to rigid control.

I felt for the keys in the ignition.

"Where'd they take my son?"

"They didn't tell me."

"You lying *bitch*! I'll tell *you* then." He dropped his voice and I could feel the force of his words against my cheek. The sexuality was back, the same tickle of desire that rises when you dance with a man for the first time—some awareness of the flesh and all the possibilities that wait. He was calm again, confident, his throaty laugh nearly jubilant. "Rochelle's got a twin brother flies a plane," he said. "She knows better than to take Eric back to her place because I'd find him first thing and she'd be dead before she shut the door. She'll try to get him out by air, take him off and hide him somewhere till things cool down." He moved the gun away from my head, gesturing with the barrel. "Back out on the street and take a left. We'll head out to the airport, there's a charter place out there. Drive carefully, okay?"

I nodded dumbly, my mood shifting as abruptly as his. So far, I was alive, not maimed or disabled. I was grateful he hadn't hurt me, thrilled I wasn't dead. I did as I was told. I felt absurdly happy that his manner was pleasant, his tone nearly friendly as I backed out of the drive. He'd reduced my habitual cockiness to humility. There was still hope. There was still a chance. Maybe they'd already left. Maybe they were gone. Maybe I could kill him before he killed me. I had a flash of Rochelle being shot in the chest. He'd kill her as carelessly as he'd killed Patrick Bronfen, with the same matter-of-factness, the same casualness, the same ease. Dietz would die. Messinger would trade me for Eric at the outset and then kill us all. Rochelle, Dietz, and me, in whatever order would maximize the horror. I focused on the road, suddenly conscious of the car. I could smell leather seats, the fresh rose in a crystal vase. The car glided in silence. I turned right on 101 and flew north. There was not a highway patrol car in sight.

My mouth was dry. I cleared my throat. "How did you know where I was?"

"I put a bug on the Porsche the first night it was parked in front of your place. See this? My receiver. I've been following you guys everywhere in a couple of different rental cars."

"Why'd you kill Patrick?"

"Why not. He's a dickface."

I glanced over at him curiously. "Why'd you spare Ernie?"

"That old fart? Who knows? Maybe I'll go back and do him now you mention it," he said. His tone was teasing. A little hit-man humor to show what a devil-may-care kind of guy he was. He'd taken the gun away from my head and it rested now on his knee. "What's the story with this body-guard? He's a pain in the ass. Two times I nearly had you and he stepped in."

I kept my eyes on the road. "He's good at his job."

He looked over at me. "You makin' it with him?"

"That's none of your business."

"Come on . . ."

"I've only known him four days!" I said, righteously.

"So what?"

"So I don't jump into bed with guys that quick."

"You should have done while you had the chance. Now he's a dead man. I'll make you a deal. How's this? Him or you. Better yet, Rochelle or him. Take your pick. If you don't choose, I kill all three of you."

"You're only getting paid for one."

"True, but I'll tell you, the money doesn't mean that much. When you do what you love, you'd do it for free, am I right?" He leaned toward the tape deck. "Want some music? I got jazz, classical, R&B. No heavy metal or reggae. I hate that shit. You want Sinatra?"

"No thanks." I saw the off-ramp for the university and the airport and eased right. The road curved up and to the left, crossing the freeway, which now passed underneath. It was gone and we hit the straightaway. Two more minutes to the airport and what was I going to do? The digital clock on the instrument panel showed that it was 8:02. A mile farther on, the access ramp to Rockpit Road came into view on the right. I took the turn. I knew the ocean was close by, but all I could smell was the rotten-egg odor of the slough that hugged the road. A fog was rolling in, a dense bank of white against the blackened sky. The university sat up on the bluffs like a walled city, all lights and buff-colored towers. I'd never gone to college. I was strictly blue-collar lineage—like this guy, come to think of it. Like Dietz.

I took Rockpit for half a mile until the hangars and assorted outbuildings of Neptune Air appeared on the left. "Here," he said. I slowed the Rolls and turned in. Messinger sat forward, peering through the windshield, which had been spritzed with fine mist.

There were four miscellaneous vehicles parked in the lot, but there was no sign of Rochelle's rental car. Messinger had me park the Rolls in the lee of a metal-sided hangar. Under the inverted V of the roofline, illuminated by a single bulb, the sign read: FLIGHT INSTRUCTION, FAA REPAIR STATION, 24 HOUR CHARTERS, PIPER DEALER, and AVIONICS SALES & SERVICES. The perimeter fence was made of chain link, wrapped with barbed wire on top, and padlocked. Warnings were posted at intervals. Floodlights on the far side of the hangar glowed blankly on the empty runway.

We left the car. It was cold and a wind whipped along the tarmac, blowing my hair in all directions. As we crossed the parking lot, Messinger took me by the elbow in a gesture so reminiscent of Dietz that the air caught in my throat.

The offices of Neptune Air were closed, the interior darkened, one dim light shining through the plate glass. We circled the building. A broad redwood deck stretched out across the rear. A picnic table and two benches had been set up for those waiting for their charter flights. I pictured the Neptune employees (all three of them) eating lunch out here, watching planes land, drinking canned sodas from the vending machine. To the right, there was a line of small private planes tied down on the tarmac. Beyond them, half a mile away, I could see the Santa Teresa Airport, the upper portion of its tower peeking up above a row of storage sheds. On one of the runways, a United 737 was lumbering across the field in preparation for takeoff. Messinger gestured and we sat down on opposite sides of the picnic table. "It's fuckin' cold out," he said.

I heard voices behind me. I turned and watched as two workmen, probably fuelers, locked the exit door to the hangar and moved off toward the parking lot. Messinger rose to his feet, peering in their direction. He pulled the nose of the .45 up and pointed, making little noises with his mouth . . . *pow, pow.* He blew imaginary smoke away from the barrel and then he smiled. "They don't know how lucky they are, do they?"

"I guess not," I said.

He sat down again.

His hair had dried into ringlets and the wind lifted them playfully. His eyes glinted in the light from a bulb at the upper corner of the building. He was watching me with interest. "Your daddy ever bring you out here to watch planes?"

"He died when I was five."

"Mine didn't either. Cocksucker. No wonder I turned out bad."

"What, he didn't show up to watch you play Little League?"

"He didn't do much of anything except drink, fornicate, and kill folk. That's where I got all my talent. From him."

My fear had receded and in its place, I was beginning to feel a characteristic crankiness settle in. It was one thing to die, and quite another being forced to sit around in a cold wind making small talk with a fatuous ass like Messinger. I'd been thinking I better make nice. Now I wondered what the point was. In the meantime, he was staring at my face. I stared back, just to see what it would feel like.

He nodded judiciously. "Your black eye's looking better."

I ran a finger along my orbital ridge. I kept forgetting what I must look like to the uninitiated observer. The last time I'd assayed my various injuries, I'd noticed the bruises had changed hues dramatically. A lemon-yellow backdrop now blended into lime-green, which was overlaid with plum. "You nearly got me that round."

He waved the compliment away. "That was just a warm-up. I wasn't serious."

"What'd Eric think of it?"

"Didn't bother him. Look at cartoons. Kids see violence all the time and it doesn't count for shit. People don't really die. It's all special effects."

"I doubt he's going to feel that way if you shoot his mom."

"Not *if* I shoot her—when." I saw his gaze shift.

Out on the runway, a tiny plane had landed, sounding like a VW in need of a new fan belt. I lost sight of the aircraft behind some outbuildings and then the plane appeared again, puttering toward us. He got to his feet. "I bet this is him. Come on. And keep your mouth shut or I'll pop you one."

The plane reached the concrete apron beside the hangar and the pilot made a miniature U-turn so that he was now facing out toward the runway. He cut the engine, doused the lights. Messinger had gripped me across the back of the neck, marching me toward the plane in quickstep. I imagined the pilot taking off his headset, writing in his logbook, loosening his seat belt. If this was Rochelle's brother, he was going to recognize Messinger as soon as he caught sight of him.

A column of fear wafted up my spine like smoke. I tried to hang back, resisting, but Messinger's fingers dug into my neck with excruciating pain. We had picked up the pace, almost trotting side by side until we reached the tail unit of the plane. Just in front of us, the door to the cockpit opened and the pilot stepped down. We were less than six feet away.

254

Messinger said, "Hey, Roy?"

I screamed a warning.

The pilot turned in surprise.

Spwt!

Roy dropped to his knees. He toppled forward on his face. His nose had been shattered by the bullet, which took out a chunk of skull when it exited. I cried out in horror, recoiling from the sight. I felt tears like a stinging blow. A quick cloud of gunpowder perfumed the night air. I put a hand against the plane for support. Messinger had already lifted the dead man by the arms and he was dragging him backward across the tarmac toward the slanted shadows of the hangar.

I pushed away from the plane. I took off, running for dear life. I headed toward the parking lot, hoping to reach the road.

"Hey!"

I could hear Messinger behind me, pounding hard. I didn't dare look. He was faster than I and he was gaining. I felt the shove that sent me tumbling forward on my hands. I tried to roll, but I wasn't quick enough to save myself. I was down and he was on me, winded and raging. He pulled me over on my back. I kept my arms up to ward off the blows he aimed at me.

Something caught his attention and his face jerked up. A car was approaching from the direction of the slough. He pulled me to my feet, half-dragging, half-hauling me across the concrete toward the shelter of the building. He backed up against the stucco, my body clamped against his, half tucked under his armpit. He had his one hand across my mouth, the barrel of the gun at my temple again. I was close to suffocation, both of us breathing hard.

The car pulled into the parking lot. I heard two car doors slam, one right after the other, and then the murmur of voices. I saw Rochelle first, heard her heels tapping on the pavement, saw the pale cheeks, the pale hair above the turned-up collar of her trenchcoat. Eric walked beside her, his face tilted toward hers. The two were holding hands. Dietz was locked up close to her, his attention focused on the

255

surrounding darkness. When he spotted the plane, he hesitated. I could almost see his puzzled squint. He put an arm out to stop Rochelle's progress and Eric halted in his tracks.

Messinger pushed us away from the building. "Hey, pal. Over here. Look what I got."

For a moment, the five of us formed a tableau. I felt like we were part of a pageant, some community theater group acting out a well-known scene from history. No one moved. Messinger had removed his hand from my mouth, but none of us said a word.

Finally, Eric seemed to perk up. "Daddy?"

"Hey, big fella. How're you doin'? I came to pick you up."

Rochelle said, "Mark, let me have him back. I beg you. You've had him eight months. Let him stay with me. Please."

Despite the distance between us, the voices carried easily.

"No way, babe. That's my kid. Tell you what, though. I'll make a deal. I get Eric. You get Kinsey. Fair enough?"

Dietz glanced at Rochelle. "He won't hurt Eric—"

Rochelle lashed out at Dietz. "Shut up! This is between us."

"He'll kill her," Dietz said.

"I don't give a shit!" she snapped.

Messinger cut in. "Excuse me, Dietz? I hate to interrupt, but you're never going to win an argument with her. She's a hardheaded bitch. Believe me, I know."

Dietz was silent, looking at him. Rochelle had put her arms around Eric possessively, holding him against her, much as Messinger held me.

Messinger was concentrating on Dietz for the moment. "I'd appreciate your taking your gun out, pal. Could you do that? I don't want to have to blow this lady's brains out quite yet. I thought you might like to say good-bye to each other first."

"How serious are you about a deal?" Dietz said.

"Let's do the gun first, okay? Then we'll negotiate. I have to tell you I'm feeling tense. I got a .45 with the safety off and the trigger only takes two pounds of pressure. You might want to move kind of slow."

Dietz seemed to proceed in slow motion, removing his gun from the middle-of-the-back holster he was wearing under his tweed sport coat. He held the barrel upright and removed the magazine, which he tossed out on the pavement. I could hear the metal clatter on concrete as he kicked it away. He tossed the gun over his shoulder into the dark. He held his hands up, palm out.

Dietz and I exchanged a look. I could feel Messinger's tension through the bones of my back. I was warmer, laid up against him, and if I didn't move my head, I was hardly aware of the gun barrel. The length of it, with the suppressor attached, prevented him from pointing it, end on, at my head. He was forced to hold it at an angle. I wondered if the sheer weight of it wasn't becoming burdensome.

Messinger was apparently watching Dietz with care. "Very nice. Now why don't you persuade Rochelle to cooperate. See if you can talk her into it because if not, I'm about to collect on this fifteen-hundred-dollar hit."

Rochelle said, "Why don't you ask Eric what he wants to do?"

Messinger's tone was condescending. "Because he's too young to make a decision about his own custody. Jesus Christ, Rochelle. I don't believe some of the shit you come up with. That's just the kind of attitude makes you a terrible parent, you know that? If he stayed with you, you'd turn him into some kind of little fruit. Now let's cut the horseshit and make a little trade here. Just send Eric over and we'll see what we can do."

Dietz looked at Rochelle. "Do what he says."

She said nothing. She stared at Messinger and then her gaze shifted over to me. "I don't believe you. You'll kill her anyway."

"No, I won't," he said, as if falsely accused. "That's why I brought her out here, to trade. I'd never welsh on a deal where my kid is concerned. Are you nuts?"

Dietz said to her, "You'll have another chance to get Eric back. I promise. We'll help you. Just do this for now."

Even at that distance, I could see her face crumple. She gave Eric a little push. "Go on . . ." She was starting to cry, hands shoved down in her coat pockets.

Eric hesitated, looking from her face to his father's.

"It's all right, angel," she said. He began to walk toward us rapidly, head down, his face hidden.

Messinger's grip on me tightened and I could smell the tawny sweat of sex oozing out of his pores. Time seemed to slow as the kid crossed the pavement. All I could hear was the sound of the wind chuffing across the runway.

Eric reached us. I'd never really seen him up close. His face was like a valentine, all pink cheeks, blue eyes, long lashes. So vulnerable. His ears stuck out slightly and his neck seemed too thin. "Don't hurt her, Daddy."

"I wouldn't do that," Messinger said. "The car's parked on the far side of the hangar. You can wait for me over there. Here's the keys."

"Mark?" Rochelle's voice sounded faint against the distant droning of an incoming plane. Tears were streaming down her face. "Can I kiss him good-bye?"

I heard him mutter. "Christ." He raised his voice. "Come ahead then, but make it quick." To Eric, he said, "You wait here for your mommy and then you go get in the car like I said. You eat any supper?"

"We stopped at McDonald's and had a Big Mac."

"I don't believe it. You remember what I told you about junk food?"

Eric nodded, his eyes filling with tears. It was hard to know which parent he was supposed to listen to. In the meantime, Rochelle was walking toward us along a straight line, setting her high heels down one in front of the other as if in modeling school. Over her shoulder, Dietz's gaze locked down on mine. I thought he smiled his encouragement. I didn't want to see Dietz die, didn't think I could bear it, didn't want to live myself if it came down to that.

I looked at Rochelle. She'd stopped a few feet away. Eric walked over and buried his face against her. She leaned forward and laid her cheek against the top of his head. She was weeping openly. "I love you," she whispered. "You be a good boy, okay?"

He nodded mutely and then pulled away, hurrying toward the Rolls without a backward look. His father called after him.

"Hey, Eric? There's some tapes in the glove compartment. Play anything you like."

Rochelle stared at Mark. She pulled the derringer out of her pocket, aimed it straight at his head and pulled the trigger. The blast was remarkably loud for a weapon so petite. I heard his scream. He dropped the .45 and clutched his right eye with both hands, toppling sideways onto the pavement where he lay writhing in pain. Rochelle, with an efficiency she must have learned from him, stepped in close, and fired again. "You son of a bitch. You never honored a deal in your fuckin' life."

Messinger lay still.

Dietz began to cross the tarmac, moving toward me. I went out to meet him.

Epilogue

When the cops finally tore up the area around Bronfen's potting shed, four bodies came to light. The one buried in the footing was tagged as a former resident of the board-and-care, whose pension checks Bronfen had been cashing for a good five months. The pathologists are still working to identify the remaining dead, but one is most assuredly Bronfen's wife, Sheila. Irene is doing better now that she knows the truth. She's found a good therapist who's helping her sort it all out. It may take her years yet, but at least she's on the right path.

A third (and final) hired assassin was apprehended in Carson City shortly after Messinger was killed. Yesterday, I spoke to Lee Galishoff, who told me Tyrone Patty died of a knife wound, the result of a dispute with an inmate half his size.

As for Dietz, he was with me until August 29 when the job he was hoping for materialized. He's in Germany now, filming mock infiltrations of military bases. He swears he's coming back. I'd like to believe him, but I'm not sure I dare. In the meantime, I have work of my own to do and a life that feels richer for his having been a part of it.

Respectfully submitted,
Kinsey Millhone

H is for Homicide

For the Women's Group in all its incarnations:

Florence Clark
Sylvia Stallings
Penelope Craven
Mary Lynn

Caroline Ahlstrand
Mary Slemons

Susan Dyne
Joyce Dobry

Margaret Warner
Georgina Morin
and Barbara Knox

sharing tears and triumphs, rage and laughter,
for the last five years of Monday nights.

The author wishes to acknowledge the invaluable assistance of the following people: Steven Humphrey; Ron Warthen, chief investigator, Fraud Division, California Department of Insurance; Robert Chambers, regional manager, and Michael Fawcett, special agent, Insurance Crime Prevention Institute; Lt. Tony Baker, Lt. Terry Bristol, Sgt. Tom Nelson, and Carol Hesson of the Santa Barbara County Sheriff's Department; Sgt. Dave Hybert, Santa Barbara Police Department; Traffic Officer Rick Crook, California Highway Patrol; Lucy Thomas, Reeves Medical Library, and Tokie Shynk, R.N., nursing director, Coronary Care Unit, Santa Barbara Cottage Hospital; Judianne Cooper; Joyce Mackewich; Irene Franotovich; Steven Stone, presiding justice, Ventura County Court of Appeals; Eric S. H. Ching; Austin Duncan, Gold Coast Auto Salvage; and Carter Blackmar.

The author also wishes to extend a special thank-you to Adam Seligman and to Muriel Seligman, national publicity director, Tourette Syndrome Association.

one

Looking back, it's hard to remember if the low morale at California Fidelity originated with the death of one of the claims adjusters or the transfer of Gordon Titus, an "efficiency expert" from the Palm Springs office, who was brought in to bolster profits. Both events contributed to the general unrest among the CF employees, and both ended up affecting me far more than I would have imagined, given the fact that my association with the company had been, up to that point, so loose. In checking back through my calendar, I find a brief penciled note of the appointment with Gordon Titus, whose arrival was imminent when Parnell was killed. After that first meeting with Titus, I'd jotted, "s.o.b. extraordinaire!" which summarized my entire relationship with him.

I'd been gone for three weeks, doing a consumer investigative report for a San Diego company concerned about a high-level executive whose background turned out to be something other than he'd represented. The work had taken me all over the state, and I had a check in my pocket for beaucoup bucks by the time I wrapped up my inquiry on a Friday afternoon. I'd been given the option of remaining in San Diego that weekend at the company's expense, but I woke up inexplicably at 3:00 A.M. with a primal longing for home. A moon the size of a dinner plate was propped up on the balcony outside my window, and the light falling across my face was almost bright enough to read by. I lay there, staring at the swaying shadow of palm fronds on the wall, and I knew that what I wanted most was to be in my own bed. I was tired of hotel rooms and meals on the road. I was tired of spending time with people I didn't know well or expect to see again. I got out of bed, pulled my clothes on, and threw everything I had in my duffel bag. By 3:30 A.M. I'd checked out, and ten minutes later I was on the 405 northbound, heading for Santa Teresa in my new (used) VW bug, a 1974 sedan, pale blue, with only one wee small ding in the left rear fender. Classy stuff.

At that hour, the Los Angeles freeway system is just beginning to hum. Traffic was light, but every on ramp seemed to donate a vehicle or two, people pouring north to work. It was still dark, with a delicious chill in the air, a ground fog curling along the berm like puffs of smoke. To my right, the foothills rose up and away from the road, the tracts of houses tucked into the landscape showing no signs of life. The lights along the highway contributed a nearly ghostly illumination, and what was visible of the city in the distance seemed stately and serene. I always feel an affinity for others traveling at such an hour, as if we are all engaged in some form of clandestine activity. Many of the other drivers had oversize Styrofoam cups of coffee. Some were actually managing to wolf down fast food as they drove. With the occasional car window rolled down, I was treated to bursts of booming music that faded away as the cars passed me, changing lanes. A glance in my rearview mirror showed a woman in the convertible behind me emoting with vigor, belting out a lip-sync solo as the wind whipped through her hair. I felt a jolt of pure joy. It was one of those occasions when I suddenly realized how happy I was. Life was good. I was female, single, with money in my pocket and enough gas to get home. I had nobody to answer to and no ties to speak of. I was healthy, physically fit, filled with energy. I flipped on the radio and chimed in on a chorus of "Amazing Grace," which didn't quite suit the occasion but was the only station I could find. An early morning evangelist began to make his pitch, and by the time I reached Ventura, I was nearly redeemed. As usual, I'd forgotten how often surges of goodwill merely presage bad news.

The usual five-hour drive from San Diego was condensed to four and a half, which put me back in Santa Teresa at a little after eight. I was still feeling wired. I decided to hit the office first, dropping off my typewriter and the briefcase full of notes before I headed home. I'd stop at a supermarket somewhere along the way and pick up just enough to get me through the next two days. Once I unloaded my duffel at home, I intended to grab a quick shower and then sleep for ten hours straight, getting up just in time for a bite of supper at Rosie's down the street from me. There's nothing quite as decadent as a day in the sack alone. I'd turn my phone off, let the machine pick up, and tape a note to the front door saying "Do Not Bother Me." I could hardly wait.

I expected the parking lot behind my office building to be deserted. It was Saturday morning and the stores downtown wouldn't open until ten. It was puzzling, therefore, to realize that the area was swarming with people, some of whom were cops. My first thought was that maybe a movie was being shot, the area cordoned off so the cameras could roll without interruption. There was a smattering of onlookers standing out on the street and the same general air of orchestrated boredom that seems to accompany a shoot. Then I spotted the crime scene tape and my senses went on red alert. Since the lot was inaccessible, I found a parking place out at the curb. I removed my handgun from my purse and tucked it into my briefcase in the backseat, locked the car doors, and moved toward the uniformed officer who was standing near the parking kiosk. He turned a speculative eye on me as I approached, trying to decide if I had any business at the scene. He was a nice-looking man in his thirties with a long, narrow face, hazel eyes, closely trimmed auburn hair, and a small mustache. His smile was polite and exposed a chip in one of his front teeth. He'd either been in a fight or used his central incisors in a manner his mother had warned him about as a child. "May I help you?"

I stared up at the three-story stucco building, which was mostly retail shops on the ground floor, businesses above. I tried to look like an especially law-abiding citizen instead of a free-lance private investigator with a tendency to fib. "Hi. What's going on? I work in that building and I was hoping to get in."

"We'll be wrapping this up in another twenty minutes. You have an office up there?"

"I'm part of the second-floor insurance complex. What was it, a burglary?"

The hazel eyes did a full survey and I could see the caution kick in. He didn't intend to disseminate information without knowing who I was. "May I see some identification?"

"Sure. I'll just get my wallet," I said. I didn't want him to think I was whipping out a weapon. Cops at a crime scene can be edgy little buggers and probably don't appreciate sudden moves. I handed him my billfold flipped open to my California driver's license with the photostat of my P.I. license visible in the slot below. "I've been out of town and I wanted to drop off some stuff before I headed home." I'd been a cop myself once, but I still tend to volunteer tidbits that are none of their business.

His scrutiny was brief. "Well, I doubt they'll let you in, but you can always ask," he said, gesturing toward a plainclothes detective with a clipboard. "Check with Sergeant Hollingshead."

I still didn't have a clue what was going on, so I tried again. "Did someone break into the jewelry store?"

"Homicide."

"Really?" Scanning the parking lot, I could see the cluster of police personnel working in an area where the body probably lay. Nothing was actually visible at that remove, but most of the activity was concentrated in the vicinity. "Who's been assigned to the case, Lieutenant Dolan, by any chance?"

"That's right. You might try the mobile crime lab if you want to talk to him. I saw him head in that direction a few minutes ago."

"Thanks." I crossed the parking lot, my gaze flickering to the paramedics, who were just packing up. The police photographer and a guy with a notebook doing a crime scene sketch were measuring the distance from a small ornamental shrub to the victim, whom I could see now, lying face-down on the pavement. The shoes were man-size. Someone had covered the body with a tarp, but I could still see the soles of his Nikes, toes touching, heels angled out in the form of a V.

Lieutenant Dolan appeared, heading in my direction. When our paths intersected, we shook hands automatically, exchanging benign pleasantries. With him, there's no point in barging right in with all the obvious questions. Dolan would tell me as much or as little as suited him in his own sweet time. Curiosity only makes him stubborn, and persistence touches off an inbred crankiness. Lieutenant Dolan's in his late fifties, not that far from retirement from what I'd heard, balding, baggy-faced, wearing a rumpled gray suit. He's a man I admire, though our relationship has had its antagonistic moments over the years. He's not fond of private detectives. He considers us a useless, though tolerable, breed and then only as long as we keep off his turf. As a cop, he's smart, meticulous, tireless, and very shrewd. In the company of civilians, his manner is usually remote, but in a squad room with his fellow officers, I've caught glimpses of the warmth and generosity that elicit much loyalty in his subordinates, qualities he never felt much need to trot out for me. This morning he seemed reasonably friendly, which is always worrisome.

"Who's the guy?" I said finally.

"Don't know. We haven't ID'd him yet. You want to take a look?" He jerked his head, indicating that I was to follow as he crossed to the body. I could feel my heart start to pump in my throat, the blood rushing to my face. In one of those tingling intimations of truth, I suddenly knew who the victim was. Maybe it was the familiar tire-tread soles of the running shoes, the elasticized rim of bright pink sweat pants, a glimpse of bare ankle showing dark skin. I focused on the sight with a curious sense of déjà vu. "What happened to him?"

"He was shot at close range, probably sometime after midnight. A jogger spotted the body at six-fifteen and called us. So far we don't have the weapon or any witnesses. His wallet's been lifted, his watch, and his keys."

He leaned down and picked up the edge of the tarp, pulling it back to reveal a young black man, wearing sweats. As I glanced at the face in side view, I pulled a mental plug, disconnecting my emotions from the rest of my interior processes. "His name is Parnell Perkins. He's a California Fidelity claims adjuster, hired about three months ago. Before that, he worked as a rep for an insurance company in Los Angeles." The turnover among adjusters is constant and no one thinks anything about it.

"He have family here in town?"

"Not that I ever heard. Vera Lipton, the CF claims manager, was his immediate supervisor. She'd have his personnel file."

"What about you?"

I shrugged. "Well, I haven't known him long, but I consider him a good friend." I corrected myself into past tense with a small jolt of pain. "He was really a nice guy . . . pleasant and capable. Generous to a fault. He wasn't very open about his personal life, but then, neither am I. We'd have drinks together after work a couple of times a week. Sometimes the 'happy hour' stretched into dinner if both of us happened to be free. I don't think he'd really had time to form many close friendships. He was a funny guy. I mean, literally. The man made me laugh."

Lieutenant Dolan was making penciled notes. He asked me some apparently unrelated questions about Parnell's workload, employment history, hobbies, girlfriends. Aside from a few superficial observations, I didn't have much to contribute, which seemed strange to me somehow, given the sense of distress I was feeling. I couldn't take my eyes off of Parnell. The back of his head was round, the hair cut almost to the scalp. The skin of the back of his neck looked soft. His eyes were open, staring blankly at the asphalt. What is life that it can vanish so absolutely in such a short period of time? Looking at Parnell, I was struck by the loss of animation, warmth, energy, all of it gone in an instant, never to return. His job was done. Now the rest of us were caught up in the clerical work that accompanies any death, the impersonal busywork generated by our transfer from aboveground to below.

I checked the slot where Parnell usually parked his car. "I wonder where his car went. He has to drive in from Colgate, so it should be here someplace. It's American made, a Chevrolet, I think, eighty or eighty-one, dark blue."

"Might have been stolen. We'll see if we can locate the vehicle. I don't suppose you know the license number off-hand."

"Actually, I do. It's a vanity plate—PARNELL—a present to himself on his birthday last month. The big three-oh."

"You have his home address?"

I gave Dolan the directions. I didn't know the house number, but I'd driven him home on a couple of occasions, once when his car was being serviced and once when he got way too tipsy to get behind the wheel. I also gave Dolan Vera's home number, which he jotted beside her name. "I've got a key to the office if you want to see his desk."

"Let's do that."

for the next week, the killing was all anybody talked about. There's something profoundly unsettling when murder comes that close to home. Parnell's death was chilling because it seemed so inexplicable. There was nothing about him to suggest that he was marked for homicide. He seemed a perfectly ordinary human being just like the rest of us. As far as anyone could tell there was nothing in his current circumstances, nothing in his background, nothing in his nature, that would invite violence. Since there were never any suspects, we were made uncomfortably aware of our own vulnerability, haunted by the notion that perhaps we knew more than we realized. We discussed the subject endlessly, trying to dispel the cloud of anxiety that billowed up in the wake of his death.

I was no better prepared than anyone else. In my line of work, I'm not a stranger to homicide. For the most part, I don't react, but with Parnell's death, because of our friendship, my usual defenses—action, anger, a tendency to gallows humor—did little to protect me from the same apprehensiveness that gripped everyone else. While I find myself sometimes unwittingly involved in homicide investigations, it's nothing I set out to do, and usually nothing I'd take on without being paid. Since no one had hired me to look into this one, I kept my distance and minded my own business. This was strictly a police matter and I figured they had enough on their hands without any "help" from me. The fact that I'm a licensed private investigator gives me no more rights or privileges than the average citizen, and no more liberty to intrude.

I was unsettled by the lack of media coverage. After the first splash in the papers, all reference to the homicide seemed to vanish from sight. None of the television news shows carried any follow-up. I had to assume there were no leads and no new information coming in, but it did seem odd. And depressing, to say the least. When someone you care about is murdered like that, you want other people to feel the impact. You want to see the community fired up and some kind of action being taken. Without fuel, even the talk flared and died, leaving melancholy in its place. The cops swept in and packed up everything in his desk. His active caseload was distributed among the other agents. Some relative of his flew out from the East Coast and closed his apartment, disposing of his belongings. Business went on as usual. Where Parnell Perkins had once been, there was now empty space, and none of us understood quite how to cope with that. Eventually, I would realize how all the pieces fit together, but at that point the puzzle hadn't even been dumped out of the box. Within weeks, the homicide was superseded by the reality of Gordon Titus—Mr. Tight-Ass, as we soon referred to him—the VP from Palm Springs, whose transfer to the home office was scheduled for November 15. As it turned out, even Titus played an unwitting part in the course of events.

two

cf had been buzzing about Gordon Titus since June when the quarterly report showed unusual claim activity. In an insurance office, any time the loss ratio exceeds the profit ratio by ten percent, the board begins to scrutinize the entire operation, trying to decide where the trouble lies. The fact that ours was the California Fidelity home office didn't exempt us from corporate abuse, and the general feeling was that we were headed for a shake-up. Word had it that Gordon Titus had been hired by the Palm Springs branch originally to revise their office procedures and boost their premium volume commitment. While he'd apparently done an admirable job (from the board's point of view), he'd created a lot of misery. In a world presided over by Agatha Christie, Gordon Titus might have ended up on the conference room floor with a paper spindle through his heart. In the real world, such matters seldom have such a satisfactory ending. Gordon Titus was simply being transferred to Santa Teresa, where he was destined to create the same kind of misery.

In theory, this had little or nothing to do with me. My

office space is provided by CF, in exchange for which I do routine investigations for them three or four times a month, checking out arson and wrongful death claims, among other things. On a quarterly basis, I put together documentation on any suspect claim being forwarded to the Insurance Crime Prevention Institute for investigation. I was currently pursuing fourteen such claims. Insurance fraud is big business, amounting to millions of dollars a year in losses that are passed on to honest policy holders, assuming there are still a few of us left out here. It's been my observation, after years in the business, that a certain percent of the population simply can't resist the urge to cheat. This inclination seems to cut across all class and economic lines, uniting racial and ethnic groups who otherwise might have little to say to one another. Insurance is regarded as equivalent to the state lottery. In return for a couple of months' premiums, people expect to hit the jackpot. Some are even willing to tamper with the odds to assure themselves of a payoff. I've seen people falsify losses on burglary claims, indicating goods stolen that were never, in fact, in their possession. I've seen buildings burned down, medical claims inflated, wounds self-inflicted, workmen's compensation claims extended far beyond any actual disability. I've seen declarations of property damage, lost earnings, accidents, and personal injuries that occurred only in the inflamed imaginations of the claimants. Happily, insurance companies have been wising up fast and have now instituted measures for sniffing out deceit. Part of my job entails laying the foundation for prosecution of these fraudulent claims. With Gordon Titus due to arrive any day, there'd been a sudden flurry of cases thrown in my direction and I was under pressure to produce quick results.

Vera passed along the latest of these questionable claims on a Sunday afternoon in late October. I had stopped by the office to pick up some estimated income tax files that had to go to my accountant first thing Monday morning. I parked my VW in the back lot as usual, entering the building by way of the rear stairs. I passed the darkened CF offices, let myself into my office, where I checked my answering machine for messages, did a quick sorting of Saturday's mail, and tucked the tax forms in the outside pouch of my leather shoulder bag. As I passed the CF offices on my way out again, I noticed there were lights on. I paused to peer through the glass doors, wondering if a thief was making off with all the office equipment. Vera crossed my line of vision, papers in hand, apparently on her way to the copy machine. She caught sight of me and waved, veering in my direction. She's thirty-eight, single, and the closest thing to a "best" friend I'm likely to have. The cluster of office keys was still in the lock and they jingled and clanked as she opened the door. "Hey, babe. I was looking for you Friday afternoon, but you'd already left. Must be nice knocking off at two," she said as she let me in.

"Where did you come from? The place was dark when I passed by a minute ago."

She relocked the door and continued toward the copier with me trailing along behind. She was talking over her shoulder, her manner relaxed. "I just popped by to use the Xerox machine. Don't tell anyone. This is personal business. A list of guests for the reception." She raised the lid on the Xerox machine and placed a paper on the glass, punching in instructions. She pressed the "print" button and the machine fired up. She was wearing black tights and knee-high boots with an oversize sweat shirt that hit her just below the crotch. She caught my look. "I know. It looks like I forgot to put on my pants. I'm on my way to Neil's, but I wanted to grab this while I could. What are you up to? You want to join us for a drink?"

"Thanks, but I better not. I have some work to do."

"Well, you missed the big excitement. The legendary Mr. Titus showed up Friday afternoon with three of his own hand-picked lieutenants. Two reps and a claims adjuster got canned to make room for them."

"You're kidding! Who?"

"Tony Marsden, Jack Cantheas, and Letty Bing."

"Letty? She'll sue!"

"I sincerely hope so."

"I thought he wasn't due here for another three weeks."

"Surprise, surprise. I'll probably be fired next."

"Oh, come on. You're doing a great job."

"Yeah, right. That's why claims posted six hundred thousand in losses."

"That was Andy Motycka's fault, not yours."

"Oh, who cares? I'm getting married. I can do something else. I never liked the job that much anyway. How's goes the shopping so far?"

"The shopping?" I said blankly. I was still trying to cope with the disaster at CF.

"For the wedding. A dress."

"Oooh. For the wedding. I've got a dress."

"Bullshit. You only own one dress and it's black. You're the maid of honor, not a pallbearer." Vera and her beloved were getting married in eight days, on Halloween. Everyone had given her infinite grief over her choice of dates, but Vera was adamant, claiming her natural cynicism was at war with sentiment. She'd never thought to marry. She'd been dating (she said) since she was twelve years old and had gone through countless men. Despite the fact that she was absolutely nuts about her fiancé, she was determined to turn tradition on its ear. I thought a black dress would be perfect for Halloween nuptials. Once the reception was over we could go trick-or-treating together and maybe pool the take. I wanted dibs on the Hershey's Kisses and Tootsie Rolls.

"Besides, you've had that damn dress for five years," she went on.

"Six."

"And last time you wore it you said it still smelled like a swamp."

"I washed it!"

"Kinsey, you cannot wear a six-year-old smelly black dress in my wedding. You swore you'd get a new one."

"I *will*."

She gave me a flat look, filled with skepticism. "Where will you go to shop? Not K mart."

"I wouldn't go to *K mart.* I can't believe you said that."

"Well, where?"

I looked at her uneasily, trying to come up with an answer that would satisfy. I knew the hesitation was just an invitation for her to step in and boss me around, but to tell you the truth, I hadn't the faintest idea what kind of dress to buy. I've never been a maid of honor. I don't have a clue what such maidens wear. Something useless, I'm sure, with big flounces everywhere.

She stepped in. "I will help you," she said, as though to a half-wit.

"You will? That's great."

Vera rolled her eyes, but I could tell she was thrilled that I was yielding control. People like to take charge of my personal life. Many seem to feel I don't do things right. "Friday. After work," she said.

"Thanks. We can have dinner afterward. My treat."

"I don't *want* a Quarter Pounder With Cheese," she said.

I waved at her dismissively and headed toward the door. "See you in the morning. You want to let me out?"

"Hang on a minute and I'll go, too. Why don't you go ahead and pick up the case I tried to give you Friday. It's in the file in my out box. The woman's name is Bibianna Diaz. If you can nail her, maybe all of us will end up looking good."

I detoured into the glass cubicle she now occupied as claims manager, spotting the Diaz file, which was right on top. "Got it," I called.

"You can talk to Mary Bellflower once you've had a chance to review it. It was Parnell's to begin with, but she's the one who flagged it."

"I thought the cops took all his files."

"This wasn't in with the files on his desk. He'd given it to Mary the month before, so the cops never saw it." She emerged with her photocopies clamped between her teeth while she fished out her car keys.

"I'll see if there's a way to check the woman out before I talk to Mary. At least I can get the lay of the land that way first," I said.

"Suit yourself. You can work it out any way you want." Vera flipped the lights off and let us out of the office, locking the doors behind her. "If you have any questions, I'll be home by ten."

We left the building together, chatting idly as we trotted down the stairs. Ours were the only two cars in the lot, parked side by side. "One more thing," she said as she unlocked her car door. "Titus has asked to see you first thing tomorrow morning."

I stared at her across the top of her car. "Why me? I don't work for him."

"Who knows? Maybe he sees you as an 'important part of the team.' He talks like that. All this rah-rah horsepuckey. It's obnoxious." She opened the door and slid into the driver's seat, rolling the window down on the passenger side. "Take care."

"You too."

I let myself into my car, my stomach already churning. I didn't want to see Gordon Titus at all, let alone tomorrow morning. What a way to start the week. . . .

The parking lot was empty and the downtown was quiet. We pulled out at the same time, turning in opposite directions. All the stores were closed, but the lights along State Street and the smattering of pedestrians gave the illusion of activity in the otherwise deserted business district. Santa Teresa is a town where you can still window-shop after hours without (too much) fear of attack. During tourist season the streets swarm with people, and even in the off months there's a benign air about the place. I was tempted to grab some supper in one of the little restaurants in the area, but I could hear a peanut-butter-and-pickle sandwich calling me from home.

The neighborhood was fully dark by the time I parked the car and entered my gate. Henry's kitchen light was on, but I resisted the temptation to pop in to see him. He'd want to feed me dinner, ply me with decent chardonnay, and catch me up on all the latest gossip. At the age of eighty-two, he's a retired commercial baker, involved now in catering tea parties for little old ladies on our block. As a sideline, he writes those little crossword puzzle booklets you see in supermarket checkout lines, filled with puns, bons mots, and spoonerisms. When he's not doing that, he's usually chiding me about my personal life, which he thinks is not only dangerous, but much too uncivilized.

I let myself into my apartment and flipped on one of the table lamps. I dropped my handbag on the counter that separates my kitchenette from the designated living room. The place had been completely redone after a bomb blast had flattened it. I'd stayed with Henry until the construction was finished, moving back into the apartment on my birthday the previous May. And what a gift it was, like a pirate ship, all teak and brass fittings, a porthole in the door, a spiral staircase leading up to a loft where I could sleep now beneath a skylight salted with stars. My bed was a platform with drawers built into the base. Downstairs, I had a galley for a kitchen, an alcove for a stacking washer/dryer, a living room with a sofa that doubled for company, and a small guest bath. Upstairs, a second bathroom had a sunken tub with a jungle of houseplants on the windowsill and a glimpse of the ocean through the treetops.

The entire apartment was fitted with little nooks and crannies of storage space, cupboards, and hidey-holes, pegs for my clothes. The design was all Henry's, and he'd taken a devilish satisfaction out of shaping my surroundings. The carpet was royal blue, the furnishings simple. Even after six months, I walked around the place as if blind, touching everything, marveling at the feel of it, the scent of the wood. After my parents died, I'd been raised by a maiden aunt, a woman whose relationship with me entailed more theory than affection. Without ever actually saying so, she conveyed the impression that I was there on approval, like a mattress, subject to return if the lumps didn't smooth out. To give her credit, her notions of child raising, if eccentric, were sound, and what she taught me in the way of worldly truths has served me well. Still, for most of my life, I've felt like an intruder and a transient, merely marking time until I was asked to move on. Now my interior world had undergone a shift. This was home and I belonged here. While the apartment was rented, I was a tenant for life. The sensation was strange and I still didn't quite trust it.

I turned on my little black-and-white TV, letting the sound keep me company while I puttered around, making supper. I sat at the counter, perched on a barstool, munching on my sandwich as I leafed through the file Vera'd given me. There were copies of the initial claim—a single-car accident with personal injuries—a sheaf of medical bills, some correspondence, and an attached summary of the salient points. The adjuster, Mary Bellflower, had flagged the claim for a variety of reasons; the injury itself was "soft tissue" and subjective, impossible to verify. Ms. Diaz was complaining of whiplash, headaches, dizziness, lower back pain, and muscle spasms, among other things. The repairs to the car were estimated at fifteen hundred dollars, with additional medical bills (all third-generation photocopies, which would permit a bit of tampering with the figures) totaling twenty-five hundred dollars. She was also claiming twelve hundred dollars in lost wages, for a total of fifty-two hundred dollars. There was no police report from the accident scene, and the adjuster was astute enough to pick up on the fact that the collision had occurred shortly after Ms. Diaz's vehicle had been registered and insured. Also questionable was the fact that the claimant was using a post office box as an address. Mary had ferreted out an actual street address, which she'd included in her notes. I noticed she'd been careful to retain copies of the envelopes (showing date stamps) in which the claim forms had been returned. If charges were filed, these would provide evidence that the U.S. mails had been used, thus opening the matter to federal investigation under mail fraud statutes. In fraudulent cases, the claimant will often hire an attorney whose job it is to stick the screws to the claims representative, pressuring for a quick settlement. Ms. Diaz hadn't (yet) engaged the services of an attorney, but she was being pushy about reimbursement. I couldn't imagine why Parnell had turned the case over to Mary Bellflower. On a case this size the temptation is to approve payment fairly quickly to avoid any suggestion of "bad faith" on the part of the insurance company. However, because California Fidelity had recently chalked up such big losses, Maclin Voorhies, the company vice president, was taking a dim view of rubber stamping. Thus, the matter had been referred to me for follow-up. With Titus on the scene, it might turn out to be too little too late, but that's where matters stood.

It was ten when I finally turned the lights out and went up to bed. I opened one of the windows and leaned my head against the frame, letting the cold air wash across my face. The moon was up. The night sky was clear and the stars were as piercing as pinpricks. A weak storm front was moving in, and a chance of showers was being predicted sometime in the next couple of days. So far, there was no sign of rain. I could hear the muffled tumble of the surf a block away. I crawled under the covers and flipped on the clock radio, staring up at the skylight. A country song began to play, Willie Nelson in a wistful account of pain and suffering. Where is Robert Dietz tonight? I asked myself. I'd hired myself a private investigator the previous May when my name showed up as one of the four finalists on somebody's hit list. I'd needed a bodyguard and Dietz turned out to be it. Once the situation was defused, he'd stayed on for three months. He'd been gone now for two. We were neither of us letter writers and too cheap to call each other very often since he'd left for Germany. His departure was wrenching, the banal and the bittersweet mingling in about equal parts.

"I'm not good at good-byes," I'd said the night before he left.

"I'm not good at anything else," he'd replied with that crooked smile of his. I didn't think his pain was any match for mine. I might have been wrong, of course. Dietz was not the sort of man given to unrestrained expressions of anguish or distress, which is not to say such feelings didn't exist for him.

The hard part about love is the hole it leaves when it's gone . . . which is the substance of every country-and-western song you ever heard. . . .

The next thing I knew, it was 6:00 A.M. and my alarm was peeping like a little bird. I rolled out of bed and grabbed my running clothes, pulling on sweat pants, sweat shirt, crew socks, and Adidas. I paused to brush my teeth and then headed down the spiral stairs to my front door. The sun hadn't risen yet, but the darkness had eased up to a charcoal haze. The morning air was damp and smelled of eucalyptus. I clung to the front gate and did a couple of stretches—more form than content—using the walk over to Cabana Boulevard as a way of warming up to some extent. Sometimes I wonder why I continue to exercise with such diligence. Paranoia, perhaps . . . the recollection of the times when I've had to run for my life.

When I reached the bike path I broke into an awkward trot. My legs felt like wood and my breathing was choppy. The first mile always hurts; anything after that is a snap by comparison. I shut my mind off and tuned in to my surroundings. To the right of me, the ocean was pounding at the beach, a muted thunder as restful as the sound of rain. Sea gulls were screeching as they wheeled above the surf. The Pacific was the color of liquid steel, the waves a foamy mass of aluminum and chrome. The sand became a mirror where the water receded, reflecting the softness of the morning sky. The horizon turned a salmon pink as the sun crept into view. Long arms of coral light stretched out along the horizon, where clouds were beginning to mass from the promised storm front. The air was cold and richly scented with salt spray and seaweed. Within minutes, my stride began to lengthen and I could feel a mindless rhythm orchestrate all the moving parts. As it turned out, this was the last time I'd have a chance to jog for weeks. Had-I-but-known, I might have enjoyed it a lot more than I did.

three

Somehow I sensed, long before I actually laid eyes on the man, that my relationship with Gordon Titus was not going to be a source of joy and comfort to either one of us. Since he'd proposed the meeting, I figured my choices were obvious. I could avoid the office, thus postponing our first encounter, or I could comply with his request and get it over with. Of the two, the latter seemed the wiser on the face of it. After all, it was possible the meeting was a mere formality. I didn't want my lack of enthusiasm to be misinterpreted. Better, I thought, to appear to be cooperative. As my aunt used to say: "Always keep yourself on the side of the angels." It was only after she died that I began to wonder what that meant.

When I got to the office at nine, I put a call through to Darcy Pascoe, the receptionist in the California Fidelity offices next door to mine. "Hi, Darcy. This is Kinsey. I hear Gordon Titus wants to meet with me. From what Vera says, the guy's a real prick."

"Good morning, Miss Millhone. Nice to hear from you," she said in a pleasant singsong voice.

"Why are you talking like that? Is he standing right there?"

"That's correct."

"Oh. Well, would you ask him what time he wants me over there? I've got a few minutes now if it works for him."

"Just one moment, please."

She put me on hold long enough to convey the question and elicit a response. She clicked back in. "Right now would be fine."

"I'm so thrilled."

I hung up the phone. I can handle this, I thought. All of us are subjected to somebody else's power at some point. So once in a while you kiss ass. So what? Either you make your peace with that early, or you end up living your life as a crank and a misfit. As I headed for the door, I passed the wall-hung mirror and paused to check my reflection. I looked fine to me. Jeans, turtleneck, no dirt on my face, nothing green between my teeth. I don't wear makeup, so I never have to worry about caking or smears. I used to cut my hair myself, but I'd been growing it out of late, so it was now shoulder length, just the teeniest bit uneven. Fortunately, all I had to do was cock my head at a slight angle and it straightened right up.

It was with my head thus tilted that I entered the glass cubicle Gordon Titus was apparently using for his little get-acquainted meetings with the staff. Vera's office was located right next to his and I could see her at her desk, shooting me a profoundly cross-eyed look. She was wearing a subdued gray business suit with a plain white blouse, her hair tucked back in a bun. Mr. Titus stood up to meet me and we shook hands across the desk. "Miss Millhone."

"Hi. How are you? Nice to meet you," I said.

His grip was appropriately macho, firm and hearty, but not crushing, the contact maintained just long enough to show that his purpose was sincere. At first glance, I have to say he was a pleasant surprise. I pictured dry and gray, someone all tucked in and proper. He was younger than I expected, forty-two at most. He was smooth-faced, clean-shaven, his eyes blue, his hair prematurely gray and stylishly cut. Instead of a suit, he wore chinos and a blue Izod shirt. He didn't seem all that taken with me. I could tell from his glance that my professional attire was a bit of a shock. He covered it well, perhaps imagining that I'd come in to assist the charwoman with the floors before work.

"Have a seat," he said. No smile, no small talk, no social niceties.

I sat.

He sat. "We've been taking a look at the reports you submitted over the past six months. Nice work," he said. I could already sense the "but" hanging in the air above our heads. His eye traveled down the page in front of him. He leafed rapidly through the sheaf of notes clipped to the front of a manila file folder. The implication was that he had data on me going back to the first time I threw up in elementary school. There was a yellow legal pad in front of him on which he'd scribbled additional notes in ink. His handwriting was precise, the letters angular, with an emphasis on downward strokes. Occasionally, there were pits where the pen point had torn through the paper. I could picture his thoughts speeding across the page while his cursive stumped along behind, gouging out unsightly holes. He'd never forgotten how to do a formal outline. Topics were laid out with Roman numerals, subclauses neatly indented. His mind probably worked that way, too, with all the categories assigned up front and all the subordinate subjects carefully relegated to the lines below. He closed the folder and set it aside. He turned his attention to me fully.

I thought it was time to jump right in and make quick work of it. "I'm not sure if you're aware of it, but I'm not actually a California Fidelity employee," I said. "I work for the company as an independent contractor."

His smile was thin. "I understand that. However, there are several small issues we'll need to clarify for corporate purposes. I'm sure you can appreciate the fact that in a review of this sort, we need to see the whole picture."

"Of course."

He studied the first and second pages of his legal pad.

I glanced surreptitiously at my watch, under the guise of adjusting the band.

Without looking up, he said, "Have you another appointment?"

"I have a claim to investigate. I should be out in the field."

He looked up at me. His body was motionless. His blue eyes bored into mine without blinking. He was handsome, but blank, so expressionless that I wondered if he'd had a stroke or an accident that had severed all the muscles in his face.

I tried to keep my mien as dead as his. I'm a bottom-line kind of person myself. I like to cut straight to the chase.

He picked up his pen, checking item one, line one on his list. "I'm not clear whom you report to. Perhaps you can fill me in."

Oh, Jesus. "It varies," I said pleasantly. "I'm accountable to Mac Voorhies, but the cases are usually referred by individual claims adjusters." The minute I started speaking, he began to write. I'm an expert (she said modestly) at reading upside down, but he was using a shorthand code of his own. I stopped speaking. He stopped taking notes. I said nothing.

He looked up at me again. "Excuse me. I missed that. Can you describe the procedure on this? The file doesn't seem to indicate."

"Usually, I get a call. Or one of the adjusters might bring a case to my attention. I stop in the office two or three times a week." He managed to write at exactly the rate I spoke. I stopped. His pen came to a halt.

"In addition to meetings?" he asked.

"Meetings?"

"I'm assuming you attend the regularly scheduled office meetings. Budgets. Sales . . ."

"I've never done that."

He checked his notes, flipping back a page or two. A frown formed, but I could have sworn his confusion was pure theatrics. "I can't seem to find your 206's."

"Really," I said. "That surprises me." I hadn't the faintest idea what a 206 was, but I thought it should be his responsibility since he brought it up.

He passed a form across the desk to me. "Just to refresh your memory," he said.

There were lots of slots to be filled in. Dates, times, corporate numbers, odometer readings; clearly a formal report in which I was supposed to detail every burp and hiccup on the job. I passed the form back to him without comment. I wasn't going to play this game. Screw him.

He'd begun to make notes again, head bent. "I'll have to ask you to supply the carbons from your files so we can bring our files up to date. Drop them off with Miss Pascoe by noon, if you would. We'll set up an appointment to go over them later."

"What for?"

"We'll need documentation of your hours so we can calculate your rate of pay," he said as if it were obvious.

"I can tell you that. Thirty bucks an hour plus expenses."

He managed to convey astonishment without even raising a brow. "Less rental monies for the office space, of course," he said.

"In *lieu* of rental monies for the office space."

Dead silence.

Finally, he said, "That can't be the case."

"That's been my arrangement with CF from the first."

"That's absolutely out of the question."

"It's been this way for the past six years and no one's complained of it yet."

He lifted his pen from the page. "Well. We'll have to see if we can straighten this out."

"Straighten what out? That's the agreement. It suits me. It suits them."

"Miss Millhone, do you have a problem?"

"No, not at all. What makes you ask?"

"I'm not sure I understand your attitude," he said.

"My attitude is simple. I don't see why I have to put up

with this bureaucratic bullshit. I don't work for you. I'm an independent contractor. You don't like what I do, hire somebody else."

"I see." He replaced the cap on the pen. He began to gather his papers, his movements crisp, his manner abrupt. "Perhaps we can meet some other time. When you're calmer."

I said, "Great. You too. I have a job to do, anyway."

He left the cubicle before I did and headed straight for Mac's office. All the CF employees within range were hard at work, their expressions studiously attentive to the job at hand.

I put the entire exchange in a mental box and filed it away. There'd be hell to pay, but at the moment I didn't care.

The address I'd been given for Bibianna Diaz turned out to be a vacant lot. I sat in my car and stared blankly at the parcel of raw dirt, crudely landscaped with weeds, palms, boulders, and broken bottles twinkling in the sunlight. A condom dangled limply from a fallen palm frond, looking like a skin shed by some anemic snake. I double-checked the information listed in the file and then scanned the house numbers on either side. No match. I flipped open the glove compartment and pulled out a city map, which I spread across the steering wheel, squinting at the street names indexed alphabetically on the back. There was no other road, drive, avenue, or lane listed with the same name or one that even came close. I'd dropped the Diaz file off at the CF offices before my meeting with Titus, so all I had with me were a few penciled notes. I figured it was time to check back with Mary Bellflower to see what else she might have in the way of a contact. I started the car and headed toward town, feeling strangely gratified. The nonexistent street address added fuel to the notion that Ms. Diaz was telling fibs, a prospect that excited the latent felon in me. In California jargon, I can "resonate" with crooks. Investigating honest people isn't half the fun.

I spotted a pay phone on the far side of a gas station. I pulled in and had my tank topped off while I called Mary at the CF offices and told her what was going on. "You have any other address for this woman?" I asked.

"Oh, Kinsey, poor thing. I heard about your meeting with Gordon Titus. I can't believe you gave him such a hard time. He was screaming at Mac so loud I could hear it back here."

"I couldn't help myself," I said. "I really meant to behave and it just popped out."

"Oh, you poor dear."

"I don't think it's that bad," I said. "Do you?"

"I don't know. I saw him go off with the corporate vice president and he seemed pretty upset. He told Darcy to take his calls. The minute he walked out the door, the tension level dropped by half."

"How can you guys put up with that stuff? He's a jerk. Has he talked to you yet?"

"No, but Kinsey, I can't afford to lose this job. I just qualified for benefits. I'm hoping to get pregnant, and Peter's group plan doesn't cover maternity."

"Well, I wouldn't take any guff," I said. "Of course, I'll be fired, but what the hell. I'll live."

Mary laughed. "If you can pull this one off, it might help."

"Let's hope so. Do you have any other address in the file?"

"I doubt it, but I can look. Hang on a sec." I listened to Mary breathe in my ear while she leafed through the file. Reluctantly, she said, "No, I don't see anything. You know, we never got a copy of the police report. Maybe she gave them the correct address."

"Good thought," I said. "I can stop by the station as long as I'm out. What about the telephone number? Can we check the crisscross?" I had the latest Polk directory in my office, detailing addresses sequentially by street and house number, a second section listing telephone numbers sequentially. Often, if you have one good piece of information, you get a line on a subject by cross-referencing.

She said, "Won't help. It's unlisted."

"Oh, good. A crook with an unlisted number. I love that. How about the license plate on the car? DMV might have something."

"Well, that I can help you with." Mary scouted out the plate number of Bibianna's Mazda and recited it to me. "And Kinsey, if you get the address, let me know right away. I have some forms I want to send her and Mac's having a fit. You can't send registered mail to a post office box."

"Right," I said. "By the way, how come Parnell didn't handle this one himself?"

"Beats me. I assumed he was just too busy with his other cases."

"Maybe so," I said with a shrug. "Anyway, I'll call as soon as I know anything. I'm planning to pop by the office later with an update for the files."

"Good luck."

I scribbled a few hasty notes to myself after we hung up. I fished out another couple of dimes and tried Bibianna's work number, a dry cleaning establishment on Vaquero.

The man who answered the telephone was terse and impatient, probably his chronic state. The excess stomach acid was audible in his voice and I pictured him tossing Tums in his mouth like after-dinner mints. When I asked for Bibianna Diaz, he said she was out. Period.

When there was no other information forthcoming, I gave him a prompt. "Do you expect her back soon?"

"I don't expect nothin'," he shot back. "She said she'd be out all week. Back problems, she says. I'm not gonna argue anybody has a bad back. First thing you know I get slapped with a goddamn workmen's comp claim and I'm out big bucks. Nuts to that. Who's this?"

"This is her cousin, Ruth. I'm passing through town on my way to Los Angeles and I promised I'd stop and see her. Is there any way you could give me her home address? She gave it to me last week when we chatted on the phone, but I walked off without my address book so I don't have it with me."

"Nope. Sorry. No dice. And you wanna know why? Because I don't know you. You could be anyone. Nothing personal, but how do I know you don't go around slashin' young girls with a butcher knife? You see what I mean? I give out an employee's address and I'm liable for anything happens after that. Burglary, harassment, rape. Unh-hunh. No way. That's my policy." He sounded like he was in his sixties, a man besieged with lawsuits.

I started to say something else, but he plunked the phone down in my ear. I made a face at the receiver, a mature and effectual way of handling my irritation, I thought. I paid for the gasoline, got back in the VW, and drove over to the police station, where I paid eleven bucks for a copy of the accident report. The address listed was the same nonexistent street address I'd started with. The clerk working at the desk wasn't one I knew and I couldn't get her to run a check on Bibianna for me.

I left my car parked out front and walked the half block to the courthouse, where I tried the superior court clerk's office, scanning the dockets for some sign of Ms. Diaz. Not there. Too bad. It would have cheered me up enormously to learn she had a felony conviction lurking in her background. By now, without ever having laid eyes on the woman, I was operating on the assumption that she was up to no good. I wanted her address and I couldn't believe there wasn't a paper trail somewhere. I pulled up negative results from municipal court records, nothing from voter registration. I checked with the DA's office, where a pal of mine assured me Bibianna wasn't passing bad paper or late with any child support payments. Well, shoot. I'd just about exhausted the sources I could think of.

I picked up my car and hit the freeway, heading for the county sheriff's department. I parked in the small lot out front and pushed through the glass doors into a small reception area, where I signed my name in the logbook. I walked down the hall a short distance to a cubbyhole marked "Records and Warrants." The civilian clerk on duty didn't seem like a promising source of confidential information. I judged her to be in her early thirties, roughly my age, with a frizzy pyramid of tightly kinked blond hair and way too much gum for the size of her teeth. She caught me surveying her dental misfortunes and pulled her lips together self-consciously. I checked for a name tag, but she wasn't wearing one.

"Can you run a computer check and see if this woman has ever been arrested in Santa Teresa?" I reached for the pad of scratch paper on the counter and jotted down Bibianna's name and her date of birth. I took out my wallet, laid the photostat of my P.I. license next to the note.

Her pale eyes came to rest on mine with the first real sign of recognition. "We're not allowed to divulge that information. The Department of Justice has very strict guidelines."

"Well, good for them," I said. "Why don't I tell you my situation and see if it helps. I'm investigating Bibianna Diaz for possible insurance fraud, and the company I work for, California Fidelity, needs to know if she's got a record."

She processed what I'd said and I watched her formulate a reply with care. She was not quick, this one. She operated with the sort of bureaucratic caution guaranteed to infuriate the honest citizen (also people like me). "If she's been tried and convicted, you can get that information from the court clerk's office. It's a matter of public record."

"I'm aware of that. I've already checked their files. What I'm wondering is whether she's ever been arrested or booked without being formally charged."

"If she was never charged or convicted, then the fact that she was arrested would be immaterial. It's a matter of the individual's right to privacy."

"I appreciate that. I understand," I said. "But suppose she's been picked up for burglary or theft and the DA's decided he can't make a case. . . ."

"Then it's none of your business. If she was never formally charged with a crime—"

"I get the drift," I said. It never pays to deal with the

flyweights of the world. They take far too much pleasure in thwarting you at every turn. I was silent for a moment, trying to compose myself. Situations like this bring up an ancient and fundamental desire to bite. I could envision a half-moon of my teeth marks on the flesh on her forearm, which would swell and turn all colors of the rainbow. She'd have to have tetanus and rabies shots. Maybe her owner would elect to put her to sleep. I smiled politely. "Look. Why don't we simplify life to some extent. All I really need is a current address. Could you check that for me?"

"No."

"Why not?"

"Because we can't give out that information."

"What about the Freedom of Information Act?" I said.

"What about it?"

"Is there anyone else here I could talk to?"

She didn't like my persistence. She didn't like my tone. She didn't like anything else about me, either, and the feeling was mutual. Her and Gordon Titus. God. Some days it doesn't pay to get out of bed. She left the desk without another word and returned moments later with a female deputy who was pleasant but unyielding. I went through the same tiresome routine again and got nowhere.

"Well, thanks anyway. This has really been fun," I said.

I sat in my car out in the parking lot, trying to decide what to do next. This is what happens when I tell the truth, I thought righteously. No wonder I'm forced to lie, cheat, and steal. Honesty will get you nowhere, especially with these law-and-order types. I glanced down at the police report sitting on the passenger seat beside me. I waited for my flush of frustration to subside and then I picked it up.

According to the account she'd given to the officer at the scene, Bibianna had been proceeding south on Valdesto at 30 MPH when she'd been forced to slam on her brakes, swerving to avoid a cat that streaked across her path. Her car had skidded sideways and she'd plowed into a parked car. There were no witnesses, of course. Paramedics called to the scene had administered first aid for superficial contusions and abrasions and then transported her to St. Terry's emergency room for X-ray examination when she complained of neck and back pain. I wondered if the hospital billing department had a good address for her. There was probably a second insurance company, representing the owner of the vehicle she'd hit, and it was always possible that the other claims adjuster had something in his files. Bibianna lived *somewhere* and I was determined to get a line on her. I went back to the office and made the requisite phone calls, which netted me nothing. I gave Mary Bellflower a quick call next door and told her I was still working on it.

At two-fifteen, aggravated, I set the matter aside and spent the rest of the day on routine paperwork. I knew I could ill afford to get obsessed with Bibianna Diaz. Now that I had Gordon Titus breathing down my neck, I was going to have to cover some ground. I plowed on, but even while I was concentrating on other cases, finishing off the paperwork, I could feel the pull. Something was bothering me. It's not like passing a file along to another adjuster is any big deal, but Parnell was dead and that seemed to make all the difference.

four

the next morning, I showered and donned my generic uniform. I had this outfit done up for me years ago by an ex-con who learned to sew working the big machines in some federal penitentiary. The slacks were blue gray and unflattering, with a pale stripe along the seam. The matching pale blue shirt had a circle of Velcro sewn on the sleeve, which usually sported a patch that read "Southern California Services." The shoes, left over from my days on the police force, were black and made my feet look like they'd be hard to lift. Once I added a clipboard and a self-important key ring, I could pass myself off as just about anything. Usually, I pretend I'm reading a water meter or checking for gas leaks, any officious task that necessitates crawling through somebody's bushes and tampering with their security systems. Today, I slapped on an FTD patch and headed for the nearest florist, where I laid out thirty-six dollars for a massive bouquet. I bought a syrupy get-well card, scribbled an illegible name, and put in a quick call to the dry cleaning establishment where Bibianna worked. A woman answered this time.

"Oh, hi," said I. "May I speak to the owner, please?"

"This' the plant. He just left on his way over to the other place," she said. "You want that number?"

"Sure."

She recited the number to me carefully and I recited it back as if I were writing it down. What did she know? She couldn't see what I was doing anyway.

"Thanks," I said. I hung up and hopped in my car, flowers on the seat beside me. I drove over to the plant. There was a nice green length of curb out in front, fifteen minutes of free parking. I locked the car and went in. I stood at the counter briefly, waiting for service. The place smelled of soap products, damp cotton, chemicals, and steam. The area behind the counter was a forest of clothing in clear plastic bags. On my left, an elaborate electronic tram moved hanging garments in a tortuous track that snaked up and around, returning to the point of origin so that any garment on board could be delivered to the station when the proper number was punched in.

To the right, a maze of overhead pipes supported garments in the process of being pressed. There were ten women within my visual range, most of them Hispanic, working machines whose function one could only guess. A radio had been tuned to a Spanish-language station that was blasting out an up-tempo cut from a Linda Ronstadt album. Two of the women sang as they worked, moving men's shirts expertly across the machines in front of them. With the syncopated rhythm of the irons, the shirt machines, the clouds of billowing steam, the place looked like the perfect setting for a musical number.

One of the two singing women finally noticed me. She left her machine and came over to the counter where I was waiting. She was short and compact, with a round face, eyes the color of chocolate M&M's, and coarse dark hair pulled into a snood. The loose gold satin blouse she wore was sprinkled with sequins. She glanced at the bouquet. "Those for me?"

I checked the attached florist's card. "Are you Bibianna Diaz?"

"Nah. She's off this week."

"She won't be in at all?"

The woman shook her head. "She hurt her back in this accident . . . mmm, about two months ago, and it's still botherin' her. The pain flares up, she says, real bad. She can't hardly walk. Boss told her, No way, don't come in. He don't want no kind of lawsuit. She got a boyfriend?"

I turned the card over, holding it up to the light. "Looks like a get-well card, actually. Shoot. Now what am I supposed to do?"

"Take 'em to her house," she said.

"I can't. This is the only address he gave. You don't happen to have her home address, do you?"

"Nah. I never been there myself," the woman said. She turned to one of the other women. "Hey, Lupe. Where's Bibianna live?"

The second woman shook her head, but a third piped up. "On Castano. I don't know the number, but it's this big brown house in front and her place in back. She's got this little bungalow. Real cute. Between Huerto and Arroyo."

The woman at the counter turned back to me. "You know the block she's talkin' about?"

"I'll find it," I said. "Thanks. You've been a big help."

"I'm Graciela. Tell the guy to look me up he gets tired of her. I got all the same equipment, just arranged different."

I smiled. "I'll do that."

the second address on Bibianna turned out to be a dank-looking brown cottage at the back of a dank brown house, located in a midtown neighborhood distinctly down at the heel. I spotted the house in passing, then circled the block and parked across the street. I sat and scanned the premises. The lot was long and narrow, sheltered by the overhanging branches of magnolia, juniper, and pine trees. There was not a shred of grass anywhere and what vegetation there was seemed in desperate need of a trim. A cracked concrete drive cut along the property to the right. In the larger house in front, someone had nailed sagging floral print bedsheets across the windows in lieu of drapes.

There were no cars in the drive. According to the claim form, her 1978 Mazda was still in the body shop, having the right side panel replaced (among other things). I waited twenty minutes, but there was no visible activity. I torqued myself around, reaching into the backseat for the locked briefcase where I keep assorted false ID's for occasions such as this. I pulled a set for "Hannah Moore," neatly tucked into a plastic accordion file: California driver's license with my stats and a photo of me, Social Security, and credit cards for Visa and Chevron gasoline. "Hannah Moore" even had a library card since I wanted her to appear literate. I shoved my shoulder bag under the front seat and tucked the ID in my trouser pocket. I got out, locked my car, crossed the street, and made my way down the driveway.

The tall trees on the property shaded it to an unpleasant chill, and I found myself wishing I'd brought a windbreaker or a sweat shirt. The exterior of Bibianna's vintage cottage was a shaggy brown shingle, the perfect little snack for a swarm of hungry termites. I climbed two wide creaking wooden steps to a tiny porch piled with junk. A casement window on the right side had a length of red cotton hung across the glass. I tried to peek in, but I really couldn't see much. The interior seemed quiet and there were no lights visible. I knocked on the front door, taking advantage of the moment to survey my immediate surroundings. A metal mailbox was nailed to the siding near the front door. Seven addressed and stamped envelopes were loosely tucked in the catch rack, awaiting pickup by the mailman. So far no one had answered my knock. The cottage had an unoccupied air, and I fancied I could already pick up the faintly musty scent generated by some dwellings with even the briefest of absences. I knocked again, waiting an interminable few minutes before concluding there was really no one home. Casually, I looked toward the big house, but there were no signs of life, no accusing faces peering out the windows at me. I reached over and let my fingers tippy-toe through the envelopes. When no alarms went off, I picked up the whole batch and sorted through them at my leisure. Four were bills. She was paying telephone, gas, electricity, and a department store. There were two number ten envelopes, one addressed to Aetna Insurance and one to Allstate, both with "Lola Flores" listed on the return address. Oh, gee, wonder what that could be, I thought. Cheaters never quit. It looked like the scam extended beyond the claim against California Fidelity. The seventh piece of mail was a personal letter addressed to someone in Los Angeles. I plucked it out of the stack, folded it, slipped it down the waistband of my trousers and into my panties. Shame on me. That's a federal crime—the stealing part, not the underpants. I returned the rest of the letters to the catch rack. Suppressing the impulse to run, I sauntered off the porch, ambled up the drive, and crossed the street to my waiting car.

I opened the car door on the passenger side, tossed the clipboard on the front seat, barely missing the bouquet, and locked up again. I could see a minimarket at the corner of Huerto and Arroyo, about ten houses down on the right. I headed in that direction in hope of finding a telephone. The market was a tiny mom-and-pop operation, the front windows papered over with hand-lettered advertisements for beer, cigarettes, and dog food. The interior was dimly lighted and there was sawdust on the uneven wooden floor that looked like it had been there since the place was built. The shelves were a jumble of canned goods in no particular order that I could discern. Free-standing shelves formed two narrow aisles crowded with everything from Pampers to Jell-O to lawn care products. Near the front, there was a refrigerated soft drink case and an ancient crypt-style freezer filled with frozen vegetables, fruit juices, and ice-cream bars. "Mom" was standing at the front counter in a white wraparound apron, a half-smoked cigarette in one hand. She was probably sixty-five with a stiffly sprayed flip of blond hair and a wide scab mustache where she'd had the wrinkles dermabraded off her upper lip. The skin on her face had been hiked up and tacked behind her ears, and her eyes had been stitched into an expression of permanent amazement.

"You have a pay telephone?"

"Back by the stockroom," she said, pointing with her cigarette. A half-inch of ash dropped off and tumbled down the front of her apron.

I dropped four nickels into the coin slot and called Mary Bellflower, giving her Bibianna Diaz's hard-won address.

"Thanks. This is great," she said. "I've got a packet of forms I can ship right out. Are you coming back to the office?"

"Yeah, I'll be there in a bit. I thought I'd hang around for a while and see if Bibianna shows."

"Well, stop in later and we'll figure out where we go from here."

"Has Gordon Titus come back?"

"Nope. Not yet. Maybe it was a rout."

"I doubt that," I said. When I hung up the receiver, a nickel tumbled down into the return coin slot. My lucky day. On my left, there was a meat counter with a slanted glass front. A sign above it advertised the lunch special: chili beans, coleslaw, and a tri-tip sandwich for $2.39. The smell was divine. Tri-tip is apparently a regional phenomenon, some cut of beef nobody else has ever heard of. Periodically, a local journalist will try to trace the origin of the term. The accompanying article will show a moo-cow in profile with all the steaks drawn in. Tri-tip is on the near end, opposite the heinie bumper. It's usually barbecued, sliced, and served with homemade salsa on a bun or wrapped in a tortilla with a sprig of cilantro.

"Pop" emerged from the walk-in freezer. A breath of winter wafted out. He was a big man in his sixties, with a benign face and mild eyes. "What can I get you?"

"How about the tri-tip to go."

He winked at me, smiling slightly, and prepared it without a word.

Sandwich in hand, I grabbed a Diet Pepsi from the cooler and paid at the front register. I returned to my car, where I dined in style, being careful not to spill salsa down the front of my uniform. The flowers, getting limper by the minute, filled the VW's interior with the smells of a funeral home. I kept an eye on Bibianna's driveway for two hours, perfecting my surveillance Zen. In many P.I. firms, surveillance work is charged off at a higher rate than any other service offered because it's such a yawn. There were no signs of activity, no visitors, no lights coming on. It occurred to me if I intended to watch the place for long, I'd better contact the beat officer and let him know what was going on. Also, it might be smart to borrow another vehicle and maybe cook up some reason to be loitering in the vicinity. The postman came by on foot and picked up the letters waiting in Bibianna's box, replacing them with a handful of mail. I would have given a lot to see who was writing to her, but I didn't want to press my luck. Where was the woman? If her back hurt so bad, how come she was out all day? Maybe she was at the chiropractor's getting all her vertebrae lined up or her head replaced. At three I started up the car and headed back toward town.

When I arrived at the California Fidelity offices, I gave the bouquet to Darcy at the front desk. She had the good taste not to mention my little run-in with Titus. Her gaze rested briefly on my uniform. "You join the air force?"

"I just like to dress like this."

"Those shoes look like they'd be lethal in a kick-boxing contest," she remarked. "If you're here for Mary, she's got some clients with her, but you can probably mosey on back."

Mary had been hired as a CF claims representative in May, when Jewel Cavaletto retired. She'd been assigned the desk Vera had occupied before her promotion to the glass-enclosed office up front. Mary was smart but inexperienced, a young twenty-four, with the kind of face just pretty enough to net her second runner-up in a regional beauty contest. I gave her credit for the fact that she had flagged the Diaz claim. She had a good eye and if she could hang in long enough, she'd be a real asset to the company. She'd been married for three months to a salesman for the local Nissan dealership and was taking an avid interest in Vera's wedding plans. One of Mary's own wedding invitations (gauzy pink background depicting daisies blowing in a field) had been framed in brass and propped up on her desk. Where Vera had always tucked the latest issue of *Cosmopolitan* magazine under the stacks of claim folders on her desk, Mary read *Brides,* whose influence apparently extended from the engagement through the first year of marriage. Mary had once appealed to me for my recipe for chicken divan until Vera set her straight. Now she tended to regard me with the pity of the newly married for those of us determined to stay single.

I chatted with Darcy for a few minutes more and then made my way back to Mary's work station, pausing to say "hi" to a couple of other claims adjusters en route. Word of my skirmish with Titus had apparently spread and I'd been accorded celebrity status, which I figured would last until I got fired, one day at best. Mary's clients, a man and a woman, were just leaving as I reached her cubicle. The woman was in her thirties with a shaggy mane of bleached hair, the styling faintly punk. Her eyes were lined with harsh black, her lashes clearly false. Her patterned black hose and the trashy slingback pumps with spike heels seemed at odds with the severe cut of her business suit. She seemed far less aware of me than I was of her, barely glancing in my direction as she passed by in the narrow aisle between cubicles. Her companion followed at a leisurely pace, an attitude of arrogance displayed in the very way he walked. He had his hands in his pockets as if he had all day, but I could have sworn he was keeping a tight rein on himself. His dark hair was combed away from his face. He had thick brows above big, dark eyes, high cheekbones, and a mustache cut so that it seemed to trail down around his mouth. He was well over six feet tall, the heft of his broad shoulders exaggerated by the padding in his plaid sport coat. He looked like the bad guy's ominous sidekick in a prime-time television show. As he came abreast of me, he tried to sidestep but bumped me in the process. He caught my arm apologetically and murmured a "Hey, sorry" as he headed on down the corridor. I caught a whiff of the hair tonic he was using to subdue the wave in his dark pompadour. I found myself staring after them as I moved into Mary's cubicle.

She wasn't at her desk, but she appeared a half second later, eyes pinned on a Dixie cup filled with water to the brim. She wore a red cashmere sweater with the sleeves pushed up. Her complexion was fresh and clear, her skin shiny with good health. Her coloring was the stuff of magazine ads. "Here we are," she said, and then she glanced up at me with some surprise. "Oh. Did they leave? The pair that was here?"

"They went that-a-way. You missed them by a half a second."

She peered out into the corridor, but there was no sign of them. "Well, that's weird. She said she wasn't feeling good, so I went to get her this."

"She looked okay to me."

Mary's mouth pulled down with puzzlement and she set the cup of water on her desk. "I wish they'd hung around. I was hoping you could talk to them."

"About what?"

She shook her head. "They're investigators from the Insurance Crime Prevention Institute. She was, at any rate. He's a special agent with the California Department of Insurance." She handed me the woman's business card.

"*Him?* Are you sure?"

"He was hired last month. She's been showing him the ropes."

"He looked like a hood."

She laughed uncomfortably as if she were somehow responsible for his appearance now that I'd mentioned it. "He did, didn't he? It's that tacky coat, I'm sure. I'd never let Peter out in public in a thing like that. Have a seat. Did you talk to Bibianna Diaz? God, now where'd I stick her file?" She sat down and began to sort through a stack of fat manila folders on her desk.

"Nope. She's still out. I may take my camera with me next time I go over there. Maybe I can snap a picture of her doing backflips on the lawn." I passed on the information about "Lola Flores" and the two other insurance companies. "Bibianna has to be running a second scam as Lola Flores. There's no telling how many other claims she's filed concurrently."

Mary was properly incensed. "Oh, God, I don't believe this. I'll get on it right away and let 'em know what's going on."

"Just make sure they start documenting any dealings they have with her. When we send the files to ICPI, they can send theirs along, too. It should make quite a splash."

I was still half distracted by the couple who'd just left. I checked the woman's business card. The ICPI logo was legitimate, looking somehow like a place mat complete with cutlery. According to the card, she was Karen Hedgepath from an office in Los Angeles. The problem was she didn't look like any ICPI investigator I'd ever met. Most of them are real button-down types—ties, white shirts, dark conservative business suits. This woman looked like a rock star in civilian clothes. I couldn't believe the regional manager would tolerate the punk hairstyle, let alone the spike-heeled shoes.

"Here we go," Mary said, extracting a file from the middle of the stack. The folder was marked "Diaz," a piece of scratch paper with the new address clipped to the front. She reached for an invoice stapled to the envelope it had arrived in. "I just got a whole new sheaf of bills. I guess she saw a chiropractor."

"Probably a subluxation specialist," I said, using the only chiropractic term I'd ever heard.

She punched some holes in the invoice and pronged it in

the file. "Actually, they were here about Bibianna. That's why I wanted them to talk to you. I guess ICPI got wind she'd moved up here. She ran a couple of scams in Santa Monica last year and they were hoping to track her down."

"Well, that's nice. Insurance scams?"

"They didn't spell it out, but it almost has to be insurance-related, don't you think?"

I considered the situation briefly, wondering why an ICPI employee would "show the ropes" to someone working for another agency. It's not as though the ICPI and the Department of Insurance don't cooperate, but the Insurance Crime Prevention Institute isn't a law enforcement agency. And why would investigators make the trip up here in the first place? Why not put a call through to CF instead of driving the hour and a half? It just made no sense. Unless they lied. "Did you give them this address?" I asked, indicating the penciled note.

"I didn't give 'em anything. That's why I was so surprised when you said they'd left. All I did was confirm we were checking on a claim here. Why?"

"They could have spotted this while you were off at the water cooler. All they had to do was rifle the stack of files on your desk."

"Oh, come on. You don't think they'd really do that."

"Who knows? Let's just hope they were legitimate."

She put her hand on her chest like she was about to recite the Pledge of Allegiance. "Oh, Lord. What's that supposed to mean?"

"Well, you know how it is. You can hand out a business card that says anything. I've done it myself."

Mary seemed affronted, suddenly shifting from anxiety into action mode. "Give me that," she said. She snatched the woman's business card and laid it on the desk with a snapping sound. I watched her pick up the phone and punch in the telephone number with its 213 area code. "I'm going to kill myself if she isn't who she said she was." She listened for a moment and then her expression changed. She held up the receiver, which was emitting a sound like a garbage disposal grinding up a live duck.

"Maybe you dialed it wrong," I said helpfully.

"God, I can't believe I'd fall for something so obvious, but it never *occurred* to me to question her identity. How could I be so dumb?"

"Well, you don't have to be so hard on yourself. After years in the business, I can still be conned. It's human nature to trust, especially if you're honest to begin with. Not that I'm that honest, but you know what I mean."

"What do you think they were up to?"

"Beats me," I said. "Obviously, they knew Bibianna and they were aware of her inclination to cheat. The real question is, how'd they get to us? There must be a hundred insurance agencies in Santa Teresa. Why CF?"

"This is terrible. I'm just sick. What could they want with her?" Mary's cheeks had turned a bright, wholesome pink.

"Probably nothing pleasant or they would have played it straight."

"What should we do?"

"I don't see what we can do until we know what's going on. Why don't you track down the current phone number for ICPI and ask if they're investigating her." I held the note up. "In the meantime, I'll try to catch up with her and we'll fake it out from there."

five

i went home and stripped off the uniform. I transferred the fake ID from the pocket of my uniform pants to my blue jeans, which I pulled on with a navy turtleneck. I slipped into gym stocks and tenny bops and headed back to Bibianna's.

I hoped Mary Bellflower's naïveté hadn't put Ms. Diaz at risk. There were still no cars in the drive and no sign of the couple I'd seen at the CF offices. Had they already looked up the address and hightailed it over here? They had maybe thirty minutes on me, so it was always possible that they were in the cottage right now or had been and gone. *If* they'd actually been quick enough to nick off her address. A few cars passed on the street, but no familiar faces peered out. For the second time that day, I left my car, locked, on the street and moved down Bibianna's driveway. It was now four thirty-five, and I could see lights on in the cottage. As I approached, I caught a tantalizing whiff of onions and garlic being sautéed in olive oil. I climbed the wide wooden steps. From inside, this time, I could hear the jaunty theme song of a television sitcom, probably a cable station doing reruns.

I knocked on the front door, which was opened moments later by a Hispanic woman of perhaps twenty-five. She was barefoot, dressed in a red satin teddy with a short red satin robe pulled over it and tied at the waist. She was slim—nay, petite—with flawless olive skin and big dark eyes in a heart-shaped face. She had two tortoiseshell hairpins clamped in her teeth as if I'd caught her in the midst of redoing her hair. Dark hair trailed halfway down her back like a shawl, a few silken strands spilling across her right shoulder. As I watched, she gathered the length of it and made a compli-cated knot, which she secured with the two hairpins. "Yes?"

My true inclination was to stand on tiptoe so I could peer over her shoulder at the space beyond. The interior of the cottage was essentially one big room, divided into living areas by the use of brightly dyed cloth panels that swayed with the eddy of moving air from the open door. A vibrant green panel separated the living room from the kitchen, an electric blue shielded most of a brass bed frame from view. The windows were draped in the bolt ends of purple cotton twisted across brass hooks. I'd seen the same idea in a wom-en's magazine in the dentist's office but had never seen it used to such effect. The furniture was a mismatched collec-tion of wicker and castoffs, swathes of navy-and-purple cot-ton distinguishing the worn arms, lending continuity to the look of the place. The effect was striking and seemed to suggest boldness and confidence.

I realized, belatedly, that I hadn't come up with a cover story. Happily, I'm an old hand at lying, and I could feel one bubble up. "Sorry to disturb you," I said. "I'm, uhm, looking for an apartment in the area and someone said you might be giving notice."

Her look was cautious and her tone was blunt. "Who said?"

"Gee, I don't remember. A neighbor, I guess. I've been knocking on doors for days, it feels like."

"Why you want to live around here? It's depressing."

"It's close to where I work," I said, praying she wouldn't ask where that was. I'd probably pretend to be a waitress, but I couldn't, for the life of me, remember any restaurants close by.

She stared at me. "Actually, I'm hoping to move in a couple of weeks," she said. "I got some money coming in that I should hear about pretty soon."

"That's great. Do you mind if I keep in touch?"

She pulled her mouth down in a shrug. "Sure. I'd let you see the place, but it's kind of a mess. It's only one room, but it's fine if you're by yourself. You got furniture?"

"Well, some."

"The landlord's pretty good about stuff like that. Most of this I'll leave when I move out. You'd need a bed."

"I got that," I said. "You have a pen I could use? I'll make a note of your name and number and maybe give you a call in a couple of weeks."

"Just a minute," she said. She closed the door, returning moments later with a scrap of paper and a pen. I looked at her expectantly.

She tilted her head so she could watch me write. "Diaz. Bibianna with two *n*'s."

"Thanks."

I left Bibianna and went home, where I finally had a moment to examine the letter I'd stolen from Bibianna's mailbox. I made a note of the name and address of the recipient, a Gina Diaz in Culver City, California. Bibianna's mother or a sister, by my guess. From my desk drawer, I pulled out an aerosol can of some chemical concoction that turns opaque paper translucent for thirty to sixty seconds. Spray it on an envelope and you can read what's inside without going to the trouble of steaming it open. Clearly marked on the can, of course, is a stiffly worded warning, reminding the user that tampering with written communications while in United States Postal Service channels is punishable by up to five years in prison and/or a $2,000 fine. God, I should really open up a little savings account in case I get caught doing stuff like this.

I depressed the nozzle and dampened the surface of the

envelope with a fine mist, then held it up to the light. The note said: "Hi, Ma. I'm fine so far. $$ should come threw any time. Please don't let Raymond know you've heard from me. Love, B."

I watched the envelope become opaque again without any visible mark, discoloration, or odor. I took it out to the street and tucked it in my mailbox for tomorrow's pickup. I returned to my apartment and put a quick call through to Mary Bellflower. I caught her just as she was getting ready to close up her desk for the day. "Have you heard anything from ICPI?"

"Not really. I'm still waiting for a call back."

"Keep me posted," I said.

"Right."

I put on a pot of coffee and went up the spiral stairs to the loft. I changed clothes again, this time pulling on a black tank top, tight ankle-high black pants, short white socks with an edging of lace, and scuffed low-heeled black pumps. I ratted my hair, securing one hunk of it in a rubber band so that it stuck straight up like a little hair spout. I applied (inexpertly, I'll admit) eyeliner, mascara, blushers, and gaudy red lipstick, then clipped on big dangle earrings replete with red stones that no one in their right mind would mistake for rubies. Then I sprayed my entire upper body with cheap scent. I stared at myself in the bathroom mirror. I half turned away from the mirror and looked back, pulled one shoulder up, and pursed my lips. What a vamp . . . what a tramp! I didn't know I had it in me.

I clomped down my spiral stairs to the kitchenette and made myself an olive–pimento cheese sandwich, which I packed in a metal lunch box with an apple, some graham crackers, a Thermos of hot coffee, and a Dick Francis paperback. I grabbed my black leather jacket, tucked the fake "Hannah Moore" ID in my pants pocket, and snagged my car keys. I drove back over to Bibianna's neighborhood and parked a few doors away. I got out of the car and hiked down to the minimarket to use the pay phone. The meat counter was locked up and the guy was stocking shelves. I didn't see "Mom."

I dropped in two dimes and dialed Bibianna's number. When she answered after two rings, I held my nose and asked for Mame. I sounded like a cold sufferer on a TV commercial for an antihistamine.

"Who?"

"Mame?"

"You got a wrong number."

"Sorry," I said. I returned to my car and settled in.

From my position, I could see the mouth of the driveway, much of the big brown house, and a portion of the yard, but nothing of Bibianna's cottage, which was located in the rear. My assumption was that if she left the premises, she'd surface somewhere in front and I could follow by car or on foot, whichever seemed more appropriate. I had no idea if she intended to go out or where she might go if she did, but she struck me as the restless type, and I was hoping she'd find some reason to stir, even if her purpose was no more important than a run to the corner market for a six-pack. I turned on the car radio just in time for the five-thirty news. The talk of rain was beginning to sound like something more than mere rumor. I stuck my head out the car window and stared upward. A ceiling of darkening clouds was creating the illusion of sudden twilight. The wind was picking up, blowing a dried palm frond along the street. Secretly I wished I could go back to my place and lock myself in for the night instead of spying on Bibianna Diaz. I switched from station to station, listening to a rotating selection of popular songs that all seemed to sound the same. I kept one eye on the driveway and one on my book, but the dark came so quickly I wasn't able to read much. The streetlights popped on and I could see that the tree leaves had taken on a patent-leather sheen, a deep, glossy green that seemed to shimmer in the darkness. At suppertime, the neighborhood began to stir with life, people coming home from work, houselights coming on.

A single-car surveillance is usually considered the least productive technique in any private investigator's little bag of tricks. In order to be discreet, you have to keep so much distance between yourself and the subject that visual contact is tough to maintain without being "made." Then, too, if Bibianna was picked up by car, I had a fifty-fifty chance of being headed in the right direction. If I'd guessed wrong, I was sunk. A sudden U-turn in a residential neighborhood is a conspicuous move and one almost guaranteed to alert the driver of the car you're following. With a two-car surveillance you can at least trade off positions and the subject is less likely to become suspicious. Unfortunately, I hadn't been authorized to hire outside help on this. For all I knew, Gordon Titus had fired me in absentia. It certainly seemed like the wrong time to ask for a cash advance. I was operating on the cheap, trying to establish a relationship with the woman so I could find out what she was up to. A well-documented claim file is fundamental to successful prosecution under "theft by deception" statutes. Before handing over the files to the Insurance Crime Prevention Institute, CF would want to provide proof of a material false representation, proof of intent to defraud, evidence that the claims adjuster relied upon representations by the claimant in paying the claim, and evidence of payment. If Bibianna was scamming Aetna and Allstate along with California Fidelity, it would probably mean hiring a handwriting expert to establish the links, though there might well be matching fingerprints on all the claim forms she'd sent. With fraud, as with most crimes, the perpetrator's job was a lot easier than ours.

At seven twenty-five, to relieve the boredom, I ate my sandwich and two graham crackers. It was now fully dark, and a pale mist filled the air, a rain so fine that it scarcely dampened the pavement. I turned the engine on twice, letting it run for brief periods until the car warmed up. A pizza was delivered to a nearby apartment complex. The passing scent of pepperoni and melted mozzarella nearly brought tears to my eyes. An old lady walked by in a robe and a shawl with her cocker spaniel on a leash. Cars passed, moving in both directions, but none slowed down and there was no sign of Bibianna. By nine, I found myself slouched down on my spine, knees propped up against the steering wheel, trying to keep from nodding off. The couple from the CF offices had never made an appearance and I was about to write them off. Either they had no idea where Bibianna Diaz now lived or they had no compelling interest in her in the first place. I couldn't imagine why they'd gone to the trouble of tracking her down if they didn't mean to pursue the point. Maybe something had scared them off. Idly, I wondered if they were in a parked car nearby, waiting for her themselves.

At nine forty-five, quite suddenly, Bibianna appeared in the driveway. She was wearing red again, a body-hugging chemise that hit her midthigh. Dark hose and red spike heels. For someone so petite, her legs looked incredibly long and shapely, giving an impression of height when she was probably barely five feet one. She had one hand tucked in the pocket of a cracked brown leather bomber jacket that she'd left unzipped. With the other hand, she held a section of newspaper above her head, shielding her hair from the drizzle. She had her face turned in my direction, scanning the street, but she didn't seem to register the fact that she was being observed. Five minutes later, a Yellow Cab passed and came to a stop in front of her. She got in. I started my VW while she slammed the taxi door and settled herself in the backseat. I eased out into the street, flipping my headlights on as the taxi pulled away, hoping my appearance behind it would seem part of the natural flow of traffic in the area.

We traveled sedately on surface streets, heading toward Cabana Boulevard, the wide avenue that parallels the beach. This was my turf and I had to imagine she was heading toward the big restaurant/bar out on the wharf, or perhaps to one of the bawdy bars at the lower end of State Street. It turned out to be the latter. The cab slowed in front of a lowlife bar called the Meat Locker. The ABC had shut the place down twice in the past for serving alcohol to minors, and the previous owner had consequently lost his liquor license. The bar had been sold and was open now under new management. I drove on past. Through my rearview mirror, I watched as Bibianna emerged from the cab, paid the driver, and headed toward the entrance. I hung a left, drove around the block, and returned to the parking lot, where I squeezed the VW into a quasi-legal parking spot against the wall. As I locked the car, ducking my head against the sprinkle of rain, I could feel the pavement vibrate with the music from the bar. I took my last breath of fresh air and walked into the place.

Just inside the door, I paid the five-dollar cover charge and had the back of my hand stamped in purple with a USDA designation of "choice." The Meat Locker looked like it had been designed originally for industrial purposes and converted to commercial use without much concession to aesthetics. The room was cavernous and drab, with a concrete floor and metal beams showing high up in the shadowy reaches of the ceiling. A nineteen-foot bar ran along the wall to the right, packed three deep with guys whose faces looked like they belonged on the post office wall. The place smelled of beer and cigarette smoke, corn tortillas fried in lard, with an occasional whiff of dope wafting through the side door from the alleyway. All the houselights were blue. There was a live band, five guys who looked like junior high school thugs and sounded like they should still be practicing in someone's garage. The music was a raunchy blend of thumping bass, pulsing synthesizers, relentlessly repeated chords, and lyrics that were vile if you managed to discern the words above the piercing electronic howls. The dance floor was a portable wooden pallet, maybe twenty feet on a side, jammed with bouncing bodies, faces lathered in sweat.

This was where the C- singles came to hunt. There were no yuppies, no preppies, no slumming execs, no middle-class, white-bread college types. This was a hard-core pickup place for bikers and hamburger hookers, who'd screw anyone for a meal. Bar fights and knifings were taken as a matter of course, uniformed beat cops strolling through so often they were assumed to be customers. The noise level was intolerable, punctuated by an intermittent *bam!* and bursts of raucous laughter. The bar was famous for a drink called a "slammer": tequila and 7-Up in an old-fashioned glass. When the drink was served, a cloth napkin was placed across the mouth of the glass, which was then slammed down on a wooden board the waitress carried. The blow forced the tequila and 7-Up together in a high-test infusion, which the patron was expected to toss down in one gulp. Usually the limit was two slammers per customer. After two, most women had to be helped, toes dragging, to the car. After three, men had the urge to break wooden chairs or bash a hand through glass.

As I inched my way across the bar, I murmured, "Pardon me," "Excuse me," and "Oops, sorry," as I progressed, sensing an occasional anonymous hand on my ass. I found an unoccupied spot and claimed temporary ownership, leaning against the wall like everybody else. I ordered a beer from a passing barmaid who was decked out in an orange Day-Glo leotard that was cut straight up her crack in the rear. Her buns were hanging out like water-filled balloons. There was no place to sit, so I stood where I was, wedged in against a beam, while I surveyed the crowd.

I spotted Bibianna on the dance floor, undulating with remarkable energy and grace to some grinding sex tune. Men's eyes seemed to follow every shimmy, every bump. The blue lights reacted with the olive tones of her skin to create an unearthly radiance that emphasized the smooth oval of her face above the bulging breasts in the low-cut chemise. The dress seemed to glow more purple than red, pulled taut across the flat belly, slim hips, and trim thighs. When the music ended, she gave her dark hair a toss and moved away from the dance floor without a backward glance. Her partner, visibly winded, looked after her with admiration.

She began to make the rounds. She was apparently well known, pausing to exchange laughing comments with a number of guys. I made myself conspicuous, pretending to be oblivious when, by my calculations, her path would soon be intersecting mine. Foiled. Before she reached me, she changed directions, and I could see her inching toward the short corridor where the restrooms were located. I headed in that direction, risking rude remarks as I pushed my way through.

By the time I reached the ladies' room, she had entered one of the stalls. I stood at the mirror, fussing with my top-knot until the toilet flushed and Bibianna emerged. She moved to the sink beside mine, glancing at me idly in the mirror. I sensed more than saw the little jolt of recognition. She said, "Hey."

I gave her a blank look.

"Didn't you stop by this afternoon to ask about my place?"

I looked over at her politely and then allowed myself the same double take. "Oh, hi! I didn't realize it was you. What a coincidence. That's amazing. How are you?"

"I'm fine. How'd the house hunting go? Did you find anything?"

I made a face. "Not really. I got a line on an apartment about a block away from yours, but it isn't half as nice."

Bibianna took out her lipstick. She applied an arc of red to her lower lip, rubbing it against the upper lip until the color had spread uniformly across her mouth. I made a few little gestures of my own, imitating hers.

She capped the lipstick. "You ever been here before?"

I shrugged. "Couple of times. Before this new management. It's kind of unnerving, isn't it? I don't appreciate guys grabbing my butt every time I make a move."

She studied me briefly. "Depends on what you're used to, I guess. Doesn't bother me." She turned her attention from my reflection to hers, leaning forward to adjust the wisps of hair around her face. She checked her eye makeup for flaws, staring at herself gravely before she glanced back at me. "I hope you don't mind my saying this, but that hair and the getup are completely wrong."

"They are?" I looked down at myself, a feeling of despair washing over me. What is it about me that invites this kind of comment? Here I think of myself as a kick-ass private eye when other people apparently see me as a waif in need of mothering.

"Mind if I make a suggestion?" she asked.

"Fine with me," I said.

The next thing I knew, she'd whipped the rubber band out of my hair. She reached in her purse and took out some kind of bottled hair snot which she rubbed between her palms and then massaged through my hair. I felt like a dog being groomed, but I liked the effect. My tresses looked faintly wet now with just the suggestion of curl. The two of us checked my reflection in the mirror.

Bibianna's mouth pulled down judiciously. "Better," she said. "You got a scarf on you anywhere?"

I shook my head.

"Let me see what I got." She began to root around in her handbag, pulling out a joint in the process. "You want a smoke?" she asked idly.

I shook my head. "I already toked up out in the parking lot before I came in."

She tucked the dope away without further comment, intent on her search through the various compartments of her voluminous bag. "Here we go. How's this?" She pulled up a square of lime-green silk and then made a face. "Eh, no good. Color's not right for you. Dump the earrings. That'll help."

How do women know these things? More important, how come I don't? I removed the gaudy baubles from my ears and massaged my lobes with relief.

Meanwhile, she'd managed to unearth a second scarf, this one hot pink. She held it near my face, squinting at it critically. I thought she was going to make me dampen it with spit so she could wash my face, but she did some kind of tricky fold and tied the thing around my neck. Immediately, my color seemed to improve.

"That looks great. Now what?"

"You come on with me. I'll keep the worst of these shit-heads away from you."

six

i followed her into the crowd like a rookie soldier into battle. Male eyes surveyed us from head to toe, grading us according to the size of our tits, how much butt we had hanging out, and how available we seemed. Bibianna netted a lot of mouth noises, a hand gesture, and some disgusting propositions which she seemed to find amusing, tossing casual insults at the guys most vocal in their appreciation. She was easygoing, good-natured, with a quick, infectious laugh.

The music started up again and she began to dance as she walked, snapping her fingers, working her way through the crowd with an occasional crotch-activating bump and grind. She was scanning faces and I wondered who she was looking for. It didn't take long to find out. Her animation kicked up a notch, like the sudden surge in electric current preceding a blackout. Her body seemed to suffuse with a palpable heat.

"Stick around," she said. "I'll be back."

A blond guy separated himself from the pack of studs at the bar. He was curly haired, with wire-rimmed glasses, a mustache, strong chin, a slight smile turning up the corners of his mouth. I found myself making note of his physical

characteristics like a beat cop on patrol at the sight of a suspect. I knew the guy. He was of medium height, broad shoulders, narrow hips, dressed in jeans and a tight-fitting black
Polo shirt with short sleeves pushed up by well-developed
biceps. Tate. Crazy Jimmy. How many years had it been since
I'd seen him? He looked at Bibianna possessively, his thumbs
tucked into his belt loops so that his hands seemed to bracket
the bulge in the front of his pants. His manner was tempered
with self-mocking, an irresistible blend of humor and awareness. I watched as he moved in her direction, already engaging her in some kind of wordless foreplay. No one else
seemed to be aware of them. They approached the dance
floor from adjacent sides, meeting somewhere in the middle
as if every move were choreographed. This was mating behavior.

A table opened up and I snagged one of the empty chairs,
putting my jacket across the back of the chair beside me to
ward off any poachers. By the time I looked back at the
dance floor, I'd lost sight of Bibianna, but I caught a flash of
her red dress in the pulsating mass of dancers and occasional glimpses of her partner's face. I had known him in
another context altogether, and I couldn't quite reconcile the
incongruity of my past perception of him with the setting in
which I now saw him. His hair had been shorter then and the
mustache was new, but the aura was the same. Jimmy Tate
was a cop—probably an ex-cop by now if the rumors were
correct. Our paths had crossed the first time in elementary
school—fifth grade, where for half a year we were soulmates,
bound by a pact we'd sealed by touching tongues. Solemn
stuff. Jimmy was into what they call "acting out." I'm not sure
what had happened to his parents, but he'd lived in foster
homes all his life, getting kicked out of first one, then another. He was a kid who'd been labeled "incorrigible" by the
age of eight, rebellious, prone to fistfights and bloody noses.
He was frequently truant, and since I was given to truancy
myself back then, we formed an odd bond. In many ways I
was a timid child, but I had a wild streak of my own born of

grief at the loss of my parents when I was five. My mutiny originated in fear, Jimmy's in rage, but the net result was the same. I could see that under his defiance, there was such pain and such sweetness. I may even have loved him in my own innocent, prepubescent way. He was twelve years old to my eleven when I met him, a bewildered boy who had no concept of self-control. More than once he came to my defense, beating the snot out of some bullying fifth-grade boy who'd tried pushing me around. I could still recall the exhilaration I felt every time we raced away from the schoolyard, giddy with freedom, knowing how short-lived our liberation would be. He introduced me to cigarettes, tried getting me high on aspirin and Coke, showed me the difference between boys and girls. I can still remember the mix of mirth and pity I felt when I realized all boys were afflicted with a doo-dad that looked like an ill-placed thumb stuck between their legs. Eventually, Jimmy's foster mother declared him out of control and sent him back to wherever it was unwanted kids were sent in those days. Juvenile hall, I guess.

I didn't see him for eight years, and then I was astonished when he showed up my first day at the police academy. By then, his toughness had a manic edge. He was a pretty boy and a boozer, out until all hours. How he got accepted into the academy, I'll never know. Candidates are put through rigorous psychological evaluation, at which point the unsuitable and the unstable are quickly eliminated. He must have eluded the wily probing of his examiners, or maybe he was one of those rare individuals whose personality flaws don't show up under scrutiny. His academy grades were usually borderline, but he never missed a class and his competitive nature kept him in the game. He was savvy enough to turn the heat down when he had to, but he never kept himself in check for long. He did manage to graduate with the rest of us, but he was always skirting disaster in some form. I'd kept my distance, too invested in my own career at that point to risk the taint of his reputation.

He'd applied for a job with the Santa Teresa Police Department at the same time I did, but he'd been turned down. I lost track of him for a while and then I heard he'd joined the Los Angeles County Sheriff's Department. Word of his exploits started leaking back to us. In bars after hours, the talk would start, cops trading tales about the crazy things Jimmy Tate had done. He was the kind of officer you wanted next to you any time there was trouble. In a pinch, he was absolutely fearless, oblivious of danger. In a pissing contest with the "bad guys," he was right out in front. His aggression seemed to generate a force field around him, a protective shield. Other cops had told me that watching him under fire, you became aware that in his own way, he was as dangerous as "they" were—the bank robbers, the dopers, gang members, snipers, all the lunatics who had it in for us law-and-order types. Unfortunately, his ferocity pushed him across the line more than once. I gathered he did things you didn't talk about later—things you pretended you hadn't seen because he'd saved your life and you owed him. Eventually, he was tapped as part of a special investigating unit put together to monitor the activities of known criminals. Six months later, the section was disbanded after a series of questionable shootings. Twelve officers were suspended, Jimmy Tate among them. All were reinstated after review by the police commission, but it seemed clear it was only a matter of time before something blew in a big way.

Two years ago, I'd come across his name in the *L.A. Times*. He'd been reassigned to a narcotics unit and had just been indicted, along with six other deputies, in a money-skimming scandal that was rocking the department. The details were spelled out day after day during preliminary hearings. Five of the six were bound over for trial and one of those blew his brains out. I followed the court proceedings in occasional copies of the *L.A. Times*, though I never heard the outcome. It wouldn't have surprised me to learn he was guilty as charged. He was reckless and self-destructive, but as odd as it sounds, I knew if I'd had a brother, I'd have wanted him to be exactly like Jimmy Tate, not for his conduct and the dubious underlying morality, but because of his loyalty and his passionate commitment to survival. We live in a society piously concerned about the rights of criminals when their victims' lives have been trashed without any consideration of the price in pain and suffering. With Jimmy Tate in charge, believe me, justice was served. There simply wasn't much attention paid to the technicalities involved.

He and Bibianna came off the dance floor. The band was taking a break and the noise level dropped so fast it was almost like turning deaf. I focused on Jimmy's face, knowing any minute he'd spot me and the recognition would leap in his eyes. The two of them sat down at the table, and Bibianna pulled her hair up with one hand and fanned her bare neck with the other. She was winded, laughing, the color high in her cheeks, her hair damp at the temples where the dark strands had separated into little tendrils. "This's the woman I was telling you about, came to look at my place," she said to him, indicating me. "What'd you say your name was?"

Jimmy's smile was polite as his gaze traveled from her face to mine. I held a hand out.

"Hello, Jimmy. I'm Hannah Moore," I said. "You remember me?"

Clearly he did, and I knew from his look my real name was attached to the recollection. Whatever his current status, he was still too thoroughly trained as a cop to blow my cover. He smiled as he took my hand, dosing me with the same low-voltage sexuality he'd turned on Bibianna. He lifted my hand to his mouth, kissing my knuckle affectionately. "God, babe. How are you? It's been years," he said.

"You two know each other?" she asked.

He returned my hand to me reluctantly. "We were in grade school together," he said without pause, and I felt myself flush with pleasure since that was the connection I cared about. The academy and whatever happened after that was the stuff of our grown-up years. The other had a magical quality that would always take precedence in my book.

He pulled a crumpled bill out of his pants pocket with a

glance at Bibianna before his eyes returned to my face. "I need some cigarettes, doll. Can you do me that?"

She hesitated just long enough to let him know her cooperation was a gift. Her smile was underlined with irony and the look she gave me was knowing. She tucked the bill between her breasts and walked away without a word. Jimmy's gaze traced a loving line up her legs to her hips. She was moving with the self-conscious thrust and sway of a model or a starlet, aware of her effect. She sent a slow smile back to him, puckering her mouth in a gesture that was half pout, half promise.

I felt a laugh bubble up. "I can't believe running into you this way," I said. "How do you know Bibianna?"

He smiled. "I met her in L.A. at a Halloween party a year ago. I saw her a couple times down there, then ran into her again up here."

"I had no idea you were back. What have you been up to?"

"Not much," he said. His eyes flicked across my face as he checked me out. "How about yourself? Last I heard you'd left the department and were working for some agency."

"I was. I got licensed. Now I work for myself. Are you still with the L.A. County Sheriff's?"

"Not exactly."

"What 'exactly' are you doing? Last I heard you were being tried for theft," I said.

"She's something, isn't she?" he said, avoiding my question.

"What's the story, Jimmy?"

He propped his chin on his fist, smiling at me with his eyes. "I'm retired. I sued the shit out of them—ten million bucks."

"You *sued* them?" I said. "What about the charges?"

My reaction seemed to amuse him and I watched him shrug. "I was acquitted. That's the way the system works. Sometimes you get the bear, sometimes the bear gets you. I'd been on medical leave, collecting disability for job-related pain and stress. Next thing I know, there's a bunch of us charged with conspiracy, money laundering, income tax evasion, God knows what else. They put us through hell and by the time I got from under that, all my benefits were cut and I was being asked to resign. Forget that. No way. I found a lawyer and filed suit."

"After you were cleared?"

"Shit, yes. I'm not going to let them get away with that. The way they see it, I got off on a technicality. I was the only one acquitted, but I still did the whole nine yards the same as the others, so why am I being penalized twice? A jury said I was innocent."

"Were you?"

"Of course not, but that's not the point," he said. "The prosecution had a shot at me and couldn't make it stick, so now I'm off the hook. Doesn't matter if I did it or not. Court says I'm clear, I'm clear. That's the law."

"So they fired you?"

"In effect. What they did was they axed my disability. They decided I was trouble and they wanted me outta there, which is why they cut my benefits. Said I had an attitude. No way I was going to put up with that, so I sued their asses off. We just settled last week. Seven hundred and fifty thou. Of course, when the check comes through, my attorney's going to take his cut off the top, but I'm still going to end up with three sixty-five. My retirement fund. Pretty good, yes?"

"That's great."

"Meantime, I'm flat broke, but what are you going to do?"

"What about Bibianna? Does she know you're a cop?"

"Does she know you're a P.I.?"

I shook my head to one side, his smile fading as he saw my expression shift. "You're not investigating *her*?"

I didn't answer, which was answer enough.

"What for?" he asked.

I figured I might as well level with him. He'd find a way to get it out of me eventually. "Insurance fraud," I said, watching for his reaction. If I'd hoped to surprise him, I was out of luck.

"Who are you working for?"

"California Fidelity."

"Can you make a case?"

"Probably. By the time I'm done, at any rate," I said.

He looked away from me then, eyes straying toward the jukebox. I followed the line of his gaze, catching sight of Bibianna. A rainbow of lights played across her face. There was something about her—a dusky beauty, a physical perfection, that must have been irresistible, judging by the way he watched her. I saw her throw her head back and laugh, though the sound didn't carry. She was flirting with the drummer, one hand resting lightly on his arm in a gesture both intimate and casual. The drummer was tall and skinny with a face like a collie, his eyes close together and glittering with chemical substances the human body doesn't manufacture naturally. He was staring at her breasts, probably emitting the high-pitched, hopeful whine of a pup hoping for a Milk-Bone. She wasn't looking at us, but every phrase in her body language conveyed her awareness of Jimmy. Tit for tat, as it were. She turned to the jukebox and dropped in some coins, making her selection carelessly. After a moment, the pounding began, some popular song that was all bass and percussion. Bibianna moved out onto the dance floor with the drummer in tow. He was practically wetting himself, he was so excited by her attention.

"I always hated undercover," Jimmy said, raising his voice to be heard. He was still watching Bibianna, who'd begun to move with the beat, pelvis rolling like she was doing aerobic exercises to develop her glutes.

I took a sip of my beer, making no response. I'd never actually done undercover work myself, but I'd heard plenty, none of it good.

His eyes came back to mine. "Tell her what you're up to," he said.

"And blow this? You're crazy. I'm not going to do that. And you better not tell her, either. This is my turf."

"I understand that."

"Then what's the hesitation, Jimmy? I know that look."

"I'm crazy about this lady and I don't want to see her hurt.

I've been telling her for months she's going to get caught. If she knows you're on to her, she'll clean up her act."

"That's not my concern. She filed a fraudulent claim with CF, and God knows how many phony claims she's filed with other carriers. I'm going to turn her ass in."

"She's getting out of the business."

"I'll bet."

"No, she really is. She filed that claim months ago, but I talked her out of it. She's going straight, I swear."

"Dream on, Tate. Why not drop the claim, then, if she wants out?"

"She did."

"Bullshit! She's got a request for payment pending right this minute. I saw the damn thing myself. She's sticking it to us, putting the pressure on for a quick settlement. That's why the case was passed to me in the first place."

"I don't believe it."

"Ask her."

His smile was pained. "I can't very well do that without telling her what's going on."

"Then you better find a way around it before I wrap this thing up."

"There's more here than meets the eye."

"There's always more than meets the eye. It's usually crooked," I replied.

Jimmy's troubled gaze strayed back to Bibianna. He watched her with absorption, rubbing his thumb across his lower lip. He didn't want to believe me. His infatuation with the girl (and that's what she was, a girl) had apparently clouded his perception. After years of dealing with scammers, he'd suddenly decided that this one could change her wicked ways like magic if it suited her. He'd forgotten just how addictive crime can be. Repeat offenders are motivated more by withdrawal symptoms than necessity.

I'd never seen him caught up like this. In the past, his relationships with women had been easy to track, light-hearted forays with no emotional strings attached. A few laughs, some quick sex, a couple of weeks of companionship. I'm not sure how it appeared from their perspective. The women he dated were often smart but self-deluding, announcing up front that all they were looking for was fun and games when in fact they bonded with him at the drop of a hat and quickly shifted into emotional bait and switch. The turnabout became apparent in the way they looked at him, in their determination to be understanding, nonpossessive, compliant, and considerate. I'd watched eight or ten of these women pass through his life in a period of ten months. All were slim, attractive, bright, and competent—professional women with careers in advertising, sales, graphic arts, TV production. Each would become fixated, hooked by his availability, his casual charm, the sexuality that hovered in the air around him. They'd begin to service him, cooking meals, ironing shirts, subtly demonstrating how much better his life could be if they were somewhere on the premises. They'd begin to quiz him about his past relationships, trying to figure out what the last woman did wrong, trying to delete from their own behavior the qualities that had generated their predecessor's demise. This phase was brief because Jimmy's behavior would remain exactly the same throughout. Personal sacrifice netted these women nothing except, perhaps, a case of housemaid's knee. He was irresponsible, as promiscuous as ever, though he tried to be polite. He never flaunted his indiscretions, but he made no secret of them, either, since nonexclusivity was the agreement he and this latest girlfriend had started out with. Their anger would begin to surface because there was no payoff to the subservience. Each woman, in turn, would start to feel victimized, and Jimmy was the obvious target of the discontent. This, of course, provided him with the perfect justification to pull away from them. Within a month, never much more than two, they'd make some demand, perhaps complain, voicing barely controlled expressions of disappointment and rebuke. The minute that happened, Jimmy Tate was out the door without so much as a "Thank you, ma'am." I'd never seen him look at one of them the way he looked at Bibianna Diaz.

She returned to the table, where she arranged herself provocatively on Jimmy's lap, straddling him, with her skirt hiked up to her crotch, her breasts so close to his face I thought he'd munch on them like cupcakes. I spent the next half hour having my hearing impaired by the music while Jimmy Tate and Bibianna Diaz exchanged steamy glances, (more or less) making love in an upright position with their clothes on, the resulting friction scorching all the layers of fabric between them. The air smelled of desire, like the sweet perfume of wet grass after a rainstorm. That or cat spray.

The band finished one number and began the next, the only slow song I'd heard all night. Bibianna went off to dance with someone else. Jimmy didn't seem to mind. The fact that other men in the bar were seeking out her company apparently lent him stature. It also gave me time to figure out where his head was and whether he represented a help or a hindrance in my attempt to get close to Bibianna. Jimmy held his hand out. "Dance with me," he said.

seven

i put my hand in his and followed. He was one of those men who can make you feel like Ginger Rogers on the dance floor, conveying an entire set of suggestions in the way he applied pressure to the small of my back. He moved automatically while he scanned the bar, his gaze shifting restlessly across the room. It was behavior I recognized. There's really no such thing as an "ex-cop" or a cop who's "off-duty" or "retired." Once trained, once indoctrinated, a cop is always alert, assessing reality in terms of its potential for illegal acts. Whatever Jimmy's failings as a police officer, corruption being foremost, I couldn't picture him doing anything else with his life. It was hard for me to believe he'd sabotaged himself so thoroughly, cutting himself off from the only work he'd ever cared about. It wasn't really out of character for him, but it wasn't smart. What was he going to do now? Retire to what?

He sensed my preoccupation and refocused his attention. "Why so quiet?"

"I was thinking about the trial, wondering how you got caught up in that stuff to begin with."

"I started out as a JD," he reminded me.

"You were twelve. You didn't have anything at stake back then. I know you've had problems, but I never thought you were dirty."

"Lighten up. What's that supposed to mean? I'm no dirtier than anybody else. Come on, Kinsey. You know how it is. I palmed cash sometimes. Hell, everybody does. I saw guys palming cash the first day I ever went to work. So it's not like this was anything new—it just wasn't organized. I didn't cheat little old ladies out of their Social Security checks. These were fuckin' coke dealers—human garbage. The worst. The money wasn't even legal, but there it sat. You have any idea what it's like to make a bust like that? You could have two hundred thousand—hell, half a million dollars—layin' on the table in these nice neat stacks, all tied up with rubber bands. It doesn't even seem real. It's like funny money. Props. So who's gonna point a finger if a stack of bills disappears? The launderers? Get real. Those guys repudiate cash on the spot because then you got no hard evidence. By the time it gets booked in, there's twenty thousand less. Who knows where it went? Who even gives a shit?"

"You were skimming off more than twenty thousand, from what the papers said. Didn't it ever occur to you that you were being set up?"

"Sergeant Renkes was rakin' off four times the money we were, so why would I think he was setting us up? On the face of it, he had more to lose than we did."

"But why all the conspicuous consumption?" I said. "The newspapers talked about speedboats and condos . . . luxury cars. On a cop's salary? Didn't you think anybody'd notice?"

Jimmy laughed. "Nobody said we were smart. I wanted the perks. We all did, and why not? So it turns out the whole thing was a setup. Maybe we shoulda guessed. Anyway, that's why Bosco blew his brains out. Because we'd been stung and he couldn't see any other way out. Renkes headed up the unit we were working . . . he set the game up, invited us to play, and then he turned us in. It was all departmental housecleaning, and Danny Renkes was the janitor."

"Did you know the bust was coming?"

"In some ways, sure. There were rumors for months. Nobody really wanted to believe it. I was on disability by then, so I wasn't an active player when the bust went down. I'd done my share, of course, and Renkes knew that. First time I heard the scuttlebutt, I started asking around. Everybody said the same thing. Run for cover, dude. Bail out. Get a lawyer before the shit hits the coast like a hurricane. I hired the smartest motherfucker in the business. Had to hock everything I owned to pay the man's retainer, but it was worth every penny. Wilfred Brentnell. You ever heard of him?"

"Who hasn't? I was told the only case he ever lost was up here. Nikki Fife, remember her? I guess the Santa Teresa courts weren't that impressed with his expertise."

"That's the price you pay for living in the provinces. The man's a whiz. First rate. They call him 'Bent Willy' because he's got a finger crooked like that from some kind of accident."

"What about Renkes? Aren't you bitter about him?"

"I don't hold it against him. I mean, I understand why the man did it. I wouldn't have done it myself, but then I wasn't caught first like he was. I didn't have the DA breathin' down my neck, cuttin' deals."

"Deals?"

"Shit, yes. They got him on another rap. You knew that, didn't you?"

I shook my head. "I only caught the story in fragments."

"Oh, yeah. They had that dude cold. Thing about Renkes is he sold out cheap. He got burnt. He should have taken it on the chin instead of blowin' the whistle on the rest of us. But that's life, right?"

The music ended. We moved toward the table, passing Bibianna. Jimmy uttered a low growl and gripped her by the back of the neck, claiming her with his touch. She turned with a smile and he pulled her in against him in a

hip-grinding embrace, probably meant to reassert his proprietary rights. Bibianna pushed him away, but she was
laughing as she did it and the gesture had no force. He
slung an arm across her shoulder in an affectionate ham-
merlock. They kissed again. I could feel my eyes roll heavenward. We sat down and ordered yet another round of
beers.

The noise level was rising, alcohol unleashing a manic bab-
ble of laughter and loud talk, with quarrelsome undertones.
The air was gray with cigarette smoke, the sharp report of
slammers coming down one after another in steady succession, like a trio of carpenters with hammers. The music
started up again, this time with lighting effects added, guaranteed to send you into seizures. Out on the dance floor, a
drunk toppled backward, crashing into a table. A shriek went
up, a chair broke, glasses flew in a spray of glass shards and
tequila. Jimmy and Bibianna didn't seem to notice. They
were doing a sit-down version of the dirty-boogey, imitating
all those terrible movie scenes where couples tongue each
other on the screen and chew each other's lips. Being with
lovers can be such a trial to those of us who are celibate. The
very air was charged, sparks leaped between them in a nearly
imperceptible arc. Every time their eyes locked, I could sense
their underwear getting damp.

I glanced at my watch: eleven-fifteen. Enough of this. I
scraped my chair back. "That's it for me," I said. "Time to go.
Good night. It's been great." It took a while to get their
attention. Jimmy managed to pull out of a nosedive of a kiss.
He looked up at me with heavy-lidded surprise, still breathing hard.

"Hope I didn't interrupt anything," I said.

Lust had slowed his responses and I could see him grope
for his speaking voice. "Don't go," he croaked. "Stick around.
We need to talk."

"About what?"

Bibianna had to lean forward in order to be heard, but she
seemed pretty cool by comparison. "Too noisy here. We're

going next door to grab a bite to eat. Why don't you come with us?"

I was torn, I confess. I'd spent much of the day setting up the contact and I knew I'd be smart to cement the relationship. There was a possibility, of course, that Jimmy Tate might reveal the truth about my identity, but I thought I could trust him to keep his mouth shut. At the moment, he seemed more concerned about getting laid. They were teasing themselves, postponing the inevitable, while I was only marking time. Oh, hell, I thought, I'm going to end up alone in my bed anyway, so why rush? I zipped up my leather jacket while I waited for them to disentangle all the various body parts. As we moved through the crowd toward the front door, I got a couple of offers, but I didn't take them seriously. Both were addressed to "Hey, you . . . yeah, you . . ." accompanied by much display and posturing. One kid looked like he was sixteen. The other had a big gold tooth sticking out in front.

The three of us left the bar, stepping into a light rain. Jimmy grabbed Bibianna's hand and they began to run. I trotted behind them, catching up when they reached the little restaurant three doors down. After the high-decibel racket in the bar, the cafe we entered was as quiet as a deprivation tank. Bourbon Street was small, essentially one long, narrow room that resembled a mock New Orleans alleyway. The walls were brick, broken up by a series of false windows and doorways, backlighted to create the illusion of warm interiors. A series of balconies jutted out at the level of the second floor, suggesting a gallery of apartments surrounded by wrought-iron railings, the pseudo–French Quarter setting complete with wall-mounted lamps in which tapered light bulbs flickered like windblown candles. Fake green ivy snaked its way up the wall, looking so real I could have sworn I smelled the breeze that seemed to rattle through the leaves.

The restaurant kitchen was hidden around one corner where a wall angled out. The scent of shrimp *étouffée* and blackened red fish hovered in the air as if you'd caught a whiff of someone else's Sunday dinner. There were seventeen tables in all, most of them empty, each covered with white butcher's paper. Hurricane lamps provided illumination that flattered the patrons, at the same time dispensing light sufficient to eat by.

Jimmy ordered Cajun popcorn—crawfish parts fried crisp with a spicy sauce—and then a pot of jambalaya for the three of us. Bibianna wanted oysters on the half shell first. I watched them negotiate the meal, feeling strangely passive myself. They argued the issue of wine versus beer and finally ordered both. They'd become nearly playful, while I felt myself disconnect. I picked at a cornbread muffin, trying to figure out what time it was in Dietz's life. Germany was what, eight hours ahead of us? I entertained a few wicked fantasies about Dietz, while observing Bibianna and Jimmy idly as if through a two-way mirror. It seemed clear to me that there was more going on here than a quick fling. Jimmy Tate was a good-looking guy with all the sunny charm of a California surfer, wire-rimmed glasses adding interest to a face that might otherwise have been too handsome to warrant serious consideration. Handsome men have never held a fascination for me, but he was an exception, probably because of our shared history. He'd played hard in his life—booze and drugs, late nights, bar fights—and at thirty-four was just beginning to show evidence of self-abuse. I could see fine lines near his eyes, deeper lines around his mouth. Bibianna's youth and her dark Latina beauty were a perfect counterpoint to his blond, blue-eyed attractiveness. They seemed suited for one another, a crooked cop and a con artist . . . both willing to cut corners, both manipulating the system, looking for a fast buck. Neither was malicious but they must have recognized the lawlessness in each other's natures. I wondered what had drawn them together in the first place, whether they had sensed the shared bonds of mutiny and trespass. The similarities certainly weren't apparent on the surface, but I suspect lovers have some unerring instinct for the qualities that both attract and condemn them in relationships.

When the food arrived, they fell on it with the same lusty appetites they exhibited for one another, killing a bottle of red wine between them. I wasn't interested in anything more to drink. I concentrated on the meal in front of me with the kind of gusto that can only be thought of as sexual sublimation. After the beers I'd had, it was nice to have the opportunity to clear my head for the drive home. The place was beginning to fill up with the late night crowd. The noise was on the rise, but it couldn't begin to compete with the bar we'd just left. Dimly, I was aware of the front door behind me, opening at intervals as the midnight rush began—people looking for hot coffee, a wedge of sweet potato pie. Nature called again in response to all the beers I'd drunk. "Where are the restrooms?"

Bibianna pointed toward the rear. She and Tate were both bombed and I began to wonder jf I'd have to ferry them both back to her place in the interests of safety.

"Be right back," I said.

I wound my way through the tables, spotting the posted sign that indicated the location of the restrooms and the public telephones. I pushed through hurricane shutters and found myself in a short corridor, lighted by the same flickering bulbs. At the end of the hallway, there were two pay phones flanking an exit with a sign above it reading THIS DOOR MUST BE KEPT UNLOCKED DURING BUSINESS HOURS. To my right were two doors marked M and W. I pushed into the W. The light was better. There was a two-sink counter to my left with a mirror running above it, a paper towel rack above a metal trash bin, and two stalls, one of which was in use. I entered the other. Under the raised partition between the stalls, I could see the feet of the other's occupant, whose copious urination sounded like a quart of lemonade being poured from a great height. I glanced idly at her shoes: patterned stockings, sling-back pumps with spike heels. I squinted, bending for a closer look. I'd seen the same shoes or a pair just like them on the blonde at the CF offices earlier. I heard the toilet flush. I reassembled myself in haste while she washed her hands and snatched a towel from the dispenser. I heard the rustle of paper as she dried her hands. I flushed the toilet in my cubicle, stalling for time. I didn't dare leave the cubicle until I knew she was gone because she might well recognize my face. I heard the tip-tap of her heels crossing the tile floor. As soon as the door closed behind her, I emerged and moved swiftly to the door. I poked my head out into the corridor. I caught sight of her at one of the pay phones, inserting numerous coins into the slot. She turned away slightly as if to insure privacy. It was the woman who called herself Karen Hedgepath: spiky, punk blond hair, severely cut business suit. She kept herself in profile with her right hand pressed to her ear to block out noises from the restaurant. From the shift in her posture, I guessed that her call had been picked up. She began to speak rapidly, making gestures with her free hand. I did an about-face and returned to the main part of the restaurant while she was still occupied. A quick check revealed the presence of the big guy with the plaid sport coat. He was seated with his back to me at a two-top on the side wall, but I recognized his jacket and the set of his shoulders. He was smoking a cigarette, a bottle of red wine visible on the table in front of him.

At our table, the seats were arranged so that I was facing the restrooms, my back to the front door, with Bibianna on my right and Jimmy Tate across from me. I kept my voice down, one eye cocked in case the blonde returned unexpectedly. Bibianna looked at me with curiosity, sensing my alarm. I handed her the menu and said, "I would like for you, very discreetly, to check that doorway leading to the restrooms. A blonde is going to make an appearance in a moment. See if you know her, but don't let her know you're looking. You got that?"

"Why? What's going on?" Bibianna said to me.

"I heard her on the pay phone outside the john and she was talking about you."

"About me?"

Jimmy leaned forward. "What is this?"

The blonde appeared, coming through the shutters from the corridor. Her gaze settled lightly on our table and moved on. "Do not crank your head around," I sang under my breath.

Bibianna's eyes flicked to the woman. The reaction was subtle, but I could see the animation fade from her face. "Oh, hell. I gotta get out of here," she said.

I handed her an open menu, pointing to the first item in the dessert list, which was the key lime pie. Conversationally, I said, "Take your handbag and go to the ladies' room. Go out through the door at the end of that hall and wait at the mouth of the alley. One of us will pick you up. Leave your jacket draped across the chair. We don't want it to look like you're really going anywhere, okay?"

Jimmy's gaze shifted from my face to Bibianna's. "What's going on?"

Bibianna got to her feet, groping blindly for her handbag. Too late. The couple converged on us. The blond woman placed a firm hand on my shoulder, effectively nailing me to the chair. The guy pressed a Browning .45 against Bibianna's spine as if he might be an orthopedist probing for a herniated disk. I saw Jimmy reach for his .38, but the guy shook his head. "I got the option to smoke her if there's any problem whatsoever. Your choice."

Jimmy put both hands flat on the table.

Bibianna picked up her jacket and her handbag. Jimmy and I watched helplessly as the three of them moved toward the back door. Jimmy had better instincts about these things than I did. The minute they were out of sight, he bolted for the front, attracting startled looks from all the patrons he bumped in passing. He didn't bother to be polite. The front door banged open and he was gone. I threw some money on the table and headed after him.

By the time I hit the street, he was already pounding toward the corner, elbows pumping, gun drawn. The streets were damp, the air filled with a fine mist. I ran after him, plowing straight through a puddle on the walk. In the distance, I could hear tires squeal in the alleyway where the couple must have had a car parked. I reached the intersection moments after Jimmy did. A Ford sedan shot out of the mouth of the alley three doors down. Jimmy, as if moving in slow motion, took a stance and fired. The back window shattered. He fired again. The right rear tire blew and the Ford took a sudden fishtailing detour into a van parked at the curb. There was the gut-wrenching *wham!* of metal objects colliding. The Ford's front bumper clattered to the pavement, and glass fragments showered down with a delicate tinkling. The few pedestrians within range were running for cover, and I could hear a woman's protracted scream. The front doors of the Ford seemed to open simultaneously. The blond woman emerged from the passenger side, the big guy from the driver's side, taking cover behind the yawning car door as he turned and took aim. I hit the pavement and flattened myself in the shelter of a line of trash cans. The ensuing shots sounded like kernels of popcorn in a lidded saucepan. I hunched my shoulders, tasting grit, sucking up the mixed smell of garbage and rain-wet cement. I heard three more shots fired in succession, one of them plowing into the pavement near my head. I feared for Jimmy, felt a sick sense of dread for Bibianna, too. Someone was running. At least somebody was still alive—I just wasn't sure who. I heard the footsteps fade, then silence. I pulled myself up onto my hands and knees and scrambled toward a parked car, peering over the hood. Jimmy was standing across the street. Abruptly, he sank down on the curb and put his head on his knees. There was no sign of the blonde. Bibianna, apparently unhurt, clung to the Ford's rear fender and wept hysterically. I rose to my feet, puzzled by the sudden quiet. I approached her with care, wondering where the guy in the plaid sport coat had gone.

I could hear panting, a labored moan that suggested both anguish and extreme effort. On the far side of the Ford, I caught sight of him, dragging himself along the sidewalk. There was a wet patch of bright blood between his shoulder blades. There was blood streaming down the left side of his face from a head wound. He seemed completely focused on the journey, determined to escape, moving with the same haphazard coordination of a crawling baby, limbs occasionally working at cross-purposes. He began to weep with frustration at the clumsiness of his progress. He must have been a man who'd always counted on his physical strength to carry him through, who'd enjoyed a certain unquestioned supremacy by reason of his size. Now the sheer bulk of his body was an impediment, a burden he couldn't quite manage. He laid his head down, resting for a moment before he inched forward again. A crowd had collected, like the spectators at the finish line of a marathon. No one cheered. The faces were respectful, uncertain, perplexed. A woman moved toward the injured man and dropped beside him, reaching out tentatively. At her touch, a deep howl seemed to rise from him, guttural and pain-filled. There is no sound so terrible as a man's sorrow for his own death. The woman looked up, dazed, at the people standing nearby.

"Help," she called hoarsely. She couldn't get any volume in her voice. "Please help this man. Can't anybody help?"

No one moved.

Already, there were sirens. Jimmy Tate lifted his head.

eight

i crossed to the Ford. The left rear door was open and Bibianna sat sideways in the backseat, leaning forward with her elbows on her knees. She was shaking so hard that she couldn't keep her feet flat on the pavement. Her spike heels seemed to do a little tap dance as she pressed her hands together and clamped them between her thighs. I thought she was humming, but it was a moan she was trying to suppress through tightly clamped teeth. Her face was starchy white. I hunkered beside her, placing one hand on the icy skin of her arm. "You okay?"

She shook her head, a hopeless gesture of terror and resignation. "I'm dead meat. I'm dead. This is my fault. There's going to be hell to pay." Her gaze strayed vaguely toward the street corner, where a crowd had gathered. Tears rose in her eyes, not from sorrow as much as from desperation.

I gave her arm a shake. "Who *is* that?"

"His name is Chago. He's the brother of this guy I was living with before I came up here. He said Raymond sent him up here to bring me back."

"Bullshit, Bibianna. They weren't going to take you any-place. They were going to kill you."

"I wish I could have gotten it over with. If anything happens to Chago, Raymond's going to kill me anyway. He'll have to. Like a blood debt. My life's not worth shit."

"I thought Jimmy was the one who shot him. Why is it your fault?"

"What difference does it make? Raymond doesn't care about that. It's my fault I left. It's my fault he had to send Chago up here. It's my fault the *car* got wrecked. That's how he sees things."

"I take it the blonde was Chago's girlfriend," I said.

"His wife. Her name's Dawna. D-a-w-n-a. Do you love that? Shit, she'll kill me herself if Raymond doesn't kill me first."

Jimmy Tate approached and put his hand on the back of Bibianna's neck. "Hey, babe. How are you?"

She took his hand and pressed it against her cheek. "Oh, God, oh, God . . . I was scared for you."

He pulled her to her feet and took her in his arms, enfolding her, murmuring against her hair.

"Jesus, what am I going to do?" she wailed.

An emergency vehicle came barreling around the corner, orange light flashing as the siren ground abruptly to a halt. Two paramedics got out, one of them toting a first-aid kit. I rose to my feet, watching over the hood of the Ford as the two of them crossed rapidly to the guy, who was lying face-down on the sidewalk. His lurching journey to the corner had come to a sudden halt. I noticed he'd left a long, smeared trail of blood in his wake like a snail. The woman who knelt beside him was crying uncontrollably. I was certain she was a stranger, only connected to him by the quirk of fate that had placed her at the scene. Her two companions tried to coax her away, but she refused to relinquish her hold.

One of the paramedics knelt and placed his fingers against the guy's carotid artery, trying to get a pulse. He and the other paramedic exchanged one of those looks that in a television episode replaces six lines of dialogue. Two squad cars

(

swung into view, tires squealing, and pulled up behind the emergency vehicle. A uniformed patrolman got out of the first car and Jimmy Tate walked over to meet him. The beat officer in the second turned out to be a woman, tall, sturdily constructed, her pale hair skinned away from her face and secured in a small, neat knot at the back of her neck. She was hatless, in dark regulation pants and a dark jacket with Santa Teresa Police Department patches on the sleeves. She crossed to the paramedics and had a quick conversation. I noticed that none of them jumped into any emergency procedures, which suggested the guy in the sport coat had already departed this life. The beat officer moved back to her patrol car and radioed the dispatcher, asking for someone from the coroner's office, the CSI unit, and backup on a Code 2—no sirens. She was going to need help securing the crime scene. The rain had begun again, drizzle lending the night air a softening haze. The crowd was subdued and there was no suggestion of interference, but someone was going to have to begin interviewing witnesses, collecting names and addresses, before people got restless and started leaving the area.

Bibianna slumped back into the backseat of the car again. Long minutes passed. Bibianna had lapsed into silence, but when the first backup unit arrived, she stirred, shooting a dark look in the direction of the two officers emerging from the black-and-white. "I don't want to talk to any cops," she said. "I hate cops. I don't want to talk to them."

"Bibianna, you're going to have to talk to them. Those people tried to kill you. There's a dead man on the sidewalk. . . ."

Fury flashed across her face and her voice rose several notches. "Just leave me alone!"

Several people turned to look at us, including the beat officer, who began to walk in our direction. She put a hand on her left hip, touching her nightstick like a talisman. As she approached, I checked the name on her tag. Officer D. Janofsky. Probably Diane or Deborah. She didn't look like a Dorothy. Up close, I could see that she was in her late twenties, probably new to the department. I knew most of the officers who worked in this area, but she was not one I'd met. Her manner was cautious, her expression alert. Like many cops, she'd learned to disconnect her emotions. "Everything okay here?"

She scarcely had the words out when a third patrol car skidded around the corner. All three of us turned as the car came to a halt some distance away. Tuesday night in Santa Teresa is usually very quiet, so aside from the obvious desire to assist a fellow officer, the officer responding must have been thrilled to see some action. This was better than rousting the homeless down at the railroad tracks. Janofsky turned her attention to Bibianna, whose face had darkened. I was keeping tabs on Tate out of the corner of my eye, and I realized, as had Bibianna, that he had been taken into custody.

"Keep her away from me," Bibianna said.

"We're fine," I said, hoping to defuse the situation.

Janofsky ignored me, fixing Bibianna with a testy look. "I'd like to see your driver's license." She reached for her flashlight as if she meant to examine the license once Bibianna had produced it. I knew from experience a flashlight that size could serve as a powerful protective weapon. I watched apprehensively.

"What for?" Bibianna asked.

"Ma'am, could you show me some identification?"

"Fuck you," Bibianna said. She managed to infuse the two words with maximum boredom and maximum contempt. Why was she being so belligerent? I could feel my own temper climb and I knew the policewoman was close to blowing. This was no time to fool around. For all Janofsky knew, Bibianna had shot the man herself.

"Her name is Diaz," I interjected. "She's upset about the shooting. Can I answer any questions for you? My name's Hannah Moore." I was babbling like an idiot, trying to offset some of the tension in the air. The patrol car with Tate in it pulled away from the curb, easing through the crowd of curiosity seekers that was milling about.

Bibianna turned on me. "Keep out of this. Where are they taking Tate?"

"Probably to the station. He'll be fine. Don't worry about it. Just cool it. You've already got enough trouble on your hands."

"Could you get out of the car, please?" the officer said. She backed up half a step and planted her feet.

I said, "Goddamn it, Bibianna. Would you just do what the lady says? You've got your tit in a wringer. Don't you get that?"

Bibianna bolted from the car abruptly and gave me a shove that nearly knocked me over backward. I caught myself on the open car door, grabbing at the handle to retain my balance. Bibianna drove a shoulder into Officer Janofsky, catching her off-guard. Janofsky barked out an expletive, startled by the assault. Bibianna punched her in the face, swung around, and punched at me, too, grazing my temple with a fist the size and shape of a broken rock. That sucker *hurt*. For someone so petite, she really managed to pack a wallop.

Officer Janofsky went into combat mode. Before the other two officers even understood what was going on, she slammed Bibianna up against the car, grabbing one wrist in the process. Cops know how to pinch little hurt places on the human body that'll drop you in your tracks. I saw Bibianna stiffen and her face twist with pain as a pertinent nerve was tweaked beyond endurance. Janofsky jerked Bibianna's arms back and snapped a set of cuffs on her. I felt my heart sink. They'd march her off to jail and keep her there for life. I could see, in a flash, that if I wanted to maintain our connection, I only had one choice here. I grabbed Officer Janofsky by the arm. "Hey, get offa her. You can't treat her that way!"

Janofsky leveled me with a look. She was trembling with rage, in no mood to take any sass from the likes of me. "Back up!" She snapped.

"You back up!" I snapped back. Out of the corner of my eye, I could see two male cops coming up on my right. Here goes "assault on a police officer," I thought. I hauled off and socked Officer Janofsky in the face. The next thing I knew, I was flat on the pavement, my wrists handcuffed behind me, the right side of my face being ground into the concrete. Some cop had his knee in the middle of my back. I could hardly breathe, and for a moment I worried he'd crush my rib cage. It hurt like hell, but I couldn't even get out a "guff" of protest. I'd been effectively incapacitated, not in pain, but certainly penitent. Having made his point, the guy got up. I stayed where I was, reluctant to risk a crack in the head with a nightstick. As an addendum to my discomfort, the drizzle was suddenly upgraded to a dainty pitter-patter. I groaned involuntarily. I heard Bibianna shriek, a sound more related to outrage than pain. I inched up my head in time to see her kick Janofsky in the kneecap. The officer's adrenaline was already up and I was afraid she'd go after Bibianna with the flashlight. She grabbed her by the throat, trying to get a choke hold. One of Janofsky's fellow officers intervened at that point, which was fortunate. I laid my cheek down against the pavement, waiting for the melodrama to play itself out. The raindrops, as they hit the sidewalk, rebounded in my face. I stared at the tiny pebbles embedded in the concrete, using auditory cues to re-create the activities taking place around me. It was like listening to a sporting event on the radio. I grew weary trying to visualize the play as it progressed. Drops of water began to slide down the side of my face, collecting on the pavement in a shallow pool near my cheek. I felt like one of those protesters whose pictures you see in the paper. I craned my head around, resting my chin on the walk.

"Uh, excuse me," I said. "Hey!" It was a strain to try to hold my head in that position, so I laid it down again. Several pairs of regulation cop shoes appeared in my line of vision. I hoped none of them belonged to Lieutenant Dolan. Somebody gave an order. Suddenly, there was an officer on either side of me. I felt myself hooked under the armpits and I was lifted to my feet, levitating into an upright position effortlessly. After a quick pat-down, I was hustled off to a squad car and shoved into the backseat. The door was slammed shut.

An unmarked car came down the street from the opposite direction, sliding to a halt on the rain-lubricated asphalt. I saw Bill Blair, the coroner's deputy, get out on the driver's side, taking a moment to shrug himself into his raincoat. Head bowed against the rain, he moved over to the body without looking in my direction. All the various crime scene personnel had begun to assemble: two guys from the Public Works Department setting up barricades, running tape around the perimeter, the CSI unit, along with the supervisor in a separate vehicle. As in the early moments of a play, the actors were appearing on stage, each with the necessary props, each with a bit of business to perform. Little by little, the drama of homicide was being played out again.

I sat forward slightly, peering through the metal screen that separated the front of the squad car from the rear. It was 1:17 A.M. and my head had begun to ache. The rain now formed a hazy curtain that seemed to blow against the streetlights, sending up whiffs of steam. The sound was homely, like uncooked rice grains falling on a cookie sheet. Within minutes, the precipitation increased rapidly to a steady drumming on the roof of the black-and-white. Ordinarily, I like sitting in a parked car in a downpour. It seems cozy and safe and surprisingly intimate, depending on the circumstances, of course. The same smattering of people stood outside on the darkened street, avoiding the sight of me as if I were leprous. Anyone sitting in the rear of a cop car looks guilty somehow. The emergency vehicle had been moved to one side to allow the coroner's deputy access to the body. Chago had been covered with a length of yellow plastic to shield him from the rain. Blood had coagulated on the sidewalk like a sticky patch of motor oil, and I could still smell cordite. The police radio was squawking incomprehensibly. There was a time in my life—during my days in uniform—

when I under..ood every word. Not so, tonight. I'd lost my ear for it, like a foreign language I no longer had a use for.

Bibianna was being questioned by the police inspector, who'd appeared at some point. She was being pelted by the rain, the red dress clinging to her stained to a dark bloody hue. She looked like she was complaining, though I couldn't hear a word she said. Judging from the inspector's expression and the set of Bibianna's shoulders, she was subdued, but uncooperative. The inspector waved a hand at her impatiently. The same officer who'd ushered me to the patrol car steered Bibianna in my direction. She was frisked for weapons, a ludicrous formality under the circumstances. In the little mini she was wearing, what kind of weapon could she possibly conceal? The rear door of the squad car was yanked open and the officer pushed her head down and shoved her into the backseat beside me. She'd recovered some of her energy, jaws snapping at the guy's hand like a rabid dog. "Get your fuckin' hands offa me, you cocksucker!" she screamed.

Nice talk, huh? When you get arrested, these are the kind of people you're forced to associate with. Because of the handcuffs, her arms were pinioned awkwardly behind her, which meant she ended up lying halfway across my lap. Before the officer could close the door, she lashed a kick at him with one of her spike heels. He was lucky she missed. She'd have torn a hunk of flesh out of his thigh if she'd caught him right. He was amazingly polite—probably heartened by the fact that he could look up her dress—but I noticed he managed to get the door shut before she could kick at him again. She was a firecracker, absolutely fearless. For a minute, I thought she'd lie there and kick the windows out. She muttered something to herself and straightened up.

She flicked her hair away from her face with a shake of her head. A few drops of water flew off on me. "Did you see that? I could have been killed tonight! Those assholes tried to kill me!" She was referring to the cops, not Chago and the blonde.

"The cops didn't try to kill you," I said irritably. "What did you expect? You haul off and sock a cop, what'd you think was going to happen?"

"Look who's talking. You hit that bitch twice as hard as me." She turned a calculating look on me and I could see now that I had garnered a spark of admiration for my pugilistic skills. She began a staring contest with one of the cops standing near the car. "God, I hate pigs," she remarked.

"They don't seem all that fond of you," I said.

"I mean it! I could sue. That's police brutality."

"What's your problem?"

"Forget it. It's none of your business."

She peered out of the car window and I followed her gaze. Two cops were conferring, probably in preparation for removing us to the station. I wished they'd get on with it. I was cold. My tank top was soaked and my pants were soggy, clinging to my thighs like a lapful of wet sheets. I wasn't sure what had happened to my leather jacket. Somebody would steal it if I'd left it in the restaurant. Both my scruffy pumps and little white socks were mud-spattered and made squishing sounds every time I moved my feet. I could still smell the sooty cologne of secondhand cigarette smoke that permeated my hair. With my hands cuffed from behind, I had metal bracelets digging into the bruised flesh of my wrists.

Bibianna's mood underwent a shift. Her manner now seemed completely matter-of-fact, as if shoot-outs, death, and resisting arrest were an everyday occurrence. She held a foot up, inspecting her shoe. "Fuckin' shoes are ruined," she remarked. "That's the trouble with suede. One wet night and you're wearing slime. I wish I had a cigarette. You think they're going to bring my bag?"

"You better hope not. I thought you had a joint in there."

That warranted a half laugh. "Oh, yeah. I forgot. That's how my luck runs, you know? What's the point trying to straighten out your life if it's all going to turn to worms again?"

She peered out at the various law enforcement types milling around in the rain. "Hey! Let's pick up the pace, frog-lips. What's the delay?" It was pointless yelling with the windows rolled up. One of the beat cops turned and looked at her, but I was sure he hadn't heard a word she'd said. "Pig," she said to him pleasantly. "Yeah, you, dick-head. Get an eyeful." She stuck a leg up in the air. He looked away and Bibianna laughed.

nine

even with the harsh lights playing on her face, that fine dusky skin looked almost luminous. Thick lashes, dark eyes, a wide mouth still lush with flame-red lipstick. How'd she keep the stuff on like that? Anytime I tried lipstick, it ended up on the rim of the first glass I drank from. Hers looked fresh and wet, lending color to her face. Despite the foul talk, her dark eyes glinted with amusement. "I can't believe those guys get paid to stand around like that," she remarked with a glance at me. "How are you holding up?"

"I've been better. You have any idea where Dawna disappeared to?"

"She probably went to call Raymond. Oh, man, he's gonna have a fit when he finds out Chago's dead."

"Who are they?"

"Don't ask."

"What'd you do to piss 'em off so bad?"

"It's what I didn't do that counts."

"You owe 'em money?"

"No way, baby! They owe me. What I can't figure out is

how they got a line on me in the first place. What'd you say your name was?"

For a minute, I couldn't remember which set of fake ID's I'd brought. "Hannah Moore."

There was a calculated silence. "What's the rest of it?"

"The rest?"

"You have a middle name?"

"Oh. Sure," I said. "Uhm, Lee."

Her tone of voice turned flat. "I don't believe it."

I felt my heart do a quick flip, but I managed a noncommittal murmur.

"I never met anyone with three pairs of double letters in their name. Two *n*'s in Hannah. Two *e*'s in Lee and the two *o*'s in Moore. Plus, 'Hannah' is a palindrome, spelled the same way forward as it is backward. You ever had your numbers done?"

"Like numerology?"

She nodded. "It's a hobby of mine. I can do a chart for you later . . . all I need is your date of birth, but I can tell you right now, your soul number's six. Like you're big in domestic harmony, right? People like you, your mission is to spread the idea of the Golden Rule."

I laughed in spite of myself. "Oh, really. How'd you guess?"

A uniformed officer, toting Bibianna's handbag, moved over to the squad car and let himself in, locking eyes with me in the rearview mirror as he slammed the door shut. It was apparently his job to transport us out to the jail. He held the bag up. "This belong to one of you?"

"Me," Bibianna said, rolling her eyes in my direction. It was anybody's guess whether the joint in her bag would come to light or not. She was in deep doo-doo if it did.

He plunked the bag down on the seat beside him. "How you doin' back there?" He was in his late twenties, cleanshaven, his dark hair clipped close. The back of his neck looked vulnerable above the collar of his uniform.

None of this was lost on Bibianna. "We're great, sport. How're you?"

"I'm cool," he said.

"You have a name?"

"Kip Brainard," he said. "You're Diaz, right?"

"Right."

He seemed to smile to himself. He started the car and eased it away from the curb, radioing the dispatcher that he was on his way in with us. There was no more conversation. The rain had begun to sound like a pile of nails being dropped on the car roof, windshield wipers flopping back and forth without much effect, the monotonous calls from the car radio punctuating the silence. We reached the freeway and headed north. The windows were fogging over. In the warmth of the vehicle and the lulling drone of the engine, I nearly nodded off.

We took the off ramp at Espada and turned left onto the frontage road, proceeding about a half a mile. We turned right onto a road that cut around to the rear of the Santa Teresa County Correctional Facility, better known as the jail to those of us about to be incarcerated. On the far side of the property, the complex shared a parking lot with the Santa Teresa County Sheriff's Department. We pulled up at the gate. Kip pushed a button for the intercom. The master control regulation officer responded, a disembodied female voice surrounded by static.

"Police officer coming in with two," he said.

The gate swung open and we passed through. Once we were inside the fence, he honked the horn and the gate swung shut behind us. We pulled into a paved stretch enclosed by a chain-link fence. The whole area blazed with lights, the rain creating a misty aureole around each flood. A county sheriff's car had pulled in just ahead of us, and we waited in silence until the deputy was admitted with his prisoner, a vagrant who was visibly drunk and much in need of assistance.

Once they'd disappeared, Kip shut the engine off and got out. He opened the rear door on my side and helped me out, a clumsy procedure with my hands cuffed behind my back. "You gonna behave yourself?" he asked.

"No problem. I'm fine."

He must not have trusted me because he continued to hold on to my arm, walking me around to Bibianna's side of the car. He opened the door and helped her out of the backseat and then walked us toward the gate. A female jail officer came out to assist him. The rain was constant, unpleasant, a chill assault on my body, which was already trembling with accumulated tensions. Never had I so longed for a hot shower, dry clothes, my own bed. Bibianna's dark hair was plastered to her head in long dripping strands, but it didn't seem to bother her. All the earlier hostility had faded, replaced by a curious complaisance.

Reception at the county jail is approached through an exterior corridor of chain-link fencing that resembles a dog run. We were buzzed in, passing yet another checkpoint complete with electronic locks and cameras. Kip walked us along the passage, raindrops splashing up around us as our heels tapped across the wet pavement. "You know the routine?" he asked.

"Yeah, yeah, yeah. It's all the same, stud," Bibianna said.

"Let's make that 'Officer.' Can we do that?" he said dryly. "I take it you're an old hand at this."

"You got that right . . . Officer Stud," she said.

He decided to let it pass. I kept my mouth shut. I knew the drill from the old days in uniform. It was odd how differently I perceived the whole process now that I was the perp.

We reached a metal door. Kip pushed a button, announcing once more that he was bringing in two of us. We waited while the cameras inspected us. I've seen the big console where the MCR operator sits, surrounded by black-and-white monitors showing the equivalent of twelve totally boring Andy Warhol movies simultaneously. The operator buzzed us in. In silence, we walked down one corridor and then turned into a second, emerging eventually into the reception area where the male prisoners are booked in. I was hoping to see Tate, but he'd apparently been processed and taken to a cell. The vagrant, weaving on his feet, was emptying the pockets of his ragged sport coat. I knew him by sight, one of the town's perennial characters. Most afternoons he hung out around the courthouse having heated arguments with an unseen companion. His invisible chum was still giving him a hard time. The booking officer behind the desk waited with benign patience. I knew the deputy, too, though I couldn't remember his name. Foley, maybe. Something like that. I wasn't close enough to read his name tag and I didn't want to call attention to myself by squinting at his chest.

I turned my head, staring off to the left to avoid any visual contact. It had been a good ten years since I'd last seen the guy, but I didn't want to chance his recognizing me, blowing the cover I'd set up. I probably flatter myself. I looked as respectable as the bum they were booking. I fancied I smelled better, but perhaps not. I've noticed that most of us don't have a clue what we smell like to other people. It's almost as though our noses blank us out in self-defense.

Kip buzzed at yet another locked door, and after a brief wait another female jail officer emerged from the women's side. Bibianna and I had our pictures taken in the kind of booth you see in Woolworth's, a sorry strip of poses appearing moments later in the outside slot. In mine, I looked like a suspect in a teen porno ring, the kind of woman who'd lure the young girls with glib promises of modeling gigs. We moved into the women's booking area, where we approached a row of holding cells. I went into the first and Bibianna the second. The officer with me did a quick pat-down and then removed the handcuffs.

"Lean up against the wall," she said. Her tone wasn't unfriendly, but it was devoid of real warmth. And why not? I was just one more in an endless stream of jailbirds as far as she knew.

I faced the wall, arms straight out in front of me, leaning my weight on my hands, which were spaced about four feet apart. She did a second, more thorough, pat-down, making sure I didn't have any tiny lethal weapons concealed in my hair. She allowed me to take a seat on a bench along the wall while the proper papers were assembled at the counter to my right. When the booking officer was ready, I emptied my pockets, passing my phony driver's license, my keys, my watch, my belt, and my scruffy shoes through the window slot. There was something pathetic about the sight of my personal possessions, which were not only meager, but cheap as well. We began to go through the catechism that accompanies the loss of freedom. Personal data. Medical. Employment. I said I was out of work, claiming "waitress" as my occupation. We went through the litany of facility and arrest data. I was being charged with assault, a misdemeanor, and battery on a police officer, which is a felony with a five-thousand-dollar bail attached. I assumed Bibianna was being booked on similar charges. I was offered the chance to post bail, but I declined, operating on the premise that Bibianna would do likewise. All I needed was to be stuck in jail while she found a way to get herself bailed out. I kept waiting for the booking officer to realize that my driver's license was a fake, but she didn't seem to notice. My few pieces of personal property were itemized and placed in a clear plastic boiling pouch, like a Seal-A-Meal. The whole procedure took about fifteen minutes and left me feeling unsettled. Oddly enough, I didn't feel humiliated so much as I felt misunderstood. I wanted to assert myself, wanted to assure them that I wasn't what I appeared to be, that I was really a decent, law-abiding citizen . . . on *their* team, in effect.

The booking officer completed her process. "You want to make any calls, there's a pay phone in the next cell."

"I can't think who I'd call anyway," I said, absurdly grateful that everyone was so polite. What had I expected, curses and abuse?

Padding along in my sock feet, I was taken down the corridor to the ID bureau to be fingerprinted. A second set of photographs were taken, front and profile this time. At this rate, I could put together a little album for Mother's Day. It was 2:13 A.M. by the time I was escorted to the drunk tank, a cell maybe fifteen by fifteen feet. A skinny white woman, with her back turned, slept on a mattress in the far corner of the room. There were no outside windows. The entire front wall was barred, with a lidless commode tucked into an alcove on the right. I've seen cells where the toilet seats are removed as well. I had to guess we were being trusted not to try to hang ourselves with this one. The floor was beige vinyl tile, the walls painted cinder block. There was a built-in bench running the width of the room with some one-inch mattresses rolled up and arranged haphazardly against the wall. I snagged one for myself and spread it out on the floor.

Bibianna arrived moments later, along with two other prisoners, a black woman and a weeping white girl in formal dress.

"Hey, Hannah," Bibianna said. "Old home week. This is Nettie." She turned to the second woman. "What's your name, babycakes?"

"Heather."

Bibianna said, "Heather, this is Hannah."

"Nice to meet you," I murmured dutifully. I didn't have a clue about jailhouse etiquette. The skinny woman in the far corner stirred restlessly in her sleep.

Bibianna pulled a mattress off the bench and dragged it over toward me. "Nettie and me did a little county time about a month ago, right?" No response.

Nettie, the black woman, looked to be in her late thirties. She was tall, with broad shoulders and breasts the size of torpedoes. Her hair was big and brushed over to the right, where the bulk of it stuck out stiffly as if blown by a hard wind. The black strands had a gray cast from all the split ends. She wore blue jeans, an oversize white T-shirt, and white crew socks. Bibianna arranged her mattress beside mine and took a seat, watching Nettie with respect. "She was charged with 'attempt to inflict bodily injury' and 'assault with a deadly weapon.' She attacked a wino with an uprooted palm tree. I guess it was a little one, but can you believe that?"

The other inmate, the white girl, was scarcely more than twenty, wearing an ankle-length organza dress and a corsage on one wrist. She was crying so hard it was impossible to figure out what her story was. She sank in a huddle and buried her face in her hands. She and Nettie both reeked of booze. The black woman paced restlessly, staring at Heather, who kept wiping her nose on the hem of her dress. Finally, Nettie stopped pacing and nudged her with a foot. "What's the matter with you, blubbering away like that? Hush up a minute and tell me what's wrong here."

The girl lifted a tear-streaked face, blotchy with embarrassment. Her nose was pink, her makeup smeared, her fine, pale hair coming loose from a complicated arrangement on top that looked like it had been done professionally. There were little sprigs of baby's breath tucked here and there like pale dried twigs. She paused to lick at a tear trickling toward her chin and then told a garbled tale of her boyfriend, a fight, being left penniless on the side of the freeway, too drunk to stand, picked up by a CHP cruiser and arrested on the spot. This was her twenty-first birthday and she was spending it in the county jail. She'd barfed on her dress, which she'd had on layaway for six months at Lerner's. Her daddy was on the city council and she didn't dare call home. By the time she got to this point, she burst into tears again.

The skinny woman on the mattress made a muffled response. "B.F.D. Big fuckin' deal."

Nettie, offended, turned on the woman, whom she apparently knew. She fired a dark look at the huddled form. "Mind your own business, bitch." She patted Heather awkwardly, unaccustomed to mothering but identifying with her plight. "Poor sweet baby. That's all right. That's just fine. Now don't you be upset. Everything's going to be all right. . . ."

I stretched out on my side, my head propped up on my hand. Bibianna had her back against the wall, her arms crossed for warmth. "What a crock of shit. People out there killing each other and they arrest someone like her. I don't get it. Call her old man and have him come get her out of here. He's going to call anyway once he figures out she's not home."

"How come you're so down on the police?" I asked.

Bibianna ran a hand through her hair, giving it a toss. "They killed my pop. My mom's Anglo. He was Latino. They met in high school and she was crazy about him. She gets knocked up and they got married, but it worked out okay."

"Why'd the cops kill him?"

"It was just something dumb. He was in a little market and lifted something minor—a package of meat and some chewing gum. The store manager caught him and they got into a tussle. Some off-duty cop pulled his gun out and fired. All for a pack of ground beef and some Chiclets for me. What a waste. My mother never got over it. God, it was awful to watch. She married some guy six months later and he turned out to be a real shit, knockin' her around. Talk about bad karma—the cops killed him, too. She'd kick him out. He'd disappear and then show up again, all contrite. Move in, take her money, beat the crap out of us. He's drunk half the time, doing 'ludes and coke, anything else he could get his hands on, I guess. If he wasn't pawing at her, he was pawing at me. I cut him once, right across the face—nearly took his eye out. One night, he got caught breaking into an apartment building two doors away from us. He barricaded himself in the place with a twelve-gauge. The cops swarmed all over the neighborhood. Television crews. SWAT teams and tear gas. Cops shot him down like a dog. I was eight. It's like how many times I gotta go through this, you know?"

"Sounds like they did you a service on that one," I said. Her smile was bitter, but she made no response.

"Your mother still alive?"

"Down in Los Angeles," Bibianna said. "What about you? You got family somewhere?"

"Not anymore. I've been on my own for years. I thought you were going to do my numbers," I said.

"Oh, yeah. What's your birthday?"

The date I was using on the fake ID was a match for mine. "May fifth," I said, and gave her the year.

"And me without a pencil. Hey, Nettie? You got something to write with?"

Nettie shook her head. "Not unless you count ChapStick."

Bibianna shrugged. "What the hell. Look here." She licked her finger and drew a big tic-tac-toe grid on the floor. She wrote the number 5 in the center and raised it to the third power. The lights in the cell were dim, but the floor was so grimy I could read the spit graph without squinting. She said, "This is great. See that? Five is the number of change and movement. You got three of them. That's hot. You know, travel and like that. Growth. You're the kind of person has to be out there doing things, moving. The zero out here means you don't have any limits. You can do anything. Like whatever you tried, you'd be good at, you know? But it can scatter you. Especially with all these fives here. Makes it tough to pick the thing you want to do. You'd need to have the kind of job that would never be the same. Know what I mean? You have to be in the middle of the action. . . ."

She looked at me for confirmation.

"Weird," I said, for lack of anything better.

Nettie shot us a look. She had one arm around Heather, who had leaned against her for warmth. "We're trying to get some sleep here. Could you keep it down?"

"Sorry," Bibianna said. She abandoned the reading and stretched out on the mattress, making herself comfortable. The gridwork she'd drawn seemed to glow in the half-light. The bulb in the cell remained bright, but we were reasonably warm. There was the sense of ongoing activity in the corridors beyond: a phone ringing, footsteps, the murmuring of voices, a cell door clanging shut. At intervals, the smell of cigarette smoke seemed to drift through the vents. Somewhere on the floor below us were the dormitory rooms that housed the fifty to sixty women doing county time in any given period. I could feel myself begin to drift. At least we were out of the rain and the bad guys couldn't get us. Unless "they" were somebody locked in the cell with us. Now, there was a thought.

"One good thing," Bibianna murmured drowsily.

"What's that?"

"They didn't find that joint. . . ."

"You are one lucky chick."

After that, there was quiet except for the occasional rustling of clothes as one of us turned on the mattress. The skinny white woman began to snore softly. I lay entertaining warm thoughts about Bibianna, realizing that from here on out, I'd remember her as the person I first got jailed with, a form of female bonding not commonly recognized. I'd have felt a lot better if Jimmy Tate had come to our rescue, but I really wasn't sure what he could have done to help. Right now, he was probably sitting in a cell over on the men's side in roughly the same fix. Crazy Jimmy Tate and Bibianna Diaz, what a pair they made. . . .

ten

the next thing I knew, there was a jingling of keys. My eyes popped open. One of the female jail officers was unlocking the door. She was short and solid, built like she spent a lot of time at the gym. The other four women in the cell were still asleep. The jail officer pointed at me. Bleary-eyed, I propped myself up on one elbow, pushing the hair out of my face. I pointed at myself—did she want me? Impatiently, she motioned me over to the door. I curled forward, rising to my feet as quietly as I could. There was no way to judge what time it was or how long I'd been asleep. I felt groggy and disoriented. Without a word, she opened the door and I passed through. I followed her down the corridor in my sock feet, wishing with all my heart that I could brush my teeth.

I once dated a cop who had an eight-by-eleven-foot desk built for himself, boasting that the surface was the same size as the two-man cells in Folsom prison. The room I was ushered into was about that size, furnished with a plain wood table, three straight-backed wooden chairs, and a bulb covered with a milky globe. I would have bet money there was recording equipment in there somewhere. I peered under the table. No sign of a wire. I sat down on one of the chairs, wondering how best to comport myself. I knew I was a mess. My hair felt matted, probably sticking straight up in places. I was sure my mascara and eyeliner now circled my eyes in that raccoon effect women so admire in themselves. The trampy outfit I'd concocted was not only wrinkled, but still felt faintly damp. Ah, well. At least if I were subjected to police brutality, I wouldn't mind bleeding on myself.

The door opened and Lieutenant Dolan appeared in company with another (I was guessing) plainclothes detective. I felt a spurt of fear for the first time since this ghastly ordeal had begun. Dolan was the last man I wanted to have as a witness to my current state. I could feel a blush of embarrassment rise up my neck to my face. Dolan's companion was in his sixties, with a thick shock of silver hair brushed away from a square face, deep-set eyes, and a mouth that pulled down at the corners. He was taller than Dolan and in much better shape, substantially built with wide shoulders and heavy-looking thighs. He wore a three-piece suit in a muted glen plaid with a denim blue shirt and a wide maroon tie with a floral pattern more fitting for a couch cover. He wore a gold ring on his right hand, a watch with a heavy gold band on his left. He made no particular attempt to be polite. If he had an opinion of me, nothing registered on his face. Together, the two men seemed to fill the room.

Dolan leaned out into the hall and said something to someone, then closed the door and pulled a chair up, straddling it. The other man sat down at the same time and crossed his legs at the knee with a slight adjustment of his trousers. He held his big hands loosely in his lap and made no eye contact.

Dolan seemed positively perky by comparison. "I'm having some coffee brought in. You look like you could use some."

"How'd you know I was here?"

"One of the deputies recognized you when you were booked in and called me," he said.

"Who's this?" I asked with a glance at the other man. I didn't think he should have the advantage of anonymity. He clearly knew who I was and enough about me to adopt an attitude of disinterest.

"Lieutenant Santos," Dolan said. Santos made no move. What was this, my week to meet hostile men?

I got up and leaned across the table with my hand held out. "Kinsey Millhone," I said. "Nice to meet you."

His reaction was slow and I wondered briefly just how rude he intended to be. We shook hands and his eyes met mine just long enough to register a stony neutrality. I had thought at first he disliked me, but I was forced to amend that assessment. He didn't have an opinion of me at all. I might be useful to him. He hadn't decided yet.

There was a rap at the door. Dolan leaned over and opened it. One of the deputies passed him a tray with three Styrofoam cups of coffee, a carton of milk, and a few loose packets of sugar. Dolan thanked him and closed the door again. He set the tray on the table and passed a cup to me. Santos reached forward and took his. I poured some milk in mine and added two packs of sugar, hoping to jump-start myself for the questions coming up. The coffee wasn't hot, but the flavor was exquisite, as soft and sweet as caramel.

"What happened to Jimmy Tate?" I asked.

"Right now, he's looking at homicide, murder two. A good attorney might get it knocked down to voluntary manslaughter, but I wouldn't count on it, given his history," Dolan said. "You want to fill us in on the shooting?"

"Sure," I said glibly, knowing I'd have to stretch the truth a bit. "California Fidelity asked me to investigate Bibianna Diaz for possible fraud in a claim she filed. I've been trying to get close enough to pick up concrete evidence, but so far all I've netted are some fashion tips. The dead man's name is

Chago. He's the brother of Raymond Something-or-other, who's an old flame of Bibianna's. I gather Raymond sent Chago and his wife, Dawna, up here to abduct Bibianna for reasons unknown. I can't get Bibianna to tell me what's going on, but they're clearly pissed. . . ."

Santos spoke up. "She and Raymond Maldonado were supposed to get married. She backed out. He doesn't take kindly to that sort of thing."

"I believe it," I said. "He apparently gave Chago instructions to 'smoke' her if she didn't cooperate."

Santos shifted in his chair, his voice flat. "That's all bluff. Raymond wants her back."

I looked from one to the other. "If you already know all this stuff, why ask me?"

Both men ignored me. I could see there wasn't going to be any point in getting crabby about the situation.

Dolan consulted a small spiral-bound notebook, leafing back a page. "What's the story on Jimmy Tate? How'd he get involved?"

"I'm not sure," I said. "I gather he and Bibianna have been embroiled in some kind of heavy-duty sexual relationship for the past couple of months. It seems to be serious—for the moment, at any rate." I went on, detailing the day's work, filling in as much as I knew about the dead man, which wasn't much, and about Jimmy Tate, which was considerable. As fond as I was of Tate, I couldn't see any reason to shield him from police scrutiny when it came to the shooting. There were other witnesses at the scene, and for all I knew, Dolan had already talked to them.

When I finished, there was a silence. I looked down at my hands, realizing that I'd systematically destroyed my now empty cup in the course of my narrative. I placed fragments on the table.

"And Tate did the shooting," Dolan said at length.

"Well, I didn't actually see that, but it's a fair assumption. He fired twice at the car, and after I hit the pavement, there were several more shots fired. I don't think Bibianna was armed."

"What about the other woman, Dawna? She have a gun?"

"Not that I saw, at least not in the restaurant. She could have had one stashed in the car, I suppose. Hasn't she turned up?" I didn't think Dolan was going to answer, but I liked pretending we were equals. Just us law enforcement types having a friendly little tête-à-tête here at the county jail.

Dolan surprised me with a response. "She took a hit. Nothing serious. Looks like a bullet ricocheted off something and grazed her collarbone. We picked her up in a phone booth a few blocks away. Probably interrupted a call to Raymond, though she wouldn't admit it."

"She's in the hospital?"

"For the time being. We'll hang on to her if we can, just to see what she has to tell us."

"About what?"

Dolan slid a look to Santos, like he was checking his hole card in a game of poker. I had the feeling Santos was making a decision. His expression didn't seem to change, but something must have been communicated between the two of them.

"I guess we better tell you what's happening," he said. His voice was rumbling and his delivery methodical. "You've stumbled into a bit of a sticky situation here."

"Oh, yeah, tell me about it."

Santos tipped his chair back against the wall and laced his hands across his head. "I head a task force made up of a number of agencies working to uncover what we believe is one of the biggest auto insurance fraud operations ever mounted in Southern California. You've worked in this business long enough to know what I'm talking about. Los Angeles County is the nation's automobile insurance fraud capital. Now it's spreading through Ventura and Santa Teresa counties. This particular ring is only one of dozens that generate an estimated five hundred million to a billion in phony claims every year. In this case, we're looking at fifteen lawyers, two dozen medical doctors, half a dozen chiropractors. On top of that, a rotating pool of some fifty to sixty individuals recruited to participate in the trumped-up incidents that comprise the claims." He pushed away from the wall, sitting upright, the front legs of the chair hitting the floor with a chirp. "You with me so far?"

"Oh, I'm here," I said.

He leaned forward, resting one arm on the table. I noticed his manner toward me was warming somewhat. He was a man animated by his work. I had no idea where he was going with the explanation, but it was clear he hadn't driven all the way up from Los Angeles in the dead of night just to deliver this deadpan rendition of his professional concerns. "We've put this case together bit by bit, piece by piece, over the last two years, and we're still not in a position to shut them down."

"I don't see the connection," I said. "Bibianna isn't part of the ring, is she?"

"She was. Raymond Maldonado started out as a 'capper.' At this point, we believe he's one of the kingpins, but we can't prove it yet. You know how these rings operate?"

"Not really," I said. "The people I'm used to dealing with are strictly amateurs."

"Well, the methods probably overlap to some extent," he said. "These days, the pros tend to avoid the big kill in favor of submitting fairly innocuous small claims that can be converted into large sums of money. They collect compensation for hard-to-disprove injuries like whiplash and lower back pain . . . you know the MO on that." He didn't really seem to require a response. "It's the capper's job to recruit the owner of a vehicle, usually someone unemployed who's hard up for cash. They take out an assigned-risk insurance policy on the car through the ring's agent. The capper then gives the car owner the names of two 'passengers'—totally fictitious—who 'ride' with the owner. He also comes up with names of people allegedly in the second car. We're talking about six or seven claims per incident. There's a variation on that one called 'bulls and cows,' where both cars are part of the scam. The 'bull'—the car with insurance—rams into the 'cow,' which is the uninsured car filled with passengers, all of whom suffer fictitious injuries. Most of the time the insured vehicle is some junker that's been insured without being examined."

"I've handled some claims where it's all faked—where there's not even a staged accident," I said.

"Oh, we got those, too. In Maldonado's case, some are paper accidents and some are staged. We got a line on this ring in the first place because the same set of names kept cropping up on supposedly unrelated claims. Same insurance agent, same attorney. The investigator finally had the names run through the computer and found links to twenty-five previous cases. Most of those were fictitious. One claimant's address turned out to be the La Brea tar pits. Another was an abandoned bus depot."

"What's their setup?" I asked.

"The ploy is called a 'swoop and squat,' which requires the use of two cars. They pull this maneuver out on one of the surface roads, probably five or six times a week. . . ."

"I'm surprised they don't try the freeways," I remarked.

He shook his head. "Too dangerous. These guys aren't interested in getting killed. What they do is choose a 'mark'—usually someone in an expensive vehicle or a commercial van—anything with a likelihood of being well insured. A vehicle they call the 'squat' car positions itself in front of the mark. These drivers are tooling down the road at thirty-five miles an hour, everybody minding his own business. At a signal, a second car, called a 'swoop,' cuts in front of the squat car, which brakes sharply, forcing the mark to rear-end it. The swoop car takes off. The squat and the mark pull over to the side like good citizens and exchange license numbers. At this point, the mark is usually pretty upset. Here, he's rear-ended another vehicle and he knows the responsibility is his. The driver in the squat car is full of sympathy—hell, he can afford to be—confirming just what the mark wants to believe, that it wasn't his fault."

"But his insurance company pays anyway," I said.

"Has to. You rear-end somebody, you're liable in this state. Turns out the squat's got all these 'problems' resulting from the accident. He sees a lawyer, who tells him he better see a doctor. Or he might be referred to a chiropractor. . . ."

"All of them in cahoots. . . ."

"All in cahoots," Lieutenant Santos said.

"And Bibìanna got involved in the ring through Raymond?"

"It looks that way. From the information we've pieced together, Raymond recruited her two years ago, though he's known her much longer. They were all set to get married about a year ago, but for some reason she pulled out. March, she did a disappearing act and a short time later surfaced in Santa Teresa. It looks, on the face of it, like she meant to go straight, but she had a hell of a time finding work. She finally picked up a job with a dry cleaning establishment, but it doesn't pay much, and in the end, I guess she couldn't resist trying a little scam or two of her own."

I was beginning to see how it all fit together. "And now my investigation has jeopardized yours."

"Not yet, but it looks like you're getting close. We can't afford to have you blundering in unawares, which is not the only problem we face. It looks like we've got a leak somewhere, critical information spilling through the pipeline into Raymond's ear. On at least three occasions, we've had raids set up . . . most recently on an auto body shop he owns in El Segundo. We have arrest and search warrants up the yin-yang. By the time we get there, the whole operation's been shut down and we walk into an empty facility—nothing left on the premises but a tire iron and a Pepsi can."

"I don't get it. What are you looking for?"

Lieutenant Santos paused to clear his throat. "Files, records. You follow the paper and it leads right to Raymond. We can pick him up, but by then the evidence has either been moved or destroyed and the DA throws the case out."

"So it was all for nothing, this raid you talked about?"

"Not quite. We took out the guy at the top, plus half a dozen other players—couple of attorneys and some MD's, two chiropractors. Raymond just turned around and expanded his piece of the operation. He used the bust to move himself up into the slot we cleared for him. We're going after him again, of course, but we have to track down this snitch first or it's the same story all over. In the meantime, we're trying another angle we think might work. The problem is, since we don't know where the leak is, it's hard to know who we can trust."

Dolan stirred restlessly, speaking up for the first time since Santos had started filling me in. "As much as I hate to say this, the breach might originate in one of the departments up here. We think that's how Raymond found out Bibianna was in Santa Teresa. She got arrested here a month ago and somebody dimed her out."

I could feel a quick spark of recollection. "Oh, yeah. I remember now she mentioned that. She's worried sick about Raymond finding her."

"She's got reason to worry. The man's got serious problems," Santos remarked. "I've seen the results of some of his handiwork."

"I still don't quite understand why you're telling me this stuff."

There was a brief silence and then Dolan spoke up. "If we can move you into position with these people, we might have another shot at them."

I stared at him blankly. "Oh, come on. You're not serious."

I looked from one to the other, but neither of them said a word. "How do you propose to do that?"

Dolan smiled with no particular mirth. "You've already done the hard part. You've established a relationship with Bibianna, which is something we can't do."

"What good is that? I thought you said she was finished with Raymond."

Dolan shrugged. "But he's not done with her. If Dawna managed to get word through to him, he's probably on his way up. Just stick with Bibianna, especially if he wants to take her back to L.A. with him. We want you on the inside."

"Wait a minute. I ran into Dawna over at the CF offices. What if she remembers me?"

"Don't worry about Dawna. We'll keep her out of circulation."

I ran a hand through my hair, which was so tricked out with hairspray, it felt like a wig. "Oh, man, you guys are really nuts," I said. "I don't know beans about undercover work."

"We're not asking you to go in there cold. . . ."

"Oh, that really sets my mind at rest."

He ignored that. "You'd be thoroughly briefed. We'd have backup in place, somebody who'd know where you were at all times."

I found myself looking from one to the other. I didn't trust them. I kept thinking there was a missing piece in here somewhere, something they were holding back. "Somehow I'm assuming you've tried it before."

"Without much luck," Santos said. "In this situation, we think a female could be effective. These guys don't credit women with much intelligence. You'd have some protective coloring despite the fact that you're not Hispanic yourself. Are you interested?"

"No."

Dolan put a hand behind his ear as if he hadn't heard right.

"I'm not going to do it, Lieutenant Dolan. It's been ten years since I was a police officer, and even then, I never did undercover work. Forget it. I'm not trained for that stuff and it's too damn dangerous."

"Sometimes it's the only option," Santos said.

"It might be your only option, but it's not mine."

Santos broke off eye contact. "You're looking at a year of

county jail time on this battery. Assaulting a police officer is a felony. We can have your license pulled."

I stared at him. "So now you're going to threaten me? Oh, great. I love that. Well, guess what? I'm not going to do your dirty work. I don't give a shit about Raymond Maldonado." I could feel the heat flash through my frame. "I hate to be bullied and I don't relish being beaten with a stick as the motivation for my behavior. You want a performance out of me, you better start someplace else."

Santos apparently intended to pursue the point, but Dolan made an impatient gesture, silencing him. "Let's just discuss it before you say anything."

"The answer's no."

Again, the two men exchanged a look I couldn't quite read. It seemed clear they were working every angle in the book, which was laughable in my view because I wasn't going to yield.

Dolan sat forward in his chair and his voice dropped a notch. "One more thing you should know and then you can do anything you want. Your friend Parnell Perkins was one of Raymond's employees. We think Raymond killed him, but we don't have any proof."

"I don't believe it."

"Perkins's real name was Darryl Weaver. He was working for an insurance company down in Compton. Raymond was running all his claims through Weaver until the two had a falling-out. Weaver left Los Angeles and moved up here, changed his name, and went to work for California Fidelity."

Suddenly I understood why he'd passed Bibianna's file on to Mary Bellflower. He probably assumed that Raymond and Bibianna were back together, that Raymond would be on his trail if he didn't do something quick. The sight of Bibianna's name must have made his heart stop. . . .

Santos came to life again, taking up the thread. "He came to us about a month ago and offered to cooperate. After he was killed, Santa Teresa Police Department ran the prints and notified us, which is why I'm here."

"That's why you buried the homicide investigation," I said, "to protect the larger one."

"That's right," Dolan replied. "We can't afford to have Raymond find out what we're up to. We haven't dropped the investigation, we're just pursuing it quietly."

The room was suddenly still. They let the silence accumulate. I took my time, stalling long enough to consider the implications. A little voice inside sang, Don't do it. Don't do it. "What's the timetable?" I said cautiously. I was hooked and they knew it.

Dolan looked at Santos. "Tight. Half a day at best."

"What are you really asking me to do?"

"Three things. Find the leak. Find out where the files are, and find us proof that Raymond killed your buddy."

Santos chimed in again, the two of them working me like sheepdogs. "You just tell us what you need. We'll give you anything you want."

Dolan said, "The object is to get yourself recruited. You can take it from there, with or without Bibianna's cooperation."

I thought it over briefly, all the time wondering at the wisdom of my consenting. I could feel my mental processes kick in despite the lingering misgivings. "If you're talking about staged accidents . . . it seems like it'd be smart to have a dummy policy in the name of Hannah Moore."

"Could you arrange that through CF?" Dolan asked.

"I could, but it'd be better if it came from you. You'd have to clear it with Mac Voorhies and it'd probably still have to go through channels."

"The fewer people who know the better, and we have to work fast," Dolan said.

"Is that going to present a problem?" Santos asked me.

I said, "I think CF would be willing to cooperate."

"We'll ask you to wear a wire," Santos said. "We can get a tech here by nine this morning and get a unit on you then."

"Won't Raymond and his cronies search me?"

Santos said, "I doubt it, but if they do, we'll be in earshot, don't forget."

Dolan seemed to sense I wasn't comforted. "If you're wired, we can have a car full of plainclothes parked half a block away. We want you to have all the protection you can get. This may be the best opportunity we have to get at these folks and we don't want to blow it. Any questions?"

"I'm sure I'll think of some."

Santos said, "We'll have another chance to brief you. Right now, we're going to put you back in with Bibianna. Morning comes, we'll get the two of you bailed out. Take the credit yourself. It's good to have the woman in your debt. We'll delay your release until the wire tech comes in."

"Won't she be suspicious if she's out and I'm not?"

"I'm sure you'll find a way to cover," Dolan said dryly. "In the meantime, make arrangements to connect with her later in the day."

"What if Raymond shows up before then?"

"We'll think of something else. Oh, and while we're on the subject . . ." Dolan jotted down a special telephone number where he could be reached at any hour. I tucked the slip of paper in my sock. He glanced at his watch and then got up as a signal to end the meeting.

I got to my feet. Santos and I shook hands. "What time is it?" I asked.

"Two minutes after four."

"I'm too old to be up at this hour," I said, and then glanced at Dolan. "Can you do me a favor? I left my black leather jacket in the restaurant and my VW's still parked in the Meat Locker side lot. I probably can't get over there until this afternoon. Could you ask about the jacket and warn the meter maid? I don't want to get towed or ticketed."

"Will do. You don't want to screw around with those meter gals," Dolan said. He flashed a smile and then held out his hand to me. "Thanks."

"I haven't done anything yet."

The female corrections officer took me back to the drunk tank and locked me in. I felt nearly sick with fatigue, my brain buzzing from the coffee, body dragging from the lack of sleep. I moved over to my mattress and sank down gratefully, curling up on my side with my face turned toward the others. Bibianna was awake, her eyes pinned on me suspiciously. "Where have you been?"

"The homicide detective had some questions about the shooting."

"Has Dawna been picked up?"

"She's in the hospital at the moment with superficial injuries. Tate's here on the men's side. They're talking about charging him with murder, but I don't see how they can. Manslaughter's more like it."

"Bastards."

"He'll survive."

"Yeah, I suppose." Bibianna seemed on the verge of drifting back to sleep.

I hesitated briefly, then held my nose and plunged right in. "By the way, while I was out there I put a call through to my bail bondsman, who's posting bail for both of us. He'll be over here at eight."

Her eyes flew open. "You're bailing me out, too? Why would you do that? I don't have no kind of money like that. You're talkin' five hundred bucks!"

"So you can owe me. Don't sweat it."

Her look was puzzled. "But why now? How come you didn't do that in the first place?"

"I just remembered I had money in a savings account. My car's in the shop. I was saving to get the tranny fixed. What the hell. Let it sit. It's not doing me any good here."

She hadn't bought my story yet. "I can't believe you'd do that."

The skinny woman piped up from the mattress in an aggravated tone of voice. "What's the matter with you, crazy? Take the money and shut your mouth."

Bibianna flicked a look at the woman and smiled in spite of herself. She studied me for a moment and then murmured a

"Thank you." Her eyes closed again. She turned over on her stomach and tucked her arms under her for warmth. Within minutes, she'd dozed off.

The air in the cell was permeated with the scent of sleeping bodies: damp socks, stale breath, unwashed hair. I had thought my cellmates might waken with my return, but no one else stirred. The light in the corridor shone dimly. The quiet became absolute. On the floor, I could still see the numerology grid Bibianna'd drawn for me with spit. Movement and change. Well, now wasn't that the truth?

eleven

What happened next was the result of a bureaucratic error for which responsibility was never assigned. The paperwork came down at six and Bibianna and I were mustered out. Just like that. There was no word from Dolan and Santos, no sign of the tech who was supposed to fit me with a wire. I kept waiting for the jail officer to call me back, take me aside under some pretext or other for the promised briefing. What was the deal here? Had there been a change of plans? For the life of me, I couldn't think of a reason to delay my release. I'd just have to play the situation as it came to me. I was carrying my personal property, still sealed in the clear plastic pouch. They'd returned our shoes, belts, and other potentially death dealing items, like tampons. I was feeling vile, but the first breath of fresh air restored my good spirits to some extent. After a mere four hours in the slammer, the freedom had a giddiness attached to it.

The morning was cold and foggy, the ground still saturated from the rain the night before. The scruffy hills around the jail looked serene. Little birdies sang. The passing traffic out on the freeway seemed to ebb and surge, rhythmic white noise, very restful, like the ocean at high tide. I longed for a shower, for breakfast, for privacy. I'd have to conjure up an excuse to separate from Bibianna, contact Dolan, and find out what the hell was going on. In the meantime, I was going to have to stick to her like glue.

The first order of business, of course, was to find a ride home. I checked my plastic pouch, feeling like a mental patient just released from the institution. I had ten bucks in cash, which I decided to blow on a taxi. I'm too cheap for cabs as a rule, but I really felt I deserved this one. Bibianna and I clopped down the long drive that led away from the jail. I was a sight to behold, tank top and wrinkled black pants, my little white socks turning black where the dye on my wet pumps had rubbed off. Bibianna wasn't looking all that hot herself. The red of her dress was unflattering by day, a mismatch for the spike heels, which the rain had pulled out of shape. She was applying a fresh coat of lipstick, open compact held in front of her face as she walked. She'd stripped off her panty hose, which had been riddled with runs after our adventures of the night before. Her legs looked pale and scrawny in the harsh light of day, and her dress was as pleated across the lap as the bellows of an accordion. Oh, well. I suppose there are times when you rejoice just to find yourself on the move again. Behind us were the chain-link fences, incessant lights, the locks, the barred windows. In spite of our liberation, I couldn't think of a thing to say to her. "Thanks . . . it's been fun . . . we'll have to do this again sometime soon." The simple rules of etiquette didn't seem to apply.

Bibianna tucked her compact in her purse, her manner anxious.

"Did they ask you about the shooting?" I asked.

"Not yet. Some homicide cop is supposed to come around to my place later today."

"What are you going to tell them?"

"Who cares about that? I gotta find a way to get outta here before Raymond shows up. . . ."

I felt an anxiety of my own. What the hell was going on here? Where was Dolan? What was I supposed to do?

Suddenly, Bibianna clutched my arm, digging her nails into my flesh. "Sweet Jesus," she whispered, staring dead ahead.

I followed her gaze, realizing belatedly that her attention was riveted on a dark green Ford that was parked down the road, its rear end lowered until the pan nearly scraped the ground. Her fear was so palpable that the hair rose up on the back of my neck.

"Who's that?"

"It's Raymond. Oh, God." Her voice broke. Tears leapt to her eyes and she made a peculiar squeaking sound in her throat. I assessed the situation rapidly, without knowing quite what to do. Of all the bad luck. Apparently, Dawna had managed to put a call through to him.

He'd been leaning on the front fender, watching cars pass on the frontage road. When he caught sight of us, he began to amble in our direction.

"Bibianna, cool it. Just calm down. Let's head back to the jail. . . ."

She shook her head. "Even if the cops took us home, he'd catch up eventually. Don't leave me. Swear you won't. Whatever happens, just go along with it. Don't set him off or he'll tear the place apart and you along with it."

"All right, all right. Come on now. Just be cool. I'm not going anywhere."

"Promise you won't leave me."

"I promise," I said.

At first, I didn't get it. At that distance, the guy looked like anybody else. He was tall and very slender, with wide shoulders and a narrow waist. From what I could see of him, he was dressed like a fashion plate: leather sport coat, pleated trousers, pointy black patent-leather shoes capped with silver at the toes, mirrored sunglasses. He could have been Latino or Italian, dark hair and olive skin. I placed him in his early thirties. He had his hands in his pockets and his manner seemed relaxed.

Bibianna's fingers were ice cold. She clung to my hand the way a friend might in the middle of a horror movie just before the guy with the butcher knife leaps out. I couldn't see anything in his appearance that would warrant her response.

When he reached us, he took his sunglasses off. He had dark thick lashes, a full mouth, a dimple in his chin. Once he was in close range, I realized there was something wrong. His eyes had rolled back in his head, leaving narrow slits of white along the lower rims. His face and body underwent a series of convulsive movements; he blinked his eyes, the corner of his mouth jumped involuntarily, his lips opened wide, then his head jerked back twice. The effect was weird—a sequence of behaviors that set his whole body in motion, culminating in a sound that was half shout, half cough. He moved his right arm, rolling it in its socket as if to loosen tension. In memory, a buzzer sounded dimly, and I recalled the existence of some medical condition that produced just this effect—tics and shouts. He made no reference to it, nor did Bibianna, who seemed more concerned about his reaction to Chago's death.

"I didn't do it. I swear to God. I didn't kill him. I'm sorry. It was an accident. Oh, please. Raymond, I didn't have anything to do with it. . . ."

His expression had softened, becoming nearly wistful as he took her by the shoulders and pulled her in close to him, rubbing his hands up and down her bare arms. "You don't know how happy I am to see you. . . ."

I could see her tense up, holding herself away from him slightly, though she couldn't do much without perhaps risking some kind of outburst. He began to nuzzle her hair. "Oh, baby. Angel. Sweet thing, I'm glad to see you," he murmured, his voice soft. "This is beautiful. I really missed you, you know that?" He drew back from her then, clamping his fingers around her jaw so that she was forced to look at him. "Hey, it's all right. Everything's okay. Don't worry." His gaze moved across to me. "Who is this?" His head jerked twice.

"Hannah Moore," I said.

She flicked a look at him. "This is Raymond Maldonado."

He held his hand out. "Nice to meet you. Sorry about all this. My brother was killed last night."

We shook hands. His were warm and soft, his grip firm. "I'm sorry about your brother. That's terrible." The pleasantries created an air of unreality.

Raymond glanced at Bibianna. "You ready?"

"I'm not going. Raymond, I mean it. I'm done with all that. I don't want to go back to Los Angeles. I told you. I didn't have anything to do with . . ." He took her arm and began to walk her toward the car. I could see her mouth twist and his fingers dug into her elbow painfully. She babbled on. He raised a hand as if to silence her, warding off the spill of words. She pressed a hand to her lips. He turned his head to one side. He hunched a shoulder, did a neck roll, and took a deep breath, eyes sliding up in his head. His face jerked to the right, once, twice. His eyes came open, the irises sliding into view—large, dark brown, and clear. He continued toward the car.

I followed without invitation, calculating rapidly. Here was my quarry, Raymond Maldonado in the flesh. I knew I was being offered the perfect opportunity, but I'd had no prep time. If I went in without a briefing, I could blow the whole operation. I couldn't afford to start playing undercover cop, but what choice did I have? He was walking so rapidly, I had to do a quickstep to keep up.

Bibianna was getting into passive resistance, slowing down, hanging back. "Listen, Raymond. Maybe I could go another time, okay? Hannah's been talking about going home with me," she said. "And we do have plans. . . ."

He turned and smiled at me. "We're getting married."

"Today?"

He shook his head. "Soon, though. It was all set up, but she said she wasn't ready. Next thing I know she takes off. Just like that, she's gone. Doesn't even leave me a note. I wake up one morning and she's disappeared. . . ."

Bibianna's face was drawn and pale. "I'm sorry. I didn't mean to hurt you, Raymond, but what could I do? What was I going to say to you? I tried to tell you. . . ."

He raised a finger to his lips and then he pointed it at her reprovingly. "You don't leave a guy, Bibianna." He turned to me, one hand out, palm up, arguing his case. "I've been in love with this woman for how many years now? Six? Eight? What am I going to do with her, huh?"

Bibianna was silent, her eyes full of dread. I couldn't believe the change that had come over her. All the confidence was gone, the high energy, the sexiness. My own mouth was getting dry, and a whisper of fear tickled me in the small of the back.

We reached the car. Another fellow stepped out, a Latino with a dark knit watch cap pulled down to his ears. His eyes were black, as flat and dull as spots of old paint. He had acne scars on his cheeks and a mustache made up of about fourteen hairs, some of which looked like they were drawn on by hand. He was my size. He wore sharply pressed khaki pants with numerous pleats across the front and an immaculate white undershirt. Tufts of underarm hair were visible, straight and dark. His bare arms were muscular, tattoos extending from his shoulders to his wrists—a graphic rendition of Donald Duck on his right and Daffy Duck on his left.

"That's a copyright violation," I remarked, nearly giddy with anxiety.

"That's Luis," Raymond said.

He had a gun. He held the rear car door open, like a well-mannered chauffeur.

Bibianna balked, one arm braced against the car. "I'm not going without Hannah."

Raymond seemed taken aback. "Why not?"

"She's my friend and I want her with me," she said.

"I don't even know this girl," he said.

Bibianna's eyes flashed. "Goddamn it! This is just like you, Raymond. You say you love me. You say you'll do anything. First thing I ask for, all I get is an argument. Well, I'm sick of it!"

"Okay, okay. She can go if she wants. Anything you say."

Bibianna turned to me with a look filled with mute pleading. "Please. Just for a few days."

I felt myself shrug. "I got nothing else to do," I said.

Bibianna got in first, sliding across the backseat. Raymond slid in beside her. I hesitated briefly, wondering at the wisdom of it.

Luis turned the gun so that it was pointing at my chest. It clarified my thinking most emphatically.

I got into the backseat. The dashboard was covered in white terrycloth with "Raymond and Bibianna" machine-stitched in glossy green script across the face of it. A rosary hung from the rearview mirror along with a Sacred Heart of Jesus, bleeding. The interior of the car, including front and back seats, was upholstered in white acrylic teddy bear fur. There was a Radio Shack car phone on the front seat. All the car lacked was a collection of bobbleheads on the rear . . . or a four-inch Virgin Mary with little magnetized feet. The minute I got in, I knew I'd made a mistake.

Luis started the engine without a word. The mufflers sounded like distant jackhammers as he pulled out onto the road. He kept both hands on the steering wheel with his arms fully extended, his trunk and head inclined back. He made a U-turn and sped toward the freeway. Raymond's ticcing recurred at perhaps three-minute intervals, sometimes less. I found myself unnerved at first, especially in the absence of any explanation. The others seemed to take it for granted. At first, I would jump every time he did it, but I found myself adjusting, marveling that anybody had to live like that. Was there no help for him?

Bibianna now seemed to be in the mood for an argument, maybe to forestall any amorous intentions. "How'd you find out about last night?"

"Dawna called and told me some of it before the cops picked her up. Who's the guy?"

"What guy?"

"The guy last night shot Chago."

"How do I know who he was? Just somebody in the restaurant with a gun."

"Dawna said you were with him."

"I was there by myself."

"Not what she says."

"She said that? It's bullshit. What'd he look like? She tell you that?"

"She didn't have a chance. Squad car pulled up and she hung up. Said some chick was there, too."

"She's blowin' smoke up your skirt. What a bitch! I was there by myself when Chago showed up with a gun. Maybe the guy was an off-duty cop or just your average citizen with a gun."

Raymond's face darkened. "That would really piss me off. What's the matter with people? Too many fuckin' handguns around." He turned and looked at me. "Every day in the paper, somebody gets blown away. *L.A. Times*. You read Metro? Scares the shit out of me." He held a hand up, blocking words in. "You know that slogan says, 'Guns don't kill people. People kill people.'? What a crock that is."

"Luis has a gun," I remarked helpfully.

"That's different. He's a lieutenant. He's like a bodyguard to me. I can't believe some joker in a restaurant shoots my brother for no fuckin' reason."

All the little birdies had flown out of this man's tree. I sat with my eyes straight ahead and my mouth shut, remembering what Bibianna had told me about his temper.

Raymond turned to Bibianna and started kissing her, his hands moving across her breasts with an intimacy I found embarrassing. She was compliant, but she rolled an eye at me frantically across his shoulder. I looked out the window.

I leaned forward and tapped Luis on the shoulder, trying the only Spanish phrase I'm familiar with. "Uh, *habla usted inglés?*"

"Shit, lady. What do I look like, a retard?" he said. His English wasn't even spoken with an accent, and I had to wonder if the gangbanger outfit was an affectation.

"Oh. Well, could you pull over at this next corner and let me the fuck out? I gotta make a quick phone call."

This did not produce the desired results.

I kept my tone conversational as I turned to Raymond, placing my mouth up close to his ear. "Excuse me, Raymond. Could you have the guy let me out up here?"

Raymond had run his hand up under Bibianna's skirt, pushing the fabric back, running a finger under the rim of her underpants. There was nothing remotely sexual about it. He was claiming his rights. I could hear her murmuring, "Fantastic . . . oh, baby, that's great," anything to appease and placate his neediness. The driver caught my eye in the rearview mirror and winked at me conspiratorially. He flipped on the car radio to mask the escalating sounds. Salsa music filled the car. This was repellent.

I was fully prepared to fling myself out, risking concussion and broken bones, just to escape from this brothel of faux fur and religious artifacts. I waited until the car slowed as we approached the on ramp to the freeway, then I slid my hand under the door handle and gave it a yank. Nothing happened. Both of the window cranks had been removed in the rear. I leaned my forehead against the tinted glass, staring out the window. Behind me, I could hear Raymond fumble with his belt buckle and the zipper to his pants. This was worse than an X-rated video. I turned and stared at them.

"God, *Bibianna*," I said loudly. "How *rude*! How do you

think I *feel* sitting here while you *screw* some stud! Why don't you keep your hands to yourself, okay?"

Raymond turned a sex-groggy face toward me, his eyes at half-mast. His mouth seemed gorged, his chin laved in lipstick, his hair standing straight up. The whole car smelled like hormones, sex juice, and underpants. Luis, all asmirk, tried to peer into the backseat through the rearview mirror.

I turned on him savagely. "Hey, Jack. What are *you* lookin' at?" And then to Raymond. "I'm sorry, Raymond. I know it's not your fault how these people act."

Bibianna pushed herself into an upright position, doing what she could to pull her skirt back into place. She murmured, "Sorry." She had a big hickey on her neck where Raymond had been slurping away on her.

Raymond actually seemed embarrassed, tucking in his shirt. He went through a sequence of behaviors that included the head jerking and the neck rolls.

I plowed right on. "I told her I got a steady boyfriend in the slammer," I said to him. "The last thing I need is watching you two get it on. God. She's got no class." I sat back in the seat, brushing imaginary lint off my black pants.

Raymond pulled out a handkerchief and wiped some of Bibianna's lipstick off his chin. His smile was sheepish. "Take it easy. It's not her fault. She can't help it," he said.

"Well, I get sick of hearing her brag about you. Why can't she keep her opinions to herself?"

"She brags about me?"

"No, Raymond. I'm just saying that to hear myself talk," I said. "I don't suppose I could trouble anybody for some grub. We haven't had breakfast and I'm starving to death."

Raymond leaned forward and gave Luis a thump on the head. "What's the matter with you? Pull off here. Didn't you hear what the lady said?"

Raymond studied me with amusement, talking to Bibianna

over his shoulder. "I like your friend, here. She's got some spunk."

"This isn't *spunk*, Raymond. This is irritation," I said. Bibianna eyed me uneasily, but I was really on a roll. I was making up Hannah's character as I went along, and it was liberating as hell. She was short-tempered, sarcastic, outspoken, and crude. I could get used to this. License to misbehave.

Raymond smiled at me.

"This okay, boss?" Luis, of the handsomely tattooed arms, was slowing near the entrance to a McDonald's on upper State Street.

"This okay with you?" Raymond said to me. He seemed genuinely concerned that the restaurant meet with my approval.

"Raymond, this is perfect. Way to go."

I ate three Egg McMuffins. If it had been 10:00 A.M., I'd have had a couple of QP's with cheese instead. Bibianna couldn't eat. She sat and picked at an apple Danish while Luis and Raymond, with a flair for the Gallic, ordered French toast and French fries, with a side of maple syrup. I had spotted a telephone in the narrow corridor leading to the ladies' room, but the wall-mounted instrument was in plain view of the table where the four of us sat. Raymond kept his arm loosely draped around Bibianna's shoulders, rubbing her upper arm in a manner meant to be sexy. Guys learn to do that in high school and it's very irritating. She was back to being passive, obsequious, and subdued. I wanted to see her sass him. Resist. I wanted her to thumb her nose at him. It was not going to help her to act like a whipped dog. It was time she stood up for herself again. If she acted like a victim, the guy was going to treat her like one.

I got up from the table. "I gotta go to the can. Come with me, Bibianna. You can rat my hair."

"I'm fine."

"Well, I'm not. Could you pardon us, Raymond? We have to go do some girl stuff."

"Have at it," he said.

I kissed my fingertip and placed it on the tip of his nose. "You're a peach."

He slid out of the booth so Bibianna could get up.

twelve

In the ladies' room, she turned on the faucet and splashed some cold water in her eyes. I pulled out a paper towel and passed it to her. She buried the lower half of her face in the paper toweling, staring at herself in the mirror above the sink. She wiped her hands and threw the paper away. "Thanks for what you did in the car. God, I can't stand this. I really hate his guts."

"He's certainly crazy about you," I said.

She moved into one of the stalls, trying the window above the toilet. "Shit. This is nailed shut. Do you think there's another way out of here?"

"I don't know. I'll check," I said. I was in a bit of a bind with Bibianna, wanting to help her without actually giving up proximity to Raymond Maldonado. I went over to the door and opened it a crack, making a show of searching for a rear exit. All I caught sight of was Raymond doing one of his head jerks. The public pay phone on the wall was tantalizingly near, but Luis was bound to spot me if I tried to use it. I closed the door again. "What's the matter with Raymond?"

"He's getting worse," she said morosely. "I never saw him so bad."

"Yeah, but what *causes* that?"

"It's called Tourette. TS, whatever that is. It's like something in his nervous system—neurological and like that. All I know is he does that stuff over and over and sometimes he gets into uncontrollable rages. He's got pills he won't take because he can't stand the side effects."

"He's had it all his life?"

"I guess so. He doesn't ever talk about it much."

"But he's not doing anything for it?"

"Smokin' dope helps, he says, and he sometimes shoots up."

"Is that why you left, because of the Tourette?"

"I left because he's a jerk! The other I could live with, but the guy's turning mean. It's got nothing to do with his condition," she said. "Jesus, we gotta figure out how to get out of here." She moved into the second stall and tried the window there. Also locked. "The hell with it. We're going to have to make a break for it some other way. I wish Tate were here."

I said, "You and me both, kid. You think Raymond knows you're involved with him?"

"God, I hope not. He's so jealous, he can't see straight."

"How'd you meet Tate?"

"He crashed a costume party last Halloween. Dressed as a cop. Everybody thought it was a joke, except me. I can smell a cop a mile off." She took a brush from her handbag and ran it through her hair. "It's really different with Jimmy."

"Well, that's obvious," I said. "I take it you're in love with him."

She smiled fleetingly for the first time since we'd left the jail. "I better be. We got married week before last. That's why my place is coming up for rent. I'm moving in with him."

The door flew open. I must have jumped a foot. It was Luis with his .45 and his little smirking mustache. "All right, ladies. Time to go. Speed it up. Raymond says you been in here long enough."

I waved at him dismissively. "Oh, come off it, Luis. What is it with you? Running around acting like an idiot. I still have to tee-tee and so does she."

He colored faintly. "Snap it up."

"Right," I said, moving over to the first stall. Out of the corner of my eye, I saw him shove the gun in his waistband and back out of the room.

Ten minutes later we were on the road.

So that's how I came to be speeding down 101 in a low-rider Wednesday morning, October 26. Vera's wedding was coming up on Monday and I was going to miss it, sure as shit. If Raymond killed Bibianna, he was going to have to kill me, too. By Halloween, I'd probably be in the long-term parking lot at LAX, crammed in the trunk of some stranger's vehicle. Even in the hot sun, it can sometimes take days before anybody picks up the scent.

Luis drove while Raymond sat in the front seat fiddling with the radio. At irregular intervals, he would go through his ticcing sequence. If he was talking to Luis, the tics would seem to subside, only to assail him with a vengeance as soon as his mouth was shut. Bibianna had curled up on the backseat in a troubled sleep. At least now she wouldn't have to worry about being quizzed by the Santa Teresa cops. I was feeling wired. In the past couple of hours, I'd passed through fatigue to exhaustion and out to the other side. God knows my work exposes me to an occasional unsavory character, but I really don't like violence or danger or threats to my health. My semiannual visit to the dentist is as masochistic as I care to get. Yet here I was in the company of these *vatos*, wondering how I could get to the telephone number Dolan had given me. I missed my beloved handbag, my jacket, and my gun. At the same time, I confess, I felt extraordinarily alive. Perhaps I was merely experiencing one of life's peak moments before the bottom dropped out.

At Oxnard, we left the freeway and continued south on Highway 1, winding our way through the southeastern section of town. We passed the Naval Construction Battalion Center at Port Hueneme (pronounced "Y-knee-me"). The road began to parallel the deep blue green of the ocean, which was far off to our right. The beaches were deserted except for an occasional fisherman casting his line out into the water. The sand had been packed down and darkened by the rain, but the sky was now cloudless, a clear azure blue. The morning sun had burned the fog away, and I could see straight out to the horizon. On the landward side, loose sand swept down to the highway from rosy beige cliffs creased into folds by erosion, hills flattening out to pale gray scrub, freckled with vegetation.

After we passed Point Dume, houses began to appear, filling the widening strip of land between the road and the ocean, properties piling up rapidly as the miles accrued. In the parking lane, RVs and pickups were lined end to end. Guys in shorts and wet suits unloaded surfboards and windsails. By the time we reached Malibu, apartments and condos and single-family dwellings were crowded cheek by jowl, the architectural mix ranging all the way from chateaus to beach shacks, Italian villas, Tudor mansions, Cape Cod, and concrete. The rich folk with taste had apparently been elsewhere the day the planning commission took a vote. (What planning commission?) As a consequence, the road was densely lined now with retail businesses, signs advertising Texaco, Malibu Lumber, Crown Books, Shoes, Fast Frame, Jack-in-the-Box, Motel, Malibu Inn, Liquor, Jimmy's Ribs at the Beach, Budget Cars, Palm and Card Reading, Shell Gas, Realty, Arco AM/PM, Malibu Travel, Motel, Liquor, Pizza, Real Estate, Locksmith, Shoe Repair, Malibu Fish Market . . . a vulgar hodgepodge of neon, billboards, and blinking lights. Traffic was piled up in a perpetual gridlock of Mercedeses, BMWs, and Jaguars.

We hit the light where Sunset Boulevard dead-ends at Pacific Coast Highway. The woman in the little sports car idling next to us turned an uneasy eye on Luis with his watch cap and his Walt Disney arms. He had a truly vile suggestion he was kind enough to share with her. Raymond gave his head a censoring thump. Maybe that's why he wore the watch cap, to keep the brain damage to a minimum.

Luis rubbed his head irritably. "Hey, man. Take it easy."

"You take it easy," Raymond shot back with an apologetic glance at me. It was clear he'd pegged me as the refined one in the crowd.

When the light changed, Luis pulled out with a series of jerks that left the rear suspension bucking. Within minutes we had passed from prosperity to privation.

Our destination was a beach town a few miles south of the airport in an area tainted with poverty. To the east, the ghetto communities of Compton, South Gate, and Lynwood were rigidly subdivided into gang turfs where some fifteen to twenty homicides marred the average weekend. Here, there were only endless drab buildings decorated with angular territorial declarations thrown up by the taggers with cans of black spray paint. Wait until future cryptographers resurrect those stone tablets. Even the passing city buses were defaced, mobile messengers bearing insults from one gang to the next. The streets were littered with trash and old tires. The winos had already plucked up all the bottles and cans, anything that could be recycled in exchange for Thunderbird revenues. A dilapidated sofa sat on the curb as if waiting for a bus. Listless ghetto warriors loitered near a corner market. On the island side of the four-lane boulevard, every third storefront had been boarded up. Those still doing business were protected by steel bars across plate-glass windows papered over with advertisements.

I saw a Burger King, a Sav-On drugstore, a corner record shop with a big sign reading CLOSED, a post office branch with a U.S. flag drooping from its pole. On the ocean side of the street, there was a tired mix of small frame houses and boxy apartment buildings. All the yards seemed to be raw dirt surrounded by chain-link fences. The poor sections of every city I've seen have the following elements in common: sagging porches, flaking paint, grass that's tenacious if it grows at all, vacant lots filled with rubble, Pepsi-Cola signs, idle children, cars with flat tires permanently parked at the curb, abandoned houses, lethargic men whose eyes turn vacuously as you pass. Violence is a form of theater that only the disenfranchised can afford. Admission is cheap. The bill of fare is an ever-changing drama of life and death, drugs and stick-ups, drive-bys, retaliations, the fearfulness of mothers who look on in anguish from the sidelines. As often as not, it's the bystanders who fall prey to the spray of random bullets.

We cut inland, driving past six square blocks of housing projects. I could feel anxiety stir like a boiling sickness.

By the time we reached Raymond's place, I had no idea what part of Los Angeles we were in. We parked the Ford out in front of a three-story apartment building, across the street from an automobile salvage yard. There were probably forty units in the apartment complex, arranged in tiers around a concrete courtyard. At first glance, it didn't seem all that shabby to me. The neighborhood itself wasn't nearly as impoverished as some we'd traversed.

It was midmorning, and even with a nip still in the air, most of the apartment doors stood open. The interiors I glimpsed were crowded, overfurnished, and dismal. The televisions all seemed to be tuned to the Anglo soaps, while the radios, sitting atop the sets, played Hispanic music, curiously at odds with the gringo images. There were Halloween decorations everywhere, but some had been up so long, the pumpkins were getting soft and the crepe-paper skeletons were powdered with dust.

The four of us clambered up a rear staircase to the second floor, where we turned left, proceeding to an apartment that overlooked the street. "Is this your place we're going to?" I asked Raymond. He was walking with Bibianna, the two of them just ahead of me. Luis was bringing up the rear in case I tried to bolt.

"This is for when we get married," Raymond said with a shy glance at her. He felt in his pocket in a sudden recollection. He pulled out a key on a metal ring with a big plastic M attached, probably for Maldonado. He handed it to Bibianna. My guess was he'd meant it to be a ceremonial moment, but she shoved it in her handbag, barely honoring it with a look. Her face was stony and he seemed embarrassed that she showed no enthusiasm for matters that obviously obsessed him.

The problem with real life is there's no musical score. In movies, you know you're in danger because there's an ominous chord underlining the scene, a dissonant melodic line that warns of sharks in the water and boogermen behind the door. Real life is dead quiet, so you're never quite sure if there's trouble coming up. A possible exception is stepping into a strange apartment full of guys in hairnets. Personally, I've never understood how wearing a hairnet ever came to symbolize the baddest of the bad-asses on the street. There were five of them, all Hispanics in their late teens or early twenties, all wearing heavy wool Pendleton shirts buttoned up to their chins. Three were sitting around the kitchen table, one with his girlfriend on his lap. A second girl sat with her bare legs outstretched, tight skirt hiked up to midthigh. She was smoking a cigarette, practicing smoke rings through pouty lips painted bright red. Two guys lounging against the wall came to attention as Raymond came in the door. On the wall was a large handmade sign with "R.I.P." at the top and Chago's name in caps below, a pair of praying hands and a crucifix drawn in the space between. Someone had tacked several snapshots of Chago on the wall nearby, along with what looked like a testimonial of some kind. Among the piles of papers on the table was a stack of homemade flyers, reproductions of the same neatly hand-lettered prose. From the somber expressions and the number of beer bottles evident, I gathered these were Chago homies and that we'd interrupted an impromptu wake. I checked for Raymond's reaction, but he had none. Did he feel no sorrow for his brother's death?

I willed myself to behave casually, assuming an air of nonchalance. What did I have to fear? After all, I wasn't a prisoner, I was Raymond's guest. I could pick up the information for Lieutenant Dolan and then head on home. Granted, I don't usually hang out on gang turf, but I try to be openminded. There were cultural differences here that I couldn't even guess at, let alone define. That didn't make anybody bad, right? So why expect the worst? *Because you don't know what the hell you're doing,* a little voice inside me said.

The air was gray with smoke, some of it marijuana, a substance I haven't abused since I was in high school (except for that brief period when Daniel Wade was in my life). The decor, at a glance, consisted of royal blue shag carpeting and the kind of furniture sold on the roadsides across the border in Mexico. (Also in Orange County on Euclid, south of the Garden Grove Freeway.) It looked like Raymond had made an attempt to upgrade the place, covering the entire large wall to my left with smoky gold mirrored tiles. Unfortunately, the tiles had recently been smashed with a kitchen chair, which had been tossed to one side, its chrome legs askew. Most of the glass had been swept up, but I could see signs of blood on the bare wall behind. It wasn't bright red or dripping, but it was clear something frightful had taken place here not long ago. No one referred to the destruction. Raymond showed no curiosity at the sight, which lent support to the notion that he was responsible. Bibianna took it in at a glance but said nothing. Maybe she knew better than to mention the fact. I tore my gaze away.

On the right, the L of a kitchen was visible, every surface in it piled high with used paper plates, beer bottles, ashtrays, empty cans of Rosarito refrieds. The air smelled of cilantro, corn tortillas, and hot lard. Five brown grocery sacks bulged with refuse, grease showing through in big dark polka dots. On one bag, a quicksilver something disappeared from view.

One of the guys at the metal-topped kitchen table labored over a form he was filling out in pencil. His face was dark with frustration. His handgun rested casually on a stack of completed forms, serving as a paperweight. Fleetingly, I wondered if he was an illegal alien filling out fake INS documents. Behind him, daylight poured through a big picture window that cast him in silhouette. In the event of a drive-by, he'd be picked off like a metal bear in a shooting gallery. I heard Raymond call him Tomas, but I couldn't catch the rest of the conversation.

Of the two fellows leaning against the wall, one was wearing a Sony Walkman, a handgun shoved down in his waistband. The other played a hollow note across the mouth of an empty Dos Equis beer bottle. Both bore a passing resemblance to Raymond, and I wondered if they were related—his brothers or cousins. Apparently they all knew Bibianna, but none made eye contact. The two women seemed uneasy at her arrival, exchanging a guarded look.

I wasn't introduced, but my presence generated a sly interest. I was surveyed by several pairs of male eyes, and somebody made a remark that amused those who heard it. Luis appeared again, a Dos Equis in hand. He took up a squatting position, hunkering against the wall, body thrust forward slightly, his head thrown back, staring down his nose at me. There was something arrogant in his bearing, suggesting the sexual superiority of renegades and outlaws. Whatever his purpose, its effect was to establish his claim on me. The other guys seemed to posture for one another but displayed no plumage.

At the table, an argument broke out among the three who seemed to be speaking some *cholo* mix of Spanish and fractured English. I couldn't understand a word, but the prevailing tone was quarrelsome. Raymond shouted something I was glad I couldn't translate. The guy with the pencil and paper went back to work with a sulkiness that didn't bode well.

Bibianna, unimpressed with the lot of them, flung her purse in a chair and slipped out of her high-heeled shoes. "I'm taking a shower," she said, and padded out of the room. Raymond moved to the telephone, where he punched in numbers with his back half-turned. "Alfredo, it's me. . . ." He dropped his voice into a range I couldn't hear. From the rear, as he talked, I saw him go through a series of rapid tics, almost like a pantomime or a game of charades.

I thought I'd make myself inconspicuous while I decided what to do next. I looked around for a seat and changed my mind abruptly. Just inside the door, about three feet away, there was a pit bull. I don't know how I'd missed the mutt, but there he was. The dog had a brindle coat with a white chest and white legs. His head was wide and thick, ears uncropped, but tucked in close like a bat's. There was a leather collar around his thick neck with metal spikes sticking out. Was the blood on the wall connected with the dog? A length of slack chain was attached to his collar, extending about three feet, the other end wrapped around the leg of the oversize royal blue couch. The dog emitted a low humming growl while it stared at my throat. Dogs and I don't get along that well in the best of circumstances. I'm hardly ever smitten with a beast that looks like it's prepared to rip out my carotid artery.

One of the guys snapped at the dog in Spanish, but the animal didn't seem to understand the language any better than I did. The guy jerked his head in my direction, the knot of his hairnet sitting in the middle of his forehead like a spider in a web. "Don't make no sudden moves and don't never touch his head. He'll tear your arm off."

"I'm sorry to hear that. What's his name?" I asked, praying it wasn't Cujo.

"Perro," he said. And then with a grin, "Means 'dog' in Spanish."

"You think that up all by yourself?" I said mildly.

Everybody laughed. Ah, they do speak English, I thought. His smile was thin. "He hates gringas."

I glanced at the dog again and shifted my weight, trying to ease away. How could the dog know my nationality? He flattened his ears and exposed his teeth. His upper lip curled back so far, I could see up his nose.

"Hello, Perro," I sang. "Nice dog. Good doggie." Slowly, I allowed my gaze to drift, thinking the eye contact was perhaps too aggressive for the little fellow's taste. Wrong move. The dog lunged, erupting into a savage barking that shook his entire body. I shrieked involuntarily, which the guys seemed to think was hilarious. The couch humped about four inches in my direction, bringing him almost in range of me. I could actually feel the hot breath of his bark against my leg like little puffs of wind. "Uh, Raymond?"

Raymond, still talking on the phone, held a hand up, impatient at the interruption.

"Could somebody call the dog, please?" I repeated the request, this time audibly.

Raymond snapped his fingers and the dog sat down. The guy with the Sony Walkman smirked at my relief. Raymond put a hand across the mouth of the receiver and jerked his head in the guy's direction. "Juan. Take the dog out." And then to me, "You like a beer? Help yourself. Soon as Bibianna's done, you can shower if you want." He returned his attention to the phone. I didn't move.

Grudgingly, Juan removed the handgun from his waistband and laid it on the table. He picked up a chain leash from the arm of the couch and attached it to Perro's collar. The dog made a quick snapping feint at his hand. Juan pulled his fist back and for a minute the two locked eyes. Juan must have been Alpha male because Perro backed down, reinforcing my contention that dogs aren't that smart. A drop of sweat began a lazy trickle down the small of my back.

Once the dog had been removed, I helped myself to a beer and then took a seat in a wide-armed upholstered chair on the far side of the room. I pulled my feet up under me just in case there were vermin cruising at floor level. For now, there was nothing to do except sip my beer. I laid my head against the chair back. The false high I'd experienced in the car had now drained away, replaced by a thundering weariness. I felt heavy with fatigue, as if tension had generated a sudden weight gain.

thirteen

i must have dozed off because the next thing I knew, some-one had removed the half-empty beer bottle from my hand and was giving my arm a gentle shake. I woke with a start, turning to stare at the woman blankly, trying to reorient myself. Oh, yeah. Bibianna. I was still caught up in the af-termath of the shoot-out between Chago and Jimmy Tate. Luis and Raymond were still in the apartment, but the others had gone.

Bibianna was looking better, some of the old confidence in evidence. She was wearing a thick white terrycloth robe, her hair wrapped in a towel. She smelled of soap. Her face had been scrubbed, shining now with the wholesome look of youth. She went into the kitchen and fetched herself a beer. Raymond, still on the phone, followed her with his eyes. I felt a surge of pity. He was a good-looking man, but his longing was unabashed and gave him a hangdog appearance. Now that Bibianna's cockiness had resurfaced, his uncertainty had surfaced, too. He seemed needy and insecure, qualities most women don't find that appealing. The macho swagger I'd seen earlier had been undercut by pain. He must have known she didn't give a rat's ass about him. The power had shifted, lodging now with her where it had once lodged with him.

"Come on. I got some clothes you can borrow," she said.

"I'd kill for a toothbrush," I murmured as we moved toward the bedroom.

She stopped, glancing back at Luis, who was now perched up on the kitchen counter. "Run over to the Seven-Eleven and pick up a couple of toothbrushes."

He didn't respond to the request until Raymond snapped impatient fingers at him. Luis hopped down and crossed to Raymond, who shoved some crumpled bills at him. As soon as he'd left, Raymond turned on Bibianna. "Hey. You don't talk to him like that. Guy works for me, not you. You treat him with a little respect."

Bibianna rolled her eyes and motioned me into the bedroom with her.

The room had been furnished with more of Raymond's roadside taste. The bed was king-size with red satin sheets and a big puffy comforter. The bed tables and chest of drawers looked like wood veneer over particleboard, in a "Spanish style," which is to say lots of black wrought-iron hinges and pulls. Bibianna slid the closet door open. "He moved all of my clothes from my other place. He didn't even ask me," she said. "Look at this. He thinks he can buy me, like I'm up for sale."

The wooden rod was crammed with hanging clothes, the long shelf above stacked with sweaters, handbags, and shoes. She crossed to the bureau and started opening drawers full of underwear, most of it new. She found me a pair of red lace underpants with the store tags still attached. She offered me a bra, which I declined. No point in putting apples in a sack meant for cantaloupes. In addition to the underwear, she rounded up some sandals, a red miniskirt with a matching red leather belt, and a white cotton peasant blouse with puff sleeves and a drawstring at the neck.

As she handed me the garments, she murmured, "Get out if you have the chance."

"What about Raymond?"

"Don't worry about it. I can handle him."

"Everything okay?"

Raymond was standing in the doorway. He'd taken off his sport coat and his shoulders looked narrow without its bulk.

She turned on him in a flash. "Do you fuckin' mind? We're having a private conversation here *if* it's any of your business."

He flicked a look at me, embarrassed.

"I think I'll take a shower," I murmured.

He held out a package. "Here's your toothbrush."

"Thanks."

I took the bag and moved past him, eager to escape. There's nothing worse than being present when a couple gears up for battle. Both were making covert attempts to enlist my sympathy, and the nonverbal recruitment process was making my stomach churn.

I went into the guest bathroom and locked the door behind me. I hung my tank top over the doorknob to discourage anyone from peeping through the keyhole. My toes started curling at the state of the bathroom, which had all the charm one might picture in a military latrine. I've never been good at walking around barefoot in public locker rooms, where the floors always seem to be littered with hair, rusted bobby pins, and disintegrating clumps of spongy wet Kleenex. I won't describe the sink. The glass shower door had been cracked and mended with plumber's tape, and the metal track in which the door slid was crusty with soap scum. A long pointed stain extended from the shower head to the top of the tub itself. There was a plastic bottle of generic shampoo in the corner and I picked it up gingerly, my lips pursing with distaste.

I put paper on the rim of the toilet and availed myself of the facilities. While I was sitting there, I extracted Dolan's telephone number from my right sock. I committed it to memory, tore the slip of paper in tiny pieces, and tossed them in the bowl, flushing it afterward. The water wouldn't go down. The tiny pieces of paper, like confetti, whirled around and around with an agonizing laziness while the water level rose dangerously close to the rim. Oh, great. The toilet was going to overflow. I began to wave my hands, whispering, "Get back . . . get back." Finally, the water subsided, but I didn't care to try to flush again until the tank refilled. I cupped a hand to my ear without picking up any indication that this was happening. If Raymond burst in, would he fish out the pieces of the note and try to paste them all together? Surely not.

I opened the toilet tank. There were plastic packets taped along the sides of the tank . . . probably heroin or cocaine. Now there's a concept. If the cops ever raided the place, they'd sure be fooled by *that*. One of the pouches was jammed up against the ball cock machine. I pushed it aside and rattled the lever. The tank began to fill. Finally, the toilet flushed with gallumphing sounds—a triumph of personal ingenuity and low-grade plumbing skills. My Dick Tracy secret code was safely washed out to sea.

The shower water was tepid to begin with, but I managed to lather myself with a tiny bar of soap that said "Ramada Inn." I shampooed my hair and was just rinsing it when the hot water ran out. I finished in haste. The only towel in the bathroom was thin, stiff, and dingy from use. I patted myself dry with my tank top and got dressed.

When I emerged from the bathroom, dirty clothes in hand, the apartment was quiet. I peered into the living room. Luis had apparently gone home. Raymond and Bibianna were nowhere in sight. The door to the master bedroom was closed, and I could hear voices raised heatedly in Spanish. I leaned my head close, but I really couldn't understand a word of it. I returned to the living room. Perro had been secured to the couch again, and he was chewing happily on the leather portion of the chain leash that restrained him. The minute he saw me, he rose to his feet, the hair standing up along his back in a ridge. He lowered his head and began to hum down in his chest. To reach the front door, I'd have to pass within inches of him. Skip that, I thought.

The telephone, a touch tone, had been sitting on the coffee table. Now there was no sign of it. I scanned the room without result. Apparently, Raymond had unplugged the instrument at the jack and had taken it into the bedroom with him. That wasn't very trusting. I backed up, turning left into a short hallway. The other bedroom contained a dilapidated brown couch and a bare mattress with a couple of pillows minus the cases.

I went to the window overlooking the street. I flipped open the locking mechanism and pushed at the aluminum-framed sliding window, which I managed to hump back in its track with a minimum of squeaks. It's not that I was looking for an immediate avenue of escape. I just like to know where I am and what's possible in the event of an emergency. I leaned close and angled my head so I could see in all directions.

To my right, the face of the building was shabby and plain, a sheer drop of some twenty-plus feet to bare sidewalk. No balconies, no wood trim, and no trees within range. From what I could see, this was a neighborhood of *tacquerías* and strip joints, auto body shops and pool halls, all of it as torn and deserted as a war zone. I checked to my left and was heartened to see a zigzagging metal stairway. At least in a pinch, I'd have access to the world at large.

I surveyed the room behind me, so exhausted I could hardly stand. I opted for the lumpy couch, which was slightly too short to stretch out on fully. The cushions smelled of dust and stale cigarette smoke. I pulled my knees up and crossed my arms, hugging them in against me for solace. I didn't care what was happening, I had to get some sleep.

When I woke, I could tell from the slant of light in the room that it was close to four o'clock. The days had already begun to seem truncated, the premature darkness signaling the sudden onset of winter. At this point, annually, all the furnaces are turned on. The new cord of oak is delivered and stacked. This is the season when Californians, by agreement, begin to bring out their woolens, complaining loudly of the cold when it's only fifty degrees out—as close to freezing temperatures as we're likely to get.

The apartment was still quiet. I got up and tiptoed out to the living room. Perro was snoring, but I figured it was just a ruse. He was hoping I'd try to sneak past him so he could leap up and tear my ass off. I edged to my left, into the dining area, which formed a straight line with the galley-style kitchenette. I'd popped in there briefly when I helped myself to a beer, but I hadn't been able to check for exits. I was hoping for a back door, but the kitchen was a dead end and there didn't appear to be any other way out.

I glanced over at the kitchen table, which was still covered with stacks of papers. I picked up a sheaf and sorted through. What ho! Well, at least now I knew what had made the guy so cross. These vicious-looking *batos locos* had been licking their pencil points, trying to fill out insurance forms for a series of bogus injuries they couldn't even spell right. "Wiplash" and "bruces" and "panes in my looer and uper bake." One had written: "Were drivin north wen this car hit us from behine and nockt us into a telepone phole. I bump my hed on the winsheld, suffrin bruces. Ever sins the accident, I hadve wiplash and panes in my nek. Also, bad hedakes, dobull vishun and shoot-in panes in my bake."

The attending physician on most forms was a Dr. A. Vasquez, with a chiropractor named Fredrick Howard running a close second in popularity. Now that I looked closely, I realized that all the "victims" had given identical accounts of their "accidents." What Tomas had been doing was copying out the same information on form after form. Properly briefed or not, my investigative instincts began to stir and I could feel my excitement mount. This was part of what Dolan and Santos were looking for, grand theft in progress with the names of the players spelled out nice and neat. There was no sign of a file cabinet, from what I'd seen so far, but Raymond had to keep all the paperwork somewhere. I chose a completed claim form at random, folded it quickly, and shoved it down my blouse front, patting it into place. I left the remaining papers as I'd found them and returned to the spare room, crackling faintly as I walked. When I reached the doorway, I spotted Raymond standing near the window, going through the pouch of personal possessions I'd brought with me from the jail.

"Help yourself. All I got on me is ten bucks," I said from the doorway.

If he was embarrassed to be caught, he gave no indication of it. There was a brief pause while he went through a series of tics we both ignored. "Who's Hannah Moore?"

"Excuse me?"

"Hannah Moore's not your real name."

"It isn't? Well, that's news to me." I tried for a tone somewhere between facetious and perplexed.

"This driver's license is a fake." He tossed the license on the floor and turned his attention to the other items in the bag.

"If it's any of your business, my license was suspended about a month ago," I said snappishly. "A friend of mine put this one together for me. You have a problem with that?" I crossed the room and snatched it from the floor, plucking the plastic pouch from him in the same agitated movement.

"I don't have a problem," he said. He seemed amused by my display of temper. "How'd you get your license yanked?"

"I was picked up on a DUI. Two of 'em since June."

I could see him digest the information, undecided at this point whether he believed me or not. "What happens if you get stopped by a cop and he runs the fake?"

"I'll end up in jail again. What difference does it make?"

"So what's your real name?"

"What's yours?"

"Where's your car at?"

"Out of commission. I need some work done on the tranny, but I don't have the bucks."

We locked eyes. His were large and darker than I remembered. He needed a shave, his jaw shadowed by a day's growth of beard. He'd changed into casual slacks and a short-sleeved silk shirt in a teal shade that made his eyes look very warm. His taste in clothing was sure classier than his taste in household furnishings. I had to guess he was making money, especially if what Santos said was true. Raymond's neck jerked, after which he turned his head and yelled something with his hand against his mouth as if coughing.

I heard the door to the master bedroom open. A moment later, Bibianna padded into the room. She was barefoot, wearing a short white silk shift that made her skin seem dark by contrast. She stood in the doorway while she lit a cigarette, watching me with interest, her eyes unreadable. She had her hair pulled up in a slatternly knot on the top of her head. Her gaze slid over to Raymond. "Where's the telephone?"

"It's broken."

"It's not broken. I saw you using it a little while ago."

"Now it is. You don't need it."

"I want to call my mother."

"Some other time," he said.

She pushed away from the doorframe and turned on her heel, disappearing down the hall toward the living room.

He stared after her. A nearly imperceptible tic had started near his mouth. He did a neck roll and moved his right arm in its socket to ease the tension. The man had to be exhausted at the end of a day. He shook his head. "I don't get it. I've done everything for her. Bought her clothes. I take her fancy places, get her anything she wants. She doesn't have to lift a finger. She doesn't even have to work. I took her on a big cruise. Did she tell you about that?"

I shook my head.

"You ask her. She'll tell you. All the food you could eat. They had a six-foot swan made of ice, this fountain pouring champagne. I get her this apartment. You know what she says to me? It's trash. She hates the place. What's the matter with her?" His bafflement was mixed with belligerence. "Tell me what I did wrong. Tell me what I have to do yet."

"I'm not exactly an expert on what makes a relationship work."

"You know the problem? I'm too nice. It's the truth. I'm too good to the woman, but I can't help myself. That's just how I am. We were all set to get married. Did she tell you about that?"

"You mentioned it, I think."

"She broke my heart and I can't figure out why she did it. . . ."

"I got news for you, Raymond. You can't hang on to someone who doesn't want to be here."

"Is that it?" He studied me so intently that for a moment I thought I might actually persuade him to let go of her. He shoved his hands in his pockets, his look brooding in the fading light.

"Raymond?" Bibianna called him from the living room. "What's this?"

"What."

A moment later, she reappeared. She had a knife in her hand, a narrow switchblade with a bone handle. The blade was dark with dried blood.

His eyes settled on the knife. "Where'd you get that?"

"It was on the kitchen counter. This is yours. I recognize it."

He held his hand out, ignoring the original question. I thought about the smashed mirror tiles and the broken chair leg, blood splattered on the wall. Hesitantly, Bibianna placed the knife in his hand, her expression troubled. Again, the power had shifted. He pressed a button on the handle, easing the blade into its slot. He tucked it in his pants pocket. He blinked. He jerked his head to the side and his mouth opened wide.

She watched him with caution. "Where'd all the blood come from?"

"Put your clothes on. I'll take you out to dinner. We can bring something back for her," he replied.

I felt a momentary stir of excitement, longing for a short period of unsupervised time.

"Why can't Hannah go? She's probably starving."

"She can have a bowl of chili until we get back. There's a big pot on the stove."

I spoke up casually. "Really, Bibianna. I'm fine. I'll just keep the dog company." Like me and Perro were old pals. I was dying to be alone, eager to get a call through to Dolan while I could.

The two of them went through a long debate—where to go, what to wear, whether they should wait for Luis and make a foursome out of it. I could feel my stomach shrivel from anxiety, but I didn't want to seem too impatient for their departure. Raymond was all in favor of waiting for Luis, but Bibianna said she didn't want to eat a meal with him and Raymond didn't press. I could feel myself mentally shifting from foot to foot.

fourteen

They didn't leave until nearly seven, after an agony of argument and indecision. Perro remained in his usual place by the door, gnawing on his chain. He had the kind of teeth you might see on a dinosaur skeleton, perfect for grinding up alligators and other modest-size mammals. Once the door closed behind them, I headed for the spare bedroom, where I took a minute to fish the claim form out of my bodice and tuck it under one of the couch cushions for safekeeping. Then I began to search for the missing telephone. I started in the master bedroom, checking every drawer. I couldn't believe he'd have stashed the phone among her possessions, so I skipped her chest of drawers and concentrated on his. She'd probably gone through a brief search herself without luck.

His top drawer on the left was a mass of unmatched socks, clumsily folded handkerchiefs. The drawer on the right held the sorts of odds and ends you can't bear to throw out: matchbooks, cuff links, tie tacks, a roach clip, loose change, a wallet in good shape but emptied of credit cards. A flat brown bank book for a savings account showed a balance of forty-three thousand bucks. Down a drawer were folded shirts and under them the sweaters. In a box, near the back of the drawer, I found two handguns. One was a semiautomatic, a .30-caliber broomhandle Mauser in an imprinted case, with an extra magazine, cleaning brush, test target, and a box of bottleneck cartridges. I bent my head and sniffed the barrel, without touching it. It hadn't been cleaned, but it hadn't been fired recently, either. The second gun was a SIG-Sauer P220 .38 Super, which probably cost three hundred and fifty bucks. Did I dare steal one for my very own? Nah, not at this point. It wouldn't be smart. Under the box was a jumbled collection of California driver's licenses with assorted ID's. I made a mental note to go through them later if I could find an opportunity. I put the guns back on top of the documents.

I checked the closet, top and bottom, sorting through any pile of articles large enough to conceal an unplugged telephone. I peered under the bed, searched the drawers in the bed tables. I went into the master bathroom, which was larger than the other but not any cleaner. The medicine cabinet was too small to hide anything. I dug through the clothes hamper. The telephone was tucked down in the bottom. I emitted a little yelp and pulled it out from under a mound of dirty underwear. I knew there was a jack in the living room, but I was too nervous to plug in the phone out there. Luis was due any minute. I didn't want him to find me with my mouth against the receiver.

I scanned the baseboards in the bedroom for another jack. There were none in the immediate vicinity. I got down on my hands and knees and crawled around the perimeter, toting the telephone along with me as I peered behind the chest of drawers and the bed table. I finally spotted a jack on the wall behind the king-size bed, just about dead center. By stretching out on my belly and extending my arm through the dust bunnies and the woofies, I contrived to press the little gizmo on the phone into the matching hole in the jack. I was lying on the floor between the bed and the closet when the dog began to bark. Luis. Shit! I snicked the line from the jack and jerked the length of it out from under the bed. Perro was barking so loud, I couldn't tell if Luis had let himself in or not. I made a beeline to the master bathroom, wrapping the cord and the phone as I went.

"Hey! Where is everybody?" He was in.

"Luis? Is that you? I'm in the bathroom," I called.

I shoved the phone to the bottom of the hamper and piled the dirty clothes on top. I checked my reflection in the mirror and picked a dog hair off my lip. I just had time to wrap a bath towel around my head, turban style, when Luis appeared in the bathroom doorway. He'd pulled a flannel shirt on. Long sleeves now concealed the handsome tattoos on his arms, but I could still see the two pairs of duck feet sticking out of his sleeves. He surveyed the room. His look flicked to me, his eyes chilly with suspicion.

"Where's Raymond?"

"He and Bibianna went out."

"What are you doing in here?"

"Bibianna said I could borrow her hair dryer," I said, praying she really had one. I glanced at the hamper. A length of telephone cord was dangling down the side, coiled in a tiny noose. I shifted my weight, effectively blocking his view. "I'll be out in just a second."

He stared. His face was an oval with high cheekbones and a little pointed chin. His teeth were in good shape, but he had a thin, mean-looking mouth, accentuated by that pathetic mustache. His dark hair was straight, slicked back in a ponytail, previously concealed by his watch cap. He had to be in his late twenties. "What time did they say they'd be back?"

"Could we talk about this in a minute? I'd like to do my hair," I said. I moved to close the bathroom door, which forced him to back up a foot. I shut the door emphatically, waited half a second, and then jerked the door open again. He straightened up, embarrassed. He tucked his thumbs in his belt loops and ambled casually toward the living room.

"You are too considerate," I called after him, and slammed the door shut for emphasis. I found the hair dryer and turned it on, then laid it on the toilet lid and let it run while I wrapped the cord around the phone and placed it carefully down in the hamper where I'd found it. I rearranged the clothes on top. With the lid in place, I turned and checked my hair in the mirror. I picked up the wheezing dryer and bent over at the waist until my head was upside down. I blew a jet of hot air through my mop for about a minute. When I straightened up, it didn't look any better, but it did look different, like a sticker bush without leaves. I flipped the hair dryer off and went out into the living room.

The evening was spent peaceably. Luis didn't seem to be plagued by intellect or curiosity, so there was little conversation. He sat on the nondoggie end of the couch while I sat in the chair. He turned on the television set. He had a limited attention span and very little patience for complexity. Once in a while, he'd do something that indicated a curious awareness of me, nothing overt, but palpable nevertheless. His sexuality was oppressive, like the smell of orange blossoms on a humid summer night. He watched several shows simultaneously, using the remote control to switch from channel to channel. The dog stared at me intently through the car chases and canned laughter, and if I chanced to glance at him, he seemed to squint his little eyes.

At ten-twenty, Raymond and Bibianna came back with a bucket of parts from some Kentucky Fried Chicken rip-off. I was so hungry by then that I devoured five pieces, along with a carton of mashed potatoes with brown sludge, a squat container of coleslaw, three misshapen biscuits, and a fried pie with hardly any filling. Luis ate right along with me and finished up any food that was left. At midnight, Bibianna found me a blanket and a nightie. I trundled off to what I now considered my bedroom. I shut the door, stripped my clothes off, slipped into the nightie, and settled down on the lumpy couch.

I awakened with a start. At first I had no idea where I was or what was happening. It was the dead of night. I strained against the gloom, doing a visual search of the room I was lying in, caught in a moment of sleep-induced amnesia. A pale wash from the streetlight cast a plank of yellow on the ceiling. A thin scent of lard-fried tortillas hung in the air. I remembered Raymond. Had I heard something? Whatever the noise, I must have incorporated it into a murky dream which had evaporated on waking. Only the feeling of the dream remained—heavy, anxious. I could sense a presence in the room. My eyes were becoming accustomed to the dark. I divided my visual field into sections, which I studied one by one. My heart lurched. The door to my room now appeared to be open a crack. Luis? I struggled, trying to see if I could distinguish a silhouette against the paler gray of the corridor. The door swung open, a widening gap filled the shadows. I whispered, "What do you want?"

Silence.

I heard a tapping, the sound of metal being trailed across the floor. Fear flared in me like a match. It was the dog. I remembered him chewing the leather strap that connected his leash with the chain securing him. God only knew how long he'd been free, roaming the apartment. I could see the glint of his dark eyes, his head low. I had no weapon in range, no way to protect myself. He seemed to be sifting the air for human scent. If I could remain absolutely still, he might lose interest and turn away, heading for the room where Raymond and Bibianna slept. I held my breath. The pit bull advanced toward the couch where I was lying rigidly, his toenails tap-tapping on the bare wooden floor. I was on my right side, my face almost level with his. I had my right arm tucked under me, but my left was hanging off the edge of the couch since there was no place else to put

it. The dog extended his snout until the leath
touched the fingers of my left hand. I coul
bristles on his muzzle brush against my wr
moving. Finally, with infinitesimal care, I
hand away. I heard him growl low in his
daring to retract my fingertips. He e
was resting his chin on the edge of
level with mine. He made a whining
go blank. Within seconds, he had so
couch with me, crowding me agai
bony front legs pinning me in
placed a hand on his head betw
palm.

"I thought you hated havi
indignantly. Clearly not. I b
ear. The dog panted happ
oped me from chest to k
though he did exude a
first time I'd ever had
pork. When I woke a

It's amazing how
roundings and al
place seemed fam
lent me a clean T-s
breakfast, Luis made
we washed down with Pe
streak in my nature had en
sponge and some Comet and a
bathroom, scouring the floor, the sink,
the grubby tile around the shower. I p
anna to get the bags of garbage removed fr
and then I scoured the sink, the stove top, an
Perro, the pit bull, was back in his position by t
standing guard. Like a one-night stand, the surly ing
was acting as if he didn't know me from a lamppost, and
he growled ominously every time I made eye contact. It

question. "What's the story on Chago?
Luis concentrated on his saucepan, wondering
until the autopsy's done. Might be as early as tomorrow, t
won't say."
"Does he have other brothers?" They won't release the bod
"Juan and Ricardo. They were here yesterday."
"What about parents?"
"His father was sent to prison for child abuse
killed in prison when they heard what he did to
"Which was what?"
Luis looked up at me. "He don't talk about th
ask." He went back to his saucepan, stirring
"His mother ran off and left when he was s
"He's the oldest?"
"Of the boys. There's three older sisters
think it's his fault what happened to the
"Another happy childhood," I said.
known him?"
"Six, eight months. I met him th
named Jesus."
Bibianna appeared in the doo
shoulders like an Indian. "Raym
Luis shook his head.
She disappeared again, and
shower water running. Luis
stove and prepared to take
picked up the chain, he di
tion of the leash. Under
worried, "Shit." I kept
engender a sense of lo
way to attach the leas
apartment.

Bibianna reappeared, fully dressed this time. She found a dog-eared deck of cards and sat on the floor next to the coffee table, where she laid out a game of solitaire. I considered hunting for the phone, but I didn't want to call Dolan with Bibianna close by. The less she knew about who I was, the better. I flipped on the television set. The day already had an odd feel to it—idle, unstructured, without purpose or appeal—like a forced vacation in a cut-rate resort.

Bibianna seemed preoccupied and I hated to cut into that, but we seldom had time alone and I needed information.

"How often does he get violent?" I asked.

She turned a dark look on me. "Not every day. Sometimes two or three times a week," she insisted. "I talked to Chago about it once and he told me it started when Raymond was just a little kid. He'd blink his eyes and then the twitches started and pretty soon he was barking and coughing. His father figured he was doing it on purpose, just to get attention, so he used to beat him up. He did some other stuff, too, which got him thrown into prison. Poor Raymond. He was hyperactive in school, in trouble all the time. It's probably why his mother left. . . ."

"And he's done it ever since? The whole time you've known him?"

"He got better for a while, but then it started up again, worse than before."

"Can't the doctors do anything?"

"What doctors? He doesn't see doctors. Sometimes sex calms him down. Booze or sleep, dope. Once he got the flu and had a fever a hundred and three? He was fine, no problem, never even had a twitch. He was great for two days. Flu went away, he was at it again, this time licking his lips, doing this weird thing with his hands. I don't want to talk about it anymore. It's depressing."

Raymond returned just before lunch with a folded newspaper and a bag of doughnuts. Luis and the dog came in right behind him. If Raymond was in mourning for his brother, I saw no signs of it. The ticcing seemed less evident today, but I couldn't be sure. He left the room at intervals and I began to suspect he was venting in the other room. That or shooting up. I was just getting into a really trashy soap, my bare legs thrown over the arm of the chair, sandal flapping on one foot, when he and Luis sat down at the kitchen table, talking softly in Spanish. During the next commercial, I went into the kitchen and got myself a glass of water. I paused, peering over Raymond's shoulder to see what they were up to. It was pure nosiness on my part, but he didn't seem to mind. What I'd thought was the daily paper turned out to be a throwaway rag filled with classifieds. Luis flipped to the automobile section and folded back the pages. I checked the dateline. Thursday, October 27. These were probably new listings for the weekend coming up. Luis skipped over the trucks, vans, and imports and concentrated on the domestic cars for sale.

"Here's one," Luis said. With a Magic Marker, he circled an ad for a 1979 Caddy. I leaned closer, reading, "Good condition. $999. OBO."

"What's OBO?" I asked. I knew, but I wanted to demonstrate some interest and I thought showing ignorance was the safest bet.

"Or best offer," Raymond said. "You want a Cadillac?"

"Who, me? Not especially."

"I like that Chrysler Cordoba," Raymond said to Luis, pointing to the next box. Luis drew a wobbly-sided egg around the ad for a " '77 white. runs/looks great. $895/obo." A telephone number was listed on both ads.

Raymond got up and left the room, returning with the telephone, which he plugged into the wall jack. I pulled up a chair and sat down. Luis continued to circle ads while Raymond placed call after call, inquiring about each car that interested them, making note of the address. When this exercise was complete and they'd culled out the ads of interest, Luis made a list on a separate piece of paper.

Raymond glanced at me. "You have car insurance?"

"Sure."

"What kind?"

I shrugged. "Whatever the state of California requires. I've been thinking I should drop it since my car's dead. Why?"

"You have liability *and* collision?"

"How do I know? I don't walk around with the details of my car insurance memorized. The policy's up in Santa Teresa."

"Can't your insurance company give you the information?"

"Sure. If they looked it up."

"Might be worth it to get your car fixed if you got collision coverage." Raymond lifted the telephone receiver and held it out to me. "Call 'em."

"Right now?"

"Is that a problem?"

"Not at all," I said with an uneasy laugh. I could feel my heart start to bang in my chest. The thumping felt so conspicuous I checked to see if my T-shirt was pulsating in the front. For a moment my mind went blank. I couldn't remember California Fidelity's number, I couldn't remember the contact number Dolan had given me, and I couldn't decide which to try in any event. I took the receiver.

I punched in the 805 area code, hoping for the best. Automatically, my fingers moved across the face of the telephone, dialing CF in a medley of musical tones that sounded like "Mary Had a Little Lamb." I wondered if Dolan had been in touch with Mac Voorhies. Was I going to have my cover blown right here on the spot?

The number rang twice. Darcy answered. I hoped I didn't sound like myself when I said, "May I speak to Mr. Voorhies?"

"Just a moment, please. I'll ring his office."

She clicked off. Music played in the background, filling

telephone limbo with an orchestrated rendition of "How High the Moon." Inexplicably, the lyrics popped into my head unbidden. I thought about Dawna, wondering how long the cops could hold her. Wounded or not, she was dangerous.

fifteen

Mac came on the line. "Voorhies."

"Mr. Voorhies, my name is Hannah Moore. I have car insurance with your company and I wanted to check on my coverage."

There was dead silence. I knew he recognized my voice. Raymond leaned his head close to mine, angling the phone so he could listen to the conversation.

Mac hesitated. I could hear him grope with the request, trying to figure out what was going on and what he could say without jeopardizing my situation, whatever that might be. He knew me well enough to realize I wouldn't make such a call without a good reason. "Is this regarding an automobile accident?" he asked cautiously.

"Well, no. I, uhm, might be driving a friend's car and he doesn't like the idea unless he knows I'm covered." Raymond's face was six inches away from mine. I could smell his after-shave and feel the warm, slightly adenoidal character of his breath.

"I can understand that. Is your friend there now?" Mac asked.

"That's right."

"Do you have the policy number handy?"

"Uh, no. But the agent is Con Dolan."

Raymond drew back and reached for a piece of paper, scratching out a note. "Ask about collision." I hate it when people coach me when I'm on the phone. He pointed significantly. I waved at him with irritation.

"Uh, it's really the collision I need to know about," I amended.

Another awkward pause. I smiled at Raymond wanly while Mac cleared his throat. "I tell you what I'll do, Miss . . ."

"Moore."

"Yes, all right. Why don't I see if I can get in touch with Mr. Dolan. He's no longer with the company, but I'm sure he's still in town. I can check our files for the coverage and get back to you. Is there a number where you can be reached this afternoon?"

Raymond pulled his head back and put a finger to his lips.

I said, "Not really. I'm staying with this guy in Los Angeles, but I'm not sure how long I'll be here. I could call again later if you'll tell me what time."

"Try five this afternoon. I should have the information by then."

"Thanks. I'd appreciate it." I handed Raymond the receiver and he hung it up.

"What'd he say?"

"He's going to check. I'm supposed to call him back this afternoon at five."

"But as far as you know the insurance is in effect."

"I told you it was."

Raymond and Luis exchanged a look. Raymond looked over his shoulder at Bibianna, still intent on her game of solitaire. "Get your jacket. We're going out." And then to me. "You need a jacket? She'll give you one."

"What's happening?"

"We're going on a drive-down."

"Whatever *that* is," I said.

We took Sepulveda Boulevard up to Culver City, with Luis at the wheel. Bibianna was being sullen, sitting silently in the backseat with her arms crossed while Raymond either made calls on the car phone or rubbed, petted, and generally annoyed her, rambling on about all the money he meant to make, all the things he'd done, and all the big plans he had for the two of them. I had to give that guy some lessons. He was going about this all wrong. Aside from the fact that (unknown to him) she was already Mrs. Jimmy Tate, she was never going to tumble to all the smoke he was blowing. Women don't want to sit around listening to guys talk about themselves. Women like to have conversations about real things, like feelings—namely, theirs. Raymond seemed to think he just hadn't persuaded her yet of the depth of his affection. I wanted to scream, "She knows that, you dummy! She just doesn't give a shit."

We pulled up at the first address.

The '79 Caddy was parked at the curb, a black Seville, being offered by a muscular black guy with a pink shower cap, a tattooed teardrop on his cheek, and a gold hoop through his left ear. Honestly, I'm not making this stuff up. He wore a T-shirt and low-slung jeans, with his Calvin Kleins sticking out above his belt. He was actually very cute with a mustache and goatee, a mischievous smile, and a little space between his teeth. Bibianna stayed in the car, but I got out and stood around with the guys, shifting from foot to foot while the three of them entered into a long and tedious negotiation. Raymond went through several sequences of ticcing, but the black guy didn't react except to stop making eye contact. I could see that in some circles, Raymond would be treated like a walking basket case. I wanted to speak up protectively and say, "Hey, the guy çan't help it, okay?"

The OBO turned out to be a hundred dollars less than the $999 listed in the paper. Raymond turned his body slightly and took out a fat cylinder of bills with a rubber band wrapped around them. He slipped the rubber band over his wrist while he peeled off the right denominations. The pink slip was signed and changed hands, but I couldn't believe Raymond was actually going to take it down to the DMV. Habitual criminals never seem to be troubled about things like that. They do anything they please while the rest of us feel compelled to play by the rules.

The black guy strolled off as soon as the transaction was completed. Raymond and Luis made a study of the car, which seemed to be in reasonable shape. Chrome flakes were peeling off the bumper and the right rear taillight had been smashed. The tires were bald, but the body didn't show any major dents. The interior was gray, a rip in the passenger seat neatly sutured with black thread. The floor, front and back, was littered with fast-food containers, empty soft drink cans, crushed cigarette packs, newspapers. Luis took a few minutes to shove it all into the gutter, emptying the ashtray in a little mountain of cigarette butts.

"What do you think?" Raymond asked me.

I couldn't imagine why my opinion mattered. "Looks better than anything I ever drove."

He stuck a finger in the key ring and flipped the keys into his palm. "Hop in. Bibianna goes with him."

I glanced over at the dark green Ford where Bibianna sat. She was perched up on the backseat, using the rearview mirror to braid her dark, glossy hair. "Fine with me," I said.

I got into the Caddy.

Raymond got in on the driver's side and slipped his seat belt on. "Buckle up," he said. "We're going to have an accident."

"Is this car insured? We just bought the damn thing," I said with surprise.

"Don't worry about that stuff. I can call my agent later. He does anything I want."

I buckled up, trying to picture myself in a neck brace.

The transmission was automatic. The car had power locks and power brakes, power windows. Raymond started the engine, which thrummed to life. He adjusted the rearview mirror and waited while a silver Toyota passed at cruising speed before he pulled into the lane of traffic.

I tried the power windows, which went up with a quiet hum. "How do we do this?" I asked.

"You'll see."

We seemed to drive randomly, taking Venice Boulevard through Palms, turning right on Sepulveda into an area called Mar Vista. These were neighborhoods of small stucco bungalows with small yards and tired trees with leaves that were oxygen-starved from all the smog in the air. Raymond watched the streets like a cop looking for the telltale indications of a crime in progress.

"What makes this a drive-down?"

"That's just what we call it when we're out cruising for an accident. Car's called a bucket. I got a fleet of buckets, a whole crew of drivers doing just what we're doing. You're a ghost."

I smiled. "Why's that?"

"Because you don't get paid, therefore you don't exist."

"How come I don't get paid?"

"You're a trainee. You're just here to beef up the head count."

"Oh, thanks," I said. I turned and looked out the window on the passenger side. "So, what are we looking for?"

Raymond glanced at me sharply, suspicion etched in his face.

"I'm just trying to learn," I said.

"A victim. We call 'em vics," he replied in belated answer to my question. "Somebody running a stop sign, backing out of a drive into the right-of-way, pulling out of a parking space . . ."

"And then what?"

He smiled to himself. "We hit the guy. You want to catch the rear quarter panel because the damage shows up nice and nobody gets hurt."

We drove around for an hour, unable to conjure up a traffic offender for the life of us. I could see that Raymond was impatient, but oddly enough, there was no twitching whatever during the time in the car. Maybe work was soothing to his battered nervous system. "Let me try," I said.

"You serious?"

"If I score, I want the money. What's it pay?"

"A hundred bucks a day."

"You're full of shit. I bet you make a fortune and I want a fair shake."

"Pushy bitch," he said mildly.

We traded places. I took a moment to slide the front seat a little closer to the gas pedal and the brake. I eased the Caddy into traffic. By then, we'd worked our way up Lincoln Boulevard to the outskirts of Santa Monica. At Pico, I cut left, picking up Ocean Avenue at San Vicente. Raymond hadn't paid much attention, but when he saw the direction I was taking, he looked at me with surprise. "What's wrong with Venice?"

"Why not Beverly Hills?" I asked. At first the idea seemed to unsettle him, but he could see the possibilities. We worked our way up to Sunset Boulevard and headed east, passing the northern perimeter of the sprawling UCLA campus. Just past the Beverly Hills Hotel, I took a right onto Rexford. I found it soothing to cruise along the wide tree-lined streets. This was an area known as the "flats" of Beverly Hills. The houses were oversize and filled the lots from side to side. All the lawns were green, the shrubs trimmed, gardeners blowing errant leaves down the driveways. Shade trees were planted along the grassy stretch between sidewalk and street, sycamores interspersed with oaks. High fences shielded the backyard tennis courts from sight. Now and then, I caught a glimpse of a swimming pool and cabana. The stoplight at Santa Monica Boulevard was green. I drove the Caddy sedately into the heart of the Beverly Hills shopping district.

Technically, I knew I was skating on thin ice with this drive-down. The only thing I remembered about undercover work from police academy days is that it's against "public policy" for an officer of the law to participate in the commission of a crime or incite someone to do so. Happily, I wasn't actually an officer of the law, and if it ever came right down to it, it would be Raymond's word against mine. Helping Raymond stage a few fraudulent accidents seemed to me the quickest way to persuade him I was on the up-and-up.

Raymond stared out the window, his manner uneasy. "You're never going to find any business up here."

"Want to bet?" I had just spotted a late-model Mercedes pulling out of a parking lot in the middle of the block, left turn signal blinking. The car was a four-door sedan, a conservative black with a vanity plate that read BULL MKT. The woman driving was probably forty years old, with a cap of blond hair and big round sunglasses pulled down toward the tip of her nose. I slowed the Caddy, mentally apologizing for my sins in advance. I came to a full stop and politely waved her out. She gave me a quick wave and a smile, showing perfect caps.

"What are you *doing*?"

"Yielding the right-of-way," I said with innocence.

As soon as the Mercedes eased into my path, I gunned the Caddy and rammed the left rear quadrant with a thump. It was just like bumper cars and I felt the same sick charge, half guilt, half thrill. The indentation was nicely placed. The woman shrieked and turned to look at me openmouthed with astonishment.

Raymond was out of the Caddy in a flash. "What the fuck are you doing? You pulled out right in front of us!"

I got out and moved to the front of the Caddy, where I checked the broken headlight and flaking bumper. Not bad. The damage to the other car was six grand at least. The blonde had recovered from her initial dismay. She got out of the Mercedes and slammed the car door. She was dressed for tennis, little white skirt, green-and-white-striped Polo shirt, long, tan legs, little socks with jaunty green pom-poms sticking out above her spotless white tennis shoes. The Mercedes's left rear quadrant, recently a pristine shiny black, now sported a dent of substantial proportions, fender crumpled, chrome sticking out like a horizontal antenna. The rear door would have to be pried open with a crowbar. I could see the color rising in her face as she surveyed the damage. She turned and jabbed an angry finger in my face. "You fucking asshole! You sat there and motioned me out!"

"She did not!" Raymond said.

"She did, too!"

"Did not," I inserted to show where my loyalties lay.

Raymond said, "Look at my car! We just bought this car and now look what you've done!"

"*Your* car! Look at *mine*!"

I put a hand against my neck and Raymond turned to me with concern.

"Are you okay, hon?"

"I guess so," I said without conviction. The neck roll I did was accompanied by a wince.

Raymond dropped his irate manner and substituted an air of studied calm that was more effective in its way. "Lady, I hope you got good insurance coverage. . . ."

The afternoon was marked by Raymond's intermittent demolition derby, surreal in its fashion, depressing in its effect. We backtracked from Beverly Hills into Brentwood, through Westwood, and then south into Santa Monica again. We sought out areas congested with traffic, watched for minor violations, inattentiveness, and lapses in judgment. Raymond kept a meticulous record of each accident we staged— four in all—noting time and location, the other driver's name and insurance company.

The Caddy performed like a first-rate battering ram, sustaining very little damage for the losses we inflicted on other unsuspecting motorists. The victims seemed so gullible somehow, distressed, apologetic, sometimes irate, but usually worried they'd be slapped with ruinous lawsuits. I played my part—righteous and upset, pretending sudden shooting pains in my neck or back—but I couldn't bear to look at them. This was not a kind of cheating I did very well, and I could proceed only by employing the same mental detachment I adopt when I enter a morgue. Raymond, of course, was only interested in filing phony claims for vehicular damage and whatever injuries we could fake as a consequence. His skills at manipulation were honed by long practice.

At four, much to my relief, he decided we'd done enough. I'd been at the wheel for the first couple of accidents. Then Raymond had taken over. He found an on ramp for the 405 and headed south, toward the apartment. I felt like a traveling salesperson, on the road with my boss. My questions to Raymond had the same banal thrust you'd imagine from a Fuller Brush trainee. "What's your background for this?" said I, much as if I were inquiring about his qualifications for a career with *Encyclopaedia Britannica.*

"Some guy taught me the business when I was first starting out. He's in the slammer, so it's my operation."

"Like a promotion."

"Yeah, right. Exactly. I got a stable of doctors and attorneys who do the actual paperwork. I'm strictly supervision. Times are slow I do a little work like this. I like to keep a hand in."

"Your job is what, supplying the claimants?"

"Well, yeah. What do you think we been doing all afternoon? Right now, I got a crew of ten, but that goes up and down. It's hard to get good help."

I laughed. "I bet."

"I'll tell you a little secret. And this is the key to sound business management. Be careful of the guy right below you on the pyramid. You don't tell him jackshit."

"Because he might want to take over?"

"That's right. He's the dude wants to put a knife in your back. You take Luis. I love the guy like a brother, but certain things I don't tell him, people he doesn't see. That way I don't have to worry, know what I mean?"

"The money must be good."

Raymond shook his head. "Are you kidding? The money's great. I make maybe a thousand a case, depending on the nature of the 'injury.' The GP or the chiropractor probably clears another fifteen hundred."

"God, that's amazing. What do they do, pad the fees?"

"Sometimes they do. Or they charge for services never rendered. The insurance company doesn't know the difference, and either way, the doc makes out. Plus, you have the attorney on top of that," he said. He smiled wryly. "Of course, the biggest chunk goes to me."

"Because you take all the risks?"

"Because I put up all the dough. Bankroll the cars, pay all the cappers up front. I probably shell out five or six grand per crew to get 'em rolling. Multiply that by ten, twenty crews working seven days a week? It adds up."

"Sounds like it," I said, and let the subject drop.

A long silence followed. I still didn't have a fix on the mental arithmetic, but the money was clearly huge. I laid my head back against the seat. It wasn't hard to see the appeal. For a guy like Raymond, the money was a lot better than an honest day's work. Hell, I could make more money crashing cars than I did as a P.I. Of course, there was a downside. With all the bumps, smacks, and minor episodes of whiplash, my head was pounding and my neck was seizing up. I massaged the muscles along one shoulder, feeling tense.

"What's the matter?"

"My neck's stiff."

"You and me both," he said in a moment of self-mockery. He looked at me closely. "For real?"

"Raymond, we've just been in four auto accidents! That last one we had, I nearly slid off the seat. You could have warned me."

"You want to see a doctor? I can set it up. Heat treatments, ultrasound, anything you want. It's one of the perks."

"Let me see how I feel when we get back to the apartment. Where's Bibianna? I hope I'm not the only one out here risking my neck."

"Her and Luis are doing a drive-down same as us."

"Good. I'm glad to hear it."

He looked over at me, trying to gauge my mood. "You like it so far?"

"It sure beats working for a living."

He flashed a smile, eyes returning to the road. "Doesn't it?"

We stopped briefly at Buddy's Auto Body Shop across the street and two doors down from the apartment where Raymond lived. The garage itself sat in one corner of a property that extended from street to street. In the far corner, there was a corrugated metal shack surrounded by chassis, fenders, bumpers, engines, tires. A dilapidated chain-link fence enclosed maybe two full acres of wrecked cars and assorted parts. A sign read: BUDDY'S AUTO SALVAGE OPEN 6 DAYS TOP $$ FOR YOUR CAR OR TRUCK. ONE OF THE LARGEST SELECTIONS OF USED PARTS IN SOUTHERN CALIFORNIA. A big black rottweiler, with a head as craggy as a tree stump, was asleep in the dirt beside a pickup truck.

I said, "Does Buddy work for you?"

"*I'm* Buddy. Guy runs the place is Chopper. Back in a minute," he murmured as he got out. Raymond apparently operated his "repair" business in conjunction with an auto wrecking and salvage company, probably dismantling vehicles once he'd maximized the insurance potential.

I waited until he went into the garage and then I got out myself and ambled over to the Pepsi machine just inside the door. I took my time tucking coins in the slot, extracting a can of Diet Pepsi. I popped the top and downed it, idly taking in my surroundings. There was not another soul in sight and no indication of any work being done. The late afternoon sun slanted onto the cracked concrete floor in tawny yellow strips. The air smelled of oil, old tires, and hot metal. A pyramid of bright blue metal barrels had been laid on their sides and served now as storage bins for a jumble of rusted car parts. I could see Raymond through the open doorway of an area marked off as office space. The flat-roofed building appeared to be converted from a very small stucco house. Additional office space was provided by a single-wide trailer tucked between the fence and the building. The horizontal panes of a pair of dusty louvered windows were slanted open to let in some air. A wooden pallet was leaning up against the trailer. There was an alarm company sign affixed to the side of the trailer, but I didn't take it seriously. This didn't look like an establishment famous for its security.

Raymond finished his business and emerged from the garage with a guy at his side whom he introduced as Chopper. He was an Anglo in his forties, balding and squat. His breathing was labored and his face freckled, with sweat.

I said, "Great dog," hoping to ingratiate myself with his owner.

"That's Brutus." Chopper gave a piercing whistle and Brutus awoke obligingly and lumbered to his feet. The poor dog was ancient, so crippled by arthritis that he walked with a rocking motion, approaching by degrees. Up close, I could see his black hair was dusted with white. He paused beside me, his manner humble. I put my hand down near his nose and he licked me. I felt embarrassingly dewy-eyed about the damn beast.

Raymond and Chopper finished their business and we walked on back to the apartment building, leaving the car where it was.

sixteen

bibianna was already home, seated at the kitchen table, applying a coat of bright red polish to her nails. She was wearing red shorts and a halter top in a vivid jungle print, red, black, olive green, and white. Her hair was pulled up in a glossy coil on top. Luis was out somewhere walking the dog. I marveled that Bibianna hadn't escaped while she could. Raymond had forgotten to return the telephone to its hiding place. He didn't seem aware of it, but Bibianna sure was. She ignored the instrument so studiously I had to guess she'd used it. I caught her eye with a visual query, but she kept her expression blank. I wondered who she'd called. Her mother? Jimmy Tate? Could he be out of jail yet?

Raymond glanced at his watch. "Hey. It's nearly five. Time to call your insurance agent."

My conversation with Mac was brief. Raymond let me handle the transaction without his ear pressed to the phone along with mine. I identified myself as Hannah Moore and Darcy put me through to Mac, who spelled out the particulars of my insurance coverage, making sure the message would sound benign to anybody listening. "Mr. Dolan assured me you were covered in case of accident. Do you still have his number?"

"Yes, I've got it. Thanks for the information. I appreciate your help.".

"Anytime," he said. "And keep safe."

"I hope to."

Once I'd hung up, I finished jotting down notes: policy number, my deductible, liability, collision, major medical, and death benefits. I was assuming Mac had set up a special policy under the name "Hannah Moore," with a flag on the computer so he'd be alerted if a claim came in. I gave Raymond the policy number and the data Mac had relayed.

Shortly thereafter, I heard Perro tapping along the walkway outside, his breathing hoarse and wheezy as he strained against the leash. Luis opened the door and the dog bounded in. Somewhere, in a brain about the size of a BB, this beast had suddenly decided he remembered me. He charged at me joyfully, knocking into Bibianna as he vaulted across her lap. When he reached me he jumped up, propping his paws on my shoulders so we could stare into each other's eyes. I leaned sideways against the kitchen table while he slopped a tongue across my mouth. Bibianna had leapt away from him with a shriek, her fingers held aloft so he wouldn't screw up her nails. Raymond snapped his fingers, but the dog was too intent on true love to obey. Raymond yelled something, which he covered with a cough. I caught a glimpse of his face just as his eyes began to roll back. A tic was tugging at his mouth, his lower lip pulling down grotesquely. His head jerked twice to the left, mouth coming open. His temper seemed to snap and he went for the dog, landing an ill-aimed blow at Perro's meaty shoulder. The dog snarled and lunged. Raymond punched at the dog again, catching him in the nose. Perro yelped and scrambled away from him, cowering submissively. I moved into the path of Raymond's fist, blocking his next punch while Bibianna threw herself against him. Raymond shoved her out of the way. He knocked me aside and would have punched the dog again, but Luis hauled Perro by the choke chain and dragged him toward the door. Raymond stood and panted, eyelids fluttering, white slits visible along the rim. The rage and cruelty in his face were frightening, especially since his outburst was directed at the poor dog. Pit bull or no, Perro had a goofy innocence about him and all of us felt protective.

Bibianna pushed Raymond into a chair. "What's the matter with you!"

Raymond rubbed at his fist, his self-control returning by degrees. Luis and the dog disappeared. My heart began to pump belatedly. Raymond was breathing hard. I saw his head jerk. He eased his right arm in its socket and did a neck roll to relax. The tension drained from the room.

His gaze focused on Bibianna, who was pinning him to the chair, pressing down on his shoulders to prevent his getting up. She straddled his lap, the long, flawless legs anchoring him into place. It was the same move I'd seen her use with Tate the night before last. Hard to believe that less than forty-eight hours ago, she'd been with him.

Raymond stared up at her. "What's the matter? What's happening?"

"Nothing. Everything's fine," she said tersely. "Luis took the dog for a walk."

The moment passed. I was beginning to recognize the shifts in his moods. The spill of rage stirred sexuality. Before he could slide his hands up along her thighs, she removed herself from his lap as if she were getting off a horse. She smoothed her shorts and crossed to the television set, where she scooped up the deck of cards that was sitting on top. "Let's play gin rummy," she said. "A nickel a point."

Raymond smiled, indulging her, probably thinking he would nail her later.

When Luis came back with the dog, Bibianna lent me some jeans, a T-shirt, and some tennies so we could go out to dinner. The four of us left on foot and headed into the dismal commercial district that bordered the apartment complex. We crossed a vacant lot and went in through the rear entrance of a restaurant called El Pollo Norteño, which by my translation meant the North Chicken. The place was noisy, vinyl tile floor, the walls covered in panels of plastic laminate. The room felt close, nearly claustrophobic from the flame grills in the rear. Countless chickens were trussed on a rotating spit, brown and succulent, skins crisp and glistening with sputtering fat. The noise level was battering, mariachi music punctuated by a constant irregular banging of the cleavers whacking whole chickens into quarters and halves. The menu was listed on a board behind the register. We ordered at the counter, picked up four beers, and then canvassed, looking for a booth. The place was crowded, patrons spilling out onto a makeshift wooden deck that was actually an improvement. It was quieter out there and the chill California night air was a distinct relief. Moments later, a waitress appeared with our order on a tray, setting down paper plates and plastic flatware. We tore the chicken with our hands, piling shreds of grilled meat onto soft corn tortillas, spooning pinto beans and fresh salsa on top. It was a three-paper-napkin extravaganza of messy hands and dripping chins. Afterward, we adjourned to a bar two doors away. It was nine by then.

The Aztlan was smoky, cavernous, ill lighted, occupied almost exclusively by Hispanic men whose eyes, at that hour, were turning slippery from all the alcohol they'd consumed. The laughter came in constant, raucous bursts that were sly and assaultive, very worrisome. There was, on the surface, a thin veneer of control. Under it, and unpredictable, was the boiling violence of youth. The Spanish music was cranked up to a feverish pitch, forcing loud talk in aggressive tones that even merriment couldn't mask. I took my cue from Bibianna, who seemed watchful, her sexuality under wraps. Here, there was none of the familiar bantering I'd seen in the Meat Locker. Raymond was too easily set off and her intentions were too readily misunderstood. Luis seemed right at home, sauntering to the bar with his macho attitude. In his snowy white undershirt, his bare arms were a moving cartoon, Daffy Duck and Donald Duck in aggressive black and yellow.

While Luis fetched four more beers, we pushed through the crowd toward the back. In a second room about half the size of the first, there were three pool tables, two of them occupied. The felt surfaces looked as green as grassy islands under hot hanging lights. The dark of the ceiling was broken up by the blinking of multicolored Christmas tree lights that were probably strung up year-round. Raymond found an empty booth and Bibianna slid in. I was bringing up the rear, sidetracked by the jostling of the intervening mob. I felt a hand on my arm, impeding my progress.

"Hey, babe. You play pool?"

I knew the voice.

I turned and it was Tate.

I could feel my heart do a flip-flop, fearing Raymond's reaction. I glanced back at Bibianna automatically. She was squeezed into the booth, facing in my direction. She must have recognized Tate about the time I did because her face seemed to pale.

"Let's just mosey over to the pool table," Tate said under his breath. "Has Raymond figured out yet it was me killed Chago?"

"If he did, you'd be a dead man. Dawna got picked up before she could tell him everything. Why don't you get out while you can," I murmured.

Tate took my arm, moving me toward the pool table. "Aren't you happy to see me?"

I closed my eyes briefly. "Jesus, Tate. Get away from me. What are you *doing* here?"

He took my hand. I was forced to follow as we crossed to the rack of pool cues, where I watched Tate select one. "I had to see Bibianna. She tell you about us?"

"Of course. You could have told me yourself if you'd trusted me."

"Who had time? I'se busy shooting bad guys." He raised

the cue to shoulder height and sighted down the length of it like a rifle. "Boom."

"How'd you know where we'd be?"

"Pick a cue stick," he said.

I chose one at random, too distracted to be particular, not that I have a clue about the qualities of a good cue.

"Not that one." He handed me another cue stick and then continued casually. "This is Raymond's hangout. You don't have to be Sherlock Holmes to figure out where he'll be. By the way, if Raymond comes over and wants to know what's going on, tell him the truth—we went to grade school together."

"How'd you get out of the slammer? I thought you were broke. What's bail on a murder charge, two hundred thousand bucks?"

"Two fifty. I got a friend in Montebello who put up his house. My attorney got bail knocked down to a hundred grand. I'm out on OR plus bail. . . ."

"And they let you leave the county?"

"Quit worryin'. It's legitimate. I talked my probation officer into an eight-hour turnaround. My wife's sick, I said. I'm due back in Santa Teresa by six A.M. or they'll throw me in the can again." Tate arranged the balls in the rack and broke. Balls scattered everywhere with a satisfying crack.

"What are we doing? I haven't played pool for years."

"Eight-ball. It's your shot."

"You're very cute," I said without much conviction. "Just tell me what to hit and let's get on with it."

"You think I can have time alone with her?"

"No."

"Would you give her a message? Would you tell her I'm doing everything I can to get her out of here?"

"Sure."

We played pool. Jimmy Tate pretended to tutor me and I took instruction, all in the interest of conducting a tense conversation overlaid with bright smiles. From a distance, I hoped we'd look like potential bedmates to someone who would kill us if he figured out what was actually happening. Tate loved it, of course. This was just the sort of situation he thrived on—out there on the front line, taking flak, taking risks in the name of I don't even know what. I was feeling that same sick sensation that prefaces a tetanus shot. Something bad was going to happen and I couldn't figure out how to escape it.

Tate said, "You taking good care of her for me?"

"I'm a real champ," I said. "This is the last time I'm ever doing shit like this for anyone."

He smiled. "That's because you'd rather kick butt."

"You got *that* right."

Tate cleaned up the table and we joined the other three, who were bunched into the booth. Luis got up and I slid in beside Tate, who remained carefully attentive to me in the process. Luis found an empty chair and pulled it over to the table. I think it was the first time I ever served as a "beard" in a dangerous liaison. Liar that I am under ordinary circumstances, I found it a tricky business to fake a flirtation. I felt awkward and false, reactions not lost on Raymond, whose radar was telling him enemy aircraft were somewhere in the area. I felt his eyes scan my face with a half-formed question. Maybe he'd write me off as a hopeless social oaf. Certainly the woodenness of my response to Tate was obvious.

Tate proceeded to tease me outrageously under Bibianna's watchful gaze. She was feigning indifference, but her interest was obvious. Aside from the fact the situation scared me silly, I was glad to have Tate on the scene. I hadn't realized, before he showed up, how isolated I was feeling. I was still vulnerable, of course—more so with him there—but at least I had a friend, and I knew, from my long experience, he'd lay down his life for me if it came to that.

Bibianna, in range of Jimmy Tate again, began to do the ritual dance. There was nothing overt in her behavior. She went out of her way to cater to Raymond, tucking her arm in his, leaning against him so that her breast brushed his arm enticingly. She and Tate avoided eye contact, ignoring one another so pointedly I'd have thought them rude if I hadn't known their true relationship. As it was, the game they played was far riskier. The color crept up in her cheeks unbidden. I watched the sexuality emerge, some ancient, unspeakable response to her mate. I couldn't believe Raymond didn't pick up on it. The only clue I had about his inner state was the eruption of the tics, which were running once a minute.

He was clearly feeling territorial. Whether he was sensitive to what was actually going on or not, Tate was still a male, not only on Raymond's turf, but in close proximity to his woman. Raymond seemed to swell, trying to engage Tate in a shoving match of boasts and braggadocio, a verbal pissing match. I don't know what, among women, would constitute an equivalent. I tuned out the talk because it was all chest-thumping bullshit, fueled by alcohol and testosterone. I couldn't even begin to compute what Tate's response might be when he found out Bibianna was sleeping with Raymond. The whole situation might have amused me if I hadn't been so eaten up with tension.

Luis was watchful. The usual blank mask fell away and I saw, for the first time, a wily intelligence at work. Behind his dead eyes, a lively animal lurked, all the more dangerous for its cunning at concealment. The spark died. He slouched in his seat, flinging an arm across the back of the chair. He lifted his beer bottle by the neck and drank deeply. By the time he looked at me again, the arrogance was back, the superiority of the male lording it over lesser mortals.

I thought the night would never end. The Spanish music was jarring, either loud and frenetic or emotionally oppressive. The air was cloudy with smoke and the smell of beer. The only thing I cared about was staying very close to Tate, whose sun-weathered face was the only refuge I could see. I made him dance with me, in part to keep him away from Raymond, who was no fool. In the stress of the moment, we all drank way too much. I'd be sick in the morning, but I didn't care at this point. Maybe I could carve out a quiet life for myself on the bathroom floor, head hanging over the toilet bowl.

We closed the place down at 2:00 A.M. Outside the bar, we parted company with Tate. I was just relieved to get out of the situation in one piece, with no fisticuffs, no confrontations, no tears. Luis left the three of us out in front of the apartment, peeling off in the Cadillac. I preceded Raymond and Bibianna up the stairs, waiting while Raymond unlocked the door and let us in. The dog lay in the doorway like a sentinel, lifting his heavy bony head to give me a look as I passed. At least he had the good grace not to growl.

I went into my room and slipped into my nightie, then headed for the bathroom. The door to the master bedroom was closed. I knew from the way Raymond had been looking at Bibianna that his desires were at a peak again. In the interest of keeping peace, she was going to have to submit. I felt for her. What could be worse than making love to someone you didn't want to be with, caught up in a situation that dictated intimacy? I washed my face and brushed my teeth, turned the bathroom light out, and padded barefoot into my room. I opened one of the windows and leaned out, gazing briefly along the street, first in one direction, then the other. No one was stirring. In the quiet of the hour, by the pale wash of moonlight, even poverty can look appealing. The shabbiness is cleansed, all the broken parts made whole. The concrete sidewalk seemed to glow with silver, the street a darker tone. A car passed, driven slowly. Jimmy Tate, perhaps? Was he wild with the notion of Bibianna in bed with someone else? I remembered Daniel, my second ex-husband, whose sexual betrayal had been a source of such anguish once. Later, after love dies, it's hard to remember how it could have ever mattered so much.

From the other room, I heard the muffled thumping as the king-size bed banged into the wall. I lifted my head, suddenly sobered by the realization that this was the perfect time to get some work done if I moved fast enough. I peeled off my nightie and pulled on some jeans. I yanked a T-shirt over my head and slipped my bare feet into Bibianna's tennis shoes, which I tied in haste. I unlocked the sliding glass window and shoved it open, aluminum frame rasping in its track.

The night air was cold and a light breeze whipped across my face. Below, the passageway between buildings looked dark and empty. I could smell smog and briny ocean in a heady mix. I boosted myself up onto the windowsill and scrambled out onto the metal landing between flights of stairs. The alcohol I'd consumed was acting as a sedative for any anxiety I might have felt. My heart was pumping hard and the effect was energizing. I was thrilled to be on the move again, excited to be looking at some action after all the enforced passivity.

seventeen

My tennis shoes made hardly any sound as I eased past Raymond's darkened window. I held my breath, but the closed bedroom drapes were still being flattened rhythmically as the headboard banged against them. I felt my way down the stairs, my footsteps making soft tinking sounds where my rubber soles touched the metal. At the bottom of the steps, I paused to orient myself. I was sheltered in the dark shadow of the apartment complex. It was close to 3:00 A.M., the street deserted, the neighborhood cloaked in silence. Even traffic on the big boulevard half a block away was only intermittent. The moon was full and rode high in the night sky. The Los Angeles city lights projected an ashen reflection across the heavens, blotting out the stars. As my eyes became accustomed to the dark, I began to distinguish the clear, pale light being cast by the moon. I emerged from the gap between Raymond's building and the apartment complex next door. I turned left, clinging to the shadows as I crossed the street, moving toward the auto salvage yard. I touched the fence and felt my way along the perimeter, sometimes traversing the circular glow of streetlights. I chose a spot halfway down the block where a driveway cut through the fence. A cluster of tall weeds and ratty shrubs flanked the gate. By day, the dirt lane was used by the tow trucks bringing in disabled vehicles. At night, when the yard closed, a wide gate was rolled across the opening, looped with a chain, and secured by a padlock. I pushed at the gate, forcing it open as far as the chain would permit. A ten-inch gap appeared. I hunkered, holding to the gatepost with both hands as I slid my right leg through. By pushing back with my hips, I could force the fence post back by another couple of inches. I rotated my shoulders, slipped my head through the gap, and then pivoted on my feet, neatly inserting myself into the yard on the other side.

The chunky mountains of rusted metal were lightly frosted by moonlight. I felt as if I'd entered a charnel house of wrecked autos. Some cars had flipped, their tops squashed flat. Some had been torn in two on impact with trees, bridge abutments, and telephone poles. The roll call of destruction conjured up awesome images of the attendant human suffering: ripped chrome and cracked glass, smashed fenders, splayed and flattened tires, engines rammed through hoods, steering columns crammed up against broken front seats. Every vehicle I saw represented a chapter in somebody's life—sometimes the last—sirens and flashing lights signaling injury and death, the loss of a loved one, or the opening scene in a nightmare of mending and medical expenses.

I waited until my heart had stopped pounding in my ears and then I picked my way down the dirt lane toward the offices of Buddy's Auto Body Shop. The pickup truck I'd seen earlier was no longer parked near the trailer, but Brutus had been left behind to stand guard over the property. I could see him, black and bulky near the single-wide, keeping watch as I approached. I sank down on my heels, calling to him softly, making little kissing sounds in the quiet. He gathered his hind feet under him, launched himself into a standing position, and began to toddle toward me carefully. He seemed to tiptoe, bones creaking, his forward motion fueled by memories of a vigorous youth.

I held my hand out and he sniffed it, making hoarse sounds of joy and recognition. I spent a few minutes with him, assuring him of my benign intentions. When I rose to my feet, he accompanied me to the trailer and watched politely while I removed all the louvers from the window. I stuck a hand through the opening and felt a solid wooden surface, which I guessed was a desk shoved up against the wall just below the window. I stacked the louvers neatly on the desk top inside.

I hoisted myself up, whispering compliments to Brutus, who wagged his tail so hard he nearly toppled sideways in the process. "Back in a flash," I said. I swung my feet through the window and eased myself into the pitch black of the office. I was now sitting on a desk. I could feel an adding machine, the telephone, and miscellaneous office supplies. I replaced the glass louvers in the metal brackets made for them.

I eased down off the desk. I stood there for a few minutes until I got used to the darkness. I usually don't do these breaking-and-entering gigs unless I have my little tool kit in tow: flashlight and lockpicks, adhesive tape, and jimmies. Here, I was empty-handed and I felt distinctly disadvantaged. All I wanted was to check the file cabinets to see if Raymond kept his papers on the premises. Once I established the whereabouts of the records, I was out of here. I was going to have to risk a light. I kept in mind the sign I'd seen, indicating an alarm system. Would Raymond actually have such a system, or was he the kind who thought he could deter all the burglars and vandals by pretending to have security? Hard to say with him. He was so righteous about the law when it suited his purposes.

I felt along the wall until I found the switch. I hesitated for a moment and then flipped the light on. The forty-watt bulb revealed an inner office maybe ten feet by twelve, wall paneled halfway up with sheets of fake knotty pine. Girlie calendars from the last six years were tacked up above a work bench where some front windshields had been piled. Three extension cords were plugged into a socket in the inner office and looped through the doorway to service the outer office. Every surface in the room was a jumble of cardboard boxes and greasy car parts. Two gray metal file cabinets were tucked into the corner on the far side of the room. As I crossed the open door leading to the outer office, I caught a blink of light out of the corner of my eye. The passive infrared "seeing eye" of Raymond's alarm picked up my body heat and set off the entire system.

A horn, probably adequate to announce the end of the world, began a great whooping noise that alternated between high notes and low notes and seemed to include some kind of bell clanging in between. We are programmed from birth to react to sudden loud noises. Of course I jumped and my heart kicked up into high gear. At the same time, I could feel my emotions disconnect as they do in certain emergencies. I wondered belatedly if Raymond's alarm was set up to signal the police. I better count on it, I thought. I glanced at my watch. It was 3:12 A.M. I figured I had about five minutes max before the black-and-whites showed up. Might have been a charitable estimate on my part. Maybe the LAPD didn't even bother with alarms. Maybe they'd respond in their own sweet time. What did I know about the machinations of big-city police procedure? While the alarm system bleated and shrieked and pointed an auditory finger, I crossed to the file cabinet and opened the first drawer. Invoices, car parts. I shut that one and tried the next. More invoices, financial records, correspondence, blank forms. Drawer three was a repeat. I skipped to the next file cabinet and started with the top, working my way down. The bottom three drawers were packed with manila folders full of claim forms. I glanced at dates in haste, noting that the claims seemed to extend back about three years. Outside, Brutus was offering up an occasional hoarse bark, apparently overjoyed that I had hit the jackpot. I closed the file drawers, checked to see that the louvered window was shut, tidied some papers on the desk, and brushed some dirt off the Month-at-a-Glance that was lying there. I walked into the outer office, moved around the corner to the front door, which I opened, ducked back to the inner office, and flipped out the light there, then felt my way in the dark to the front door again. I stepped out and gave the door a hard pull behind me, effectively locking it again. The alarm clamoring against the night air seemed to have aroused no particular interest among the neighbors. I wondered if Raymond could hear it from across the street and two doors down.

I set off at a run, jogging down the dirt path toward the gate, with Brutus bringing up the rear. I could hear him loping along behind me, panting happily as he maneuvered his legs in some dimly remembered sequence. I glanced back. For an old pooch, he was really truckin', determined to keep up with me in my little nighttime ramble. I reached the gate and pushed it, reversing the procedure by which I angled my way in. I heard a car squeal around the corner and looked back just in time to see the black-and-white appear on the scene. I shoved back hard on the fence post and pivoted my way through the narrow opening.

I heard a sound like the equivalent of a canine rebuke. When I looked over I saw that Brutus had his head stuck in the gap between the gate and the fence post. He was yanking backward, his bony head and the thick muscular neck pinched in a vise of fencing. Car doors slammed and one uniformed cop headed toward the front entrance while the second one walked in my direction.

"Oh, God," I said. I jerked the gate forward and pushed the dog's head to free him. Then I plunged into the bushes and crouched down. I was shielded temporarily by a tangle of shrubbery, but the oncoming cop was scanning every inch of the fence with a heavy-duty flashlight. Meanwhile, inside the fence, Brutus had discovered what I was doing. He put his nose against the chain link and made a worried sound, half growl, half celebration of our newly cemented friendship.

The cop down the block near the office gave a whistle and the officer closer to me turned and headed back the way he'd come. I pulled myself to my feet and extracted myself from the bushes, inching away from the squad car as inconspicuously as I could. Brutus began to bark, unwilling to be abandoned just when the game was getting good. There was a line of parked cars at the curb. I reached the first and ducked behind it, using the cars as concealment until I reached the corner. I crossed the street at an angle and doubled back toward Raymond's, cutting into the heavy shadows between apartment buildings. Above me, the window in his bedroom blazed with light. I took the metal stairs three at a time, pulling myself up by the railing. Out of breath, I eased past the bedroom, found my open window, and plunged into the bedroom again. I whipped my shoes off, pulled my jeans down, and stuck my head out the door, squinting at the lights that were now flipped on in the hall. Bibianna, in a silk robe, was just emerging from the bedroom. I could hear Raymond in the living room on the phone with someone.

"What's happening?" I asked.

Bibianna rolled her eyes. "It's the body shop. False alarm. Sometimes the damn thing goes off. Chopper's on his way over, but the cops say it's nothing. Go back to bed."

I closed the door. Sleep was a long time coming.

I woke at nine-thirty to the smell of coffee. I showered and dressed. The door to the master bedroom was open and I caught a glimpse of the broad king-size bed, neatly made. No sign of Raymond or Bibianna. I wandered into the living room to find that Luis was the only one on the premises, except the dog, of course. Luis paid no particular attention to me. He placed a clean mug on the counter and I poured myself some coffee.

"Thanks," I murmured. I sat down at the kitchen table, doing a quick inspection first to make sure it had been wiped clean. "Where's Bibianna?"

"They went off someplace."

"What are you, the baby-sitter?"

He made no reply. A carton of eggs sat open on the counter. In the day since I'd cleaned the kitchen, it had fallen into disarray again. Trash bags were lined up against the cabinets, bulging with beer bottles and discarded paper plates. The sink was piled high with dirty pots and pans, ashtrays spilling butts. Who smoked? I never saw anyone with a cigarette. Luis had pulled out the only clean skillet. He set it on a burner. He began to remove items from the refrigerator: peppers, onions, chorizo. "You want breakfast?"

"Sure, I'd love it. You need any help?"

He shook his head.

It seemed like the perfect opportunity to pump him for information, but I didn't want to start with the fraud ring itself lest I seem too inquisitive. "I hope this doesn't seem too personal," I said. "I thought Raymond would be upset about Chago's death, but he hasn't said a word about it. Weren't they close?"

Luis sliced the peppers into rings and then chopped onions, making no reference to the chemically induced tears rolling down his cheeks. His gaze came up to meet mine. "Chago was all he had. Raymond's sisters kicked him out when he was fourteen on account of his temper. He was on his own after that and he's done okay, considering. Kids in school used to mock him, making fun of his disease."

"You knew him then?"

"Juan told me about it. I kind of wish he'd go to the doctor, get some help for himself, but he won't do it. He thinks Bibianna's all the help he needs."

I watched him, expecting more, but apparently he felt what he'd said should suffice. He used the knife to mound the onions, then walked the blade through the pile, mincing them. He crossed to the stove. I waited as he tilted the skillet, watching a hunk of melting butter circle lazily. He tossed in the onions and peppers. Finally, he spoke up again. "How you know Jimmy Tate? I saw his picture in the papers. He's a cop," he said, rendering the word with venom.

"An ex-cop. From grade school. We were kids together in Santa Teresa a long time ago."

"He's a snitch."

"That's bullshit. L.A. County Sheriff's Department just fired the guy and he turned around and sued. They're not going to hire him to do anything!"

Luis turned, pointing at me with the knife. "Let me tell you something. Tate's got no business with us. He shows up and I smell a snitch. Don't tell me bullshit. I know what I'm talking about."

I could feel myself hesitate, backing up a step. The idea of Tate undercover had crossed my mind, too. In the interview with Dolan and Santos, I'd asked twice if they had a man in and both times they'd been nonresponsive. Tate's suit against the department and his Tuesday night arrest might be part of his cover. If Luis was suspicious, then Raymond would be, too, and every move Tate made would be subject to scrutiny. "What's Raymond say?"

"He's checking out a source."

"Well, that's good," I said. "Then he can find out for sure, right?" My heart did a rat-a-tat-tat from fear. The possibility of a department leak was already a source of concern. If word trickled out about me, I was dead.

Luis retreated again. He sliced into the skin of a Mexican sausage and squeezed out the meat in a gesture surprisingly ominous. Soon I could smell the chorizo sizzling away with the onions and peppers. Luis broke eight eggs into a bowl with one hand, then whipped them into a froth with a fork.

I didn't want to defend Jimmy Tate too vigorously because it might backfire. Somebody might begin to wonder what made me such an expert. Best not to protest too much when you're tampering with the truth. Besides, Tate's cover had to be deep—if, indeed, that's what was happening. Dolan and Santos were both aware of the need for secrecy. I let the subject drop. I had thought to probe for information about the fraud ring. Now, I decided to bypass the quiz. All I needed was Luis turning his steely gaze on me.

We ate the omelet in silence. I'm forced to report it was one of the best I've ever eaten. The few bites I couldn't finish, I put down for the dog. Perro snapped the eggs up in one bite with a jerk of his head that propelled food down his throat. After breakfast, Luis scrubbed the skillet. My job was to fold the plates and throw them in the trash.

"What's the program for the day?"

"I take you to the chiropractor as soon as Raymond gets back."

"How come we have to wait? Can't we do anything on our own?"

Luis said nothing. I decided it wasn't wise to press. Raymond didn't seem to trust him much more than he trusted me.

At noon Raymond and Bibianna returned to the apartment. Her face was haggard, the look she turned on me full of dread. She was signaling something, but I wasn't sure what. In contrast, Raymond's mood seemed expansive, though I noticed the twinkle of a tic in his blinking. Bibianna took her jacket off and tossed it on the couch. There was a Band-Aid across the crook of her right arm. Raymond grabbed her from behind in a bear hug, an odd hostility disguised as affection.

He caught my look, which had touched on the Band-Aid and glanced off. "She had a blood test. We're getting married as soon as the license comes through. Three days max."

"Congratulations," I said weakly. "Really, that's great."

Luis extended his hand. He and Raymond went through some complicated series of palm slaps and grips, signifying great gang joy at the nuptials of another. Bibianna's happiness was so overwhelming that she had to leave the room, a reaction not lost on the ever-vigilant Raymond. I could see the tic pick up, his mouth coming open, his neck jerking back. Luis broke out a couple of beers, ostensibly to celebrate. My guess was he hoped to head off one of Raymond's attacks. "Get her out here. Luis is going to get us some champagne. We'll drink a toast."

"I'll be right back," I murmured, and went into the bedroom. Bibianna was sitting on the edge of the bed, her head in her hands.

I sat down on the bed beside her, watching her without a word. What could I say? She was married to Jimmy Tate. There was no way she was going to end up married to Raymond, too. Finally, I said, "What are you going to do?"

She looked at me bleakly. "Kill myself or kill him." She reached out and took my hand, giving it a squeeze.

"I'll hang in," I said.

"I know that," she replied.

eighteen

Luis parked the Ford in a small weedy lot adjacent to a strip mall that had probably been built in the early fifties judging by the architectural style, which was of the cinder block and glass brick variety. The chiropractor's office was located in a storefront, wedged between a barbecue joint and a barbershop. Dusty beige drapes covered the plate-glass windows, protecting the interior from the curious stares of those passing on the street. Not that there was much to see inside. The walls were flat blue, lined with metal folding chairs. A television set in the corner ran a Spanish-language tape extolling the virtues of the chiropractic arts. A tattered illustration on the wall labeled "Chart of the Eye" showed the split circles with radial divisions essential to iridiagnosis, by which one could accurately identify diabetes mellitus, typhoid, aortic regurgitation, and other alarming conditions. The floor was covered in marbled beige vinyl tiles, through which a damp mop had been trailed recently, leaving tracks of yesterday's dirt. A counter separated the reception area from the examining rooms in the rear. There were sixteen people waiting to see Dr. Howard and no magazines. One of the other patients was a fellow I thought I'd seen in Raymond's apartment the day I arrived. I filled out a rudimentary medical history, automatically printing the first three letters of "Millhone" before I caught myself, converting the *i* and *l* to the double *oo*'s of my current alias, "Moore." The form itself took two minutes to complete, after which we all sat and looked at one another while two babies cried and eleven people smoked thirty-four cigarettes between them. The inhalation of passive smoke in conjunction with my boredom was enough to make me want to flee the premises. I checked my watch. I'd been sitting for an hour and a half. I didn't feel I could complain since I was only there to cheat the insurance company. I imagined all the other people, blacks, Hispanics, the elderly, the weekend athletes, being variously cracked, pummeled, pounded, and popped into alignment in the back room while I awaited my turn. People coming out to pay for treatment did appear to be relieved. Their backs seemed straighter, shoulders squared. They moved with more energy, taking with them enormous jars of pills which I assumed were expensive vitamins or calcium supplements. Many soft and crumpled dollar bills were passed over to the bilingual receptionist, a woman in her forties, quite possibly the doctor's wife.

When my turn came, I checked her name tag, but all it said was Martha. She walked me down a short corridor, past the open door of what must have been Dr. Howard's office. I caught a glimpse of a scarred oak desk covered with stacks of charts and small standing picture frames, probably showing him with loving family members, thus establishing his marital status and firmly declaring him off limits to women patients with designing minds. I was ushered into the adjoining examining room, noting with interest the door between the two rooms, which stood ajar. I could see through the doctor's office right back out into the hallway, where a passing patient turned and looked at me with curiosity. Martha opened a cabinet and removed a print smock that seemed to be made of two oblong cotton panels stitched together at the side and secured with elastic at the neck.

"Take your shoes off and strip down to your panties," she said, handing me the gown. "He'll be with you in ten minutes."

"Thanks. Uhm, could we close that other door?" I asked.

"Certainly." She moved through the doctor's office to the hall door, closing it as she went out.

I could feel my fingers start to itch.

My, my. All by myself and the office records of a scofflaw, insurance-defrauding bone cracker not ten feet away. I checked the door to the examining room, which had a thumb button on the knob, which I pressed, locking it. I stripped my clothes off in haste and pulled the gown over my head, then padded barefoot into the doctor's office, locking his door, too. The walls were so thin and so poorly constructed that it wasn't hard to run an auditory check of what was going on around me. I heard the doctor enter the room across the hall, greeting the patient by name as he closed the door behind him. Their murmurs were audible, though the content of the consultation was lost as he proceeded to his adjustment. I kept one ear cocked while I searched as thoroughly as I could in the eight minutes allotted me, uncovering a drawerful of claims that were a cursory match to the insurance forms I'd seen at Raymond's. I heard the door across the hall come open, the doctor's voice growing more distant as he gave a few final words of counsel and advice. I closed the desk drawer and crossed rapidly to the office door, grabbed the knob, and twisted. The button popped out. I was heading toward the examining room again when one of the little framed family photos on his desk caught my eye.

I stopped and squinted, peering at a bridal photo of a young woman I could have sworn I'd seen before. I snatched up the double frame, quickly rearranging the remaining frames to conceal the sudden gap. I eased into the examining room and had just tucked the picture frame in the handbag I'd borrowed from Bibianna when I heard the doctor try the door.

"Just a minute," I called. I popped the lock and opened the door for him with a sheepish smile. "Sorry," I said. "I didn't realize it was locked. Are you Dr. Howard?"

"That's right." He came into the room, closing the door behind him.

I resisted the impulse to shake hands with the man. It seemed inappropriate since I'd just burgled something from his desk. He was in his sixties, very clean looking. He wore white pants and a white jacket, with a snowy dress shirt underneath, starched shirt collar standing up so high it seemed to pleat his neck. His dark hair looked soft on top. His hairline was receding, which left him with a long expanse of unlined forehead. He had cold eyes, a mild brown, behind square tortoiseshell frames, a humorless mouth that turned down slightly at the corners. He managed a perfunctory smile with his lips while the rest of his face remained fixed. His gaze was intense, giving him the look of a man capable of seeing straight from his own felonious heart into mine. The fragrance of crushed spices wafted into the room behind him, some faded Oriental blend of musk and sandalwood.

He glanced at my chart. "Miss Moore. What seems to be the trouble? Why don't you hop up on the table."

"It's my neck," I said as I hiked myself onto the table. "I was in a little accident and Raymond Maldonado suggested I have you check it." He crossed to a corner sink and washed his hands with a virulent-looking red liquid soap from a wall dispenser. The gaze he turned on me was brief, but sharply focused. "You should have mentioned that to Martha. We'll need an X ray," he said. "I'll have my assistant take it. You can come back here when you're done." He moved to the door and held it open for me. Instinct told me to take my handbag, which I picked up and tucked under one arm, a gesture of distrust not lost on him.

"Your purse is safe, if you'd care to leave it," he said.

"It's no trouble," I murmured, not volunteering to put it back. I had visions of his searching it in my absence, discovering the photo I'd swiped before he arrived. My memory warbled a little tune, too faint to identify. I was certain I'd seen the woman in the picture, but I had no idea where.

Barefoot, I followed him down the corridor to a makeshift X-ray laboratory, partitioned off by a few temporary plywood screens. The equipment looked like some I'd seen in a doctor's office when I was a kid: bulky and black, with a cone the size of a zoom lens. I imagined 1950s-style rays, thick and clunky, piercing my body in poorly calibrated doses. The assistant, a young guy with a cigarette bobbing in his mouth, took two views—a full spine and a close-up of the cervical vertebrae. I'm wary of unnecessary X-ray procedures, but again, since I was cheating, it was hard to protest. I returned to the examining room, where I had another long wait, this time sitting dutifully on the paper-covered table. For all I knew Dr. Howard was observing me through a hidden peephole. He returned in due course, snapping the developed film onto a wall-mounted viewer. He explained patiently, in chiropractic terms, how misshapen my spine was. Happily, my neck wasn't broken, but almost every other part of my back was in want of improvement. He put me facedown on the table and did something divine, crunching my bones in a manner that sounded like someone chewing ice. He prescribed a lengthy series of adjustments, writing out his diagnosis with a fountain pen. He was left-handed, wrist curving atop the sentences as he sketched out his recommendations. The pen made a scratching sound as it angled across the page. Even his writing looked expensive, I thought. California Fidelity was going to pay dearly for my ills.

"What's your relationship to Raymond?" he asked without looking up. Something about the nonchalance of his tone sounded a note of caution.

"I'm a friend of Bibianna's, his fiancée."

"Have you known her long?"

"Two days," I said. "We did an overnight together in the Santa Teresa County Jail."

The sharp gaze shifted and I thought I detected a nearly

imperceptible pursing of his lips. He disapproved of lowlifes like Bibianna and me, probably Raymond Maldonado, too. "How long have you had your offices down here?" I asked.

"Since my license was reinstated," he said, surprising me with his candor. Maybe I'd misjudged the man. He opened a drawer and took out a number of ink pens, of various types and colors. He passed me a sheet of paper with a series of slots in the left-hand column. "Sign each line with a different pen, rotating them randomly. We'll fill the dates in later when we go to bill your insurance company. Who's the carrier?"

"California Fidelity. I called the office up north and they said they'd send the claim forms down."

"Good," he said. "And what sort of work do you normally do?"

"Waitress."

"Not good. I don't want you on your feet and no lifting heavy trays. File for disability. Nice to meet you," he said. He snapped my chart shut, got up, and left the room. Half a minute later, I heard him entering the examining room next to mine.

It was two fifty-five by the time I left his office. The day was hot for late October, the air perfumed with the yeasty smell of warm exhaust fumes. The neighborhood we were in wasn't much of an improvement over the one where Raymond lived. As I approached the Ford, Luis leaned over and opened the car door. I slid into the front seat. Whatever Dr. Howard had done in the way of adjustments, my hangover was at least gone. I tilted my head this way and that, taking inventory of my neck. Not bad. No stiffness, no more aches or pains.

The interior of the car smelled of fast-food burgers and cold French fries. There was an empty milk shake container on the dashboard and a white paper bag sitting on the front seat. "Oh, goody, for me?" I asked. I peered into the bag, hunger rising suddenly. "Luis, there's nothing in here but trash!"

"I thought you'd ate."

"You thought I'd ate?" I said pointedly.

Luis seemed embarrassed. "Eaten."

"Yeah, well, I eaten the same time you did and I'm starving again." I revised my tone. There was no point in being a bitch about this. "Isn't there any way we could stop and pick up some lunch for me on the way home?"

He started the car, checking the flow of traffic in the rear-view mirror. "Raymond said come back as soon as you got done. We got work to do."

"How come we have to do everything he says?"

Luis turned a flat look on me.

I thought about Raymond's temper. "Good point," I said.

When we got back to the apartment, the dog was tied to the railing out on the balcony and the apartment door was standing open. There were six or eight young Hispanics on the premises, most of whom I hadn't seen before. Bibianna sat on the couch, bending over a game of solitaire which she'd laid out on the coffee table. Luis went into the kitchen and fetched himself a beer. I excused myself with a murmur and went into my room, where I removed the stolen pictures from my handbag. I moved over to the window and opened it quietly. The frame was a bifold, two photographs in matte gold, hinged in the middle. I dismantled the frame and tossed it out the window, checking first to make sure I wouldn't be clunking anybody in the head with it. I studied both photographs closely, holding them up to the light. These were formal wedding portraits. The first was one of those group shots taken at the church altar afterward, people lined up in a semicircle with the bride and groom in the center. In addition to the newlyweds, there were six young women in lavender, fanning out to the left, and six guys in gray tuxedos with lavender cummerbunds on the right. Dr. Howard was clearly the father of the bride, whose mother didn't look a thing like the receptionist. I'd guessed wrong there. The second photograph was a full-length shot of the bride herself. She was the woman I thought I recognized. She was standing in three-quarter profile, her eyes lifted solemnly toward the stained-glass window above her head, bridal bouquet held at her waist. The dress was a close-fitting satin with a train that had been spread out around her feet as if the material had melted to form a pool. Her blond hair was pulled back, secured in some kind of netting like a bridal snood. The face was tantalizing, not pretty by any stretch, but she'd clearly hired a team of makeup experts to enhance her every feature. I was sure I'd seen her recently, but not looking nearly as good as this. I squinted, perplexed. It was like seeing your mailman at a cocktail party in fancy dress. I had to shrug and forget it for the moment. It would come to me, probably popping into my head when I was in the middle of something else.

I crossed to the closet, slid the door back, and pulled up a corner of the dark blue shag wall-to-wall carpet. I slipped the pictures under it and pressed the carpet back in place.

I returned to the living room, where Bibianna was studying the run of solitaire she'd laid out. I settled into the chair. I tucked my feet up under me and watched Bibianna play, keeping a discreet eye on the gangbangers, who had formed a rough line near the kitchenette. It must have been payday. Raymond sat at the table, collecting hand-held slips of paper, counting out bills in return. He was all business, conducting transactions in Spanish. Without appearing to pay much attention, I took note of the faces, wondering if I'd be able to identify them later from mug shots, if required. The only two I recognized were Raymond's brother, Juan, and the sulky fellow, Tomas, who'd had so much trouble with his paperwork the day I arrived. Raymond glanced over at me and I dropped my gaze to the solitaire laid out on the table.

I'd watched her set it up so many times by now, I was almost ready to try it myself. This one wasn't the usual red queen on a black king strategy but ran in suits so that if you won, you ended up with only four piles, one for each suit, cards in numerical order from aces up to kings. She went through all the cards in her hand by threes without coming up with a play. She tossed the hand in and pulled the cards together in a pile.

"You want to do my chart?" I asked.

She shook her head. "The stuff's at my mother's and Raymond won't let me talk to her. I tried to call her last night, but he caught me with the phone and nearly beat the shit out of me. What an ass. . . ." She glanced over at Raymond, who had stopped what he was doing so he could stare at her. Bibianna stirred uneasily and glanced at me. She said, "I can read your palm instead. Put your hands on the table."

"Palm down?"

"Yeah. Just put 'em down on the tabletop."

I eased my feet out from under me and leaned forward so I could rest my palms flat on the table as instructed. Raymond must have realized she was into her palmistry and he went back to work. Bibianna's look became intent. She scrutinized the backs of my hands, then lifted both and turned them over. She took my right hand in hers and examined it with care, saying nothing. Her manner was as professional as a doctor's. I don't believe in palmistry, any more than I believe in numerology, astrology, the Easter bunny, or the tooth fairy, but there was something in her expression that piqued my curiosity. "What?" I said.

She ran an index finger across my right palm, took up my left palm, and looked at it again. "You like action. You know how I know that? When you put your hands down on the table, you left a lot of space between. Insecure people put 'em close together. Short nails indicate you're aggressive. No ridges or spots, which is good. Means you're healthy. Skin type is medium, doesn't say much, but look at this . . . how wide the space is between your thumb and the fingers on this hand. You think for yourself. . . ."

Her voice was hypnotic and I found myself listening to her with great seriousness. I'd expected a lot of talk about life lines and love lines, but she didn't have a chance to get to that. The trouble broke out so suddenly, I never knew what started it. I heard a shout, the banging as a chair fell over backward. By the time I looked up, Raymond had Tomas down on the floor. He was clutching the guy by the throat, the switchblade against his cheek. Raymond's face was contorted by rage, his hands shaking as he squeezed his fingers into Tomas's windpipe. Tomas was burbling, his eyes wide as he struggled to free himself. Sweat had beaded his forehead. I saw the blade of the knife slip into his cheek, sinking into the flesh, blood welling up. Raymond seemed almost hypnotized by the process. No one else made a move. It seemed to be one of those moments where retaliatory violence would only jeopardize Tomas's chance of survival.

Bibianna whispered, "My God . . ." She crossed the room, kneeling beside Raymond, where she began to murmur in his ear. I could see him struggle for control. He made a sound like a sob, very tight and ancient, almost a squealing at the back of his throat. Bibianna touched his hand, talking to him earnestly. "Don't do this, Raymond. I beg you. Let him go. He didn't mean nothing by it. You're hurting him. Please . . ."

He lifted the knife. Bibianna extracted it from his hand while his victim rolled away, blood pouring down his face. Raymond seemed to cough and his rage shifted from Tomas to Bibianna. He grabbed her by the arms and hauled her upright, shoving her up against the wall so hard her head banged a piece of plaster loose. He put his face an inch away from hers, the now familiar ripple of tics tugging half the muscles in his face. His eyes rolled up in his head so that he seemed to look at her with the milky, blind slits. His voice was a whisper. "I'll kill you, you ever interfere with me again, you got that?"

Bibianna nodded frantically. "I won't. I'm sorry. I didn't mean to . . ."

He stepped away. The ritual cough and bark began and I could see him jerk his head, rolling his shoulder in its socket. Luis had grabbed a kitchen towel and was pressing it against the cut in Tomas's cheek, issuing orders in Spanish. Blood soaked through instantly. Two of the guys came to Tomas's assistance, helping him out the door. The apartment cleared rapidly. My heart was pounding. Bibianna sank down on the couch, white-faced. She put her head between her knees, close to fainting. I moved over and sat down beside her, patting her and murmuring words of encouragement as much for my own benefit as for hers. Moments later, Luis returned. I gathered that someone was taking Tomas off to the emergency room. In the meantime, Raymond seemed to have regained control. Bibianna composed herself and picked up her cards again with shaking hands. Luis wiped blood off the kitchen floor. All of us understood how important it was to get past the moment. To avoid any further upset, we acted as if nothing had happened, which made us co-conspirators. No reference was made to Tomas or what he'd done to precipitate Raymond's reaction.

Raymond paced the room, snapping his fingers restlessly as he turned to Bibianna. "Hey. Get your jacket. We're going out. Hannah, you too."

I got my jacket. Hell, I wasn't going to argue with the man.

This time Raymond and I took the Ford, while Luis followed us in the Cadillac, Bibianna in the passenger seat. I turned halfway, looking through the back window at the Caddy, which kept pace with us. Luis and Bibianna were only dark silhouettes. "How come she always goes with him on these runs?"

"We fight," he said.

I studied him with interest. He seemed relaxed, his manner open and easy. I was beginning to understand that for a short period of time just after an "attack," he was really rather benign, as if soothed by the outburst. For a brief interlude, he would be completely approachable, even loving. He was not a bad-looking guy. He could probably find a woman who'd care for him if he wasn't fixated on Bibianna.

He caught my look. "What are *you* lookin' at?" His words were belligerent, but the tone was mild.

"I was just trying to figure out why you're so obsessed with Bibianna. Why insist on marriage when she's clearly not that hot for it?" I held my breath, but he didn't seem to take offense.

"She can't mess with me. No way. People who screw with my head have to learn they can't. She hasn't got the word yet."

"About what? You have her back. What else do you want?"

"I have to make sure she stays."

"How can you do that?"

"I did already," he said. "She just doesn't know it yet."

nineteen

nineteen

that afternoon at the Southern California College of Auto Fraud, I took a "crash" course in "Swoop and Squat," which Lieutenants Dolan and Santos had summarized so neatly in our little jailhouse chat. We drove up into West L.A., on the border of Bel Air, running Sunset Boulevard from Sepulveda to Beverly Glen. Afternoon traffic was hellish and the drivers familiar with that stretch of road seemed to drive with their eyes shut, shifting lanes without notice, exceeding the speed limit by thirty and forty miles per hour.

Once we found a mark, Raymond and I, as the "squat" car, would position ourselves in front of it while Luis and Bibianna would pull up beside us. Luis would "swoop" suddenly into our lane. Raymond would slam on the brakes and the hapless mark behind us, caught by surprise, would plow right up our tailpipe. Luis would speed off while Raymond and I, in our car, and the mark in his, would pull over to the curb, all of us dismayed and outraged by the unexpected turn of events. There was no danger of the mark's turning around and calling the cops, because we all knew the LAPD wouldn't respond to the scene of an accident unless there was bodily injury involved. It was strictly up to us to exchange names, addresses, telephone numbers, and the names of our various insurance companies, after which we'd take off, connect up with Luis and Bibianna again, and go looking for the next vic. We ran the scam four times, with Raymond assuring me we'd racked up maybe thirteen thousand dollars' worth of business.

What troubled me, aside from the fact that I was whipping the hell out of my neck, was a worrisome little shift in my attitude. What idiots, I thought. People deserve anything that happens to them. I was beginning to believe it was all the mark's fault for being gullible and stupid, for not recognizing the game in progress, for being foolish enough to take our assurances at face value. I could feel that secret sense of superiority every con artist must have when the bait goes down and the victim snaps it up. Mentally, I had to shake myself off, though I suppose it never hurts to be reminded that none of us are that far away from larceny. Actually, it's the people who make the most righteous moral noises that I worry about the most.

We packed it in at five after a quick conference in a little pocket park where we'd pulled off to compare notes. Several nannies in uniform murmured together while the toddlers in their keeping cavorted on the play equipment. We sat on the grass, Bibianna with her shoes off, while Luis and Raymond stretched out in the fading sunlight and relived every thrilling moment. It was like hearing men talk about a golf game or a hunting trip, the two of them rehashing the experience in amazing detail. There was a quick debate about whether to try one more quick accident, but none of us were really interested. All I wanted was some aspirin and a trip back to Dr. Howard's office, where I could look forward to a back cracking that would liberate my neck.

Raymond said he had an errand to run, so he and I got back in the car. Luis peeled off in the Caddy with Bibianna while Raymond turned onto Beverly Drive and headed into the heart of the Beverly Hills business district. Two blocks down, he took a right on Little Santa Monica, which runs parallel to Santa Monica Boulevard. As we approached Wilshire Boulevard, he slowed, looking for a parking space. The meters had all been taken. With an expression of impatience, he turned into the entrance to an underground parking garage that serviced a twenty-story office building. We paused at the electronic kiosk, which buzzed, clunked once, and presented him with a ticket. The electronic "arm" shot up and Raymond slid into the nearest parking spot, clearly marked for the handicapped. He left the keys in the ignition and opened the door on his side.

"Wait here. Somebody hassles you, move the car. I'll be right back."

A vertical sign on the wall indicated that the elevators were located through the double glass doors. He walked rapidly in that direction, heels tapping on the concrete, the sound echoing against the ramps sweeping up to the left. What was he up to?

The minute he was gone, I took the keys out of the ignition and slipped around to the rear of the car, where I opened the trunk. It was empty except for the spare tire and jack. Rats. I slid into the front seat again and returned the keys to the ignition. I leaned over and checked the door pocket on Raymond's side of the car, but all I came up with were a torn Los Angeles street map and some discount coupons for a local pizza joint. The pocket on my side of the car was empty, which I knew because I'd checked it slyly while we were driving around. I popped open the glove compartment, crammed with junk. I began to sort through the wad of old gas receipts, defective ballpoint pens, successive years of car registrations, the service manual, work orders from the mechanic who did the routine maintenance. Raymond was conscientious about upkeep, I had to give him that. At regular thirty-second intervals, I checked the underground reception area where I'd seen him disappear. I was assuming he'd gone up in the elevators to one of the executive offices above.

I sorted through the mess of papers in my lap, uncovering rags, a beer flip, a moldy Hershey's bar suffering from heat prostration, a foil-wrapped condom. Did we once keep our gloves in our automobile glove compartments? Now, the space seemed to rank right up there with the refrigerator as a resting place for animate and inanimate debris, evidence of a lack of personal cleanliness you'd just as soon your friends never found out about. I returned the odds and ends to the glove compartment, being careful not to be too tidy about it. Frustrating. I'd hoped to come up with something. Oh, well. With snooping, you can't expect to score every time out. An illegal search might net results in four cases out of ten. The rest of the time, it simply satisfies your basic nosiness.

By the time I heard Raymond's heels tap-tapping against the concrete, everything was back in place and I was ratting my hair in the rearview mirror, which I'd swiveled around to face me. This "Hannah Moore" persona was having a distinct effect. My "do" now consisted of some really nifty spikes on top. I looked like a punker, but it was kind of fun, if you want to know the truth. Next thing I knew I'd be getting my ears pierced and chewing gum in public, social sins my auntie had always warned me about, along with red nail polish and dingy bra straps.

Raymond opened the car door and tossed the automated parking ticket on the dashboard while he shrugged out of his jacket and tucked it in the backseat. I picked up the ticket and held on to it for him, taking advantage of my little helping girl impulse to glance down at it casually. On the back, in lieu of parking validation stickers, there was the stamped imprint from the firm of Gotlieb, Naples, Hurley, and Flushing. Attorneys? Accountants? Raymond whipped the ticket out of my hand and stuck it in his mouth, clamping it between his teeth while he started the car and backed out of the space. What was his problem? Gosh, the man just didn't seem to trust me. As we turned left out of the parking garage, I silently repeated the name of the firm, like a mantra, until I'd committed it to memory. I'd have Dolan check it out if I could get a call through to him.

We drove back to the apartment through rush-hour traffic: six lanes of the Indy 500, featuring business execs and other control freaks. I was tense, but Raymond didn't seem affected. External stresses didn't seem to disturb him the same way emotional matters did. He flipped the radio on to a classical station and turned the volume up, treating the cars on either side of us to a sonata that sounded like it was made up almost entirely of mistakes. This stretch of the 405 was flat, a sprawling expanse of concrete, riddled with factories, dotted with oil derricks, power lines, and industrial structures designed for no known purpose. In the distance, an irregular fence of chimneys was silhouetted against the skyline, which had browned down to an eerie sunset of green-and-orange light.

It was after seven o'clock and fully dark by the time we pulled into a parking space out in front of the apartment building. Walking up to the second floor, I was struck by the sounds of apartment life. As usual, many front doors stood open, televisions blaring. Children were running along the balconies, engrossed in a game of their own devising. A mother leaned over the railing and yelled at a kid named "Eduardo," who looked to be about three years old. He was protesting in Spanish, probably complaining about the indignity of an early bedtime.

Luis took the dog and went home soon after we got to the apartment. He'd been baby-sitting Bibianna, making sure she didn't bolt the minute Raymond's back was turned. The television set was on, tuned to a cable rerun of "Leave It to Beaver," which Bibianna watched halfheartedly while she laid out another hand of solitaire. Nobody seemed to feel like fixing dinner since we'd all spent a hard day smashing up cars and cheating California motorists. Bibianna's depression was exacerbated by cramps, and she went off to bed with a hot-water bottle. Raymond conjured up the telephone from its latest hiding place and sent out for

Chinese. His tics were back, though they'd ceased to bother me. The guy's personal problems were much larger than the Tourette's, which I suspect other people probably learn to cope with pretty well. His sociopathology was a different matter altogether.

While the two of us sat at the kitchen table, waiting for the guy to deliver the order, Raymond rolled and smoked a joint. I picked up a couple of the half-completed insurance forms I'd seen earlier. Time to make myself useful, I thought. I looked from the first form to the second. "What's this?" I said, a laugh bubbling up again. I can't help it—some spelling errors tickle me. "Suffering from a bad case of 'bruces'?" As I reached for a third form, Raymond snatched the papers away from me.

"Raymond, come on. What's the matter with you? You can't send that to an insurance company. Both of those claims say exactly the same thing." I went ahead and pulled a third claim form from the pile. "Here's another one. Same date, same time. Don't you think they check this stuff? They're going to pick up on that. Here, look. If you want to have those guys fill out the forms, at least use a little imagination. Set up a few different stories. . . ."

"I was going to do that," he said with irritation.

"Let me have a turn. It'd be fun," I said.

At first, I didn't think he'd do it, but his gaze had settled on my face and I could see I'd piqued his interest. Reluctantly, he relinquished the form we'd been wrestling over. I picked up a pencil stub and began to print out the narrative for an auto accident.

"Don't make it sound too smart," Raymond said.

"Trust me."

I proceeded to invent, off the top of my head, several variations of the accidents I'd participated in that afternoon. I had to pat myself on the back. I was really good at this. I'd make a fortune if I ever turned my hand to crime in earnest. Raymond apparently thought so, too. "How you know all this stuff?"

"I'm a person of many talents," I said, licking my pencil point. "Quit peeking. You make me nervous."

Raymond got us both a cold beer and we chatted while I wrote up fictional fender-benders and minor wrecks. Raymond hadn't managed to graduate from high school, whereas I attended three whole semesters of junior college before I lost heart.

"Why'd you quit, though? You're smart."

"I never liked school," I said. "High school, I was smokin' too much dope to do well. College just seemed to be made up of all this stuff I didn't like. I was too rebellious back then. And it's not like I had a 'career' goal in mind. I couldn't see the point in learning things I didn't want to know. Poly sci and biology. Who needs it? I don't give a damn about xylem and phloem."

"Me neither. Especially phloem, right?"

"Yeah, right," I said, laughing on the assumption he was making a joke.

He smiled at me, rather sweetly. "I wish Bibianna were more like you," he said.

"Forget it. I'm a mess. Divorced twice. I'm not any better at relationships than she is."

He cleared his throat. "You know, in my experience? Women are no fuckin' good. The average woman will take you for everything you got. Then, you know what they do? They leave your ass and walk off. I don't get it. What'd I ever do?"

"I don't know what to tell you, Raymond. Guys have left me and that doesn't make 'em bad. That's just the way life goes."

"They break your heart?"

"One or two."

"Well, now see . . . that's the difference. You get your heart broke like I do, it's hard to trust, you know that?" He stared at his beer bottle, peeling a strip of the label with his thumbnail.

I felt myself go still and I chose my words with care. "I'll tell you what somebody told me once. 'You can't make anyone love you and you can't keep anyone from dying.' "

He stared at me, his dark eyes nearly luminous. There was a silence while he digested that. He shook his head. "Here's what I say. Somebody don't love me? They die."

At eight forty-five, our dinner arrived in six white cartons, complete with tiny flat plastic pillows of soy sauce and Chinese mustard strong enough to cause a nosebleed. I forked up my food with the voracious appetite generated by secondhand marijuana smoke, which was probably fortunate under the circumstances as the dishes themselves seemed remarkably similar. All of them were tossed together in a flurry of bok choy and bamboo shoots, one smothered in a sauce that looked like Orange Crush thickened with cornstarch. Both Raymond and I made little snuffling noises as we ate, polishing off everything except a golf-ball-size clot of steamed rice. The strip of paper in my fortune cookie read, "Your sunny disposition brightens everything around you." Raymond's read, "No two roads ever look alike," which made no sense whatever. He seemed to think it was profound, but by then the whites of his eyes had turned pink and he'd started eating a dope-inspired snack that he had devised—grape jelly scooped up with stale corn chips. I went to bed, but before I turned off the light, I took out the stolen bridal photo and took one more look. Who was this woman? I knew it would come to me. Her identity might also turn out to be unrelated to the investigation, but I didn't think so.

I settled down for the night on my lumpy couch. I longed to be at home in the safety of my own bed. I could feel anxiety whisper at the base of my spine. There was an ancient, familiar physical sensation I couldn't at first identify—some piece of my childhood being stirred up by circumstance. I felt a squeezing in my stomach—not an ache, but some process that was almost like grief. I closed my eyes, longing for sleep, longing for something else, though I couldn't think what. My eyes came open and in a flash, I knew. I was homesick.

My aunt had sent me off to summer camp when I was eight, claiming that it would be good for me to "get away." I see now maybe she was the one who needed the relief. She told me I'd have a wonderful time and meet lots of girls my own age. She said we'd swim and ride horses and go on nature walks and sing songs around the campfire at night.

In dizzying detail, memories passed across my mental screen. It was true about the girls and all the activities. What was also true was that after half a day, I didn't want to be there. The horses were big and covered with flies, hot straw baseballs coming out their butts at intervals. Their muzzles were as soft and silky as suede with little prickles embedded in it, but when you least expected it, they would whip their heads up quick and try to bite you with teeth the size of piano keys. Nature turned out to be straight uphill, dusty and hot and itchy. The part that wasn't dry and tiresome was even worse. We were supposed to swim in a lake with an Indian name, but the bottom was vile and squishy. Half the time I worried there'd be broken bottles buried in the ooze. One false step and I knew my tender instep would be slashed to the bone. When I wasn't worried about slime and sharp rocks, I worried about the creatures gliding through the murky depths, tentacles trailing languidly toward my pale skinny legs. The first night around the campfire, after we sang "Kumbayah" about six times, they told me about this poor girl camper who had drowned two years before, and one who'd had an allergic reaction to a bee sting and nearly died, and another who broke her arm falling out of a tree. Also one of the girl counselors had been parked with her boyfriend necking when the radio announcer told about this escaped raving maniac and after they rolled the car window up and drove away quick, there was his *hook* right in the window. That night I cried myself to sleep, weeping in utter silence so as not to disgrace myself. In the morning, I discovered that I had all the wrong kind of shorts and I was forced to endure a lot of pitying looks because mine had elastic around the waist. At breakfast, the scrambled eggs were flabby and had white parts this girl in my cabin said were made out of unborn baby bird. After I was sick and got sent to the infirmary, there was a twelve-year-old girl who was bleeding, but they said wasn't really hurt. It was just a dead baby coming out of her bottom every month. At lunch, there was carrot salad with dark spots. The next day, I went home, which is where I wanted to be now. I slept poorly.

twenty

early the next morning, the Santa Teresa cops called to say Chago's autopsy had been completed. Raymond went off to the funeral home to make arrangements to have the body brought down. The funeral director had apparently assured him by phone that he could have Chago ready for viewing that evening. Rosary would be recited Sunday evening at the funeral chapel. A mass would be said at 10:00 A.M. Monday morning at Blessed Redemption, with interment following at Roosevelt Memorial Park in Gardena.

When Raymond got back he conferred with Luis, who left soon afterward with the dog. Word was apparently out on the street. The same two girls I'd seen the first day showed up and sat down at the kitchen table, where they began putting together paper booklets with a stapler and some colored marker pens. I could see "R.I.P. CHAGO" in ornate Gothic letters on the front. A stack of Xeroxed photographs were being collated with printed matter. Within an hour, Chago's old homies began to arrive in twos and threes, some accompanied by wives or girlfriends. Most of them seemed too old to be active gang members at this point. Drugs, cigarettes, and booze had taken their toll, leaving bloated bellies and bad coloring. These were the survivors of God knows what turf wars, guys in their late twenties who probably considered themselves fortunate to be alive. The mood of the gathering was one of muted uneasiness, a community of mourners assembling to honor a fallen comrade. All I'd known of Chago was his last inching journey toward a Santa Teresa street corner. In the rain and the darkness, he'd set his failing sights, hunching toward home. I saw no sign of Juan or Ricardo, Raymond's two remaining brothers, but Bibianna assured me they'd be at the funeral home later. I gathered visiting hours would extend through the evening and both of us would have to be there. In the meantime, I was feeling awkward. I hadn't known Raymond's brother and didn't know any of the people who'd come to pay their respects. I was looking for the opportunity to excuse myself discreetly and retire to my room. There was a little flurry by the front door and the priest arrived in clerical black, a hyphen of snowy white collar visible at his neck.

Bibianna leaned close and murmured, "Father Luevanos. He's the parish priest."

Father Luevanos was in his sixties, a spare man with a withered face and a frizzy cloud of white hair. He was small and trim, shoulders narrow, his hands long and thin. He seemed to hold them away from his body, palms facing outward, like St. Francis of Assisi only minus the birds. He moved through the crowd, talking softly to each of his parishioners. He was treated like royalty, people parting to let him through. Raymond crossed to his side. Father Luevanos took his hands and the two murmured together in a mixture of English and Spanish. I could see Raymond's grief surface in response to the priest's compassion. He didn't weep, but his face underwent a curious series of tics that, from a distance, looked like the fast-forward sequence of a man in tears. I gathered Chago had been one of Raymond's anchors, perhaps the only family member who really loved Raymond and was loved in return. Raymond caught my eye. He beckoned me over and introduced me to the priest. "She's from Santa Teresa."

Father Luevanos held on to my hands while we talked. "Nice to meet you. You have a lovely community in Santa Teresa. How long have you known Valensuelo?"

"Who?"

"Chago," Raymond murmured.

"Oh." I could feel my cheeks color. "Actually, I'm a friend of Bibianna's."

"I see."

As if on cue, Bibianna moved forward to greet the priest. She had changed into a black skirt, a white blouse, and black spike heels. She had tucked a red satin rose in her hair. Her face was very pale, makeup looking stark against the pallor of her cheeks. "Father . . ." she whispered. She was close to tears and her mouth began to tremble when he took her hands. He leaned toward her, murmuring something in Spanish. She must have felt an almost overwhelming impulse to unburden herself.

Once Father Luevanos had departed, the mood of the place began to lighten. The afternoon had a lazy feel to it, despite the occasion. The front door stood open and the crowd spilled out onto the balcony. Some of the guys had brought six-packs, chips, and salsa. Conversations were punctuated by the hiss of pop-tops. There was muted laughter and cigarette smoke. Somebody brought a steel-string guitar and picked out intricate melodies. A nine-month-old baby named Ignatio toddled five steps and then sank down on his diapered behind, thoroughly satisfied with the applause his journey had netted him.

At five-thirty, the crowd began to thin. We were expected over at the funeral home early so Raymond could view the body before the others arrived. We headed out for the funeral home at six. Bibianna and I sat together in the backseat. Luis drove. Raymond sat in the passenger seat, silent and distraught, clutching a bundle he'd carried out of the bedroom with him, wrapped loosely in the folds of a white satin scarf. His emotional distress had set off a whole galaxy of symptoms, jerks and twitches that seemed all the more wrenching for the look on his face. In the space of an hour, he'd gone from a vicious hoodlum to a scared-looking kid, overwhelmed by the ordeal that lay ahead of him.

The funeral home was housed in an extravagant Victorian mansion, one of the rare remaining structures from the early grandeur of Los Angeles. The onetime single-family residence was three stories tall, the roofline broken up by towers and chimneys. The face of it was smoke-darkened stone and brown shingle, ancient tattered palms and cedars overpowering the lot, which was flanked on either side by squat concrete office buildings. The facade jarred my sense of reality, placing me for a split second in the year 1887, past and future trading places briefly.

The interior was a cavernous collection of hushed rooms with high ceilings, dark varnished woodwork, textured wallpaper, and indirect lighting. The muted chords of an organ were barely audible, creating a subliminal mood of sorrow and solemnity. The furniture was Victorian, damask and ornately carved wood, except for the metal folding chairs that had been arranged around the "parlor," where Chago had been laid out. The pearly gray coffin rested in a bay at the far end of the room, half lid open to reveal a white satin interior and a portion of his profile. The bier was surrounded by big sprays of white gladioli and wreaths of white carnations, white rosebuds, baby's breath. Raymond had apparently spared no expense.

Luis, Bibianna, and I lingered discreetly near the entranceway while Raymond approached the coffin, bearing his bundle like an offering. I gathered this was the first time he'd seen Chago since his death on Tuesday night. He bowed his head, staring into the coffin, his expression not visible from where we stood. After a moment, he crossed himself. I saw him unfold the white satin scarf and lean close to Chago's body, but it was hard to tell what he was doing. Moments later, he backed away from the coffin and crossed himself again. He took out a handkerchief and blew his nose. He mopped at his eyes and tucked the handkerchief away, then turned and walked the length of the room in our direction. When he reached us, Luis put out a hand and clasped him by the shoulder, giving him a consoling pat. "Hey, man. It's rough," he said his voice barely audible.

Bibianna moved away from us. She approached the coffin reluctantly, her apprehension apparent. She looked at the body briefly, then crossed herself. She went over and took a seat, fumbling in her handbag for a Kleenex.

"You want to see him?" Raymond asked. His eyes were clouded by a pleading impossible to resist. It seemed like an intimate moment, observing the dead, and since I hadn't known the man, it seemed inappropriate that I'd join his friends and family at the head of his coffin. On the other hand, it seemed insulting to refuse.

Raymond picked up on my indecision, smiling sweetly. "No, come on. It's okay. He looks good."

That was a matter of opinion, of course. I'd actually seen Chago twice: once on Tuesday at the CF offices when he bumped into me in the hall, and again that night at the Bourbon Street restaurant when he'd abducted Bibianna at gunpoint. He'd seemed like a big man then, but death had pressed him flat. He looked like a Ken doll on display in an oversize carrying case. He was probably four or five years younger than Raymond, with the same good looks. His face was smooth and unlined, chin and cheekbones prominent. His hair had been blown into a dark glossy pompadour that made his head seem too large for the width of his shoulders. Raymond's satin-wrapped packet had apparently contained religious items. An oversize Bible, bound in textured white, had been clumsily propped up against the chalky pink of Chago's folded hands. A rosary had been laid across his fingers and a framed photograph of him as a small boy placed on the small white pillow on which he lay. The pillow was satin and looked like the sort women use when they don't want to mess up an expensive salon hairdo. Luis and I studied Chago as attentively as one watches an infant in the company of a proud parent.

At seven, some of the homeboys I'd seen at the apartment began to arrive. They seemed ill at ease in Raymond's presence, unaccustomed to seeing him in a sport coat and tie. Chago's buddies had all donned specially made up black T-shirts with "In Loving Memory of Chago—R.I.P." on the back and their own names on the front.

I sat down beside Bibianna, the two of us saying little. Occasionally someone would make eye contact, but no one talked to me. Most of the conversations taking place around me were in Spanish anyway, so I couldn't even eavesdrop decently.

The crowd was swelling. There was no sign of either of Raymond's brothers, but I did see three women I took to be his older sisters. They seemed remarkably similar with their large dark eyes, full mouths, perfect skin. They sat in a cluster, beautiful women in their forties, heavy and dark, looking like nuns with their black mantillas and their rosaries. They would exchange occasional comments, but not a word to Raymond, who was making an elaborate show of not giving a damn. In an unguarded moment, I saw him flick a look in their direction. I understood then that Bibianna was just another version of his sisters, exquisite and rejecting just as his mother must have been. Poor Raymond. No matter how many versions of the story he managed to create, he would never win her love and he'd never make it come out happily.

A cluster of three mourners approached Bibianna, Chicanas in their twenties, one with a baby on her hip. I got up and eased toward the door, wondering if there was any way I could get to a telephone. Before I reached the doorway, Luis appeared at my side and took my arm. I leaned close. "Do you think there's a ladies' room upstairs?"

"You're not going anywhere."

"Oh. Well, I guess it doesn't matter then if there's one upstairs or not."

I sat back in my chair and glanced at my watch. It was ten after eight. I was hungry. I was bored. I was restless. I was scared. I'd been living for too long with high doses of fight-or-flight anxiety and it was making my head pound and my stomach churn. Luis stuck to me like a burr. For the next fifty minutes, I squirmed on my folding chair, crossing and un-crossing my legs, fiddling with my hair. To amuse myself, I memorized faces, just in case later I'd have to identify some-one on the witness stand. Finally, at nine-twenty the dark-suited staff person assigned to our viewing room made an appearance and glanced pointedly at his watch. Raymond got the message and began to circle the room, saying good night to the last of the visitors.

On the way home, we dropped Luis off at his place. As soon as we reached the apartment, Raymond disappeared into the bedroom while Bibianna and I began to tidy up the place. It's not like either of us cared much, but it was some-thing to do. In the background, without being fully conscious of it, we could hear the rattle of change on the wooden chest of drawers as Raymond emptied his pockets. We tossed empty beer cans in a plastic garbage bag, dumped out laden ashtrays. Raymond emerged from the bedroom and moved into the bathroom usually designated for my use. Moments later, I heard the squeak of the faucets. Pipes began to thun-der and water splashed against the shower tiles like a sudden autumn rain.

I glanced over at Bibianna. "How come he's showering in my bathroom?"

"It'll give him a chance to . . ." She made a gesture toward the crook of her left arm.

"He's shooting up?"

It dawned on me first, the significance of the rattle of metal in the bedroom. I felt my head come up. Luis wasn't here. There was no dog at the threshold. She caught my sharp intake of breath and looked over at me.

I said, "Jesus, what's wrong with us?" I moved swiftly into the bedroom and grabbed the car keys off the top of the dresser where he'd dumped them. I hesitated and then jerked open the drawer with the handguns in it. The box was where I remembered it, miscellaneous ID's under it. I lifted the lid. The SIG-Sauer was still there, along with the Mauser and the cartridges. I tucked the SIG-Sauer in my waistband. To hell with being unarmed. I'd just as soon walk naked through an airport terminal. I was back seconds later with the keys, which I tossed to her. The shower had been turned off. Deftly, I transferred the gun to my handbag. We heard the bathroom door open. "Bibianna?"

She was struggling to separate out the keys to the Caddy, attached to the ring on a circle of wire. Her hands were shaking badly, keys jingling between her fingers like castanets.

"Take the whole friggin' thing!" I hissed. "Go!"

The telephone rang and we both jumped, in part because the sound was so unexpected. The instrument sat on the floor under the kitchen table, plugged into the wall jack. I gave her a push toward the door and snatched up the receiver. "Hello?"

On the other end of the line, a woman with a tremulous voice said, "Bibianna, thank God. Lupe told me you were back. I tried to reach you up in Santa Teresa. I've been at the hospital . . . I've been—" She broke down.

"Excuse me. I'm sorry. I'm Hannah, Bibianna's friend. Hold on a sec. She's right here." There was something in the woman's tone that went beyond distress.

Bibianna had stopped midway across the room and was staring at me. I held out the receiver.

She approached like a sleepwalker. I wanted to hurry her, anxiously aware that Raymond must have heard the phone ring, too. She took the phone from me. "Hello?"

I stared at her, mesmerized.

She said, "Mom? Yes . . ."

Raymond appeared in the doorway, his hair still tousled

where he'd toweled it in haste. "Bibianna?" He'd pulled on a pair of chinos, hands still busy with his belt buckle. I found myself checking his bare arms for the injection site. He said, "What's going on? Who's on the phone?"

Bibianna turned away and pressed a hand to her ear so she could hear over Raymond's questions. A frown formed and she said, "What?" with disbelief.

The remainder of her mother's message to her was played out on Bibianna's face. Her eyes strayed to the wall of broken mirror tiles, plaster showing through in irregular patches where the glass had been shattered. Her lips parted and a sound escaped. She put a hand up to her cheek. Something in her expression made my stomach churn with dread.

No more than fifteen seconds had passed when Raymond strode across the room, snatched the receiver, and slammed it into the cradle. He ripped the phone cord from the jack and flung the instrument at the wall. The plastic housing cracked, splitting open to expose the internal mechanism. Bibianna's horrified gaze jumped from the telephone to his face. "I know what you did to her. . . ."

"To who?"

"My mother's in the hospital."

Raymond hesitated, sensing from the break in her voice that he was losing control. "What I did? What'd I do?"

Bibianna's lips moved. She was repeating a phrase . . . a mere murmur at first, gradually raising her voice. "You cut her face, you son of a bitch. You cut her face! *You cut my mother's face right here in this apartment!* You cut her beautiful face, you son of a bitch. *You bastard. . . .*"

She flew at Raymond, her fingers curved as claws digging into his face. She plowed into him, the force of her fury driving him back against the table. One of the kitchen chairs tipped over backward with a clatter. Bibianna reached the kitchenette in two steps, caught a kitchen drawer by the handle, and gave it a yank. Raymond lunged and grabbed her from behind. He half lifted her off her feet and dragged her back, Bibianna clinging to the drawer by the handle. The whole drawer was jerked free, a jumble of utensils flying everywhere. Raymond dropped, pulling her down on top of him. She struggled, half turning, kicking at Raymond with her spike-heeled shoes, long legs flashing. He tried to punch her and missed. She caught him in the chest with a kick and I heard the "oof" as the air was knocked out of him. She torqued around to her hands and knees, scrambling back into the kitchenette, where she snatched up a butcher knife that had skittered across the kitchen floor. She swung around, bringing the knife down. Raymond's hand shot out. He locked her wrist in an iron grip, squeezing so hard I thought he'd crush the bone. She cried out. The knife dropped. For a moment, they lay together. His body half covered hers and both were panting hard.

Her face began to crumple, tears welling up in her eyes. "Get offa me, you bastard," she said. Raymond seemed to think the worst of it was over. He lifted himself away from her and extended his hand, pulling her to her feet again. The moment she was upright, she lashed a kick at his groin, the pointed toe of her spike heel making contact slightly off center, but with sufficient force to cause him to grab at himself, hunching forward protectively. The sound he made was a churlish mix of pain, surprise, and fury.

I had lost track of the car keys, which must have sailed out of Bibianna's hand at some point in the struggle. I scanned the floor in haste, spotted them near the wall, and scooped them up. I tossed them to her underhand, a perfect throw. She caught the keys and took off. The front door banged back and she was gone, high heels pounding rapidly toward the stairs and out of earshot. I headed for the door at a dead run myself.

Raymond tackled me from behind. I stumbled, flinging my hands out, and he brought me down. We grappled, making grunting sounds. He pounded me with his fist, venting his fury in a succession of blows, which I warded off with my arms raised in an X across my face. He grabbed me by the hair and hauled me to my feet. He whipped my right arm behind my back and jerked upward, propelling me out the door and along the gallery. All he had on was a pair of pants. His chest was rosy from blows that had been landed on his bare skin. I longed to stomp his bare feet, but I knew he'd break my arm in retaliation.

Out in front of the building, I could hear Bibianna revving up the Cadillac, which peeled out with a shriek of tires. Raymond marched us to the Ford. He popped open the trunk lid with one hand and grabbed a tire iron, pulling me around with him to the driver's side. He smashed backward at the window until enough glass was gone to allow him to reach in and pull up the door lock. He yanked the door open and shoved me into the car. He pulled a set of keys from under the front seat, along with a handgun. He cocked it and pointed it at me, then reached under the steering column with his left hand and started the car.

twenty-one

We took off. Bibianna had no more than a two-minute head start. Raymond placed the handgun between his thighs. At fifty miles an hour, he really didn't have to worry that I'd bolt from the moving vehicle. He jammed down on the accelerator, pushing the shimmying Ford to sixty, sixty-five. Streetlights streamed by. I hung on for dear life, my eyes pinned to the road with all the horrified fascination of a funhouse ride. Judging from the consternation of the drivers on all sides of us, Bibianna must have been cutting through red lights at the intersections just ahead.

Raymond didn't seem nearly as concerned as I was with the cars or pedestrians, with the niceties of stoplights or the sanctity of crosswalks. People were diving out of his path, a string of honking horns and curses flying up in our wake. He picked up the car phone and held it against the steering wheel so he could punch in a number with his thumb. He listened for one ring, two. Someone picked up on the other end.

He said, " 'Ey, Chopper! Bibianna just took off in the Caddy and I need some help. . . . Right. She'll hit the 405 northbound at Avalon. If you miss us at the Harbor, try Crenshaw or Hawthorne."

There was obviously a question being posed from the other end.

"I'll leave that up to you, man," Raymond said. He hung up. He set the phone down and retrieved the gun from the fleshy holster of his thighs, holding it in his right hand while he steered with his left.

We were still on Avalon Boulevard, screaming toward the freeway. By the time we reached Carson, the light was green and we sailed through. Raymond had eased back to sixty miles an hour, squeezing out a lane of his own between parked cars and the moving vehicles crawling toward the on ramp. I braced myself, one hand on the dashboard, one hand clutching the seat back. I could see drivers in cars just ahead spotting us in their rearview mirrors—first the casual glance, then the double take as they calculated our speed, realizing that we would shortly be climbing up their rear bumpers. Some cars would speed up, crowding left to allow us room to pass. Some would take the first avenue of escape they could find, squealing into driveways, up onto the sidewalk— anything to avoid the inevitable rear-end collision. I found myself gritting my teeth in silence, then warbling out a cry of fear and distress as we overtook each car and managed, some- how, to get past.

Raymond's face was totally composed, his concentration intense. I could see now that his pupils had been reduced to pinpoints, but he showed no other signs of heroin intoxica- tion. Maybe he had his doses so carefully calibrated that he could function normally even with his veins full of smack. He sideswiped a parked car and I shrieked involuntarily, my head jerking back as the impact bounced us into the oncom- ing traffic. He corrected our course. If he was aware of my vocalization, he gave no indication of it. The irony wasn't lost on me, that in this situation of high stress, I was exhibiting all of Raymond's symptoms. Maybe in his neurological makeup, some part of him was forever reacting to high-speed chases and phantom crashes, narrowly averted disasters from which he saved himself with quick action and spontaneous yelps of horror, dismay, and surprise.

We careered to the right, up the on ramp to the 405, northbound. I had no idea how he knew she'd be there, but I spotted Bibianna just ahead of us in the black Caddy the moment we merged with freeway traffic. It was late Saturday evening, so we weren't looking at the usual jam and crawl of the rush hour. I kept my eyes glued to the road, praying mutely for her safety. She probably thought she was free, not realizing he was already there behind her only eight cars back. He tucked the handgun between his thighs again and picked up the car phone, punching in the number with his thumb. He spoke rapidly to Chopper, giving our coordinates. I could hear them calculate the projected point of interception. My heart was still pounding and I watched the Caddy fearfully, scanning the freeway for some sign of the CHP.

We had just passed the on ramp at Rosecrans when I heard the chirp of a car horn next to us. I looked over at the next lane. The car was a Chevy, dark blue. Chopper was driving. Raymond pointed at the Caddy and then sliced his index finger across his throat. Chopper grinned and gave Raymond the thumbs-up. Raymond eased his foot off the accelerator, dropping back to normal speed, while the guy in the Chevy eased into our lane and sped up. The last I saw of Bibianna, the Chevy was just beginning to overtake her. That's when I caught a glimpse of the vanity license plate. A chill puckered my scalp and rippled down my spine, the cold wedging like a pillow in the small of my back. The plate read PARNELL. Raymond must have had Parnell Perkins's car ever since his death, probably using it to collect phony damage and injury claims.

Raymond spotted a black-and-white in the southbound

lane. It was possible somebody'd called the cops to report his erratic driving because the officer gave the Ford a quick startled look as we passed. Raymond cut over two lanes to the right and took the nearest off ramp. Even if the cop circled back, we'd be gone. He found a darkened side street, pulled over to the curb, and parked. He sat back and expelled a breath of air.

I had started to shake, from fear, from relief, from visions of Bibianna's fate and bloody images of Bibianna's mother, whom I'd never even laid eyes on. I thought about Parnell facedown in the parking lot with a bullet in his head. I pressed my hands between my knees, teeth chattering, my breath coming in gasps.

Raymond was looking at me with puzzlement. "What's the matter with you?"

"Shut up, Raymond. I don't want to talk to you."

"I didn't do nothing. What'd I do?"

"You didn't *do* anything? I don't believe this. . . ."

"Chick stole my car and I chased her. What'd you expect?"

"You're crazy!"

"*I'm* crazy? Why? Because I won't let that bitch take me for everything I'm worth? You better believe it."

"What's going to happen?"

"Beats me."

I sat up, irritated with his attitude. "Don't play dumb, Raymond. What's Chopper going to do to her?"

"How do I know? I'm not a fuckin' psychic. Don't worry about it. It's got nothing to do with you."

"What about her mother?"

"What do you care? Quit acting like this is *my* fault."

I looked at him with astonishment. "Who's fault is it, then?"

"Bibianna's," he replied, as if it were self-evident.

"Why is it her fault? You're the one who cut the woman."

"Who, Gina? She's alive, isn't she? Which is more than you can say for Chago. I got a brother dead, and who do you think did that?"

"Not her," I shot back.

"That's my point," he replied patiently. "She didn't do nothing. She's innocent, right? Just like him. Tit for tat. It says so right in the Bible—an eye for an eye—and that's all this is about. Lookit, I could have killed the bitch, but I didn't, did I. And you know why? Because I'm a good guy. Nobody gives me credit. Bibianna has to learn not to fuck with me, I told you that. You think I like this? She'd done what I said to begin with, we wouldn't be here."

"Which is what?"

"Quit horsing around and get serious. She shoulda married me when I asked her. I'm not stupid, you know. I don't know what's going on, but I've been as patient as I'm gonna be. And that goes for you, too. You got that?"

I stared at him, at a loss for words. His view of the world was so skewed there was no reasoning with him. He really seemed to see himself as innocent, the victim of a circumstance in which everyone was responsible for his behavior except him. Like every other "victim" I've known, he clung to his "one-down" position as justification for his abuse of other people.

Raymond picked up the car phone and punched in a number. " 'Ey, Luis. Raymond. Put some clothes on, we're swinging by to pick you up." He glanced at his watch. "Ten minutes. And bring the mutt."

He started the car then and pulled out, hanging a left onto a main artery as we headed south again. I glanced out the window. Raymond was driving at a sedate forty miles an hour. We were now on Sepulveda, not far from the airport. Not a wonderful neighborhood, but I thought I'd be safe until I could get a call through to the cops. I opened the car door. Raymond speeded up.

"Please stop the car. I'm getting out," I said.

He picked up the gun again and pointed it at me. "Close the door."

I did as I was told. He turned his attention to the road again. In the glow from the streetlights, I studied his profile, hair still damp from the shower, the tousle of curls, dark eyes, long lashes, the dimple in his chin. He was bare-chested, barefoot, his skin very pale. I could see the faint scarring in the crooks of his arms. My guess was that after the intensity of the chase and the rush of adrenaline, the euphoric effects of his shooting up were beginning to wane. His ticcing had returned. The mysterious connections in his neurological circuitry were touching off a series of reactions, as if he were enduring tiny jolts of electricity. His mouth came open and he jerked his neck to the right. His body jumped with the same irrepressible response I've felt when a doctor pops with his rubber hammer on my patellar reflex. In that quick tap, there isn't any way to prevent my foot from flying out. Raymond seemed to live with the constant assault of invisible rubber hammers, which rapped him randomly at all hours of the day, testing every reflex . . . little elves and fairies tapping on him like a boot. If his gun hand jerked the wrong way, he was going to plug me full of holes. My own adrenaline had seeped away, leaving me depleted.

"Oh, God, Raymond. Please. I just want to go home," I said wearily.

"I'm not going to let you out here. It's too dangerous. You wouldn't last a block."

I wanted to laugh at the absurdity of his concern. There he was, holding me at gunpoint, probably willing to kill me if it came to that, but he didn't want me out on the streets in a questionable neighborhood. Raymond punched in another number. He really reminded me of some high-powered business exec.

Someone answered on the other end.

"Hey, yeah," he said. "I got a problem. Somebody just stole my car. . . ."

I slouched down on my spine, knees propped against the dashboard, listening with wonder as Raymond availed himself of city police services in the matter of his missing Cadillac. From his end of the conversation, I gathered he was going to have to go over to the 77th Division and file a stolen vehicle report, but he was the soul of cooperation, Mr. Righteous Citizen rallying the forces of law and order to his cause. He hung up and we drove in silence as far as Luis's place.

We pulled over at the curb and Raymond gave a quick beep. A moment later, Luis appeared with Perro at his side. Raymond pulled on the emergency brake and got out on the driver's side. "You drive," he said to Luis.

Luis put the dog in the front seat between us and got behind the wheel. "Where we going?"

"Police station."

Luis took off. Perro leaned against me, panting bad breath. I could tell he would have preferred the window seat himself so he could hang his head out and let his ears flap in the passing breeze.

Luis watched Raymond in the rearview mirror with guarded interest. "So what's happening?"

"Bibianna stole the Caddy. We gotta file a report."

"Bibianna stole the Caddy?"

"Yeah, can you believe that? After all I've done for her? I called Chopper and sent him after her. I don't have time for that shit, you know what I'm talking about?"

Luis made no comment. I saw him slide a look in my direction, but what was I going to say?

We reached the 77th Division police station. Luis parked on the street and got out of the car, peering into the backseat while Raymond gave him instructions about the stolen Caddy. "What about the registration?" he asked.

"It's in the car," Raymond said irritably.

"You want me to give 'em your telephone number?"

"How else are they going to notify me when they find the car?"

"Oh."

"Yeah, 'oh,'" Raymond said.

Luis disappeared.

"Guy's a fuckin' pinhead," Raymond said to himself. He

kicked the back of my seat. "I still got a gun on you," he said. "I ain't forgettin' it was you helped Bibianna get away."

I waited in the car with Raymond, pinned in place by Perro's weight, wishing a cop would saunter by so that I could scream for help. Several patrol cars gunned past us, but no one seemed to realize that this tacky-looking Anglo was Nancy Drew in disguise. I stared out at the police station not fifty feet away.

Luis came back to the car and got in without a word. He took a quick look in the rearview mirror. I turned around and looked myself, realizing belatedly that Raymond had nodded off.

Once we reached the apartment complex, Luis had to help him up the stairs. I went up first, with the dog bringing up the rear. Raymond was awake but seemed groggy and out of it. When we reached the apartment, Luis unlocked the door. For a moment, the exterior lights fell on Raymond's bare back and I saw that his skin was crisscrossed with scars, like a webbing of white diamonds. The old cuts had healed but had never entirely gone away. The even spacing suggested quite methodical work.

Inside the apartment, I scanned the living room, searching for the handbag I'd left behind earlier. I spotted it on the floor, shoved halfway under the upholstered chair. It had apparently been kicked to one side during the struggle with Raymond and the top was now yawning open. Luis held Raymond's gun and he motioned me toward the couch. I took a seat. From that angle, the butt of the SIG-Sauer was clearly visible in the handbag. I willed myself to look away. I didn't dare make a move for it for fear Luis would catch sight of it. Raymond staggered off to bed.

I was forced to sleep on the couch that night. Perro guarded the front door while Luis dozed in the chair, keeping watch over me, Raymond's gun in hand. The kitchen bulb glowed like a nightlight. Now and then, Luis and I would stare at each other across the dimly lighted room, his dark eyes devoid of any feeling whatsoever. It's the same look you get from a lover when he's moved on to someone new. Whatever moments you might have shared get buried under layers of hostility and indifference.

I was jolted awake at eight by a banging on the front door. Perro started barking savagely. I swung my feet off the couch and got up, automatically moving toward the door. Luis beat me to it. He had the dog by the collar. He opened the door and I saw Dawna on the threshold in a nifty black suit. Oh, great. This was what Dolan and Santos called "Don't worry about Dawna, we'll keep her out of circulation." Raymond emerged from the master bedroom, pulling his shirt on. He was still barefoot, wearing his wrinkled chinos from the night before. "What's happening?" he asked.

"It's Dawna," Luis said.

As Raymond moved to the door, I leaned over the upholstered chair and eased my handbag out from under it, closing the flap across the butt of the gun.

Luis had turned. "Sit down."

"I'm sitting," I said irritably. I took a seat in the upholstered chair, feigning boredom while Raymond and Dawna went through murmured greetings. Her face had crumpled at the sight of him. Raymond put his arms around her and rocked her where they stood. Wait till she got a load of me. The only comfort I had was the handbag, which now rested to the right of the chair, just beyond my fingertips. Luis had moved into the kitchen and he was leaning against the kitchen counter, rolling a joint with complete absorption. Stoned on Sunday morning. Just what we all needed. Dawna sat down on the couch, still crying into Raymond's handkerchief.

Her face was Kabuki white, her mouth a pout of bright red. Her hair had been newly bleached to the color of typing paper, standing up in spikes as if somebody'd folded it in quarters and cut it with a pair of scissors. The effect was of an albino rooster. Where her suit jacket gaped open, I caught sight of a thickly padded gauze bandage, secured with adhesive tape. She didn't look so hot and my guess was her injury had taken its toll. I could see Perro lying on the floor near the couch, staring at the juicy part of Dawna's leg. I studied her with dread and anxiety. Once she regained her composure, she was going to notice me. There was a fair chance she'd remember me from the CF offices, but what was I going to do?

twenty-two

the tricky part of any lie is trying to figure out how you'd behave if you were innocent. I couldn't act like I didn't know Dawna Maldonado at all. We'd both been there Tuesday night when Chago was killed. Should I treat her as a friend or foe? Under the circumstances, it seemed wise to keep my mouth shut and let the scenario play out as it would, like improvisational theater. As there was no escaping, I tucked the handbag under my arm and moved over to the kitchen table. I sat down, placing the bag casually near one leg of my chair. I picked up Bibianna's ragged deck of cards. I shuffled the cards, trying to remember how Bibianna set up the solitaire she always played.

Meanwhile, conversation between Raymond and Dawna had turned to the shooting. It was just at that point that Dawna finally caught sight of me. "What's she doing here?"

Oh, well, I thought, here we go.

Raymond seemed startled by her reaction, which had a distinctly hostile tone to it. "Oh, sorry. This is Hannah. She's a friend of Bibianna's."

Dawna's eyes were ice blue, lined with black, her gaze calculating. "Why don't you ask *her*? She was with 'em that night."

"*She* was?"

"She was there at the restaurant, sitting at the table with 'em when I got off the phone."

Raymond seemed confused. "You're talking about Hannah?"

"God, Raymond. I just got done sayin' that, didn't I?"

He turned to me. "I thought you met Bibianna in jail. I thought you said you were cellmates."

I started laying cards out like this was no big deal. Seven stacks, first card up, the other six facedown. "I never said that. We got thrown in the slammer together, but I'd met her before that, at a singles bar. I figured she'd told you or I'd have said something myself."

Next round, skip the first pile. The face-up card went on the second pile, the other five facedown. Just playing solitaire here, casual as all get-out. Luis was eavesdropping, being careful not to call attention to himself lest Raymond take off after him.

"What the fuck were you doin' there with her and Jimmy Tate?"

Ah, he'd figured out it was Tate, probably from the description Dawna'd given him of the guy. "I wasn't doing anything. We'd just gone next door for a bite to eat when those two showed up."

"Bibianna was with Jimmy Tate?"

Dawna snorted. "Jesus, Raymond. What's the matter with you? You sound like a parrot." Out of the corner of my eye, I could see how much she was enjoying herself. In her family dynamic, she was probably the kid who puffed up her self-importance by tattling on all her siblings.

Raymond ignored her, focusing on me. "How come you never told me she was with him that night?"

"Jimmy Tate was with me. We ran into Bibianna at the

bar and asked her to join us for a bite to eat. What's the big deal?"

"I don't believe it."

I stopped dealing out the cards. "You don't believe me?"

"I think you're lying."

"Wait a minute, Raymond. I've known you all of five days. So how come I'm suddenly accountable to you for my behavior?"

Raymond's eyes were glittering, his voice too soft to suit me. "Dawna says Tate was the one killed my brother. Did you know that?"

Oops. Actually I did know that. I said nothing, wondering why my mouth was suddenly so dry. I couldn't think of an adequate response and for once the glib lie didn't spring that readily to mind.

"Answer me," he said. "Tate killed my brother?"

I picked my way through the possibilities, not wanting to commit myself to a course of action just yet. "I don't know," I said. "When the shooting started, I hit the pavement."

"You didn't see Tate with a gun?"

"Well, I knew Tate had a gun, but I don't know what he did with it because I wasn't looking."

"What about Chago? You knew he was hit. Who you think did that?"

"I have no idea. Honestly. I didn't have a clue what was happening. All I know is Tate and I run into Bibianna, we go next door for a bite to eat, and next thing I know these two goons show up and take Bibianna off at gunpoint. Shooting breaks out, cops show up. Bibianna and I are hauled off to jail. . . ."

I was on slightly safer ground here because I knew Dawna had disappeared about the time Chago was hit. I was working on the assumption that she didn't have any idea what had gone on after that. Actually, I wasn't as nervous about the current subject as I was about the possibility of her remembering she'd seen me at the California Fidelity offices.

She'd been studying my face, her brow furrowed with one of those quizzical looks that indicate a marine layer blanking out memory. Any minute now the fog might begin to lift. "She's bullshitting you, Raymond."

"Just let me handle this," he said irritably. He turned away and lit a cigarette, watching my face as he took the first drag of smoke.

The phone rang. The four of us turned and stared. Luis moved first, picking up the receiver. "Hello?" He listened briefly, then covered the mouthpiece with his right palm. "Cop on the line says they found the car."

Raymond took the phone. "Hello? . . . Yeah, this is him. . . . Anybody hurt? Oh, really. Well, I'm sorry to hear that. Where is that? Uh-huh . . . yeah. Where's the car now? Yeah, right. I know the place. . . . Huhn, he did? Hey, that's too bad."

Raymond got off the phone with a glance at Luis. "Bibianna had an accident up in Topanga Canyon. Chopper pushed the Caddy off a cliff, from what this guy says."

"No shit," Luis said.

I could feel my heart beating in my throat. "What happened to Bibianna? Is she okay?"

Raymond waved dismissively. "Don't worry about it. She's at St. John's. Get a jacket, baby-doll. We got work to do." He flashed a grin at Luis. "This is great. Caddy's totaled. We're talking twenty-five hundred bucks." He caught sight of my face. "What are you lookin' at? I got a legitimate auto claim here," he said self-righteously.

"What about me?" Dawna said, protesting.

"You can come with us if you want or you can stay here and sleep. You look beat. We'll be back in an hour and then go over to the funeral home."

She stared indecisively, then conceded. "You go on. I'll grab some rest."

Raymond drove way too aggressively for traffic conditions. I was sandwiched between him and Luis in the front seat, one hand braced on the dashboard, making small involuntary sounds each time Raymond changed lanes without warning or pushed the Ford up within a few feet of somebody's back bumper before he pulled out and around, passing them with a dark backward scowl. His jaw was set, his tics almost constant, and everything in life was someone else's fault. Even Luis began to react, murmuring, "Jesus," at one of Raymond's hair-raising near misses.

The two talked across me as if I were empty space, so it took me a moment to realize what they were saying.

Raymond said, "Stupid bitch must have got off the 101 at Topanga. God, how dumb can you get? That's the middle of nowhere. You know that road?"

"Hey, that's rugged," Luis said.

"The worst. Mountains sticking straight up. Sheer drops off the sides. She should have stayed in the populated areas and found a cop. She's not going to get any help out there. All Chopper had to do was wait till she hit one of those hairpin turns and *boom!*" Raymond gestured his contempt. "Cop says he must have rammed into the Caddy's rear end and got himself hung up but good." He made a diving motion with his hand.

I glanced at Raymond. "*He* went off, too?"

Raymond gave me a look like I'd suddenly started speaking English. "What do you think we've been talking about? Chopper's dead and she's not that far from it. Serves her right. You didn't figure that out? Bibianna's in whatchacallit . . . intensive care."

"Oh, no," I said.

"What is it with you? You gonna make that my fault, too? Bibianna steals my car and totals the fuckin' thing and *I'm* to blame?"

"Oh, for God's sake, Raymond. Take responsibility. This is all your doing and you know it."

"Don't push your luck, bitch. I didn't do nothin'!" Raymond's face darkened and he drove in stony silence. I could feel anxiety seeping into my chest wall, squeezing my digestive system.

We got off the 405 at the Santa Monica Freeway, heading west as far as the Cloverfield exit, which we took and then turned right. I'd been to St. John's some years ago, and by my recollection, it was not far away, somewhere around 21st or 22nd Street, between Santa Monica Boulevard and Wilshire. It was ten-thirty by now. Hospitals are rigorous about visits to ICU, but Raymond would no doubt bull his way in.

We parked in one of the visitors' lots and crossed to the main entrance, passing under an arch. A fountain lined with blue-green tile splashed noisily in the center of a brick-paved court. Beyond the fountain was a bronze bust of Irene Dunne, the first lady of St. John's. The place was massive, cream-colored blocks that had probably once been a fairly straightforward chunk of concrete. Now a portico jutted out in front, two wings flanked the building on either side, with a multistory addition looming up in the rear. It looked like most of the available land had been devoured by new construction, surrounding properties annexed as the space needs of the hospital grew. The rest of the neighborhood was a modest assortment of single-family dwellings, 1950s style. An ambulance passed us, emitting an occasional short howl. Its yellow lights were flashing, sirens off, as it headed for the emergency entrance.

Wheelchair ramps swept up to the front on either side of the main entrance with a central staircase. We moved up the center steps and into the lobby with its muted maroon carpet and the spicy scent of carnations. To the left, an entire wall was devoted to listing the names of those who'd made significant financial contributions to St. John's, the range extending from benefactors, to patrons, to fellows, to donors too miserly for categorization. On the far side of the wall, Admitting was dominated by a large oil painting of a curly-haired person looking heavenward in torment.

Raymond inquired at the Patient Information desk for the whereabouts of ICU. I comforted myself that she must have been conscious when they brought her in or the cops never would have found out who she was. As far as I could tell, she'd had no identification with her.

Behind me, I overheard a fragment of conversation. A woman said, ". . . so I says to this chick at the sheriff's department, 'What business is it of yours? If he ain't been charged with nothing, how come you're talkin' to his probation officer about it?' That's like a violation of his civil rights or something, isn't it? . . ."

Two wires connected in my brain, completing a circuit. I made the kind of "oh" sound that escapes your lips when you spill ice water down your front. I knew who Dr. Howard's daughter was, the bride in the photograph. She was the civilian clerk who'd given me such a hard time at the S.T. County Sheriff's Department when I was trying to get Bibianna's address. Oh, hell, I had to get to a telephone. No wonder Dolan thought he had a leak!

Raymond marched us to the elevator, which we took up to the second floor. When the doors opened, we turned right, passing the maternity ward, where a recently delivered mother, in robe and slippers, proceeded at half speed, touching the wall gingerly as she walked. Raymond was on his best behavior, moving quickly, his gaze front and center. I could see Luis's eyes flick into an occasional empty room. I did likewise, unable to resist, though there wasn't that much to see. The air already smelled of lunch.

The wing designated 2-South housed Intensive Care, Coronary Care, the Cardiac Surgery Unit, and Intermediate Care behind closed double doors. A sign said AUTHORIZED PERSONNEL ONLY, with a wall-mounted telephone nearby. Apparently, you had to call in and get permission to enter the department itself. Four women sat in the adjacent waiting room, variously conversing and reading magazines. I could see a public pay phone, a magazine rack, a color television set. In the hallway, there were a water fountain and, in a niche, a statue of a male saint supporting baby Jesus by his bare bottom. The floor was made up of polished marble chips in squares with thin metal seams between.

Luis took a seat on a beige leather bench, his knee jumping. A lab tech walked by with a fat tube of dark red blood. Luis got up and moved to the wall, where he studied three lines about the visiting hours. It was the first time I'd seen the two of them in a situation they couldn't handle with machismo.

Like Luis, Raymond was apparently one of those people made uneasy by illness. He was subdued, respectful. The ticcing had started up, the head jerk reminding me of the sort of startle reaction I sometimes experience when I'm on the verge of sleep. Hospital staff, catching sight of him, seemed to diagnose him in passing, thinking no more about it than I did at this point. From Raymond's manner, I had to guess he'd been hospitalized as a child, subjected to medical processes that had left him edgy and alert. Almost imperceptibly, he slowed, shoving his hands in his pockets while he decided what to do next.

He was just picking up the telephone when the double doors opened and a nurse emerged. She was a redhead, in her thirties, white pants suit, thick-soled white shoes, wearing a nursing school pin but no cap. "Can I help you?"

"Yeah, uhm, I got a . . . my fiancée was brought in last night. She was in this automobile accident? The cops said she was here. It's Diaz, the last name . . . I was just wondering, you know, if I could see her."

She smiled pleasantly. "Just a minute, I'll check." She moved on to the waiting room, where she stuck her head in, beckoning to one of the visitors. The woman set her magazine aside and followed the nurse back through the double doors. I took the liberty of peering through the glass, but all I could see was an extension of the corridor and, at the far end of the hall, a glass-enclosed room furnished with monitoring equipment. The patient was barely visible and there was no way of knowing if it was Bibianna or not.

Luis was shifting from foot to foot, fingers snapping softly. "Oh, man, I hate this. I'm going down to the lobby. You can pick me up on the way out. Maybe I'll find the coffee shop and get me something to eat."

"Do it," Raymond said.

Luis crossed his arms and hugged himself casually. "You want me to get you some coffee, something like that?"

"Just get outta here, Luis. I don't give a shit."

"Maybe I'll come back in a while," he said. He glanced at me and then walked backward for a few steps, waiting to see if Raymond had any serious objections. Raymond seemed to be fighting his own inclination to bolt. Luis turned and headed toward the elevators.

As soon as he was out of sight, I touched Raymond's arm. "I think I'll look for a ladies' room, okay?"

The nurse returned. "It'll be a few minutes. The neurologist just left, but I think he's still in the hospital. Would you like to have him paged?"

"Uh, yeah. Could you do that?"

"Of course. You can have a seat, if you like," she said, indicating the waiting room.

"She going to be okay?"

"I really couldn't say," the nurse said. "I can have Dr. Cherbak talk to you about her condition as soon as he gets here. Your name is?"

"Raymond. I'll just wait. I don't want to interrupt nobody. . . ."

"There's a vending machine if you want to have some coffee."

"Can you tell me where the restrooms are?" I asked. God, couldn't I think of any more imaginative way of getting away from these guys?

The nurse pointed toward the corridor. "First door."

I went into the waiting room with Raymond. As soon as he sat down on the couch, I said, "I'll be right back."

He could hardly pay attention, he was so uneasy by then. I

walked away from him, trying to control myself, trying not to break into a run. I passed the restroom and kept going, looking for a place I could have a little privacy and the use of a telephone.

Two-South segued back into 2-Main without any noticeable shift in floor covering or the wall colors, which were pale blue and pale beige, with a pattern of cattails or full-foliage trees in silhouette. I became aware that I had moved from near death to near birth, the signs on the wall pointing to Labor, Delivery, the Newborn Nursery, and the Fathers' Waiting Room. I was looking for a pay phone, fumbling aside the gun in my bag for loose change, feeling panic mount as the seconds ticked away. Once I got the relevant information back to Dolan, I was out of there.

I passed the desk on 2-Main. There was a counter to my left with wall-mounted monitors that showed green lines I assumed were vital signs.

A black nurse coming out of a room marked "Staff Lounge" nearly bumped into me. She was wearing an ankle-length white gown that tied in the back, a mask pushed up on the middle of her forehead like a pale green hump. She was in her forties, slim, with dark eyes and a clear, unlined face. "Can I help you?"

"I sincerely hope so," I said. "This is my situation and you just have to trust me on this. I'm a private investigator from Santa Teresa. I'm working undercover on an auto insurance fraud case and I'm here in the company of a thug who's going to start looking for me any minute. I have to get a call through to Lieutenant Dolan up in Santa Teresa. Do you have a telephone I could use? I swear it won't take long and it could save my life."

She looked at me with the blank contemplation of somebody assessing information. It must have been something in the tone I used, pure desperation overlaid with "earnest." It certainly wasn't anything in the way I looked. For once, I was telling the truth, using every cell in my being to convey. my sincerity. She listened, brown eyes intent on my face as I spoke. It's possible the tale I told was so preposterous she just didn't think me capable of making it up. Without a word, she pointed toward a telphone on the desk behind the counter.

twenty-three

i went through the hospital operator, placing a person-to-person call to Dolan at the number he'd given me. While I waited for the call to be patched through, I read the bulletin board, which seemed devoted in equal parts to medical cartoons, notices of classes coming up, and menus for neighborhood fast-food restaurants offering free delivery. I was starving to death.

When I heard Dolan's voice, I closed my eyes and put a hand on my chest, patting myself with relief. "Lieutenant Dolan, this is Kinsey Millhone. I'm calling from St. John's Hospital and I don't have long."

"What's up?"

I started talking, my mind racing ahead, trying to organize the information as I spoke. "First of all, Bibianna Diaz is in ICU down here. She was run off the road last night—"

"I heard," Dolan interjected.

"You know about that?"

"One of Santos's men called me the minute the report came through. Hospital has orders to be polite to Raymond without letting him get anywhere near her hospital bed. They know what to do."

"Well, thank God for *that*." I filled him in quickly on the situation to date, including the file I'd seen at Buddy's Auto Body Shop. "I think I've figured out who the leak is up there." I told him about Dr. Howard, the chiropractor, and the photo of his daughter. I had no idea what her married name was, but I gave him an accurate (though acid) description of her. As a civilian clerk working for the county sheriff's department, she was in a perfect position to funnel information to her father, and through him to Raymond. The minute Bibianna was first arrested in Santa Teresa, Raymond would have known her whereabouts. A sudden thought occurred to me. "Lieutenant, do you know anything about the gun Parnell was murdered with? Raymond's got a thirty-caliber broomhandle Mauser. I saw it in his dresser drawer."

Dolan cut in. "Forget Parnell for now and do me a favor. I want you to hang up and get the hell out of there."

"Why, what's happening?"

"Tate's probably already on the premises. Hospital notified him late last night and he took off, heading south. If Raymond finds out he's there, they'll have a showdown for sure."

"Oh, shit."

Behind me, a woman doctor came into the nurses' station, wearing surgical greens. She pulled off her cap and shook her hair out wearily. She paused to study me, hair rumpled, lines of exhaustion weighting down her face. I couldn't tell if she wanted the telephone or the chair.

Dolan was saying, "I got somebody down there who can help you out. Hold on. I got a call coming in. . . ."

I saw Raymond pass the desk, heading toward the elevators, probably in search of me. I couldn't wait for Dolan. "I gotta go," I said into dead air, and hung up. Every brain cell in my head was screaming at me to get out, but I couldn't leave Jimmy Tate here without backup. I left the nurses' station and trotted down the hall behind Raymond, finally catching up with him.

I tapped him on the shoulder. "Hi, where did you go?"

He turned and looked at me irritably. "Where the hell have you been? I'm off lookin' for you."

"I went over to the nursery to see the newborns," I said.

"What for?"

"I like babies. I might want to have one of my own some-day, you know? They're really cute, all tiny and puckery. They look like Cornish game hens—"

"We ain't here for that," he said gruffly, though he seemed mollified by my explanation. He grabbed my arm and turned me, walking us back down the corridor toward ICU.

"Why don't we take a break and get some coffee," I said.

"Forget that. I'm jumpy enough as it is."

We reached the ICU waiting room and Raymond sat down again. He took a magazine from a nearby stack and flipped through it with an air of distraction. The pages made little snapping sounds in the quiet of the room. Two women seated at the other end of the room stared at him, frankly curious about his tics.

Raymond glanced up, catching them in the act, and stared back at them until they broke off eye contact. "Jesus, I hate it when people stare at me. They think I like doing this?" He gave me an exaggerated jerk, glaring darkly at the two women, who were stirring with self-consciousness.

I said, "How's Bibianna doing? Has anybody said?"

He shifted restlessly. "Doctor's supposed to show up any minute and talk to us."

I had to get him out of there. A color television in the corner, sound off, was tuned to one of those nature films where they show half of one species being eaten by another.

Raymond leaned forward. "Jeez, what's *taking* them so long?"

"You want some lunch? Why don't we go down to the coffee shop and find Luis. I'm starving."

He hung his head, shaking it, and then looked over at me, his expression bleak. "What if she doesn't make it?"

I bit back a retort. I couldn't think of an answer that didn't seem quarrelsome. I revised my reaction. On reflection, it seemed perfectly in keeping with the depth of his denial that he'd now be worried sick about a woman he'd tried to have assassinated less than twenty-four hours before. If Raymond found out Jimmy Tate was here, he'd bring the whole place down.

I said, "We're both going to go crazy if we hang around here. It won't take long. We can grab a quick lunch and come right back up. The doctor might not be back on the ward for an hour."

"You think?"

"Come on. Get a cup of coffee, at least."

Raymond tossed the magazine aside and got up. We moved into the corridor and he slowed his step. "Maybe I should tell the nurse where we are in case he shows."

"Or I can do that if you like. Why don't you go ahead and buzz the elevator for us?"

Two Hispanic nurses approached from down the corridor. There was some activity in the hallway and both of us looked over. A doctor appeared from the Rehab wing, heading for ICU. He was wearing a calf-length white duster over a gray suit. He had his full name stitched above his pocket in blue script. A stethoscope coiled up out of his pocket like a length of narrow-gauge garden hose. He was in his fifties with closely clipped gray hair, rimless glasses, and a limp. His right foot was strapped into a walking cast that looked like a ski boot. He noticed my glance and smiled apologetically, though he offered no explanation. I pictured a sports-related mishap, which might have been his hope. He probably tripped on a sprinkler head while he was pinching suckers off his roses. "Can I help you folks?"

Raymond said, "I'm here about Bibianna Diaz. Are you the doctor?"

"Absolutely. Nice to meet you, Mr. Tate. I'm Dr. Cherbak." He reached out to Raymond and the two of them shook hands. "Nurse said you were here. Sorry it took me so long. . . ."

Raymond's smile slipped a notch. "The name is Raymond Maldonado. What's Tate got to do with it?"

Dr. Cherbak blinked with uncertainty and then checked Bibianna's chart. "Sorry. She asked to have her husband notified, and naturally, I thought . . ."

From where I stood, I could see the big pink notice reading PC, protective custody, affixed to the front. Raymond seemed to spot it about the same time I did.

"Her husband?" he repeated. He stared at the doctor, who must have realized he'd committed an egregious error.

I touched Raymond's arm, murmuring, "Raymond, there's been a misunderstanding, that's all. Maybe she has a head injury. Who knows what she might have said? She might be hallucinating—"

Raymond jerked away from my touch. "Shut up!" he said. And then to the doctor: "She told you that? Jimmy Tate's her *husband*? That's bullshit. I'll rip your fuckin' face off, you say that."

The two nurses, in conversation, were suddenly attentive, watching the encounter as if it were a soap opera. I could feel the dread suffuse me like a fever. "Let's come back later. . . ."

"How's she doing?" Raymond asked. He was being pugnacious, jaw working with tension.

"I'm not at liberty to—"

"I asked you how she's doing. You want to answer me, you dick?"

Dr. Cherbak stiffened. "I can see I've made a mistake," he said. "If you're not related to the patient, I'm limited in the amount of information I can give you. . . ."

Raymond gave him a push. "Fuckin' A you made a mistake! I'm going to marry this woman, get it? Me. Raymond Maldonado. You got that straight?"

Dr. Cherbak turned on his heel and moved toward ICU at a brisk clip, pushing through the double doors. I heard him on the other side. "Get Security up here. . . ."

Raymond banged through the doors after him and grabbed him from behind. "Where's Bibianna?" he screamed. *"Where is she?"*

The doctor stumbled off-balance and one of the duty nurses started to run. A second nurse picked up a phone to call Security. Raymond pulled out a gun and pointed it at her, his arm stiff, his intent murderous. She lowered the phone. He swung the gun back and forth as he made his way down the hall. I pulled out the SIG-Sauer, but the doctor was in my way. Hospital staff seemed to be everywhere.

I screamed, *"Tate!"* I started running.

Bibianna was in the second room. Tate was on his feet, his gun out. Raymond fired. I saw Tate go down.

Raymond doubled back, heading right at me.

I held the gun with both hands and yelled, "Stop!" but he knew I wouldn't fire under the circumstances. There were too many people in the vicinity to risk shooting. He shouldered me aside and took off at a dead run, his heels clattering as he plowed through the double doors and down the corridor. He still had his gun, but he was moving too fast to take aim or fire with any accuracy. I banged through the doors behind him and pounded down the hallway after him. Heads appeared in doorways, people attracted by all the commotion, disappearing again quickly when they spotted the guns. Raymond reached an Exit sign and grabbed the knob, flung the door open, and headed down the stairs. I caught the door as it swung shut and forced it back with a crash. I could hear Raymond's descent, his footsteps echoing rapidly in a spiral below me. I was jumping down three steps at a time, trying to cut his lead, when I heard him reach the exterior door below. His exit set off an alarm bell that began to peal shrilly.

I doubled my pace, hitting the door with one hand, the SIG-Sauer in the other, nearly recoiling at the sudden blast of bright sunlight in my face. I could see Raymond tearing across a stretch of lawn just ahead of me. We'd emerged from one end of the hospital, close to Arizona Avenue in an area of small stucco houses with an occasional three-story medical building. Raymond ran toward the street, feet flying, arms pumping. I was vaguely aware of someone running behind me, but I couldn't afford to look. I was narrowing the gap, calling on the last of my physical reserves. I had to be in better shape than Raymond, but I could feel myself wheezing, lungs on fire. Six days without exercise had taken the edge off, but I still had some juice.

Raymond took a quick look behind him, gauging the distance between us. He got off a shot that smacked into a palm tree to my left. He tried to goose up his pace, but he really didn't have it in him. I was close enough now that the sound of his heavy breathing seemed in concert with mine and the heels of his shoes nearly touched my pumping knees. I had a tight grip on the gun. I reached out and pushed him hard in the back. He stumbled, arms flailing as he tried to regain his balance. He went down in a sprawl and I landed, knees first, in the middle of his back. His breath left him in a *whoosh* and the gun flew out of his hand. I was up and on my feet, panting heavily. He turned over as I raised the barrel of the gun and placed it between his eyes. Raymond had his hands up, inching away from me. For ten cents I would have blown that motherfucker away. My rage was white hot and I was out of control, screaming *"I'll kill your ass! I'll kill your ass, you son of a bitch!!"*

Behind me, I heard, *"Freeze!"*

I whipped around.

It was Luis.

The gun in his right hand was pointed directly at Raymond. In his left hand was a badge. He was LAPD.

epilogue

by the time I got back upstairs, the emergency room crew was already working on Jimmy Tate, who was whisked into surgery within the hour. The bullet had caught him in the abdomen and he'd apparently suffered a ruptured spleen. Bibianna wasn't in much better shape, but both survived. Whether they lived happily ever after or not, I really couldn't say, as all this happened just three weeks ago. I made it back to Santa Teresa in time for Vera's wedding on Monday night, which was Halloween. Naturally, as I hadn't had time to shop, I was forced to wear my faithful all-purpose dress, which in my opinion suited the occasion to a T. Vera was urging me to bring a date, so I took Luis with me, Donald and Daffy Duck arms and all.

Raymond Maldonado has hired himself a top-notch attorney. At this point the charges against him range from murder one, in the case of Parnell Perkins, to grand theft, insurance fraud, mail fraud, all the way down to petty larceny. I gather that certain cases involving individuals with Tourette's syndrome present a serious challenge to the criminal justice system. My guess is he'll work out a deal, naming some of the other key figures in the fraud ring including three attorneys from the law firm of Gotlieb, Naples, Hurley, and Flushing.

The cops never did come up with my black leather jacket. Somebody in the restaurant probably lifted it the minute my back was turned. I'm tellin' you, people are crooks! And it's not just the ordinary man in the street. I haven't been paid for all the work I did. I billed the Santa Teresa Police Department for services rendered. Dolan tells me he forwarded the invoice to the LAPD, who'll probably turn around and try to lay it off on the Department of Insurance. I'll give those turkeys ninety days to "process" my money and then I'm calling my attorney.

The only other matter that needs clearing up has to do with Gordon Titus and that's simple enough. The sucker fired me.

I is for
Innocent

For my granddaughter, Erin,
with a heart full of love

The author wishes to acknowledge the invaluable assistance of the following people: Steven Humphrey; Sam Eaton, Attorney-at-Law; B. J. Seeboll, J.D.; John Mackall, Attorney-at-Law; Debra Young, Attorney-at-Law; Joe Driscoll, Joe Driscoll & Associates Investigations; Lieutenant Terry Bristol and Sergeant Carol Hesson, Santa Barbara County Sheriff's Department; Detective Lawrence Gillespie, Coroner's Bureau, Santa Barbara's Sheriff's Department; Eric S. H. Ching; Debbie Davidson, KEYT-TV; Richard Dodge, Far West Gun County; Charles Sunderlin, Premier Products Manager, Heckler & Koch; George E. Rush; Florence Michel; David Elder; and Carter Blackmar.

I feel compelled to report that at the moment of death, my entire life did not pass before my eyes in a flash. There was no beckoning white light at the end of a tunnel, no warm fuzzy feeling that my long-departed loved ones were waiting on The Other Side. What I experienced was a little voice piping up in an outraged tone, "Oh, come on. You're not serious. This is really *it*?" Mostly, I regretted I hadn't tidied my chest of drawers the night before as I'd planned. It's painful to realize that those who mourn your untimely demise will also carry with them the indelible image of all your tatty underpants. You might question the validity of the observation since it's obvious I didn't die when I thought I would, but let's face it, life is trivial, and my guess is that dying imparts very little wisdom to those in process.

My name is Kinsey Millhone. I'm a licensed private investigator operating out of Santa Teresa, which is ninety-five miles north of Los Angeles. For the past seven years, I'd been running my own small agency adjacent to the home offices of California Fidelity Insurance. My agreement with the company entitled me to the use of an attractive corner suite in exchange for the investigation of arson and wrongful death claims on an "as needed" basis. In early November, that arrangement was abruptly terminated when a hotshot efficiency expert was transferred to Santa Teresa from the CF branch office in Palm Springs.

I hadn't thought I'd be affected by the change in company management since I was operating as an independent contractor instead of a bona fide California Fidelity employee. However, at our first (and only) meeting, this man and I took an instant dislike to each other. In the fifteen minutes that constituted our entire relationship, I was rude, pugnacious, and uncooperative. The next thing I knew I was out on the street with my client files packed up in assorted cardboard boxes. Let's not even mention the fact that my association with CF had culminated in the wholesale bust-up of a multi-million-dollar auto insurance scam. All *that* netted me was a surreptitious handshake from Mac Voorhies, the company vice-president and avowed chickenheart, who assured me he was just as appalled by this guy as I was. While I appreciated the support, it didn't solve my problem. I needed work. I needed an office in which to do the work. Aside from the fact that my apartment was too small to serve the purpose, it felt unprofessional. Some of my clients are unsavory characters and I didn't want those bozos to know where I lived. I had troubles enough. With the recent sharp rise in property taxes, my landlord had been forced to double my rent. He'd been more upset about the hike than I had, but according to his accountant, he'd had no choice. The rent was still very reasonable and I had no complaints, but the increase couldn't have come at a more awkward time. I had used my savings to pay for my "new" car, a 1974 VW—this one pale blue, with only one minor ding in the left rear fender. My living expenses were modest, but I still didn't have a sou left at the end of the month.

I've heard that no one gets fired without secretly hoping for the liberation, but that sounds like the kind of pronouncement you make before you've been given the boot. Being fired is the pits, ranking right up there with infidelity in its brutalizing effect. The ego recoils and one's self-image is punctured like a tire by a nail. In the weeks since I'd been terminated, I'd gone through all the stages one suffers at the diagnosis of a soon-to-be-fatal disease: anger, denial, bargaining, drunkenness, foul language, head colds, rude hand gestures, anxiety, and eating disorders of sudden onset. I'd also entertained a steady stream of loathsome thoughts about the man responsible. Lately, however, I'd begun to wonder if it wasn't true, this notion of a repressed desire to be unceremoniously shit-canned. Maybe I was bored with CF. Maybe I was burned out. Maybe I was simply longing for a change of scene. Whatever the truth, I'd begun to adjust and I could feel the optimism rising through my veins like maple syrup. It was more than a matter of survival. One way or another, I knew I'd *prevail*.

For the time being, I was renting a spare room in the law offices of Kingman and Ives. Lonnie Kingman is in his early forties, five foot four, 205 pounds, a weight-lifting fanatic, perpetually pumped up on steroids, testosterone, vitamin B_{12}, and caffeine. He's got a shaggy head of dark hair, like a pony in the process of shedding a winter coat. His nose looks like it's been busted about as often as mine has. I know, from the various degrees framed and hung on his wall, that he received a B.A. from Harvard and an M.B.A. from Columbia, and then graduated *summa cum laude* from Stanford Law School.

His partner, John Ives, while equally credentialed, prefers the quiet, nonglamorous aspects of the practice. His forte is appellate civil work, where he enjoys a reputation as an attorney of uncommon imagination, solid research, and exceptional writing skills. Since Lonnie and John established the firm some six years ago, the support staff has expanded to include a receptionist, two secretaries, and a paralegal who doubles as a runner. Martin Cheltenham, the third attorney in the firm, while not a formal partner, is Lonnie's best friend, leasing office space from him in the same way I do.

In Santa Teresa, all the flashy cases seem to go to Lonnie Kingman. He's best known for his criminal defense work, but his passion is complex trials in any case involving accidental injury or wrongful death, which is how our paths crossed in the first place. I'd done some work for Lonnie in the past and, aside from the fact that I'm occasionally in need of his services myself, I figured he'd be good for the referrals. From his point of view, it didn't hurt to have an investigator on the premises. As with California Fidelity, I was not an employee. I worked as an independent contractor, providing professional services and billing accordingly. To celebrate the new arrangement, I went out and bought myself a handsome tweed blazer to wear with my usual jeans and turtleneck. I thought I looked pretty snappy in the outfit.

It was a Monday early in December when I first got involved in the Isabelle Barney murder case. I'd driven down to Cottonwood twice that day, two ten-mile round-trips, trying to serve a subpoena on a witness in a battery case. The first time, he wasn't home. The second time, I caught him just as he pulled into his driveway from work. I handed him the papers, disregarding his annoyance, and took off again with my car radio thundering to mask his parting remarks, which were rude. He used a couple of words I hadn't heard in years. On my way into town, I did a detour past the office.

The Kingman building is a three-story stucco structure, with parking tucked in at ground level and two floors of of-

4

fices above. Across the facade, there are six pairs of floor-to-ceiling French doors that open inward for ventilation, each flanked by tall wooden shutters painted the soft verdigris of a greening copper roof. A shallow wrought-iron bracket is secured across the lower half of each set of doors. The effect is largely decorative, but in a pinch might prevent a suicidal dog or a client's sulky child from flinging itself out the window in a fit of pique. The building straddles the property and has a driveway that passes through an arch on the right, opening up into a tiny parking lot in the rear. The one drawback is the parsimonious assignment of parking spaces. There are six permanent tenants and twelve parking spots. Since Lonnie owns the building, his law firm had been allotted four: one for John, one for Martin, one for Lonnie, and one for Lonnie's secretary, Ida Ruth. The remaining eight places were parceled out according to the individual leases. The rest of us had a choice of street parking or one of the public lots three blocks away. The local rates are absurdly cheap, given big-city standards, but on my limited budget the tab mounts up. Street parking downtown isn't metered, but it's restricted to ninety minutes and the meter maids are quick to ticket you if you cheat by so much as a minute. As a consequence, I spent a lot of time either moving my car or cruising the area trying to ferret out a spot that was both close by and free. Happily, this exasperating situation only extends until 6:00 P.M.

It was then 6:15 and the third-floor windows along the front were dark, suggesting that everyone had already gone home for the day. When I drove through the arch, I saw Lonnie's car was still in its slot. Ida Ruth's Toyota was gone so I eased my car into her space, next to his Mercedes. An unfamiliar pale blue Jaguar sedan was parked in John's slot. I hung my head out the car window and craned my neck. Lonnie's office lights were on, two oblongs of pale yellow against the slanting shadows from the roof. He was probably with a client.

The days were getting steadily shorter, and a gloom settled over the town at that hour. Something in the air generated a longing for a wood fire, companionship, and the kind of cocktail that looks elegant in the print ads and tastes like liniment. I told myself I had work to do, but in truth it was just a way to postpone going home.

I locked my car and headed for the stairwell, which was tucked into a hollow core that extended up the center of the building like a chimney flue. The stairs were inky, and I had to use my little keychain flashlight to break up the darkness. The third-floor corridor was in shadow, but I could see lights in the reception area through the frosted glass in the front door. By day, the whole third-floor complex was cheerful and well lighted, with white walls, burnt orange carpeting, a forest of greenhouse plants, Scandinavian furniture, and original artwork in bright crayon tones. The office I was renting had served as a combination conference room and kitchen, and was outfitted now with my desk and swivel chair, file cabinets, a small flop-out couch that could double as a bed in an emergency, a telephone, and my answering machine. I was still listed in the yellow pages under Investigators, and people calling the old number were advised of the new. In the weeks since the move, while some business had trickled in, I'd been forced to resort to process serving to make ends meet. At twenty bucks a pop, I was never going to get rich, but on a good day I could sometimes pick up an extra hundred bucks. Not bad, if I could sandwich it in with other investigative work.

I let myself in quietly, not wanting to disturb Lonnie if he was in the middle of a conference. His office door was open and I glanced in automatically as I went past. He was chatting with a client, but when he caught sight of me, he raised his hand and beckoned. "Kinsey, could you spare a minute? There's someone here I want you to meet."

I backtracked to his doorway. Lonnie's client was seated in the black leather wing chair, with his back to me. As Lonnie

6

stood up, his client stood, too, turning to look at me as we were introduced. His aura was dark, if you buy that kind of talk.

"Kenneth Voigt," Lonnie said. "This is Kinsey Millhone, the private investigator I was telling you about."

We shook hands, going through the usual litany of greetings while we checked each other out. He was in his early fifties with dark hair and dark brown eyes, his brows separated by deep indentations that had been set there by a scowl. His face was blunt, his wide forehead softened by a tongue of thinning hair that was brushed to one side. He smiled politely at me, but his face didn't brighten much. A pale sheen of perspiration seemed to glimmer on his forehead. While he was on his feet, he shed his sport coat and tossed it on the couch. The shirt he wore under it was dark gray, a short-sleeved Polo with a three-button placket open at the neck. Dark hair curled from his shirt collar and a mat of dark hair covered his arms. He was narrow through the shoulders and the muscles in his arms were stringy and undeveloped. He should have worked out at a gym, for his stress levels, if nothing else. He took out a handkerchief, dabbing at his forehead and his upper lip.

"I want her to hear this," Lonnie was saying to Voigt. "She can go through the files tonight and start first thing in the morning."

"Fine with me," Voigt said.

The two sat down again. I folded myself into one corner of the couch and pulled my legs up under me, considerably cheered by the prospects of a paycheck. One advantage in the work for Lonnie is he screens out all the deadbeats.

Lonnie offered me a word of explanation before the conversation continued. "The P.I. we were using just dropped dead of a heart attack. Morley Shine, you know him?"

"Of course," I said, startled. "*Morley* died? When was this?"

"Last night about eight. I was gone over the weekend and

didn't get back till after midnight so I didn't hear about it myself until this morning when Dorothy called me."

Morley Shine had been around ever since I could remember, not a close friend, but certainly a man I could count on if I found myself in a pinch. He and the fellow who'd trained me as a P.I. had been partners for years. At some point, they'd had a falling-out and each had gone into business for himself. Morley was in his late sixties, tall and slump-shouldered, probably eighty pounds overweight, with a round, dimpled face, wheezing laugh, and fingers yellowed from all the cigarettes he smoked. He had access to snitches and informants in every correctional facility in the state, plus contacts in all the relevant local information pools. I'd have to quiz Lonnie later about the circumstances of Morley's death. For the time being, I concentrated on Kenneth Voigt, who had backed up his narrative so he could get a running start.

He stared down at the floor, hands clasped loosely in his lap. "My ex-wife was murdered six years ago. Isabelle Barney. You remember the case?"

The name meant nothing. "I don't think so," I said.

"Someone unscrewed the fisheye in the middle of the front door. He knocked, and when she flipped on the porch light and peered out, he fired a thirty-eight through the spyhole. She died instantly."

My memory kicked in with a jolt. "That was her? I do remember that much. I can't believe it's been six years." I nearly added my only other recollection, that the guy alleged to have killed her was her estranged husband. Apparently not Kenneth Voigt, but who?

I made eye contact with Lonnie, who interjected a comment, picking up on my question as if with ESP. "The guy's name is David Barney. He was acquitted, in case you're curious."

Voigt changed positions in his chair as if the very name made him itch. "The bastard."

Lonnie said, "Go on with your story, Ken. I didn't mean

8

to interrupt. You might as well give her the background as long as she's here."

It seemed to take a few seconds for him to remember what he'd been saying. "We were married for four years . . . a second marriage for both. We have a ten-year-old daughter named Shelby who's off at boarding school. She was four when Iz was killed. Anyway, Isabelle and I had been having problems . . . nothing unusual as far as I knew. She got involved with Barney. She married him a month after our divorce became final. All he wanted was her money. Everybody knew that except poor, dumb Iz. And I don't mean any insult to her when I say that. I loved the woman, truly, but she was gullible as they come. She was bright and she was talented, but she had no sense of self-worth, which made her a sitting duck for anybody with a kind word. You probably know women like that. Emotionally dependent, no self-esteem to speak of. She was an artist, and while I had tremendous admiration for her ability, it was hard to watch her throw her life away. . . ."

I found myself tuning out his analysis of her character. His generalizations about women were obnoxious and he'd evidently told the same story so often his rendering of events was flat and passionless. The drama was not about her anymore, it was the tale of his reaction. My eye wandered over to the pile of fat manila folders on Lonnie's desk. I could see VOIGT/BARNEY written across the spine. Two cardboard boxes stacked against the wall contained additional files, judging by the labels affixed to one side. Everything Voigt was saying was going to be right there, a compilation of facts without all the editorials attached. It seemed weird to me—what he said might be true, but it wasn't necessarily believable. Some folks are like that. The simplest recollection just sounds false in the rendering. He went on for a bit, speaking in closely knit paragraphs that didn't yield the opportunity for interruption. I wondered how often Lonnie had served as his audience. I noticed he'd disconnected, too. While Kenneth

Voigt's mouth was moving, Lonnie picked up a pencil and began to turn it end over end, tapping on his legal pad first with the point and then with the eraser. I returned my attention to Ken Voigt.

"How'd the guy get off?" I asked as soon as he paused for breath.

Lonnie jumped in, apparently impatient to get down to the meat of the matter. "Dink Jordan prosecuted. What a yawn that was. Jesus. I mean, the man is competent but he's got no style. He thought he could win on the merits of the case." Lonnie snorted at the absurdity of the assumption. "So now we're suing the shit out of David Barney for wrongful death. I hate the guy. Just hate him. The minute he pled not guilty, I told Ken we should jump on the son of a bitch with hobnail boots. I couldn't talk him into it. We filed and got him served, but then Ken insisted we sit on it."

Voigt frowned uncomfortably. "You were right, Lon. I see it now, but you know how it is. My wife, Francesca, was opposed to our reopening the investigation. It's painful for everyone . . . me more than most. I simply couldn't handle it."

Lonnie crossed his eyes. He didn't have a lot of sympathy for what people could or couldn't handle. *His* job was to handle it. Voigt's job was to turn him loose. "Hey, okay. Skip that. It's water under the bridge. It took a year to get him tried and acquitted on the criminal charges. In the meantime, Ken here watches David Barney work his way through Isabelle's money. And believe me, there's plenty of it, most of which would have gone to his daughter, Shelby, if Barney'd been convicted. Finally, the family reaches a point where they can't stand it anymore, so Ken comes back to me and we get into gear. Meanwhile, Barney's attorney, guy named Foss, files a discretionary motion to dismiss for lack of prosecution. I whip into court and tap-dance my tiny heart out. The motion was denied, but the judge made it clear he wasn't happy with me.

"Now, of course, David Barney and this jerk who represents him are using every delay they can think of, and then some. They dicker around and dicker around. We're going through all the discovery, right? The guy's been acquitted in criminal court so what difference does it make what he says at this point? But he's tight-lipped. He's tense. That's because he's guilty as hell. Oh, and here. Check this. Ken here has a guy shows up . . . turns out he shared a cell with David Barney. This guy's been following the case. He sits in on the trial, just to see what's going on, and he's telling us Barney as good as admitted he killed her as he's walkin' out the courtroom *door*. The informant's been hard to nail down, which is why I want to get the sucker served first thing."

"What good's it going to do?" I asked. "David Barney can't be tried again on the murder one."

"Exactly. Which is why we kicked it over to the civil side. We've got a much better shot at him there, which he damn well knows. The guy's really dragging his feet, doing everything he can to hinder and obstruct. We file a motion. He's got thirty days to answer so his attorney—what a geek—waits until day twenty-nine and then files a demurrer. Anything to string it out. He's throwing up roadblocks left and right.

"We bring Barney in for a deposition and he pleads the Fifth. So we take him into court and force him to testify. The judge *orders* the guy to answer because he has no Fifth Amendment rights. There's no danger of prosecution because jeopardy has attached. Back we go on the depo. So now he takes the Fifth again. We take him in on the contempt, but in the meantime we're running up against the court statute—"

"Lonnie?" I said.

"We're humming and humming and it's not working for us. We're coming up to the five-year statute and we really need to make the case happen. We're on the master calendar and we've been given priority, and now *Morley* drops dead—"

"Looonnnnie," I sang. I raised my hand to get his attention.

He stopped.

"Just tell me what you need and I'll go out and get it for you."

Lonnie laughed and tossed his pencil at me. "This is why I like her. No bullshit," he said to Voigt. He reached over and pushed the stack of files in my direction. "This is everything we got, though it's a bit disorganized. There's an inventory on top—just make sure it's all in there somewhere before you start work. Once you're familiar with the basics, we can figure out where the gaps are. In the meantime, I want you two to get acquainted. You're going to be seeing a lot of each other in the next month."

Voigt and I smiled politely at Lonnie without looking at one another. He didn't seem to feel any more excited about the prospects than I did.

2

I ended up staying at the office until midnight. The accumulated files on Isabelle Barney spilled over the tops of the two cardboard cartons, each of which weighed over forty pounds. I nearly developed a hernia hauling the boxes from Lonnie's office to mine. There was no way I could get through all the data at one sitting so I figured I might as well take my time. Lonnie wasn't kidding when he said the files were disorganized. According to the inventory, the first box should have contained copies of police reports, transcripts from the murder trial, the complaint Lonnie'd filed in the civil action in the Santa Teresa County Superior Court, all the demurrers, answers, and cross-complaints. I couldn't even be sure that the trial transcripts were complete. What files I could spot were lumped together in one of those annoying hodgepodges that make finding anything a chore.

The second box supposedly contained copies of all of Morley Shine's reports, affidavits, transcripts from the numerous depositions taken, and pages of supporting documentation. Fat chance. I could see the list of witnesses that Morley had talked to—he'd been billing Lonnie on a regular monthly basis since June 1—but not all of the corresponding written reports were in evidence. It looked like he'd served about half the subpoenas for the upcoming trial, but most of those seemed to be repeat witnesses from the criminal proceedings. Eight signed civil subpoenas, with instructions for service attached, were clipped together in a folder. I didn't see that he'd served any new witnesses . . . unless the yellow server's copies were filed somewhere else. From a scribbled note, I gathered that the informant's name was Curtis McIntyre, whose telephone number was a disconnect and whose last known address was no good. I made a note to myself to track him down first as per Lonnie's request.

I leafed through page after page of interrogatories and responses, making an occasional note to myself. As with a jigsaw puzzle, what I hoped to do was to familiarize myself with the picture on the box lid and then proceed to put the pieces together one section at a time. I knew I'd be repeating some of Morley Shine's investigation, but his approach tended to be a bit ham-fisted and I thought I'd do better if I started from scratch, at least in the sensitive areas. I wasn't sure what to do about the gaps in the files. I hadn't finished going through the boxes yet and I could tell I was going to have to empty everything out and repack the data so they would match the index. Certain avenues Morley'd pursued appeared to be dead ends and could probably be eliminated unless something new cropped up. He'd probably been keeping all the current files in his office or at home, which I did myself if I was still in the process of transcribing notes.

The bare bones of the story were much as Kenneth Voigt had indicated. Isabelle Barney died sometime between 1:00 and 2:00 A.M. on December 26 when a .38-caliber weapon was fired at point-blank range through the peephole in her front door. The ballistics expert called it "a near-contact shooting," with the hole in the door acting almost like an extension of the barrel and Isabelle's eye almost touching the door. The wood around the hole was blown out at right angles to the hole and toward Isabelle, with some fragments probably blown back toward the killer as well. In a dry parenthetical note, the ballistics expert suggested that the blast might well have forced "material" back into the barrel itself, perhaps jamming the gun, and thus making a second shot problematic, if not impossible. I skipped the rest of that paragraph.

The muzzle flash had singed the wood inside the hole, charring it slightly. The report noted powder residue on the outside of the door around the hole, inside the hole, and also around the hole on the inside of the door. Much of the area was splintered by the gas pressure. The bird shot and the remnants of blue plastic cap removed from the wound indicated that the bullet was a Glaser Safety Slug, a light, high-velocity round consisting of bird shot suspended in a viscous medium encased in a copper jacket with a plastic nose cap. When the slug hits a medium like flesh with a high water content, the plastic cap separates, the copper jacket peels back, and the bird shot spreads out rapidly, transferring all of the energy in the slug to the flesh. Because each piece is small and of low mass, it dumps its energy quickly and stays in the body, hence the name Safety Slug. Bystanders are not endangered by an overpenetrating bullet, and since the Safety Slug also disintegrates against hard surfaces (such as skulls . . .), ricochets are minimized as well. No getting around it, I thought, this killer was just too considerate.

According to the pathologist, the bullet, along with fragments of metal and wood, entered the victim's right eye. The autopsy report spelled out in highly technical detail the destruction to soft tissue left in its wake. Even with my sketchy knowledge of anatomy, it was clear death was instantaneous and therefore painless. The machinery of life had shut down long before the nervous system had a chance to register the agony such a wound would inflict.

It's hard to have faith in your fellow man when you're forced to look at some of his handiwork. I disconnected my emotional machinery while I studied the autopsy X rays and photographs. I work best when I'm armed with an unflinching view of reality, but the detachment is not without its dangers. Unplug yourself often and you risk losing touch with your feelings altogether. There were ten color photographs, each with a nightmarish quality of violated flesh. This is what death is, I reminded myself. This is what homicide really looks like in the raw. I've met killers—soft-spoken, pleasant, and courteous—whose psychological denial is so profound that their perpetration of a killing seems inconceivable. The dead are mute, but the living still have voice with which to protest their innocence. Often their objections are noisy and pious, impossible to refute since the one person who could condemn them has been silenced forever. The final testimony from Isabelle Barney was framed in the language of her fatal injury, a devastating portrait of waste and loss. I tucked the pictures back in the envelope and moved on to a copy of the case notes Dink Jordan had sent over to Lonnie.

Dink's real name was Dinsmore. He referred to himself as Dennis, but nobody else did. He was in his fifties, bland and gray, a man without energy, humor, or eloquence. As a public prosecutor he was competent, but he had no sense of theater. His delivery was so slow and so methodical it was like reading the entire Bible through a microscope. I'd once watched him lay out his closing arguments in a spectacular felony murder trial with two jurors nodding off and two more so bored they were nearly comatose.

David Barney's attorney was a man named Herb Foss,

whom I didn't know at all. Lonnie claimed he was a jerk, but you had to give him credit for getting David Barney off.

While there had been no witnesses to the shooting and the murder weapon was never found, evidence showed that Barney had purchased a .38-caliber revolver some eight months before the murder. He claimed the gun had been removed from his bed table at some point during the Labor Day weekend, when the couple had given a large dinner party in honor of some friends from Los Angeles, Don and Julie Seeger. When he was questioned about his reasons for not filing a police report, he maintained that he'd discussed it with Isabelle, who'd been reluctant to confront her guests with the alleged theft.

During the trial, Isabelle's sister testified that the couple had been talking for months about a separation. David Barney contended that the breach between them wasn't serious. However, the gun theft incident precipitated a quarrel, which culminated in Isabelle's ordering him to move out. There seemed to be much disagreement about the prognosis for the marriage. David Barney claimed the relationship was stable but stormy, that he and Isabelle had been in the process of negotiating their differences. Observers seemed to feel that the marriage was dead, but *that* might have been wishful thinking on their part.

Whatever the truth, the situation deteriorated rapidly. David Barney moved out on September 15 and then proceeded to do everything in his power to regain Isabelle's affections. He made frequent phone calls. He sent flowers. He sent gifts. When his attentions became annoying, instead of giving her the breathing space she requested, he redoubled his efforts. He left a single red rose on the hood of her car every morning. He left jewelry on her doorstep, sent her sentimental cards in the mail. The more she rejected him, the more obsessed he became. During October and November, he called her day and night, hanging up if she answered. When she had her number changed, he managed to acquire the new unlisted number and continued phoning her at all hours. She got an answering machine. He continued to call, leaving the line open until the message tape ran out. She told friends she felt she was under siege.

In the meantime, he leased a house in the same stylish section of Horton Ravine. If she left the house, he followed her. If she stayed home, he parked across the road and watched the house through binoculars, keeping track of visitors, repairmen, and the household help. Isabelle called the police. She filed complaints. Finally, her attorney had a restraining order issued, prohibiting phone calls, written communication, and his approach anywhere within two hundred yards of her person, her property, or her automobile. His determination seemed to subside, but by then the harassment had taken its toll. Isabelle was terrified.

By the time Christmas came, she was a nervous wreck, eating little, sleeping poorly, subject to anxiety, panic, and tremors. She was pale. She was haggard. She was drinking too much. She was agitated by company and frightened to be alone. She sent the four-year-old Shelby to live with her father. Ken Voigt had remarried, though some witnesses suggested that he'd never quite recovered from his divorce from her. Isabelle took tranquilizers to get through the day. At night, she popped down sleeping pills. Finally, the Seegers prevailed on her to pack her bags and accompany them on a trip to San Francisco. They were en route to Santa Teresa to pick her up when the electronic fuel injection on the car went out. They called and left a message to let her know they'd be late.

From midnight until approximately 12:45, Isabelle, feeling anxious and excited about the trip, had a lengthy telephone conversation with a former college roommate who lived in Seattle. Some time after that, she heard a rap at the door and went downstairs, assuming the Seegers had arrived. She was fully dressed, smoking a cigarette, her suitcases already lined up in the foyer. She flipped on the porch

18

light and put her eye to the spyhole before opening the door. Instead of seeing visitors, she was staring down the bore of the .38 that killed her. The Seegers showed up at 2:20 and realized something was wrong. They alerted Isabelle's sister, who was living in a cottage on the property. She used her key to let them in through the rear. The alarm system was still armed at the perimeter. As soon as they spotted her, the Seegers called the police. By the time the medical examiner arrived at the scene, Isabelle's body temperature had dropped to 98.1. Using the Moritz formula and adjusting for the temperature in the foyer, her body weight, clothing, and the temperature and conductivity of the marble floor on which she lay, the medical examiner placed the time of death roughly between 1:00 A.M. and 2:00 A.M.

At noon the next day, David Barney was arrested and charged with first-degree murder, to which he entered a plea of not guilty. Even that early in the game, it was clear that the evidence against him was largely circumstantial. However, in the state of California, the two elements of a homicide—the death of the victim and the existence of "criminal agency"— may be proved circumstantially or inferentially. A finding of murder in the first degree can be sustained where no body is produced, where no direct evidence of death is produced, and where there is no confession. David Barney had signed a prenuptial agreement that limited his financial settlement if they divorced. At the same time, he was listed as the prime beneficiary on her life insurance policies, and as her widower he stood to inherit the community property portion of her business, which was estimated at two point six million bucks. David Barney had no real alibi for the time of her death. Dink Jordan felt he had more than enough evidence to convict.

As it happened, the trial lasted three weeks, and after six hours of closing arguments and two days of deliberations, the jury voted for acquittal. David Barney walked out of the courtroom not only a free man, but very rich. Interviewed later, some jurors admitted to a strong suspicion that he'd killed her, but they hadn't been persuaded beyond a reasonable doubt. What Lonnie Kingman was attempting, by filing the wrongful death suit, was to retry the case in civil court, where the burden of proof is based on a preponderance of evidence instead of the "reasonable doubt" formula of a criminal prosecution. As I understood matters, it would still be necessary for the plaintiff, Kenneth Voigt, to establish that David Barney killed Isabelle, and, further, that the killing was felonious and intentional. But the onus would be eased by the shift to proof by preponderance. What was at stake here was not Barney's freedom, but any profits he'd garnered from the crime itself. If he'd killed her for money, at least he'd be stripped of his gains.

I realized I was yawning for the third time in a row. My hands were filthy and I'd reached the point in my reading where my mind was wandering. Morley Shine's methodology had really been slipshod and I found myself irritated with the poor man in death. There's nothing quite as irksome as someone else's mess. I left the files where they were and locked my office door. I let myself out into the third-floor corridor and locked the door behind me.

Mine was the only car left in the parking lot. I pulled out of the driveway and turned right, heading toward town. When I reached State Street, I hung a left and headed home, cruising through the empty, well-lighted downtown area of Santa Teresa. Most of the buildings are only two stories high, the Spanish-style architecture of the ground-hugging variety due to frequent earthquakes. In the summer of 1968, for instance, there was a swarm of sixty-six tremors, ranging in severity from 1.5 to 5.2 on the Richter scale, the latter being strong enough to slop half the water out of a swimming pool.

I felt a surge of regret when I passed my old building at 903 State. By now, someone new had probably moved into the space. I ought to talk to Vera, the CF claims manager, to find out what had happened in the weeks since I'd been gone. I hadn't seen her since she and Neil got married on Halloween night. As a side effect of being fired, I was losing touch with a lot of people I knew—Darcy Pascoe, Mary Bellflower. The notion of Christmas in the new office setting seemed strange somehow.

I narrowly missed the light at the intersection of Anaconda and 101. I came to a stop and turned my engine off, waiting the four minutes for the light to turn green again. The highway was deserted, empty lanes of asphalt stretching out in both directions. The light finally changed and I zoomed across, turning right at Cabana, the boulevard paralleling the beach. I took another right onto Bay and a left onto my street, which was narrow and treelined, mostly single-family dwellings with an occasional condo. I found a parking spot two doors away from my apartment. I locked my car and scanned the darkened neighborhood by habit. I like to be out by myself at this hour, though I try to be vigilant and exercise appropriate caution. I let myself into the side yard, lifting the gate on its hinge to avoid the squeak.

My apartment was once a single-car garage attached to the main house by a breezeway, which had been converted to a sunroom. Both my apartment and the sunroom had been reconstructed after a bomb blast and I now had an additional loft sleeping space with a second bath built in. My outside light was on, compliments of my landlord, Henry Pitts, who never goes to bed without peering out his window to see if I'm safely home.

I locked the door behind me and went through my usual nighttime routine, securing all the doors and windows. I turned on my little black-and-white TV for company while I tidied my apartment. Since I'm usually gone during the day, I find myself doing personal chores at night. I've been known to vacuum at midnight and grocery shop at 2:00 A.M. Since I live alone, it isn't hard to keep the place picked up, but every three or four months I do a systematic cleaning, tackling one small section at a time on a rotating basis. That night, even taking time to scrub the kitchen, I was in bed by 1:00.

Tuesday, I woke at 6:00. I pulled on my sweats and tied the laces of my Nikes in a double spit knot. I brushed my teeth, splashed some water on my face, and ran wet fingers through my sleep-flattened hair. My run was perfunctory, more form than content, but at the end of it I was at least in touch with some energy. I used the time to tune into the day, a moving meditation meant to focus my mind as well as coordinate my limbs. I was dimly aware that I hadn't been taking very good care of myself of late . . . a combination of stress, irregular sleep, and too much junk food. Time to clean up my act.

I showered and dressed, ate a bowl of cereal with skim milk, and headed back to the office.

As I passed Ida Ruth's desk, I paused for a quick chat about her weekend, leisure she usually fills with backpacking, horse trails, and hair-raising rock climbs. She's thirty-five and unmarried, a robust vegetarian, with windswept blond hair and brows bleached by the sun. Her cheekbones are wide, her ruddy complexion unsoftened by makeup. While she's always dressed well, she looks like she'd prefer wearing flannel shirts, chinos, and hiking boots. "If you want to talk to Lonnie, you better scoot on in. He's got a court appearance coming up in ten minutes."

"Thanks. I'll do that."

I found him at his desk. He'd shed his coat and had his shirtsleeves rolled up. His tie was askew and his shaggy hair stood out around his head like wheat in need of threshing. Through the windows behind him, I could see clear blue skies with a scrim of mauve-and-gray mountains in the background. It was a gorgeous day. A thick tumble of vivid magenta bougainvillea camouflaged a white brick wall two buildings away.

"How's it going?" he asked.

"All right, I guess. I haven't finished going through the boxes yet, but it seems pretty disorganized."

"Yeah, well, filing was never Morley's strong suit."

"Girls just naturally do that so much better," I said dryly.

Lonnie smiled as he jotted a note to himself, presumably concerning the case he was working on. "We ought to talk fees. What's your hourly rate?"

"What was Morley charging?"

"The usual fifty," he said idly.

He had opened a drawer and was sorting through his files so he couldn't see my face. Morley was getting fifty? I couldn't believe it. Either men are outrageous or women are fools. Guess which, I thought. My standard fee has always been thirty bucks an hour plus mileage. I only missed half a beat. "Bump it up five bucks and I won't charge you mileage."

"Sure," he said.

"What about instructions?"

"That's up to you. Carte blanche."

"Are you serious?"

"Of course. You can do anything you want. As long as you keep your nose clean," he added in haste. "Barney's attorney would love nothing better than to catch us with our pants down, so no dirty tricks."

"That's no fun."

"But it allows you to testify without being thrown out of court and that's critical."

He glanced at his watch. "I gotta run." He grabbed his suit coat from a hanger and shrugged back into it. He straightened his tie and snapped his briefcase shut and was halfway out the door.

"Lonnie, wait a minute. Where do you want me to start?"

He smiled. "Find me a witness who can put the guy at the murder scene."

"Oh, right," I said to the empty room.

I sat down and read another five pounds of garbled information. Maybe I could sweet-talk Ida Ruth into helping me reconstruct the files. The first box seemed immaculate by comparison to the second. My first chore was going to be to stop by Morley Shine's house to see what files he had there. Before I left the office, I made a few preliminary calls. I had a pretty good sense of who I wanted to talk to and it was then a matter of setting up some appointments. I got through to Isabelle's sister, Simone, who agreed to talk to me around noon at her place. I also had a quick chat with a woman named Yolanda Weidmann, who was married to Isabelle's former boss. He was tied up in his home office and would be until three, so she suggested I stop by later in the afternoon. The third call I placed was to Isabelle's longtime best friend. Rhe Parsons wasn't in, but I left a message on her machine, giving her my name and telephone number, indicating that I'd try again.

Since the police station was only a block away, I decided to start with Lieutenant Dolan in Homicide. He was out with the flu, but Sergeant Cordero was there. I spotted Lieutenant Becker in the corner deep in conversation with someone I took to be a suspect, a white guy in his twenties, looking sullen and uncooperative. I knew Becker better than Cordero, but if I waited until he was free, he'd end up quizzing me about my relationship with Jonah Robb in Missing Persons. I hadn't seen Jonah in six or eight months and I didn't want to generate any contact at this point.

Sheri Cordero was an oddity in the department. Being a female and Hispanic, she man-

3

aged to fill two minority slots simultaneously. She was twenty-nine, short, buxom, smart, tough, somewhat abrasive in ways that I could never quite define. She never said anything offensive, but the guys in the department were not entirely at ease with her. I understood what she was up against. The Santa Teresa Police Department is better than most, but it's never easy being a woman and a cop. If Sheri erred on the side of being humorless, it was no surprise. She was in the middle of a phone conversation, which she converted to Spanish the minute I arrived. I sat down in the Leatherette-and-metal chair beside her desk. She held up a finger, indicating she'd be with me momentarily. She had a little artificial Christmas tree on her desk. It was decorated with candy canes and I helped myself to one. The nice thing about being in the presence of someone on the telephone is that you can study the person at your leisure without being thought rude. I unwrapped the candy cane and tossed the cellophane in the trash. She was clearly engaged in the subject at hand, gesturing vigorously to make her point. She had a good face, rather plain, and she wore little makeup. One of her two front teeth had a corner clipped off and it added a whimsical note to an otherwise stern expression. While I watched, she began to doodle on a legal pad—a cowboy stabbed in the chest with a cartoon knife.

She finished her conversation and turned her attention to me without any visible transition. "Yes?"

"I was looking for Lieutenant Dolan, but Emerald tells me he's out sick."

"He's got that bug that's been going around. Have you had that thing? I was out for a week. It's the pits."

"So far I've been spared," I said. "How long's he been out?"

"Just two days. He'll come dragging back in looking like death. Is there something I can help you with?"

"Probably. I've been hired by Lonnie Kingman in a wrongful death suit. The defendant is David Barney. I was curious about the scuttlebutt. Were you here back then?"

"I was still a dispatcher, but I've heard 'em talk. Man, they were pissed when he walked. He looked good for the shooting, but the jury wasn't buying. Talk about frustrated. Lieutenant Dolan was mad enough to bite through nails."

"From what I hear, David Barney's former cellmate claims he as good as confessed once the verdict came down."

"You're talking about Curtis McIntyre. Guy's in the county jail, and if you want him, you better make it quick. He gets out this week after doing ninety days on a battery," she said. "Did you hear about Morley Shine?"

"Lonnie mentioned that last night, but I didn't hear the details. How'd it happen?"

"What I heard he just keeled over dead. He'd been in bed with the same damn flu, but I guess he was feeling better. He was having dinner Sunday night? You know Morley. He hated to miss a meal. Got up from the table and dropped in his tracks."

"He had heart trouble?"

"For years, but he never took it serious. I mean, he was under doctor's care, but it never seemed to faze him. He was always joking about his ticker."

"That's too bad," I said. "I'm really sorry to see him go."

"Me, too. I can't believe how terrible I feel. Roll call somebody told me Morley Shine died? I busted out crying. I swear to God, I surprised myself. It's not like we were close. We used to talk over at the courthouse if I was waiting to testify on a case. He was always hanging around there, chain-smoking Camels, munching Fritos or something from the vending machine. It bums me out all those old guys are dropping dead. How come they didn't take better care of themselves?"

Her phone rang and she was quickly caught up in another matter. I gave her a quick wave and moved away from her desk. In essence, she'd told me what I'd wanted to know. The cops were convinced David Barney was guilty. That didn't make it true, but it was another precinct heard from.

I stopped off in Records and asked Emerald if I could borrow the phone. I called Ida Ruth and had a quick chat with her, asking her to set up an interview for me with Curtis McIntyre at the jail later in the morning. Visiting hours are ordinarily limited to Saturday afternoons, 1:00 to 3:00, but since I was working as Lonnie Kingman's representative, I could talk to him at my convenience. Oh, the joys of the legitimate endeavor. I'd spent so many years skulking through the bushes, I could hardly get used to it.

With that taken care of, I asked her for Morley Shine's home address. Morley had lived in Colgate, the township bordering Santa Teresa on the north. Colgate consists largely of "lite" industry and tract housing with assorted businesses lined up along the main street. Where the area was once farmland and citrus groves, the uninhabited countryside has now given way to service stations, bowling alleys, funeral homes, drive-in theaters, motels, fast-food restaurants, carpet outlets, and supermarkets, with no visible attention paid to aesthetics or architectural unity.

Morley and his wife, Dorothy, owned a modest three-bedroom home off South Peterson in one of the older housing developments between the highway and the mountains. My guess was the house had gone up in the fifties before the builders really got clever about differentiating exteriors. Here, the Swiss-chalet-style trim was painted either dirt brown or blue, the two-car garages designed so they stuck out in front, overpowering the entrances. Wooden shutters matched the wooden flower boxes planted with drooping pansies, which on closer inspection turned out to be entirely fake. The whole neighborhood seemed dispirited, from the patchy lawns to the cracked concrete driveways where every second house had a car up on blocks. Somehow the Christmas decorations only made things worse. Most of the houses were trimmed now in multicolored lights. One of Morley's neighbors seemed to be in competition with the house across the street. Both had covered every available stretch of yard with seasonal items, ranging from plastic Santas to plastic wise men.

This was now Tuesday morning. Morley had died on Sunday night, and while I was uneasy about intruding, it seemed important to retrieve what I could of the paperwork before some well-meaning relative went through and trashed everything he had. I knocked at the front door and waited. Morley had never cared much for detail and I noticed his house had the same slapdash quality. The blue paint on the porch rail, uneven to begin with, had begun to peel with age. I had the depressing sensation of having been here before. I could picture the shoddy interior: cracked tile on the kitchen counters, buckling vinyl tile on the floors, wall-to-wall carpeting trampled into traffic patterns that could never be cleaned of soil. The aluminum window frames would be warped, the bathroom fixtures corroded. A battered green four-door Mercury had been pulled off onto the side grass. I pegged it as Morley's, though I wasn't sure why. It was just the sort of clunker that he'd have found appealing. He had probably purchased it new in the year oughty-ought and would have driven it resolutely until the engine died. A new red Ford compact was parked in the driveway, the frame on the license plate advertising a local car rental company; probably someone from out of town. . . .

"Yes?" The woman was small, in her midsixties, looking energetic and competent. She wore a pink floral-print blouse with long sleeves, a tweed skirt, hose, and penny loafers. Her gray hair was honest and her makeup was light. She was in the process of drying her hands on a dish towel, her expression inquiring.

"Hi. My name is Kinsey Millhone. Are you Mrs. Shine?"

"I'm Dorothy's sister, Louise Mendelberg. Mr. Shine just passed away."

"That's what I heard and I'm sorry to disturb you. He was in the middle of some work for an attorney named Lonnie Kingman. I've been asked to take over his caseload. Did I come at a bad time?"

"There's never going to be a good time when someone's

just died," she replied tartly. This was a woman who didn't take death seriously. In its aftermath, she'd come along to do the dishes and tidy up the living room, but she probably wouldn't devote a lot of time to the hymn selection for the funeral service.

"I don't want to be more of a bother than I have to. I was sorry to hear about Morley. He was a nice man and I liked him."

She shook her head. "I've known Morley since he and Dorothy met in college back in the Depression. We all adored him, of course, but he was such a fool. The cigarettes and his weight and all the drinking he did. You can get away with a certain amount of that when you're young, but at his age? No, ma'am. We warned him and warned him, but would he listen? Of course not. You should have seen him on Sunday. His color was awful. The doctor thinks the heart attack was aggravated by the flu he had. His electrolyte balance or something of the sort." She shook her head again, breaking off.

"How's she doing?"

"Not that well, to tell you the truth, which is why I came down from Fresno in the first place. My intention was to help out for a couple of weeks just to give him some relief. You know she's been sick for months."

"I didn't know that," I said.

"Oh, my, yes. She's a mess. She was diagnosed with stomach cancer this last June. She had extensive surgery and she's been taking chemotherapy off and on ever since. She's just skin and bone and can't keep a thing down. It's all Morley talked about and here he up and went first."

"Will they do an autopsy?"

"I don't know what she's decided about that. He just saw the doctor a week ago. Dorothy wanted him on a diet and he finally agreed. An autopsy's not required under the circumstances, but you know how they are. Doctors like to get in there and poke and pry. I feel so sorry for her."

I made some sympathetic sounds.

She gestured briskly. "Anyway, enough said. I suppose you came to take a look at his study. Why don't you step on in here and let me show you where it is. You just take what you want, and if you need to come back, you can help yourself."

"Thanks. I can leave you a list of any files I take."

She waved off the suggestion. "No need to do that. We've known Mr. Kingman for years."

I moved into the foyer. She proceeded down a short hallway with me following. There was no sign of Christmas. With Mrs. Shine's illness and now Morley's death, there might have been a sense of relief that no such effort would be required this year. The house smelled of chicken soup. "Does Morley still have an office here in Colgate?" I asked.

"Yes, but with Dorothy so sick, he did most of his work here. I believe he still went in most mornings to pick up his mail. Did you want to look there as well?" She opened a door to what had clearly once been a bedroom, converted now to office space by the addition of a desk and file cabinets. The walls were painted beige and the beige shag carpeting was just as shabby as I'd imagined it.

"That's what I was thinking. If I can't find the files here, it probably just means he had them out at the office. Is there some way I could get a key?"

"I'm not sure where he kept them, but I'll check with Dorothy. My goodness," she said then as she looked around. "No wonder Morley didn't want anyone in here."

The room was faintly chilly, the disorder that of a man who operates his affairs according to no known system. If he'd realized he was going to drop dead, would he have straightened up his desk? Unlikely, I thought. "I'll Xerox what I need and bring the files back as soon as possible. Will someone be here in the morning?"

"What's tomorrow, Wednesday? As far as I know. And if not, just go around to the back and set them on the dryer in

31

the service porch. We usually leave that door open for the cleaning woman and the visiting nurse. I'm going to find you a key to Morley's office. Dorothy probably knows where it is."

"Thanks."

While I waited for the woman to return, I did one circuit of the room, trying to get a feel for Morley's methods of paper management. He must have tried to get himself under control at intervals because he'd made up files labeled "Action," "Pending," and "Current." There were two marked "To Do," one marked "Urgent," and an accordion folder he'd designated as his "Tickler" file. The paperwork in each seemed outdated, mismatched, as disorderly as the room itself.

Louise stepped back into the study from the hall with a ring of keys in hand. "You better take this whole batch," she said. "Lord only knows which is which."

"You won't need these?"

"I can't think why we would. You can drop them off tomorrow if you'd be so kind. Oh. And I brought you a grocery bag in case you need to load things up."

"Will there be a service?"

"The funeral's Friday morning at the Wynington-Blake here in Colgate. I don't know if Dorothy will be able to manage it or not. We held off on it because Morley's brother is flying in from South Korea. He's a project engineer with the Army Corps of Engineers at Camp Casey. He can't get to Santa Teresa until late Thursday. We scheduled the service on Friday for ten o'clock. I know Frank will be jet-lagged, but we just couldn't delay it any longer than that."

"I'd like to be there," I said.

"That would be lovely," she said. "I know he'd appreciate that. You can let yourself out when you're done. I have to give Dorothy her shot."

I repeated my thanks, but she was already moving on to the next chore. She smiled at me pleasantly and closed the door behind her.

I spent the next thirty minutes unearthing every file that seemed relevant to Isabelle's murder and the subsequent civil suit. Lonnie would have had a fit if he'd known how haphazardly Morley went about his work. In some ways, the measure of a good investigation is the attention to the paperwork. Without meticulous documentation, you can end up looking like a fool on the witness stand. The opposing attorney loves nothing better than discovering that an investigator hasn't kept proper records.

I packed item after item in the grocery bag—his calendar, his appointment book. I checked his desk drawers and his "in" and "out" boxes, making sure there wasn't a stray file stashed somewhere behind the furniture. When I was confident I'd lifted every pertinent folder, I put his key ring in my shoulder bag and closed the study door behind me. At the far end of the hall, I could hear the murmur of voices, Louise and Dorothy conversing.

As I returned to the front door, I passed the archway to the living room. I made an unauthorized detour to what had to be Morley's easy chair, upholstered in ancient cracked leather, the cushions conforming to his portly shape. There was an ashtray that had been emptied of cigarette butts. The end table still bore the sticky circles where his whiskey tumblers had sat. Snoop that I am, I checked the end-table drawer and felt down in the crevices of the chair. There was nothing to find, of course, but I felt better for it.

Next stop was Morley's office, located on a little side street in "downtown" Colgate. This whole residential section had been converted into small businesses: plumbers' shops, auto detailing services, doctors' offices, and real estate brokerages. The former single-family dwellings were identical frame bungalows. The living room in each now served as the front office for an insurance company or, in Morley's case, a beauty salon from which he rented a room with a bath at the rear. I went around to the outside entrance. Two steps led up to a small concrete porch with a small overhanging roof. The office door had a big pane of frosted glass in the upper half, so I couldn't see in. Morley's name was engraved on a narrow plaque to the right of the door, the kind of plate I could imagine his wife having made for him the day he went into business. I tried key after key, but none of them fit. I tried the door again. The place was locked up tighter than a jail. Without even thinking about it, I walked around to the rear and tried the window back there. Then I remembered I was playing by the rules. What a bummer, I thought. I'd been hired to do this. I was entitled to see the files, but not allowed to pick the lock. That didn't seem right somehow. What were all the years of breaking and entering for?

I went back around to the front and entered the beauty salon like a law-abiding citizen. The windows had been painted with mock snowdrifts, two of Santa's elves holding a painted banner reading MERRY X-MAS across the glass. There was a big decorated Christmas tree in the corner with a few wrapped boxes under it. There were four stations altogether, but only three were occupied. In one, a plastic-caped woman in her forties was having her hair permed. The beautician had divided the damp strands into sections, inserting small white plastic rollers as dainty as chicken bones. The permanent wave solution filled the air with the scent of spoiled eggs. In the second station, the woman in the chair had her head secured in a perforated bathing cap while the beautician pulled tiny strands through the rubber with what looked like a crochet hook. Tears were rolling down the woman's cheeks, but she and the beautician were chatting away as if this were an everyday occurrence. To my right, a manicurist worked on a client, who was having her fingernails painted a bubblegum pink.

On the back wall, I spotted a paneled door that was probably connected to Morley's office. There was a woman in the rear folding towels into tidy stacks. When she saw my hesitation, she moved up to the front. Her name tag said: Betty. Given her occupation, I was surprised she didn't have a bet-

34

ter cut. She'd apparently fallen into the hands of one of those cruel stylists (usually male) who delight in mismanaging the hair of women over fifty. The particular cut that had been inflicted on this woman consisted of a shaved backside and a frizzy pouf along the front that made her neck look wide and her facial expression fearful. She fanned the air, her nose wrinkling. "Pee-yew! If they're smart enough to get a man on the moon, why can't they make a perm lotion that don't stink?" She picked up a plastic cape from the nearest chair and assessed me with a practiced eye. "Boy oh boy. You sure do have a hair emergency. Take a seat."

I looked around to see who she was talking to. "Who, me?"

"Aren't you the one who just called?"

"No, I'm here on some business for Morley Shine, but his office is locked up."

"Oh. Well, I hate to be the one to tell you, honey, but Morley passed away this week."

"I'm aware of that. Sorry. I guess I should have introduced myself." I took out my identification and held it out to her.

She studied it for a moment and then frowned, pointing to my name. "How do you pronounce that?"

"Kinsey," I said.

"No, the last name. Does that rhyme with *baloney?*"

"No, it doesn't rhyme with *baloney.* It's *Mill*-hone."

"Oh. *Mill*-hone," she said, mimicking me dutifully. "I thought it was Mill-*hony*, like the lunch meat." She looked back at the photocopy of my private investigator's license. "Are you from Los Angeles, by any chance?"

"No, I'm a local."

She looked up at my hair. "I thought maybe that was one of those new mod cuts like they do down on Melrose. Asymmetrical, they call it, with a geometrical ellipse. Something like that. Usually looks like it's been whacked off with a ceiling fan." She laughed at herself, giving her chest a pat.

I leaned back to catch a glimpse of myself in the nearest mirror. It did look kind of weird. I'd been growing my hair for several months now and it was definitely longer on one side than it was on the other. It also seemed to have a few ragged places and a stick-up part near the crown. I experienced a moment of uncertainty. "You think I need a cut?"

She hooted out a laugh. "Well, I should hope to shout. It looks like some lunatic hacked your hair off with a pair of nail clippers!"

I didn't think the analogy was quite as funny as she did. "Maybe some other time," I said. I decided to get down to business before she talked me into a haircut I would later regret. "I'm working for an attorney by the name of Lonnie Kingman."

"Sure. I know Lonnie. His wife used to go to my church. What's he got to do with it?"

"Morley was doing some work for him and I'm taking over the case. I'd like to get into his office."

"Poor guy," she said. "With his wife sick and all that. He moped around here for months, doing nothing as far as I could tell."

"I think he did a lot of work from his home," I said. "Uh, can I get into his office through here? I saw the door back there. Does that connect to his suite?"

"Morley used to use it when he had a bill collector on his doorstep." She began to walk me toward the back, which I took as cooperation.

"Was that often?" I asked. It was hard for me to mind my own business when I had someone else's business within range of me.

"It was lately."

"Would you mind if I stepped in and picked up the files I need?"

"Well, I don't see why not. There's nothing in there worth stealing. Go ahead and help yourself. It's just a thumb-lock on this side."

"Thanks."

I let myself in through the connecting door. There was one room, the back bedroom in the days when the bungalow was used as a residence. The air smelled musty. The carpeting was a mud brown, a color probably chosen because it wouldn't show dirt. What showed up instead was all the lint and dust. There was a small walk-in closet that Morley used for storage, a small bathroom with a brown vinyl tile floor, a commode with a wooden seat, a small Pullman sink, and a fiberglass shower stall. For one depressing moment, I wondered if this was how I'd end up: a small-town detective in a dreary nine-by-twelve room that smelled of mold and dust mites. I sat down in his swivel chair, listening to the creak as I rocked back. I snagged his Month at a Glance. I checked his drawers one by one. Pencils, old gum wrappers, a stapler empty of staples. He'd been sneaking fatty foods on the sly. A flat white bakery box had been folded in half and shoved down in the wastebasket. A large grease stain had spread across the cardboard and the remains of some kind of pastry had been tossed in on top. He probably came into the office every morning to sneak doughnuts and sweet rolls.

I got up and crossed to the file cabinets on the far wall. Under "V" as in VOIGT/BARNEY, I found several manila file folders stuffed with miscellaneous papers. I removed the folders and began to stack them on the desk. Behind me the door banged open and I felt myself jump.

It was Betty, from the beauty shop. "You find everything you need?"

"Yes. This is fine. Turns out he kept most of his files at home."

She made a face, tuning in to the musty odor in the room. She went over to the desk and picked up the wastebasket. "Let me get this out of here. The trash isn't picked up until Friday, but I don't want to risk the ants. Morley used to order his pizzas here where his wife couldn't check on him. I know he was supposed to diet, but I'd see him in here with cartons of take-out Chinese, bags from McDonald's. I tell you, the man could eat. Of course, it wasn't my place to make a fuss, but I wished he'd taken a little bit better care of himself."

"You're the second person who's said that today. I guess you have to let people do what they're going to do." I picked up the files and the calendar. "Thanks for letting me in. I imagine someone will come over in a week or so and clean the place out."

"You're not looking for office space yourself?"

"Not this kind," I said without hesitation. It occurred to me later she might have taken offense, but the words just popped out. The last I saw of her, she was opening his front door so she could stick the wastebasket out on the porchlet.

I returned to my car, dumped the stack of files in the backseat, and backtracked into town, where I turned into the parking garage adjacent to the public library. I grabbed a clipboard from the backseat, locked my car, and headed for the library. Once inside, I went down to the periodicals room, where I asked the guy at the counter for the six-year-old editions of the *Santa Teresa Dispatch*. In particular, I wanted to look at the news for December 25, 26, and 27 of the year Isabelle Barney was murdered. I took the reel of tape to one of the microfilm readers and threaded it through the viewer, patiently cranking my way back through time until I reached the period that interested me. I made notes about the few significant events of that weekend. Christmas had fallen on a Sunday. Isabelle had died very early on Monday. Maybe it'd be helpful to jog people's memories with a few peripheral facts. A storm had dumped heavy rain over most of California, resulting in a major pileup on the northbound 101 just south of town. There'd been a minor crime wave that included the hit-and-run fatality of an elderly man, who'd been struck by a pickup out on upper State Street. There was also a market robbery, two household burglaries, and a suspected-arson fire, which destroyed a photographer's studio in the early-morning hours of December 26. I also jotted down a reference to an incident in which a two-and-a-half-year-old boy suffered minor injuries when he fired a .44-caliber revolver left in the car with him. As I read the news accounts, I could feel my own memory ignite briefly. I'd forgotten all about the fire, which I'd actually caught sight of as I drove home at the close of a stakeout. The harsh glow of the blaze had been like a torch against the lowering night sky. The rain had contributed a surreal misty counterpoint and I'd been startled when James Taylor's rendition of "Fire and Rain" suddenly came on my car radio. The fragment of memory terminated as abruptly as a light going out.

I combed the rest of the reel, but nothing much stood out. I went back to the beginning and made copies of everything except the print ads and the classifieds. I rewound the film and tucked the reel of tape back in the box. I paid for the copies at the main desk on my way out, thinking about the people whose whereabouts I'd have to question for those couple of days. How much would I remember if someone quizzed me about the night Isabelle was killed? One fragment had been restored, but the rest was a blank.

4

I retrieved my car from the public lot and drove out to the Santa Teresa County Sheriff's Department Detention and Corrections Facility. Morley's interview with Curtis McIntyre was one of the documents I'd found in the proper file, though the subpoena had never been served. He'd apparently spoken to Curtis mid-September and no one had talked to him since. According to Morley's notes, McIntyre had been in a holding cell with Barney his first night in the can. He claimed they'd established a friendship of sorts, more on his part than Barney's. He'd found himself intrigued because Barney was a man who seemed to have everything. Curtis, accustomed to doing jail time with losers, had followed the case in the papers. When the trial came up, he'd made a point of being in attendance. He and Barney hadn't talked much until the day he was acquitted. As David Barney left the courtroom, Curtis McIntyre had stepped forward to offer his congratulations. At that point, according to the informant, David Barney made the remark that implied he'd just gotten away with murder. I couldn't tell if Curtis had elaborated on that or not.

I parked out in front of the jail, across the lot from the Santa Teresa County Sheriff's Department with its fleet of black-and-whites. I moved up the walk and pushed through the front door into the small reception area, approaching the L-shaped counter with the glass partition along the top. I'd done an overnight at the jail nearly six weeks before and I was glad to be returning in a legitimate guise. It felt much better walking in the front door than it had going in the back in the company of an arresting officer.

I signed in at the desk and filled out a jail visitation pass. The woman at the counter took the information and disappeared from the window. I waited in the lobby, perusing the bulletin board while she called down for someone to bring Curtis up to the interview room. On the wall near the pay phone, all the better bail bondsmen were listed, along with the Santa Teresa taxicab companies. Getting yourself arrested is usually an unexpected piece of misery. Once your bail's been posted, if your car's been impounded, you find yourself stuck out in the boonies—an added element of distress after a night of humiliations.

The woman behind the counter caught my attention. "Your client's coming up in a minute. Booth two."

"Thanks."

I traversed the short hallway and passed through the door leading to the visitors' booths. There were only three in that section, set up so that inmates could confer in private with their attorneys, probation officers, or anyone else they had a legitimate reason to consult. I let myself into the second "room," which was maybe four feet wide, furnished with a glass window, a four-foot length of counter, and a footrail of the sort you'd find in a bar. I hied myself up to the counter and put my foot up, leaning on my elbows. Beyond the glass was a roomette that mirrored the one I was in, with a door in the back wall through which the inmates were brought. Within minutes, the door opened and Curtis McIntyre was ushered in. He seemed puzzled at the unscheduled visit, perplexed at the sight of me when he'd probably expected his attorney.

He was twenty-eight, lean and long-waisted with hips so narrow they hardly held his pants up. He looked good in jail blues. His shirt was short-sleeved, showing long, smooth arms, the perfect epidermal canvas for a dragon tattoo. My guess was that somebody'd once told Curtis he had soulful eyes because he seemed determined to make deep, meaningful eye contact with me. He was clean-shaven, with an innocent-looking face (for a convicted felon). His hair was ill cut, which was no big surprise as the man had been in jail for months. I didn't picture his having a regular salon cut and blow-dry in the best of circumstances.

I introduced myself, explaining my purpose, which was to get his written statement. "From Mr. Shine's notes, I gather you met David Barney in a holding cell the first night after his arrest."

"You single?"

I checked behind me. "Who, me?"

He smiled the kind of smile you'd have to practice in the mirror, eyes boring into mine. "You heard me."

"What's that got to do with it?"

His voice softened to the coaxing tone reserved for stray dogs and women. "Come on. Just tell me. I'm a nice guy."

I said, "I'm sure you're very nice, but it's none of your business."

This amused him. "How come you're afraid to answer? Are you attracted to me? Because I'm attracted to you."

"Well, you're very forthcoming and I appreciate that, Curtis. Uh, now, could you tell me about the time you spent with David Barney?"

He smiled faintly. "All business. I like that. You take yourself serious."

"That's right. And I hope you'll take me serious, too."

He cleared his throat, sobering, clearly trying to make a good impression. "Him and me were in a cell together. He was arrested on a Tuesday and we didn't go before the judge until Wednesday afternoon. Seemed like a nice guy. By the time his trial come up, I'se out, so I figured I'd sit in on it and see what all the fuss was about."

"Did the two of you talk about the murder at the time of his arrest?"

"Naw, not really. He was upset, which I could understand. Lady got shot in the eye, that's ugly. I don't know what kind of person'd do a thing like that," he said. "Turns out it was him, I guess."

"What did you talk about?"

"I don't know. Nothin' much. He was asking what all I was in for and stuff like that, what judge I thought we'd pull for the arraignment the next day. I give him a rundown on which ones are tough, which is most of 'em. Well, that one guy's a pussy, but the rest is mean."

"What else?"

"That's about it."

"And on the basis of that, you sat through the whole trial?"

"Not the whole trial. You ever sit through a whole trial? It's boring, idn't it? I'se glad I never went to law school."

"I'll bet." I checked through my notes. "I've read the deposition Mr. Kingman took—"

"You single?"

"You asked me that before."

"I bet you are. You know how I know?" He tapped himself on the temple. "I'm psychic."

"Well, then, you can probably tell me what I'm going to ask you next."

43

He flushed happily. "Not really. I don't know you that well, but I'd like to."

"Maybe you'll be able to intuit the answers to some questions I have."

"I'll try. Absolutely. Go ahead. I'm all ears." He lowered his head and his expression became serious.

"Tell me again what he said to you once the acquittal came down."

"Said . . . let's see now. He goes, something like . . . 'Hey, dude. How you doin'? How about that? Now you see what a high-priced attorney buys?' And I'm like, 'Way to go, man. That's great. I never thought you done her.' He just got this big shi—pardon me—this big grin. He kind of leaned over close and said, 'Ha ha ha, I guess the joke's on them.'"

This seemed like an improbable conversation to me. I'd never met David Barney, but I couldn't believe he'd talk like that. I watched Curtis's face. "And from that, you concluded what?"

"I concluded he done her. You have a boyfriend?"

"He's a cop."

"Bullshiiiit. I don't believe you. What's his name?"

"Lieutenant Dolan."

"What's he do?"

"Homicide. STPD."

"Don't you never date anybody else?"

"He's too jealous for that. He'd rip your head right off your neck if he found out you were hustling me. Did you talk to David Barney any other time?"

"Besides jail and court? I don't think so. Just them two occasions."

"It seems odd that he'd say that."

"How come? Let's discuss that." He put his chin on his fist, ready to engage me in protracted discourse.

"The man hardly knows you, Curtis. Why would he confide something so significant? And right there in court. . . ." I cupped a hand to my ear. "With the sound of the judge's gavel still ringing in the air."

Curtis frowned thoughtfully. "You'd have to ask him that, but if you're asking me, I'd say he knows I'm a jailbird. He might have felt more comfortable with me than all his high-tone friends. Anyhow, why not? Trial was over. What's anybody going to do? Even if they heard him there's no way they can touch him on account of double jeopardy."

"Where were you when this conversation was taking place?"

"Outside the door. It was Department Six. He come out and I clapped him on the shoulder, shook his hand—"

"What about reporters? Wasn't he being mobbed at that point?"

"Oh, God, yes. They was everyplace. Yelling his name, stickin' microphones in his face, asking how he felt."

I could feel the skepticism rise. "And in the middle of it he stopped and made that remark?"

"Well, yeah. He leaned over and spoke in my ear just like I said. You're a private detective? Is that really what you do?"

I shrugged to myself and began to print his account of events. "That's really what I do," I said.

"So like when I get out, if I have a problem, I can look you up in the phone book?"

I wasn't paying much attention to him since I was in the process of converting his version into a written statement. "I guess so." If you can read.

"How much do you charge for a service like that? What's that cost?"

"Depends on what you want."

"But about what?"

"Three hundred bucks an hour," I said, lying automatically. At fifty bucks an hour he might possibly afford me.

"Go onnn. I don't believe it."

"Plus expenses."

"Goddamn, I can't believe it. Are you shittin' me or what? Three hundred an *hour*. Every hour you work?"

"It's the truth."

"You sure make a lot of money. For a girl? Lord," he said.

"How about if you lend me some? Fifty dollars, or a hundred. Just till I'm out and then I can pay you back."

"I don't think men should borrow money from women."

"Who else you gonna borrow from? I mean, I don't know dudes with dough. Unless they're drug kings, something like that. Santa Teresa, we don't even get the kings. We get more like the jacks." He snorted out a laugh. "You have a gun?"

"Sure I do," I said.

He rose halfway off his seat and peered down through the glass like I might have a six-shooter strapped to one hip. "Hey, come on. Let me see."

"I don't have it with me."

"Where's it at?"

"My office. I keep it down there in case somebody should refuse to pay a bill. Could you read this and see if it accurately reflects your recollection of your conversation with Mr. Barney?" I passed it under the glass partition, along with a pen.

He barely glanced at it. "Close enough. Hey, you print pretty good."

"I was a whiz in grade school," I said. "Could I ask you to sign it?"

"How come?"

"So we'll have a record of your testimony. That way if you forget, we can refresh your memory in court."

He scribbled a signature and passed the statement back. "Ask me something else," he said. "I'll tell you anything."

"This is fine. Thanks a lot. If I have any other questions, I'll be in touch."

After I left Curtis, I sat out in the parking lot watching cop cars come and go. This was too good to be true. Here's Curtis McIntyre driving nails into David Barney's coffin and it just didn't sound right. David Barney refused to talk now, nearly five years after the fact, two years since his acquittal. From what Lonnie'd said, extracting the most benign information from the man had been like pulling teeth. Why would he

46

blab a makeshift confession to a dimwit like Curtis? Oh, well. It's hard to reconcile the inconsistencies in human nature. I started the car and pulled out of the parking lot.

According to the files, Isabelle Barney's sister, Simone Orr, was still living on the Barney property in Horton Ravine, one of two exclusive neighborhoods favored by the Santa Teresa well-to-do. Promotional materials from the Chamber of Commerce refer to Horton Ravine as a "sparkling jewel in a park-like setting," which should give you some idea how puffed up these pamphlets can get. To the north, the Santa Ynez Mountains dominate the sky. To the south lies the Pacific Ocean. The views are always described as "breathtaking," "stunning," or "spectacular."

In the real estate ads describing the area words like *serenity* and *tranquillity* abound. Every noun has an adjective attached to give it the proper tone and substance. The "lush, well-manicured" lots are large, maybe five acres on average, and zoned for horses. The "elegant, spacious" homes are set well away from the roads, which wind through hills "dotted" with bay, sycamore, live oak, and cypress. Lots of *dotted*s and *amid*s.

I found myself rhapsodizing in salespeak as I drove up the long, circular drive to the stately, secluded entrance to this classic Mediterranean home with its sweeping, panoramic views of serene mountains and sparkling ocean. I drove into the splendid flagstone courtyard and parked my used VW amid a Lincoln and a Beamer. I got out and entered a walled garden, passing along the handsome paved gallery. The entire four-acre parcel was dotted with seasonal perennials, lush ferns, and imported palms. Also, two gardeners trailing four hundred yards of hose between them.

I'd put a call through to Simone in advance of my arrival and she'd instructed me carefully how to reach her little cottage, which was situated on the lower terrace amid lush lawns and assorted outbuildings, like the poolhouse and the tool-shed. I rounded the eastern wing of the house, which I'd been told was designed by a well-known Santa Teresa architect whose name I'd never heard. I crossed the Spanish tiled entertainment terrace, complete with custom-built, black-bottom swimming pool, lava rock waterfall, spa, wading pool, and koi pond surrounded by short, perfectly trimmed hedges of lantana and yew. I descended a flight of stairs and followed a flagstone path to a wooden bungalow tucked up against the hillside.

The house was tiny, built of board and batten, with a steeply pitched shingle roof and wooden decking on three sides. The exterior was Shaker blue, the trim painted white. Wood frame windows formed the upper portion of the walls on all sides. The top half of the Dutch door stood open. December in Santa Teresa can be like spring in other parts of the country—gray days, a bit of rain, but with a lot of blue sky shining through.

I stopped in my tracks, completely smitten with the sight. I have a special weakness for small, enclosed spaces, a barely disguised longing to return to the womb. After the death of my parents, when I first went to live with my maiden aunt, I established a separate residence in an oversize cardboard box. I had just turned five and I can still remember the absolute absorption with which I furnished this small corrugated refuge. The floor was covered with bed pillows. I had a blanket and a lamp with a fat blue ceramic base and a sixty-watt bulb that heated the interior to a tropical pitch. I would lie on my back, reading endless picture books. My favorite was about a girl who discovered a tiny elf named Twig who lived in an overturned tomato-juice can. Fantasies within fantasies. I don't remember crying. For four months, I hummed and I read my library books, a little closed-circuit system designed to deal with grief. I ate cheese-and-pickle sandwiches like the ones my mother made. I fixed them myself because they had to be just right. Some days I substituted peanut butter for the cheese and that was good. My aunt went about her business, leaving me to work through my feelings without intrusion. My parents died Memorial Day. That fall, I started school. . . .

"Are you Kinsey?"

I turned to look at the woman as if waking from a sleep. "That's right. And you're Simone?"

"Yes. Nice to meet you." She carried a pair of gardening scissors and a shallow wicker basket piled with cut flowers, which she set down. Her smile was brief as she held out her hand for me to shake. I judged her to be in her late thirties or very early forties. She was slightly shorter than I with wide shoulders and a stocky build, which she managed to minimize by the clothes she wore. Her hair was a reddish-blond, a fine flyaway shade much darker at the roots, cut shoulder length and crinkled from a perm. Her face was square, her mouth wide. Her eyes were an unremarkable shade of blue with mascara-darkened lashes and fine reddish brows. The outfit she wore was a black-and-white geometric print, a washable silk jacket over a long black tunic top, her long loose skirt brushing the tops of black suede boots. Her fingers were blunt and there was clear polish on her nails. She wore no jewelry and very little makeup. Belatedly, I noticed that she used a cane. I watched while she transferred it from her left hand to her right. She adjusted her stance and shifted some of her weight to the cane as she leaned down and picked up the basket at her feet.

"I have to get these in water. Come on in." She opened the bottom portion of the Dutch door and I followed her in.

I said, "Sorry to have to trouble you again on this. I know you talked to Morley Shine several months ago. I suppose you heard about his death."

"I spotted his obituary in this morning's paper. I called Lonnie's office first thing and he said you'd be in touch." She moved over to the small tiled kitchen peninsula that served as both a work surface and a breakfast bar, with two wooden stools tucked under it. She hooked the cane over the edge of the counter and took out a clear glass pitcher, which she filled with tap water. She bunched the flowers nicely and stuck them in the makeshift vase, then set the arrangement on the windowsill and dried her hands on a towel.

"Have a seat," she said. She pulled out one stool and perched on it while I took the other.

"I'll try not to take too much of your time," I said.

"Listen, if it helps convict the shitheel, you can take all the time you want."

"Isn't it a bit awkward, your living on the property just a hundred yards away from him?"

"I hope so," she said. The depth of bitterness in her voice seemed to affect its very pitch. She looked up in the direction of the big house. "If it's awkward for me, think how it must feel to him. I know it galls him that I refuse to be driven off. He'd love nothing better than to force me out."

"Can he do that?"

"Not as long as I have anything to say about it. Izzy left me the cottage. It was part of her will. She and Kenneth bought the property many years ago. They paid a small fortune for it. When that marriage folded, she got it as part of the financial settlement. She had it listed as her sole and separate property when she and David got married. She also made him sign prenups."

"Sounds very businesslike. Did she do that with the others?"

"She didn't have to. The first two had money. Kenneth was number two. With David, it was different. Everybody told her he was after her money. I guess she thought the prenups would prove he wasn't. What a joke."

"So he'll never get title to this place?"

Simone shook her head. "She rewrote her will, leaving him a life interest. When he dies—which I hope is real soon, I might add—it goes to her daughter, Shelby. The little house is mine—as long as I'm alive, of course. When I die, it reverts."

"And you're not afraid?"

"Of David? Absolutely not. He got away with murder once, but the man's not a fool. All he has to do is sit tight. If he wins this civil suit, it's all his, isn't it?"

"It looks like it."

"He could come out of the whole deal smelling like a rose. So why in the world would he jeopardize that? Something happened to me, he's the first place they'd look."

"What if he loses?"

"My guess is he'd head straight for Switzerland. He's probably salting away money in a secret bank account. He's too clever to kill again. What would be the point?"

"But why did Isabelle set it up like that? Why tempt the Fates? As I understand it, between the prenuptial agreement and the terms of the will, she might as well have gone ahead and stuck her head in the noose."

"She was in love with the guy. She wanted to do right by him. She was also a realist. He was husband number three and she didn't want to get ripped off. Look at it from her perspective. You marry some guy, you don't think he's going to *kill* you. If you really thought that, you wouldn't marry him in the first place." Her eyes strayed to her watch. "Jesus, it's nearly one. I don't know about you, but I'm starving. Have you had lunch?"

"You go ahead," I said. "I shouldn't be too much longer. I'll grab a bite on the way back to the office."

"It's no problem. Please join me. I'm just making sandwiches. I'd like the company."

The invitation seemed genuine and I smiled in response. "All right. That'd be nice."

5

She moved into the tiny kitchen area and began to take items from the tiny fridge.

"Can I do anything to help?"

"No, thanks. There isn't really room enough for two of us to work. Guys love it, unless it turns out they have a passion for cooking. Then they take over here and I sit out there where you are."

I half turned on the stool, checking out the room behind me. "Great house," I remarked.

She flushed with pleasure. "You like it? Isabelle designed it . . . the start of her career."

"She was an architect? I didn't know that."

"Well, she wasn't really, but she passed for one in some respects. Look around if you like. It's only three hundred square feet."

"Is that all? It seems bigger." I stepped out onto the front porch, curious to see how the general layout related to the interior. Since the windows were cranked open, I could talk to her easily as I rounded the structure. The cottage felt as if it had been miniaturized, scaled down from human-size dimensions to a little playhouse for grown-ups. Every comfort seemed attended to, without flourish or wasted space. There was even a small chimney. I stuck my head in the window so I could peer at the compact fireplace. Many interior surfaces, including the hearth, sills, and countertops, were covered with hand-painted blue-and-white tiles in a flower motif. "This is wonderful."

Simone flashed me a smile.

I withdrew from the window and circled the perimeter. Herbs had been planted in every sunny spot. I could smell rosemary and thyme when the breeze whiffled through. The house was situated on an apron of grass that spread out in a half-moon. Below, the hillside fell away steeply into a tangle of live oak and chaparral. The view was to the mountains across the town of Santa Teresa. I reentered the only door, which opened into the kitchen. "You'll have to see my place sometime. It has a similar feel to it. A perfect little hideaway."

I continued my survey while she cut several slices from a loaf of wheat bread. The place was so small I could tour without moving far. The furnishings were antique: a crude pine table, two cane-bottom chairs, a corner cabinet with wavy, blue-tinted glass panes, a brass bed with a patchwork quilt, white on white. The bathroom was small, the only portion of the house that was fully enclosed. The rest was essentially one large room, with areas defined according to function. Everything was open, airy, tidy, full of light. Every detail was perfect, like a series of illustrations for a glossy household magazine. There were views from the front and side windows, but none from the back, where the slope rose again sharply to the main house above.

I pulled a stool up to the counter and watched her make sandwiches. She'd assembled plates, cutlery, and blue-and-white cloth napkins, which she passed to me. I set two places at the table. "If she wasn't an architect, how'd she do this?"

"She was like an unpaid apprentice to a local architect. Don't ask me how she managed it or why he agreed. She sort of went in when it suited her and did what she pleased."

"Not a bad deal," I said.

"That's where she met David. He came to work for the same firm. Her boss's name was Peter Weidmann. Have you talked to him yet?"

"No, but I intend to, as soon as I leave here."

"Oh, good. He and Yolanda live close by. About a mile from here. He's a nice man, retired now. He really taught Isabelle a lot. She was an artist by nature, but she didn't have the discipline. She could do anything she wanted, but she was always such a dilettante—full of great ideas, but lousy at development. She lost interest in most things—until she started doing this."

"This, meaning what?"

"She designed tiny houses. Mine was the first. Somehow *Santa Teresa Magazine* heard about it and did a big photo spread. The response was incredible. Everybody wanted one."

"For guests?"

"Or for teens, in-laws, art studios, meditation retreats. The beauty is you can tuck one into any corner of your property . . . once you get past the zoning sharks. She and David pulled out of Peter's firm when this whole thing took off. The two of them went into business and made a fortune overnight. She was written up everywhere, from the snooty publications to the mundane. *Architectural Digest, House & Garden, Parade.* Plus, she won all these design awards. It was astonishing."

"What about David? How did he fit in?"

"Oh, she had to have him. She was such an airhead about

business. She originated the designs, did preliminary sketches, and roughed out the floor plans. David had a degree and he was AIA, so he was responsible for drafting, all the blueprints and specs, things of that sort. He also did the marketing, advertising . . . the grunt work, in effect. Hasn't anybody told you this?"

"Not a bit," I said. "I met Ken Voigt last night and he talked about Isabelle briefly. As I said on the phone, I've read all the files, but this is the first time I've heard the particulars. How did Barney feel about her getting all the glory?"

"He probably resented it, but what could he do? His career had gone nowhere. The same was true of Peter Weidmann."

Simone moved to the table with a pitcher of iced tea and a plate of sandwiches. We sat down to eat. The coarse-textured bread was thinly sliced and lightly buttered. Leaves hung out of the sandwich like the trimmings from a garden.

"Watercress," she said when she caught my expression.

"My favorite," I murmured, but it turned out to be good—very peppery and fresh. "You have a picture of her?"

"Oh sure. Hang on and I'll get it."

"No hurry. This is fine," I said with my mouth full, but she was up and moving over to the bed table, returning seconds later with a photograph in an ornate silver frame.

She passed me the picture and sat down again. "She and I were twins. Fraternal, not identical. She was twenty-nine when that was taken."

I studied the picture. It was the first glimpse I'd had of Isabelle Barney. She was prettier than Simone. She had a softly rounded face with glossy dark hair that fell gracefully to her shoulders, silky strands forming a frame for her wide cheekbones. Her eyes were a clear brown. She had a strong short nose, a wide mouth, muted makeup, if any. She seemed to be wearing some kind of scoop-necked T-shirt, dark brown like her hair. I found myself nodding. "I can see the resemblance. What's your family background?"

I passed the picture back and she propped it up at one end of the table. Isabelle watched us gravely as the conversation continued. "Both our parents were artists and a bit eccentric. Mother had family money so she and Daddy never really did much. They went to Europe one summer on a six-week tour and ended up staying ten years."

"Doing what?"

She took a bite of sandwich, chewing some before she answered. "Just bumming around. I don't know. They traveled and painted and lived like Bohemians. I guess they hung out on the fringes of polite society. Expatriates, like Hemingway. They came back to the States when World War Two broke out and somehow ended up in Santa Teresa. I think they read about it in a book and thought it sounded neat. Meanwhile, money was getting tight and Daddy decided he'd better pay more attention to their investments. He turned out to be a whiz. By the time we were born, they were rolling in it again."

"Who was the oldest, you or Isabelle?"

She took a sip of her iced tea and dabbed her mouth with a napkin. "I was, by thirty minutes. Mother was forty-four when she had us and nobody had a clue she was carrying twins. She'd never been pregnant so she assumed she was in menopause when she first stopped having periods. She was a Christian Scientist and refused to see a doctor until the last possible minute. She'd been in labor fifteen hours when she finally agreed to have Daddy take her to the nearest hospital. They barely got her upstairs when I arrived. She was all set to hop off the table and go home again. She figured that was the end of it and the doctor did, too. He was expecting the placenta when Isabelle slid out."

"Your parents still living?"

She shook her head. "Both died within a month of each other. We were nineteen at the time. Isabelle got married for the first time that year."

"Are you married?"

"Not me. I feel like I've been married, watching her go through hers."

"Voigt was the second?"

"Right. Number one was killed in a boating accident."

"What was it like being twins? Were the two of you alike?"

"Unh-unh. No way. God, we couldn't have been more different. She inherited the family talent and all the vices that went with it. Artwise, she excelled, but it all came so easily she didn't take it seriously. The minute she mastered a skill, she lost interest. Drawing, painting. She did a little bit of everything. She made jewelry, she sculpted. She got into textiles and did incredible work, but then she got restless. She wasn't satisfied. She always wanted to do something else. In a way, the tiny houses saved her, though she might have gotten bored if she'd lived long enough."

"I gather, from what Ken says, she had a problem with low self-esteem."

"Among other things. She had all the inclinations of an addict. She smoked. She drank. She took pills any chance she got. She toked two or three joints a day. For a while, she dropped acid."

"How'd she get any work done? I'd be a basket case."

"It didn't affect her in the least. Besides, she could afford all that stuff, which is too bad in a way. She never really had to work because we inherited money. Fortunately, she never got into cocaine or she'd have gone through every cent."

"Wasn't that hard on you, her being out of control?"

"It was hard on all of us. I was always the heavy—parental, responsible. Especially since we were so young when our parents died. Isabelle got married, but I still felt like her mother. I admired her tremendously, but she was difficult. She couldn't sustain a relationship. She had nothing to give on a day-to-day basis. She was very self-involved. It was 'me, me, me.'"

"Narcissistic," I supplied.

"Yes, but I don't want to give the wrong impression. She

had some wonderful qualities. She was warm and witty and she was terribly bright. She was fun. She had a good time. She really knew how to play. She taught me a lot about how to lighten up."

"Tell me about David Barney."

"David. That's a tough one," she said and then paused to consider. "I'll try to be fair. I'd say he's handsome. Charming. Trivial. He and his wife moved up here from Los Angeles when he joined Peter's firm."

"He was married?"

"Not for long."

"What happened to his ex?"

"Laura? She's still around someplace. After David dumped her, she was forced to go to work, like every other ex-wife in town. God, women are getting screwed in divorces these days. For every guy who claims he's been 'taken' by some babe, I can show you six, eight, ten women who've been 'had' financially. Anyway, I'm sure she's in the book."

"Go on."

"Yes, well, David was a snob. He didn't want to work for a living any more than Isabelle did, except she was loving every minute of the work, not surprisingly. I mean, she had this sudden celebrity status and she ate it up. He was pushing her to sell the business while it was hot, before it peaked. He had some cockamamie scheme about prefabs and franchises. I'm not really sure what his idea was, but she hated it. By then, she was disenchanted with the marriage anyway, feeling bullied and suffocated. She wanted out from under."

"If they'd divorced, the business would have been considered community property, wouldn't it?"

"Sure. It would have been divided in half and he'd have lost really big. What'd she need him for? She could find half a dozen guys to fill his slot, but that wasn't true for him. Without her, he had zip. On the other hand, if she *died*, the business came to him intact . . . more or less. Her portion would go to Shelby, but he didn't have to worry about a four-year-old. At that point, Isabelle had already come up with so many preliminary sketches he could afford to coast and survive on the proceeds. Plus, with her dead, he must have counted on collecting the insurance. Again, some would go to Shelby, but he's still going to rake in a bunch."

"*If* he wins," I said. "Where's the house he leased when they separated?"

She flapped her hand toward the ocean. "As you leave the drive you turn left and it's down half a mile. A big white monstrosity, one of those contemporary houses made out of glass and concrete. It's so ugly, you can't miss it."

"Within easy walking distance?"

"He could have crawled it's so close."

"Were you here at the cottage the night she was killed?"

"Well, yes, but I didn't hear the shot. She'd phoned down here earlier to tell me the Seegers would be arriving late. They'd called about the car trouble and she didn't want me to worry if I saw lights on in the house. We chatted for a while and she sounded great. She'd been such a mess."

"Because of his harassment?"

"And the quarrels and the threats. Her life was a nightmare, but she was excited about San Francisco, looking forward to a little shopping, the theater, and the restaurants."

"What time did you talk to her?"

"About nine, I guess. It wasn't late. Isabelle was a night owl, but she knew I was usually in bed by ten. The first time I realized there was something wrong was when Don Seeger came down. He said they were worried because they couldn't get Isabelle to answer the door. They could see the fisheye was missing from the door and the hole looked burned. I grabbed a robe, got my key, and went up to the main house with him. We went in through the back door and found her in the foyer. I felt like a zombie. I was absolutely numb. So cold. It was awful, the worst night of my life." I could see tears for the first time and her face was suffused with pain.

She fumbled in her pocket for a Kleenex and blew her nose. "Sorry," she murmured.

I studied her for a moment. "And you really think he killed her?"

"There's not a doubt in my mind. I just don't know how you're going to prove it."

"Me neither," I replied.

It was 2:34 when I left Simone and returned to my car. A heavy marine layer had begun to settle in, obscuring the view. The afternoon light already had the gray feel of twilight and the air was chilly. There was something distinctly unpleasant about having to pass the main house. I glanced quickly at the windows that looked out over the courtyard. There were lights burning in the living room, though the rooms upstairs were dark. No one seemed to be aware of my passing. The BMW was still parked where it had been when I arrived. The Lincoln was gone. I unlocked my car and slid under the steering wheel. I tucked the key in the ignition and paused to scan the house again.

On this side, a loggia ran along the second story, the red tile roof supported by a series of white columns. A vine had grown up the pillars and trailed now along the overhang, lacy green with a white blossom, probably fragrant if you got close enough. The front door was bisected by a shadow from the balcony overhead, the view further eclipsed by the branches of the live oaks that crowded the walled garden. Because the driveway was long and curved up at such an angle, the house wasn't visible from the road below. A passerby might have caught sight of someone, approaching or departing, but at 1:30 in the morning, who'd be up and about? Teenagers, perhaps, getting home from a date. I wondered if there'd been a concert or a play that night, some charitable event that might have kept the area residents out after midnight. I'd have to check back through the papers and find out what was going on, if anything. Isabelle had been killed in the early morning hours on the day after

Christmas, which didn't sound promising. The fact that no one had ever stepped forward with information made the possibility of a witness seem even more remote.

I started the car and shifted into reverse, backing around to my left so I could head down the driveway. David Barney had claimed he was out for a night jog when Isabelle was shot. Night jogging, right, in a neighborhood dark as pitch. Much of Horton Ravine had a rural feel to it—wooded stretches without streetlights and no sidewalks at all. While no one could corroborate his story, there was no one to contradict it either. It didn't help matters that the cops had never come up with a single piece of evidence tying Barney to the scene. No witnesses, no weapon, no finger-prints. How was Lonnie going to nail the sucker if he had no ammunition?

I eased the VW down the driveway and hung a left at the bottom. I kept one eye on the odometer and the other on the road, cruising past several houses until I spotted the one that I was looking for—the place David Barney leased when he left Isabelle's. The house in question was the architectural equivalent of a circus tent: white poured concrete, with a roof line broken into wedges that fanned out from a center pole. Each triangular section was supported by three gaily painted metal pipes. Most of the windows were irregularly shaped, angled to catch some aspect of the ocean view. My guess was that inside the floors would be aggregate concrete, with the plumbing and furnace ducts plainly visible and raw. Add some corrugated plastic panels and an atrium done up in wall-to-wall Astroturf and you'd have the kind of house *Metropolitan Home* might refer to as "assured," "unsparing," or "brilliantly iconoclastic." "Unremittingly tacky" would also cover it. Pay enough for anything and it passes for taste.

I parked my car on the berm and hiked back along the road. I reached Isabelle's driveway in exactly seven minutes. Walking up the drive might take another five at best. If you made the trip at night and didn't want to be seen, you'd have to step off into the bushes if a car went past. At that hour, you weren't likely to find anyone else out on foot. Returning to my car, I timed myself again. Eight minutes this round, but I wasn't really pushing it. I made a note of the numbers on the mailboxes by the road. The neighbors might know something that would be of help. I'd have to do a door-to-door canvass to satisfy myself on that point.

I'd scheduled my appointment with the Weidmanns for 3:30, which gave me twenty minutes to spare. In most investigations I'm hired for, the object of the exercise is to flush out culprits: burglars, deadbeats, embezzlers, con artists, perpetrators of insurance fraud. Occasionally, I take on a missing-persons search, but the process is much the same—like picking at a piece of knitting until you find a loose thread. Pull at the right point and the whole garment comes unraveled. This one was different. Here, the quarry was known. The question wasn't who, but how to bring him down. Morley Shine had already done a thorough (though poorly organized) investigation and he'd come up with zilch. Now it was my turn, but what was left? I made some doodles on the page, hoping something would occur to me. Most of my doodles looked like great big goose eggs.

6

It's been my observation that the rich like to subdivide into the haves and the have-mores. What's the point in achieving status if you can't still be compared favorably with someone else in your peer group? Just because the wealthy band together doesn't mean they've relinquished their desire to be judged superior. The circle is simply more select and the criteria more exotic. The assessment of personal real estate is a case in point. Mansions, while easily distinguished from middle-income tract houses, can be further classified according to a few easily remembered yardsticks. The size and location of the property should be given first consideration. Additionally, the longer the driveway, the more points will be accorded. The presence of a private security guard or a pack of attack-trained dogs would naturally be counted more discerning than mere electronic equipment, unless of an extremely sophisticated sort. Beyond that, one must factor in such matters as guesthouses, spiked gates, reflecting pools, topiary, and excessive outdoor lighting. Obviously the fine points will vary from community to community, but none of these categories should be overlooked in assessing individual worth.

The Weidmanns lived on Lower Road, one of Horton Ravine's less prestigious addresses. Despite the pricey tone of the neighborhood, half the homes were nondescript. Theirs was unremarkable, a one-story pale green stucco, adorned with wrought-iron porch supports and topped with a flat rock-composite roof. The lot was large and nicely landscaped, but the house was too close to the road to count for much. Given the fact that Peter Weidmann was an architect, I'd expected a lavish layout, an entertainment pavilion or an indoor pool, embellishments that would reflect the full range of his design talents. Or maybe this one did that.

I parked on a concrete apron to one side of the house. Once on the porch, I rang the bell, and waited. I half expected a maid, but Mrs. Weidmann came to the front door herself. She must have been in her seventies, smartly turned out in a two-piece black velour sweatsuit and a pair of Rockport walking shoes.

"Mrs. Weidmann? I'm Kinsey Millhone," I said, holding out my hand politely.

She seemed disconcerted by the move and there was one of those embarrassing delays until we actually shook hands. There was something in the hesitation—distaste or prudery —that caused me to bristle inwardly. Her hair was a stiff cap of platinum blond, parted down the middle, the strands separating into two tense curls, like rams' horns in the center. She had bags under her eyes and her upper lids had begun to droop, reducing the visible portion of her irises to mere hints of blue. Her skin was a peachy color, her cheeks tinted a hot pink. She looked like she'd just flunked a stress test, but a closer examination showed she was simply wearing foundation and blusher in a shade far too vivid for her coloring.

She stared at me, as if waiting for a little door-to-door salesmanship. "What was this regarding? I'm afraid it's slipped my mind."

"I work for Lonnie Kingman, Kenneth Voigt's attorney in his suit against David Barney—"

"Oh! Yes, yes, yes. Of course. You wanted to speak to Peter about the murder. Terrible. I believe you said the other fellow died. What was his name, that investigator. . . ." She tapped her fingers on her forehead as if to stimulate thought.

"Morley Shine," I said.

"That's the one." She lowered her voice. "I thought he was dreadful. I didn't like him."

"Really," I said, feeling instantly defensive. I'd always thought Morley was a good investigator and a nice man besides.

She wrinkled her nose and the corners of her mouth turned up. "He smelled so peculiar. I'm sure the man drank." Her expression was one of perpetual pained smiles superimposed on profound disapproval. Age plays cruel tricks on the human face; all our repressed feelings become visible on the surface, where they harden like a mask. "He was here several times, asking all these silly questions. I hope you don't intend to do that."

"I will have to ask some, but I hope not to be a bother. May I come in?"

"Of course. Please excuse my bad manners. Peter's in the garden. We can chat out there. I was going out for my walk when you knocked, but I can do that in a bit. Do you exercise?"

"I jog."

"Jogging's very bad. All that pounding is much too hard

on the knees," she said. "Walking's the thing. My doctor is Julian Clifford . . . do you know him?"

I shook my head.

"He's a top orthopedic surgeon. He's also a neighbor and a very dear friend. I can't tell you how often he's warned me about the harm people do in their determination to jog. It's absurd."

"Really," I said faintly.

She went on in this vein, her tone argumentative though I offered no resistance. I had no intention of altering my regimen for a woman who thought Morley smelled bad. Her shoes made no sound as we crossed the marble-tiled foyer and moved down a hallway to the rear of the house. While the exterior was strictly fifties ranch style, the interior was furnished in an Oriental motif: Persian carpets, matching silk-paneled screens, ornate mirrors, a black lacquer chest inlaid with mother-of-pearl. She had two matching cloisonné vases the size of umbrella stands. Many items seemed to come in pairs, one placed on either side of something grotesque.

I followed her through the kitchen and out the back door, where a concrete patio ran across the rear of the house. Four low steps led down to a brick walk that extended into a small formal garden. Toward the rear of the property, I could see a woody area peppered with toadstools, some growing singly, some in fairy rings. The air smelled damply of dead leaves and mosses. A few forlorn birds were still perched in the treetops, their singing disconsolate as winter crept closer.

The patio furniture was wrought iron and canvas, the seat cushions fading from exposure to the weather. Peter Weidmann was napping, a thick hardback book lying open in his lap. I'd glanced at a copy in a bookstore recently: Part One of some celebrity's boring autobiography "as told to" some writer who'd been hired to render it intelligent. It looked as if he'd read all the way to page five. A sprinkling of cigarette butts surrounded his chair. He was probably not allowed to smoke in the house.

He looked like a man who'd lived all his life in a business suit. Now retired, he wore dark, stiff jeans and a new plaid flannel shirt, packing creases still showing, two buttons open to expose a portion of his white undershirt. Why does a man like that look so vulnerable in leisure clothes? He was narrow through the face, with black unruly eyebrows and short-cropped white hair. He and Yolanda had reached that stage in their fifty-year marriage where she looked more like his mother than his wife.

"This is called active retirement," she said with a laugh. "I wish I could retire, but of course, I never had a job." Her tone of voice was jocular, though her comment was bitter. The pretended humor barely served to mask the bite underneath. She nudged his shoulder, relishing the excuse to disturb his peace and quiet. "Someone to see you, Peter."

"I can come back a little later. There's no need to wake him."

"He won't mind a bit. It's not as if he's done any hard work today." She leaned close and said, "Peter."

He roused himself with a start, disoriented by the depths of his sleep and the sudden voice in his ear.

"We have company. It's about Isabelle and David. This young woman is Mr. Kingman's secretary." She turned to me with a sudden worry. "I hope that's right. You're not an attorney yourself, are you?"

"I'm a private investigator."

"I didn't think you looked like an attorney. Your name again is what—?"

Mr. Weidmann set his book aside and rose to his feet. He extended his hand. "Peter Weidmann."

We shook hands. "I'm Kinsey Millhone. Sorry to disturb you."

"That's quite all right. Would you like some coffee or a cup of tea?"

"Thanks, but I'm fine."

Yolanda said to him, "Well, it's much too chilly to be out on the porch." And then to me, "He's had the flu twice this winter and I'm not about to go through that again. I was exhausted from all the fetching and carrying. Men are such babies when it comes to being sick." The complaint was accompanied by a wink to me. She'd claim she was teasing if Peter took offense.

"I'm afraid I don't make a very good patient," he said.

"It's not something you'd want to be good at," I replied.

He made a gesture toward the house. "We can talk in the den."

We formed a little three-person procession into the house, which seemed nearly stuffy after the damp air outside. The den was small and the furniture had the same shabby feel as the porch chairs. I suspected the house was divided into "his" and "hers." "Her" portion was well appointed—expensive, overdecorated, filled with objects probably collected from various trips to foreign ports. She'd co-opted the living room, the formal dining room, the kitchen, the breakfast room, and most probably all the bathrooms, the guest bedroom, and the master suite. He'd been accorded the back porch and the den, where he'd carefully hoarded all the household items she was threatening to throw out.

As soon as we entered the paneled den, she began to wave her hands in the air, making a face about the smell of cigarette smoke. "For heaven's sake, Peter, this is dreadful. I don't see how you can stand it." She moved over and cranked a window open, fanning the air with a magazine she'd picked up.

I'm not all that fond of cigarette smoke myself, but with her making such a scene, I found myself coming to his defense. "Don't worry about it. It doesn't bother me," I said.

She picked up a filled ashtray and made a face. "Well, it might not bother you, but it's disgusting," she said. "Just let me fetch the Airwick." She moved out of the room taking the offending ashtray with her. The tension level dropped a notch. I turned my attention to the wall above the fireplace, which was hung with framed "celebrity" photographs. I moved closer to have a look. "These are you?"

"In the main," he said.

There were pictures of Peter Weidmann with the mayor at a groundbreaking ceremony, Isabelle Barney in the background; Peter at a banquet receiving some kind of placard; Peter at a construction site, posed with the contractor. The latter photo had apparently been run in the local newspaper because someone had clipped it, framed it, and hung it beside the original. The caption identified the occasion as the dedication of a new recreational facility. From the various cars visible in the background, I judged the majority of the pictures had been taken in the early seventies. Along with the commercial projects, there were photographs of residential sites. Two photographs featured minor-level "movie stars" whose homes he'd apparently designed and built. I took a moment to view the whole gallery, as interested in seeing Isabelle as I was in seeing him. I like to watch people at work. Our occupations bring out aspects of our personalities no one would ever dream of if they met us in "civilian" settings.

In his hard hat and coveralls, Peter looked young, very sure of himself. It wasn't simply that the pictures had been taken years ago when he was, in fact, younger. This must have been the apex of his career, with everything going right. He had had big projects in the works. He must have had recognition, influence, money, friends. He looked happy. I glanced over at the man beside me, so lusterless by comparison.

I caught him watching my reaction. "This is great," I said.

He smiled. "I've been very fortunate." He pointed to one of the photos. "Sam Eaton, the state senator," he said. "I did a house for him and his wife, Mary Lee. This is Harris Angel, the Hollywood film producer. You've probably heard of him."

I said, "The name sounds familiar," though it didn't at all.

Yolanda returned with the Airwick. "Maria put this in the refrigerator of all places," she said. She set the bottle on the table and exposed the wick. The scent that wafted out, a cross between Raid and shoe polish, made me long for the smell of cigarette smoke instead.

I took in the rest of the room at a glance. There was a stack of newspapers on the floor beside Peter's leather wing chair, a smaller pile of papers on the ottoman, magazines on the end table, and evidence of lunch dishes. There was a library table arranged under the windows that overlooked the backyard. On it was an old portable typewriter, a stack of books, and a second ashtray filled with cigarette butts. An old dining-room chair was pulled up to the table, with a second chair nearby piled high with paperbacks. The wastebasket was full.

She caught my eye. "He's working on a history of Santa Teresa architecture." I realized in a flash that in spite of her hostility, she was also proud of him.

"Sounds interesting."

"It's just something I'm fooling around with," he put in.

She had to laugh again. "I've got plenty for him to do if he gets tired of that. Have a seat if you can find a place. I hope you can stand the mess. I won't even let the cleaning woman in here. It's too far gone. She can do the whole house in the time it takes her to get this one room straightened up."

He smiled uncomfortably. "Now, Yolanda. Be fair. I clean the place myself . . . sometimes as often as twice a year."

"But not this year," she said, topping him.

He let the subject matter drop. He cleared his leather wing chair for her and pulled over a dining-room chair for me. I pushed some files aside, making room to sit.

"Just put those files on the floor," she said.

"This is fine." I was already tired of the game they played

—her put-downs, his collusion, my *pro forma* reassurances. "Did you want to get your walk in? I didn't mean to hold you up."

Her expression shifted. Being brittle herself, she was easily injured. "I can certainly do that if you think I'm in the way."

"Now, now, now. You stay right where you are," he said. "I'm sure she's here to talk to both of us."

"I suppose we could have some sherry," she said hesitantly.

He waved her into the chair. "I'll do that. You just have a seat."

"Please don't go to any trouble. I have to be somewhere else shortly." This was not entirely true, but I wasn't sure how much more I could endure. I took my notebook out of my handbag and leafed through the pages. "Let me ask a couple of questions and then I can get out of here. I don't want to take any more of your time than I have to."

Peter sank into a chair. "Exactly what is it you're doing?"

Yolanda adjusted one of the rings she wore, making sure the square-cut diamond was properly centered on her finger. "You'll have to pardon Peter. I only explained it to him twice."

"This is a follow-up to Morley Shine's investigation," I said, ignoring her. "Frankly, we're hoping to strengthen the plaintiff's case. Did you have contact with David or Isabelle on the day she died?"

He said, "I don't remember anything specific, but it seems unlikely."

"Well, of course it's unlikely. You were in the hospital, don't you remember? Your heart attack was December fifteenth that year. You were at St. Terry's until January second. I was afraid to tell you about Isabelle because I didn't want you upset."

His look was blank. "I suppose that's right. I'd forgotten that it all happened in that same period," he said to her. And

71

then to me, "They'd pulled out of the firm by then and set up offices of their own."

"Taking any client they could," she inserted with acid.

"Was there bad blood about that?"

She fiddled primly with her ring. "Not to hear him tell it, but of course there was."

"Now, Yolanda, that's not true. I wished her all the best."

"Peter hates to make a fuss. He won't confront anyone, least of all someone like her. After all he'd done."

"As I understand it, Isabelle came up with the idea for tiny houses while she was working for you."

"That's right."

"What about . . . what's it called . . . proprietary rights? Wouldn't the idea actually belong to you?"

Peter started to answer, but Yolanda broke in. "Of course. He never even asked her to sign the form. The woman walked out with everything. He wouldn't even press the point, though I begged him to. In effect, Isabelle stole millions from him—literally millions. . . ."

I formed my next question with care. I could already tell Peter was much too circumspect to be of any use in my investigation. Yolanda, the spite queen, was going to serve me well if I could set her up right. "You must have been furious."

"And why wouldn't I be? She was a self-indulgent, degenerate—" She bit off the sentence.

"Go on," I said.

"Yolanda," Peter said with a warning look.

She amended her stance. "I wouldn't want to speak ill."

"It won't hurt her at this point. I understand she was excessive—"

"Excessive doesn't *begin* to cover it. She was downright dishonest!"

Peter leaned toward his wife. "I don't think we should present a totally biased view. You may not have been fond of her, but she *was* talented."

"Yes, she was," Yolanda said, coloring. "And I suppose—to be fair about it—her problems were not all her fault. Sometimes I almost felt sorry for her. She was neurotic and high-strung. The woman had everything but happiness. David latched onto her like a parasite and he sucked her dry."

I waited for more, but she seemed to have run down. I looked at Peter. "Is that your analysis?"

"It's not my place to judge."

"I'm not asking you to judge her. I'd like your point of view. It might help me understand the situation."

He thought about that one briefly and apparently decided it made sense. "She was unfortunate. I don't know what else to say."

"How long did she work for you?"

"A little over four years. An informal apprenticeship."

"Simone told me she didn't actually have an architectural degree," I said.

"That's correct. Isabelle had no formal design training. She had wonderful ideas. She bubbled over with enthusiasm. It was almost as if the same reservoir fed both her creativity and her destruction."

"Was she a manic-depressive?"

"She seemed to live with very high levels of anxiety, which is why she drank," he said.

"She drank because she was an alcoholic," Yolanda put in.

"We don't know that," he said.

She had to laugh at that, patting herself on the chest to curb her merriment. "You'll never get a man to admit a beautiful woman is flawed."

I could feel the tension collecting again at the back of my neck. "What sort of man is David Barney? I gather he's an architect. Is he talented?"

Yolanda said, "He's a carpenter with pretensions."

Peter brushed her response aside. "He's a very good technician," Peter said.

"Technician?"

"That's not meant as criticism."

"He's the defendant. You can criticize all you like."

"I'm reluctant to do that. After all, we're in the same profession even though I'm retired. It's a small town. I don't feel it's my place to comment on his qualifications."

"What about the man himself?"

"I never cared for him personally."

"Oh, for God's sake, Peter. Why don't you tell her the truth? You can't stand the man. Nobody can abide him. He's sly and dishonest. He manipulates left and right—"

"Yolanda—"

"Don't you 'Yolanda' me! She's asked for an opinion and I'm giving her mine. You're so busy being nice you forget how to tell the truth. David Barney is a spider. Peter thought we should all socialize, and we did, over my protest. I felt it was going too far. When the two of them were in Peter's firm, I tried to be pleasant. I didn't care for David, but I did what was expected. Isabelle had brought in a great deal of business and we were appreciative of that. Once she got involved with David . . . he was not a good influence."

I refocused my attention. She'd be great on the witness stand if she could keep from losing it. "How'd she manage to bring in so much business?"

"She had a lot of money and she traveled in the right circles. People looked up to her because it was clear she had exquisite taste. She was very stylish. Whatever she took up, everyone else followed suit."

"When she and David left, they took a lot of clients with them?"

"That's not unusual," Peter said hastily. "It's unfortunate, of course, but it happens in every business."

"It was a disaster," Yolanda said. "Peter retired shortly afterwards. The last time we saw them was the dinner party they gave Labor Day weekend."

"When the gun disappeared?"

The two exchanged a look. Peter cleared his throat again. "We heard about that later."

"We heard about it at the time. There was a frightful quarrel upstairs in the master bedroom. Of course, we didn't know the subject, but that's certainly what it was."

"What's your theory about who might have taken it?"

"Well, *he* did, of course," Yolanda said without the slightest hesitation.

7

I stopped by the office briefly and typed up my notes. The light on my answering machine was blinking merrily. I punched the Replay button and listened to the message. It was Isabelle's friend Rhe Parsons, sounding harried and dutiful, the kind of person who returns a phone call just to get it over with. I tried her number, letting the phone ring while I leafed through one of the files sitting on my desk. Where was I going to find a witness who could put David Barney at the murder scene? Lonnie's suggestion was facetious, but what a coup that would be. Four rings . . . five. I was just about to hang up when someone answered abruptly on the other end. "Yes?"

"Oh, hi. This is Kinsey Millhone. May I speak to Rhe Parsons?"

"You're doing it. Who's this?"

"Kinsey Millhone. I left a message—"

"Oh, right, right," she cut in. "About Isabelle. I don't understand what you want."

"Look, I know you talked to Morley Shine a couple of months ago."

"Who?"

"The investigator who was handling this. Unfortunately, he had a heart at—"

"I never talked to anyone about Isabelle."

"You didn't talk to Morley? He was working for an attorney in the lawsuit filed by Kenneth Voigt."

"I don't know about any of this stuff."

"Sorry. Maybe I was misinformed. Why don't I tell you what's going on," I said. I went through a brief explanation of the lawsuit and the job I'd been hired to do. "I promise I won't take any more of your time than I have to, but I would like to have a quick chat."

"I'm swamped. You couldn't have called at a worse time," she said. "I'm a sculptor with a show coming up in two days. Every minute I've got is devoted to that."

"What about coffee or a glass of wine later this afternoon? It doesn't have to be nine to five. I can come at your convenience."

"But it has to be today, right? Can't it wait a week?"

"We have a court date coming up." We're all busy, I thought.

"Look, I don't mean to sound bitchy, but she's been gone for six years. Whatever happens to David Barney, it won't bring her back to life. So what's the point, you know?"

I said, "There's no point to anything if you get right down to it. We could all blow our brains out, but we don't. Sure, she's gone, but her death doesn't have to be senseless."

There was a silence. I knew she didn't want to do it and I hated to press, but this was serious.

She shifted her position, still annoyed, but willing to bend a bit. "Jesus. I teach drawing at Adult Ed from seven to ten o'clock tonight. If you stop by, we can talk while the students work. That's the best I can do."

"Great. That's perfect. I appreciate your help."

She gave me directions. "Room ten, at the back."

"I'll see you there."

I arrived home at 5:35 and saw that Henry's kitchen light was on. I walked from my back door to his, peering in through the screen. He was sitting in his rocker with his daily glass of Jack Daniel's, reading the paper while his supper cooked. Through the screen, I was assailed by the heady scent of frying onions and sausage. Henry set his paper aside. "Come on in."

I opened the screen door and stepped into the kitchen. A big pot of water was just coming to a boil and I could see tomato sauce simmering on the back burner. "Hi, babe, how are you? Whatever you're cooking, it smells divine."

He'd be handsome at any age, but at eighty-three he was elegant—tall, lean, with snowy white hair and blue eyes that seemed to burn in his tanned face. "I'm putting together a lasagna for later. William gets in tonight." Henry's older brother William, who was eighty-five to his eighty-three, had suffered a heart attack in August and hadn't been doing well since. Henry had debated a trip back to Michigan to see him, but had decided to postpone the visit until William's health improved. Apparently he was better because Henry'd received a call to say he was coming here.

"That's right. I forgot. Well, that should be an adventure. How long will he stay?"

"I agreed to two weeks, longer if I can stand him. It'll be a pain in the ass. Physically, he's recovered, but he's been depressed for months. Really down in the dumps. Lewis says he's totally self-obsessed. I'm sure Lewis is sending him out here to get even with me."

"What did you do to him?"

"Oh, who knows? He won't say. You know how parental Lewis gets. He likes to have me think about my sins in case there's one I haven't told him about. I stole a girl from him once back in 1926. I think this is to retaliate for her, but maybe not. He's got a long memory and not a shred of benef-icence." Henry's brother Lewis was eighty-six. His brother Charlie was ninety-one, and his only sister would be ninety-four on the thirty-first of December. "Actually, I'll bet it wasn't his idea at all. Nell's probably throwing William out. She never liked him that much and now she says all he does is talk about death. She doesn't want to hear it with a birth-day coming up. Says it's bumming her out."

"What time's his plane get in?"

"Eight-fifteen, if it doesn't crash, of course. I thought I'd bring him back here for salad and lasagna, maybe go up to Rosie's for a beer after that. You want to join us for supper? I made a cherry pie for dessert. Well, actually, I made six. The other five go to Rosie to pay off my bar tab." Rosie's is the local tavern, run by a Hungarian woman with an unpro-nounceable last name. Since Henry's retirement from com-mercial baking, he's begun to barter his wares. He also caters tea parties in the neighborhood, where he's much in de-mand.

"Can't do it," I said. "I've got an appointment at seven and it may run late. I thought I'd grab a quick bite up at Rosie's before I head out."

"Maybe you can catch us tomorrow. I don't know how we'll spend the day. Depressed people never do much. I'll probably sit around and watch him take his Elavil."

The building that houses Rosie's looks as if it might once have been a grocer's. The exterior is plain and narrow, the plate-glass windows obscured by peeling beer ads and buzzing neon signs. The tavern is sandwiched between an appliance repair shop and an ill-lighted Laundromat whose patrons wander into Rosie's to wait out their washing cycles, chugging beer and smoking cigarettes. The floors are wooden. The walls are plywood, stained a dark mahogany. The booths that line the perimeter are crudely built, destined to give you splinters if you slide too fast across the seat. There are eight to ten tables with black Formica tops, usually one leg out of four slightly shorter than the rest. Mealtime at Rosie's is often spent trying to right the wobble, with the endless intervention of stacked paper matchbooks and folded napkins. The lighting is the sort that makes you look like you've been abusing your Tan-in-a-Bottle.

Dinner was uneventful once I knuckled under and ordered what Rosie told me. She's a formidable presence: in her sixties, Hungarian, short, top-heavy, a merciless enforcer for the food Mafia. The special that night was called *gulyashus*, which had to translate to "beef stew."

"I was thinking of a salad. I need to clean up my act after too much junk food."

"Salad is for after. The *gulyashus* comes first. I make very authentic. You're gonna love it," she said. She was already penciling the order in the little notebook she'd begun to carry. I wondered if she kept a running account of all the meals I'd eaten there. I tried to peek at the page once and she rapped me with her pencil.

"Rosie, I don't even know what *gulyashus* is."

"Just hush and I'm telling you."

"Tell me then. I can't wait."

She had to get herself all settled for the recital, like a concert violinist with her feet placed properly. She makes a point of speaking lumpy English which she apparently thinks contributes to her authority. "In Hungarian, the word *gulyás* means 'herdsman.' Like a shepherd. This dish originate in ninth century. His very good. The shepherd cook up these cubes of meat with ongion, very little moisture. No paprika then so I don't use myself. When all the liquid is boil out, the meat is dried in the sun and then stored in this bag made of the sheep's . . . how you say . . ."

"Balls?"

"Estomach."

"Previously digested. Very tasty. I'll take it. I don't want to hear the rest."

"Good choice," she said complacently.

The dish she brought was actually what my aunt used to call "galoshes," cubes of beef simmered with onion and thickened with sour cream. It really was wonderful and the tart salad afterward was the perfect contrast. Rosie allowed me to have a glass of mediocre red wine, some rolls and butter, and a cheese tray for dessert. The dinner cost only nine dollars so I couldn't complain. Dimly I wondered if, for total obedience, I'd sold out too cheap.

While I drank my coffee, she stood by my table and complained. Her busboy, Miguel, a sullen lad of forty-five, was threatening to quit if she didn't give him a raise. "Is ridiculous. Why should he get more? Just because he learned to wash a dish like I teach him? He should pay me."

"Rosie!" I said. "The man started washing dishes when Ralph quit six months ago. Now he's doing two jobs and he ought to be paid. Besides, it's nearly Christmas."

"Is easy work," she remarked, undismayed by the notions of fair play, justice, or seasonal generosity.

"It's been two years since his last raise. He told me that himself."

"You taking his side, I see."

"Well, of course I am. He's been a good employee. Without him, you'd be lost."

Her look was stubborn. "I don't like men who pout."

The Adult Education facility where Rhe Parsons was teaching was located on Bay Street, on the far side of the freeway about two blocks from St. Terry's Hospital. Once an elementary school, the complex consisted of some offices, a small auditorium, and countless portable classrooms. Room ten was at the rear of the parking lot, an oversize art studio with a door on either end. Light poured out onto the walkway. I have a natural aversion to educational institutions, but drawing seemed benign—unlike math or chemistry. I peered in.

The interior was unfurnished except for easels and a few straight-backed wooden chairs. In the center of the room there was a low platform where a woman in a bathrobe, presumably the model, was perched on a tall wooden stool, reading a magazine. Students milled about, their ages ranging from late thirties into the seventies. In Santa Teresa, most adult education courses are offered free of charge. In a lab class like this there might be a two-dollar fee for materials, but most enrollment is open and costs the students nothing. I stood in the back of the studio. Behind me, cars were still pulling into the parking lot. It was 6:52 and people were still arriving, chatting as they entered the classroom. I watched as several women dragged additional easels from a small supply room. A coffee urn had been set up and I could see a big pink bakery box, probably filled with cookies to have with coffee during the break. A tape of Kitaro's *Silk Road* was playing, the sound low, infiltrating the room with a seductive tone. I could smell oil paint and chalk dust and the first bubbling evidence of strong coffee perking.

I spotted the woman I assumed to be Rhe Parsons emerging from a small supply closet with a roll of newsprint and a box of pencils; jeans, a denim work shirt with the sleeves rolled up, a pack of cigarettes visible in her left breast pocket. No makeup, no bra. She wore heavy leather sandals and a hand-tooled leather belt. Her hair was dark, pulled back in a French braid that extended halfway down her back. I placed her in her late thirties and wondered if she'd been at Woodstock once upon a time. I'd seen clips of the concert and I could picture her cavorting barefoot through the mud, stark naked, with a joint, her hair down to her waist and daisies painted on her cheek. Growing up had made her crabby, which happens to the best of us. She set the pencils on the counter and carried the newsprint to a big worktable where she began to cut off uniform sheets, using an industrial-size paper cutter. Several students without sketch pads formed a ragged line, waiting for her to finish. She must have sensed my scrutiny. She looked up, catching sight of me, and then went on about her business. I crossed the room and introduced myself. She couldn't have been more pleasant. Perhaps, like many habitually cranky people, her irritation passed in the moment, to be replaced by something sunnier.

"Sorry if I seemed short with you on the telephone. Let me get these guys going and we can talk out in the breezeway." She checked her watch, which she wore on the inner aspect of her wrist. It was seven straight up. She clapped her hands once. "Okay, people. Settle down. We're paying Linda by the hour. We're going to start with quick sketches, one minute each. This is to loosen up so don't worry about the small stuff. Think big. Fill the paper. I don't want any tight-ass tiny images. Betsy's going to be the timekeeper. When the bell rings, grab the next sheet of newsprint and start again. Any questions? Okay, then. Let's have some fun with this."

There was a bit of a scramble while the late students found empty easels. The model hopped off the stool, dropped her robe, and struck a pose, leaning forward with her hands on the wooden stool, a graceful curve to her back. It was comforting to see that she looked like an ordinary mortal—round and misproportioned, her torso softened by motherhood. The woman working next to me studied the model briefly and began to draw. Fascinated, I watched her capture the line of the model's shoulder, the arch of her spine. The quiet in the room was intense against the lyrical meandering of the music.

Rhe was watching me. Her eyes were a khaki green, her brows ragged. She moved toward the rear exit and I followed. The night air was fifteen degrees cooler than the room itself. She reached for a cigarette and lit it, leaning against one of the supports. "You ever draw? You seemed interested."

"Can you really teach people how to do that?"

"Of course. You want to learn?"

I laughed. "I don't know. It makes me nervous. I've never done anything remotely artistic."

"You ought to try it. I bet you'd like it. I teach the basics fall semester. This is life drawing, for people with a little drawing experience. Do what I tell you, you could pick it up in no time." Her gaze strayed out across the parking lot.

"Are you expecting someone?"

She looked back at me. "My daughter's stopping by. She wants to borrow my car. Hang around long enough and I may bum a ride home."

"Sure, I could do that."

She went back to the subject, maybe hoping to postpone any talk of Isabelle. "I've been drawing since I was twelve. I can remember when it happened. Sixth grade. We were out on a field trip in a little park with a pond. Everybody else drew the fountain with these flat stick people at the edge. I drew the spaces between the chicken wire in the fence. My drawing looked real. Everybody else's looked like sixth graders on a field trip. It was like an optical illusion . . . something shifted. I felt my brain do a sudden quickstep and it made me laugh. After that, I was like this art prodigy . . . the star of my class. I could draw anything."

"I envy you that. I always thought it'd be neat. Can I ask about Isabelle? You said your time was in short supply."

She looked away from me then, her voice dropping somewhat. "You might as well. Why not? I talked to Simone this afternoon and she filled me in."

"Sorry about the confusion over Morley Shine. According

to the files, he'd already talked to you. I was just going to fill in the blanks."

She shrugged. "I never heard a word from him, which is just as well. I'd have *really* been annoyed if I had to have the same conversation twice. Anyway, what is it you want to know?"

"How'd you meet?"

"Out at UCST. We took a printmaking class. I was eighteen, unmarried, with a kid on my hands. Tippy was two. I knew who the father was. He's always pitched in with her and helped me out with the money, but he's not the kind of guy I'd ever marry. . . ."

I pictured a dope dealer with his nose pierced, a tiny ruby sitting on his nostril like a semiprecious booger, long, unwashed hair tumbling halfway down his back.

". . . Isabelle had just turned nineteen and she was engaged to the guy who was later killed in a boat. We were both way too young for the shit that was coming down, but it bonded us like cement. We were friends for fourteen years. I really miss her."

"Are you close to Simone?"

"In some ways I am, but it's not like Isabelle. For sisters, they were very different . . . remarkably so. Iz was special. She really was. Very gifted." She paused to take the last drag from her cigarette, which she flipped into the parking lot. "Tip adored Isabelle, who was like a second mother to her. She told Iz the secrets she didn't have the nerve to tell me. Which is just as well, in my opinion. There are things I'm not sure any mother needs to know about her kid." She interrupted herself by holding an index finger up. "Let me take a break here and see how the class is doing."

She moved to the doorway and looked in on the class. I saw one of the students, a man in his sixties, turn a befuddled face toward her. He put a tentative hand up. "Hang on a sec," she said, "I better earn my paycheck."

The man who'd summoned her launched into a long-winded question. Rhe used hand gestures as she made her response, almost like American Sign Language for the deaf. Whatever her point, he didn't seem to get it at first. The model had changed her pose and was perched again on the stool, one bare foot resting on the second rung. I could see the angle of her hip and the line where her buttock was flattened out by the wood. Rhe had moved on. I waited while she completed the circuit, making her way from one easel to the next.

I heard footsteps behind me and I turned, glancing back. A young woman was approaching in tight jeans and high-heeled cowboy boots. She wore a Western-cut shirt and a big leather bag slung across her shoulder like a mail pouch. Her face was a clumsier version of Rhe's, though I suspected the maturation process would refine her features somewhat. At the moment, she looked like a rough pencil sketch for a portrait in oil. Her face was wide, her cheeks still rounded with the last vestiges of baby fat, but she had the same green eyes, the same long, dark hair pulled up in a braid. I placed her in her late teens or very early twenties. Bright-looking, good energy. She flashed me a smile.

"Is my mother in there?"

"She'll be out in a minute. Are you Tippy?"

"Yes," she said, surprised. "Do I know you?"

"I was just talking to your mom and she said you'd be stopping by. My name is Kinsey."

"You teach here, too?"

I shook my head. "I'm a private investigator."

She half smiled, getting ready for the punch line. "For real?"

"Yep."

"Cool. Investigating what?"

"I'm working for an attorney on a case going into court."

Her smile faded. "Is this about my aunt Isabelle?"

"Yes."

"I thought that already went to court and the guy got away with it."

"We're trying again. A different angle this time. We may nail him if we're lucky."

Tippy's expression seemed to darken. "I never liked him. What a creep."

"What do you remember?"

She made a face . . . reluctance, resistance, a touch of regret perhaps. "Nothing much, except we all cried a bunch. Like for weeks. It was awful. I was sixteen when she died. She wasn't my real aunt, but we were really close."

Rhe emerged from the classroom with her key ring in her hand. "Hi, baby. I thought that was you out here. I see you met Miss Millhone."

Tippy gave her mother's cheek a kiss. "We were just waiting for you. You look tired."

"I'm okay. How was work?"

"Work was fine. Corey says I might get a raise, but it's only like three percent."

"Don't knock it. Way to go," Rhe said. "What time are you picking Karen up?"

"Fifteen minutes ago. I'm already late."

Tippy and I watched while Rhe slipped the car key from the ring and then pointed toward the parking lot. "It's in the third row, to the left. I want the car back by midnight."

"We're not even out until quarter of!" Tippy yelped in protest.

"As soon as possible after that. And don't run me out of gas the way you did last time."

"It was empty when you gave it to me!"

"Would you just do what I say?"

"Why, you have a date?" Tippy asked impishly.

"Tippy . . ."

"I'm just teasing," she said. She plucked the key from her mother's hand and started off across the parking lot, bootheels clacking.

" 'Gee, Mom, I hope this isn't inconvenient,' " Rhe called toward her departing form. " 'Thank you, darling mother.' "

"You're welcome," Tippy called back.

Rhe shook her head with the kind of mock disgust that only a totally smitten parent indulges in. "Twenty years they're totally self-involved, then they turn around and get married."

"I know people must say this to you all the time, but you really don't look old enough to be her mother."

Rhe smiled. "I was sixteen when she was born."

"She seems like a neat kid."

"Well, she is, thanks to AA, which she joined when she was sixteen."

"Alcoholics Anonymous? Are you serious?"

"The drinking started when she was ten. I was working to support us and the baby-sitter was a lush. Tip would go there after school and guzzle beer every chance she got. I never had a clue! Here I am thinking it's neat because my child is so docile and obedient. She never once complained. She never whined if I was late or had to leave her overnight. I had other friends who were single moms like me. They had a bitch of a time. Their kids ran away, or caused trouble. Not my little Tippy. She was so easy to get along with. She didn't do well in school and she had the 'flu' a lot, but otherwise she seemed fine. I guess I was in denial, because I know now she was drunk or hung over half the time."

"You're lucky she straightened out."

"Part of that was Izzy's death. It did us in. It made us closer. We lost the best friend we ever had, but at least it brought us back together."

"How'd you find out about her drinking?"

"She reached a point where she was drinking so much I couldn't miss it. By the time she reached high school, she was really out of control. Popping pills. She smoked dope. She'd had her driver's license six months and she'd already had two wrecks. Plus, she stole anything that wasn't nailed down. This was actually the autumn before Isabelle's murder at Christmastime. She'd started her junior year, cutting classes, flunking tests. I couldn't handle it. I kicked her out, so she went to live with her father. When Iz died, she came back." She stopped to light another cigarette. "Jesus. Why'm I telling you this stuff? Look, I gotta get back to class. Do you mind hanging out? I really do need a ride home if you can do me that."

"Sure. I'd be happy to."

8

I drove her home at 10:30 after class had ended. Most of the students were gone by five after ten, cars spilling out of the darkened parking lot with the sweep of headlights, engines thrumming. I offered to help her tidy up, but she said it'd be quicker if she did it herself. I wandered around the room, doing an idle survey while she emptied the coffee urn and rinsed it out, put away the drawing supplies, and then flipped out the lights. She locked the doors behind us and we headed for my VW, which was the only car left in the parking lot.

As we drove through the gated driveway, she said, "I live in Montebello. I hope that's not too far out of your way."

"Don't worry about it. I'm on Albanil, near the beach. I can come back along Cabana and it's no big deal."

I turned right onto Bay, and then right again on Missile, picking up the freeway about two blocks down. She gave me directions to her place and for two miles we chatted idly, while I tried to decide what I could learn from her. "How'd you first hear about Isabelle's death?"

"The cops called about two-thirty and told me what had happened. They asked if I'd come over there and just sit with Simone. I threw some clothes on, hopped in the car, and barreled over there right away. I was just in shock. The whole time I was driving, I képt talking to myself like some kind of nut. I didn't cry till I got there and saw the look on Simone's face. The Seegers were a mess. They kept telling the same story over and over again. I don't know which of us was in worse shape. Actually, I think I was. Simone was numb and out of it until David showed up. Then she lost it completely. She really came unglued."

"Oh, that's right. He claimed he was jogging in the middle of the night. Did you believe him?"

"God, I don't know. I did and I didn't. He'd been doing night runs for years. He said he liked it because it was quiet and he didn't have to worry about all the traffic and exhaust fumes. I guess he suffered from insomnia and roamed the house at all hours."

"So he used the jogging to wind down when he couldn't sleep?"

"Well, yeah, but on the other hand, the night of the murder, it seemed awfully contrived." She twisted a finger in an imaginary dimple in her cheek like a ditzy blonde. " 'What a coincidence. I was just passing by on my two A.M. run.' "

"Simone tells me he was living down the road at that point."

She made a face. "In that awful house. He told the cops he was just getting back from a run when he saw the lights up at Isabelle's and stopped to see what was going on."

"Did he seem upset?"

"Well, I wouldn't say that, but then nothing seemed to move him. It was one of her big complaints. He was an emotional robot."

"You mentioned Simone going nuts. What'd you mean by that?"

"She got hysterical when he showed up, convinced he'd killed Isabelle. She always maintained the story about the stolen gun was pure bullshit. We'd all been in the house on countless other occasions. Why would any one of us suddenly sneak upstairs and steal David's thirty-eight, for God's sake? She figured it was part of a setup. I guess I'd have to agree."

"So, you were at the dinner party Labor Day weekend when the gun disappeared?"

"Sure, I was there and so was everybody else. Peter and Yolanda Weidmann, the Seegers, the Voigts."

"Kenneth was there? Her ex-husband and his wife?"

"Hey, current etiquette. One big happy family, except of course for Francesca. That's Kenneth's wife, the long-suffering. What a martyr she was. Sometimes I think Isabelle just invited them to bug her. All Francesca had to do was refuse to go."

"What was her problem?"

"She knew Ken was still hung up on Isabelle. After all, Iz was the one who gave Kenneth the boot. He married Francesca on the rebound."

"Sounds like a soap opera."

"It gets worse," Rhe said. "Francesca's beautiful. Have you met her?" I shook my head and she went on. "She's like a model, perfect features and a body to die for, but she's insecure, always choosing men who withhold. You know what I mean? Ken was ideal because she knew she'd never really have his full attention."

I said, "Let me ask you this. I heard his version last night and he claims Isabelle was the one who was insecure. Is that true?"

"Not from my point of view, but she may have shown a different side of herself to men," she said. She pointed to a series of driveways coming up on the left. "It's this first one," she said.

We were in the section of Montebello known as the slums, where the houses only cost $280,000 each. I pulled up in front of a small stucco cottage painted white. She opened the car door on her side, getting out. "I'd ask you in for some wine, but I really do have to get to work. I'll be up half the night."

"Don't worry about it. That's fine. I'm bushed. I appreciate your time," I said. "By the way, where's the show?"

"The Axminster Gallery. There's a champagne reception Friday evening at seven. Stop by and see it if you can."

"I'll do that."

"And thanks for the ride. If you think of any other questions, you can let me know."

Henry's house was dark by the time I got home. There were no messages on my machine. As a way of unwinding, I tidied up the living room and scrubbed the downstairs bath. Cleaning house is therapeutic—all those right-brain activities, dusting and vacuuming, washing dishes, changing sheets. I've come up with many a personal insight with a toilet brush in hand, watching the Comet swirl around in the bowl. Tomorrow night I'd dust my way up the spiral staircase, then tackle the loft and the upstairs bathroom.

I slept well, got up at 6:00 A.M., and did my usual run, whizzing through my morning routine on automatic pilot. On my way into the office, I stopped off at the bakery and bought a huge Styrofoam container of *caffè latte* with a lid. I had to park my car two blocks away, and by the time I got to my desk the coffee was the perfect drinking temperature. While I sipped, I sat and stared at the file folders strewn across every available surface. I was going to have to straighten things up just to figure out what was what. I drained half the coffee and set the cup aside.

I pushed my sleeves up and went to work, getting organized. I emptied both boxes, plus the brown grocery bag full of files I'd picked up at Morley's house, adding in the few additional files from his office. I rearranged the piles alphabetically and then painstakingly reconstructed the sequence of reports, using Morley's invoices as a master index. In some instances (Rhe Parsons being a case in point), I had a name itemized on his bill without a file to match. For "Francesca V.," whom I took to be the current Mrs. Voigt, I found a file folder neatly labeled, but there was no report in it. The same was also true of a Laura Barney, who I assumed was David's ex-wife. Had Morley talked to them or not? The former Mrs. Barney apparently worked at the Santa Teresa Medical Clinic in some capacity. Morley'd noted a telephone number, but there was no way to tell if he'd gotten through to her. He'd been paid for sixty hours' worth of interviews, in some cases with accompanying travel receipts, but the corresponding paperwork didn't add up to much. I made a penciled notation of any name without attendant notes or a written report.

By 10:30, I had a list of seventeen names. Just as a spot check, I tried two. First, I placed a call to Francesca, who answered after one ring, sounding cool and distant.

I identified myself and verified, first of all, that she was married to Kenneth Voigt. "I'm reorganizing some files and I wondered if you remember what date you talked to Morley Shine."

"I never talked to him."

"Not at all?"

"I'm afraid not. He called and left a message about three weeks ago. I returned his call and we agreed to meet, but then he canceled for some reason. As a matter of fact, I asked Kenneth about it just last night. It seemed odd somehow. Since I testified at the first trial, I assumed I'd be called the second time around."

I glanced down at Morley's memo, which seemed to indicate they'd had a meeting. "We better set up an appointment as soon as possible."

"Hang on a minute and I'll get my book." She put the phone down on her end and I heard the tap of heels across hardwood. She returned to the telephone with a rustle of paper. "I'm busy this afternoon. What's this evening look like for you?"

"That sounds fine to me. What time?"

"Could we make it seven? Kenneth usually doesn't get home until nine, but I'm assuming you don't need him to sit in."

"Actually, I'd prefer to have the time alone."

"Good. Then I'll see you at seven."

I tried the clinic next and found myself connected with what I guessed was the reception desk. The person who answered was female and sounded young.

"Santa Teresa Medical Clinic, this is Ursa. May I help you?"

I said, "Can you tell me if you have a Laura Barney working at the clinic?"

"Mrs. Barney? Sure. Hang on and I'll get her."

I was placed on hold briefly.

"This is Mrs. Barney."

I introduced myself, explaining, as I had with Francesca, who I was and why I was calling. "Can you tell me if you talked to Morley Shine in the last couple of weeks?"

"As a matter of fact, I had an appointment with him last Saturday, but he never showed up. I was very annoyed because I'd canceled some plans in order to make time for him."

"Did he give you any indication what he meant to ask?"

"Not really, but I assumed it was in conjunction with this lawsuit coming up. I was married to the man acquitted of the criminal charges."

"David Barney."

"That's right. We were married for three years."

"I'd like to talk to you. Can we set up a time this week?" In the background, I could hear another line begin to ring insistently.

"I'm usually here until five. If you stop by tomorrow I can probably make some time."

"Four-thirty or five?"

"Either one is fine."

"Good. I'll stop by as close to four-thirty as I can make it. I'll let you pick up your other call."

She said thanks and clicked off.

I went back to my list and called nine other names at random. Not one of them had ever heard from Morley Shine. This was not looking good. I buzzed Ida Ruth in the outer office. "Is Lonnie still in court?"

"As far as I know."

"What time's he get back?"

"Lunchtime, he said, but he sometimes skips lunch and heads for the law library instead. Why, what's up? You want to get a message to him?"

A low-level dread had begun to churn in my chest. "I better go over there and have a chat with him myself. Which courtroom, did he say?"

"Judge Whitty, Department Five. What's going on, Kinsey? You sound very strange."

"I'll tell you later. I don't want to commit myself quite yet."

I walked over to the courthouse, which was only two blocks away. The day was sunny and clear, with a mild breeze ruffling the grass on the courthouse lawn. The architecture of the building itself is Mediterranean, complete with towers, turrets, sandstone arches, and open-air galleries. The exterior landscaping is a bright mix of magenta bougainvillea, red bottlebrush, junipers, and imported palms. A low growing fringe of ground cover along the sidewalk threw out a heady perfume.

I went up the wide concrete steps, through ornate wooden doors. The corridor was empty. The floor was paved with glossy irregular stone tiles the color of old blood. The lofty ceilings were hand-stenciled and crisscrossed with dark beams. The lighting fixtures were wrought-iron replicas of Spanish lanterns, the windows secured by sturdy grillwork. The place might have been a monastery once; all cold surfaces, stripped of ornament. As I passed, the door to the jury assembly room opened and prospective jurors poured out into the hallway, filling the air with the tap-tapping of footsteps and the murmur of voices. Soon I could hear the incessant squeaking of stall doors in the rest rooms across the hall. Department 5 was located another two doors down the hall on the right, the lighted sign above the door indicating that court was still in session. I eased the door open and slipped into a seat in the rear.

Lonnie and opposing counsel were involved in a case management conference, their voices droning on the warm air like big fat bumblebees. The judge was in the process of referring the case to judicial arbitration, setting the dates for both the completion of the arbitration and a future case management conference. As usual, I wondered how individual fates could be decided through a process that sounded, on the face of it, so dull. When the judge broke for lunch, I waited by the door, catching Lonnie's eye as he turned and headed through the little swinging gate that separated the spectators' "pews" from the court. He took one look at my face and said, "What's the matter?"

"Let's go outside where it's private. You're not going to like this."

We walked side by side without a word, footsteps clattering, down the corridor, down the concrete steps, out the front entrance to the sidewalk. We struck off across the grass just far enough to ensure that we wouldn't be overheard. He turned and looked at me and I plunged in.

"I don't know a nice way to say this so I'll get right to the point. It turns out Morley's files are more than disorganized. Half the reports are missing and what he's got there is suspect."

"Meaning what?"

I took a deep breath. "I think he was billing you for work he never did."

Lonnie's face went blank as the news sank in. "You're shittin' me."

"Lonnie, he had a heart condition and his wife is very sick. From what I gather, he was hard up for money, but he didn't have the time or the energy to do much."

"How'd he think he could get away with that? I got a court date in less than a month. Did he think I wouldn't *notice*?" he asked. "Hell, what's the matter with me? I *didn't* notice, did I?"

I shrugged. "In the past, from what I've heard, his work was always great." Small comfort to an attorney who could end up in court with nothing in his hand but his dick.

Lonnie seemed to pale, apparently conjuring up the same image of himself. "Jesus, what was he thinking of?"

"Who knows what he was thinking? Maybe he was hoping he could get caught up."

"How bad is it?"

"Well, you still have the witnesses from the criminal trial. It looks like most of them have been subpoenaed, so you're cool on that score. I'm guessing maybe half the witnesses on the new list never heard from him. I could be wrong. All I did was a spot check. I'm really judging by the number of reports I can't find."

Lonnie closed his eyes and wiped his face with one hand. "I don't want to hear this. . . ."

"Look, we still have some time. I can go back and fill in, but if we run into a snag, we're up shit creek. Some of these people may not even be available."

"Jesus, this is my fault. I've been tied up with this other matter and it never occurred to me to question his paperwork. What I saw looked okay. I knew he was backlogged, but what he gave me seemed fine."

"Yeah, what's there *is* fine. It's what's not there that worries me."

"How long will it take?"

"Two weeks at the very least. I just wanted you to be aware of what you're up against. With the holidays coming up, a lot of people are going to be tied up or out of town."

"Do what you can. At two, I'm taking off for Santa Maria for a two-day trial. I get back late on Friday, but I won't come into the office until Monday morning. We can talk about it then."

"Will you be staying up there?"

"Probably. I could come home at night if I had to, but I hate losing the hour drive time each way. After a full day in court, I just want to grab a quick bite somewhere and then hit the sack. Ida Ruth will have the motel number if there's an emergency. In the meantime, do what you can, okay?"

"Sure."

I went back to the office. As I passed Lonnie's office door I spotted Ida Ruth talking on the telephone. She caught sight of me and waved frantically, motioning me back. She put the party on hold and then put her hand across the receiver, as if to further muffle her side of the conversation in progress. "I don't know who this guy is, but he's asking for you."

"What's he want?"

"He just read Morley's obituary. He says it's urgent he talk to whoever's taking over for him."

"Let me get back to my desk and I'll pick it up in there. Maybe he's got some information for us. What line's he on?"

She held up two fingers.

I trotted down the hall, closed the office door behind me, dumped my handbag, and reached across my desk, punching line two, which was blinking steadily. "This is Kinsey Millhone. Is there something I can help you with?"

"I read in the paper Morley Shine died. What happened?" The voice was well modulated, the tone cautious.

"He had a heart attack. Who is this?"

There was a pause. "I'm not sure that's relevant."

"It is if you want to talk to me," I said.

Another pause. "My name is David Barney."

My heart did one of those sudden hard bangs. "Excuse me. I'm the wrong person to ask about Morley Shine—"

He cut in, saying, "Listen to me. Now, just listen. There's something screwy going on. I talked to him last Wednesday—"

"Morley called you?"

"No, ma'am. I called him. I heard some ex-con named Curtis McIntyre is set to testify against me. He claims I told him that I killed my wife, but that's bullshit and I can prove it."

"I think we should stop this conversation right here."

"But I'm telling you—"

"Tell it to your attorney. You have no business calling me."

"I've told my attorney. I told Morley Shine, too, and look how he ended up."

I was silent for half a second. "What's that supposed to mean?"

"Maybe the guy was getting too close to the truth."

I rolled my eyes. "Are you implying he was murdered?"

"It's possible."

"So is life on Mars, but it's not likely. Why would anybody want to murder Morley Shine?"

"Maybe he'd found something that exonerated me."

"Oh, yeah, really. Such as what?"

"McIntyre claims he talked to me outside the courtroom the day I was acquitted, right?"

I said nothing.

"Right?" he asked again. I hate guys who insist on a line-by-line response.

"Make your point," I said.

"The fucker was in jail then. It was May twenty-first. Check his rap sheet for that year. You'll see it plain as day. I told Morley Shine the same thing Wednesday morning and he said he'd look into it."

"Mr. Barney, I don't think it's a good idea for us to talk

like this. I work for the opposition. I'm the enemy, you got that?"

"All I want to do is tell you my side of it."

I held the phone out and squinted at the receiver in disbelief. "Does your attorney know you're doing this?"

"To hell with that. To hell with him. I've had it up to here with attorneys, my own included. We could have settled this years ago if anybody'd had the decency to listen." This from a man who shot his wife in the eye.

"Hey, you have the legal system if you want someone to listen. That's what it's all about. You say one thing. Kenneth Voigt says something else. The judge will hear both sides and so will the jury."

"But you won't."

"No, I won't listen because it's not my place," I said irritably.

"Even if I'm telling the truth?"

"That's for the court to decide. That isn't my job. My job is to gather information. Lonnie Kingman's job is to put the facts before the court. What good is it going to do to tell me anything? This is stupid."

"Jesus Christ! Someone has to help me." His voice broke with emotion. I could hear mine getting colder.

"Talk to your attorney. He got you off a *murder* rap . . . so far, at any rate. I wouldn't mess with success if I were you."

"Could you meet with me . . . just briefly?"

"No, I can't meet with you!"

"Lady, I'm begging you. Five minutes is all I ask."

"I'm going to hang up, Mr. Barney. This is inappropriate."

"I need help."

"Then hire some. My services are taken."

I put the phone down and jerked my hand back. Was the man nuts? I'd never heard of a defendant trying to enlist the sympathies of the opposition. Suppose, in desperation, the guy came after me? I snatched up the phone again and buzzed Ida Ruth.

"Yessum?"

"The guy who just called. Did you give him my name?"

"Of course not. I'd never do such a thing," she said.

"Oh, shit. I just remembered. I gave it to him myself."

I picked up the phone again and placed a call to Sergeant Cordero in Homicide. She was out, but Lieutenant Becker picked up. "Hi, this is Kinsey. I need some information and I was hoping Sheri could help."

9

"She won't be back until after three, but maybe I can help. What's the scoop?"

"I was going to ask her to call the county jail and have someone check the jail release forms for a fellow named Curtis McIntyre."

"Wait a minute. Let me grab a pencil. That was McIntyre?"

"Right. He's an informant set to testify on a case for Lonnie Kingman. I need to know if he was incarcerated on May twenty-first, five years ago, which is when he claims he talked to the defendant. I can get the information by subpoena, but it's probably just a wild-goose chase and I hate to go to all the trouble."

"Shouldn't be hard to check. I'll call you back when I've got it, but it may take a while. I hope you're not in any crashing hurry."

"The sooner the better."

"Ain't that always the way?" Lieutenant Becker said.

Once I hung up the phone, I sat and thought about the situation, wondering if there was a quicker means of verifying the information. I could certainly wait until midafternoon, but it would prey on my mind. David Barney's call had left me feeling restless and out of sorts. I was reluctant to waste time checking out what was probably pure fabrication on his part. On the other hand, Lonnie was counting on Curtis McIntyre's testimony. If Curtis McIntyre was lying, we were sunk, especially with Morley's investigation coming unraveled at the same time. This was my first job for Lonnie. I could hardly afford to get fired again.

In my head, I reran the conversation I'd had with Curtis at the jail. In his account, he'd intercepted David Barney in the corridor just outside the courtroom on the day he was acquitted. I didn't think I could count on Barney's attorney, Herb Foss, to corroborate Curtis's claim, but could there have been another witness to their encounter? Just the countless reporters with their Minicams and mikes.

I grabbed my jacket and my shoulder bag. I left the office and dogtrotted the two blocks to the side street where I'd finally managed to squeeze my car into a bare stretch of curb. I took Capilla Boulevard across town, through the heart of the commercial district, and headed up the big hill on the far side of the freeway.

KEST-TV was located just this side of the summit. From the bluff where the station sat, there was a 180-degree living mural of the city of Santa Teresa: mountains on one side, the Pacific Ocean on the other. There was parking for about fifty cars and I pulled into a spot designated for visitors. I got out of the car and paused for a moment to take in the view. The wind was buffeting the dry grasses along the hill. In the distance, the pale ocean stretched to the horizon, looking flat and oddly shallow.

I remembered the story I'd once heard from a marine archaeologist. He told me there was evidence of primitive offshore villages, underwater now, located at the mouths of ancient sloughs or arroyos. Over the years, the sea had offered up broken vessels, mortars, abalone spangles, and other artifacts, probably eroding from former cemeteries and middens along the now-submerged beach. In legend, the Chumash Indians recount a time when the sea subsided and remained that way for hours. A house was exposed at the far reaches of the low tide . . . a mile out, or two miles . . . this miraculous shanty. People gathered on the beaches, murmuring with amazement. The waters receded further and a second house appeared, but the witnesses were too frightened to approach. Gradually the waters returned and the two structures vanished, covered by the slow swell of the incoming tide.

There was something eerie about the tale, Holocene ghosts offering up this momentary vision of a tribal site lost from view. Sometimes I wondered if I'd have dared venture out across that stretch of exposed channel. Perhaps half a mile out, it plunged downward like the sides of a mountain, underwater cliffs tumbling ever deeper to the canyon below. I pictured the sediment on the ocean bottom, glistening, dead gray from the lack of light, cobbled and pockmarked with all its blunt and stony treasures. Time covers the truth, leaving scarcely a ripple on the surface to suggest all the plains and valleys that lie below. Even now, dealing with a six-year-old murder, much was hidden, much submerged. I was left to gather artifacts washed up like rubble on the shores of the present, uneasy about the treasures, undiscovered, lying just out of reach.

I turned and went into the station. The building itself was a one-story stucco structure, painted a plain sand color, bristling with assorted antennae. I went into the lobby with its pale blue carpeting, furnished with the kind of "Danish Modern" furniture an affluent college student might rent for a semester. Christmas decorations were just going up: an artificial tree in one corner, boxes of ornaments stacked in a chair. On the wall to my right, numerous broadcast awards were mounted like bowling trophies. A color television was tuned to a morning game show, the gist of which seemed to be identifying a series of celebrities whose first names were Andy.

The receptionist was a pretty girl with long dark hair and vivid makeup. The name on the placard read Tanya Alvarez. "Rooney!" she called, her eyes pinned to the set. I turned and looked at the picture. "Andy Rooney" was correct and the audience was applauding. The next clue came up and she said, "Oh, shoot, who is that? What's-his-face? Andy Warhol!" Right again, and she flushed with pleasure. She looked over at me. "I could make a fortune on that show, except probably the day I got on it'd be some category I never heard of. Blowfish, or exotic plants. Can I help you?"

"I'm not sure. I'd like to look at some five-year-old news footage, if you have it."

"Something we taped?"

"That's what I'm assuming. This was the verdict on a local murder trial and I'm pretty sure you'd have covered it."

"Hang on a minute and I'll see if somebody back there can help you." She rang through to "somebody" in the bowels of the building, briefly describing the nature of my quest. "Leland'll be out in five minutes," she said.

I thanked her and spent the mandatory waiting period wandering from the front entrance, which looked out onto the parking lot, to the sliding glass doors on the far side of the reception area, which looked out onto a wide concrete patio furnished with molded white plastic chairs. A three-dimensional view of the city wrapped around the patio like a screen. I could imagine the station employees having lunch out in the hot sun—women with cotton skirts discreetly pulled up, men without shirts. A big dish antenna dominated the view. The air looked hazy from up here. . . .

"I'm Leland. What can I do for you?"

The fellow who'd appeared through the doorway behind me was in his late twenties and had to be a hundred pounds overweight. He had a mop of curly brown hair surrounding a baby face, with wire-rimmed glasses, clear blue eyes, flushed cheeks, and no facial hair. With a name like Leland, he was doomed. He looked like the kind of kid who'd been tormented by his schoolmates since the first day of school, too bright and too big to avoid the involuntary cruelties of other middle-class children.

I introduced myself and we shook hands. I explained the situation as succinctly as possible. "What occurred to me was that with local reporters present on the day Barney was acquitted, there were probably Minicams rolling as he emerged from the courtroom."

"Okay," he said.

" 'Okay' wasn't really the response I was looking for, Leland. I was hoping you had a way to go back and check the old news tapes."

Leland gave me a blank look. I wish a P.I.'s job were half as easy as they make it look on television. I've never opened a dead bolt with a pass of my credit card. I can't even force mine into a doorjamb without breaking it off. And what's it supposed to do once you slide it in there? Most of the latch bolts I've seen, the slanted angle is on the *inside* so it's not as though you could slip a credit card along the face of it and force the latch to move back. And where the angle faces the outside, the strike plate resists the insertion of even the most flexible object. Leland seemed to be taking the same implacable position.

"What's the matter? Don't you keep that stuff?"

"It's not that. I'm sure there's a copy of the footage you're looking for. The master tapes are catalogued by subject matter and date, cross-referenced and cross-filed on three-by-five index cards."

"You don't have it on computer?"

He shook his head, with just a hint of satisfaction. "The logistics of the system don't really matter much because I can't let you see the master tape without a properly executed subpoena."

"I'm working for an attorney. I can get a subpoena. This is no big deal."

"Go ahead then. I can wait."

"Yeah, well, I can't. I need the information as soon as possible."

"In that case, you got a problem. I can't let you see the master tape unless you have a subpoena."

"But if I could get it eventually, what difference does it make? I'm entitled to the information. That's the bottom line, isn't it?"

"No tickee, no washee. That's the bottom line," he said.

I was beginning to see why his imaginary classmates liked to torture him. "Could we try this?" I pulled out a mug shot of Curtis McIntyre. "Why don't you look at the tape and tell me if he's on it. That's all I want to know."

He stared at me with that blank look all petty bureaucrats assume while they calculate the probabilities of getting fired if they say yes. "Why do you want to know? I really wasn't listening before."

"This fellow claims he had a conversation with the defendant in a murder trial shortly after he was acquitted. He says the cameras were rolling as the guy left the courtroom, so if what he says is true, he ought to be clearly visible on the tape, right?"

"Yeeess," he said slowly. I could tell he thought there was some kind of trick to it.

"This isn't a violation of anybody's civil rights," I said reasonably. "Could you just look?"

He held his hand out. I gave him Curtis's mug shot. He continued to hold his hand out.

I stared for a moment. "Oh," I said. I opened my handbag and took out my wallet. I peeled off a twenty and put it in his palm. His expression didn't actually change, but I knew he was insulted. I'm sure it's the same look you'd get from a New York taxi driver if you tipped him a dime.

I peeled off another twenty. No reaction. I said, "I really hate corruption in someone so young."

"It's disgusting, isn't it?" he replied.

I added a third.

His hand closed. "Come with me."

He turned and headed back through the doorway and into a narrow corridor. I followed without a word. Offices opened up on either side of us. Occasionally, we passed other station employees wearing jeans and Reeboks, but no one was doing much. The spaces seemed cramped and irregular, with too much knotty pine veneer paneling and too many cheaply framed photographs and certificates. The whole interior of the building had been done up with the sort of do-it-yourself home improvements that later make a house impossible to sell.

At the rear, we passed into a tiny concrete cul-de-sac with a wood-and-metal stairway leading up to an attic. Just to the right was an old-fashioned wooden file cabinet, with a smaller wooden file sitting on top. He opened the drawer for the year we wanted and began to sort through the index cards, starting with the name Barney. "We won't have the actual field tapes," he remarked while he looked.

"What's a field tape?"

"That would be like the whole twenty minutes of tape the guy shot. We keep the ninety seconds to two minutes of edited footage that actually goes on the air."

"Oh. Well, even that would help."

"Unless the guy you're looking for stepped up and spoke to your suspect after the cameras finished rolling."

"True enough," I said.

"Nope. Nothing," he said. "Well, let's see here. What else could it be under?" He tried "Murder," "Trials," and "Courtroom Cases," but there was no reference to Isabelle Barney.

"Try 'Homicides,' " I suggested.

"Oh, good one." He shifted to the *H*'s. There it was, with a numerical designation that apparently referred to the number of the tape on file. We went up the narrow stairs and through a door so low we were forced to duck our heads. Inside, there was a warren of tiny rooms with six-foot ceilings, lined with videocassette containers, neatly labeled and filed upright. Leland located and retrieved the cassette we were looking for and then led me downstairs again and around to the right where there were four stations set up with monitoring equipment. He flipped on the first machine and inserted the tape. The first segment appeared on the screen in front of us. He pressed Fast Forward. I watched the news for that year whiz by like the history of civilization in two minutes flat, everybody very animated and jerky. I spotted a still of Isabelle Barney. "There she is," I yelped.

Leland backed the tape up and began to run it at normal speed. An anchorperson I hadn't seen for years was suddenly doing the voice-over commentary as snippets of the case, neatly spliced together, spelled out the highlights of Isabelle's death, David Barney's arrest, and the subsequent trial. The acquittal, in condensed form, had the speedy air of instant justice, well edited, swiftly rendered, with liberty for all. David Barney emerged from the courtroom looking slightly dazed.

"Hold it. Let me look at him."

Leland stopped the tape and let me study the image. He was in his forties with light brown wavy hair combed away from his face. His forehead was lined and there were lines radiating from the corners of his eyes. He had a straight nose and a tense grin over artificially even teeth. His chin was strong and I could see that he had strong hands with blunt-cut nails. He was slightly taller than medium height. His attorney looked very tall and gray and somber by comparison.

"Thanks," I said. I realized belatedly that I'd been holding my breath. Leland pushed Play and the coverage quickly switched to another subject altogether. He handed me Curtis McIntyre's mug shot. "No sign of him."

For the money I'd given him, he could have feigned disappointment. "Could it be the camera angle?" I asked.

"We got a wide and a close. You saw 'em come through the door alone. Nobody approached in the footage we caught. Like I said, the guy might have stepped up and spoken once the press conference was over."

"Well. Thanks," I said. "I guess I'll have to rely on my other source."

I went back to my car, not sure what to do next. If I got verification of Curtis McIntyre's incarceration, I intended to confront him, but I couldn't do that yet. In theory, I had numerous interviews to conduct, but David Barney's phone call had thrown me. I didn't want to spend time shoring up David Barney's alibi, but if what he said was true, we'd end up looking like a bunch of idiots.

I took the winding road down the backside of the hill and turned right on Promontory Drive, following the road along the ocean and through the back entrance to Horton Ravine. I used the next hour and a half canvassing the old neighborhood to see if anybody had been out and about on the night Isabelle was murdered. It didn't thrill me to be in range of David Barney, but I couldn't see a way around it and still get the information I wanted. A canvass by telephone is the same as not doing it. It's too easy for people to hang up, tell fibs, or shine you on.

One neighbor had moved and another had died. A woman on the adjacent property thought she'd heard a shot, but she hadn't paid much attention to the time and she'd later wondered if it hadn't been something else. Like what, I thought. I wasn't sure if it was my paranoia or not, but any time I heard what sounded like a gunshot, I checked the clock to see what time it was.

Of the eight remaining homeowners variously peppered along that stretch of road, none had been out that night and none had seen a thing. I got the impression that it had all happened far too long ago to bear worrying about at this point. A six-year-old murder doesn't engage the imagination. They'd already told their versions of the story one too many times.

I went home for lunch, stopping off at my apartment just long enough to check for messages. My machine was clear. I went next door to Henry's. I was looking forward to meeting William.

I found Henry standing in his kitchen, this time up to his elbows in whole wheat flour, kneading bread. Pellets of dough clung to his fingers like wood putty. Usually, Henry's kneading has a meditative quality, methodical, practiced, soothing to the observer. Today, his manner seemed faintly manic and the look in his eyes was haunted. Beside him, at the counter, stood a man who looked enough like him to be a twin; tall and slim, with the same snowy white hair and blue eyes, the same aristocratic face. I took in the similarities in that first glance. The differences were profound and took longer to assimilate.

Henry wore a Hawaiian shirt, white shorts, and thongs, his long limbs sinewy and tanned as a runner's. William wore a three-piece pin-striped suit, a starched white shirt, and a tie. His bearing was erect, nearly stiff, as if to compensate for the underlying feebleness I'd never known Henry to exhibit. William held a pamphlet in a slightly shaking hand and he pointed with a fork to a drawing of the heart. He paused for introductions and we went through the proper litany of inaugural sentiments. "Now where was I?" he asked.

Henry gave me a bland look. "William's been detailing some of the medical procedures associated with his heart attack."

"Quite right. You'll be interested in this," William said to me. "I'm assuming your knowledge of anatomy is as rudimentary as his."

"I couldn't pass a test," I said.

"Nor could I," William replied, "until this episode. Now Henry, you'll want to pay attention to this."

"I doubt that," Henry said.

"You see, the right side of the heart receives blood from the body and pumps it through the lungs, where carbon dioxide and other waste products are exchanged for oxygen. The left side receives the blood full of oxygen from the lungs and pumps it out into the body through the aorta. . . ." The diagram he was using looked like the road map of a park with lots of one-way roads marked with black-and-white arrows. "Block these arteries and that's where you have a problem." William tapped on the diagram emphatically with the fork. "It's just like a rockslide coming down across a road. All the traffic begins to pile up in a nasty snarl." He turned a page in the pamphlet, which he held open against his chest like a kindergarten teacher reading aloud to a class. The next diagram showed a cross section of a coronary artery that looked like a vacuum cleaner hose filled with fluffies.

Henry interrupted. "Have you had lunch?"

"That's why I came home."

"There's some tuna in the refrigerator. You can make us some sandwiches. Do you eat tuna, William?"

"I've had to give it up. It's a very fatty fish to begin with and when you add mayonnaise . . ." He shook his head. "Not for me, thanks. I'll open one of the cans of low-sodium soup I brought with me. You two go ahead."

"Turns out William can't eat lasagna," Henry said to me.

"Much to my regret. Fortunately, Henry had some fresh vegetables I was able to steam. I don't want to be a bother and I said as much to him. There's nothing worse than being a burden to your loved ones. A heart condition doesn't have to be a death sentence. Moderation is the key. Light exercise,

113

proper nutrition, sufficient rest . . . there's no reason to believe I couldn't go on into my nineties."

"Everyone in our family lives into their nineties," Henry said tartly. He was slapping loaves into shape, plunking one after another into a row of greased pans.

I heard a dainty ping.

William removed his pocket watch and flipped the case open. "Time for my pills," he said. "I believe I'll take my medication and then have a brief rest in my room to offset the stress of jet lag. I hope you'll excuse me, Miss Millhone. It's been a pleasure meeting you."

"Nice to meet you, too, William."

We shook hands again. He seemed somewhat invigorated by his lecture on the hazards of fatty foods.

While I put the sandwiches together, Henry put six loaves of bread in the oven. We didn't dare say a word because we could hear William in the bathroom filling his water glass, then returning to his room. We sat down to lunch.

"I think it's safe to say this is going to be a very long two weeks," Henry murmured.

I moved over to the refrigerator and took out two Diet Pepsis, which I brought back to the table. Henry popped both tops and passed one back to me. While we ate, I filled him in on the investigation, in part because he likes hearing about the work I do, and in part because I find it clarifies my thinking when I hear what I have to say.

"What's your feeling about this Barney fellow?" he asked.

I shrugged. "The man's a creep, but then I don't think much of Kenneth Voigt, either. Talk about grim. Fortunately for them, the judicial system doesn't seem to hinge on my personal opinions."

"You think the informant is telling the truth?"

"I'll know a lot more when I find out where he was on May twenty-first," I said.

"Why would he lie? Especially when it's so easy to check? From what you've said, if he was actually in jail, all you have to do is go back and look at his paperwork."

114

"But why would David Barney lie about it when the same possibility applies? Apparently, nobody's thought to verify the date so far—"

"Unless Morley Shine checked it out before he died." Henry imitated the "significant moment" music on a radio drama: "Duh-duh-duh."

I smiled, mouth too full of sandwich to articulate a reply. "Oh, great. That's all I need," I said when I could. "I do my job right and I die, too." I wiped my mouth on a paper napkin and took a sip of Pepsi.

Henry gestured dismissively. "Barney's probably generating some kind of smoke screen."

"I hope that's what it is. If some of this shit checks out, I don't know what I'm going to do."

Famous last words. Before I left, I put in a call to Lieutenant Becker to see if he'd heard from Inmate Records.

"I just got off the phone with them. The guy was right. Curtis McIntyre was being arraigned that day on a burglary charge. He might have passed Barney in the hall on his way to see the magistrate, but he'd have been shackled to the other prisoners. There's no way they could have talked."

"I better find out what's going on here," I said.

"You better do it quick. McIntyre got out of jail this morning at six."

10

I headed back to the office and called Sergeant Hixon, a friend of mine out at the jail. She checked Curtis McIntyre's records and gave me the address he'd provided his last parole officer. Curtis seemed to spend a portion of each year taking advantage of the rent-free accommodations provided by the Santa Teresa County Sheriff's Department, which he probably considered the equivalent of a Hawaiian condominium vacation time-share. When he wasn't enjoying the free meals and volleyball at the local correctional facility, he apparently occupied a room at the Thrifty Motel ("Daily, Weekly, Monthly . . . Kitchens") on upper State Street.

I parked my VW across the road from this establishment, which quick calculation told me was within walking distance of the jail. Curtis didn't even have to spring for a taxi on release. I imagined that his was that one room without a ratty car parked out front. The occupants of the other units boasted Chevies and ten-year-old Cadillacs, vehicles favored by auto insurance defrauders, which is what they might have been. Curtis hadn't been out of jail long enough to engage in any illegal activities. Well, maybe littering, lewd conduct, and public spitting, but nothing *major*.

The Thrifty Motel looked like the sort of "auto court" where Bonnie and Clyde might have holed up. It was L-shaped, built of cinder block, and painted the strange green that yolks turn when they've been hard-boiled too long. There were twelve rooms altogether, each with a tiny porch a little bigger than a doormat. Someone had planted marigolds in matching coffee cans arranged in twos and threes by the front steps. The office at the entrance was dominated by a Coke machine and the front window was obscured by mock-ups of all the credit cards they took.

I was just about to cross the road and verify his presence when I spotted him emerging from the very room I'd mentally assigned him. He looked rested and freshly shaved, wearing jeans, a white T-shirt, and a denim jacket. He was in the process of running a pocket comb through his hair, which was damp from the shower and formed a curly fringe around his ears. He was simultaneously smoking and chewing gum, a refreshingly aromatic combination for the breath. I fired up the VW and followed at a distance.

I kept him in sight as he headed west, passing numerous small businesses: a pizza parlor, a gas station, a U-Haul rental, a home improvement "emporium," and a garden shop. Beyond these, where the road curved around to the left, was a combination bar and grill called the Wander Inn. The door was standing open. Curtis flipped his cigarette toward the pavement and disappeared through the front. I pulled into the gravel parking lot around at the back and left my car in one of ten empty slots. I entered the rear door, passing the rest rooms and the kitchen, where I could see the fry cook shaking the oil from a wire basket piled with golden fries.

The interior of the bar was all polyurethane and beer smell, illuminated by a wide shaft of daylight coming in the front. Already, the cigarette haze gave the room the misty quality of an old photograph. The only colors I could see were the vibrant primary hues of the pinball machine, where a cartoon spacewoman with big conical breasts straddled the earth in a formfitting blue space suit and thigh-high yellow boots. Behind her, a big red dildo-shaped spaceship was just blasting off for the moon.

At the bar, six men turned to look at me, but Curtis wasn't one. I spotted him in a booth, a beer bottle to his lips, Adam's apple thrusting up and down like a piston. He set the empty bottle on the table and paused to produce several noisy burps in succession, like a furious sea lion barking at his mate.

A waitress in a white blouse, black slacks, and crepe-soled deck shoes emerged from the kitchen with a tray of hot food, which she took to his booth. I waited until he'd been served a cheeseburger and a mound of fries, all of which he doctored with liberal doses of salt and ketchup. He piled lettuce, tomato, pickle, and onion on the burger, put the top of the bun back, and mashed it into place. He had to hold it with both hands in order to bite in. I approached the booth and slid into the seat across from him. He expressed as much enthusiasm as he could muster with his mouth full and his lips smeared with ketchup. "Hey, how are you? This is great! Glad to see you. I don't believe this. How'd you know I'd be here?" He swallowed his cheekful of burger and wiped the bottom half of his face with a paper napkin. I handed him a second napkin from the dispenser and watched him as he cleaned up his fingers, after which he insisted on shaking hands with me. I didn't see a polite way to refuse, though I knew my palm would smell like onions for an hour afterward.

I folded my arms, leaning on my elbows, to discourage any further contact. "Curtis, we have to talk."

"I got time. You want a beer? Come on and let me buy you one."

Without waiting for assent, he signaled the bartender by holding up his beer bottle and two fingers. "You want some lunch, too? Have some lunch," he said.

"I just ate."

"Well, have some fries. Help yourself. How'd you know I was out? Last time you seen me I'se in jail. You look great."

"Thanks. So do you. That was yesterday," I pointed out.

Curtis popped up and crossed to the bar to get the beers. While he was gone, I ate a couple of his french fries. They were wedge cut, with the skins on, and perfectly cooked. He returned to the booth with the beers and I saw him make a move as if to slide in on my side.

"No way," I said. He was acting like I was his date and I could see the guys at the bar begin to eye us with speculation.

I refused to give him room and he was forced to sit down again where he'd been. He handed me a beer and grinned at me happily. Curtis seemed to think that along with all the beer, cigarettes, and saturated fats, he might just get lucky and get laid this afternoon. He put his chin in his fist and tried his soulful, puppy-dog gaze on me. "You're not gonna be mean to me, now, are you, hon?"

"Finish your lunch, Curtis, and don't give me any more of that hangdog look. It just makes me want to hit you with a rolled-up newspaper."

"Damn, you're cute," he said. Love had apparently diminished his appetite. He pushed aside his plate and lit a cigarette, offering me a drag, like we were postcoital.

"I'm not cute at all. I'm a very cranky person. Now could we get down to business? I'm having a little problem with the story you told me."

He frowned to show he was serious. "How come?"

"You said you sat in on David Barney's trial—"

"Not the whole thing. I told you that. Crime might be exciting, but the law's a bore, right?"

"You said you talked to David Barney as he left court just after he'd been acquitted."

"I said that?"

"Yes, you did."

"Don't remember that part. What's the problem?"

"The problem is you were in jail at the time, waiting to be arraigned on a burglary charge."

"Nooo," he said with disbelief. "*I* was?"

"Yes, you were."

"Well, I'm burnt. You got me there. I forgot all about that. I guess I got my dates wrong, but the rest of it is gospel." He held his hand up as if he were taking an oath. "Swear to God."

"Cut the horseshit, Curtis, and tell me what's going on here. You didn't talk to him. You're lying through your teeth."

"Now wait. Just wait. I did talk to him. It just wasn't where I said."

"Where then?"

"At his house."

"You went to his *house*? That's baloney. When was this?"

"I don't know. Couple weeks after his trial, I guess."

"I thought you were still in jail."

"Naw, I'se out by then with time served and all that. My attorney cut a deal. I, like, copped to the lesser plea."

"Forget the jargon and tell me how you ended up at David Barney's house. Did you call him or did he call you?"

"I don't remember."

"You don't *remember*?" I said in a scathing tone of skepticism. I was being rude, but Curtis didn't seem to notice. He was probably accustomed to being addressed that way by all the hard-nosed prosecuting attorneys he'd faced in his short, illustrious career.

"I called him."

"How'd you get his telephone number?"

"Called Information."

"What made you think to get in touch with him?"

"It seemed like to me he wouldn't have many friends. I been there myself. Get in trouble with the law, a lot of people won't fool with you much after that. It's like they don't want to hang out with a jailbird."

"So you thought he needed a best friend and you were going to be it. What's the rest of it?"

His response was sheepish and he had the good grace to squirm. "Well, now, I knew where he lived—out in Horton Ravine—so I figured he was good for a meal or a couple drinks. We'd been cellmates and all and I thought he'd at least be polite."

"You went to borrow money," I said.

"You might put it that way."

So far, it was the only thing he'd said that rang true.

"I'd just got out. I didn't have no funds to speak of and this guy had lots. He's loaded—"

"Skip that. I believe you. Describe the house."

"He's living in the dead wife's house by then—up a hill, Spanish, with this courtyard and a terrace with this big black-bottom swimming pool—"

"Got it. Go on."

"I knock on the door. He's there and I say I was in the area and stopped by to congratulate him on gettin' off a murder rap. So he asks me in and we have a couple drinks—"

"What'd you drink?"

"He had some kind of pussy drink, vodka tonic with a twist. I had bourbon straight up with a water back. It was classy bourbon, too."

"So you're having drinks . . ."

"That's right. We're having these drinks and he's got this little old gal in the kitchen making up a tray of snacks. That green stuff. Guacamole and salsa and these triangle-shape chips that're gray. I said, 'What the hell are them?' and he said, 'They're blue corn tortilla chips.' Looked gray if you asked me. We set there and drank and carried on until almost midnight."

"What about dinner?"

"Wasn't any dinner. Just snacks is all, which is how we got so loaded."

"And then what?"

"And that's when he said what he said, about he done her."

"What'd he say exactly?"

"Said he knocked on the door. She come downstairs and flipped on the porch light. He waited until he seen her eye block the light in the little peephole? Then he fired away. Boom!"

"Why didn't you tell me this story to begin with?"

"It didn't look right," he said righteously. "I mean, I went up there to ask if he'd lend me some money. I didn't want it to seem like I was mad he turned me down. Nobody'd believe me if I told the story that way. Besides, he was nice about it and I didn't want to look like a dick. Pardon my French."

"Why would he admit he killed her?"

"Why not? Once he's acquitted, he can't be retried."

"Not in criminal court."

"Shoot. He's not going to worry about a damn civil suit."

"And you're prepared to go into court with this?"

"I don't mind."

"You will testify under oath," I said, trying to make sure he understood what this was about.

"Sure. Only . . . you know."

"Only you know what?"

"I'd like a little something back," he said.

"As in what?"

"Well, fair is fair."

"Nobody's going to pay you money."

"I know that. I never said money."

"Then what?"

"I'd like to see a little time off my parole, something like that."

"Curtis, nobody's going to make a deal with you. I have no authority whatsoever to do that."

"I never said make a deal, but I could use some consideration."

I looked at him long and earnestly. Why didn't I believe what he was telling me? Because he looked like a man who wouldn't know the truth if it jumped up and bit him. I don't know what made me blurt out the next question. "Curtis, have you ever been convicted of perjury?"

"Perjury?"

"Goddamn it! You know what perjury is. Just answer the question and let's get on with this."

He scratched at his chin, his gaze not quite meeting mine. "I never been *convicted*."

"Oh, hell," I said.

I got up out of the booth and walked away from him, heading for the rear of the restaurant. Behind me, I could hear him spring to his feet. I glanced back in time to see him fling some bills on the table as he hurried after me. I stepped out into the parking lot, nearly recoiling from the harsh sunlight on the white gravel.

"Hey! Now, wait up! I'm telling you the truth."

He grabbed at me and I pulled my arm out of reach. "You're going to look like crap on the stand," I said, without breaking stride. "You've got a record a mile long, including charges of perjury—"

"Not 'charges.' Just the one. Well, two, if you count that other business."

"I don't want to hear it. You've already changed your story once. You'll change it again the next time somebody asks. Barney's attorney is going to tear you apart."

"Well, I don't see why you have to take that attitude," he

said. "Just because I told one lie doesn't mean I can't tell the truth."

"You don't even know the *difference*, Curtis. That's what worries me."

"I do know."

I unlocked my car door and opened it, rolling down the window to break the air lock when I shut it. I got in the front seat and slammed the door smartly, nearly catching his hand on the doorpost where he was resting it. I reached over and flipped open the glove compartment. I got out one of my business cards and thrust it through the window at him. "Give me a call when you decide to tell the truth."

I started the car and pulled away from him, flinging up dust and gravel in my wake.

I drove back to the office with the radio blasting. It was 3:35 and, of course, parking was at a premium. It didn't occur to me that with Lonnie driving up to Santa Maria, his space would be free. I circled the area, increasing one block with each round, trying to snag a spot within reasonable walking distance of the office. Finally, I found a semiquestionable slot, with my rear bumper hanging out into somebody's driveway. It was an invitation for a parking ticket, but maybe all the meter maids had gone home by then.

I spent the rest of the afternoon doing busywork. My appointment with Laura Barney was coming up within the hour, but in truth, I was marking time until I had a chance to talk to Lonnie, who Ida Ruth kept assuring me was temporarily out of service. I found myself loitering in the vicinity of her desk, hoping I'd be nearby if he should happen to call in. "He never calls when he's working," she said patiently.

"Don't you ever call him?"

"Not if I'm smart. He gets annoyed when I do."

"Don't you think he'd want to hear about it if his prime witness turned sour?"

"What does he care? That's this case. He's tied up doing

something else. I've worked for him six years and I know what he's like. I can leave a message, but he'll just ignore it until this trial is over with."

"What am I supposed to do till he gets back? I can't afford to waste time and I hate spinning my wheels."

"Do whatever you want. You're not going to get anything from him until nine o'clock Monday morning."

I glanced at my watch. This was still Wednesday. It was 4:05. "I've got an appointment near St. Terry's in half an hour. After that, I think I'll go home and clean house," I said.

"What's with the cleaning? That doesn't sound like you."

"I spring clean every three months. It's a ritual I learned from my aunt. Beat all the throw rugs. Line-dry the sheets. . . ."

She looked at me with disgust. "Why don't you go on a hike up in Los Padres?"

"I don't hang out in nature if I can help it, Ida Ruth. There are ticks up in the mountains as big as water bugs. Get one of those on your ankle, it'd suck all your blood out. Plus, you'd probably be afflicted with a pustular disease."

She laughed, gesturing dismissively.

I dispensed with a few miscellaneous matters on my desk and locked my office in haste. I was curious about David Barney's ex-wife, but somehow I didn't imagine she'd enlighten me much. I went downstairs and hoofed it the three and a half blocks to my car. Happily, I didn't have a ticket sitting on my windshield. Unhappily, I turned the key in the ignition and the car refused to start. I could get it to make lots of those industrious grinding noises, but the engine wouldn't turn over.

I got out and went around to the rear, where I opened the hood. I stared at the engine like I knew what I was looking at. The only car part I can identify by name is the fan belt. It looked fine. I could see that some little doodads had come unhooked from the round thing. I said, "Oh." I stuck 'em back. I was just getting in the front seat when a car pulled halfway into the drive. I tried the engine and it fired up.

"Can I help?" The guy driving had leaned across the front seat and rolled the window down on the passenger side.

"No, thanks. I'm fine. Am I blocking your drive?"

"No trouble. There's room enough. What was it, your battery? You want me to take a look?"

What was this? The engine was running. I didn't need any help. "Thanks, but I've already got things under control," I said. To demonstrate my point, I revved the engine and shifted into neutral, temporarily perplexed about which way to go. I couldn't pull forward because of the car parked in front of me. I couldn't back up because his car was blocking my rear.

He turned his engine off and got out. I left mine rumbling, wondering if I had time to roll up my window without seeming rude. He looked harmless enough, though his face was familiar. He was a nice-looking man, in his late forties with light brown wavy hair graying at the temples. He had a straight nose and a strong chin. Short-sleeved T-shirt, chinos, deck shoes without socks.

"You live in the neighborhood?" he asked pleasantly.

I knew this guy. I could feel my smile fade. I said, "You're David Barney."

He braced his arms on the car and leaned toward the window. Subtly, I could feel the man invading my turf, though his manner remained benign. "Look, I know this is inappropriate. I know I'm way out of line here, but if I can just have five minutes, I swear I won't bother you again."

I studied him briefly while I consulted my internal warning system. No bells, no whistles, no warning signs. While the man had annoyed me on the telephone, "up close and personal" he seemed like ordinary folk. It was broad daylight, a pleasant middle-class neighborhood. He didn't appear to be armed. What was he going to do, gun me down in the streets with his trial a month away? At this point, I had no idea where my investigation was going. Maybe he'd provide some inspiration for a change. I thought about the professional implications of the conversation. According to the State Bar Rules of Court, an attorney is not permitted to communicate directly with the "represented party." A private investigator isn't limited by the same stringent code.

"Five minutes," I said. "I have to be somewhere after that." I didn't tell him the appointment was with his ex-wife. I turned the engine off and remained in my car with the window rolled down halfway.

He closed his eyes, letting out a big breath. "Thank you," he said. "I really didn't think you'd do this. I don't even know where to begin," he said. "Let me admit to something right up front. I pulled your distributor caps. It was a sneaky thing to do and I apologize. I just didn't think you'd agree to talk to me otherwise."

"You got that right," I said.

He looked off down the street and then he shook his head. "Did you ever lose your credibility? It's the most amazing phenomenon. You know, you live all your life being an upright citizen, obeying the law, paying taxes, paying your bills on time. Suddenly, none of that counts and anything you say can be held against you. It's too weird. . . ."

I tuned him out briefly, reminded of a time, not that long ago, when my own credibility went south and I was suspected of taking bribes by the very company that had trusted me with its business for six years.

". . . really thought it was over. I thought I'd come through the worst of it when I was acquitted on the criminal charges. I just got my life back and now I'm being sued for everything I own. I live like a leper. I'm shunned. . . ." He straightened up. "Oh, hell, let's not even get into that," he said. "I'm not trying to generate sympathy—"

"What are you trying to do?"

"Appeal to your sense of fair play. This guy McIntyre, the informant—"

"Where'd you get that name?"

"My attorney took his deposition. I was floored when I heard what he had to say."

"I'm not at liberty to discuss this, Mr. Barney. I hope you understand that."

"I know that. I'm not asking. I just beg you to consider. Even if he'd actually been in the courthouse when the verdict came down, why would I say such a thing to him? I'd have to be nuts. Have you met . . . what's his name, Curtis? I was in a cell with the man less than twenty-four hours. The guy's a schmuck. He comes up to me on acquittal and I confess to murder? The story's crazy. He's an idiot. You can't believe that."

I was feeling oddly protective of Curtis. There was no way I was going to tell Barney the informant had changed his account. Curtis's testimony might still prove useful if we could ever figure out what the truth was. I didn't intend to discuss the details of his statement, however shaky it might appear. "This isn't such a hot idea," I said.

Barney went on, "Just think about it, please. Does he strike you as the type I'd confide my darkest secrets to? This is a frame-up. Somebody paid him to say that—"

"Get to the point. The talk about a frame-up is horseshit. I don't want to hear it."

"Okay, okay. I understand where you're coming from. That wasn't my intention anyway," he said. "When we spoke on the phone, I mentioned the business about this guy Shine. I was thrown by his death. It really shook me, I can tell you. I know you didn't take me seriously at the time, but I'm telling the truth. I talked to him last week and told him the same stuff I'm telling you. He said he'd check into a couple of matters. I thought maybe the guy was going to give me a break. When I heard he was dead, it scared the hell out of me. I feel like I'm playing chess with an invisible opponent and he just made a move. I'm getting boxed in here and I don't see a way out."

"Wait a minute. Did you think Morley Shine would do something your own attorney couldn't manage?"

"Hiring Foss on this one was a big mistake. Civil work doesn't interest him. Maybe he's burned out or maybe he's just tired of representing me. He's strictly painting by the numbers, doing what's expected, as far as I can see. He's got some investigator on it—one of those guys who generates a lot of paper, but doesn't inspire much confidence."

"So why don't you fire him?"

"Because they'll claim all I'm doing is impeding due process. Besides, I've got no money left. What little I have goes to pay my attorney, plus the upkeep on the house. I don't know what Kenneth Voigt thinks he's going to get out of the deal even if he makes this thing stick."

"I'm not going to argue the merits of the case. This is pointless, Mr. Barney. I understand you have problems—"

"Hey, you're right. I didn't mean to get off on that stuff. Here's the point: This case goes into court, all it's going to do is make both these attorneys rich. But Voigt's not going to back off. The guy's after my blood, so there's no way he'll agree to walk off with a handshake and a check for big bucks, even if I had it. But I'll tell you one thing—and here's what I do have—I've got an alibi."

"Really," I said, my voice flat with disbelief.

"Yes, really," he said. "It's not airtight, but it's pretty solid."

"Why didn't it come up during the criminal trial? I've read the transcripts. I don't remember any mention of an alibi."

"Well, you better go back and read the transcripts again because the testimony's right there. Guy named Angeloni. He put me miles from the crime scene."

"And you never testified in your behalf?"

He shook his head. "Foss wouldn't let me. He didn't want the prosecution to get a crack at me and it turned out he played it smart. He said it'd be 'counterproductive' if I took the stand. Hell, maybe he thought I'd alienate the jury if I got up there."

"Why tell me about it?"

"To see if I can put a stop to this before it goes to trial. The meter's ticking. Time is short. I figure my only chance is to make sure Lonnie Kingman knows the cards he's got out against him. Maybe he can talk to Voigt and get him to drop his suit."

"Have Herb Foss talk to Lonnie! That's what attorneys are supposed to do."

"I've asked him to do that. The guy is jerkin' me around. I finally decided it's time to circumvent the man."

"So you're tipping me off to your own attorney's *defense?*"

"That's right."

"Are you suicidal?"

"I told you I'm desperate. I can't go through this again. You don't have to take my word for it. Check the facts yourself," he said. "Now, do you want to hear me out or not?"

What I wanted was to bang my forehead against the steering wheel till it bled. Maybe the self-inflicted pain would help me clear my thought processes. Actually, I have to confess I was hooked. If nothing else, knowing Herb Foss's strategy would give Lonnie a big advantage, wouldn't it? "Jesus, all right. What's the story?" I said.

11

"Look, I know people don't believe I was out jogging the night Isabelle was killed, but I can tell you where I was. At one-forty, I was at the southbound off-ramp at San Vicente and the One-oh-one, which is probably eight miles from the house. If Iz was killed between one and two, there's no way I could have done it and still ended up at that intersection when I did. I mean, I've been running for years and I'm in pretty fair shape, but I'm not *that* good."

"How can you be so sure of the time?"

"I was running for time. That's how I train. And I'll tell you who else was there: Tippy Parsons, Rhe's daughter, driving a little pickup, and she was very upset. She came barreling down the off-ramp and turned left on San Vicente."

"Did she see you?"

"She nearly ran me down! I'm not sure she realized it, but she nearly knocked me ass over teakettle coming off the exit. I looked at my watch because I knew my times would be screwed up and it pissed me off."

"Did *anyone* see you?"

"Sure. Some guy working on a busted water main. They had a crew out there. You probably don't remember, but we had some heavy rainstorms over Christmas that year. With the ground saturated, the soil was shifting and those old pipes were disintegrating everyplace."

"You said the alibi wasn't airtight. What's that supposed to mean?"

He smiled slightly. "If you're dead or in federal custody, *that's* airtight. A hotshoe like Kingman can always find a way to twist facts. All I'm saying is, I was miles away and I've got a witness. And he's an honest, hardworking guy, not some piece of shit like what's-his-face, McIntyre."

"What about Tippy? She's never said a word about this as far as I know. Why didn't you confront her?"

"What the hell for? I figured if she'd seen me, she'd have spoken up by now. And even if she spotted me, it's my word against hers. She was sixteen years old and hysterical about something. She might have just broken up with her boyfriend, or her cat might have died. The bottom line is, I was miles from the house when Isabelle was killed. I didn't even know what had happened until an hour later when I jogged past the house again. All the cop cars were there, the place was blazing with lights—"

"What about the repair crew? Will they support your claim?"

"I don't see why not. The guy took the stand before. Fellow by the name of Angeloni. He's on the list of witnesses, probably right up at the top. He saw me for sure and I know he saw her truck. She scared me so bad I had to sit on the curb and get my heart back to normal. It took me five or six minutes until I was okay again. By then, I said to hell with it and headed on home."

"And you told the cops this?"

"Go read the report. Cops figured me for the murder so they didn't pursue it."

I was silent for a moment, wondering what to make of it. Two days ago, his claims would have seemed preposterous. Now I wasn't sure. "I'll pass this on to Lonnie when I talk to him. That's the best I can do." Jesus, was I going to have to go out and corroborate his alibi?

He started to say more and then seemed to think better of it. "Fine. You do that. That's really all I'm asking. I appreciate your time," he said. His eyes met mine briefly. "I thank you for this."

"It's all right," I said.

He returned to his car. I watched him in the rearview mirror while he started the engine and backed out of the drive. He pulled away and I listened to the sound of his transmission as he shifted gears. Curious story. Something rang a bell, but I couldn't think what it was. Was Tippy Parsons really at the intersection? It seemed as if there must be a way to find out. I remembered reading about the storm coming through about that time.

I started the VW and pulled away from the curb, heading for the appointment with his ex-wife.

The Santa Teresa Medical Clinic, where Laura Barney worked, was a small wood-frame structure in the shadow of St. Terry's Hospital, which was two doors away. The exterior was plain—ever so faintly shabby—the interior pleasant, but leaning toward the low-budget. The chairs in the waiting room had molded blue plastic seats and metal legs linked together in units of six. The walls were yellow, the floors a marbleized vinyl tile, tan with white streaks. There was a wide wooden counter at one end of the room. On the far side, through the wide archway, I could see four desks, straight-backed office chairs, telephones, typewriters . . . nothing high-tech, streamlined, or color-coded. The rear wall was lined with tan metal file cabinets. I gathered, from the scattering of toddlers, pregnant women, and wailing infants, that this was a combination maternity and well-baby facility. It was almost closing time and the patients still waiting had probably been backed up for an hour. Children's toys and ripped magazines were strewn across the floor.

I moved to the counter, spotting Laura Barney by her name tag, which read "L. Barney, R.N." She wore a white pants-suit uniform and white crepe-soled shoes. I judged her to be somewhere in her early forties. She had reached an age where she could still achieve the same fresh good looks she'd enjoyed ten years earlier—it just took a lot more makeup and the effect probably wore off after an hour or two. At this time of day, the layers of foundation and loose powder had become nearly translucent, showing skin underneath that was reddened from cigarette smoke. She looked like a woman who'd been forced to go out into the workplace and wasn't at all happy with the necessity.

She was currently in the process of instructing a new employee, probably the same young girl I'd spoken to on the phone. Laura was counting out money like a bank teller, flicking bills through her fingers almost faster than the eye could see, turning each bill so it was right side up. If she came across a denomination that was out of place, she would slide it into the proper sequence. "Every bill should face in the same direction and they should be arranged with the smallest bills in front. Ones, fives, tens, twenties," she was saying. "That way you'll never inadvertently make change with a ten-dollar bill when you mean to use a one. Look at this. . . ." She fanned them out like a magician performing a card trick. I almost expected her to say, "Pick a bill, any bill. . . ." Instead, she said, "Are you listening?"

"Yes, ma'am." The young woman might have been nineteen, fifteen pounds overweight, with dark curly hair, flushed cheeks, and dark eyes glinting with suppressed tears.

L. Barney, R.N., opened the cash drawer again and removed an unruly wad of bills, which she held out silently. The young clerk took them. Self-consciously, she began to sort through the handful of bills, turning one upright in an awkward imitation of Laura Barney's expertise. Several denominations were out of sequence and she held the wad against her chest while she tried to straighten them out, dropping two fives in an attempt to get them in the correct order. She stammered an apology, stooping quickly to retrieve them. Laura Barney watched her with a slight smile, eyes nearly glittering with the urge to snatch the money back and do it for her. She must have itched to demonstrate the smooth, seamless effort with which an experienced cashier could perform so elementary a task. The absorption with which she watched seemed to make the girl more clumsy.

Her own manner was brisk, efficient. She'd picked up a ballpoint pen, which she was clicking impatiently. She wasn't going to waste a lot of time and sympathy. Get 'em in, get 'em out. Payment is expected at the time services are rendered. Her smile was pleasant but fixed and probably ran only for the few seconds necessary to register the chill underneath. If you tried to complain later to the clinic doctor you'd be hard-pressed to put your finger on her failings. I'd dealt with people like her before. She was all form and no content, a stickler for detail, an avid enforcer of the rules and regulations. She was the kind of nurse who assured you your tetanus shot would feel like a little bee bite when in truth it'd raise a knot on your arm the size of a doorknob.

She looked up at me and the fixed smile returned. "Yes?"

"I'm Kinsey Millhone," I said. I half expected her to hand me a clipboard with a medical history to be completed.

"Just a moment, please," she said. Her manner suggested that I'd made an unreasonable demand for immediate service. She finished dealing with the clerk and then called two patients in rapid succession. "Mrs. Gonzales? Mrs. Russo?"

Two women rose from their respective chairs. One carried a swaddled infant, the other had a toddler affixed to one hip. Both had pre-school-age children in addition. Laura Barney held open the wooden gate that separated the waiting area from the corridor leading back to examining rooms. The two women and accompanying children passed in front of her, thus emptying the waiting room. She continued to hold the gate open. "You want to come with me?"

"Oh, sure."

She picked up two charts, like menus, and herded us into the rear, issuing instructions in rapid Spanish. Once everyone had been ushered into examining rooms, she continued on down the hall, crepe soles squeaking on the tile floor. The room she showed me into was a nine-by-nine generic office with one window, a scarred wooden desk, two chairs, and an intercom, the kind of setting where you're apt to receive the bad news about the lab tests they just ran. She shut the door and motioned to one chair while she cranked open the window and took a seat herself. She removed a pack of Virginia Slims and a pack of matches from her uniform pocket and lit a cigarette. She glanced surreptitiously at her watch, while pretending to adjust the band. "You came to ask about David. What exactly did you want to know?"

"I take it you're not on friendly terms with him."

"I get along with him fine. I hardly see the man."

"You also testified at his murder trial, didn't you?"

"Generally, I'm used to demonstrate what an unscrupulous bastard he is. You haven't read the transcripts?"

"I'm still in the process of reviewing all the paperwork. I was hired Sunday night. I've got a lot of ground to cover yet. It would be helpful if you could fill in some of the facts from your perspective."

"The facts. Well, let's see now. I met David at a party . . .

well, it was nine years ago this month. How's that for touching? I fell in love with him and we were married six weeks later. We'd been married about two years when he was offered a position with Peter Weidmann's firm. Of course, we were thrilled."

I interrupted. "How did that come to pass?"

"Through a friend of a friend. We were living in Los Angeles, very interested in getting out. David heard Peter had an opening so he applied. We'd been in Santa Teresa all of two months when Isabelle came on board. David didn't even like her. I thought she was very bright and very talented. I was the one who insisted we befriend her. After all, she was the light of Peter's eye. He was her mentor, in effect. It wasn't in David's best interest to be competitive when she was assigned to work on all the high-visibility projects. I encouraged David to cultivate her both socially and professionally so I guess you could say I engineered their entire relationship."

"How did you find out about their affair?"

"Simone let something slip. I forget now what it was, but suddenly everything made sense. I knew David had been distant. It was common knowledge that Isabelle and Kenneth were having problems. It took me a while to put two and two together, that's all. None so blind, et cetera. I confronted him, like a fool. I wish now I'd kept my mouth shut."

"Why is that?"

"I forced his hand. Their relationship didn't last. If I'd had the presence of mind to ignore what was happening, the affair might have blown over."

"Do you think he killed her?"

"It had to be someone who knew her pretty well." The intercom buzzed abruptly. She depressed the button. "Yes, Doctor."

The doctor sounded like he was calling from a public telephone booth. "We're going to do a pelvic on Mrs. Russo. Could you come in?"

She said "Yes, sir" to him and then to me, "I have to go. Anything else you want is going to have to wait."

She held the door open for me and I passed through.

Within seconds she was gone and I was left to find my own way out. I went back to my car and sat there for a minute while I dug my wallet from the depths of my leather shoulder bag. I removed all the paper money and carefully rearranged the bills, turning them so they all faced in the same direction, ones in front, a twenty bringing up the rear.

I drove back to the office and parked my car in Lonnie's slot, taking the stairs two at a time up to the third floor. If Ida Ruth was surprised to see me back, she kept it to herself. I unlocked my office and started going through the files, which were somewhat better organized, but still loosely arranged on every available surface. I found the file I was looking for and moved over to the desk, where I clicked on the light and settled down in my swivel chair.

What I pulled out were the photocopies of the six-year-old newspapers I'd pulled in preparation for canvassing the Barneys' neighbors. Sure enough, for the days in question there was ample reference to the heavy rainfall over most of California. There was also mention of emergency crews from the public works department working overtime to repair the rash of burst water pipes. The same weather pattern had spawned a minor crime spree—felons running amok, apparently stimulated by the shift in atmospheric conditions. I flipped through the pages, scanning item after item. I wasn't really sure what I was looking for . . . a link, some sense of connection to the past.

The questions were obvious. If Tippy Parsons could support David Barney's alibi, why hadn't she stepped forward with the information years ago? Of course, she might not have been there. He might have seen someone else or he might have manufactured her presence to suit his own purposes. If she *was* there, she might not have seen him—there was always that chance—but placing her at the scene would certainly lend credibility to his claims. And what about the guy Barney claimed was at the scene? Where was he in all this?

I reached for the telephone and dialed Rhe Parsons, hoping to catch her in her studio. The number rang four times, five, six. On the seventh ring she answered, sounding breathless and out of sorts. "Yes?"

"Rhe, this is Kinsey Millhone. Sorry to disturb you. It sounds like I caught you right in the middle of your work again."

"Oh, hi. Don't worry about it. It's my own fault, I guess. I should get a portable telephone and keep it out in the studio. Sorry for all the heavy breathing. I'm really out of shape. How are you?"

"I'm fine, thanks. Is Tippy there by any chance?"

"No. She works until six tonight. Santa Teresa Shellfish. Is there something I could help you with?"

"Maybe so," I said. "I was wondering where she was the night Isabelle was killed."

"She was home, I'm sure. Why?"

"Well, it's probably nothing, but somebody thought they saw her driving around in a pickup."

"A pickup? Tippy never had a pickup."

"It must be a mistake then. Was she with you when the police called?"

"You mean, about Isabelle's death?" There was a moment of hesitation, which I should have taken as a warning, but I was so intent on the question, I forgot I was dealing with a m-o-t-h-e-r. "She was living with her father during that period," she said with care.

"That's right. So you said. I remember that now. Did *he* have a truck?"

Dead silence. Then, "You know, I really resent the implications here."

"What implications? I'm just asking for information."

"Your questions sound very pointed. I hope you don't mean to suggest she had anything whatsoever to do with what happened to Iz."

"Rhe, don't be silly. I'd never suggest such a thing. I'm trying to disconfirm a report. That's all it is."

"What report?"

"Look, it's probably nothing and I'd rather not get into it. I can talk to Tippy later. I should have done that in the first place."

"Kinsey, if somebody's making some claim about my daughter, I'm entitled to know. Who said she was out? That's an outrageous accusation."

"*Accusation?* Wait a minute. It's hardly an accusation to say she was driving around in a pickup truck."

"Who told you such a thing?"

"Rhe, I'm really not at liberty to divulge my sources. I'm working for Lonnie Kingman and that information is privileged. . . ." This was not true, but it sounded good. Lawyer-client privilege didn't extend to me and had nothing to do with any witnesses I might approach. I could hear her try to get a grip on her temper.

"I'd appreciate it if you'd tell me what's going on. I promise I won't ask about your sources, *if* that's really an issue."

I debated briefly and decided there was no reason to withhold the information itself. "Someone claims to have seen her out that night. I'm not saying it has any bearing on Isabelle's death, but it struck me as odd that she's never spoken up. I thought she might have mentioned something to you."

Rhe's tone was flat. "She's never spoken up because she wasn't out."

"Great. That's all I need to know."

"Even if she was, it's no business of yours."

I cupped a mental hand behind my mental ear. " 'Even if she was' meaning what?" I said.

"Nothing. It's a turn of phrase."

"Would you ask her to call me?"

"I'm not going to ask her to call you!"

"Do what you like, Rhe. I'm sorry for the interruption." I banged down the receiver, feeling my face suffuse with heat. What was her problem? I made a note about a subpoena for Tippy Parsons if there wasn't one already. I hadn't attached that much credence to Barney's claim until I heard Rhe's reaction.

I buzzed Ruth on the intercom and asked her to order me a complete new set of transcripts from the criminal trial. Then I slouched down in my swivel chair, my feet up on the desk, fingers laced in front of me, as I thought about developments. No doubt about it, things were looking bad. Between Morley's sloppy records and his untimely death, we had a mess on our hands. Lonnie's prime witness suddenly seemed unreliable and now it looked as though the defendant actually had an alibi. Lonnie wasn't going to like this. It was better that he hear it now than on the first day of the trial when Herb Foss made his opening remarks to the jury, but it still wasn't going to sit well. He was going to get home Friday night and spend a lovely weekend with his wife. He'd been married for eight months to a *kenpo* karate instructor whom he had successfully defended against charges of felonious assault. I'm still trying to find out what Maria actually did, but all Lonnie would tell me is that the court case stemmed from a rape attempt by a man now retired from active life. I pulled my wandering thoughts back to the situation at hand. When Lonnie ambled into the office Monday morning, the dog-doo would start flying. Some of it was bound to land on me.

I went back through the list of prospective witnesses Lonnie'd acquired on discovery. A William Angeloni was listed, though his deposition hadn't been taken. I made a note of his address, checked the telephone book, and made a note of his number. I picked up the receiver and then set it down again. Better to do this in person so I could see what he looked like. Maybe he was some kind of sleazeball David Barney'd hired to lie for him. I shoved some papers in my briefcase and headed out again.

The address was over on the west side, the house a small stucco bungalow undergoing an extensive remodeling. The roof had been peeled back and the walls on one side had been ripped out. Big sheets of cloudy plastic were nailed across the studs, protecting whatever portions of the house remained untouched. Lumber and cinder block were neatly stacked to one side. There was a big dark blue Dumpster sitting in the drive, filled with broken drywall and ancient two-by-fours sporting bent and rusty nails. It looked as if the laborers had all left for the day, but there was a guy standing in the yard with a beer can in one hand. I parked my car across the street and got out, crossing to the borders of his now-scruffy lawn. "I'm looking for Bill Angeloni. Is that you, by any chance?"

"That's me," he said. He was in his midthirties, extraordinarily good-looking—dark, straight hair worn slightly long and brushed to one side, dark brows, dark eyes, strong nose, dimples, and a manly chin that probably took six swipes of a razor to shave properly. He wore jeans, muddy work boots, and a blue denim shirt with the sleeves rolled up. The hair on his forearms was dark and silky. He smelled of damp soil and metal. He looked like an actor who'd star in some movie about a doomed love affair between an heiress and a park ranger. I thought it was probably inappropriate to fling myself against him and bury my nose in his chest.

"Kinsey Millhone," I said, introducing myself. We shook hands briefly and then I told him who I worked for. "I just had a chat with David Barney and he mentioned your name."

Angeloni shook his head. "I can't believe that poor son of a bitch has to go to court again." He finished his beer, crushed the can, and fired a jump shot, tossing the empty container in the Dumpster with a plunking sound. He said "Two points" and made crowd sounds with his fist against his mouth. He had a nice smile, unpretentious.

"This time it's wrongful death," I said.

"Jesus. What about double jeopardy? Isn't that what it's called? I thought you couldn't be tried twice."

"That applies to criminal. This is civil."

"I'm glad I'm not him. You want a beer? I just got home from work and I always suck down a few. This place is a mess. You better watch out for loose nails."

"Sure, I'll have one," I said and followed him toward the kitchen, which I could see clearly through the plastic. His butt was cute, too. "How long has this been going on?"

"The remodel? About a month. We're adding a big family room and a couple bedrooms for the kids."

Scratch the wedding, I thought as we pushed into the kitchen.

He took two beers from a six-pack and popped the tops on both. "I gotta fire up the barbecue before Julianna gets home with the little rug rats in tow. My turn to cook," he said, dimpling.

"How many kids?"

He held up one hand and wiggled his fingers.

"Five?"

"Plus one in the hatch. They're all boys. We're looking for a little girl this time."

"Are you still with the water department?"

"Ten years in May," he said. "You're a private investigator? What's that like?"

I talked idly about my work while he dumped the ashes from the Weber grill. He had a flat electrical starter that he plugged into an extension cord, mounding on charcoal briquettes, which he rearranged with a set of long metal pincers. I knew I should press for information. All I needed was confirmation of David Barney's whereabouts the night of the murder—the possible identification of Tippy Parsons, too—

but there was something hypnotic about all the homely activity. I'd never been with a man who'd cared enough to fire up a Weber grill on my behalf. Lucky Julianna.

"Could you tell me about the night you saw David Barney?"

"There wasn't much to it. We were out digging up the street, trying to find a broken pipe. It had been pouring for days, but it wasn't raining right then. I heard a thump and looked up to see this guy in a running suit sprawled in the street. A pickup was turning left onto San Vicente and I guess it nearly nailed him. He picked himself off the pavement, limped over to where we were, and sat down on the curb. He was shaken, but not hurt. Mostly mad, you know how it is. We offered to call the paramedics, but he wouldn't hear of it. He sat till he caught his breath and then he took off again, kind of slow and limping. The whole business lasted maybe ten minutes or so."

"Did you see the driver of the truck?"

"Not really. It was some young girl, but I didn't get a clear look at her face."

"What about the license number? Did you catch that?"

He shrugged apologetically. "I never even thought to look. The truck was white. I know that."

"You remember the make?"

"Ford or Chevy, I'd guess. American, at any rate."

"How'd you find out who David Barney was? Did he introduce himself?"

"Not at the time. He got in touch with us later."

"How'd he know who you were?"

"He tracked us down through the department. Me and my buddy James. He knew the date, time, and location so it wasn't that tough."

"Can James confirm this?"

"Sure. We both talked to the guy."

"At the time Mr. Barney got in touch with you, did you know about his wife's murder?"

"I'd been reading about it in the paper. I didn't realize the connection until he told us who he was. Jesus, that was nasty. Did you hear about that?"

"That's why I'm here. The guy still swears he didn't do it."

"Well, I don't see how he could. He was miles away."

"You remember the time?"

"About one forty-five. Might have been a little earlier, but I know it wasn't later because I looked at my watch just as he was taking off."

"Didn't it seem odd to see someone out jogging at one-thirty in the morning?"

"Not a bit. I'd seen him jog along the same path the night before. Emergency work you see all kinds of things."

"You testified at the murder trial, didn't you?"

"Sure."

"What about this round? Will you testify again?"

"Absolutely. Glad to do it. The poor guy needs a break."

I thought back through Barney's story, trying to remember what he'd told me. "What about the cops? Did the police ever interview you?"

"Some homicide detective called and I told him everything I knew. He thanked me and that's the last I ever heard from him. I tell you one thing—they didn't like him. They had him tried and convicted before they even got him into court."

"Well, thanks. I appreciate this. You've given me a lot of information. I may get back in touch if I have any other questions." I gave him my card in case he thought of anything else. I crossed back to the car and sat there, making notes while his comments were still fresh.

I thought about Tippy, searching my memory. Rhe had told me those were Tippy's teen alcoholic years. If I remembered right, Rhe had sent her off to live with her father because she and Tippy had had a falling-out. So how would Rhe know if she was in that night or not? Maybe I should just ask Tippy and be done with it. "Do the obvious" had always been a working motto of mine.

I glanced at my watch. It was 5:35. Santa Teresa Shellfish

was out on the wharf—maybe two blocks from my apartment, which was not that far away. I headed for home, across the backside of Capillo Hill. If Tippy *was* out that night, I couldn't see why she wouldn't own up to it six years later. Maybe nobody'd ever asked her. What a happy thought.

12

I parked the car in front of my place, dropped off the briefcase, plucked my windbreaker off the back of the door, and walked the two blocks to the wharf. The sun wasn't quite down yet, but the light was gray. The days were marked by this protracted twilight, darker shadows gathering among the trees while the sky remained the color of polished aluminum. When the sun finally set, the clouds would turn purple and blue and the last rays of sun would pierce the gloom with shafts of red. Winter nights in California were usually in the fifties. Summer nights were often in the fifties, too, which offered the possibility of sleeping year-round beneath a quilt.

To my right, a quarter mile away, the long slender arm of the breakwater curved around the marina, cradling sailboats in its embrace. The ocean pounded on the seawall, the force of the waves creating a plume of spray that marched from right to left. Beneath my feet, the pier seemed to shift as if nudged by the waves. The smell of creosote rose like a vapor from heavy timbers saturated to a dark gloss. The tide was high, the water looking like dark blue ink, silver pilings stained with the damp. Cars rolled down the pier, the rumble of loose boards creating a continuous tremor along the length. The fog was rolling in, bringing with it the damp cloudy smell of seaweed. Darkened boats were moored just offshore in the poor man's marina.

On the wharf itself the lights were bright and cold against the deep shadows of the ocean. The Marina Restaurant was ablaze, the air around it scented with the savory aroma of char-grilled fish and steaks. One of the parking valets jogged toward the end of the small lot to retrieve a vehicle. Gulls rested on the peaked roof of the bait-and-tackle shop, the shingled slopes banked with snowy white where the bird droppings had collected. The fishermen were packing up, tackle boxes clattering, while a pelican waddled about beady-eyed, still hoping for a handout.

Looking back toward the town, I could see the dark hills carpeted in pinlights. The 101 was laid out parallel to the beach, the California coastline running an unexpected east to west in this stretch. Across the four lanes of the freeway, the one- and two-story buildings in the business district marched away up State Street, diminishing in size like a drawing lesson in perspective. The palm trees were a dark contrast to the artificial light that was just beginning to bathe the downtown with its pale yellow glow.

The sun had now dropped from sight but the sky wasn't completely dark, more the ashen charcoal gray of a cold hearth. I reached the brown-painted board-and-batten building that housed the Santa Teresa Shellfish Company. Eight wooden picnic tables and benches were secured to the pier out in front. The three employees inside were young, late teens—in Tippy's case, early twenties—wearing blue jeans and dark blue Santa Teresa Shellfish T-shirts, each emblazoned with a crab. Along the front of the booth, seawater tanks were filled with live crabs and lobsters, stacked on one another like sullen marine spiders. A glass-fronted display case was lined with crushed ice, fish steaks and fillets arranged in columns of gray and pink and white. A counter ran along the back. Beyond it, through a doorway, I could see an enormous fish being gutted.

They were in the process of closing up, cleaning off the counters. I watched Tippy for almost a minute before she spotted me. Her motions were brisk, her manner efficient as she waited to take an order from a fellow standing at the display case. "Last order of the day. We gotta close in five minutes."

"Oh, right. I'm sorry. I didn't realize it was so late." He scooted down toward the tank, pointing to the hapless object of his appetite. She tucked her order pad in her pocket and plunged her arm into the murky water. Deftly, she seized the lobster across its back and held it up for his approval. She plunked it on the counter, grabbed up a butcher knife, and inserted the tip just under the shell where the tail connected to the spiny body. I glanced away at that moment, but I could hear the thump as she pounded the knife and neatly severed the creature's spine. What a way to earn a living. All that death for minimum wage. She popped it in the steamer, slammed the door shut, and set the timer. She turned to me without really registering my identity.

"Can I help you?"

"Hi, Tippy. Kinsey Millhone. How are you?"

I saw belated recognition flash in her eyes. "Oh, hi. My mom just called and said you'd be stopping by." She turned her head. "Corey? Can I go now? I'll close out the register tomorrow if you can do it today."

"No problem."

She turned to the fellow waiting for his lobster dinner. "You want something to drink?"

"You have iced tea in a can?"

She took the can out of the cooler, put ice in a paper cup, and extracted a small container of coleslaw from the back of the display case. She scribbled the total across the bottom of the ticket and tore it off with a flourish. He gave her a ten and she made change with the same efficiency. The timer on the steamer began to peep. She reached in with a hot mitt and flopped the steaming lobster on the paper plate. The guy had barely picked up his order when she untied her apron and let herself out the Dutch door to one side.

"We can sit out at one of the tables unless you'd rather go somewhere else. My car's parked over there. You want to talk in the car?"

"We can head in that direction. I really just have a couple of quick questions."

"You want to know what I was doing the night Aunt Isabelle was killed, right?"

"That's right." I was sorry Rhe'd had time to call her, but what could I do? Even if I'd come straight over, Rhe would have had time to telephone. Now Tippy'd had sufficient warning to cook up a good cover story . . . if she needed one.

"God, I've been trying to think. I was at my dad's, I guess."

I stared at her briefly. "You don't remember anything in particular about that night?"

"Not really. I was still in high school back then so I probably had a lot of homework or something."

"Weren't you out of school? That would have been the day after Christmas. Most kids have the week off between Christmas and New Year's."

She frowned slightly. "I must have been, if you say so. I really don't remember."

"You have any idea what time your mother called to tell you about Isabelle?"

"Uh, I think about an hour later. Like an hour after it happened. I know she called from Aunt Isabelle's, but I think she'd been there awhile with Simone."

"Is there any chance you might have been out around one or one-thirty?"

"One-thirty in the morning? You mean, like doing something?"

"Yes, a date, or maybe just bopping around with your buddies."

"Nunh-unh. My dad didn't like me to be out late."

"He was home that night?"

"Sure. Probably," she said.

"Do you remember what your mom said when she called?"

She thought about that for a moment. "I don't think so. I mean, I remember she woke me up and she was crying and all."

"Does your dad have a truck?"

"Just for work," she said. "He's a painting contractor and he carries his equipment in the pickup."

"He had the same truck back then?"

"He's had the same truck ever since I can remember. He needs a new one actually."

"The one he has is white?"

That one slowed her down some. A trick question perhaps? "Yeah," she said reluctantly. "Why?"

"Here's the deal," I said. "I talked to a guy who says he saw you out that night, driving a white pickup."

"Well, that's screwed. I wasn't *out*," she said with just a touch of indignation.

"What about your father? Maybe he was using the truck."

"I doubt it."

"What's his name? I can check it out with him. He might remember something."

151

"Go ahead. I don't care. It's Chris White. He lives on West Glen, down around the bend from my mom."

"Thanks. This has been real helpful."

That seemed to worry her. "It has?"

I shrugged and said, "Well, sure. If your father can verify the fact that you were home, then this other business is probably just a case of mistaken identity." I allowed just the tiniest note of misgiving to sound in my voice, a little bird of doubt singing in a distant part of the forest. The effect wasn't lost.

"Who was it said they saw me?"

"I wouldn't worry about it." I looked at my watch. "I better let you go."

"You want a ride or something? It's no trouble." Little Miss Helpful.

"I walked over from my place, but thanks. I'll talk to you later."

"Night," she said. Her parting smile seemed manufactured, one of those expressions clouded with conflicting emotions. If she didn't watch it, those little frown marks were going to require cosmetic surgery by the time she was thirty. I glanced back and she gave me a halfhearted wave, which I returned in kind. I headed back down the pier, thinking "Liar, liar, pants on fire" for reasons I couldn't name.

I dined that night on Cheerios and skim milk. I ate, bowl in hand, standing at the kitchen sink, while I stared out the window. I made my mind a blank, erasing the day's events in a cloud of chalk dust. I was still troubled about Tippy, but there was no point in trying to force the issue. I turned the whole business over to my subconscious for review. Whatever was bugging me would surface in time.

At 6:40, I left for my appointment with Francesca Voigt. Like most of the principal players in this drama, she and Kenneth Voigt lived in Horton Ravine. I drove west on Cabana and up the long, winding hill past Harley's Beach, entering the Ravine through the back gate. The entire Horton property was originally two ranches of more than three thousand acres each, combined and purchased in the mid-1800s by a sea captain named Robertson, who, in turn, sold the land to a sheep rancher named Tobias Horton. The land has since been subdivided into some 670 wooded parcels, ranging from one-and-a-half-acre to fifty-acre estates, laced with thirty miles of bridal paths. An aerial view might show that two houses, seemingly miles apart, were really only two lots away from each other, separated more by winding roads than by any actual geographical distance. In truth, David Barney wasn't the only one whose property was in range of Isabelle's.

The Voigts lived on what must have been six or eight acres, if one could judge property lines by the course of the fifteen-foot hedges that snaked along the road and cut down along the hillside. The shrubs and flower beds were all carefully tended, towering eucalyptus grouped together at the fringes. The driveway was a half circle with a bed of thickly planted pansies massed together in its center, a blend of deep reds and purples, petals vibrant in the glow of the landscape lighting. Off to the right, I could see horse stalls, a tack room, and an empty corral. The air smelled faintly musty, a blend of straw, dampness, and the various by-products of horse butts.

The house was built low to the ground, white frame and white painted brick, with long brick terraces across the front, dark green plantation shutters flanking the wide mullioned windows. I left my car out in the drive, rang the bell, and waited. A stolid white maid in a black uniform opened the door. She was probably in her fifties and looked foreign for some reason—facial structure, body type . . . I wasn't really sure what it was. She didn't quite make eye contact. Her gaze came to rest right about at my clavicle and remained there as I indicated who I was and told her that I was expected. She made no reply, but she conveyed with body language that she comprehended my utterings.

I followed her across the polished white marble foyer and then trudged with her across white carpeting as thick and pristine as a heavy layer of snow. We passed through the living room—glass and chrome, not a knickknack or a book in sight. The room had been designed for a race of visiting giants. All the furniture was upholstered in white and oversize: big plump sofas, massive armchairs, the glass coffee table as large as a double-bed mattress. On a ponderous credenza, there was a bowl filled with wooden apples as big as softballs. The effect was strange, re-creating the same feelings I had when I was five. Perhaps, unbeknownst to myself, I'd begun to shrink.

We walked down a hallway wide enough for a snowplow. The maid paused at a door, knocked once, and opened it for me, staring politely at my sternum as I passed in front of her. Francesca was seated at a sewing machine in a room proportioned for humans, painted buttery yellow. One entire wall was covered by a beautifully organized custom-built cabinet that opened to reveal cubbyholes for patterns, bolts of fabric, trim, and sewing supplies. The room was airy, the interior light excellent, the pale hardwood floors sanded and varnished.

Francesca was tall, very slender, with short-cropped brown hair and a chiseled face. She had high cheekbones, a strong jawline, a long straight nose, and a pouting mouth with a pronounced upper lip. She wore loose white pants of some beautifully draped material, with a long peach tunic top that she had belted in heavy leather. Her hands were slender, her fingers long, her nails tapered and polished. She wore a series of heavy silver bracelets that clanked together on her wrist like chains, confirming my suspicion that glamour is a burden only beautiful women are strong enough to bear. She looked like she would smell of lilacs or newly peeled oranges.

Francesca smiled as she held her hand out and we introduced ourselves. "Have a seat. I'm nearly finished. Shall I have Guda bring us some wine?"

"That would be nice."

I glanced back in time to see Guda's gaze drop to Francesca's belt buckle. I took this to mean she had heard and would obey. She nodded and moved out of the room on crepe-soled shoes. "Does she speak English?" I asked once the door was shut.

"Not fluently, but well enough. She's Swedish. She's only been with us a month. The poor dear. I know she's homesick, but I can't get her to say much about it." She sat back down at her machine, taking up a length of gauzy blue fabric that she had gathered across one end. "I hope this doesn't seem rude, but I don't like leaving work undone."

Expertly she turned the piece, adjusted a knob, and zig-zagged a row of stitches across the other end. The sewing machine made a soothing, low-pitched hum. I watched her, feeling mute. I didn't know enough about sewing to form a question, but she seemed to sense my curiosity. She looked up with a smile. "This is a turban, in case you're wondering. I design headwear for cancer patients."

"How did you get into that?"

She added a small square of Velcro and stitched around the edges, her knee pressing the lever that activated the machine. "I was having chemotherapy for breast cancer two years ago. One morning in the shower, all my hair fell out in clumps. I had a lunch date in an hour and there I was, bald as an egg. I improvised one of these from a scarf I had on hand, but it was not a great success. Synthetics don't adhere well to skulls as smooth as glass. The idea for the business got me through the rest of the chemo and out the other side. Funny how that works. Tragedy can turn your life around if you're open to it." She sent a look in my direction. "Have you ever been seriously ill?"

"I've been beaten up. Does that count?"

She didn't respond with the usual exclamations of surprise or distaste. Given what she'd been through, merely being punched out must have been an easy fix. "Call me if it ever happens to you again. I have cosmetics designed to cover any

155

kind of bruise you might have. Actually, I have a whole line of products for the ravages of fate. The company's called Head-for-Cover. I'm the sole proprietress."

"How's your health at this point?"

"I'm fine. Thanks for asking. These days, so many of us make it. It's not like the past when any cancer diagnosis meant death." She added the other small square of Velcro, flipped the foot up, removed the garment, and clipped the threads. Deftly, she adjusted the turban around her head. "What do you think?"

"Very exotic," I said. "Of course, you could wrap your head in toilet paper and you'd look okay."

She laughed. "I like that. Disposable head wraps." She made a note to herself and then set the turban aside, shaking her hair loose. "Done. Let's go out on the terrace. We can use the heaters if it seems chilly."

The wide stone terrace at the rear of the house looked out over Santa Teresa with a view toward the mountains. In the town below, lights had come on, delineating the layout of city blocks in a grid of streets and intersections. We settled into wicker chairs padded with plump cushions in floral chintz. The pool was lighted, a glowing blue-green rectangle with a spa at one end. Wisps of steam drifted off the surface, creating a mild breeze scented with chlorine. The surrounding grass looked lush and dark, the house behind us a blaze of yellow.

Guda appeared with a bottle of chardonnay nestled in a cooler, two long-stemmed wineglasses, and a tray of assorted canapés. I put my feet up on a wicker ottoman and fed myself little treats. Guda served us water crackers as crisp and flavorless as slate, mounded with soft herb cheese infused with garlic. On the plate with the crackers, she'd arranged tuna-filled cherry tomatoes and flaky homemade cheese sticks. After a sumptuous supper of cold cereal, I had to restrain an urge to snatch at the food like a snarling mongrel. I tried a sip of the wine, a silky blend of apple and oak. Kick-ass private eyes hardly ever live like this. We're the Gallo aficionados of the jug-wine set. "Count your blessings," I said.

Francesca surveyed her surroundings as if seeing all of it through my eyes. "Odd that you should say that. I've been thinking of leaving Kenneth. I'll wait till the trial is over, but after that I can't think what would keep me."

I was surprised at the admission. "Really?"

"Yes, really. It's a matter of priorities. Winning his love used to seem so important. Now I realize my happiness has nothing to do with him. He did hang in there with me through the surgery and the chemo and I'm grateful for that. I've heard a lot of horror stories about spouses who can't handle the prolonged stresses of a battle with cancer. I'm the one who's undergone a shift. Gratitude doesn't make a marriage. I woke up one morning and realized I was out of control."

"What triggered the realization?"

"Nothing in particular. It's like being in a dark room with the lights suddenly flipped on."

"What will you do if you leave?"

"I'm not sure, but something simple. I probably feel the same sense of amazement at this place that you do. I wasn't born with money. My father was a grade-school custodian and my mother worked in a pharmacy, stocking shelves with dental floss and Preparation H."

I laughed at the image. "Well, you look like you belong here."

"I'm not sure that's a compliment. I'm a quick study. When Kenneth and I first started dating, I watched everybody in his crowd. I figured out who was really classy and did whatever they did, with embellishments of my own, of course, just to make it look original. It's just a series of tricks. I could teach you in an afternoon. It's mildly entertaining, but none of it really matters much."

"Don't you enjoy having all these things?"

"I suppose so. I mean, sure, it's nice, but I spend most days in the sewing room. I could do that anywhere."

"I can't believe you're saying this. I heard you were nuts about Kenneth."

"I thought so myself and I was, I suppose. I was totally infatuated with him in the early days of our relationship. It was like a form of craziness. I thought he was powerful and strong, knowledgeable, in charge. Very manly," she said in a deep voice. "He fit my image of what a man should be, but you know what? He turns out to be rather shallow, which is not to say I'm so profound myself. I woke up one day and thought, What am I doing? Really, it's a struggle to be around him. He doesn't read. He doesn't think about things. He has opinions, but no ideas. And most of his opinions he picks up from *Time* magazine. He's so shut down emotionally, I feel as if I'm living in a desert."

"That sounds like half the people I know," I said.

"Maybe so. It might just be me, but he's changed a lot in the last few years. He's so brooding and dark. You've met him, haven't you? What's your reaction?"

I shrugged noncommittally. "He seems okay," I said. I'd only met the man once, and though I didn't find him attractive, I'm wary about bad-mouthing one spouse to another. For all I knew, they'd reconcile later in the evening and all my remarks would be reported verbatim. I shifted the subject. "Speaking of reactions, what was yours to Isabelle? I take it that's part of what your testimony will be about."

Francesca made a face, stalling her response until she'd topped off our wineglasses. "That and the infamous gun disappearance. All of us were there. As for Isabelle, she was a bit like Kenneth in some ways—charismatic on the surface, but under that, nothing. She did have talent, but as a person she was hardly warm or caring."

"You and Kenneth connected up once she got involved with David Barney?"

"That's right. We met at a fund-raiser at the Canyon Country Club. I was there with a friend and someone introduced us. Isabelle had just left him and he was like a whipped puppy dog. You know how it is. There's nothing quite as irresistible as a man in need of help. I was smitten. I pursued him. I thought I'd die if I couldn't have him. I must have looked like a fool. People tried to warn me, but I wouldn't listen. The entire six months his divorce was in process, I nurtured and patted and petted and cooed."

"It worked, didn't it?"

"Oh, I got what I wanted for all the good it did me. We were married the minute he was free, but his heart wasn't in it. He was hung up on her, which kept me hooked for a long time. I knew he didn't love me so how could I resist the man? I had to fawn and grovel. I had to please him at any cost. Nothing worked, of course. I mean, basically he prefers women as rejecting of him as he is of me. Isn't that pathetic? He'll probably fall head over heels in love with me the day I serve him with papers."

"What changed your attitude, the cancer?"

"That was part of it. The lawsuit has had an effect on top of that. I realized, at a certain point, it was just his way of staying connected to Isabelle. He can be embroiled. He can suffer on her behalf. If he can't have her, at least he can have the money. That's what matters now."

"What about their daughter, Shelby? How does she fit into this?"

"She's a nice enough kid. He hardly sees her. She's hardly ever home. Once in a while—like, every two or three months —he goes to visit at school and takes her out for the day. They go to dinner and a movie and that's the extent of it."

"I thought the legal wrangle was for her, to make sure she's provided for."

"That's what he says, but it's ridiculous. He's heavily insured. If anything happened to him, Shelby'd get a million dollars. How much more does she need? He refuses to let go. That's all the lawsuit's about. God, do I sound like a bitch?"

"Not at all. I appreciate your candor. Frankly, I didn't think you'd tell me much."

"I'll tell you anything you want to know. I don't care about these people. I used to feel protective. There was a time I never would have said a word. I'd have felt guilty and disloyal. Now, it doesn't seem to matter much. I've begun to see them with great clarity. It's like being nearsighted and suddenly getting prescription lenses. It's all so much clearer it's astonishing."

"Such as what?"

"Just what I've been talking about . . . Kenneth and his obsession. The hard part for him was once Isabelle left him, he had to face the fact she was a flaming narcissist. With her dead, he can go back to believing she was perfect."

"She and David met at work, isn't that how it went? Peter Weidmann's firm?"

"That's right. It was 'love at first sight,' " she said, making quote marks with her fingers.

"You think he killed her?"

"David? I'm not sure how to answer that. During the trial I sure thought so, but now it doesn't make much sense to me. I mean, look at the situation. Hasn't it ever struck you how 'feminine' the murder was? It's always amazed me that no one's mentioned this before. I don't mean to sound sexist, but there's something almost 'sanitary' about shooting through a peephole. Maybe it's my prejudice, but I tend to think when men kill it's more forceful and direct. They strangle or bludgeon or stab. It's real straight-ahead stuff. Even when they shoot, there's nothing devious or sneaky. It's like BOOM! They blow your head off. They don't tiptoe around."

"In other words, men tend to kill face-to-face."

"Exactly. Shooting through a peephole, you wouldn't have to take responsibility. You wouldn't even have to *look* at the blood, let alone risk getting spattered. David may have harassed her, but he was so visible about it. Right out there in front of God and everyone. Restraining orders, cops, the two of them screaming at each other on the phone. If he really killed her, he must have known he'd be the first person they'd suspect. And that business about his jogging? What a stupid idea. Believe me, the man is smart. If he were guilty, then surely he could have come up with a better alibi than that."

"But what are you suggesting? You must have some kind of theory or you wouldn't be saying this."

"Simone's a possibility."

"Isabelle's twin *sister*?"

"Don't you know the story?"

"I guess not," I said, "but I'm sure you'll fill me in."

She laughed at my tone. "Well, look at the story. They never really got along. Isabelle did as she pleased and poor Simone was left holding the bag half the time. Isabelle had everything—ostensibly, at any rate—looks, talent, a darling child. Ah, and that was the sticking point. Simone wanted to have a baby more than anything. Her biological clock had jumped to daylight saving time. I take it you've met her?"

"I talked to her yesterday."

"And you noticed the limp?"

"Sure, but she didn't mention it and I didn't ask."

"It was a terrible accident. Isabelle's fault, I'm afraid. This was maybe seven years ago, about a year before Iz died. Iz was drunk and brought the car home and left it in the driveway without pulling the emergency brake. The car started to roll down that horrendous hill, smashing through the underbrush, picking up momentum. Simone was down at the mailbox and it crashed right into her. Crushed her pelvis, crushed her femur. They said she'd never walk again, but she defied 'em on that. You probably saw for yourself. She's really doing very well."

"But no kids."

"That's right. And what made things worse, she was engaged at the time and her fiancé broke it off. He wanted a family. End of story. For Simone, it really was the final straw."

I watched her face, trying to compute the impact of the information. "It's worth some thought," I said.

13

I stopped off at Rosie's on the way back to my place. I don't usually hang out in bars, but I was restless and I didn't feel like being alone just then. At Rosie's, I can sit in a back booth and ponder life's circumstances without being stared at, picked up, hit on, or hassled. After the wine at Francesca's, I thought a cup of coffee might be in order. It wasn't really a question of sobering up. The wine at Francesca's was as delicate as violets. The white wine at Rosie's comes in big half-gallon screw-top jugs you can use later to store gasoline and other flammable liquids.

Business was lively. A group of bowlers had come in, a noisy bunch of women who were celebrating their winning of some league tournament. They were parading around the room with a trophy the size of *Winged Victory,* all noise and whistles and cheers and stomping. Ordinarily Rosie doesn't tolerate rowdies, but their spirits were contagious and she didn't object.

I got myself a mug and filled it from the coffeepot Rosie keeps behind the bar. As I slid into my favorite booth, I spotted Henry coming in. I waved and he took a detour and headed in my direction. One of the bowlers was feeding coins into the jukebox. Music began to thunder through the bar along with cigarette smoke, whoops, and raucous laughter.

Henry slid in across from me and put his head down on his arm. "This is great. Noise, whiskey, smoke, life! I'm so sick of being with that hypochondriac of a brother. He's driving me nuts. I swear to God. His health regimen occupied our entire day. Every hour on the hour, he takes a pill or drinks a glass of water . . . flushing his system out. He does yoga to relax. He does calisthenics to wake up. He takes his blood pressure twice a day. He uses little strip tests to check his urine for glucose and protein. He keeps up a running account of all his body functions. Every minor itch and pain. If his stomach gurgles, it's a symptom. If he breaks wind, he issues a bulletin. Like I didn't notice already. The man is the most self-obsessed, tedious, totally boring human being I've ever met and he's only been here one day. I can't believe it. My own brother."

"You want a drink?"

"I don't dare. I couldn't stop. They'd have to check me into detox."

"Has he always been like that?"

Henry nodded bleakly. "I never really saw it till now. Or maybe in his dotage he's become decidedly worse. I remember, as a kid, he had all these accidents. He tumbled out of trees and fell off swings. He broke his arm once. He broke a wrist. He stuck a pencil in his eye and nearly blinded himself. And the cuts. Oh my God, you couldn't let him near a knife.

164

He had all kinds of allergies and weird things going wrong with him. He had a spastic salivary gland . . . he really did. Later, he went through a ten-year period when he had all his internal organs taken out. Tonsils and adenoids, appendix, his gallbladder, one kidney, two and a half feet from his upper intestine. The man even managed to rupture his spleen. Out it came. We could have constructed an entire human being out of the parts he gave up."

I glanced up to find Rosie standing at my shoulder, taking in Henry's outburst with a placid expression. "He's having a breakdown?"

"His brother's visiting from Michigan."

"He don' like the guy?"

"The man is driving him nuts. He's a hypochondriac."

She turned to Henry with interest. "What's the matter with him? Is he sick?"

"No, he's not sick. He's neurotic as hell."

"Bring him in. I fix. Nothing to it."

"I don't think you quite understand the magnitude of the problem," I said.

"Is no problem. I can handle it. What's the fellow's name, this brother?"

"His name is William."

Rosie said "William" as she wrote it in her little notebook. "Is done. I fix. Not to worry."

She moved away from the table, her muumuu billowing out around her like a witch's cape.

"Is it my imagination or has her English gotten worse lately?" I asked.

Henry looked up at me with a wan smile.

I gave his hand a maternal pat. "Cheer up. Is done. Not to worry. She'll fix."

I was home by 10:00, but I didn't feel like continuing my cleaning campaign. I took my shoes off and used my dirty socks to do a halfhearted dusting of the spiral staircase as I went up to bed. Works for me, I thought.

I was awakened in the wee hours with a telegram from my subconscious. "Pickup," the message read. Pickup what? My eyes came open and I stared at the skylight above my bed. The loft was very dark. The stars were blocked out by clouds, but the glass dome seemed to glow with light pollution from town. The message had to be related to Tippy's presence at the intersection. I'd been brooding about the subject since David Barney first brought it up. If he was inventing, why attach her name to the story? She might have had a ready explanation for where she was that night. If he was lying about the incident, why take the chance? The repair crew had seen her, too . . . well, not really her, but the pickup. Where else had I come across mention of a pickup truck?

I sat up in bed, pushed the covers back, and flipped on the light, wincing at the sudden glare. In lieu of a bathrobe, I pulled on my sweats. Barefoot, I padded down my spiral staircase, turned on the table lamp, and hunted up my briefcase, sorting through the stack of folders I'd brought home from the office. I found the file I was looking for and carried it over to the sofa, where I sat, feet tucked up under me, leafing through old photocopies of the *Santa Teresa Dispatch*. For the third time in two days, I scanned column after column of smudgy print. Nothing for the twenty-fifth. Ah. On the front page of the local news for December 26 was the little article I'd seen about the hit-and-run fatality of an elderly man, who'd wandered away from a convalescent hospital in the neighborhood. He'd been struck by a pickup truck on upper State Street and had died at the scene. The name of the victim was being withheld, pending notification of his next of kin. Unfortunately, I hadn't made copies of the newspapers for the week after that so I couldn't read the follow-up.

I pulled out the telephone book and checked the yellow pages under Convalescent Homes & Hospitals. The sublistings were Homes, Hospitals, Nursing Homes, Rest Homes, and Sanitariums, most of which simply cross-referenced each other. Finally, under Nursing Homes, I found a comprehensive list. There was only one such facility in the vicinity of the accident. I made a note of the address and then turned the lights out and went back up to bed. If I could link that pickup to the one Tippy's father owned, it might go a long way toward explaining why she was reluctant to admit she was out. It would also verify every word David Barney'd said.

In the morning, after my usual three-mile run, a shower, breakfast, and a quick call to the office, I drove out to the South Rockingham neighborhood where the old man had been killed. At the turn of the century, South Rockingham was all ranchland, flat fields planted to beans and walnuts, harvested by itinerant crews who traveled with steam engines, cookhouses, and bedroll wagons. An early photograph shows some thirty hands lined up in front of their cumbersome, clanking machinery. Most of the men are mustachioed and glum, wearing bandannas, long-sleeved shirts, overalls, and felt hats. Staunchly they lean on their pitchforks while a dusty noon sun beats down. The land in such pictures always looks pitiless and flat. There are few trees and the grass, if it grows at all, seems patchy and sparse. Later aerial photos show the streets radiating from a round hub of land, like the spokes of a wagon wheel. Beyond the outermost rim, the squares of young citrus groves are pieced together like a quilt. Now South Rockingham is a middle-class neighborhood of modest custom-built homes, half of which went up before 1940. The balance were constructed during a miniboom in the ten years between 1955 and 1965. Every parcel is dense with vegetation, houses crowded onto every available lot. Still, the area is considered desirable because it's quiet, self-contained, attractive, and well kept.

I located the convalescent hospital, a one-story stucco structure flanked on three sides by parking lots. From the outside, the fifty-bed facility looked plain and clean, probably expensive. I parked at the curb and climbed four concrete steps to the sloping front walk. The grass on either side was in its dormant stage, clipped short, a mottled yellow. An American flag hung limply from a pole near the entrance.

I pushed through a wide door into a comfortably furnished reception area, decorated in the style of one of the better motel chains. Christmas hadn't surfaced yet. The color scheme was pleasant: blues and greens in soothing, noninflammatory shades. There was a couch covered in chintz and four matching upholstered chairs arranged so as to suggest intimate lobby chats. The magazines on the end tables were neatly fanned out in an arc of overlapping titles, *Modern Maturity* being foremost. There were two ficus trees, which on closer inspection turned out to be artificial. Both might have used a dusting, but at least they weren't subject to whitefly and blight.

At the desk, I asked to see the nursing home director and was directed to the office of a Mr. Hugo, halfway down the corridor to my left. This wing of the building was strictly administrative. There were no patients in evidence, no wheelchairs, gurneys, or medical paraphernalia. The very air was stripped of institutional odors. I explained my business briefly, and after a five-minute wait Mr. Hugo's personal secretary ushered me into his office. Nursing home directors must have a lot of holes to fill in their appointment books.

Edward Hugo was a black man in his midsixties with a curly mix of gray and white hair and a wide white mustache. His complexion was glossy brown, the color of caramel. The lines in his face suggested an origami paper folded once, then flattened out again. He was conventionally dressed, but something in his manner hinted at obligatory black-tie appearances for local charity events. He shook my hand across his desk and then took his seat again while I took mine. He folded his hands in front of him on the desk. "What can I help you with?"

"I'm trying to learn the name of a former patient of yours,

an old gentleman who was killed in a hit-and-run accident six years ago at Christmas."

He nodded. "I know the man you're referring to. Can you explain your interest?"

"I'm trying to verify an alibi in another criminal matter. It would help if I could find out if the driver was ever found."

"I don't believe so. Not to my knowledge, at any rate. To tell you the truth, it's always bothered me. The gentleman's name was Noah McKell. His son, Hartford, lives here in town. I can have Mrs. Rudolph look up his number if you'd like to speak to him."

He went on in this manner, direct, soft-spoken, and matter-of-fact, managing in our ten-minute conversation to give me all the information I needed in a carefully articulated format. According to Mr. Hugo's account of the night in question, Noah McKell had removed his IV, disconnected himself from a catheter, dressed himself in his street clothes, and left his private room by the window.

I was surprised by that. "Aren't the windows kept locked?"

"This is a hospital, Miss Millhone, not a prison. Bars would constitute a danger if a fire ever broke out. Aside from that, we feel our patients benefit from the fresh air and a view of some greenery. He'd left the premises on two other occasions, which was a matter of great concern to us, given his condition. We considered the use of restraints for his protection, but we were reluctant to do so and his son was adamant. We kept the bed rails up and we had one of the aides look in on him every thirty minutes or so. The floor nurse went in at one-fifteen and discovered the empty bed.

"Of course, we moved very quickly once we realized he was gone. The police were alerted and the security people here began an immediate search. I received a call at home and came right over. I live up on Tecolote Road so it didn't take me long. By the time I got here, we'd heard about the hit-and-run. We went to the scene and identified the body."

"Were there any witnesses?"

"A desk clerk at the Gypsy Motel heard the impact," he said. "She ran out to help, but the old man was dead. She was the one who called the police."

"You remember her name?"

"Not offhand. Mr. McKell would be able to tell you, I'm sure. It's possible she's still there."

"I think I better talk to him in any event. If the driver was found, I won't need to take any more time with the questions."

"I'd like to think he would have told us if that were the case. Please give me a call and let me know what you find. I'd feel better about it."

"I'll do that, Mr. Hugo, and thanks for your help."

I called Hartford McKell from a public telephone booth that was located near a hamburger stand on upper State. There was no point in going back to the office when the accident site was only two blocks away. I pulled out a pen and a notepad, prepared to take notes.

The man who answered the phone identified himself as Hartford McKell. I explained who I was and the information I needed. He sounded like a man without humor—direct, impatient, with a tendency to interrupt. In the matter of his father's death, he made it clear he wasn't interested in commiseration of any sort. The story seemed to spill out, his anger unabated by the passage of time. I refrained from comment except for an occasional question. The driver of the vehicle had never been found. The Santa Teresa Police had conducted an intense investigation, but aside from the skid marks, there hadn't been much in the way of evidence at the scene. The only witness—the motel desk clerk, whose name was Regina Turner—had given them a sketchy description of the truck, but she hadn't seen the license plate. It was one of those traffic fatalities that outraged the community and he'd offered a twenty-five-thousand-dollar reward for information leading to the arrest and conviction of the driver. "I brought Pop down here from San Francisco. He'd had a stroke and I wanted him close. You know where he was headed every time he left? He thought he was still up there, just a few blocks from his place. He was trying to get home because he was worried about his cat. Animal's been dead now for fifteen years, but Pop wanted to make sure his cat was okay. It makes me crazy to think someone's gotten away with murder."

"I can understand—"

He cut me off. "No one can understand, but I'll tell you one thing: You don't run over an old man and then drive on without a backward glance."

"People panic," I said. "One in the morning, the streets are virtually empty. The driver must have figured no one would ever know the difference."

"I don't really care what the reasoning was. I want to nail the son of a bitch. That's all I care about. Do you have a line on this guy or not?"

"I'm working on it."

"You find the driver and that twenty-five thousand is yours."

"I appreciate that, Mr. McKell, but that's not my prime interest in the matter. I'll do what I can."

We terminated the conversation. I got back in the car and drove the two blocks down State Street to the intersection where the elder McKell was killed. The + formed by the two cross streets was bounded by a motel, a vacant lot, a garden-style medical complex, and a small bungalow, which looked like a private residence, converted now to real estate offices. The Gypsy was an unassuming block of units, with all the architectural grace of a two-by-four, bounded on all sides by strip parking. An accordion-pleated metal portico jutted out in front. The two-story building had probably gone up in the sixties and seemed to rely heavily on concrete and alumi-num-frame sliding doors. I parked in the portion of the motel lot set aside for registration. The office was glass-enclosed with ready-made mesh drapes blocking out the early afternoon sun. A blinking neon sign out in front alternated NO and VACANCY.

The woman behind the desk was big—not the giant but the large economy size. She had a big well-shaped nose, a large mouth rosy with lipstick, ice-blond hair pulled up in a braid on top, the coil of hair wrapped around itself until it formed a rope. She wore mauve glasses with beveled frames, the lower portion of both lenses smudged slightly with peachy foundation makeup. Her street clothing was obscured by a pink nylon smock of the sort worn by cosmetologists.

I took out a business card and placed it on the counter. "I wonder if you can help me. I'm looking for Regina Turner."

"Well, I'll try. I'm Regina Turner. Glad to meet you," she said. We shook hands. Our conversation was put on hold briefly when the telephone rang; she held one finger up as a digital marker while she verified some reservations. "Sorry for the interruption," she said when she'd hung up. She gave my card a perfunctory glance and then focused a sharp look on my face. "I don't answer questions about the folks who stay here."

"This is about something else," I said. I was halfway through my explanation when I saw her clock out. I could tell she'd already leapfrogged to the end of the conversation. "You can't help me," I said.

"I wish I could," she replied. "The police talked to me just after that poor old man was killed. I felt awful, honestly, but I told them everything I know."

"You were working that night?"

"I work most nights. Anymore, you can't get good help, especially around the holidays. I was right here at the desk when the accident occurred. I heard the squeal . . . that's an awful sound, isn't it? And then a thump. This pickup must have barreled around the big bend out there at sixty miles an hour. Truck caught the old fella in the crosswalk and flung him right up in the air. Looked like somebody been gored by a bull. You know how in the movies you see 'em get tossed like that? He came down so hard I could hear him hit the pavement. I looked out the front window and saw the truck pull away. My view of the intersection is excellent. You can see for yourself. I dialed nine-one-one and went out to see what I could do. By the time I got to him, the poor man was dead and the truck had taken off."

"Do you remember the time?"

"Eleven minutes after one. I had that same little digital clock sitting on the counter and I remember seeing that the time was one-one-one, which is my birthday. January eleventh. I don't know why, but something like that will stick with you for years afterwards."

"You didn't see the driver?"

"Not at all. I saw the truck. It was white, with some kind of dark blue logo on the side."

"What kind of logo?"

She shook her head. "That I can't help you with."

"This is good though. Every little bit helps," I said. There were probably only six thousand white trucks in California. The particular pickup involved in the accident might have been junked, repainted, sold, or taken out of state. "I appreciate your time."

"You want your card back?" she asked.

"You keep it. If you think of anything that might help, I hope you'll get in touch."

"Absolutely."

At the door, I hesitated. "Do you think you could identify the truck if I brought you some pictures?"

"I'm pretty sure I could. I may not remember it, but I think I'd recognize it if I saw it again."

"Great. I'll be back."

I returned to my car, aware of the little rush of hope I was having to subdue. I wanted to make an assumption here. I'm not a fool. I could see the probability that the white pickup truck involved in McKell's death was the same pickup that had bumped into David Barney approximately thirty minutes later and approximately eight miles away. There was too much at stake to jump to conclusions about who was driving it. Better to play it by the book as I'd been taught. The first step was to take pictures of several similar vehicles, including the truck owned by Tippy's father, Chris White. If Regina Turner could make a positive ID, then I'd have something concrete to start with. Step two, of course, was to figure out who had actually been at the wheel.

14

I went back to the office, again parking my car in Lonnie's slot. As usual, I took the stairs two at a time all the way to the third floor and spent a moment leaning against the wall gasping while I recovered my breath. I let myself into the law office through the plain unmarked door halfway down the hall from the entrance. It was an exit we used as a shortcut to the bathrooms across the hall from us. Originally, the third floor consisted of six separate suites, but Kingman and Ives had gradually assimilated all the available space except for the rest rooms, located in the corridor so as to be accessible to the public.

I unlocked my door and checked for messages. Louise Mendelberg had called, wondering if there was any way I could get Morley's keys back to them that afternoon. Morley's brother was due in and they wanted to make his car available. Any time would be fine if it was not too much trouble.

I decided to get my desk organized and then Xerox the files I'd picked up at Morley's house so I could return them at the same time. I sat down and went through the mail, putting bills in one pile and junk in the wastebasket. I opened all the bills and did some quick mental arithmetic. Yes, I could pay them. No, I couldn't quit my job and retire on my savings, which were nil anyway. I peeked at the balance in my checkbook and paid a bill or two just for sport. Take that, Gas & Electric. Ha ha ha! Foiled again, Pacific Telephone.

I gathered up the stack of folders and went down to use the copier. It took me thirty minutes to Xerox all the data and reassemble the files. I put the originals back in the grocery bag Louise had given me for the purpose, set aside a box of files to review at home, and then removed my 35-millimeter camera from the bottom drawer and loaded it with a roll of color film. I hauled out the telephone book and looked up Tippy's father in the yellow pages under Painting Contractors. Chris White's company, Olympic Painting, was featured in a substantial quarter-page box ad that listed his name, company address, telephone number, license number, and the scope of his work: "complete painting services, water blasting (we provide the water), custom colors and matching, fine wood finishing, wallpapering." I jotted down all the information relevant to my purposes. After I dropped off the files, I was going to go find five or six white pickup trucks and take pictures. I had a quick chat with Ida Ruth and then went out by the same door I'd entered, hauling the grocery bag and a cardboard box.

The drive to Colgate was pleasant enough. The day was clear and chilly and I flipped on the VW's heater so that it would blow hot breath on my feet. I was beginning to give serious thought to the possibility that David Barney might be innocent. Up to this point, we'd all been operating on the assumption that he was the one who shot Isabelle. He was the obvious suspect, with the means, the motive, and the opportunity to have killed her, but murder is an aberrant deed, often born of passions distorted by obsessiveness and torment. Emotion doesn't travel in a straight line. Like water, our feelings trickle down through cracks and crevices, seeking out the little pockets of neediness and neglect, the hairline fractures in our character usually hidden from public view. Beware the dark pool at the bottom of our hearts. In its icy, black depths dwell strange and twisted creatures it is best not to disturb. With this investigation, I was once again uncomfortably aware that in probing into murky waters I was exposing myself to the predators lurking therein.

Morley Shine's driveway was empty, the red Ford rental car nowhere in evidence. The Mercury still sat on the grass in the side yard. I stood on the porch and studied the pattern of rust spots on the fender while I waited for someone to answer my knock. Two minutes passed. I knocked again, this time louder, fervently hoping that I wasn't rousing Dorothy Shine from her sickbed. After five minutes, it seemed safe to assume that no one was home. Maybe Louise had taken Dorothy to the doctor or the two had been required to put in an appearance at the funeral home to pick out a casket. Louise had told me they left the back door unlocked so I made my way around the side of the house, passing through the breezeway between the garage and house. The door to the utility room was not only unlocked, but slightly ajar. I rapped again at the glass and then waited the requisite few minutes in case someone was home. Idly, I surveyed the premises, feeling vaguely depressed. The property looked as though it was ready for the auction block. The backyard was neglected, the winter grass dry and frost-cropped. In the weedy flower beds that bordered the yard, last autumn's annuals were still planted in dispirited clumps. Once-sunny marigolds had turned brown, a garden of deadheads with leaves limp and withered. Morley probably hadn't sat out here with his wife for a year. I could see a built-in brick barbecue, the cook surface so rusty the rods on the grill nearly touched each other.

I pushed the door all the way open and let myself in. I wasn't sure why I was being so meticulous. Ordinarily, I'd have popped right in and had a look around, just because I'm nosy and the opportunity was presented. This time I really didn't have the heart to snoop. Morley was dead and what remained of his life should be safe from trespass. I left the grocery bag of files on the washing machine as instructed. The very air smelled medicinal, and from the depths of the house I could hear the ticking of a clock. I pulled the door shut behind me and returned to the street.

As I took out my car keys, I realized with a flash of irritation that I'd meant to leave Morley's keys in the bag with the files. I turned on my heel and retraced my steps at a half trot. As I passed the Mercury, I could feel my steps slow. Wonder what he has in the trunk, my bad angel said. Even my good angel didn't think it would hurt to look. I'd been given ready access to both his offices. I had his very keys in hand and in the interest of thoroughness it seemed only natural to check his vehicle. It was hardly trespassing when I had implied permission. By the time I reached that phase of my rationalization, I had popped open the trunk and was staring down in disappointment at the spare tire, the jack, and an empty Coors beer can that looked as if it had been rolling around in there for months.

I closed the trunk and moved around to the driver's side, where I unlocked the car and searched the interior, starting with the rear. The seats were covered in a dark green suede cloth that smelled of cigarette smoke and ancient hair oil. The scent conjured up a quick flash of Morley and a sharp jolt of regret. "God, Morley, help me out here," I said.

The floor in the back netted me a gas receipt and a bobby

pin. I wasn't really sure what I was looking for . . . an invoice, a pack of matches, or a mileage log, anything to indicate where Morley had gone and what he'd done in the course of his investigation. I slid into the driver's seat and placed my hands on the steering wheel, feeling like a kid. Morley's legs were longer than mine and I could barely reach the brakes. Nothing in the map pockets. Nothing on the dashboard. I leaned over to my right to check the glove compartment, which I found crammed with junk. This was more my speed. Cleaning rags, a lady's hairbrush, more gas receipts (all local and none recent), a crescent wrench, a pack of Kleenex, a used windshield wiper blade, proof of insurance and registrations for the last seven years. I removed item after item, but nothing seemed pertinent to the case itself.

I returned everything to the glove compartment, tidying the contents in the process. I straightened up and put my hands on the steering wheel again, imagining I was Morley. Half the time when I search I don't find jackshit, but I never give up hope. I'm always thinking something's going to come to light if I just open the right drawer, stick my hand in the right coat pocket. I checked the ashtray, which was still full. He'd probably spent a lot of time in the Merc. In this business, where you're on the road a lot, your car becomes a traveling office, a surveillance vehicle, the observation post for a nightlong stakeout, even a temporary motel if your travel funds run short. The Mercury was perfect, aging and nondescript, the sort of vehicle you might note in your rearview without really seeing it. I checked the car above eye level.

On the sun visor, he'd attached a "leather-finish" vinyl utility valet with a mirror, a slot for sunglasses, and a pencil and blank memo pad that looked unused. The valet was attached to the visor by two flimsy metal clamps. I reached up and pulled the visor down. On the underside, Morley'd slipped a six-inch strip of paper under one of the clamps. It was the perfect place to tuck such things; "To Do" lists, receipts for cleaning, parking lot tickets. The strip had been torn from a perforated flap for one of the film envelopes used by a One-Hour Foto Mart in a Colgate shopping mall. The strip showed an order number, but no date, so it might have been up there for months. I slipped the paper in my pocket, got out of the car, and locked it up again. I completed the return trip to the utility porch, where I dropped the keys in the brown bag with the files I'd left.

I drove the five blocks to the mall. An Asian fellow, wearing rubber gloves, was visible through the plate glass window of the One-Hour Foto Mart, removing strips of film from the developer. Prints on a conveyor moved slowly down one side of the window and across the front. Fascinated, I paused, watching as a surprise fortieth birthday party progressed from cake and wrapped presents on a table to a crowd of grinning well-wishers looking smug and self-satisfied while the birthday boy in sweaty tennis togs pretended to be a good sport.

I was stalling, postponing the inevitable. I wanted the photo order to be pivotal. I wanted the pictures to relate to the investigation in some terribly meaningful and pithy way. I wanted to believe Morley Shine was as good a private eye as I'd always believed he was. Oh well. I pushed the door open and went in. Might as well get it over with. Chances were I'd be looking at a set of snapshots from his last vacation.

The interior of the shop smelled of acrid chemicals. The place was empty of customers and the young clerk who waited on me took no time at all coming up with the order. I paid $7.65 and he assured me that I'd be reimbursed for any prints I didn't like. I left the envelope sealed until I reached my car. I sat in the VW and rested the envelope on the steering wheel. Finally, I opened the top flap and slid the prints into the light.

I made a startled sound . . . not a real word, but something punctuated with an audible exclamation point.

There were twelve prints altogether, each marked at the bottom with last Friday's date. What I was looking at were six white pickup trucks, two views each, including one with a dark blue logo with five interlocking rings. The company was Olympic Painting Contractors; Chris White's name was printed underneath with a telephone number. Morley had been on the same track I was, but what did it mean?

I sorted back through the photographs. It looked as though he'd done exactly what I meant to do. He'd apparently visited various businesses and used-car lots around town and had taken pictures of six- and seven-year-old white pickups, some with logos, some without. In addition to Chris White's company truck, there was one utilized by a gardening firm and one used by a catering company with a camper shell on top. Clever touch. Because he'd incorporated a variety of trucks in the "lineup," it was possible that a more detailed recollection might be triggered from the one and only witness we had.

I stared out the car window, pondering the implications. If he'd talked to Regina Turner at the Gypsy Motel, she'd never mentioned it to me. Surely she'd have brought it up if she'd been queried twice about the same six-year-old fatal accident. But how else could he have known about the logo and color of the vehicle, if not from her? David Barney might have told him about the truck that nearly knocked *him* down. Morley might have thought to check old issues of the newspaper just as I had myself. Maybe he acquired a copy of the original police report on the hit-and-run and then decided to take the pictures with him when he interviewed the only witness. A description of the truck plus Regina's name and place of business would have been noted by the first officer on the scene. The problem was, I hadn't spotted the police report among the files I'd found, nor had I seen any photocopies of the newspapers to indicate that he was curious about other incidents on the night Isabelle was killed. When I'm working a case, I tend to take a lot of notes. If anything happened to me, the next investigator coming down the pike would know what I'd done and where I'd meant to go next. Clearly, Morley didn't work that way. . . .

Or did he?

I'd always given him credit for being both smart and efficient. The guy who trained me in the business was a nut about details, and since he and Morley had been partners, I'd assumed it was an attitude they shared. I suspect that's why I was so dismayed when I finally saw Morley's offices. It was the chaotic state of his paperwork that made me question his professionalism. What if he wasn't as disorganized as he seemed?

A sudden image intruded.

When I was a kid, there was a novelty item that circulated through our elementary school. It was a fortune-telling device, a "crystal ball" that consisted of a sealed sphere with a little window, the whole of it filled with dark water in which a many-sided cube floated. The cube had various messages written on it. You would pose a question and then turn the ball upside down in your hand. When you righted it, the cube in the water would float to the surface with one of the printed messages uppermost. That would be the answer to your query.

In my gut, I could feel a message begin to rise to the surface. Something was off here, but what? I thought about what David Barney'd said when he'd suggested Morley's death was a shade too convenient. Was there something to that? It was a question I couldn't stop and pursue at the moment, but it had a disquieting energy attached to it. I set the notion aside, but I had a feeling it was going to stick to me with a certain burrlike tenacity.

At least with the pictures, Morley had saved me a step, and I was grateful for that. I took comfort from the fact that we were thinking along the same lines. I could go straight back to the Gypsy and show these to Regina.

"Well, that was quick," she said when she caught sight of me.

"I was lucky," I said. "I came across a batch of snapshots that should do the job."

"I'll be happy to take a look."

"I have one question first. Did you ever hear from an investigator named Morley Shine?"

Her face clouded briefly. "Nooo, I don't think so. Not that I recall. In fact, I'm sure not. I'm good with names—my return customers like to be remembered—and his is unusual. I'd know if I'd talked to him, especially about this. What's the connection?"

"He was working on a case until two days ago. He died Sunday evening of a heart attack, which is why I was called in. It looks like he saw a link between the same two incidents."

"What was the other one? When you were here earlier, you said a near miss of some sort."

"A white pickup truck bumped a guy at an exit off the southbound One-oh-one. This was about one forty-five. He claims he knew the driver, though he had no idea there'd been a hit-and-run earlier." I held out the envelope. "Morley Shine dropped these off to be developed. If he meant to talk to you, he was probably waiting until he picked up the prints for ID purposes." I placed the envelope on the counter.

She adjusted her glasses and removed the twelve snapshots. She studied them thoughtfully, giving each picture her undivided attention before she laid it on the counter, making a line of trucks, like a motorcade that marched across the blotter. I watched for a reaction, but when Tippy's father's truck crossed her line of vision, there was no alteration in her expression, no remark indicating surprise or recognition. She studied the six trucks with care and then put an index finger on the Olympic Painting pickup. She said, "This is the one."

"You're sure of that."

"Positive." She picked up the print and held it closer. "I never thought I'd see this again." She flashed me a look. "Maybe we'll finally see someone brought to justice after all these years. And wouldn't that be nice."

I had a brief image of Tippy. "Maybe so," I said. "Anyway, you'll hear from the police as soon as I talk with them."

"Is that where you're off to?"

I shook my head reluctantly. "I have something else to do first."

I made a quick call to Santa Teresa Shellfish, but Tippy'd traded shifts and wasn't going to be in that day. I left the motel and headed for Montebello, hoping I could catch Tippy at home . . . preferably without her mother hovering in the background. In essence, I'd put the woman on notice. Rhe knew something was up, though she probably didn't have a way to guess just how serious it was.

West Glen is one of the primary arteries through Montebello, a winding two-lane road lined with tall hedges and low stone walls. Morning glories spilled over the fence tops in a waterfall of blue. The gnarled branches of the live oaks were laced together overhead, the sycamores interplanted with eucalyptus and acacia trees. Thick patches of hot pink geraniums grew by the road like weeds.

The small stucco cottage that Rhe and Tippy occupied was a two-bedroom bungalow built close to the road. I squeezed my car in on the shoulder and walked up the path to the porch, where I rang the bell. Tippy appeared almost instantly, shrugging into her jacket, purse and car keys in hand. She was clearly on her way out. She stared at me blankly with her hand on the doorknob. "What are you doing here?"

"I have a couple more questions, if you don't mind," I said.

She hesitated, debating, then she checked her watch. Her expression denoted a little impromptu wrestling match—reluctance, annoyance, and good manners doing takedowns. "God, I don't know. I'm meeting this friend of mine in about twenty minutes. Could you, like, really make it quick?"

"Sure. Can I come in?"

She stepped back, not thrilled, but too polite to refuse. She was wearing jeans and high-heeled boots, a portion of a black

184

leotard visible under her blue denim jacket. Her hair was down today and it trailed halfway down her back, strands still showing waves where the French braid had been undone. Her eyes were clear, her complexion faintly rosy. Somehow it made me feel bad that she looked so young.

I took in the cottage at a glance.

The interior consisted of a combination living room/dining room, tiny galley-size kitchen visible beyond. The walls were hung with original art, probably Rhe's handiwork. The floors were done in Mexican paving tiles. The couch was upholstered in hand-painted canvas, wide brushstrokes of sky blue, lavender, and taupe, with lavender-and-sky-blue pillows tossed carelessly along its length. The side chairs were inexpensive Mexican imports, caramel-colored leather in a barrel-shaped rattan frame. There was a wood-burning fireplace, big baskets filled with dried flowers, lots of copper pots hanging from a rack in the kitchen area. Dried herbs hung from the crossbeams. Through French doors, I could see a small courtyard outside with a pepper tree and lots of flowering plants in pots.

"Your mom here?"

"She went up to the market. She'll be back in a minute. What did you want? I'm really really in a hurry so I can't take too long."

I took a seat on the couch, a bit of a liberty as Tippy hadn't really offered. She chose one of the Mexican chairs and sat down without enthusiasm.

I handed her the pictures without explanation.

"What're these?"

"Take a look."

Frowning, she opened the envelope and pulled out the prints. She shuffled through with indifference until she came to the Olympic Paint truck. She looked up at me with alarm. "You went and took a picture of my dad's pickup?"

"Another investigator took those."

"What for?"

"Your father's truck was seen twice the night your aunt

185

Isabelle was murdered. I guess the other P.I. meant to show the pictures to a witness for identification."

"Of what?" I thought a little note of dread had crept into her voice.

I kept my tone flat, as matter-of-fact as I could make it. "A hit-and-run accident in which an old man was killed. This was on upper State in South Rockingham."

She couldn't seem to formulate the next question, which should have been, Why tell me? She knew where I was headed.

I went on. "I thought we ought to talk about your whereabouts that night."

"I already told you I didn't go out."

"So you did," I said with a shrug. "So maybe your father was the one driving."

We locked eyes. I could see her calculate her chances of squirming out from under this one. Unless she fessed up to the fact that she was driving, she'd be pulling her father right into the line of fire.

"My dad wasn't driving."

"Were you?"

"No!"

"Who was?"

"How should I know? Maybe somebody stole the truck and went joyriding."

"Oh, come on, Tippy. Don't give me that. You were out in the truck and you fuckin' know you were so let's cut through the bull and get down to it."

"I was not!"

"Hey, face the facts. I feel for you, kiddo, but you're going to have to take responsibility for what you did."

She was silent, staring downward, her manner sullen and unresponsive. Finally she said, "I don't even know what you're talking about."

I nudged her verbally. "What's the story, were you drunk?"

186

"No."

"Your mom told me you'd had your license suspended. Did you take the truck without permission?"

"You can't prove any of this."

"Oh, really?"

"How are you going to prove it? That was six years ago."

"For starters, I have two eyewitnesses," I said. "One actually saw you pull away from the scene of the accident. The other witness saw you at the southbound off-ramp on San Vicente shortly afterward. You want to tell me what happened?"

Her gaze flickered away from mine and the color came up in her cheeks. "I want a lawyer."

"Why don't you tell me your side of it. I'd like to hear."

"I don't have to tell you anything," she said. "You can't make me say a word unless I have an attorney present. That's the law." She sat back in the chair and crossed her arms.

I smirked and rolled my eyes. "No, it's not. That's *Miranda*. The cops have to Mirandize you. I don't. I'm a private eye. I get to play by a different set of rules. Come on. Just tell me what happened. You'll feel better about it."

"Why would I tell you anything? I don't even like you."

"Let me take a guess. You were living at your dad's and he was out and these friends of yours called you up and just wanted to go out for a little while. So you borrowed the truck and picked them up and the three of you or the four of you, however many it was, were just messing around, drinking a couple of six-packs down at the beach. Suddenly it was midnight and you realized you better get home before your father did so you quick took everybody home. You were barreling home yourself when you hit the guy. You took off in a panic because you knew you'd be in big trouble if you got caught. How's that sound? Close enough to suit?"

Her face was still stony, but I could see that she was fighting back tears, working hard to keep her lips from trembling.

"Did anybody ever tell you about the fellow you hit? His

name was Noah McKell. He was ninety-two years old and he'd been staying at that convalescent hospital up the street. He had the wanderlust, I guess. His son told me he was probably trying to get home. Isn't that pathetic? Poor old guy used to live in San Francisco. He thought he was still up there and he was worried about his cat. I guess he forgot the cat had been dead for years. He was heading for home to feed it, only he never got there."

She put a finger to her lips as if to seal them. The tears began. "I've tried to be good. I really have. I'm AA and everything and I cleaned up my act."

"Sure you did and that's great. But your gut must send you little messages, doesn't it? Eventually, you'll get back into booze just to silence that voice."

Her voice shifted up into the squeaky range. "God, I'm sorry. I really am. I'm so sorry. It was an accident. I didn't mean to do it." She hugged herself, bending over, the sobs as noisy as those of a child, which is what she was. I watched with compassion, but made no move to comfort her. It wasn't up to me to make life easier. Let her experience remorse, all the grief and guilt. I didn't know that she'd ever let herself assimilate the full impact of what she'd done. The tears came in uncontrollable waves, great gut-wrenching sobs that seemed to shake her from head to toe. She sounded more like a howling beast than a young girl filled with shame. I let it happen, almost unable to look at her until the pain subsided some. Finally, the storm passed like a fit of helpless laughter that peters out at long last. She groped in her purse and pulled out a wad of tissues, using one to mop her eyes and blow her nose. "God." She clutched the fistful of tissues against her mouth for a moment. She nearly lost it again, but she collected herself. "I haven't had a drop of alcohol since the night it happened. That's been hard." She was feeling sorry for herself, maybe hoping to stimulate pity or compassion or amnesty.

"I'll bet it has," I said, "and I applaud that. You've done a lot of hard work. Now it's time to tell the truth. You can't skip over that and expect recovery to work."

"You don't have to lecture me."

"Apparently I do. You've had six years to think about this, Tootsie, and you haven't done the right thing yet. I'll tell you this: It's going to look a lot better if you walk into the police station of your own accord. I know you didn't mean to do it. I'm sure you were horrified, but the truth is the truth. I'll give you some time to think, but by Friday I intend to have a conversation with the cops. You'd be smart to get your butt in there and talk to them before I do."

I got up and slung my big leather bag across my shoulder. She made no move to follow. When I reached the front door, I looked back at her. "One more thing and then I'll leave you to your conscience. Did you see David Barney that night?"

She sighed. "Yes."

"You want to expand on that?"

"I nearly ran into him coming off the freeway. I heard this thump, and when I looked out the window, he was staring right at me."

"You do understand you could have cleared him years ago if you'd admitted that." I didn't wait for her response. She was beginning to sound martyred about the whole business and I didn't want to deal with that.

15

I stopped off at my place after I left Tippy and grabbed a hasty lunch, which I ate without much interest. There was precious little in the refrigerator and I was forced to open a can of asparagus soup, which I think I bought originally to put over something else. I've been told novice cooks are chronically engaged in this hoary ruse. Cream of celery soup over pork chops, baked at 350 for an hour. Cream of mushroom soup over meat loaf, same time, same temp. Cream of chicken soup over a chicken breast with half a cup of rice thrown in. The variations are endless and the best part is you have company once, you never see them again. Aside from the aforementioned, I can scramble eggs and make a fair tuna salad, but that's about it. I eat a lot of sandwiches, peanut-butter-and-pickle and cheese-and-pickle being two. I also favor hot sliced hard-boiled egg sandwiches on whole wheat bread with lots of salt and Best Foods mayonnaise. As far as I'm concerned, the only reason for cooking is to keep your hands busy while you think about something else.

What was bugging me at this point was this question of Morley's death. What if David Barney's paranoia was justified? He'd been right about everything else. What if Morley was getting too close to the truth and had been eliminated as a consequence? I was torn between the notion of murder as too farfetched and the worry that someone was actually getting away with it. I went back and forth, exploring the possibilities. His curiosity might well have been stimulated by his conversation with David Barney. Maybe he'd inadvertently stumbled across something significant. Had he been silenced? I could feel myself shy away from the idea. It was so damn melodramatic. Morley had died of a heart attack. The death certificate had been signed by his family doctor. I didn't doubt there were drugs that could trigger or simulate the symptoms of cardiac arrest, but it was hard to picture how such a drug might have been administered. Morley wasn't a fool. Given his health problems, he wasn't going to take medications not prescribed by his own physician. It almost had to be poison, but I hadn't heard the possibility mentioned. Who was I to step in and distress his ailing widow? She had problems enough and all I had to offer was conjecture.

I finished my soup, washed the bowl, and left it in the dish rack with my solitary spoon. If I kept up this cycle of cereal and soup, I could eat for a week without dirtying another dish. I wandered idly around the apartment, feeling restless and uneasy. I wanted desperately to talk to Lonnie, but I didn't see a way to do it, short of driving the hour up to Santa Maria. Ida Ruth seemed to feel he'd resent the intrusion, but I thought he should be apprised of what was going on. Currently, his case was in complete disarray, and I didn't see a way to clean it up before he came home. He was going to love me.

This was now Thursday afternoon. Morley's funeral was on Friday, and if I had questions to raise about the cause of death I was going to have to move quickly. Once he was buried, this whole issue would be buried with him. Since his death was attributed to natural causes, my guess was that nobody'd bothered to question his activities the last couple of days of his life. I still had no idea where he'd gone or whom he'd seen. The only thing I was sure about was that he'd taken those pictures. I was assuming his actions had been prompted by his conversation with David Barney, but I couldn't be certain. Maybe he'd talked to Dorothy or Louise about the case.

I put a call through to the house. Louise answered on the first ring. "Hi, Louise. This is Kinsey. You found the bag I left?"

"Yes, and thank you. I'm sorry we weren't here, but Dorothy wanted to go over to the funeral home to see Morley. We realized you'd stopped by as soon as we got back."

"How's Dorothy holding up?"

"About as well as could be expected. She's a pretty tough old bird. We both are if it comes to that."

"Uhm, listen, Louise, I know this is an imposition, but is there any way I could talk to the two of you this afternoon?"

"About what?"

"I'd really prefer to discuss it in person. Is Dorothy up for a visit?"

I could hear her hesitation.

"It's important," I said.

"Just a minute. I'll check." She put a hand over the mouthpiece and I could hear the murmur of their conversation. She came back on the line. "If you can make it brief," she said.

"I'll be out there in fifteen minutes."

For the third time in two days, I drove out to Morley's house in Colgate. The early afternoon sun was just making an appearance. December and January are really our best months. February can be rainy and it's usually gray. Spring in Santa Teresa is like spring anywhere else in the country. By early summer, we're swathed in a perpetual marine layer so that days begin in the bright white-gray of fog and end in a curious golden sunlight. So far December had been a blend of the two seasons, spring and summer alternating inexplicably from day to day.

Louise answered my knock and let me into the living room, where Dorothy had been ensconced on the couch.

"I'm going to make us a pot of tea," Louise murmured and then excused herself. Moments later, I could hear her rattling dishes as she took them from the cupboard.

Dorothy was still dressed in a skirt and sweater from her recent outing. She'd taken off her shoes and a quilt had been tucked around her legs for warmth. One narrow foot, looking as fragile as porcelain, extended from the swaddling. She and Louise might have looked more like sisters before her illness had drained her face of color. Both were small-boned with blue eyes and fine-textured skin. Dorothy was sporting a platinum-blond wig in a blowsy bedroom style. She caught my eye and smiled, reaching up to adjust the Dynel pouf. "I always wanted to be a blonde," she said ruefully and then held out her hand. "You're Kinsey Millhone. Morley told me all about you." We shook hands. Hers felt light and cold, as leathery as a bird's claw.

"Morley talked about me?" I said with surprise.

"He always thought you had great promise if you could learn to curb your tongue."

I laughed. "I haven't quite managed that, but it's nice to hear. I was sorry he and Ben never patched up their differences."

"They were both much too stubborn," she said with mock disgust. "Morley never could remember what they fought about. Have a seat, dear. Louise will bring us some tea in just a minute."

I chose a small chair covered in a tapestry. "I don't want to be a bother. I appreciate this. You must be tired."

"Oh, I'm used to that. If I fade, you'll just have to forgive me and carry on with Loo. We were just over at the funeral home for the 'viewing,' as they refer to it."

"How does he look?"

"Well, I don't think the dead ever look *good*. They seem flat somehow. Have you ever noticed that? Like they've had half the stuffing taken out," she said. Her tone was matter-of-fact, as if she were discussing an old mattress instead of the man she'd been married to for forty-odd years. "I hope that doesn't sound heartless. I loved the man dearly and I can't tell you what a shock it was to have him go like that. This past year, we talked quite a lot about death, but I always assumed mine was the one under discussion."

Louise returned to the room. "The tea will just be another minute. In the meantime, why don't you tell us what's on your mind." She perched on the arm of Morley's leather chair.

"I need some answers to a few questions and I thought you might help. Did Morley talk to you about this case he was working on? I don't want to give you background if you already know the setup."

Dorothy adjusted her quilt. "Morley told me about every case. As I understand it, this fellow Barney had already been tried for murder. The lawsuit was an attempt on the part of the victim's ex-husband to prove him guilty of wrongful death so that he couldn't inherit the woman's estate."

"Exactly," I said. "David Barney got in touch with me twice yesterday. He said he'd talked to Morley on Wednesday of last week. He implied Morley was going to look into a couple of questions for him. Did Morley tell you what he was doing? I'm trying to piece this together and I don't want to jump to conclusions if I can help it."

"Well, let's see now. I know the fellow got in touch with him, but he never went into any detail. I had my chemo Wednesday afternoon and I was in bad shape. Usually we spent time together in the evenings, but I was completely exhausted and ended up in bed. I slept right through the evening and most of Thursday."

I glanced at Louise. "What about you? Did he talk to you about it?"

She shook her head. "Not anything specific. Just the fact that they'd talked and he had work to do."

"Did he seem to believe what David Barney had told him?"

Louise thought about that and shook her head. "I'm not really sure. He must have given him some credit or he wouldn't have done anything."

Dorothy spoke up. "Well, now that's not quite true, Loosie. Whatever the man said, he was trying to keep an open mind. Morley said it was foolish to make assumptions before all the facts were in."

I said, "That's certainly what I was taught." I reached into my shoulder bag and retrieved the pack of photographs. "It looks like he took these sometime on Friday. Did he tell you what he was up to?"

"That one I can answer," Louise said promptly. "We had an early lunch together. Since he was dieting, he liked to have his meals here at the house. Less temptation, he said. He left here about noon and went out to the office to pick up his mail. He had an early afternoon appointment and then he spent the rest of the day out looking for trucks. He dropped the film off on his way home and said he'd pick the prints up Saturday, which was when he started feeling poorly. He probably forgot all about it."

"How'd he know what to look for?"

"You mean what kind of truck it was? He didn't say anything about that. He thought the same truck might have been involved in some kind of accident, but he didn't say what it was or how he came to that conclusion. He'd picked up a description of it from the original police report."

I thought about the timing. Everything must have come on the heels of his conversation with David Barney. "What happened on Saturday?"

"With his work?" Louise asked.

"I mean with anything." I looked from Louise to Dorothy, inviting either one to answer.

Dorothy took my cue. "Nothing unusual. He went into the office and did some things out there. Mail and whatnot from the sound of it."

"Did he have an appointment?"

"If he was seeing anyone, he didn't say who. He came home around noon and just picked at his lunch. He usually took his meals in my room so we could visit while he ate. I asked him then if he was feeling all right. He said he had a headache and thought he was coming down with something. I thought that was more than Louise had bargained for—two invalids for the price of one. I sent him to bed. I couldn't believe he actually listened, but he did what I said. Turned out he had that terrible flu that's been going around. The poor thing. Nausea, vomiting, diarrhea, stomach cramps."

"Could it have been food poisoning instead?"

"I don't see how, dear. All he had for breakfast was cereal with skim milk."

"Morley really ate that? It doesn't sound like him," I said.

Dorothy laughed. "His doctor put him on a diet at my insistence—fifteen hundred calories a day. Saturday lunch, he had a little soup and a few bites of dry toast. He said he was a little nauseated and didn't have much appetite. By midafternoon, he was sick as a dog. He spent half the night with his head in the commode. We joked about taking turns if I started feeling worse. Sunday morning he was better, though he didn't look good at all. His color was terrible, but the vomiting had stopped and he was able to keep a little ginger ale down."

"Tell me about Sunday dinner. Did you fix it yourself?"

"Oh dear no, I don't cook. I haven't cooked for months. Do you remember, Loosie?"

"I made us a cold plate, poached chicken breast with salad," she said. From the kitchen came the piercing shriek of the kettle. She excused herself and headed off in that direction while Dorothy took up the narrative.

"I was feeling better by then so I came out to the table just to keep them both company. He did complain some of chest pain, but I assumed it was indigestion. Louise was concerned, but I remember teasing him. I forget what I said now, but I was sure it wasn't serious. He pushed his plate back and got up. He had his hand to his chest and he was gasping for breath. He took two steps and went down. He was gone almost at once. We called the paramedics and we tried mouth-to-mouth, but it was pointless."

"Mrs. Shine, I don't know how to say this, but is there any way you might consider having the body autopsied? I know the subject is painful and you may not feel there's any necessity, but I'd feel better if we were really sure about the cause of death."

"What's the nature of your concern?"

"I'm wondering if someone, uhm, tampered with his food or medications."

Her gaze settled on my face with a look of almost luminous clarity. "You think he was murdered."

"I'd like to have it ruled out. It may be a long shot, but we'll never know otherwise. Once he goes in the ground . . ."

"I understand," she said. "I'd like to talk it over with Louise and perhaps Morley's brother, who's arriving tonight."

"Could I call you later this evening? I'm really sorry to have to press. I know it's distressing, but with services tomorrow, time is very short."

"Don't apologize," she said. "Of course you may call. At this point, I don't suppose an autopsy would do any harm."

"I'd like to have a conversation with the coroner's office to alert them to the situation, but I don't want to do anything without your permission."

"I have no objections."

"To what?" Louise asked as she came around the corner with a fully laden tea tray. She placed the tray on the coffee table. Dorothy filled her in, summing up the possibilities as succinctly as she'd summed up the wrongful death suit.

"Oh, let her go ahead with it," Louise said. She filled a cup and passed it over to me. "If you discuss it with Frank, you'll never hear the end of it."

Dorothy smiled. "I thought the same thing myself, but I didn't want to say so." To me she said, "Go ahead and do whatever you think best."

"Thank you."

Detective Burt Walker, of the coroner's bureau, was a man in his early forties with receding auburn hair and a close-clipped beard and mustache in a blend of red and blond. His face was round, his complexion ruddy, his coloring suggestive of Scandinavian heritage. His glasses were small and round with thin metal frames. He wasn't heavyset, but he looked like a man who was becoming more substantial as the years went on. The weight looked good on him. He wore a brown tweed jacket, beige chinos, blue shirt, a red tie with white polka dots. While I detailed the circumstances surrounding Morley's death, he leaned an elbow on his desk and variously nodded and rubbed his forehead. I verbalized my suspicions, but I couldn't tell if he was taking me seriously or simply being polite.

When I finished, he stared at me. "So what are you saying?"

I shrugged, embarrassed when it came right down to articulating my hunch. "That he actually died from some kind of poisoning."

"Or maybe it was a poison that precipitated his fatal heart attack," Burt said.

"Right."

"Well. It's not inconceivable," he said slowly. "Sounds like he could have been dosed. I don't guess there's any chance he might have done it himself, despondent, depressed about something."

"Not really. His wife does have cancer, but they'd been married forty years and he knew she depended on him. He'd never abandon her. They were very devoted from what I gather. If he was poisoned, it'd almost have to be something he ingested without knowing."

"You have a theory about the chemical agent involved?"

I shook my head. "I don't know anything about that stuff. I've talked to his wife about his last couple of days and she can't pinpoint anything in particular. Nothing overt or obvious, at any rate. She said his color was bad, but I really didn't quiz her about what she meant by that."

"Couldn't have been anything corrosive or you'd know right off," he said. He sighed, shaking his head. "I don't know what to tell you. I'm not going to ask a toxicologist to run any kind of 'general unknown.' You got nothing to work with. A request like that is too broad. You look at the number and variety of drugs, pesticides, industrial products . . . man oh man . . . even the substances you handle casually at home. From what you're telling me—I mean, let's assume you're right, just for the sake of argument—the problem's compounded by the fact he was in such poor shape."

"You knew Morley?"

He laughed. "Yeah, I knew Morley. Great old guy, but he's living in the fifties when everybody thought drinking a fifth a day and smoking three packs of cigarettes was just something you did for sport. Guy like Morley whose liver or kidney functions were probably already hampered by disease will be more severely affected by any kind of toxic agent because they got no efficient way to excrete such a substance and they probably can't tolerate as much as a healthy individual. Few things we can probably eliminate right off the bat," he said. "Acids, alkalies. I take it she didn't mention any kind of smell to his breath."

"No, and she'd have noticed. They tried mouth-to-mouth resuscitation at first and then figured out it was pointless."

"Takes out cyanide, paraldehyde, ether, disulfide, and nicotine sulfate. You couldn't palm those off on a person anyway."

"Arsenic?"

"Well, yeah. Symptoms you described would fit that pretty well. Except him feeling better. I don't like that much. Too bad he never went over to ER. They'd have tagged it."

"I guess with his wife sick, he didn't want to be a bother," I said. "Everybody's had the flu. He probably thought that's all it was."

"Which it might have been," Burt said. "On the other hand, if it's something he ate and you're talking about the gastrointestinal tract as the portal of entry, then you're talking about a period of time here when you got both chemical transformation and elimination. Generally speaking, chemicals that enter a living organism are either metabolized, eliminated, or both, which means you're progressively reducing the amount of detectable poison. Digestive system goes to work. Hell, he's throwing up the evidence. If the poison kills quickly, there's almost always quantities present on autopsy. It doesn't help he's been embalmed. In a situation like that, when you've got embalming fluid injected in the circulatory system with resultant visceral profusion, toxicologist's problems are blown way bad."

"But would it still be possible to identify?"

"Probably. We'd have to analyze samples of clean embalming fluids, too, check those against whatever foreign elements and compounds are found in the viscera. I tell you what would be the biggest help if you want to get serious about this: Bring me any household products you can find on the premises. Check the garbage for suspect foods. Pill bottles, rat poison, roach powder, cleaning and disinfecting agents, garden insecticides, that kind of thing. I can have a conversation with the funeral director and see if he has anything to contribute. Those guys are pretty sharp once they know what you're after."

"So you'll do it?"

"Well, if she signs the papers, we'll give it a shot."

I could feel excitement bubble up, mixed with equal parts fear. If I was wrong, I was going to feel like a fool.

"What's the grin for?" he asked.

"I didn't think you'd take me seriously."

"I'm paid to take people seriously when it comes right down to it. Lot of times, presumption of death by poisoning only comes about because of suspicion on the part of decedent's friends and relatives. We'll bring Morley out here and take a look."

"What about the funeral?"

"They can go ahead with the services. We'll have him brought out here after that and get right on it." He paused, giving me a speculative look. "Got a suspect in mind if it turns out you're right?"

"I literally don't have a clue," I said. "I'm still trying to figure out who killed Isabelle Barney."

"I wouldn't try too hard if I were you."

"How come?"

"That kind of curiosity might have been what killed Morley."

16

I couldn't believe I had to go back to Morley's
again, but that's where I was headed. Burt
Walker had asked me to bring him any household products that were possible poison candidates. Louise was out in front, standing at the
mailbox, when I pulled up. If she was surprised
to see me she gave no indication. She waited
patiently while I parked the car and got out. We
began walking toward the house as companion-
able as old friends.

"Where's Dorothy?" I asked.

"She's gone to her room to rest."

"Was she upset?"

Her look was frank. "My sister is a realist.

Morley's gone. If someone poisoned him, she wants to know. Of course it's upsetting. Why wouldn't it be?"

"I hated to add to her burden, but I didn't see a way around it."

"There's nothing either one of us can do about that. What brings you back?"

I told her about my conversation with the coroner. "He doesn't seem optimistic, but at least he's willing to check into it if I round up some possibilities. I'm going to need some sort of carrier for the items we find."

"How about a kitchen garbage bag? Ours are the small ones with a drawstring at the top."

"Perfect," I said.

I followed her to the kitchen and together we gathered up everything that seemed pertinent. The storage area under the sink turned out to be a rich lode of toxic substances. It was sobering to realize that the average housewife spends her days knee-deep in death. Some items I declined, like the Drano, reasoning there was no way he could have sucked down a fatal dose of hair-ball solvent without being aware of it.

Louise had a sharp eye, pointing out items I might have overlooked otherwise. Into the bag went oven cleaner, Raid, Brasso, household ammonia, denatured alcohol, and a box of ant motels. I had a brief incongruous image of Morley with his head back, slipping ant motels down his gullet like a succession of live goldfish. There were several of Morley's prescriptions lined up along the kitchen window sill and we tossed those into my trick-or-treat bag.

In the bathroom, we emptied the medicine cabinet of everything with Morley's name on it, plus a few over-the-counter medications that might be lethal in quantity. Aspirin, Unisom, Percogesic, antihistamines. None of it felt particularly ominous or threatening. We checked all the wastebaskets, but came up with nothing the slightest bit suspicious. The garage netted us a few containers, but not nearly as many as I'd anticipated. "Not many insecticides or fertilizers," I remarked idly. Louise was loading my bag with turpentine and paint thinner.

"Morley hated working in the garden. That was Dorothy's bailiwick." She stood back from the shelves, doing a slow turn as she scanned the premises. "That looks like it. Well, motor oil," she said. She turned and looked at me.

"You might as well put it in the bag," I said. "I can't believe he OD'd on Sears heavyweight, but anything's possible. What about the office? Does he have a medicine cabinet in the bathroom there?"

"I hadn't even thought about that. He sure does. Here, let me rustle up his keys while we're at it."

"Don't worry about it. I can have the woman in the beauty shop let me in from her side."

We returned to the front of the house, where I got out my car keys. "Thanks for your help, Louise."

"Let us know what they find," she said.

"It'll be a while yet. Toxicology reports sometimes take a month."

"What about the autopsy? That should tell them something."

"Nothing's going to happen till after the funeral."

"Will we see you at the service?"

"As far as I know."

Driving over to Morley's office I found myself nearly overwhelmed with uncertainty. This was ridiculous. Morley wouldn't have eaten anything laced with Brasso or Snarol. He was hardly an epicurean, but he surely would have noticed the first time he slurped up a spoonful of malathion or Sevin. I couldn't speak to the issue of his medications. None of the bottles had been empty, or even low, so it didn't look as if he'd overdosed, accidentally or otherwise. The two prescriptions that came in capsule form could have been tampered with, of course. I gathered that most days the back door was left unlocked and open. Anyone could have walked in and replaced his pills with something fatal.

I reached Morley's office and parked in the driveway. I rounded the bungalow and moved toward the front door, toting my plastic garbage bag like a vagrant Santa Claus. On second viewing, the place seemed even more depressing than it had at first. The exterior siding was painted the bright turquoise of Easter eggs, the window frames and roof trim done in sooty white. Various signs in the plate glass window, tucked in among the snowdrifts, announced that the salon was now stocking Jhirmack and Redken. I went in.

This time the shop was empty and Betty, whom I took to be the owner, was having coffee and a cigarette at the back while she worked on her accounts. "Where is everybody?"

"They're all out at lunch. Jeannie has a birthday and I said I'd mind the phones. What can I do for you?"

"I need to get back into Morley's office."

"Help yourself," she said and shrugged.

Someone had pulled the shades down. The light in the room was tawny, overcast sun filtered through cracked paper. Along with the smell of mildew and carpet dust, I picked up the scent of old cigarette butts mingling with the smell of scorched coffee and fresh smoke that wafted through the heating vent from the salon adjacent.

A cursory check of the desk drawers and file cabinets netted me nothing in the way of toxic substances. In the bathroom, I found a can of Comet so close to empty the remaining cleanser had formed pellets that rattled around the bottom like dried peas. The medicine cabinet was empty except for a half-empty bottle of Pepto-Bismol. I added that to my plastic bag in case the contents had been infused with rat poison, powdered glass, or mothballs. Having staged this little melodrama, I felt obliged to play it all the way out to the end. The bathroom waste can was empty. I returned to the office to check the wastebasket under Morley's desk but there was no sign of it. I looked around in puzzlement. I'd seen it in here my first trip.

I opened the connecting door and stuck my head into the salon. "Where'd Morley's wastebasket disappear to?"

"Out on the porch."

"Thanks. Can you do me another favor?"

"I can try," she said.

"Morley's office might turn out to be a crime scene; we won't know for another couple days. Can you keep it secure?"

"Meaning what? Don't let anybody in?"

"Right. Don't touch anything and don't throw anything away."

"That's how Morley kept it in the first place," she said.

I closed the door again and retrieved the wastebasket from the front porch, where the Ho Chi Minh of ant trails now meandered across the concrete. Gingerly, I poked through, brushing ants away. I sat down on the top step and began to empty the contents. Discarded papers, catalogues, used Kleenex, Styrofoam coffee containers. The cardboard box, with the half-eaten pastry in it, had now become sole food source for the teeming colony of ants. I set the box on the porch beside me and did a quick study of the contents. Morley must have stopped off at the bakery on his way into the office, picked up a sweetie, and brought it back with him. He'd eaten half of it and then tossed the rest in the trash, probably feeling guilty about breaking his diet. I peered at the pastry closely, but I had no idea what I was looking at. It didn't appear to be fruit, but what else do you make strudel with? I gathered the remnants carefully and wrapped them in the paper that had come with the box.

There was nothing else of interest. I piled everything back in the wastebasket and tucked it just inside the door, which I locked behind me. I returned to my car and took the entire collection of detritus to the coroner's office, where I left it with the secretary to pass along to Burt.

I was ready to pack it in for the day and head home. The whole case was making my stomach hurt. I was feeling bummed out and depressed. The only thing I'd actually accomplished so far was to dismantle Lonnie's case. Thanks to my efforts, the informant's testimony had now been called into question and the defendant himself had an alibi. If I made many more of these sterling contributions, Barney's attorney would have grounds for dismissal. I could feel the anxiety begin to churn in my chest and I felt the kind of gut-level fear I hadn't experienced since grade school. Not to whine about it, but in some ways I could see that my being fired from CF was generating a crisis of confidence. I had always acted from instinct. I was often frustrated in the course of an investigation, but I operated with a sort of cocky self-assurance, buoyed up by the belief that in the end I could do the job as well as the next man. I'd never felt quite as insecure as I was feeling now. What would happen if I had my ass fired for the second time in six weeks?

I went home and cleaned my apartment like Cinderella on uppers. It was the only thing I could think of to offset my anxiety. I grabbed some sponges and the cleanser and attacked the bathroom off the loft. I don't know how men cope with life's little stresses. Maybe they play golf or fix autos or drink beer and watch TV. The women I know (the ones who aren't addicted to junk food or shopping) turn to cleaning house. I went to town with a rag and a johnny mop, mowing down germs with copious applications of disinfectants, variously sprayed and foamed across every visible surface. Any germs I didn't kill, I severely maimed.

At 6:00 I took a break. My hands smelled of bleach. In addition to sanitizing my entire upstairs bathroom, I'd dusted and vacuumed the loft, and changed the sheets. I was just about to tackle my dresser dr. wers when I realized it was time to stop and grab a bite to eat. It might even be time to knock off altogether. I took a quick shower and then donned fresh jeans and a clean turtleneck. My stab at domesticity didn't extend to home cooking, I'm afraid. I snagged my shoulder bag and a jacket and headed up to Rosie's.

I was somewhat taken aback to find the place just as busy as it had been the night before. This time, instead of bowlers, there appeared to be a softball team—guys in sweatpants and matching short-sleeved shirts that sported the name of a local electrical supply firm in stitching across the back. Much cigarette smoke, many raised beer steins and bursts of the sort of raucous laughter that drinking unleashes. The place looked like one of those beer commercials where people seem to be having a much better time than they actually do in real life. The jukebox was pounding out a cut so distorted it was difficult to identify. The television set at one end of the bar was turned to ESPN, the picture showing laps of some dusty and interminable stock car race. No one was paying the slightest attention, but the sound was turned up to compete with the din.

Rosie looked on, beaming complacently. What was happening to the woman? She'd never tolerated noise. She'd never encouraged the patronage of sports buffs. I'd always worried the tavern would be discovered by the yuppies and turned into an upscale drinking establishment for business executives and attorneys. It never crossed my mind I'd be rubbing elbows with a bunch of Ben-Gay addicts.

I spotted Henry and his brother William. Henry was wearing cutoffs, a white T-shirt, and deck shoes, his long tanned legs looking muscular and sturdy. William still wore his suit, but he'd removed the matching vest. While Henry slouched in his chair with a beer in front of him, William sat bolt upright, sipping mineral water with a slice of lemon. I gave Henry a wave and headed for my favorite back booth, which was miraculously empty. I stopped at the halfway point. Henry's gaze had settled on mine with such a look of mute pleading that I found myself opting for his table instead.

William rose to his feet.

Henry shoved a chair toward me with his foot. "You want a beer? I'll buy you a beer."

"I'd really prefer white wine if it's all the same to you," I said.

"Absolutely. No problem. White wine it is."

Since I'd seen the two of them the day before, I could have sworn they'd regressed. I could almost picture them as they'd been at eight and ten years old respectively. Henry was all elbows and knees, conducting himself with a sullen-younger-brother belligerence. He'd probably spent his youth being victimized by William's fastidious and lofty manner. Maybe their mother had assigned Henry to his brother's care, forcing the two of them into unwanted proximity. William looked like the sort who would lord it over Henry, tormenting his younger brother when he wasn't tattling on him. Now at eighty-three, Henry looked both restless and rebellious, unable to assert himself except in clowning and asides.

He was searching now for Rosie while William sat down again. I turned to William and raised my voice so he could hear me over all the ruckus in the place. "How was your first day in Santa Teresa?"

"I'd say the day was fair. I suffered a little episode of heart palpitations. . . ." William's voice was powdery and feeble.

I put a hand to my ear to indicate I was having trouble hearing him. Henry leaned toward me.

"We spent the afternoon at the Urgent Care Center," Henry yelled. "It was fun. The equivalent of the circus for those of us on Medicare."

William said, "I had a problem with my heart. The doctor ordered an ECG. I can't remember now what he called my particular condition. . . ."

"Indigestion," Henry hollered. "All you had to do was burp."

William didn't seem dismayed by Henry's facetiousness. "My brother's uncomfortable at any sign of human frailty."

"Hanging around you all my life, I ought to be used to it."

I was still focused on William. "Are you feeling okay?"

"Yes, thank you," he replied.

"Here's how I feel," Henry said. He crossed his eyes and hung his tongue out the side of his mouth, clutching his chest.

William didn't crack a smile. "Would you care to have a look?"

I wasn't sure what he was offering until he took out the tracing from his electrocardiogram. "They let you keep this?" I asked.

"Just this portion. The remainder is in my chart. I brought my medical records with me, in case I needed them."

The three of us stared at the ribbon of ink with its spikes at regular intervals. It looked like a crosscut of ocean with four shark fins coming straight at us through the water.

William leaned close. "The doctor wants to keep a very close eye on me."

"I should think *so*," I said.

"Too bad you can't take a day off work," Henry said to me. "We could take turns checking William's pulse."

"Mock me if you like, but we all have to come to grips with our own mortality," William said with composure.

"Yeah, well, tomorrow I've got to come to terms with somebody else's mortality," I said. And to Henry I added, "Morley Shine's funeral."

"A friend of yours?"

"Another private investigator here in town," I said. "He used to be pals with the guy who trained me so I've known him for years."

"He died in the line of duty?" William asked.

I shook my head. "Not really. Sunday night he dropped dead of a heart attack." The minute I said it, I wished I'd kept my mouth shut. I could see William's hand stray to his chest.

He said, "And what age was the man?"

"Gee, I'm not really sure." I was lying, of course. Morley was a good twenty years younger than William. "Golly, there's Rosie." I can "Gee" and "Golly" with the best of 'em in a pinch.

Rosie had just emerged from the kitchen and was staring

at us from across the room. She approached, her face set in an expression of determination. As she passed the bar, she reached over and muted the volume on the TV set. Henry and I exchanged significant looks. I was sure he was thinking the same thing I was: She was going to take care of William and no two ways about it. I found myself almost feeling sorry for the man. The jukebox shut down and the noise level dropped. The quiet was a blessing.

William pushed his chair back and rose politely to his feet. "Miss Rosie. What a pleasure. I hope we can persuade you to join us."

I looked from one to the other. "You've been introduced?"

Henry said, "She came over to the table when we first got here."

Rosie's gaze strayed to William and then dropped modestly. "You might be engaged in conversation," she said, fishing for reassurance as usual. This from a woman who bullies everybody unmercifully.

"Oh, come on. Have a seat," I said, adding my invitation to William's. He remained standing, apparently waiting for her to sit, which she showed no signs of doing.

Rosie barely acknowledged Henry and me. Her glance at William shifted from coquettish to quizzical. She focused on the ECG tracing. She tucked her hands beneath her apron. "Sinus tachycardia," she announced. "The heart is suddenly beating one hundred times a minute. Is horrible."

William looked at her with surprise. "That's it. That's correct," he said. "I suffered such an incident just this afternoon. I had to see the doctor at an urgent care facility. He's the one who ran this test."

"There's nothing they can do," she said with satisfaction. "I have similar condition. Maybe some pills. Otherwise is hopeless." She settled herself gingerly on the edge of the chair. "You sit."

William sat. "It's much worse than fibrillation," William said.

"Is much more worse than fibrillation and palpitations put together," Rosie said. "Let me see that." She took the tracing. She adjusted her glasses low on her nose, rearing back to see it better. "Look at that. I can' believe this."

William peered over at it again as if the strip of paper might have been injected with a whole new meaning. "It's that serious?"

"Terrible. Not as bad as mine, but plenty serious. These wavy lines and these spiky points?" She shook her head, her mouth pulling down. She handed the tracing back abruptly. "I get you a sherry."

"No, no. Out of the question. I don't imbibe spirits," he said.

"This Hungarian sherry. Is completely different. I take myself at first sign of attack. Boomb! Is gone. Just like that. No more wavy lines. No more spike."

"The doctor never mentioned anything about sherry," he said uneasily.

"And you want to know why? How much you pay to see this doctor today? Plenty, I bet. Sixty, eighty dollars. You think he don' want you come running beck? You got that kind of money? I'm telling you, do what I say and you'll be just like new in no time. You try. You don' feel better, you don' pay. I guarantee. I give you the first. On the house. Ebsolutely free."

He seemed torn, debating, until Rosie turned a steely gaze on him. He held his thumb and his index finger an inch apart. "Perhaps just a bit."

"I pour myself," she said, getting to her feet.

I raised my hand. "Could I have a glass of white wine, please? Henry's treating."

"A round of blood pressure medication for the bar," he said.

Rosie ignored his attempt at humor and moved off toward the bar. I didn't dare look at Henry, because I knew I'd smirk. Rosie had William eating out of her hand. While

Henry had been mocking and I'd been polite, Rosie was treating William with the utmost seriousness. I had no idea where she intended to go from here, but William seemed to be thoroughly disarmed by the approach.

"Doctor never said anything about spirits," he repeated staunchly.

"It can't hurt," I supplied just to keep the game afloat. Maybe she meant to get him drunk, soften his defenses so she could tell him the truth—for a man his age, he was as healthy as a horse.

"I wouldn't want to do anything counterproductive to my long-term treatment," he said.

"Oh, for God's sake. Have a drink," Henry snapped.

Under the table, I placed my foot on top of Henry's and applied some pressure. His expression shifted. "Yes, well, that just reminded me. Grandfather Pitts partook of occasional spirits. You remember that, don't you, William? I can still picture him on the front porch, sitting in his rocking chair, sipping his tumbler of Black Jack."

"But then he *died*," William said.

"Of course he died! The man was a hundred and one years old!"

William's expression shut down. "You needn't shout."

"Well, shit! People in the Bible didn't live as long as he did. He was healthy. He was hale and hearty. Everybody in our family—"

"Hennnnrrry, you're losing it," I sang.

He was abruptly silent. Rosie was returning to the table with a tray in hand. She'd brought a glass of white wine for me, a beer for Henry, plus two liqueur glasses and a small ornate bottle filled with amber liquid. William had obediently risen to his feet again. He pulled a chair out for her. She put the tray down and sent him a simpering smile. "Such a gentleman," she said and actually batted her eyes. "Very nice." She passed the wine to me, the beer to Henry, and then sat down. "Permit me, please," she said to William.

"Just the tiniest amount," he said.

"I'm telling you the amount," she said. "I'm showing you how to drink. Like this." She poured sherry to the rim of the small glass and placed it to her lips. She tossed her head back and drained the contents. She dabbed the corners of her mouth daintily with the knuckle of her index finger. "Now you," she said. She filled a second liqueur glass and handed it to William.

He hesitated.

"Do what I'm telling you," she said.

William did as she was telling him. As soon as the alcohol hit the back of his throat, he began to shudder . . . a wonderful involuntary spasm that started in his shoulders and traveled rapidly down his spine. "My stars!"

" 'My stars!' is correct," she said. She studied him slyly and her chuckle was positively lascivious. She poured them both another round, tossing her shot down like some old cowboy in a John Wayne movie. Having got the hang of it, William did likewise. A bit of color had come up in his cheeks. Henry and I were watching with mute amazement.

"Done!" Rosie banged a hand on the table and gathered herself together. She stood, placing the sherry bottle and the two glasses carefully on her tray again. "Tomorrow. Two o'clock. Is like medicine. Very strict. Now I bring you dinner. I know just what you need. Don't argue."

I could feel my heart sink. I knew dinner would consist of some incredible concoction of Hungarian spices and saturated fats, but I didn't have the nerve to flee.

William watched her depart. "That's remarkable," he said. "I believe I can actually feel my blood pressure drop."

17

I slept badly that night and jogged Friday morning in a halfhearted fashion. Morley's funeral was scheduled for 10:00 and I was dreading it. There were still too many questions up in the air and I felt as if I'd been responsible for most of them. Lonnie would be coming back from Santa Maria as soon as he wrapped up his court case. I still had a batch of subpoenas Morley'd never served, but it didn't make sense to try to get those out until I knew where things stood. Lonnie might not be going into court at all. I showered and then dug around in my underwear drawer, searching for a pair of panty hose that didn't look like kittens had been climbing up the legs. The drawer was a jumble of old T-shirts and mismatched socks. I was really going to have to get in there and get it organized one day. I put on my all-purpose dress, which is perfect for funerals: black with long sleeves, in some exotic blend of polyester you could bury for a year without generating a crease. I slipped my feet into a pair of black flats so I could walk without hobbling. I have friends who adore high heels, but I can't see the point. I figure if high heels were so wonderful, men would be wearing them. I decided to skip breakfast and get into the office early.

It was 7:28 and mine was the first car in the lot. With no access to daylight, the interior stairwell was intensely dark. The little flashlight on my keychain provided just enough illumination to prevent my tripping and falling flat on my face. When I reached the third floor, I let myself in by the front entrance. The place was gloomy and cold. I spent a few minutes turning lights on, creating the illusion that the workday had begun. I set up a pot of coffee and flipped the switch to On. By the time I'd unlocked my office, the scent of perking coffee was beginning to permeate the air.

I checked my answering machine and found the light blinking insistently. I pressed the button for messages and was greeted by an annoyed-sounding Kenneth Voigt. "Miss Millhone. Ken Voigt. It's . . . uh . . . midnight on Thursday. I just got a call from Rhe Parsons, who's very upset over this business with Tippy. I've put a call through to Lonnie up in Santa Maria, but the motel switchboard is closed. I'll be at the office by eight tomorrow morning and I want this straightened out. Call me the minute you get in." He left the telephone number at Voigt Motors and clicked off.

I checked my watch. It was 7:43. I tried the number he'd left, but all I got was a recording, advising in cultured tones that the dealership was closed and giving me an emergency number in case I was calling to announce that the building was going up in flames. I was still wearing my jacket and it didn't make sense to settle in at my desk. Might as well face the music. Ida Ruth was just arriving so I told her where I was going and left the place to her. I went back down to the parking lot, where I retrieved my car. I'd only met Kenneth Voigt once, but he'd struck me as the sort who'd enjoy being on the sending end of a good chewing out. I really didn't want to discuss the latest developments in the case. For one thing, I hadn't told Lonnie what was happening and I figured it was his place to deliver bad news. At least he could advise Voigt about the legal consequences.

Traffic on the freeway was still fairly light and I made it to the Cutter Road off-ramp by five minutes after eight. Voigt Motors was the authorized dealer for Mercedes-Benz, Porsche, Jaguar, Rolls-Royce, Bentley, BMW, and Aston Martin. I parked my VW in one of ten empty slots and moved toward the entrance. The building looked like a Southern plantation, a glass-and-concrete tribute to gentility and taste. A discreet sign, hand-lettered in gold, indicated that business hours were Monday–Friday 8:30am to 8pm, Saturday 9am to 6pm, and Sunday 10am to 6pm. I cupped a hand against the smoky glass, looking for signs of activity in the shadowy interior. I could see six or seven gleaming automobiles and a light at the rear. To the right, a staircase swept up and out of sight. I tapped a key against the glass, wondering if the tiny clicking sound carried far enough to be effective.

Moments later, Kenneth Voigt appeared at the top of the stairs and peered over the railing. He came down and crossed the gleaming marble floor in my direction. He wore a dark pin-striped business suit, a crisp pale blue dress shirt, and a dark blue tie. He looked like a man who'd built up one of the most prosperous high-end car dealerships in Santa Teresa County. He detoured briefly, taking time to flick on interior lights, illuminating a fleet of pristine automobiles. He unlocked the front door and held it open for me. "I take it you got my message."

"I was in early this morning. I thought we might as well talk in person."

"You'll have to hang on a minute. I was just putting a call through to New York." He crossed the showroom, moving toward a row of identical glass-fronted offices where business was conducted during working hours. I watched as he took a seat in somebody else's swivel chair. He punched in a number and leaned back, keeping an eye on me while he waited for his call to go through. Someone apparently picked up on the other end because I saw his interest quicken. He began to gesture as he talked. Even from a distance, he managed to look tense and unreasonable.

Don't blow this, I thought. Do not mouth off. The man was Lonnie's client, not mine, and I couldn't afford to antagonize him. I ambled around the showroom, hoping to stifle my natural inclination to bolt. Getting fired had taken some of the cockiness out of me. I focused on my surroundings, taking in the aura of elegance.

The air smelled wonderfully of leather and car wax. I wondered what it felt like to have enough in a checking account to make a down payment on a vehicle that cost more than two hundred thousand dollars. I pictured lots of chuckles and not a lot of haggling. If you could afford a Rolls-Royce, you had to know it would set you back plenty walking in the door. What was there to negotiate, the trade-in on your Bentley?

My gaze settled on a Corniche III, a two-door convertible with a red exterior. The top was down. The interior was upholstered in creamy white leather piped in red. I glanced back at Voigt. He was now fully engrossed in his telephone conversation so I opened the door on the driver's side of the Rolls and got in. Not bad. A copy of the car's specs was printed on parchment, bound in leather, and tucked in the glove box. It looked like the wine list in an expensive restaurant. There wasn't anything as vulgar as a price in evidence, but I did learn that the "kerb weight" for the motorcar was 2430 kg and the "luggage boot capacity" was 0,27 m^3. I studied all the dials and switches on the instrument panel, admiring the inlaid walnut. I did some serious driving, turning the steering wheel this way and that while I made tire-squealing noises with my mouth. James Bond in drag. I was in the process of navigating a hairpin turn on a mountainous road above Monte Carlo when I looked up to find Voigt standing beside the car. I could feel the color rise in my face like heat. "This is beautiful," I murmured. I knew I only said it as a way of sucking up to him, but I couldn't help myself.

He opened the door and slid in on the passenger side. He surveyed the dashboard lovingly and then touched the supple leather on the bucket seat. "Fourteen hides for every Corniche interior. Sometimes after closing, I come down here and sit."

"You own this place and you don't drive one yourself?"

"I can't afford it quite yet," he said. "I made up my mind if we won this lawsuit I was going to buy one of these, just for the thrill of it." His expression was pained. "From what Rhe tells me, you've stirred up a hornets' nest. She's talking about suing the shit out of you and Lonnie both."

"On what grounds?"

"I have no idea. People who sue hardly need a reason these days. God only knows how it's going to impact my case. You were hired to serve subpoenas. You weren't instructed to go off on any tangents."

"I can't assess the situation from a legal standpoint—that's really Lonnie's job. . . ."

"But how did it happen? That's what I don't get."

Trying not to sound defensive, I told him about my conversation with Barney and what I'd found out since then, detailing Tippy's involvement in the death of the elderly pedestrian. Voigt didn't let me get to the end of it.

"That's ludicrous. Absurd! Morley worked on this case for months and he never came up with any information about Tippy and this hit-and-run accident."

"Actually, that's not true. He was pursuing the same lead I was. He'd already taken pictures of her father's pickup, which was my next step. I showed the photographs to the witness, who's identified it as the vehicle at the scene."

His brow furrowed. "Oh, for God's sake. So what? After all these years, that doesn't constitute proof. You're jeopardizing millions and what's the point?"

"The point is I talked to Tippy and she told me she did it."

"I don't see the relevance. Just because David Barney claims he saw her that night? This is bullshit."

"You might not see the relevance, but a jury will. Wait until Herb Foss gets hold of it. He'll play the timing for all it's worth."

"But suppose it was earlier? You can't be sure about what time it was."

"Yes, I can. There's a corroborating witness and I've talked to him."

He wiped his face with one hand, palm resting across his mouth briefly. He said, "Jesus. Lonnie's not going to be happy. Have you talked to him?"

"He'll be back tonight. I can talk to him then."

"You don't know how much I have wrapped up in this. It's cost me thousands of dollars, not to mention all the pain and suffering. You've undone all of that. And for what? Some six-year-old hit-and-run accident?"

"Wait a minute. That pedestrian is just as dead as Isabelle. You think his life doesn't matter just because he was ninety-two? Talk to his son if you want to discuss pain and suffering."

A look of impatience flitted across his face. "I can't believe the police will press charges. Tippy was a juvenile at the time and she's led an exemplary life since. I hate to seem callous, but what's done is done. In Isabelle's case, you're talking cold-blooded murder."

"I don't want to argue. Let's just see what Lonnie says. His point of view may be entirely different. Maybe he'll come up with a whole new strategy."

"You better hope so. Otherwise, David Barney's going to get away with murder."

"You can't very well 'get away with' something if you didn't do it in the first place."

A telephone began to ring in one of the sales offices. Unconsciously, we both paused and looked in that direction, waiting for the machine to pick up. By the fifth ring, Voigt flashed a look of irritation at the rear. "Oh, hell, I must have turned off the answering machine." He got out and crossed the showroom at a quick clip, snatching up the receiver on the seventh or eighth ring. When it was clear that he'd been caught up in another lengthy conversation, I got out of the Rolls and let myself out the side door.

I spent the next hour in a Colgate coffee shop. In theory, I was having breakfast, but in truth, I was hiding. I wanted to feel like the old Kinsey again . . . talkin' trash and kickin' butt. Being cowed and uncertain was really for the birds.

The Wynington-Blake mortuary in Colgate is a generic sanctuary designed to serve just about any spiritual inclination you might favor in death. I was given a printed program as I entered the chapel. I found a seat at the rear and spent a few minutes contemplating my surroundings. The construction was vaguely churchlike: a faux apse, a faux nave with a big stained-glass window filled with blocks of rich color. Morley's closed coffin was visible up in front, flanked by funeral wreaths. There were no religious symbols—no angels, no crosses, no saints, no images of God, Jesus, Muhammad, Brahma, or any other Supreme Being. Instead of an altar, there was a library table. In lieu of a pulpit, there was a lectern with a mike.

We were seated in pews, but there wasn't any organ music. The hallowed equivalent of Muzak was being piped in, hushed chords vaguely reminiscent of Sunday school. Despite the secular tones of the environment, everybody was dressed up and looking properly subdued. The place was filled to capacity and most of those gathered were unknown to me. I wondered if the etiquette followed that of weddings

—the deceased's friends on one side, the survivor's on the other. If Dorothy Shine and her sister were present, they'd be seated in the little family alcove to the right, hidden from public view by a partial wall of glass block.

There was a quiet stirring to my left and I became aware that two gentlemen had just entered the pew from the side aisle. As soon as they'd been seated, I felt a gentle nudge to my elbow. I glanced to my left and experienced a disorienting moment when I caught sight of Henry and William sitting next to me. William was wearing a somber charcoal suit. Henry had forsaken his usual shorts and T-shirt and was quite respectably attired in a white dress shirt, tie, dark sport coat, and chinos. And tennis shoes.

"William wanted you to have support in this your hour of need," Henry murmured to me under his breath.

I leaned forward. Sure enough, William had a mournful eye fixed on me. "Actually, I could use it, but what made him think of it?"

"He loves funerals," Henry was whispering. "This is like Christmas morning for him. He woke up early, all excited—"

William leaned over and put a finger to his lips.

I gave Henry a nudge.

"It's the truth," he said. "I couldn't talk him out of it. He insisted I put on this ridiculous outfit. I think he's hoping for a really tragic cemetery scene, widow flinging herself into the open grave."

There was a rustling sound. At the front of the chapel, a middle-aged man in a white choir robe had appeared at the lectern. Under the robe, you could see he was wearing an electric blue suit that made him look like some kind of television evangelist. He seemed to be organizing his notes in preparation for the service. The microphone was on and the riffling of paper made a great clattering.

Henry crossed his arms. "The Catholics wouldn't do it this way. They'd have some boy in a dress swinging a pot of incense like he had a cat by the tail."

William frowned significantly, cautioning Henry to silence. He managed to behave himself for the next twenty minutes or so while the officiating pastor went through all of the expected sentiments. It was clear he was some kind of rent-a-reverend, brought in for the day. Twice, he referred to Morley as "Marlon" and some of the virtues he ascribed to him bore no relation to the man I knew. Still, we all tried to be good sports. When you're dead, you're dead, and if you can't have a few lies told about you when you're in your grave, you've just about run out of shots. We stood and we sat. We sang hymns and bowed our heads while prayers were recited. Passages were read from some new version of the Bible with every lyrical image and poetic phrase translated into conversational English.

"The Lord is my counselor. He encourages me to go birding in the fields. He leads me to quiet pools. He restores my soul and takes me along the right pathways of life. Yes, even if I pass by Death's dark wood, I won't be scared. . . ."

Henry sent me a look of consternation.

When we were finally liberated, Henry took me by the elbow and we moved toward the door. William lingered behind, filing with a number of others toward the closed casket, where final respects were being paid. As Henry and I passed into the corridor, I glanced back and saw William engaged in an earnest chat with the minister. We went through the front door to the covered porch that ran the width of the building. The crowd had subdivided, half still in the chapel, the other half lighting up cigarettes in the parking lot. The scent of sulfur matches permeated the air. This was funeral weather, the morning chilly and gray. By early afternoon, the cloud cover would probably clear, but in the meantime the sky was dreary.

I looked to my right, inadvertently catching sight of a departing mourner with a slight limp. "Simone?"

She turned and looked at me. Now I'm an haute couture ignoramus, but today she was wearing an outfit even I recognized. The two-piece "ensemble" (to use fashion magazine talk) was the work of a designer who'd amassed a fortune making women look ill-shapen, overdressed, and foolish. She turned away, her body rocking as she hobbled toward her car.

I touched Henry's arm. "I'll be right back."

Simone wasn't actually running, but it was clear she didn't want to talk to me. I pursued her at a hard walk, closing down the distance between us. "Simone, would you wait up?"

She stopped in her tracks, letting me pull abreast.

"What's your hurry?"

She turned on me in cold fury. "I got a call from Rhe Parsons. You're going to ruin Tippy's life. I think you're a shit and I don't want to talk to you."

"Hey, wait a minute. I got news for you. I don't make up the facts. I'm being paid to investigate—"

She cut in. "Oh, right. That's a good one. And who paid you? David Barney, by any chance? He's good-looking and single. I'm sure he'd be willing to cut you in on the deal."

"Of course it wasn't David. What's the matter with you? If she committed a crime—"

"The girl was sixteen years old!"

"The girl was drunk," I said. "I don't care what age she was. She has to take responsibility—"

"Don't try that righteous tone on me. I don't have time for this," she said and began to walk away. She reached her car and fumbled with her keys. She got in and slammed the door shut.

"You're pissed because this gets David Barney off the hook."

She rolled the window down. "I'm pissed because David Barney is a horrible man. He's despicable. I'm pissed because good people have to suffer while the bad people walk away with everything."

"You think just because you don't like some guy it's okay to see him falsely convicted of murder?"

"He hated Iz." She put the key in the ignition, turned the engine over, and released the hand brake.

"That doesn't mean he killed her. You were not exactly without a motive yourself."

"Me?"

"The accident you were involved in was her fault, wasn't it? I heard she was drunk and left the car in the drive without the brake pulled on. Because of her, you lost any hope of having children. That's a big price to pay when you'd been cleaning up after her for most of your life. It couldn't have sat well with you—"

"That's ridiculous. People don't murder other people over things like that."

"Of course they do. Pick up the newspaper any day of the week."

"David Barney's full of shit. He'd do anything to shift the blame."

"This didn't come from him. It came from someone else."

"And who was that?"

"I'd rather not go into that. . . ."

"Well, you're a fool if you believe it."

"I didn't say I believed it, but the point is a good one."

"Which is what?"

"Other people had a motive for wanting her dead. We've all been so busy believing David Barney did it, we haven't looked at anyone else."

She seemed momentarily stumped by the thought and then her gaze shifted slyly. "Well, then. Why don't you look in the right direction?"

"What are you saying?"

"I'm saying Yolanda Weidmann. Isabelle wrecked Peter's business pulling out when she did. He really promoted her career. He put in a lot of time and money when no one else would lift a finger. You have to understand just how crazy Isabelle was. Erratic, self-destructive, all the booze and the dope. She didn't have a degree. She didn't have a reputation until Peter took her up. He was her mentor and she shafted him royally. She turned her back on him after all he did. And then, that heart attack of his. That was the finishing touch. In theory, it was brought on by stress and overwork. The truth is, she broke his heart. That's the long and short of it."

"But he didn't seem bitter when I talked to him."

"I didn't say *he* was bitter. Yolanda's the one. She's really a spider, not a woman you'd want to cross."

"I'm listening."

"You've met the woman. You tell me."

I shrugged. "Personally, I couldn't stand her. I spent half an hour over there and she put him down constantly, all these barbs and zingers, little ha-has at his expense. I'd rather see a knock-down, drag-out fight. At least it's honest. She seemed . . . I don't know . . . wily."

Simone smiled slightly. "Ah, yes. She's very cunning. Under it all, I assure you, she's fiercely protective. She can treat him any way she likes, but you try it and look out! I think it makes her a very good candidate."

"But the woman must be sixty-five years old if she's a day. It's hard to believe she'd turn to murder."

"You don't know Yolanda. I'm surprised she didn't do it sooner. As for her age, she's in better shape than I am." She broke off eye contact and her manner became brisk. "I have to go. I'm sorry I blew my stack." She put the car in reverse and backed out of the slot. I stared after her with interest as she pulled away.

I retraced my steps, moving toward the entrance. I could see Henry heading off across the parking lot toward his car. The first cluster of mourners had dispersed to some extent and those who remained in the chapel were just emerging. William appeared from the cool depths of the funeral home, looking somehow offended and confused. He was holding his fedora, which he placed squarely on his head with a slight adjustment to the brim. "I don't understand what denomination that was."

"I think the service is meant to cover all bets," I said.

He looked back over his shoulder at the facade with disapproval. "The building looks like a restaurant."

"Well, you know, eating out is close to a religion these days," I said dryly. "People used to tithe to the church. Now the ten percent goes to the waiter instead."

"It wasn't very satisfactory as funerals go. In Michigan, we conduct these services properly. I understand there's not even going to be a graveside ceremony. Very disrespectful, if you ask me."

"It's just as well," I said. "From what I know of Morley, he didn't have a highly developed spiritual side and he probably wouldn't have wanted any kind of fuss made about his death. Anyway, his wife is ill and might not have been up for more than this." I didn't mention that the body would probably be whisked over to the coroner's office within the hour.

"Where did Henry go?" William asked.

"He's bringing the car around, I think."

"Will you be coming back to the house with us? We're having a light lunch on the patio and we'd be happy to have you join us. We invited Rose, hoping to reciprocate her many courtesies."

"I wish I could, but I have something to take care of. I'll stop by a little later and see what you're up to."

Henry pulled up beside us in his five-window coupe. It's a 1932 Chevrolet that he's had since it was new. It's been meticulously maintained, boasting the original paint, headliner, and upholstery. If William were driving it, I suspect the car would seem prissy. With Henry at the wheel, there was something rakish and sexy about the vehicle. You have to keep an eye on Henry as he's still very appealing to "babes" of all ages, including me. I could see people turning to admire the car, checking him out afterward to see if he was someone famous. Because Santa Teresa is less than two hours away from Hollywood, a number of movie stars live in town. We all know this, but it's still disconcerting when some guy at the car wash who looks just like John Travolta turns out to be John Travolta. I saw Steve Martin driving through Montebello once and nearly rammed into a tree trying to get a good look at him. He's Technicolor handsome, in case you're wondering.

William got into Henry's car and the two rumbled off. There was still not a hint about the trap Rosie meant to spring. Whatever her intention, it was still early in the game. William did seem less self-absorbed today. We'd actually made it through a three-minute conversation without reference to his health.

I drove back into town, taking the freeway south on 101. I got off at the Missile off-ramp and headed east until I reached State Street, where I hung a right. The Axminster Gallery, where Rhe Parsons's show would be opening that night, was located in a complex that included the Axminster Theater and numerous small businesses. The gallery itself was located along a walkway that ran behind the shops. I parked on a side street and cut through a public lot. The entrance was marked by a hand-forged iron sign. A panel truck had been backed in close to the door and I could see two guys unloading blocks wrapped in heavily quilted moving pads. The door was standing open and I followed the workmen in.

The entry was narrow, probably scaled down for effect, because I quickly passed into a large room with a thirty-foot ceiling. The walls were a stark white and light cascaded down through wide skylights, currently cranked open to admit fresh air. A complicated arrangement of canvas, cording, and pulleys was affixed at ceiling height so that the fabric shades could be drawn across the opening if the light needed to be cut. The floors were gray concrete carpeted with Oriental rugs, the walls hung with batiks and framed watercolor abstracts.

Rhe Parsons was consulting with a woman in a smock, the two of them apparently discussing the placement of two final pieces the workmen were bringing in. I circled the room while the discussion continued. Tippy was perched on a stool near the back wall, commenting on the overall effect from her vantage point. Rhe's show consisted of sixteen pieces arranged on pedestals of varying heights. She was working in resins, casting large polished pieces—maybe eighteen inches on a side—which at first seemed identical. I inspected five in range of me. I could see that the translucent material was formed into subtly tinted layers, with sometimes an object buried at the heart—a perfectly preserved insect, a safety pin, a locket on a chain, a ring of brass keys. With the light shining through, the effect was of peering through blocks of ice, except that the resin looked solid and indestructible. It wasn't hard to imagine these totems being dug up at some point in the future, along with bleach bottles, pull tabs, and disposable diapers.

Rhe must have seen me, but she gave no sign of recognition. She was wearing jeans and a heavy mohair sweater in shades of pale blue and mauve. Her dark hair was banded at the nape of her neck, a long silky tassel reaching almost to her waist. Tippy wore a jumpsuit in a lightweight denim. Unseen by her mother, she greeted me with a wiggle of her fingers, which I took to mean "Hi." It was heartening to realize that the person whose life I'd allegedly ruined was alive and well and still speaking to me.

Rhe murmured something to her companion, who turned to stare at me. The woman picked up a clipboard and clopped off across the room, stack heels resounding on the concrete floor.

"Hello, Rhe."

"What the hell do you want?"

"I thought we should talk. I didn't mean to cause you any trouble."

"Wonderful. That's great. I'll tell my attorney you said so."

Out of the corner of my eye, I saw Tippy hop down from the stool and cross the room toward us. Rhe made the kind of gesture an owner uses with a dog. She snapped her fingers and held her hand flat, meaning "Stay" or "Lie down."

Tippy wasn't that well trained. She said "Mom . . ." in a tone that embraced both outrage and insult.

"This doesn't concern you."

"It does too!"

"Wait for me in the car, baby. I'll be there in a minute."

"Can't I even listen to the conversation?"

"Just do as I tell you!"

"Well, God!" Tippy said. She rolled her eyes and sighed hard, but she did as her mother asked.

As soon as she'd left, Rhe turned on me with a chill fury. "Do you have any idea the damage you've done?"

"Hey, I came here to discuss the situation, not to take abuse. What did I do?"

"Tippy *just* got herself squared away. She's finally on track and now you come along with this trumped-up allegation."

"I wouldn't call it trumped up. . . ."

"Let's not get into semantics. The point is, even if it's true, which I greatly doubt, you didn't have to turn it into a big deal—"

"What big deal?"

"Besides which, if you're convinced she's guilty of some kind of criminal behavior, she's entitled to an attorney. You had no right to confront her without my being present."

"She's twenty-two, Rhe. In the eyes of the law, she's an adult. I don't want to see her charged with anything. There might have been an explanation, and if so, I wanted to hear it. All I did was talk to her, trying to get information, and I did that without going to the cops first, which I could easily have done. If I'm aware a crime's been committed, I can't look the other way. The minute I cover for her, I become an accessory."

"You intimidated her. You were threatening and manipulative. By the time I got home, she was hysterical. I really don't know what your story is, but you had better take a good hard look at yourself. You are not judge and jury here—"

I raised my hands. "Wait a minute. Just wait. This isn't about me. This is about Tippy, who seems to be dealing with reality a lot better than you are. I understand you feel protective—I would, too—but let's not lose sight of the facts."

"What facts? There aren't any facts!"

"Let's skip it. Never mind. Discussion isn't possible. I can see that now. I'll have Lonnie talk to your attorney as soon as he gets back."

"Good. You do that. And you better be prepared for the worst."

Trying to get the last word in was almost irresistible, but I closed my mouth and removed myself from the room before I said something I might regret later. As I left the gallery, Tippy approached and fell into step with me. "I wouldn't let your mother see us together if I were you."

"What'd she say?"

"Just about what you'd expect."

"Don't worry, okay? I know she was really mad, but she'll get over it. She's been under a lot of pressure lately, but she'll come around."

"Let's hope so for your sake," I said. "Listen, Tip, I'm really sorry this had to happen. I feel like a dog, but I didn't see a way around it."

"It's not your fault. I'm the one who fucked up. I'm the one who should feel bad about it, not you."

"How are you doing?"

"Pretty good," she said. "I talked to one of my AA counselors last night and she was really great. As soon as we finish here I'll go talk to her, and then later this afternoon I'll talk to the police."

"Your mother's right. It's probably a good idea to see an attorney before you do. You need some advice about presenting your side of it."

"I don't care about that. I just want to get it over with."

"It still might be smart. They'll want your attorney there anyway before you make a statement. You want me to go with you?"

She shook her head. "I can handle it, but thanks."

"Good luck."

"You, too." She glanced back toward the gallery reluctantly. "I better split. I don't guess we'll see you at the opening tonight."

"Probably not, but I do like her work," I said. "Call if you need me."

She smiled and waved, walking backward, then turned and went back to the gallery.

I got in my car and sat there for a minute, feeling heavy-hearted. Tippy was a good person. I wished there were some way to spare her what she would have to go through. She'd be okay in the end, I was confident of that, but I didn't relish having been the impetus for her pain. I could argue she'd actually brought it on herself, but the truth was, she'd found a way to live with the situation for six years now. I had to guess she'd experienced remorse and regret in privacy. Maybe there simply wasn't any way to avoid public penance. In the meantime, I was left with feelings of my own. I really couldn't deal with any more angry people. I'd had it with accusations, threats, and bullying. My job was to figure out what was going on and I intended to do that.

I reached for the ignition key and fired up the VW, then did an illegal U-turn. There was a drugstore a block up and I pulled into the tiny lot, ducking in just long enough to buy three packages of three-by-five index cards—one white, one green, and one a pale orange. After that, I went home. I still had a batch of files from Morley's Colgate office in my car. I found a parking spot across the street from the apartment. I unloaded the backseat and proceeded through the gate, weighted down like a pack mule. I eased around to the backyard and fumbled with my keys.

In the glass-enclosed breezeway that links Henry's place with mine, I caught sight of the luncheon in progress. The December sun was weak, but with so many windows the space functioned like a greenhouse. William and Rosie had their heads bent together in earnest conversation. The subject was probably pericarditis, colitis, or the perils of lactose intolerance. Henry's face was dark and I could have sworn he was sulking, a behavior utterly unlike the Henry I knew. I anchored the stack of files against the doorframe with my hip while I unlocked my apartment and let myself in. I dumped everything on the counter. I turned around to find Henry coming in behind me with a plate piled with food—lemon chicken, ratatouille, green salad, and homemade rolls.

"Hi, how are you? Is that for me? It looks great. How's it going?" I asked.

He put the plate down on the counter. "You won't believe it," he said.

"What's the matter? Hasn't Rosie found a way to whip William into shape?"

Henry squinted his eyes and tapped his temple with his index finger. "It's funny you should mention that. The penny finally dropped. Do you know what she's doing? She's flirting with him!"

"Rosie always flirts."

"But William's flirting back." He opened a kitchen drawer and pulled out a knife and fork, which he handed me with a paper napkin.

"Well, there's no harm in that," I said, and then saw his look. "Is there?"

"You eat while I talk. Suppose the two of them get serious? What do you think's going to happen?"

"Oh, come on. They've known each other one day." I tried a bite of roll first, tender and buttery.

"He's going to be here two weeks. I hate to think what the next thirteen days are going to bring at this rate," he said.

"You're jealous."

"I'm not jealous. I'm terrified. He was fine this morning. Obsessed with his bowels. He took his blood pressure twice. He had several mysterious symptoms that occupied him for an hour. Then we went off to the funeral and he still seemed okay. We get home and he had to go and rest for a while. Same old William. No sweat, I can handle it. I put lunch together and then Rosie shows up wearing rouge on her cheeks. Next thing I know, the two of them are in there with their heads together, laughing and nudging like a couple of kids!"

"I think it's sweet. I like Rosie." I had moved on to the chicken, tucking into lunch in earnest. I hadn't realized I was hungry until I started chowing down.

"I like her, too. Rosie's fine. She's great. But as a *sister-in-law*?"

"It won't come to that."

"Oh, it won't? You ought to go in and listen to 'em talk. It would make your stomach turn."

"Come on, Henry. You're overreacting. William's eighty-five years old. She's probably sixty-five, if she'd ever admit to it."

"My point exactly. She's too young for him."

I started laughing. "I can't believe you're serious."

"I can't believe you're not! What if they get 'involved' in some flaming affair? Can you imagine the two of them in my back bedroom?"

"Is that your objection, that William might have a sex life? Henry, you astonish me. That's not like you."

"I think it's tacky behavior," he said.

"He hasn't done anything yet! Besides, I thought you wanted him to quit harping on his health. What better way? Now he can harp on something else."

Henry stared at me, his expression suddenly tinged with uncertainty. "You don't think it's vulgar? Romance at his age?"

"I think it's great. You had a romance of your own not that long ago."

"And look how that turned out."

"You survived it."

"But will he? I keep picturing Rosie flying back to Michigan for Christmas. I hate to sound snobbish, but the woman has no class. She picks her teeth with a bobby pin!"

"Oh, quit worrying."

His mouth formed a grudging line as he reconsidered his position. "I don't suppose it would do any good to protest. They'd just act as if they didn't know what I was talking about."

I kept my mouth shut, concentrating on the food instead. "This is great," I said.

"There's some for later if you want it," he remarked. He pointed to the cards. "You have work to do?"

I nodded. "As soon as I finish this."

He blew out a breath. "Well, enough of this nonsense. I better let you get to it."

"Keep me posted on developments."

"Absolutely," he said.

We made the usual departing mouth noises and then he disappeared. I closed the door behind him and made a bee-line for the loft, where I kicked off my flats and peeled out of the all-purpose dress and panty hose. I pulled on my jeans, turtleneck, socks, and Nikes. Heaven.

I went downstairs, popped open a Diet Pepsi, and got down to business. I spread all the material on the counter: Morley's files, his calendar, his appointment book, and his rough-draft reports. I made a list of all the people he'd talked to, the dates, and the details of what was said, according to his notes. I opened the first pack of index cards and started making notes of my own, laying out the story as I understood it. I used to use this technique for every case I worked, pinning the cards on my bulletin board so I could see how the story looked. I learned the practice from Ben Byrd, who'd taught me the business when I was first starting out. Now that I thought about it, Ben had probably learned the method from Morley, who'd been in partnership with him until their falling-out. I smiled to myself. They'd called the agency Byrd–Shine; two old-fashioned gumshoes with whiskey bottles in their desk drawers and endless hands of gin rummy. Their specialty had been "matrimonial inquiries," i.e., extramarital sex. In those days, adultery was considered a shocking breach of morality, good breeding, common decency, and taste. Now you couldn't qualify for a talk show appearance on grounds that tame.

The index cards permitted a variety of approaches: time-tables, relationships, the known and the unknown, motives and speculations. Sometimes I shuffled the pack and laid the cards out like solitaire. For some reason, I hadn't employed the routine of late. It felt good to get back to it. It was restful, reassuring, a welcomed time-out in which to get the facts down.

I left my perch and went over to the storage closet, where I hauled out my bulletin board and propped it up on the counter. At this stage, I make no attempt to organize the cards. I censor nothing. There's no game plan. I simply try to record all the information, writing down everything I can think of in the moment. All the cards for Isabelle's murder were green. Tippy's accident was on the orange cards, the players on the white. I found the box of pushpins and began to tack the cards up on the board. By the time I finished the process, it was 4:45. I sat on a kitchen stool, elbows propped on the counter, my chin in my hands. I studied the effect, which really didn't look like much . . . a jumble of colors, forming no particular pattern.

What was I looking for? The link. The contradiction. Anything out of place. The known seen in a new light, the unknown rising to the surface. At intervals, I took all the cards down and put them up again, ordered or random, arranging them according to various schemes. I thought idly about Isabelle's murder, letting my mind wander. How delicious it must have been for the killer to watch this whole drama unfold. It was even possible that David Barney's harassment had suggested the possibility. Shoot Isabelle and who's the first person they'd suspect? The killer had to be someone who knew David Barney's habits, someone close enough to the scene to keep watch. Of course, half of the people who knew Isabelle were in that position, I thought. The

Weidmanns lived within a mile of the house, as did her sister, Simone, whose cottage was on the property. Laura Barney was an interesting possibility. She certainly knew David's penchant for late-night runs. On the face of it, she had little or nothing to gain. I'd tended to assume that the motive was money, but among the killing set there were probably many other satisfactions besides greed to be derived from homicide. What could be more perfect than killing the woman who'd wrecked her marriage and having the blame for it fall on her ex-husband?

There was something here. I was almost sure of it. Maybe it was the angle of approach, some elusive piece of information, some new interpretation of the facts as I knew them.

When the telephone rang, I jumped, my heart banging abruptly into cardiac arrest range.

It was Ida Ruth. "Kinsey. I hope I'm not interrupting anything, but you just got a call from the coroner's office, a Mr. Walker. I guess he left a message on your office machine and then tried this one. He wants you to call him as soon as you can."

I tucked the phone against my shoulder while I picked up a pen and reached for a scratch pad. "What's Burt's number, did he give it to you?"

She gave me the number. As soon as she hung up, I dialed his office.

238

19

"Coroner's office. Detective Walker."

"Hello, Burt. This is Kinsey. Ida Ruth said you wanted me to get in touch."

"Oh, good. Glad she found you. Hang on a second, let me grab my notes." In the background, I heard paper rustling. He put a palm across the receiver, engaging in a brief muffled conversation before he came back. "Sorry. We just finished the post on Morley. Turned out he died of acute renal failure, with evidence of liver damage, cardiovascular damage with circulatory collapse, tubular necrosis—"

"Caused by what?"

"I'm getting to that. I called Wynington-Blake after we talked yesterday? I had a chat with the funeral director. I wanted to tell him what was going on and I was curious if he'd picked up on anything. He says when Morley was brought in, he was 'markedly jaundiced.' "

"From the drinking?"

"That was my first thought, but then I did a little research. I got to picking through that bunch of household and garden items you dropped off. The pastry specimen bothered me because it was vegetable material. Most of that other stuff I couldn't see how anybody could ingest without being aware of it. I checked some reference books here and I'll tell you what popped up. The autopsy confirms this. Did you ever hear about *Amanita phalloides?*"

"Sounds like a sex act. What the hell is it?"

"The death cap mushroom. *Amanita verna* is another possibility. That's another species from the same family, also known as the fool's mushroom. Both are deadly. Judging from this pastry—whatever you want to call it—it looks like somebody baked him an *Amanita* strudel."

"Sounds grim."

"Oh, it is. Listen to this. One fifty-millionth of a gram of phalloidine injected into a mouse is fatal in one to two days. Takes less than two ounces to kill a human being."

"Jesus."

"And either type would do just about what you describe of Morley's symptoms. Interestingly enough, ingestion can be followed by what they call a latent period of six to twenty hours. Then what you'd see is nausea, abdominal pain, vomiting and diarrhea, and cardiovascular collapse."

"So if he got sick midday on Saturday, he could have conceivably eaten the stuff anywhere from early Saturday morning to some time on Friday."

"Looks like it."

"Where would somebody find the damn things? Do they grow in this area?"

"Book says eastern North America and Pacific Coast, late summer and fall. It'd be late for that, but I suppose it's possible. *Verna* is said to be common in hardwood and coniferous forests. They can grow singly, or in clumps or rings. Says they're rare on the West Coast, but somebody might have brought 'em in from some other part of the country. Dried or frozen, something like that. Where'd you find the pastry, at his house?"

"In the wastebasket in his office out in Colgate. I saw the bakery box the first time I was there, but I didn't think anything about it until I went out again."

"Any idea how he got it?"

"I didn't even think to ask. I just tucked it in the bag along with everything else. Actually, I was assuming he'd stopped at the bakery and picked it up himself. Betty, in the beauty shop, says he sneaked all kinds of food in. He'd been on a strict diet for a week, but she'd seen him with doughnuts and Chinese, all kinds of fast food, so the bakery box wasn't inconsistent. Maybe somebody brought it out to him and left it on his doorstep—"

Burt cut in. "I'll tell you something else. According to the data I'm looking at? There's a brief calm period sets in. Remember telling me he got to feeling better? With *Amanita* poisoning, it sometimes looks like the patient's condition is improving."

"You're talking about Sunday morning," I said.

"Right. The truth is, the damage would have been done by then. This toxin tears up your liver, dissolves blood corpuscles, causes hemorrhaging in the digestive tract. He was probably experiencing bloody stools and bloody vomitus, though from what you've said he never mentioned it. Either he didn't think anything about it or he didn't want to alarm his wife. Actually, even if he'd gone into the emergency room, they couldn't have done anything to save him."

"He must have felt like shit. Why didn't he try to get some help?" I asked.

"It's hard to know. Severity of symptoms probably depends on how much he ate. He might have tried some, decided it was spoiled or something, and tossed the rest in the trash. You ever watch Morley eat? He was quick. Man prided himself on how fast he could put food away."

"Somebody knew him pretty well," I said.

"Not necessarily. He made no secret of it. Same with his health. He was always talking about his heart problems and his weight."

"What about the mushrooms? Can they be identified on sight?"

"Not unless you know what to look for. I'll read you what it says. '*A. verna* is pure white. *A. phalloides* is yellowish green to greenish. Spores in both are white and not attached to the stem.' Yada, yada, yada. Let's see. This particular type of mushroom starts out enclosed in what they call a universal veil that leaves a cup at the stem base. When you're picking mushrooms, you have to dig around some because it's sometimes hidden in the dirt. The illustration looks like a toadstool busting out of an egg. Says it's slimy, too. You want more?"

"I got the basics. If the killer had a batch of 'em growing in the yard, the rest would be gone by now anyway. What happens next?"

"I've sent the pastry up to Foster City, the Chemical Toxicology Institute, for analysis. Might be a while until we hear back from them, but I have a feeling they're going to confirm our suspicion. I've put a call through to Homicide, but you might want to talk to Lieutenant Dolan yourself. Believe me, the hard work has just started. Tough thing about homicidal poisoning is proving *legally* that a crime was committed. You have to demonstrate that the death was caused by a poison that was administered with malicious and evil intent to the deceased by the accused. And that means 'beyond a reasonable doubt.' How are you going to link the killer to the crime in this case? Somebody bakes a cake and drops the damn thing off. Morley gets to his office, 'Oh, hey, is this for me?' Odds are nobody even saw where it came from, so what the whole thing's going to boil down to is all circumstantial. We don't even have a suspect."

"Yeah, I know," I said.

"Well, you have to start someplace. I'll give you a call as soon as we have more. In the meantime, I wouldn't eat anybody's home-baked goodies."

"I'll try not to. And thanks, Burt."

By the time I hung up the telephone, my hands were cold. In the past several months, Morley had talked to a number of people associated with the murder of Isabelle Barney. What had he discovered that precipitated his death, too? It must have been significant. A poisoner is considered one of the smartest and most devious of murderers, largely because poison, as a method, requires knowledge, skill, premeditation, and cunning. One doesn't poison in the heat of passion. Poisoning is not an impulsive, spur-of-the-moment crime. The covertness and deliberation suggest the kind of cruelty that makes a charge of first-degree murder nearly automatic in such cases. Morley Shine had died of an internal violence that probably left no outward mark, yet his death had been as agonizing as a stabbing or gunshot wound. I had a sudden flash of the killer with a supply of deadly mushrooms, leafing through a cookbook for a little appetizer Morley might enjoy. I pictured pastry dough being rolled out, the filling gently sautéed with butter, the strudel lovingly assembled, packed in a bakery box, and delivered to Morley's doorstep. The killer might have sat and chatted with him while he ate the lethal savory. Even if it had tasted strange, Morley might not have complained. Too hungry from his diet. Too polite to protest. And then the hours that had passed while he became aware that he wasn't feeling well. He probably didn't even associate the nausea and the stomach pain with the pastry he'd consumed so many hours before. . . .

I'd seen toadstools somewhere. The image flickered in my memory . . . a wooded area . . . toadstools growing in a circle . . .

There weren't that many places it could have been. Simone's . . . the house where David Barney had lived at the time of Isabelle's death, though I didn't remember anything about the landscaping there. The house had overlooked the ocean—few trees in the vicinity. The Weidmanns'. I'd accompanied Yolanda to the patio where Peter Weidmann was napping—a formal garden with the lawn stretching off toward the trees.

Methodically, I removed the index cards from my bulletin board and put them up again. What had Morley seen that I wasn't seeing? I pulled out his Month at a Glance from one of the stacks of files sitting on my counter. I started with the month of October, trying to get a feel for what he'd been doing the last two months. Most squares were empty. November was similarly blank except for a couple of notations: two doctor's appointments, a haircut one Wednesday afternoon. This month, December, had been slightly busier and it looked like he'd actually conducted a couple of interviews. Lonnie would be thrilled to hear he'd done *some*thing for his pay. Yolanda and Peter Weidmann's names appeared twice. The first appointment must have been canceled because he had a line drawn through the time and a big penciled arrow extended from that date to the same day and time a week later. I remembered Yolanda complaining about what a pest he'd made of himself, so he must have been there more than once.

On December 1, a week ago Thursday, he'd penciled in the initials F.V. at 1:15. Voigt? Had he talked to Francesca? She'd told me she'd never met the man. I'd come across a folder made up with her name on the tab, but the file had been empty. Of course, the F.V. could have been a witness on another case, but it didn't seem likely. The Voigts' home phone number was noted at the top of the page. Had she lied about seeing him? There was also the notation on Saturday morning of the appointment with Laura Barney. She'd told me about the appointment herself, claiming Morley never showed. But Dorothy said he'd gone out to the office to pick up his mail. If my theory was right, the fatal pastry could have been delivered as early as Friday afternoon, probably no later than Saturday morning, since he became ill shortly after lunch. Might bear checking out. Working in a medical clinic, Laura Barney would certainly have access to information about poisons. Maybe I'd start with her and work my way back through the list.

I locked up the apartment and went out to the car. I fired up the engine and headed toward the freeway overpass. I cut under the 101 on Castle, turning right on Granita and then left on Bay. It was just past 5:00 when I reached Santa Teresa Medical Clinic, which was in a pleasant treelined neighborhood of medical buildings and single-family dwellings. I was hoping I hadn't missed Laura. The clinic probably closed at 5:00, which meant I was going to arrive to find the door locked and the personnel gone for the weekend. I didn't have her home address, and though I could probably find it, I was impatient at the delay. To my astonishment, I spotted her, head bent, a light coat over her uniform, white crepe-soled shoes moving rapidly as she crossed the street in front of me. I tooted my horn. She shot me a look of annoyance, apparently assuming that I was chiding her for jaywalking.

I waved and leaned over to roll down my car window on the passenger side. "Can I talk to you?"

"I just got off work," she said.

"It won't take long."

"Can't it wait? I'm exhausted. I was looking forward to a big glass of wine and a hot bath. Come back in an hour."

"I have to be someplace else."

She broke off eye contact. I could see her debate, not really wanting to give in. She made a slight face, staring at the sidewalk with annoyance.

"It'll take five minutes if that," I said.

"Oh, hell. All right," she said. She cocked her head at the house behind her, a Victorian structure that had apparently been converted into apartments. "This is where I live. Why don't you go find a place to park and come on up. That'll give me time to get out of this uniform and take my shoes off. It's apartment six, down the hall at the back."

"I'll be right there."

She turned and walked quickly up the porch steps, disappearing through the front door. I found a parking spot six doors down, on the far side of the street. In a little flicker of paranoia, I wondered if she really lived somewhere else. I pictured her entering the building, then leaving by a back exit before I could catch up with her. I went up the wooden porch steps and opened a glass-paneled door into a shadowy hallway. The place was quiet. To the left, there was a hall table with a lamp that hadn't been turned on yet. Mail was piled up, along with several copies of the day's paper. Doors along the corridor had been closed off. What had once been the front parlor and the dining room probably now formed one unit, with a second at the back, with maybe a studio at the rear. I was guessing three apartments down, another three above. A set of stairs angled up on the right.

I went upstairs as instructed. This was not the cheeriest place I'd ever been, I thought, but it was clean enough. The wallpaper looked new, chosen for its Victorian flavor, which is to say saccharine. Nosegays and trailing ribbons led the eye on a merry chase. The effect was depressing despite all the pink and green and mauve activity.

I knocked at the door marked with an oversize brass 6. Laura appeared a moment later, tying a cotton kimono at the waist. I could see her white nursy shoes on the floor near an upholstered chair where she'd tossed her white uniform. I could hear bathwater running, which seemed pointed enough. The apartment consisted of two very large rooms with a cramped bathroom, probably converted from a linen closet. I could see the space heater from the front door and the rim of an ancient tub. The ceilings were high and there was lots of woodwork of the sort that somehow smells of shellac even if it hasn't been touched by a brush for years. The place was sparsely furnished, but what she had was good. She watched me survey the living room/bedroom combination with a trace of amusement. "Does it suit you?"

"I'm always curious to see how other single people live."

"How do you live?"

"About like this. I try to keep it simple," I said. "I don't like working just to pay a bunch of bills every month."

"I hate being single. Have a seat if you like."

"You do?"

"Of course, don't you? It's lonely. And who wants to live like this?" She made a gesture that embraced more than the physical surroundings. She moved into the bathroom and turned off the water. Belatedly, I picked up the damp herbal scent of Vitabath.

"Looks great to me. Besides, nobody's going to take care of you," I said.

She returned to the room. "Well, I hope that's not true. I'm not resigned, I must say."

"Togetherness is an illusion. We're all on our own."

"Oh, spare me. I hate talk like that," she said. "You want to tell me what you came for?"

"Sure. It's about Morley Shine. You had an appointment last Saturday."

"That's right, but he never showed."

"His wife says he went to his office that day."

"I was there at nine. I waited half an hour and then I left," she said.

"Where'd you wait? Were you actually in his office?"

"I was out in the drive. Why? What difference does it make?"

"None, I suppose. I was curious about a delivery," I said.

"That box from the bakery."

"You were there when that arrived?"

"Sure, I was out in my car. The bakery truck pulled up beside me. Some guy got out with this white bakery box. As he passed me he asked if I was Marla Shine. I told him the name was Morley and the guy was late arriving. The sucker tried to give *me* the box, but I'd waited long enough and I was out of there. I hate being stood up. I got better things to do."

"What'd the guy do with it?"

"The box? I don't know. He probably took it in the front. Maybe he left it on the porch."

"What bakery?"

"I didn't see. The truck was red. Might have been a messenger service, come to think of it. Why the quiz?"

"Morley was murdered."

She said, "Really." And her surprise seemed genuine.

"It was probably the strudel in the box you saw. I just talked to the guy in the coroner's office."

"He was poisoned?"

"Looks like it."

"Where does that leave you?"

"I don't know yet. Morley knew something. I'm not sure what it was, but I think I'm close."

"Too bad he didn't leave you the answer."

"In a way, he did. I know how his mind worked. He and the fellow who taught me the business were in partnership for years."

"What else do you need from me?"

"Nothing, at this point. I'll let you get to your bath."

I headed over to the freeway, driving north on 101 until I reached the Cutter Road off-ramp. I turned left, driving into Horton Ravine through the front gateposts. I felt as if I'd spent the whole week trekking back and forth between Colgate, downtown Santa Teresa, and the Ravine itself. The afternoon was turning gray, typical December with the temperature dipping close to fifty, the kind of cold snap only Californians could complain about. I parked in the circular drive and rang the bell. Francesca came to the door herself. She wore a wool shirtwaist dress in a chocolate brown, black tights, and boots, with a black crewneck sweater across her shoulders like a shawl.

She said, "Well, Kinsey. You're the last person in the world I expected to see." She hesitated, focusing fully on my face. "Is something wrong? You don't look right. Have you had bad news?"

"Actually, I have, but I don't want to go into it. Do you have a minute to spare? I want to talk to you about something."

"Sure. Come on in. Guda's gone off to the market to pick up a few items. I was just having coffee by the fire in the den. Let me grab a mug and you can join me. It seems nasty out."

It's nasty everywhere, I thought. I followed her to the kitchen, which was done in black and white, with oversize windows on three sides. The appliance fronts were black, as well as the cabinet facings, which were a gleaming lacquer. The counters were Corian, snow white and seamless. Racks and accessories were polished aluminum. The only touches of color were bright red dish towels and bright red oven mitts. She took a mug from the cupboard and indicated we could reach the den through the dining room. "You take cream and sugar? I've got both on the tray. There's skim milk if you prefer."

"Milk is fine," I said. I didn't want to tell her about Morley just yet. She was looking back at me with curiosity, clearly troubled by my manner. Bad news is a burden that only sharing seems to lift.

The den was paneled in birch, the furniture upholstered in saddle-colored leather. She resettled herself on the leather sofa where she'd been. She was in the process of reading a hardback, a Fay Weldon novel she'd nearly finished judging by the bookmarker. It had been ages since I was able to take a day off and shut myself in under a quilt with a good book. There was a plump pot of coffee on the brass table to one side. She poured coffee into the mug and passed it over to me. I took it with a murmured "Thank you," which she acknowledged with a wary smile. She pulled a pillow into her lap, holding on to it like a teddy bear.

I noticed she didn't press to find out why I'd stopped by. Finally I said, "I checked Morley's appointment book. According to his notes, you talked to him last week. You should have told me when I asked."

"Oh." She had the good grace to flush and I could see her debate about how to respond. She must have decided the lie wasn't worth telling twice. "I guess I was hoping you wouldn't have to know."

"You want to fill me in?"

"I'm embarrassed about it really, but I called first thing Thursday morning and set it up myself."

There was silence. I said, "And?"

She lifted one shoulder uncomfortably. "I was angry with Kenneth. I'd come across some information . . . something I'd been unaware of. . . ."

"Which was what?"

"I'll get to that in a minute. You have to understand the context. . . ."

I couldn't wait to hear this. "Context" is what you mention when you're rationalizing bad behavior. You don't need to talk about "context" when you've done something good. "I'm listening."

"I finally realized just how sick I was of Isabelle's murder. I'm sick of the whole subject and all the drama attached. It's been six years and that's all Kenneth talks about. Her murder, her money, her talent. How beautiful she was. The tragedy of her death. He's obsessed with the woman. He's more in love with her dead than he was when she was alive."

"Not necessarily. . . ."

She went on as if I hadn't spoken. "I told Morley I hated Iz, that I was thrilled to pieces when she died. I was just, you know, spewing out all this emotional . . . garbage. What's weird is when I thought about it later, I understood how twisted my thinking had become. Kenneth's, too. I mean, look at us. This is really a very neurotic relationship."

"You came to this conclusion after talking to Morley?"

"That was part of what triggered the realization that it was time to get out. If I'm ever going to be healthy, I've got to separate myself from Ken, learn to stand on my own two feet for a change—"

"And that's when you decided you were leaving him? Just last week?"

"Well, yes."

"So it had nothing to do with the cancer two years ago."

She shrugged. "I'm sure that played a part. It was like waking up. It was like suddenly understanding what my life was about. Honestly, until I talked to Morley, I thought I was happily married. Really. I thought everything was fine. I mean, more or less. After that, I understood it was all an illusion."

"Must have been a hell of a conversation," I said.

I waited briefly, but she had lapsed into silence.

"What was the 'more or less' part?" I asked.

She looked up at me. "What?"

"You want to tell me what you discovered? You said something made you angry. I gather that's why you got in touch with Morley in the first place."

"Oh. Yes, of course. I was tidying up the study and came across an account Ken had been keeping from me."

"A bank account?"

"Like that. A ledger sheet. He'd been, uhm, assisting someone financially."

"Assisting someone," I repeated blankly.

"You know. Regular cash payments from month to month. This has been going on for three years. Being a good businessman, of course he kept a record. It must not have occurred to him that I'd lay hands on it."

"What's it about? Does Kenneth have a mistress?"

"That's what I thought at first, but in a way it's worse."

"Francesca, would you just quit screwing around and tell me what's going on?"

It took her a moment. "He's been giving money to Curtis McIntyre."

"To *Curtis*?" I said. I could barely take that in. "What for?"

"That's what I asked. I was appalled of course. The minute he came home, I confronted him."

I stared at her. "And what did he say?"

"He says it was like walking-around money. To help with his rent. A few bucks to get some of his bills paid off. Things like that."

"Why would he do such a thing?" I asked.

"I have no idea."

"How much?"

"About thirty-six hundred dollars so far."

"Well, there goes that," I said. "Here I've been feeling guilty because I came up with information that throws a monkey wrench into Lonnie's case and now I find out the plaintiff has been keeping the prime witness on retainer. Wait till Lonnie hears. He's going to have a fit!"

"That's what I told Ken. He swears he was just trying to help the guy out."

"Doesn't he know how that's going to look if it comes to light? It's going to look like he's paying Curtis for his testimony. Trust me, Curtis is not that reliable as it is. How are we going to pass him off as an impartial witness doing his civic duty?"

"He doesn't see anything wrong with it. He says Curtis was having trouble finding a job. I guess Curtis told him he might have to leave the area and go somewhere else. Kenneth wanted to make sure he'd be available—"

"That's what subpoenas are for!"

"Well, don't get mad at me. Ken swears it's not what it looks like. Curtis came to him after David was acquitted—"

"Oh, stop it, Francesca. What's a jury supposed to think?

How convenient. Curtis's testimony is going to directly benefit the man who's been paying him now for three years. . . ."
I stopped where I was. Something in the way she was clutching at the pillow made me study her more closely. "What's
the rest?"

"I gave Morley the ledger. I was worried Kenneth would
destroy it so I left it with Morley for safekeeping till I could
decide what to do."

"When was this?"

"When I found the ledger? Wednesday night, I guess. I
took it over to Morley on Thursday, and when Kenneth got
home later, we had a huge fight. . . ."

"Did he know you'd taken it?"

"Yes, and he was furious. He wanted it back, but there was
no way I was going to do that."

"Did he know you'd given it to Morley?"

"I never said that. He might have figured it out, but I
don't see how. What makes you ask?"

"Because Morley was murdered. Somebody baked him a
strudel filled with poisoned mushrooms. I found the white
bakery box in the wastebasket."

Her face was blank. "Surely you don't think it was *Ken*."

"Let's put it this way: I've been through both Morley's
offices. There's no ledger at all and the files are incomplete.
I've been operating on the assumption that his housekeeping
was sloppy or he was ripping Lonnie off, billing him for work
that was never done. Now I'm wondering if someone stole
files to cover the theft of something else."

"Kenneth wouldn't do such a thing. He wouldn't do any
of it."

"What happened Thursday when you couldn't produce
the ledger? Did he drop the subject?"

"He asked me repeatedly, but I wouldn't tell him. Then he
said it didn't matter anyway because it wasn't a crime. If he
lent Curtis money, it was between the two of them."

"But doesn't it strike you as interesting? Here's Kenneth

Voigt paying Curtis McIntyre, whose testimony just happens to incriminate David Barney in a lawsuit that just happens to benefit Kenneth Voigt. Don't you see the symmetry? Or maybe it was blackmail. Now there's a thought."

"Blackmail for what?"

"Isabelle's murder. That's what all of this is about."

"He wouldn't have killed Isabelle. He loved her too much."

"That's what he says now. Who knows what he felt back then?"

"He wouldn't do that," she said without much conviction.

"Why not? Isabelle rejected him for David Barney. What could be more satisfying than to kill her and have the blame fall on *David*?"

I left her sitting there with the pillow in her lap. She'd twisted one corner until it looked like a rabbit's ear.

20

On the way back to Colgate, I stopped at a gas station and filled my tank. This crosstown driving was the equivalent of a round-trip to Idaho and I was beginning to regret the fact that I wasn't charging Lonnie for the mileage. It was just after 6:00 and traffic was heavy, most of it inbound, heading in the opposite direction. Clouds lay across the mountains like a layer of bunting.

I headed for Voigt Motors, trying to calculate the odds of Kenneth Voigt telling me the truth. Whatever his relationship with Curtis, it was time for some straight talk. If I couldn't get it out of Kenneth, I was going to track Curtis down and have a chat with him. I parked in the little strip lot in front of Voigt Motors, tucking my VW between a vintage Jaguar and a brand-new Porsche. I went in through the front door, ignoring the saleswoman who stepped forward to greet me. I went up the wide stairs to the loggia of offices that rimmed the second floor—Credit, Accounting. Apparently the salespeople were required to be on the floor until closing time at 8:00. Those working the business end were a little luckier, already in the process of going home for the day. Kenneth's office door carried his name in two-inch brass letters. His secretary was a woman in her early fifties who'd gone on being a bleached blonde way beyond the legal age for it. Time had marked the space between her eyes with a goalpost of worry. She was tidying her desk, putting files away, making sure the pens and pencils were placed neatly in a ceramic mug.

I said, "Hi. Is Mr. Voigt here? I'd like to talk to him."

"You didn't pass him on the stairs as you came up? He left two minutes ago, but he may have gone down the back way. Is there something I can help you with?"

"I don't think so. Can you tell me where he parks? Maybe I can catch him before he takes off."

Her expression had changed and she regarded me with caution. "What is this regarding?"

I didn't bother to reply.

I ducked out of the office and continued along the upper level, peering briefly into every room I passed, including the men's room. A startled-looking fellow in a business suit was just shaking himself off. God, that would be convenient. If there were any justice in the world, women would have the little hang-down things and men would get stuck with putting the paper down on the seats. I said, "Ooops. Wrong room," and shut the door again. I found the back stairs through a door marked "Fire Exit." I took the stairs two at a time going down, but when I reached the parking lot, there was no sign of Ken and there were no cars pulling out of the exit.

I went back to my VW and headed out of the lot, turning left onto Faith in the direction of upper State. Curtis McIntyre's motel was only a mile away. This section of town was devoted to fast-food restaurants, car washes, discount appliance stores, and assorted small retail establishments, with an occasional office building sandwiched into the mix. Once I was past the Cutter Road Mall, the northbound freeway entrance appeared on the right. State Street angled left, running parallel to the highway for another mile or two.

The Thrifty Motel was located near the junction of State Street and the two-lane highway that cut north toward the mountains. I hung a left into the gravel entrance to the motel parking lot. I pulled into the unoccupied slot in front of Curtis's room. The lights in most rooms along the L were blazing, the air richly perfumed with the scent of frying meats, a heady blend of bacon, hamburger, pork chops, and sausage. Television news shows and booming country music competed for airspace. Curtis's windows were dark and there was no response to my knock. I tried the room next door. The guy who answered must have been in his forties, with bright blue eyes, a bowl-shaped haircut, and a beard like a tangle of hair pulled out of a brush.

"I'm looking for the guy next door. Have you seen him?"

"Curtis went out."

"Do you have any idea where?"

The guy shook his head. "Not my day to keep track of him."

I took out a business card and a pen. I scribbled a note asking Curtis to call me as soon as possible. "Could you give him this?"

The guy said, "I will if I see him." He shut the door again.

I took out another card and jotted down a duplicate message, which I slid in behind the metal 9 tacked to his door. The neon motel sign blinked on as I crossed the parking lot to the manager's office. *Thrifty Motel* was spelled out in sputtering green, the sound of flies buzzing against a window screen. The glass-paneled office door was open and a NO VA-CANCY sign, red letters on a white ground, had been propped against one of the jalousie windowpanes.

The registration counter was bare, the small area behind it unoccupied. A door in the rear was standing ajar and there were lights on in the apartment usually reserved for the manager on the premises. He was apparently watching the rerun of a sitcom, laugh track pummeling the air with recurrent surges of mirth. Every third laugh was a big one and it wasn't difficult to visualize the sound engineer sitting at the board pushing levers up and back, up and back, WAY up and back.

A small sign on the counter said "H. Stringfellow, mgr. Ring bell for service" with an old-fashioned punch bell. I dinged, which got a big laugh from the unseen audience. Mr. Stringfellow shuffled through the door, closing it behind him. He had snow-white hair and a gaunt clean-shaven face, his complexion very pink, his chin jutting forward as if he'd had it surgically augmented. He wore baggy brown pants and a drab brown polyester shirt with a thin yellow tie. "Full up," he said. "Try the place down the street."

"I'm not looking for a room. I'm looking for Curtis McIntyre. You have any idea what time he'll be back?"

"Nope. Some fellow came and picked him up. At least, I think it was a man. Car pulled in out there and off he went."

"You didn't see the driver?"

"Nope. Didn't see the car either. I was working in the back and I heard a honk. Few minutes later, I saw Curtis passing by the window. I just happened to glance out the door or I wouldn't have seen that. Pretty soon a door slammed and then the car pulled away."

"What time was this?"

"Just a little while ago. Maybe five, ten minutes."

"Do his calls come through the switchboard?"

"Isn't any switchboard. He's got a telephone in his room. That way his phone bill's his own business and I don't have to fool with it. I don't pretend I'm dealing with a classy type of tenant. Dirtbags, most of 'em, but it's nothing to me. Long as they pay the rent in advance as agreed."

"Is he pretty good about that?"

"He's better than most. You his parole officer?"

"Just a friend," I said. "If you see him, could you ask him to give me a call?" I took out another business card and circled my number.

I unlocked the car door, just about to let myself in, when my bad angel piped up, giving me a little nudge. Right there in front of me was Curtis McIntyre's door. The lock looked respectable, but the window right next to it was open. The gap was only three inches, but the wooden frame on the window screen was warped along the bottom and actually bulged out just about far enough for me to tuck my tiny fingers in. Pop the screen out and all I'd have to do is push the sash up, reach around on the inside, and turn the thumb-lock. There was no one in the parking lot and the noise from all the television sets would cover any sound. I'd been a model citizen all week and where had it gotten me? The case was never going to get as far as court anyway, so what difference would it make if I broke the law? Breaking and entering isn't *that* big a deal. I wasn't going to steal anything. I was just going to have a teeny, tiny, little peek. This is the kind of reasoning my bad angel gets into. Trashy thinking, but it's just so persuasive. I was ashamed of myself, but before I could even reconsider I was easing the screen out, slipping the naughty old digits through the opening. Next thing I knew I was in his room. I turned the light on. I just had to hope Curtis wouldn't walk in. I wasn't sure he'd care if I tossed his place. I was more worried that if he caught me there, he'd think I was hustling him.

His mother would have been embarrassed to see his personal habits. "Pick up your clothes" was not in his vocabulary. The room wasn't very big to begin with, maybe twelve feet by twelve, with a galley-size kitchen—combination refrigerator, sink, and hot plate, all filthy. The bed was unmade, no big surprise there. A small black-and-white TV sat on one of the bed tables, pulled away from the wall for better viewing in bed. Cords trailed across the floor, fairly begging to be tripped over. The bathroom was small, draped with damp towels that smelled of mildew. He seemed to favor the kind of soap with pubic hairs embedded in it.

Actually, I didn't care how he kept his place. It was the rickety wooden desk that interested me. I began to search. Curtis didn't believe in banks. He kept his cash loose in the top drawer, quite a lot of it. He probably figured that roving bands of big-time thieves weren't going to target room 9 of the Thrifty. A few bills were tossed in helter-skelter with the cash: gas, telephone, Sears, where he'd charged some clothes. Under the windowed envelopes was a heavyweight self-sealing envelope meant for mailing checks. The address was handwritten, with no return address visible in the upper left-hand corner. I flipped it over. The personalized name and address of the sender had been printed on the back flap: Mr. and Mrs. Peter Weidmann. Well, that was interesting. I tilted the shade on the little table lamp, holding the envelope so close to the bulb I nearly scorched the paper. The envelope was lined with obnoxious stars, obscuring the field so I couldn't see the contents. Happily the heat from the bulb seemed to soften the gum seal, and by picking patiently at the flap I managed to peel it open.

Inside was a check for four hundred dollars, made out to Curtis and signed by Yolanda Weidmann. There was no explanation on the check in the space marked "Memo" and no personal note tucked into the envelope. How did she know Curtis and why was she paying him? How many more people was the guy collecting from? Between Kenneth and Yolanda, he was raking in five hundred dollars a month. Add a few more contributors and it was better than a paying job. I slid the check back and resealed the envelope. The rest of the desk drawers contained nothing of interest. I did another quick visual survey and then flipped the light out. I peered around the edge of the curtain. The parking lot was deserted. I turned the thumb-lock and eased out, pulling the door shut behind me.

I bypassed the freeway and took surface roads back into Horton Ravine. Lower Road was dark, the few streetlamps too widely spaced to offer adequate illumination. The lights that had been turned on at the Weidmanns' house were the sort you offer up to burglars in hopes they'll go elsewhere. The porch light was on and there was no car in the drive. I left my engine idling while I rang the bell. Once I was convinced there was no one home, I backed down the driveway and parked around the corner on Esmeralda. The Horton Ravine Patrol would swing by at intervals, but I thought I'd escape notice temporarily. I opened the glove compartment and took out the big flashlight. To the best of my recollection, the Weidmanns didn't have electronic fences or a big slobbering Doberman. I grabbed my jacket from a jumble in the backseat. I shrugged myself into it and zipped it up the front. Time to go walking in the woods on a little toadstool hunt.

I approached the house on foot, my flashlight raking back and forth across the path in front of me. The porch light contributed a soft wash of yellow that blended with the shadows at the edge of the yard. I moved around the side of the house to the patio in the rear, where two harsh spotlights made the property inhospitable to prowlers. I crossed the concrete slab and went down four shallow steps to the formal garden. The cushion on Peter's chaise had been folded in half, possibly to spare it further weathering. Over the years, the sun had bleached the canvas to a tired and cracking gray. I could see that snails were currently using the surface as a playground.

The grass had been cut. I could see parallel paths through the back lawn, swaths overlapping where the mower had doubled back. Where I'd seen toadstools, there was nothing. I crossed the yard, trying to remember the placement of the fairy rings. Some toadstools had grown singly and some in clumps. Now everything had been obliterated by the passing mower blades. I hunkered, touching minced vegetable matter, whitish against the dark grass. Out of the corner of my eye, I caught movement . . . a shadow passing through the light. Yolanda was home, tramping through the wet grass to the place where I was crouched. She was wearing another two-piece velour running suit, this one magenta. Her walking shoes seemed to flash with short strips of reflecting tape, the pristine leather uppers sprinkled with clippings from the mown grass.

"What are you doing out here?" Her voice was low, and in the half light her face was gray with fatigue. Her platinum-blond hair was as stiff as a wig.

"I was looking for the toadstools that were here the first time I came."

"The gardener came yesterday. I had him mow all of this."

"What'd he do with the clippings?"

"Why do you ask?"

"Morley Shine was murdered."

"I'm sorry to hear that." Her tone was perfunctory.

"Really?" I said. "You didn't seem to like him much."

"I didn't like him at all. He smelled like someone who drank and smoked, which I don't approve of. You still haven't explained what you're doing on my property."

"Have you ever heard of *Amanita phalloides*?"

"A type of toadstool, I presume."

"A poisonous mushroom of the type that killed Morley."

"The gardener puts the clippings in a big heap over there. When the pile gets big enough, he loads up his truck and takes it all to the dump. If you like, you can have the crime lab come haul it away for analysis."

"Morley was a good investigator."

"I'm sure he was. What's that got to do with it?"

"I suspect he was murdered because he knew the truth."

"About Isabelle's murder?"

"Among other things. You want to tell me why you sent a four-hundred-dollar check to Curtis McIntyre?"

That seemed to stump her. "Who told you that?"

"I saw the check."

She was silent for a full thirty seconds, a very long time in ordinary conversation. Reluctantly she said, "He's my grandson. Not that it's any of your business."

"Curtis?" I said with such incredulity that she seemed to take offense.

"You don't need to say it like that. I know the boy's faults perhaps better than you."

"I'm sorry, but I never in this world would have linked you with him," I said.

"Our only daughter died when he was ten. We promised her we'd raise him as well as we could. Curtis's father was unbearably common, I'm afraid. A criminal and a misfit. He disappeared when Curt was eight and we haven't heard a word from him since. When it comes to nature versus nurture, it's plain that nature prevails. Or perhaps we failed in some vital way. . . ." Her voice trailed off.

"Is that how he got involved in all this?"

"This what?"

"He was set to testify in the civil suit against David Barney. Did you talk to him about the murder?"

She rubbed her forehead. "I suppose."

"Do you remember if he was staying with you at the time?"

"I don't see what that has to do with anything."

"Do you happen to know where he is at the moment?"

"I haven't any idea."

"Somebody picked him up at his motel a little while ago."

She continued to stare at me. "Please. Just tell me what you want and then leave me alone."

"Where's Peter? Is he here?"

"He was admitted to the hospital late this afternoon. He's had another heart attack. He's in the cardiac care unit. If it's not too much to ask, I'd like to go in now. I came home for a bite of supper. I have some phone calls to make and then I have to go back to the hospital. They're not sure he's going to make it this time."

"I'm sorry," I said. "I had no idea."

"It doesn't matter now. Nothing really matters much."

I watched with uneasiness as she tramped back across the grass, her wet shoes leaving partial prints on the concrete. She looked shrunken and old. I suspected she was a woman who would follow her mate into death within months. She unlocked the back door and let herself in. The kitchen light went on. As soon as she was out of sight, I began to cross the grass, my flashlight picking up occasional fragments of white. I hunkered, brushing aside a clump of grass clippings. Under it was a scant portion of mower-chopped toadstool—less than a tablespoon from the look of it. The chances of its being *A. phalloides* seemed remote, but in the interest of thoroughness I took a folded tissue from my jacket pocket and carefully wrapped the specimen.

I went back to my car, feeling somewhat unsettled. I was reasonably sure I understood now how Curtis had gotten involved in the case. Maybe he'd heard the jail talk among informants and had approached Kenneth Voigt after the acquittal came down. Or maybe Ken had heard from the Weidmanns that Curtis had been jailed with David Barney. He might well have approached Curtis with the suggestion about his trumped-up testimony. I wasn't sure Curtis was smart enough to generate the scheme himself.

I sat in my car on the darkened side road. I rolled the window down so I could listen to the crickets. The feel of damp air against my face was refreshing. The vegetation along the berm smelled quite peppery where I'd trampled it. I worked for the Y as a camp counselor (briefly) the summer before my sophomore year in high school. I must have been fifteen, full of hope, not yet into flunking, rebelling, and smoking dope. We'd gone on an "overnight," the whole batch of us from day camp, me with the nine-year-old girls in my charge. We did pretty well until we settled down for the night. Then it turned out the tree under which we'd arranged our sleeping bags was a vast leafy nest full of daddy longlegs spiders that commenced dropping down on us from above. Plop, plop. Plop, plop. You've never heard such shrieks. I scared the little girls half to death I'm sure. . . .

I glanced at my rearview mirror. Behind me, a car turned the corner, slowing as it reached me. The logo on the vehicle was the Horton Ravine Patrol. There were two men in the front seat, the one in the passenger seat directing a spotlight in my face. "You having a problem?"

"I'm fine," I said. "I'm just on my way." I turned the key and put the car in gear, easing forward on the shoulder until I could pull onto the pavement in front of them. I drove sedately out of Horton Ravine, the guys in the patrol car following conspicuously. I got back on the freeway, more from desperation than from any concrete plan. What was I supposed to do? Most of the leads I'd pursued had suddenly petered out, and until I talked to Curtis I couldn't be sure what was going on. I'd left word for him to call. My only choice seemed to be to head for home, where at least he could reach me if he got one of my messages.

It was 8:15 by the time I reached my place. I locked the door behind me and turned the downstairs lights on. I transferred the tissue-wrapped toadstool to a Baggie, pausing to search through a kitchen drawer until I found a marker pen. I labeled the Baggie with a crudely drawn skull and crossbones and tucked it in my refrigerator. I peeled my jacket off and perched on a stool. I studied the bulletin board with its road map of multicolored index cards.

It was aggravating to think there might be something right in front of me. If Morley had spotted something, it had probably cost him his life. What was it? I ran my gaze up one column of information and down the next, watching the sequence of events unfold. I got up and walked around the room, came back, and peered. I went over to the sofa bed and lay down on my back, staring at the ceiling. Thinking is hard work, which is why you don't see a lot of people doing it. I got up restlessly and returned to the counter, leaning on my elbows while I scanned the board.

"Come on, Morley, help me out here," I murmured.

Oh.

Well, there was a bit of a discrepancy that I hadn't paid much attention to. According to Regina Turner at the Gypsy Motel, Noah McKell was struck and killed at 1:11 A.M. But Tippy hadn't reached the intersection at San Vicente and 101 until approximately 1:40, a thirty-minute difference. Why had it had taken her so long to get there? It was probably only four or five miles from the Gypsy to the off-ramp. Had she stopped for a cup of coffee? Filled her tank with gas? She'd just killed a man, and according to David she was still visibly upset. It was difficult to picture what she'd done with that half hour. Maybe she'd spent the time driving aimlessly around. I couldn't think why it would matter, but the question seemed easy to clarify.

I reached for the phone and punched in the Parsons number, staring at the bulletin board while it continued to ring. Eight, nine. Oh, yeah. Friday night. I'd forgotten about Rhe's opening at the Axminster Gallery. I hauled out the telephone book and looked up the number for the gallery. This time somebody picked up on the second ring, but there was such a din in the background I could hardly hear. I pressed a hand to my free ear, focusing on the sounds from the gallery. I asked for Tippy and then had to make the same request only doubling the volume and pitch of my voice. The fellow on the other end said he'd go and get her. I sat and listened to people laughing, glasses clinking. Sounded like they were having a lot more fun than I was. . . .

"Hello?"

"Hello, Tippy? This is Kinsey. Listen, I know this is a bad time to try to talk to you, but I was just thinking about what happened the night your aunt was killed. Can I ask you a couple questions?"

"Right *now*?"

"If you don't mind. I'm just curious about what happened

between the time of the accident and the time you saw David Barney."

There was silence. "I don't know. I mean, I went up to my aunt's, but that's it."

"You went to Isabelle's house?"

"Yeah. I was like really upset and I couldn't think what else to do. I was going to tell her what happened and ask her for help. If she told me to go back, I would have done it, I swear."

"Could you speak up, please? What time was this?"

"Right after the accident. I knew I hit the guy so I just took off and headed right up to her place."

"Was she there?"

"I guess so. The lights were on. . . ."

"The porch light was on?"

"Sure. I knocked and knocked but she never came down."

"Was the eyepiece in the door?"

"I didn't really look at that. After I knocked, I walked around the outside, but the place was all locked up. So I just got in my truck and headed home from there."

"You went home on the freeway."

"Sure, I got on at Little Pony Road."

"And got off at San Vicente."

"Well, yeah," she said. "Why, what's wrong?"

"Nothing really. It narrows the time of death, but I can't see that it makes any difference. Anyway, I appreciate your help. If you think of anything else, would you give me a call?"

"Sure. Is that all you want?"

"For now," I said. "Did you talk to the cops?"

"No, but I talked to this lawyer and she's going in with me first thing tomorrow morning."

"Good. You'll have to let me know what happens. How's the opening?"

"Really neat," she said. "Everybody loves it. They're like freaking out. Mom's sold six pieces."

"That's wonderful. Good for her. I hope she sells tons."

"I gotta go. I'll call you tomorrow."

I said good-bye to an empty line.

The phone rang again before I could remove my hand. I snatched up the receiver, thinking maybe Tippy had remembered something. "Hello?"

There was an odd breathy silence, very brief, and then I heard a man's voice. "Hey, Kinsey?" Then the breathiness again.

"Yes." I found myself squinting at the sound. I pressed my fingers to my ear again, listening to the quiet as I'd listened to the party noises at Rhe's opening. The guy was crying. He wasn't sobbing. It was the kind of crying you do when you want to conceal the fact. The air was bypassing his vocal cords. "Kinsey?"

"Curtis?"

"Uh-hunh. Yeah."

"What's wrong? Is somebody there with you?"

"I'm fine. How are you?"

"Curtis, what's the matter? Is someone there with you?"

"That's right. Listen, why I called? I was wondering if you could meet me so we could talk about something."

"Who is it? Are you okay?"

"Can you meet me? I have some information."

"What's going on? Can you tell me who's with you?"

"Meet me at the bird refuge and I'll explain."

"When?"

"As soon as possible, okay?"

I had to make a quick decision. I couldn't keep him on the line much longer. Anybody monitoring the call would get cranky. "Okay. It might take me a while. I'm already in bed so I'll have to get dressed. I'll see you down there as soon as I can make it, but it might be twenty minutes."

The line went dead.

It wasn't nine o'clock yet, but there wasn't much traffic around the bird refuge at night. The preserve encompasses a freshwater lagoon on a little-used access road between the freeway and the beach. The twenty-car parking lot is usually used by tourists looking for a "photo opportunity." There was a tavern across the street, but the property was currently without a tenant. I wasn't going to go down there alone and unarmed. I picked up the phone again and called the police station, asking for Sergeant Cordero.

"I'm sorry, but she won't be in until seven A.M."

"Can you tell me who's working Homicide?"

"Is this an emergency?"

"Not yet," I said tartly.

"You can talk to the watch commander."

"Just skip it. Never mind. I can try someone else." I depressed the button and tucked the telephone in against my shoulder while I checked my personal address book. The "someone else" I called was Sergeant Jonah Robb, an STPD cop who worked the missing persons detail. He and I had had a sporadic relationship that fluctuated according to the whims of his wife. Theirs was a marriage of high drama and long duration, the two having met at age thirteen in the seventh grade. Personally, I didn't think they'd progressed much. At intervals, Camilla would leave him—usually without notice or explanation—taking their two daughters and any money they had in their joint bank account. Jonah always vowed each time was the last. It was during one of these periods of domestic upheaval that I entered, stage left. I was the understudy, a role I discovered I didn't like very much. I'd finally severed the connection. I hadn't spoken to Jonah now for nearly a year, but he was still someone I felt I could call in a pinch.

A woman answered the telephone in a bedroom tone of voice, Camilla perhaps, or her latest replacement. I asked for Jonah and I could hear the receiver being passed from hand to hand. His "Hello" was groggy. God, these people went to bed earlier than I did. I identified myself and that seemed to wake him up some.

"What's happening?" he said.

"I hate to bother you, babe, but a jailbird named Curtis McIntyre just phoned and asked me to meet him at the bird refuge as soon as I can get there. My guess is the guy had a gun to his head. I need backup."

"Who's with him? Do you know?"

"I don't have an answer to that yet and it's too complicated to go into on the phone."

"You got a gun?"

"It's in my office at Lonnie Kingman's. I'm just on my way over there to pick it up. Take me fifteen minutes max and then I'll head down to the beach. Can you help?"

"Yeah, I can probably do that."

"I wouldn't ask, but I don't have anyone else."

"I understand," he said. "I'll see you there in fifteen minutes. I'll drive past and then double back on foot. There's plenty of cover."

"That's what concerns me," I said. "Don't trip over the bad guys."

"Don't worry. I can smell them puppy dogs. See you down there."

"Thanks," I said and hung up.

I grabbed my shoulder bag and my jacket with the car keys in the pocket, congratulating myself that I'd had the presence of mind to get the VW gassed up. It would take all the time I'd allotted to get from my apartment to the office and back down to the bird refuge. Whomever Curtis had with him was going to be edgy about delays, suspicious if I didn't show up in the time I'd said I would. I drove faster than the law allows, but I kept an eye on the rearview mirror, watching for cunningly concealed black-and-whites. I hoped I wouldn't have trouble laying hands on the gun. I'd moved only five weeks ago, hauling my hastily packed cardboard boxes from California Fidelity to Lonnie Kingman's office. I hadn't actually seen the gun since I bought it in May. I'd resented the necessity for the purchase in the first place, but I'd heard that my name was at the top of somebody's hit list.

A private eye named Robert Dietz had stepped into the picture when I realized I needed help. Once I accepted the fact that my life was truly endangered, I gave up any passing interest in being politically correct. It was Dietz who'd insisted that I replace my .32-caliber Davis with the H&K. The damn gun had cost me an arm and a leg. Come to think of it, I wasn't all that sure where the Davis was either.

When I got to the office, I left my car out on the street with my shoulder bag tucked down against the driver's seat out of sight. There was little or no traffic and all the nearby office buildings were locked down for the night. I moved through the darkened arch along the driveway that led back to the little twelve-car parking lot. I didn't see Lonnie's Mercedes, but there was a section of pavement washed with the light from his offices above. Well, great. He was back. I couldn't stop and explain what was going on, but it probably wouldn't be hard to talk him into going with me. Despite his professional demeanor, Lonnie's a brawler at heart. He'd love the idea of sneaking through the bushes in the dark.

I used my keychain flashlight against the pitch-black stairwell. When I reached the third-floor corridor, I could see where Lonnie'd turned the lights on in the reception area. I bypassed the front entrance and used the unmarked door that opened closer to my office. I glanced to my right toward Lonnie's office, located one door down from mine.

"Hey, Lonnie? Don't disappear on me. I need some help. I'll be there in a second and tell you what's going on."

I didn't bother to wait for a reply. I opened my office door and flipped the light switch. My office space had once functioned as the employees' lounge/kitchen, with my current closet serving as a pantry of sorts. There were five cartons still stacked against the back wall, clearly stuff I hadn't needed in the new place so far. I couldn't even remember what was in those boxes. I've heard the theory that if you still haven't unpacked a carton two years after a move, you simply call the Salvation Army and have the damn thing hauled away. I'd cleverly marked each box "Office Stuff." I pulled one out and ripped off the wide brown sealing tape. I peeled the flaps back. This box contained all my income tax files. I tried the next box and hit pay dirt. Oh, yea. The Heckler & Koch was sitting right on top, still in the box, the Winchester Silvertips in two boxes just under it.

I sat down on the floor and took the gun out. I grabbed a box of ammo and opened it, pulling out the little white Styrofoam base. I began to push cartridges into the magazine. Once we'd arrived at the gun shop, Dietz and I had had yet another fractious argument about which model I should buy: the P7, which held nine rounds, or the P9S, which held ten. Guess which one cost more? I was in a bitchy mood anyway, feeling stubborn and uncooperative. The P7 was already priced at more than eleven hundred bucks. I'd also griped about the P9S, which I felt was too much gun for me. What I meant, of course, was expensive, which Dietz guessed right away.

I'd said, "Goddamn it. I get to win sometimes."

"You win more often than you should," he'd said. I wished now he'd won a lot more arguments, especially the one about my going off to Germany with him. . . .

The lights in my office went out abruptly and I was left in the pitch-black dark. I had no exterior windows so I couldn't see a thing. Had Lonnie left without saying a word? Maybe he hadn't heard me come in, I thought. I slid the magazine into the gun and slapped it home with my palm. Navigating in the dark is like escaping from a burning building—you stay low. I tucked the gun in my waistband and crawled to the doorway with no dignity whatsoever. It beat bumping into the furniture, but it wasn't going to look good if the lights popped back on. My office door was standing open and I peered out into the hallway. All the lights in the office were out. What the hell had he done, stuck a fork in the outlet? The whole place had been plunged into blackness. I said, "Lonnie?"

Silence. How could he have disappeared so fast?

I could have sworn I heard a faint sound from the vicinity of Lonnie's office. I didn't think I was alone. I listened. The office was so quiet the silence seemed dense, thick with sub-sounds. Even in the dark, I found myself closing my eyes, hoping somehow to hear better with my visual sense shut down. I sat back on my haunches, crouched in my doorway across from the point where Ida Ruth and a secretary named Jill had their desks.

Who was in the office with me? And where? Having called out twice now in clear bell-like tones, we all knew where I was. I eased back down on all fours and started belly-crawling the ten feet across the corridor toward the space between the two secretaries' desks.

Somebody fired at me. The report was so loud I levitated like a cat, in one of those miraculous moves where all four limbs seem to leave the ground at once. Adrenaline blew through me in a sudden spurt. I wasn't aware that I had shrieked until the sound was out. My heart banged in my throat and my hands tingled from the rush. I must have leaped the distance because I found myself exactly where I wanted to be, in a crouch, my right shoulder resting against Ida Ruth's desk drawers. I put a hand across my mouth to still my breathing. I listened. The shooter seemed to be firing from the vantage point of Lonnie's office, effectively cutting me off from the reception area, where the front entrance was located. The obvious maneuver here was to back my way down the wide corridor, which was now to my left. The un-marked door, leading to the main hall, was about fifteen feet away. Once there, I could crouch beside it, try the knob to make sure the door was still open, count to three, and then voom . . . go right through. Good plan. Okay. All I had to do was get there. The problem was that I was afraid to risk the distance without cover of some kind. Where was Ida Ruth's rolling chair? That might do. . . .

I put a tentative hand out, groping my way along the floor

in search of the chair. I found myself touching a face. I jerked my hand back, emitting a sound at the back of my throat as I sucked in my breath. Someone was lying on the floor next to me. I half expected a hand to shoot out and grab me, but there was no move in my direction. I reached out again and made contact. Flesh. Slack mouth. I felt the features. Smooth skin, strong chin. Male. The guy was too thin to be Lonnie and I didn't believe it was John Ives or the other attorney, Martin Cheltenham. It almost had to be Curtis, but what the hell was he doing here? He was still warm, but his cheek was sticky with blood. I put my hand on his throat. No pulse. I placed a hand on his chest, which was dead still. His shirt was wet in front. He must have made the call from the office. He was probably shot shortly afterward in preparation for my arrival. Somebody knew me better than I thought . . . well enough to know where I kept my gun, at any rate . . . well enough to know I'd never show up at a meeting without coming down here first.

I felt behind me in the dark again, encountering one of the sturdy casters on Ida Ruth's rolling chair. I blinked in the dark as another possibility occurred to me. If I could find an open phone line, I could dial 911 and let it ring through to the dispatcher. Even if I never said a word, the address would come up on the police station computer and they'd send someone to investigate. I hoped.

I came up on my knees, peering over the top of the nearest desk. Now that my eyes were adjusting, I could distinguish greater and lesser degrees of dark: the charcoal upright of a doorway, the block form of a file cabinet. I moved my hand across the surface of the desk with incredible care, not wanting to bump into anything or knock anything over. I found the telephone. I lifted the entire instrument. I cleared the edge of the desk and lowered it to the floor. I angled the receiver upward slightly, slipping an index finger onto the cutoff button. I put the receiver against my ear and let the button come up. Nothing. No dial tone. No light coming on.

I peered up over the desk again and scanned the dark. There was no movement, no shadowy silhouette framed in Lonnie's doorway.

I eased the gun from my waistband. I'd never fired the H&K in a tight spot. I'd gone up to the range a few times with Dietz before he left. He'd put me through numerous firing drills until I refused to take any more orders from him. Usually I'm pretty good about keeping in practice, but not lately. It was the first time I'd tuned in to the fact I was depressed about his leaving. Shit, Kinsey, get a clue. The gun was reassuring. At least I wouldn't be totally at the mercy of my assailant. I squeezed the cocking lever on the grip.

I could hear breathing now, but it might have been mine.

I wished I hadn't left the relative safety of my office. My phone had a separate line and it might still be functioning. If I could cross the hall and get back to my office, I could at least lock the door and shove the desk up against it. All I'd have to do then was hold out until morning. Surely the cleaning crew would be in. I might be rescued sooner if anybody figured it out. I thought about Jonah. He'd be waiting at the bird refuge, wondering what had happened. What would he do when I didn't show up? Probably assume he got the location wrong. To my mind, the term *bird refuge* didn't contain any ambiguity. There was only one parking area. I had told him I was coming here first to pick up my gun, but he'd sounded half asleep. Who knew what he'd remember or if it would ever dawn on him to check it out.

I pulled Ida Ruth's chair closer and crouched behind it, keeping it between me and my assailant as I crept toward the unmarked door. Another shot was fired. The bullet tore through the upholstery with such force that the plastic chair back banged me right in the face. It was all I could do to keep from screaming as the blood gushed from my nose. I scooted backward, pulling the chair along in front of me as I scrambled toward the door. I eased a hand up along the door-frame until I touched the knob. Locked. Another shot was fired. A splinter of wood sailed past my face. I dove toward the wall, using the baseboard like a lane marker as I swam my way along the floor, praying the carpet would part for me and let me sink beneath the pile. The next shot ripped along my right hip as if someone were trying to strike a giant match. I jumped again, making a short exclamation of pain and astonishment. The stinging sensation told me I'd been hit. I fired back.

I rolled toward the far side of the corridor. The only protection I had at this point was the dark. If my eyes were adjusting, then so were my assailant's. I fired at Lonnie's doorway again. I heard a bark of surprise. I fired again, crawling backward down the hallway toward the kitchen in haste. My right buttock was on fire, sparks shooting down my right leg and up into my right side. I wasn't even crawling as efficiently as a six-month-old baby. I hugged the wall, feeling tears well, not from sorrow, but from pain.

I don't presume to understand how the human brain works. I do know that the left brain is verbal, linear, and analytical, solving life's little problems by virtue of sound reasoning. The right brain on the other hand tends to be intuitive, imaginative, whimsical, and spontaneous, coming up with the inexplicable Ah-ha! answer to some question you may have asked yourself three days before. There's no accounting for this. As I huddled in the blackness, gun in hand, with my lips pressed together to keep from shrieking like a girl, I knew with perfect certainty who was shooting at me. And to tell you the truth, it really pissed me off. When the next shot was fired, I flattened myself, braced the gun in both hands, and fired back. Maybe it was time to declare myself. "Hey, David?"

Silence.

"I know it's you," I said.

He laughed. "I was wondering if you'd figure it out."

"It took me a while, but I got it," I said. It was weird talking to him in the dark like this. I could barely visualize his face and that bothered me.

"How'd you guess?"

"I realized there was a gap between the time Tippy hit the pedestrian and the time she bumped into you."

"So?"

"So I called her and asked where she was for that thirty minutes. Turns out she went up to Isabelle's."

There was a silence.

I went on, "You must have just killed Isabelle when you saw Tippy coming up the drive. While she was knocking at the door, you hopped in the truck bed. She drove you away from the house when she left. All you had to do then was wait till she slowed down. Out you hop on the driver's side, giving the truck a thump with your fist as you jump. Tippy turns left and you're sprawled on the pavement in plain view of the work crew across the street."

"Yeah, with Mr. Average Citizen ready to testify in my behalf," he chimed in at last.

"What about Morley? Why'd you have to kill him?"

"Are you kidding? That old buzzard was really breathing down my neck. When I talked to him on Wednesday, he'd just about made the leap. I knew if I didn't take him down quick, I'd be in the soup. Raiding his files was a snap after that. He's kind of a slob when it came down to his paperwork."

"Where'd you get the death caps?"

"The Weidmanns' backyard. That's what inspired the notion in the first place. I went over there one night and plucked up a dozen and then paid my cook a little extra to make the pastry. She didn't know *Amanita* from her ass. She's lucky she didn't taste for seasonings as she went along."

"I gotta hand it to you. You are one clever chap," I said, thinking hard. Behind me, the corridor made a left-hand turn into a cul-de-sac with the copy room on one side and the new kitchenette on the other. If I rounded the corner, I'd be out of the line of fire, but I'd have a couple of problems I wasn't sure I could solve. One, I'd no longer have a straight line of fire myself. And two, I'd be trapped. On the other hand, I was trapped where I was. The kitchen had a small window. With luck, if I got there, I could bust out the glass and holler real loud for help. Like maybe nobody'd heard the gunfight at the O.K. Corral in here. If I could persuade him to keep talking, he might not hear me shift locations. "I'm surprised you didn't slip up somewhere along the line," I said. As long as I was stuck, I might as well fish for information.

Reluctantly, he said, "I did slip once."

"Really? When was that?"

"I got drunk one night with Curtis and flapped my big mouth. I still can't believe I did that. The minute it was out I knew I'd have to get rid of him one day."

"God," I said. "You mean to tell me he was telling the *truth* for once?"

Barney laughed in the dark. "Oh, sure. He figured it was worth some money to someone so he went straight to Ken Voigt and tattled. Sure enough, Voigt started paying Curtis to ensure his testimony. Fool."

I closed my eyes. Voigt *was* a fool. So eager to win he'd risked his own credibility. "What about me? Is there some scheme in the works or you just doing this for yucks?"

"Actually, I'd like to run you out of ammunition so I can finish you off. I killed Curtis with an H&K, like the one you've got. I'm going to shoot you with the thirty-eight I used on Isabelle and put that gun in his hand. That way, it'll look like he killed her—"

"And I killed him," I said, completing the sentence. "You ever hear about ballistics? They're going to know the gun wasn't mine."

"I'll be gone by then."

"Smart."

"Very smart," he said, "which is more than you can say of most people. Human beings are like ants. So busy, so involved in their little world. Watch an anthill sometime. Such

278

activity. You can tell everything looks so important from the ant's point of view. But it's not. In reality, it doesn't amount to anything. Haven't you ever stepped on an ant? Rubbed one out with your thumb? You don't suffer any great pangs of conscience. You think, There. I gotcha. Same thing here."

"Jesus. This is really profound. I'm taking notes over here."

That made him mad and he fired twice, slugs plowing into the carpet to my right. I matched him shot for shot just for the hell of it.

"You're so innocent," he said. "You think you're such a cynic, but you were easy to fool—"

"Let's not jump to conclusions," I said. I thought I saw his head appear in Lonnie's doorway. I fired two more times.

He disappeared. "You missed."

"Sorry to hear that." I slipped out the magazine and counted cartridges by feel. All that nice ammo in the other room.

"You have a problem over there?"

"I broke a fingernail."

He was silent for a moment. "Be careful with your ammo. You only have one shot left."

"Bullshit. I have two."

He laughed in the dark. "Oh, right. Uh-hunh."

I was quiet and then I said, "What makes you so sure?"

"I can count."

I put my head down briefly, gathering my strength. Time to move along, I thought. I slipped my left shoe off and placed it on the floor in front of me. I slipped my right shoe off, my eyes crossing at the heat in my right hip. I could feel a numbness spreading and I couldn't quite compute how pain and nothing could share the same nerve path. "That was only seven," I said.

"It was *eight*."

"I have a ten-shot," I said piously. I began to ease back toward the point at which the corridor made a left.

"A ten-shot. What crap. You're such a liar," he said.

"Oh, really? What kind of gun do you have?"

"A Walther. An eight-shot. I have two shots left."

"No, you don't. You have one. I can count, too, bird-breath." I was moving by degrees, nearing the corner, feeling backward with my foot. David Barney didn't seem to notice the change in my location.

"You can't fool me. I did my homework on you."

"Like what?" I said. I reached the corner and angled myself around until only the upper portion of my body was in the corridor. David Barney was now about twenty-five feet away. I was resting on my right side, my blue jeans wet with blood. I looked down at myself. My hip had started to glow. I lifted myself on one elbow. I'd put my weight on my key-chain, activating the little plastic flashlight that was shaped like a flattened oval and turned on when you pinched it. I eased the keys out of my jeans pocket and took the flash off the key ring. I pushed the keys to one side, uneasy about their jangling.

"Like this business about your lying. You take a lot of pride in the fact."

"Who'd you hear that from?"

"I get around. It's amazing how much information you can pick up in jail."

"I bet you tell a lot of lies yourself," I said. "You probably have a nine-shot."

He actually sounded flattered. "You never know," he said.

"What made you so sure I'd come down here tonight?" I pulled myself up onto my hands and knees.

"You didn't figure that out? You told Curtis you kept your gun here. That's why I set up the meeting at the bird refuge. I knew you'd never go down there without your gun."

Let's get this over with, I thought. I came up to a half crouch, like a runner at a starting post, painfully aware of the throbbing in my butt.

Behind me, I heard him say, "You still there?"

I didn't answer.

"Where'd you go?"

I limped in my sock feet as quickly as I could toward the kitchen door. The room glowed a faint gray from the outside light. I realized at a glance there was no place to hide. I veered out of the room and across the hall. I tiptoed to the far corner and I crouched down beside the Xerox machine with my back to the wall. Bending my right leg hurt so bad I had to grit my teeth. I made it to a sitting position, my gun in my right hand, the little flash in my left. My hands felt greasy with sweat and my fingers were cold.

"Kinsey?" From the hallway. Any minute he'd figure out I was gone and come barreling after me.

I was squeezed in beside the Xerox machine with my knees drawn up. I was hoping to keep the target area as small as possible, though crammed in a corner was probably not such a hot idea. Guy fires one bullet, he hits everything you got.

"Hey!" he said. "I'm talking to you." I could tell from his voice he was still down around Lonnie's office. The man was annoyed.

I tried to still my breathing.

He fired.

Even down the hall and around the corner, I jumped. That was eight. If the man had an eight-shot, I was doing okay. A nine-shot, I was screwed. Once he figured out where I was, I was fair game. It was really too late to go anywhere else. I was feeling clammy, that cold, sick sensation that over-whelms you when you're about to pass out. I wiped my cheek against my shirtsleeve. Fear had settled over me like an icy vapor, rippling against my spine.

The notion of dying is, at the same time, trivial and terri-fying, absurd and full of anguish. Ego clings to life. Self lets it go, willing to free-fall, willing to soar. If I regretted anything, it was simply not knowing how all the stories would turn out. Would William and Rosie fall in love sure enough? Would

Henry reach the age of ninety? With all the blood oozing out, would Lonnie ever get his carpet clean?

So many things I hadn't done. So many things I wouldn't get to do now. Dumb to die like this, but then again, why not?

I took two deep breaths, trying to keep my head clear.

In the hallway, quite close, I heard David Barney's voice. "Kinsey?" He was checking the kitchen as I had, realizing there was no place of concealment. He'd probably scouted the place while he was waiting for me to show up. He had to know the copy room was the only place left. I could hear his shallow breathing.

"Hello. You in there? Now we can have a little liar's contest. Do I have one bullet or no bullets?"

I said nothing.

"And what about the lady? She claims she has two left. Does she lie or tell the truth?"

My hands were shaking so hard I couldn't steady the gun. I pointed in the general direction of the door and fired.

His "Oh" was full of pain. He made a humming sound that told me I had hit him and he was hurting. Well, good. It made two of us. He shuffled into the room. "That makes nine," he said. His voice turned grim and silly and theatrical. He was clowning. "Are you prepared to die?"

"I wouldn't say prepared exactly, but I wouldn't be surprised." I held the small flashlight in my left hand and pinched the center. It gave off a scant tablespoon of light, but it was enough to see him with. "How about you?" I said. "Surprised?" I fired at him point-blank and then studied the effect.

This was instructional. In the movies, you shoot someone and they're either blown back a foot or they keep coming at you, up from the bathtub, up from the floor, sometimes so full of bullet holes their shirts form red polka dots. The truth is, you hit someone and it hurts like hell. I could testify to that. David Barney had to sit down with his back to the wall and think about life. A wet red stain was forming on his left side, fairly ruining his shirt and causing his expression to shift from smug superiority to consternation.

I studied him for a moment and then said, "I told you I had a ten-shot."

He didn't seem interested in that. I pulled myself into a standing position, leaving a sticky handprint on the Xerox machine. I crossed the room to the wall he was propped against. I leaned down and took his gun, which he offered up without resistance. I checked the magazine. There was one bullet left. His eyes had gone empty and his fingers opened slowly as he released his own life. Something like a moth fluttered off into the dark. I limped into the hall, raking my little flashlight across the wall until I found the fire alarm box. I busted the glass door and pulled the lever.

Epilogue

Now that I've learned how to sit down again, I suppose I
should fill in the few remaining gaps in my paperwork. The
new year has rolled over and the torrid romance between
Rosie and William continues unabated. Henry has threatened everything from a hunger strike to fisticuffs to no avail.
I can understand his concern—William would be a trial in
any event—but there's still something wonderful about love
at close range.

The police referred Tippy Parsons to the district attorney's office, where she had a lengthy and candid conversation with one of the deputy DAs. I'd thought her age might
be a mitigating factor in the hit-and-run death, but what it
came down to in the end was the simple fact that the statute
of limitations on the vehicular manslaughter had already run
out. When Hartford McKell heard the driver had been

found, he insisted on writing me a check for the twenty-five thousand bucks despite the fact that Tippy was neither arrested nor convicted. I took the money. I did the work so why not get paid? Now all I have to decide is what to do with it. In the meantime, spring is just around the corner and life is very good.

Respectfully submitted,
Kinsey Millhone